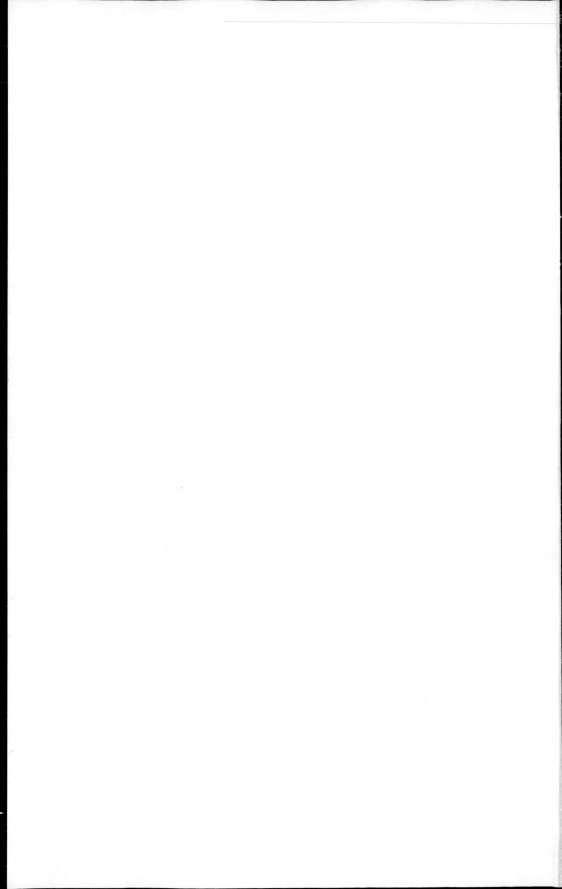

THE IRON MEN

THE IRON MEN

Leonard B. Scott

BALLANTINE BOOKS
NEW YORK

Copyright © 1993 by Leonard B. Scott
Map copyright © 1993 by Random House, Inc.

All rights reserved under International and Pan-American Copyright Con-
ventions. Published in the United States by Ballantine Books, a division of
Random House, Inc., New York, and simultaneously in Canada by Random House of Canada Limited, Toronto.

Library of Congress Cataloging-in-Publication Data:

Scott, Leonard B.
The iron men / Leonard Scott.—1st ed.
p.   cm.
ISBN: 0-345-37753-2:
I.   Title.
PS3569.C847176   1993
813'.54—dc20   92-52660
CIP

Text design by Debby Jay

Map illustration by Patrick O'Brien

Manufactured in the United States of America

First Edition: April 1993

10   9   8   7   6   5   4   3   2   1

THE IRON MEN

Is dedicated to those who have seen the glazed eyes of the fallen and heard the incessant beat of the drums calling for yet more sacrifice.

To my dad, a bomber and, later, transport pilot who did his best to destroy our country's enemy and then tried to save him.

To my mother, who picked up toy soldiers for too many years and had to pick up this soldier when he was down.

To my wife, Jammye, who has stood by me over the years.

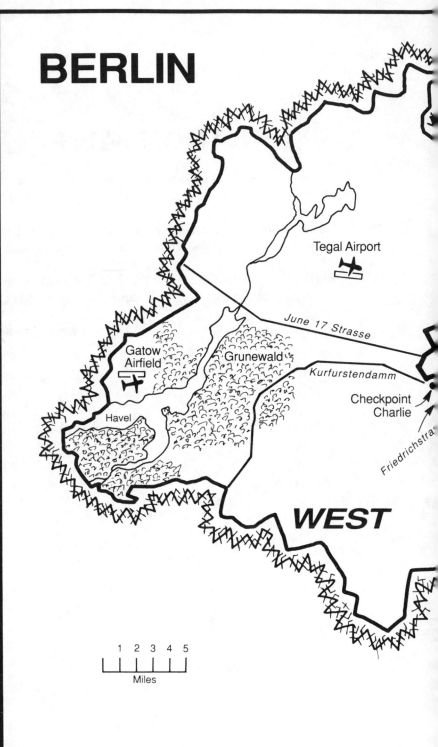

BERLIN

Tegal Airport

June 17 Strasse

Gatow Airfield

Grunewald

Kurfurstendamm

Havel

Checkpoint Charlie

Friedrichstra

WEST

1 2 3 4 5
Miles

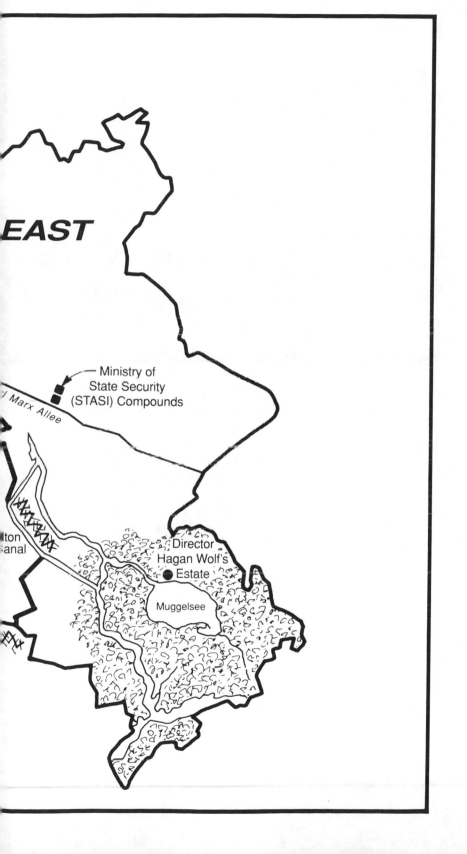

EAST

Ministry of
State Security
(STASI) Compounds

l Marx Allee

lton
anal

Director
Hagan Wolf's
Estate

Muggelsee

THE IRON MEN

PROLOGUE

6 March 1944

1306 Hours, 21,000 feet,
five miles west of Berlin, Germany

The intercom was silent. The usual chatter between crew members of *Battlin' Babe* had ended when the fighters broke off their attack. The old gal had taken a beating, but the rest of the squadron had fared far worse. Of the seventeen B-17Gs that had taken off from Huntingdonshire, England, that morning, only five remained. Flak over Enschede had claimed two fortresses, and the Luftwaffe's Messerschmitts and Focke-Wulfs over Haselünne had gotten the rest. The fighters had attacked in waves, diving like eagles, screaming through the formation at five hundred miles per hour. It had been over in two minutes. Ten flying fortresses, each with a crew of ten, were gone. There had been chutes. Some would live. But they weren't going home. Not for a long time.

Captain Jake Tallon, pilot of *Battlin' Babe,* turned his eyes forward, then carefully unwrapped a half stick of gum and put it into his mouth. Ten paces behind him two waist gunners lay dead among spent shell casings on the blood-covered catwalk. Both had been killed thirty minutes before during a Messerschmitt attack. *Babe*'s fuselage was riddled by bullets and torn and ripped by flak. One of her Wright Cyclone air-cooled radial engines had feathered and was still billowing a trail of smoke. Every surviving crew member, knowing what was ahead, sat silently, waiting.

Berlin, the sixth largest city in the world, with a population of almost four million, the capital of the Third Reich and the largest

1

industrial and commercial center on the European continent, was the target. Twelve major rail lines converged within the city, and its many canals linked it with the rich Ruhr Valley in the west and Hamburg and Stetten's ports in the north. It was also the home of the Chancellor, Adolf Hitler, and most of his staff and government administrators. And it was protected by the largest anti-aircraft defense force on the continent. Over seven hundred AA guns were trained skyward, ready for *Battlin' Babe* and the seven hundred other bombers flying formations behind her.

The navigator looked at his map. Their specific target was the Argus works in the district of Reinickendorf, where production of the pulse-jet engines of the flying bombs, the V-1s, was about to begin. The young navigator broke the silence and spoke into the interphone. "Five minutes out from target."

Captain Jake Tallon took hold of the yoke and pressed the radio talk button. "Flight, this is lead. Watch for my bomb-bay doors to open. We're less than five minutes out. Keep it in tight. Good luck. Out." He pressed the interphone. "Bombardier, how's your picture?"

"Looking good, Jake. Clear."

"Crew, this is pilot. This is it, the first daylight raid on the capital. We wanna do it right and not have to come back. We're lead for the squadron now. Make sure you've got your flak vests and steel pots on . . . we're going in. Let's show these bastards what the Army Air Corps can do."

The copilot handed Jake a flak vest and put on his own. Small black puffs appeared in the distance. "Christ, Jake, they've got our altitude already!" the copilot gasped.

"Stead-dee, Al, just keep your hands on the yoke and help me keep her on course when she starts buckin'."

The chin turret gunner scooted backward into the cupola as far as he could and brought his legs up under the two flak vests he had tied together. He peered out through the Plexiglass bubble. Ahead, the flashing detonations of countless shells were turning the sky dark. He hated flak. Against kraut fighters, he could at least shoot back, but with flak all he could do was pray and wait. When he heard the first ca-blooms over the sound of *Babe*'s roaring engines, he cringed. A moment later, *Babe* began bouncing from the concussions of twenty-pound shells exploding nearby. Jake held the yoke tightly. "Come on *Babe*, ride it out," he whispered. "You and me, ol' girl. Come on, this one is for ol' Jake."

Splinters tore through *Babe*'s skin behind the navigator's compartment. Another explosion beneath her tossed the ship up and down like a cork in rough water. Jake fought the shaking controls.

Far below, sirens wailed, and like himself, people trembled in fear. The madness had begun.

Babe bounced hard. The copilot's front windshield spider-webbed as an iron splinter shot through its center. The copilot grunted and drooped forward in his harness. Jake yelled for the radio operator just as the port wing tip disintegrated, splattered by shards of white-hot iron.

"We've lost a piece of the rudder!" the tail gunner yelled over the intercom.

"Stead-dee," said Jake. "Bombardier, how we doin'?"

"Come to heading zero-eight-five and hold. Three minutes."

The radio operator released the copilot's seat harness and dragged the man back into the cabin, leaving a deep trail of crimson blood. The 180-mile-per-hour wind screamed through the hole in the windshield, causing the blood on the seat to ripple in small waves.

"Pilot, bombardier has it."

Jake held on to the yoke and spoke calmly. "Bombardier has it." He released the yoke, giving control to the man below him, who was looking through the Norden bombsight and holding the device that would release ten armed, 500-pound incendiary bombs.

"Bomb-bay doors open," barked the bombardier. "One minute."

Babe was bucking steadily now, rattling and shaking from the beating. Jake heard the explosion and snapped his eyes to his left just as the debris of what had been twenty-eight tons of *Big Mama* scattered across the sky and disappeared. She was gone. No time for chutes, just gone.

"Thirty seconds!"

"Jake, this is tail. *Proud Mary* is going down!"

"Stead-dee. Look for chutes."

"Fifteen seconds . . . ten . . . five . . . *bombs away!*"

Babe shot skyward with the release of the weight. Jake grabbed the yoke and pushed the left rudder pedal. Come on, *Babe*, get us home, ol' girl . . . come on, get us out.

The radio operator leaned forward. "Al didn't make it."

Stead-dee, Jake told himself. He couldn't concern himself with the loss of one man now. It was still a long way home. He gripped *Babe*'s yoke as she was buffeted by the wash of explosions. We can do it, he told her. We can get 'em all home. We're a team, aren't we, ol' girl?

He pressed the radio button. "Flight, this is lead. Close it up . . . close it up."

The radio operator patted the pilot's shoulder. "There's nobody left but us, Jake. We need to join another squadron."

Jake looked far below at the smoke clouds billowing in the city.

He felt as if he could hear the pathetic screams above the crackling flames. He looked at the pool of jelled blood in the opposite seat, then closed his eyes and prayed.

"Oh shit! Jake, this is turret. We got bandits, eleven o'clock!"

"Pilot, this is tail. Never mind the bandits. I see the most beautiful sight in the world. Our fighter escorts have shown up. Hot damn, Jake! We're gonna make it home!"

Jake pushed the intercom. "Stead-dee. We're not home yet. Everybody keep your eyes peeled for leakers." He released the button and patted the yoke affectionately. "Take us home, *Babe*," he whispered.

PART I

1945–1971

CHAPTER 1

1945

14 April

The smell of death and despair hung over the battlefield like a blanket. Black, boiling clouds of smoke from the burning tanks joined in the oppressive stink of destruction. The raging sounds of battle were gone, leaving only the crackling fires from the burning tanks and the sickening screams and moans from the wounded Russian infantry soldiers. The remnants of Luftwaffe Paratroop Battalion 600 had stopped the Soviets again, but it had not been a victory for the defenders, only a prolonging of the suffering. The survivors knew the battle was not over, it was only a respite. More tanks and screaming waves of Soviet infantry would soon appear and enter the valley of death. It was just a matter of time.

Captain Axel Mader kneeled down and closed the eyelids of his dead machine gunner with a trembling, dirty hand. Exhausted from days without sleep, the young, stocky captain fell back on his buttocks among the hundreds of spent bullet casings. Too exhausted to get up, Mader leaned back against the bunker wall to mourn for his dead friend. Franz deserved at least a few moments from a friend and fellow soldier.

Mader lowered his head, remembering Franz when they had fought side by side a year before. The young, always smiling soldier had wanted only to be a poet and . . .

Mader's bearded chin dropped to his chest. The weight of his helmet forced his head over until he almost pitched forward onto the corpse. Jolted awake, Mader opened his bloodshot eyes hoping he had been sleeping and that it had all been a horrible dream. It wasn't. The dust-covered body of Franz was still there, lying in the same pool of stinking, coagulating blood.

Mader knew he had to somehow get up. The remaining survivors of his company needed him. Perhaps one of the boys or air crew mechanics-turned-soldier wanted to be a poet too. He closed his eyes again to try and find the strength and the resolve to continue believing he could make a difference by leading his men awhile longer.

A tall soldier strode across the artillery-plowed earth and tentatively entered the bunker he'd seen take a tank round during the battle. Expecting the worst, he sighed inwardly in relief, seeing his friend was still alive. Captain Jorn Furman took in a breath to calm himself and reached down, grabbing his fellow company commander's filthy tunic sleeve. "Get up, Iron Man Mader. The colonel needs reports from his commanders."

Axel's dark blue eyes misted as he looked up at the tall soldier. "Mein Gott, Jorn, I . . . I thought you were . . ."

Furman pulled the haggard soldier to his feet. "Me? Never, Axel, we made a promise, remember?"

Axel forced a weak smile, remembering it had only been a month before in a biergarten that he and his two closest friends made the promise to each other.

Hearing someone approaching from the outside, Mader and Furman snapped their heads and weapons toward the bunker entrance.

A short, round-faced officer rushed in but came to an abrupt halt seeing the two standing men. Captain Lars Kailer lowered his head as if in prayer, before lifting his eyes and snapping. "Damn you two! I ran two hundred meters to see if . . . Damn you both!"

Axel Mader's lips slowly curled back in a knowing smile. "I see you didn't forget our promise. We all have survived again."

Kailer's face tightened. "Damn the promise! We're dead men and you know it! You can't hold me to a stupid vow that can't be fulfilled."

Axel fixed Kailer then Furman with a penetrating stare and spoke fervently. "We have been through too much not to live out this war. I consider you two the brothers I never had. The promise was, we would all live, and after this war we would meet again and drink and sing the old songs. We are brothers in heart, and we damn well will *live* through this war!"

Kailer lowered his head, looking at the corpse at his feet. Slowly he raised his chin and spoke softly. "But if one of us can't keep the promise, let him die knowing he will be remembered always . . . always by his brothers."

"Always," said Axel, placing his hand on Kailer's shoulder.

Jorn Furman nodded as he placed his hand on Axel's. "Ja. Always."

Colonel Karl Haas raised his head over the lip of the command bunker to survey the battlefield. Next to him stood Regimental Sergeant Major Peter Schmidt, who had taken a bullet through the left shoulder during the fighting. Haas's sunken, lifeless eyes burned from the drifting, oily smoke, but he did not blink or tear. After six years of fighting, he had no feelings or tears left.

Six more Soviet T-34 tank hulks had joined the other fourteen wrecks smoldering in front of his battalion's defense. Between the burning iron monsters, hundreds of new bodies were stacked on top of old ones. The Russian infantry that had come behind the tanks had fared far worse than their predecessors, because they were forced to climb over human carnage and the wrecks of previous failed attacks. When their assault formation had lost its all-important forward momentum, they had ground to a halt before the defense's machine guns and Panzerfaust antitank weapons. The killing had been easy, but costly.

The colonel turned, sensing a movement to his right. His tired eyes widened in surprise. He would not have dreamed it possible, but all three of his company commanders, Mader, Furman, and Kailer, had survived the last Russian attack. Haas's dirty, lined face saddened. It had only been two years since these men and many others like them had reported for duty to his unit in Italy. My God, they had been so young when they had first come to him, lieutenants fresh from the officers' course and parachute school. Yet it was there, at Cassino, that they had won the black iron and silver medal known as the Knights Cross, Germany's highest decoration for valor. Field Marshal Goering liked to call recipients of the award his Iron Men—he had earned one himself during the First World War—and he held them in such high regard that in January he had formed an elite honor guard from their ranks among his Luftwaffe paratroop divisions. These men had done their duty in battle and he believed he was giving them a well-deserved respite from the fighting. In the spring, however, the Führer had called upon every man, woman, and child to come to the defense of Berlin against the Russians. Goering formed a special battalion made up of paratroop students, cadre, excess flight crews, and mechanics, and he called upon the Iron Men to lead them, the Luftwaffe Parachute Battalion 600, into battle. Their orders were to fight to the last man, the last breath, and the last bullet, to preserve the Fatherland. Along with other units, composed of thousands of old men and boys, they were sent to the front. They had been Germany's last hope.

The colonel felt a deep, gnawing pain in his heart. Look at them now—not one over twenty-two, and they all looked forty. They had become as close as brothers since then, and that fact alone had helped through many a difficult situation, but Haas knew it wouldn't be enough for what lay ahead.

The stout officer in the lead, Captain Axel Mader, came up and stood at attention. He had a square, prominent jaw, close-cropped blond hair, and penetrating, dark blue eyes. He was a farmer turned soldier, and one of Haas's best.

"Status?" Haas asked.

"Mein Oberst," Mader said, "first company has eighteen men who can still fight. We are out of Panzerfausts, and we have only one can of ammunition left for our remaining machine gun."

The colonel nodded without comment and waited for the next report, from Furman. Captain Jorn Furman was tall, and some competitive swimming before the war had given him broad, powerful shoulders. He had joined the army for one reason: to take his revenge on the Russians for killing his father during the first eastern offensive. He took the stub of a cigarette from his cracked lips.

"Second company has twenty-one men effective, one Panzerfaust, but no machine-gun ammunition."

The colonel's bloodshot eyes shifted to Captain Lars Kailer, who was trying not to show his pain from a bullet graze on his jaw. He had a plump, round face that often betrayed a boyish sense of humor, though since the Ardennes campaign, where there had been so much death, he seemed nothing if not mature and battle-hardened. He was the son of a rich industrialist, but no one doubted he had the heart of a warrior.

"Third company has seventeen men who can fight," he reported gravely. "We have no Panzerfausts or machine-gun ammunition."

The thin, bearded colonel glanced last at the wounded soldier standing beside him. "Sergeant Major?"

Regimental Sergeant Major Peter Schmidt painfully came to attention. "Mein Oberst, the badly wounded are consolidated behind the ridge, but are without medical attention. The surgeon was killed during the artillery barrage. The ammunition bunker is empty, and the men I sent back for resupply have not come back. Water is critical, and for the third day there is no food. That is all, mein Oberst."

The colonel looked back at the battlefield. He had to formulate a new plan.

Weeks before, he had had 540 men under his command. Strafings, bombs, and artillery had killed a quarter of the battalion before they had even reached the front lines, just forward of the Alte Oder River. Now, after six days of constant fighting, the battalion was down to less than one hundred men, and probably sixty of those were wounded.

Haas shut his eyes. He never wanted to see another dead German soldier. Neither did he want to see any more bleeding wounded or to hear any more pathetic moans and heart-wrenching screams. He could not bear to watch any more of the thousands of weary, homeless women and children who passed down rutted roads leading nowhere. The world had become too cruel. He couldn't bear giving any more orders that would add to the suffering.

He knew what he had to do. He looked fiercely into the bearded, dirty faces of his commanders and spoke with resolve. "You and your men have done all that the Fatherland could ask of its soldiers. We cannot stop tanks without Panzerfausts, and we can't stop infantry without ammunition. We will fall back across the river."

Captain Kailer immediately stepped forward to object. "But sir, our orders were to hold our position."

"To hold it *as long as possible*," the colonel snapped. "Those were General Busse's exact words. 'Hold as long as possible, then fall back and join the main defense line.' We have accomplished our mission."

Kailer persisted. "But sir, the Führer's orders were to fight to the last breath before giving up an inch of German soil."

"*The Führer is in his bunker in Berlin!* His orders were propaganda for the people, *not* for German soldiers! We cannot fight tanks with our bare hands! Think, Kailer! We can fight again when we are resupplied with ammunition and antitank weapons. The Führer's words cannot stop the Russians. German soldiers properly led, equipped, and supplied, *can!*"

Kailer felt a hand on his shoulder.

"The colonel is doing the right thing, Lars," Jorn Furman whispered softly. "Fighting without ammunition is suicide. We must pull back."

Kailer dejectedly stepped back and lowered his head.

Satisfied there would be no more objections, the colonel leaned back on the bunker wall and slid down to his buttocks. "Sergeant Major, assemble the walking wounded and lead them to the river bridge. The rest of us will cover your withdrawal. We will pull back by company in ten minute intervals. We will take as many of the badly wounded as can be carried. . . ." He swallowed hard and set his eyes to the front. "We will have to leave the rest."

Axel Mader stepped forward. "Sir, I request permission to turn my company over to my remaining platoon leader and to remain with the wounded."

The colonel's eyes softened. "An honorable request, Axel, but I must deny it. The men of your company need their commander alive." Haas searched the eyes of the other captains for doubt or unspoken questions. There were none. "That is all, then. Carry out your orders. We have no more time. The Russians will soon attack."

The three officers came to attention, then quickly departed, leaving the sergeant major alone with the exhausted battalion commander.

The old sergeant put his hand on the colonel's shoulder and spoke softly. "Mein Oberst, it is a matter of honor to remain at your side. I will order the senior medic to lead the wounded back."

Haas lifted his head and looked into Schmidt's craggy face. "No, my friend, it is not a question of honor anymore. The kind of honor you speak of is dead, like our Reich. The wounded must be cared for. The young boys they sent us are the only hope left for our country. Don't stop at the river. Take them back to the nearest aid station. Have their wounds attended and march them to the American lines to the west." Haas hoped Schmidt understood his regret and sorrow. The sergeant major had served at his side for more campaigns than he could remember. "It is my final order to you, Peter. Avoid the fanatics that would take them and throw them into the defense of Berlin. It's over. The Fatherland will need our young men to rebuild."

The veteran slowly nodded. Had his son survived Stalingrad, he would have wanted the same thing for him. He turned in silence to carry out his colonel's last command.

Ten minutes later Schmidt spoke to the assembled walking wounded. "We will move at a steady pace. We will not stop for those who fall out of the march. If we are strafed, take cover and listen for my order to form up again. Corporal Steir, lead them on."

A few yards away a junior sergeant leaned against a tree. His thigh had been badly wounded, and he could not march. Schmidt kneeled down beside the boy. He hated himself for what he had to ask of him. "Olf, you will be in charge of those wounded who are left behind. You know what must be done."

The soldier lifted his head and tried to smile. "I will miss you, Peter."

The sergeant major shook the soldier's outstretched hand. "And I you, Olf. We shall always have the old days to remember, ja?"

"Ja, the old days," Olf said reflectively. Both men exchanged a final silent farewell. The young, blond paratrooper sat up and barked to the wounded who lay about him. "Those who can, load your rifles and crawl to me."

An SS lieutenant stood on the far bank of the river and watched the approaching small unit through his binoculars until he made out the color of their uniforms. They were clearly a paratroop unit in retreat. It looked as if the company would have to get ready for action.

The new commander had to be notified. The lieutenant broke into a slow jog and crossed the road to a hastily built command post. His captain was sunning himself on a campaign chair outside of the bunker.

The young officer had to cough to gain the captain's attention. "Herr Hauptmann, deserters are approaching the bridge. I have taken the liberty to ready the company."

Captain Horst Volker sat up and raised an eyebrow. "Well done. Are the demolitions in place?"

"Jawohl, mein Hauptmann," the lieutenant answered as the tall officer stood. "The charges are ready and the detonator is in place as you ordered. Herr Hauptmann, since this is your first time dealing with deserters, may I suggest that I take care of this action for you? The senior sergeant and I have had much experience in these matters."

The captain ran his hand through his short, dark brown hair and put on his peaked cap. He gave a slight nod. "Of course, please carry on. I will accompany you and observe."

Sergeant Major Schmidt saw the SS unit deployed in full strength along the far bank and waved to them as he stepped onto the wooden planks of the bridge. It was a wonderful sight. There had been only dead men and horses to greet him along the one-kilometer march from the defense position on the ridge. By the look of them, these SS soldiers had not yet seen any battle. Their uniforms were parade clean, and their faces looked fresh and well-fed. He felt hope for the first time in a week, for surely they were part of a newly arrived division that was being regularly resupplied.

The sergeant major strode several steps before he noticed the firing wire that ran along the rail of the bridge. He warned his men to stay clear, but inwardly sighed in relief. He was thankful that the colonel had pulled the unit back before the SS could blow the bridge and trap them on the other side. He reached the far bank, turned with a smile toward his men and bellowed, "There will be hot food in your bellies tonight. Get your heads up and show this company who you are!" Still smiling, the old sergeant turned around and walked toward two approaching officers, but halted abruptly at the sight of a pistol in the lieutenant's raised hand.

The young officer stepped forward. "You and the rabble behind you are under arrest for violating the orders of the Führer. As I presume you are the most senior of them, I order you to tell the rest of the deserters to remove their tunics. They are not fit to wear the uniform of a German soldier."

Schmidt's eyes widened in shock. "But you are mistaken, Herr Leutnant. We are members of the Luftwaffe Paratroop Battalion 600 under the command of Colonel Haas. We have been fighting for six days and—"

"Enough rubbish! Follow my order."

Schmidt looked past the wild-eyed junior officer, who was obviously a fanatic, to the tall, aristocratic captain who had been watching with indifference. "Herr Hauptmann, please, surely you must understand why we are pulling back. My colonel and the rest of the battalion will be here within minutes. He can explain the orders General Busse gave to him and clear up this misunderstanding."

Volker's pale blue eyes studied the sergeant major for a moment before he stepped to within a foot of the haggard veteran. Without warning, he jammed the pistol barrel up and under Schmidt's chin. Volker's unreadable eyes, like his voice, showed not a trace of emotion. "You are a deserter," he said softly. "Obey the rules of my officer and order the others to take off their tunics."

Schmidt glared at the captain with revulsion. "We are men from the Parachute Battalion 600, we are not deser—"

Volker didn't flinch as he pulled the trigger. The sergeant major's head snapped back as the muffled discharge blew a nine-millimeter path through the roof of his mouth, brain, and the top of his skull.

The captain stepped over the body, carefully avoiding the pool of expanding blood, and pointed his Luger at the next soldier in the ranks. "Order these cowards to take off their tunics."

The stunned, wounded plane-mechanic-turned-soldier was still staring at the body of his sergeant major. He could not believe what he had just witnessed. His wide, fearful eyes shifted slowly to the captain. "Mein . . . mein Gott, Hauptmann, you have killed him. The Führer himself presented the Knights Cross to him twice.

Surely you have heard of the Iron Men who lead our battalion. We are not cowards, we are—"

Volker fired his Luger into the corporal's forehead, spraying the men behind him with blood and gray brain tissue. Volker spoke with ice-cold reserve to his shocked lieutenant. "Execute the cowards on my command."

The lieutenant raised his hand and yelled "Achtung!" to his men. He strode back with Volker to a slight rise that was safely out of the field of fire. The formation of horrified and confused wounded men could only stare as Volker said loudly, "I pronounce you guilty of desertion." He nodded, and the lieutenant dropped his hand. "Fire!"

The SS company's six machine guns burst into deadly chatter. Volker raised and fired his own pistol. The screaming and jerking of the bodies caused the lieutenant to squirm uncomfortably. His unit's orders were to gather up deserters and send them to the rear where they would be tried by the special administrative sections.

His new commander was reloading his magazine as if he had just finished target practice. The lieutenant fought back the bile rising in his throat. Some of the wounded had jumped into the river and were trying to escape. Their pathetic efforts were futile. The water around them churned with machine-gun bullets. Ten seconds later the shooting stopped.

The horrible metallic clammoring of the guns was still echoing in the lieutenant's head when he heard yet another shot. He spun around to discover Volker lowering his smoking pistol. A man who had been moaning on the ground a second before was now dead. The lieutenant felt his stomach rumbling with nausea, but he hadn't seen the end of the bloodshed yet. Volker placidly strolled over to another fallen man and shot him in the head.

"Mein Gott," the lieutenant whispered to himself, "he is enjoying it."

Captain Axel Mader heard the guns firing and moved to the front of his company's formation to join his only remaining platoon leader.

"Sir! The firing came from the direction of the bridge, and it wasn't Russian weapons," the soldier said excitedly.

Mader increased his pace and caught up to the two scouts he had sent forward. Both were gazing through binoculars toward the distant bridge. One grew pale and turned to him.

"It's a Schutzstaffel collection company, Hauptmann. They . . . they've killed our wounded. They've killed them all."

"What?" Mader snatched the glasses away from the soldier.

The scout lowered his head. "I saw such an SS collection company before on the eastern front. Sometimes they shoot or hang deserters to make an example for others."

Shaking, Mader lowered the glasses. Within seconds his emotions had gone from from shock to revulsion to seething hatred. He tossed the glasses back to the scout.

"Those SS bastards are going to pay!" he said through clenched teeth.

Colonel Haas led the remaining officers of the unit in two marching ranks over the bridge. All of them were Iron Men. He halted the formation and ordered them into a single rank which faced the road and the approaching SS captain. Each Iron Man carried a Schmeisser machine pistol at the ready, and as one they stared at the dark-haired officer with loathing, for lying grotesquely before them were the riddled bodies of their murdered comrades.

Colonel Haas took a step forward and waited for a salute.

Volker studied the colonel's worn face for a moment. "You have no rank, so do not expect any military courtesy from me. You and the rest of the rabble behind you are within the sights of my gunners, and any sudden move on anyone's part will result in the death of all of you. You will order your officers to lay down their arms, and then order the rest of your cowards to cross the bridge and do the same. You will then—"

"*Shut up, you butcher!*" Haas blurted. "I am Colonel Haas, commander of the Parachute Battalion 600. I alone am responsible for the withdrawal of my unit from the defense. You will place *me* under arrest and let the rest of my men continue to the main defense line."

The captain kept his pale blue eyes locked on the senior officer. "You dictate nothing to me. This is not a negotiation. Everyone who comes across that bridge is a traitor to the Fatherland and will be arrested and executed as an example to others."

Haas snickered and tossed his thumb over his shoulder toward the far bank. "You pompous ass, there is no one over there to make an example to, except my men and two Russian tank battalions, which are heading toward this bridge as we speak. In less than fifteen minutes you will be dead. Your lack of experience in the field shows itself in the way you positioned your company. All of your men are forward of the high ground, which is five hundred meters behind you. The Russian tanks will come and line the far bank three deep and pick you off at their leisure with their cannons. You will not kill one Russian or stop a single tank. Your men will die because of your stupidity."

The captain turned as if to reconsider the positions he had chosen. He looked back at Haas and nodded slightly. "Your assessment of our position is correct but immaterial. I am not responsible for defending this bridge, coward. I am here to stop deserters such as yourself."

Haas took another step forward. "Then arrest me and let my men cross. At this moment they are deployed on the far bank, aiming their weapons at your positions. If you execute me or my officers, my soldiers will destroy you all before the Russians come. Time is running out for you. Take me and move back while you still can."

The captain began to accuse the colonel of lying, but a faint rumbling across the river stopped him. He had heard enough panzers to know that the sound signaled a Russian advance. He glanced at the far bank, judging how much time he had, and nodded. "Very well. I arrest you . . . but you must have your officers throw their weapons into the river. Once that is done, I will allow the rest of your command to cross and continue to the Seelow defense line."

Haas stared into Volker's eyes. "Do I have your word of honor as a German officer?"

Volker raised his chin as if insulted. "You have my word of honor."

Satisfied, Haas spun around to his officers. "Follow the instructions agreed to. I will have this SS bastard before a board of inquiry once I find his superior. Hauptmann Mader, take charge and ensure that none of our men try to take revenge on these murderers as they pass. I will make sure justice is served. Good luck to all of you. I will see you at the Seelow heights."

To reach Volker, Haas had to step over the bodies of his men. He was only a few paces away when he stopped and looked down at the still form of his sergeant major. Haas shook as he whispered softly, "I'm sorry, Peter."

Volker motioned his senior sergeant forward to take the colonel into custody. "The weapons," he said in a monotone to the captain who had taken the colonel's place.

Axel Mader angrily turned and tossed his machine pistol into the river. His fellow officers did the same. He faced Volker. "Now *your* men."

Volker nodded to his lieutenant, who called out the command for the company to withdraw.

Mader waited until the SS soldiers left their positions before he raised his arm and made a circular motion to signal the rest of the battalion to cross. Then he turned again to the SS captain.

"What is your name, Hauptmann? I want to remember you."

The edges of the SS officer's lips curled up in a faint smile. "My name is Horst Volker. And may I have the pleasure to know yours? I want to remember you as well."

Mader bared his teeth as he raised his hand, pointing at Volker's face. "I am Hauptmann Axel Mader, the man who will one day kill you for what you've done."

Volker narrowed his eyes and nodded to acknowledge the challenge, but already the tall, dirty officer beside Mader had stepped forward. "I am Jorn Furman. And if Mader doesn't kill you, I will."

"Or I will!" said Lars Kailer, also stepping forward.

Volker shifted his gaze toward the bridge. He looked amused. "Ja, cowards, you will remember me."

As Mader followed his gaze to the men who were halfway across the bridge, Volker suddenly moved away and hurried to catch up with his sergeant and the prisoner, Haas.

Furman grabbed Mader's arm. "Mein Gott, Axel, *look*!"

Volker had grabbed Haas by the arm and spun him round. Now he jammed his pistol under the battalion commander's chin.

"*No*, you gave your word!" Mader screamed.

Volker smiled at Mader, then pulled the trigger.

Mader broke into a run, with the other Iron Men behind him, but Volker was already kneeling down with the handle of the detonator in his grasp. He waited until he saw the horror in Mader's eyes before he pushed down the plunger.

The bridge disappeared with an ear-shattering explosion that sent up a geyser of water and debris. The blast knocked the Iron Men to the ground and covered them in water, wood planks, and body parts of the men who had been crossing. Ahead of the others by ten meters, Mader had also been knocked down by the blast, but he had struggled to his feet again. "*Volkerrrr!*" he screamed in rage.

Volker stood and waited as the paratrooper ran toward him, closing within only a few yards before he raised his pistol and fired.

The bullet hit Mader in the chest, and he pitched sideways to the ground. Gagging, he rolled over onto his back, only to meet the gaze of Volker, who was about to put the finishing bullet into his head.

The senior sergeant came up behind Volker. "Hauptmann, there isn't time. Go on, I'll finish him and the others. The company is formed and ready to move. I'll catch up."

Volker heard the tanks rumbling closer. "Finish them all. I want no survivors."

The sergeant slapped a new magazine into his Schmeisser machine pistol. "With pleasure, mein Hauptmann." He strolled confidently toward the remaining unarmed men.

Captain Jorn Furman and the nine other Iron Men had all spaced themselves several meters apart to await the approach of the sergeant. Every man had his boot trench knife in his hand. Furman waited until the heavy sergeant was within six meters before he made his throw. The others immediately did the same.

The startled sergeant fired at Jorn, but his burst was high, for he had pulled the barrel as he ducked Furman's blade. He couldn't avoid three of the knives. None stuck, but a handle did strike him on the chin, stunning him, and he went down to his knee. It was enough.

Jorn threw himself at the man, knocking him to the ground, then pulled the Schmeisser from his hands and put a burst into the screaming sergeant's face. He was about to go after Volker, who was running in the distance, when he heard a sickening gurgling sound. "Mein Gott, Axeeeel!"

Lars Kailer finished wrapping the airtight bandage around Mader's chest and looked up at the senior captain who had taken charge of what was left of the battalion. "Jorn, he needs a doctor. I've done all I can do."

Furman looked in the direction the SS unit had gone, then back toward the river, where the first Russian tanks were coming over the bank. "Lars, I'm going after that butcher, and I'm taking Lieutenant Dieter with me. I want you and the rest of the men to take Axel to the closest field hospital. I should think to the southwest would be best and safest."

Kailer motioned to the other men to help lift the unconscious man and extended his other hand to Furman. "Take care, kamerad, remember our promise. Always."

Furman's jaw tightened. "My promise is that I will kill that murdering butcher!" His eyes lost their fire for an instant and he extended his hand. "Take care, brother. Make sure Axel fulfills his promise to us. Go, before the Russians see us."

Kailer kept his grip, looking worriedly at his tall friend. "Be careful, Jorn . . . I want our promise to come true. We will drink and sing the old songs one day, ja?"

Furman's face had turned to stone again, but he nodded as he broke Kailer's grip. "Ja, now go before it's too late." Kailer gave his friend a last parting look, then motioned his men to keep low. They began a slow run, holding the makeshift litter.

Furman watched until he was sure Kailer and the others were out of danger before looking at his last subordinate. He spoke with vengeance. "Dieter, it doesn't end until Volker dies."

The young officer nodded and tossed the SS sergeant's Schmeisser to his captain. "The hunt begins."

CHAPTER 2

1947

4 June

A black staff car emerged from the early morning Siberian mist and rolled to a stop in front of a small, dilapidated wooden building. Tired and disheveled from a four-day train ride and all-night drive, Colonel Anton Gordov opened the back passenger door and stepped out into three inches of mud. His only reception was the squeaking of a hanging sign that read:

HEADQUARTERS

CAMP VIPER

TOILING FOR THE PEOPLE

A few minutes later he was standing inside the building and facing his host. "Captain Georgi Sorokin, Internal Security Advisor for the Ministry of Foreign Affairs," the man said, smiling congenially and extending his hand.

As Gordov stepped forward and shook hands with the thin, bespectacled Sorokin, he found himself wondering about the man's rank. He had to assume he was an officer in the NKVD, the Secret Police, rather than regular military. His pale, almost feminine hands were not those of a regular army officer who had served in a line unit.

Sorokin motioned to a chair behind a small desk. Tired and irritated, Gordov took the seat and looked up impatiently at his host. "I have not had a more miserable time since the war," he said. "Perhaps you might tell me now why it was necessary for me to come all the way to this hell hole?"

Sorokin brought up a chair for himself and motioned to a stack of files on the desk. "Colonel, I apologize for not riding the train with you from Moscow, but I had to arrange for interviews and prepare these dossiers for you. Let me explain. You are here at the request of the Ministry of Defense to participate in a special project. You were selected because of your impeccable war record and your extraordinary German language skills—and, if I may speak frankly, to represent the interests of the military, so that Minister Beria will not have total control over this project. The General Secretary is aware that Beria, as head of state security, is a very ambitious man. You are, in effect, working for the Minister of Foreign Affairs, whom I represent. Your orders are to interview captured SS officers and select those you believe might be candidates for serving in governmental positions in Germany—with the understanding, of course, that they will also keep our interests in mind."

Gordov's jaw dropped open in shock. "You would use SS Nazis for this?"

Sorokin raised an eyebrow. "We have need of their experience. Most are extremely well-educated. The men now running the German government are loyal Communist party members who escaped Hitler's purges and came to us before the war, but we do not have enough of them to ensure control. That is why the General Secretary has taken a personal interest in this project."

"But why these men? There were others who were not in the SS. I must tell you, Captain, that I have two sons, and I fought in the war to protect them from animals like these."

The captain lit a cigarette and sat back in his worn leather chair. Exhaling a cloud of smoke, his eyes shifted back to his guest. "Let me tell you a story," he said. "In the closing days of the war, one of our country's young lieutenants lost his tank to a mine and so was assigned to lead a patrol into Berlin. He and his men discovered an underground storage area consisting of many interconnecting tunnels. In one of those tunnels they found files, over one hundred thousand of them, which comprised the personnel records of all the officers and enlisted men in the SS.

"They also found a complete history of the SS's Sicherheitsdienst, their notorious SD organization, which was responsible for the Nazi party's intelligence and security. They had used a historian to document all their actions, complete with eyewitness reports that included names, places, and events. This document, unlike others, was not censored. The historian, a professor of history, had an eye for detail. He was quite good. Too good. He was executed in the last days, once they learned just how precise and factual his work

had been. It was too incriminating, even for them. There were six
of these books, and all were found in a box with a firebomb attached. The documents have taken us almost two years to translate, screen, and catalog. Now we are ready to use them. The
information contained in them has helped us to identify a certain
class of SS men, all of whom we have moved into *one* labor camp.
This one. Camp Viper."

Sorokin picked up a folder from his desk and paged through it
absently. "The SS had many fanatical murderers in its ranks, but it
also had honorable men. Many SS units—the Waffen and Paratroop
SS divisions, for example—were elite organizations that selected
only the best soldiers. They fought bravely, as I'm sure you can
attest, based on your war record. Those men, however, don't interest us here. Only torturers, murderers, and the planners of such acts
are interned in this camp."

Sorokin fixed his eyes on the colonel. "We have separated the
files of our prisoners into three categories. The first two are those
who ordered or actually committed heinous crimes against the Soviet people. These will be dealt with by my own men."

The captain paused for a moment to select his next words carefully. "You, Colonel, are here to help us with the third category of
prisoner—SS officers who committed crimes solely against the German people or our wartime allies."

Sorokin patted the stack of files. "These men have the special
qualities we are looking for. they are intelligent, ruthless, and vul-
nerable to blackmail. They also happen to believe they are going to
die for what they did during the war—which will be a help to us.
During the interviews, you should talk about their crimes and
heighten their fears. Then, quickly, offer them a way out. They
shouldn't be difficult to manage. In fact, I suspect they shall be
willing to do anything we ask."

Gordov stood and looked out of the window at a row of wooden
prisoner huts covered with tar paper. "I understand the logic, but
using SS men still turns my stomach."

Sorokin handed the folder he had been holding to Gordov. "By
using men like these, we will ensure that Germany will never
again become our enemy, as she has twice in your lifetime. You
mentioned your sons. Here is the insurance that your children
will never hear the sound of German tanks upon the soil of our
Motherland."

Gordov tentatively took the file, as if he were touching something repulsive. He sat down, opened the cover and looked directly
into the smiling face of an SS captain in full uniform. The large,

glossy black-and-white photograph was obviously taken during the war. He scanned the first few pages.

> Captain Horst Volker. Present age, 26. Prussian, comes from a military family. Volker had ∴ typical youth and schooling, except that his father sent him to England for his mid-level studies. Completed only two years before the invasion of Czechoslovakia. He returned to Germany and attended the University in Dresden, and in 1942 was recruited into the SD and assigned to the counter British intelligence desk. Attended all the right military schools, including the special SS officers' training course from which he graduated at the top of his class. Served six months with the Waffen SS in Italy and was then returned to the SD, but this time in internal security. Responsible for the elimination of those who tried to assassinate Hitler in 1944, and ordered the killing of over 200 officers, enlisted men, and politically undesirable civilians. During the final months, Volker was assigned as company commander of a collection company whose duty it was to arrest, try, and execute deserters. He seemed to be particularly adept at all of his duties, for he received many decorations. He was captured after the fall of Berlin.

Gordov shook his head with a disturbed frown. "What kind of man kills front-line soldiers?"

"We shall see," Sorokin said.

Captain Horst Volker was not at all what they had expected. Instead of a broken man with downcast eyes, the tall, dark-haired prisoner came into the office with an air of arrogance. Instead of avoiding the stares of the two officers, his blue eyes bore holes through the colonel. "I am Volker," he snapped. "What is it you want with me?"

The colonel's face reddened. "*Sit down, Nazi!* I will ask the questions!"

Volker sat, but took his time about it.

"You are here because you are a criminal," Gordov said. "We are deciding your fate, so truthfully answer the questions I am about to ask."

Volker's eyes shifted to the file in front of the colonel, then back to the colonel. "It appears you already have all the information you need to make your decision. Make it, and quit wasting your time and mine."

The colonel smiled to himself as he spoke. "So you are not a criminal."

"No, I was a soldier," Volker said flatly.

"And you never killed retreating German soldiers?"

"No. I executed deserters."

"You do not believe that killing your own men was a crime?" the colonel asked, a little too loudly.

Sorokin tried to get the colonel's attention to calm him down.

Volker looked at the colonel as if he had asked a ludicrous question. "Of course it was not a crime. I followed orders."

The colonel softened his tone. "Do you ever feel guilt about it?"

"No."

"Why?"

"There is nothing to 'feel.' It is done. The deserters are dead. Now I am going to die. What is there to 'feel'?"

The colonel took out his packet of cigarettes and offered one to Volker. Volker refused. The colonel lit his own cigarette and glanced at the file.

"So you have no guilt, you have done nothing wrong, yet you believe you are going to die. Why is that?"

"I will die because someone, perhaps you, orders it. You are a soldier doing what your leaders deem necessary for your country. That is not criminal, it is honorable."

The colonel's eyes narrowed. "Are you saying what you did was honorable?"

Volker met the colonel's glare with matching intensity. "Yes."

The colonel leaped from his chair. "*You dare to call your murdering crimes honorable! You have no honor. You dirty the very word, you fanatical bastard.*"

Volker said nothing, but his eyes twinkled in victory. Sorokin had seen enough. It was time to give Gordov an opportunity to compose himself. Sorokin stood and opened the office window to distract Gordov's attention. The ploy worked. The colonel shifted his angry gaze away from Volker to his fellow officer.

Sorokin tapped his chest, signaling he would take over the questioning. The colonel didn't want to let go, but knew he must. He had violated the first rule of interrogation. Remain in control.

Colonel Gordov returned to his seat, and Captain Sorokin sat down a few feet from Volker and looked deep into his cold, blue eyes. "Captain Volker, do you know why we are here?"

"You are looking for an excuse to hang former SS officers. If you expect a signed confession from me, you will not get it."

"I see. If it makes any difference, I can assure you that we are not here looking for someone to hang. In fact, our purpose is quite the opposite."

Sorokin bent down, picked up a binder from the floor, and lifted it to his lap. He thumbed through the pages to Volker's name and scanned it to see if any of the information in the file could be useful. "Captain Volker, have you had any contact with relations in Germany since your internment?"

Volker sat immobile. "No. Your government seems to have forgotten that it too signed the agreements of the Geneva Convention."

Sorokin raised an eyebrow. "Did you know, Captain Volker, that your wife is alive?"

For the first time, Volker blinked. He began to speak, but closed his mouth, blinked again, and finally managed a whisper. "You . . . you're lying."

Sorokin smiled sincerely. "No, I'm not lying, and I am truly glad that I can bring the good news to you. Your wife, Dagmar, is living in Dresden with her mother. I'm afraid I can't tell you anything else now, for my records are incomplete, but I will find out more if you would like."

Volker sat motionless for a full ten seconds before nodding. "Thank you. Yes, I would like to know more."

The Colonel smiled inwardly. The bastard was human after all.

Sorokin avoided eye contact by looking through the file again. He did not want Volker to see the victorious twinkle he knew was in his own eyes. He turned a page. "The reports from your superiors are all quite laudatory. You are described as extremely intelligent and totally dedicated. You were particularly adept at internal security management and affairs. One of your superiors stated that you were discreet, totally reliable, and that you always completed your assignments without question. Is that true?"

Volker put his mask of coldness back on. "I believed in following the orders of my superiors, yes."

Sorokin looked again at the file. "Did you know your father and mother were killed by American bombs?"

"Yes," Volker answered flatly. "I knew they'd been killed in the firebombing of Dresden."

Sorokin nodded reflectively. "I lost my parents and my wife in the war." He looked up at Volker, speaking softly. "The war is over for us, but you and I will carry the unseen scars forever. I think maybe it's time you began living again. Your country needs you. There are elements there that are trying to cause unrest, to open old wounds caused by the war and to make them bleed again. We could use a man with your experience to help control the problem."

Volker remained motionless. He slowly shifted his gaze to the colonel. "You would permit this?"

Colonel Gordov would not look at the prisoner. He spoke while looking at his hands. "You are excused."

Volker stood and faced Sorokin. "I accept living . . . but your colonel wants my death. I accept death as well. I ask that you not inform my wife that I survived the war only to die here. She has always been fragile." He came to attention, bowing slightly to the colonel, and gave a last look at Sorokin before executing an about-face and marching out of the office.

The colonel waited until the door closed before glaring at Sorokin. "I will never initial by his name. He has no honor, no feelings, and most of all, no conscience."

Sorokin stood and walked to the window. "Colonel, we are at war again—not a war like the last one, where you led a battalion in battle, but a war nevertheless. The Americans and British have bribed the masses in their zones of occupation in Germany with money and promises of rebuilding their factories. They now try to export their capitalistic propaganda to those under our protection. They are ruthless in their attempts to undermine the government we have installed, with their constant gibberish of democracy and rights of self-determination. We must counter this threat by tightening the controls and finding those who instigate trouble and talk of rebellion. In my last assignment in Berlin, the Allies caused unrest among the people by propaganda campaigns that called for freedoms typical of a capitalistic takeover. We have need of men like Volker. With the proper training, he could be invaluable to our goals of stabilizing the situation."

The colonel stared at Sorokin as if seeing him for the first time. " 'Our goals of stabilizing.' Did I hear a slip from the captain from the Foreign Affairs Ministry or the captain who is a plant and really works for Beria? I am not a fool, Sorokin. I know what 'tightening controls' means! I am a citizen of the Socialist Republic, remember? My brother's son was a victim of 'tightening controls,' and my neighbors' son and my friend's niece!"

Sorokin glared back at the red-faced colonel. "We won the war, Colonel, but will lose what we have gained with our countrymen's blood unless actions are taken immediately to let Germans govern and control their own people. Our policies of stripping the factories and taking the resources for compensation have caused unrest. The German people are recovering from the devastation only to find no future and no hope. Our government sees its errors in the handling of the German problem and has plans to recover, but we need experienced men such as Volker. Yes, there is a plan that calls for tightening of controls, but it must be done by Germans, not Soviet soldiers."

The colonel shook his head, knowing he was arguing with a fanatic of the worst kind. Sorokin, like Volker, honestly believed he was right. The captain's true purpose was not putting SS men in governmental positions; instead he wanted them to form a nucleus of a new secret police organization that would mirror and take orders from the NKVD.

The colonel slowly shook his head. "Don't you realize what you're doing?"

Sorokin straightened his back and held up his chin. "Yes, I am preserving the Soviet Union."

Gordov sat silent for several seconds before pushing back his chair and standing. He looked at the young officer with pity. "You win, Sorokin. There is no further use for me here. I will state in my report to the General Secretary that all the Nazis were selected. *But* I will also recommend to him that Volker be sent to Berlin where his kind is needed . . . and that you should go with him. You two *deserve* each other! I would not want *you* in my homeland."

The veteran turned, picked up his coat and hat, and walked out of the office, leaving the smiling captain.

CHAPTER 3

19 June

Captain Jorn Furman lay delirious with fever in the stalag sick bay of the Tomsk Prisoner of War Camp in Siberia. Lieutenant Hans Dieter leaned over him, patting his sweat-beaded brow with a stinking rag.

"Sir, can you hear me?" Dieter asked, leaning closer and praying for a response.

"He can't hear you, son," the doctor said as he came over to the slat bed. He was an old doctor who had been captured in Berlin trying to take care of boys wounded while defending the Reichstag.

"Is there nothing you can do for him?" Dieter asked pleadingly.

The old man shook his head. "I did all I could with what we have. He's lucky to have lived this long. What happened to cause such massive injuries?"

Dieter lowered his head. "Captain Furman was in charge of off-loading logs from the railway cars. There was an accident. A ramp was jammed with a stray log. Someone didn't notice it and released an entire load. . . ."

The doctor nodded. He had heard the same story many times. The prisoners were fed so poorly and worked so hard that critical mistakes were made every day.

"Four men were crushed to death," Dieter added, "and three others were hurt badly. It took twenty men to remove the logs from Captain Furman's legs."

The doctor stepped closer to inspect the bandages where he had amputated Furman's lower legs. "They're draining nicely—but without pain reliever, his chances are very slim." He sighed and looked down the row of forty beds all filled with emaciated men whose prognoses were no better. In the past week twelve had died. He knew that in the winter months the numbers would go up to over thirty a week.

He turned to the bearded lieutenant. "Go on before the guards see you. I'll do all I can."

Dieter leaned over the bed and patted Jorn's forehead. "I'll be back, sir."

The doctor watched the young officer walk away and glanced back at his patient. "You're lucky, my friend . . . most in here have no one to grieve at their passing." The doctor checked the bandages one more time and moved down the row to check others.

One kilometer away a thin, bespectacled Soviet captain and a tall, dark-haired German wearing a black suit walked into the Soviet prison camp commander's office. The captain gave a packet of instructions to the commander and sat down to let the officer read the orders for himself. Five minutes later the commander handed the packet back. "Be back tomorrow morning for roll call and I will assemble those you requested," he said.

An hour later an orderly walked into the doctor's small office and handed the old man a piece of paper.

The doctor read the few scribbled lines and looked up. "What is this all about?"

The orderly shrugged. "I don't know. The camp commander wants all the patients who last served in paratrooper units moved to Ward One for some kind of screening. It is very unusual, ja?"

The doctor leaned back in his chair and rubbed his temples. "Ja, quite. The Russian bastards are obviously interested in our parachutists. This worries me. Have you checked to see how many we have?"

The orderly raised an eyebrow. "Of course. We have twelve not so bad, and two who are dying," the orderly said nonchalantly.

The doctor walked to the door and looked down the ward aisle. It took him only a moment to make up his mind. "The only way the Russians will know if they belonged to para units is by checking their camp identity cards. Move only cases who cannot speak to Ward One, and replace their identity cards with those of our paratrooper patients. The stupid Russians will never know the difference. I will not be a part of some kind of unit purge."

The orderly didn't argue, for the terminal cases were mere skeletons and would be much easier to move, but he had one question. "Herr Doktor, what about the double amputee you operated on this morning? Are you putting him on the terminal list?"

The old man thought about the young lieutenant who seemed to be the amputee's friend and shook his head as he walked back into his office. "Nein, we will give him another day or so. He deserves at least a chance to see if he is strong enough to survive."

20 June

Captain Georgi Sorokin thanked the camp commander for his cooperation and strode to an awaiting staff car to join Volker. Minutes later the black sedan rolled out of the camp gate followed by a small truck. Five miles down the road both vehicles rolled to a stop.

Sorokin cringed at the shot from Volker's pistol and turned just as the body of the paratrooper crumpled to the ground. He pointed at the two prisoners still in the truck. "Bury the corpse over there, just off the road." He handed the driver a pack of cigarettes. "Thank you, comrade. When the Germans are finished burying this convicted thief, return to the camp."

Minutes later the staff car was again rolling down the dirt road, leaving a cloud of red dust. Sorokin leaned back in the seat, relieved that the search was finally over. Volker had insisted on finding the survivors of a particular unit before he would start training in Moscow. He'd said it was a "matter of honor." He had explained he'd successfully completed every assigned mission for his Fatherland and wanted to clear his conscience by eliminating a few cowards who had eluded him.

Sorokin glanced at the passenger beside him. "That was the last camp. I've fulfilled my promise to you. Those you wanted eliminated have been found. Today you will be listed as dying of sickness in the camp. Your past in the SS and SD dies with you."

Volker stared straight ahead. "No, there are others. There were eleven men who crossed the bridge two years ago. I took care of their colonel and a captain that day, and we found four in your camps. That leaves five who have not been accounted for."

Sorokin shrugged. "Maybe so, but you must forget them. They are not important and can say nothing that will affect you or the project. You should not worry about five cowards, but instead concern yourself with those who knew of your activities when you were with the SD."

"I was not a fool!" Volker snapped. "I made sure there were no loose ends. I have nothing to worry about from my past, but I must finish what I should have done two years ago. Every night I see those cowards in my dreams. I must find them and their loathsome stares."

Sorokin sighed and shook his head. "You will *have* to forget them. There is no time to try and find ghosts, and it would be impossible to try and find them anyway. Germany is divided and in shambles. Nothing is like it was. Think of the future. We have erased your past and will be giving you a new identity and history, and once you've completed the training in Moscow you will be on your way to Berlin to work in the Ministry of the Interior to begin our project. The name change is necessary to save resentment from those in your government who served in concentration camps. All former SS, including those in the West, have changed their names. It is very simple. Thousands have lost or thrown away their identity papers and merely assumed new names so as not to be prosecuted. It is impossible to check, for most of the records were destroyed in the war. You will be no different, except we will give you all the documentation you will need to become another man. When your wife asks why the name change is necessary, tell her the truth. Your new duties within the government are so sensitive it requires complete secrecy to include the changing of your names. I'm sure someone will recognize you eventually and turn you in, but such a report will be seen by us and we'll take care of it. Think of me as a guardian angel who will always be there to look out for your welfare."

Volker looked at the Soviet officer with a cutting stare. "My 'guardian angel' will be ensuring his 'project' is being carried out. I am not a fool, Herr Hauptmann. I know why you will be protecting me. The survival of your nation will always come first, and so will your project."

Sorokin raised an eyebrow. "Yes, Herr Volker, I will be ensuring the survival of my country, but remember, you will be placed in a position to ensure the survival of yours. Our goals are the same, making our relationship a perfect marriage. Your country needs you. Forget the past, for it is over. Think of your future and your country's needs."

Volker nodded in silence, understanding perfectly how the communists would control him and his people, but for now it didn't matter. It was the price of defeat, he told himself. An honorable soldier understood loss and had to be patient.

• • •

Jorn Furman was shaken awake and looked up into the face of the doctor. The old physician bent closer to his patient and spoke in a whisper so as not to be overheard. "A fellow prisoner told me minutes ago your friend, Leutnant Dieter, was executed. The prisoner who talked to me was Dieter's guard. Dieter asked him to warn you 'the Butcher lives.' "

Furman's glazed eyes came into focus. The throbbing pain in his upper legs was pushed aside as he concentrated on forming his words. "The Butcher is alive?"

The doctor whispered, "Ja, he was tall and carried himself like an aristocrat. He and a Russian captain had all the prisoners who served in paratroop units assembled. The tall one read your friend's identity card and saw he had been in your old unit. He had him placed in a truck and later executed him."

Tears of rage and pain formed in the corners of Furman's eyes.

The old man patted Furman's arm. "The fever has broken, my friend. You have a chance, but the pain will become much worse in the next few days. Wanting to live will be your only medicine, for we have nothing to give you. You'll not have to worry about the tall one returning for you, even if he knew your name. I placed it on the list of men who died this week. If you recover, you can keep your old ID card. The Russians have no way to cross-check your identity."

The doctor turned and walked toward the ward door knowing he could do nothing else for the patient. There were too many others who needed him. When he had first awakened Furman, he had thought his effort was wasted. The man had the gray pallor of death. Now he wasn't so sure. The patient's color had returned and his eyes seemed to burn with fiery determination. Perhaps it would be enough. Perhaps.

Stuttgart, West Germany

A convoy of olive-drab U.S. Army trucks pulled away from the train station, leaving behind former prisoners of war. All the former soldiers of the Reich were identically dressed from the waist down with U.S. Army scuffed boots and dirty fatigue pants. Above the waist they all wore different ragged, colored sweaters and an assortment of coats and hats. Each carried a bundle formed from a fatigue shirt that was filled with all their earthly possessions: U.S. issue toothbrush, a razor, one bar of soap, a half towel, and whatever clothes and letters had been sent by relatives while in the prison camp. In their hands were a fifty-mark bill and a train pass that guaranteed a one-way trip to anywhere in the Allied zone of occupation.

The group of men quickly made their way into the station, except one. Axel Mader stood watching the trucks until they disappeared before he turned and walked up the steps toward the station doors.

He was almost to the last step when he came to an abrupt halt, realizing he was all alone. Mein Gott, I'm free! he yelled in joy to himself. After serving two years in the paratroopers during the war and two years in the American prisoner of war camp, he was finally on his own. For the first time in four years he had no responsibilities other than to himself. No more superior's orders, formations, duties, subordinates to care for, and no schedule for tomorrow. Four years . . . and all he had to show for all those wasted years were a fifty-mark note, scars on his chest, and a sweater his mother had knitted for him. The dream of the thousand-year Reich was gone, replaced with a devastated country with three and a half million dead kameraden and over three million German mothers, wives, daughters, children, and old men who had perished for Adolf Hitler's dream.

Tears welled up in the ex-prisoner's eyes as he took in a deep breath of freedom and felt the familiar pain deep in his chest. The pain from his old wound was the reminder of the other countless dead from other countries the Reich had been responsible for. So many lives . . . so much pain his country had caused, and for what?

Axel Mader lowered his head, hating what he had done in the name of the Reich, but hating his leaders more for lying and leading his beloved country to destruction and the loathing scorn of the world. The Americans had showed films in the camp of what the SS had done to the Jews and others. He had watched, not believing his people were capable of such horrors, but knew in his heart it was true. If men like Horst Volker had been allowed to kill his men, then others had surely been allowed to kill millions of Jews and others they considered subhumans.

Feeling filthy, Mader forced the films of the death camps out of his mind. The pain in his chest was deserved, and he accepted it for what others had done to countless foreigners and his countrymen. The pain was also a reminder that he had known death. Life, no matter in what form, was better than the black, cold death he had experienced. He had died for a while close to the banks of the Alte Oder River two years before. He remembered choking on his own blood, fighting for a breath to keep alive long enough to kill the blue-eyed murderer, Horst Volker; but he had failed, like his country, and slowly slipped into a cold, black void where there was no sound and no pain. He had dreamed of sunlight and smiles, only to awaken to screams. He had finally come to in the back of an open truck filled with screaming wounded. His friend and fellow company commander, Lars Kailer, had been walking alongside the truck and had cried, seeing him conscious. Lars and two other Iron Men had carried him back to a field hospital that was being pulled back to the west of Berlin. His friends had been ordered to go with the convoy as guards instead of joining units that were going to try and counterattack the Soviets who had surrounded Berlin. Axel remembered the tears of his friend and then the horror. A Russian Yak-3 fighter had dived out of clouds and roared over, strafing the convoy and dropping a single bomb. It was the last thing he remembered until he regained consciousness two days later among hundreds of wounded men lying in a muddy field. Lars and the others were gone and he had been alone without friends, thinking he was going to die, when an American half-track had clanked into the field. The first American words he had heard had come from a young officer who had gotten out of the cab and shook his head looking at the pathetic, mud-covered men. "Jee-sus H. Christ! Sergeant! Call the ol' man and tell him we need medical support up here ASAP!"

Axel turned back toward the train station doors. It was over, the war, suffering, pain, and waiting were only memories to be forgotten forever. Through the doors was the start of a new life; all he had to do was walk through the portal and forget the past. His hopes and dreams of a future were only a few steps away.

Axel bid his past farewell by wiping the tears from his eyes, and strode through the open door.

It was not over. It was just beginning. Axel Mader returned home to find his father had died of sickness only a few days before. His frail mother was so tired from working in the fields, she could not stay awake at the dinner table. There was one loaf of stale bread and a few turnips to eat, and no hay for the two skin-covered skeleton milk cows that provided her only income. Two years before, the small village where he had lived had been devastated by an American armored company when a small detachment from the SS had been left behind to fight to the death. The town looked as if the battle had occurred two months before rather than two years. Destruction, despair, and hunger were all that seemed left. His mother and the other survivors of the village were living in squalor, trying to stay alive by scavenging. The day after arriving home, Axel walked two miles to a small U.S. Army post and asked to see the commander.

The captain listened to the problems of the village and shrugged his shoulders. "I can't do much as far as giving out food because our food is rationed . . . but maybe we could work out a deal if you could organize some laborers for us. We're building additional barracks and need people who are willing to work."

The next day Axel stood outside the gate of the post with twenty men and women he had convinced to come with him from the village. The captain was good for his word and put the entire force to work that morning. Within days the village had forty people employed on the post doing everything from building new barracks to washing and pressing the commander's uniforms.

A week later Axel was promoted to supervisor of the post engineer's civilian work force. One morning the engineer captain stood watching the building of a new wing on the headquarters building and motioned to the skeleton of wood. "Axel, let me tell you a secret. That's the future. Germany needs rebuilding, and any man who knows how to build will have a job. Your country needs men who can plan, design, and build."

Axel shrugged. "I am not schooled in such things."

The captain clasped the young man's shoulder. "Axel, you may not be a builder, but you're one heck of a supervisor. You're a natural leader, and with some basic knowledge of building construction you could start your own company."

Axel glanced at the partially constructed office, then at the officer. "Will you teach me?"

The captain thought a moment and shrugged. "Hell, why not. Come on, let's go to the office and I'll give you a few books that'll explain the basics."

That evening Axel left the post with the other laborers for the two-mile walk back to the village. A young woman strolled up beside him and motioned to the books he was carrying. "Herr Mader, do you try and impress us by reading the Ami books?"

Axel blushed. He had noticed the girl the first day he had arrived in the village but had avoided her at every opportunity. The young girl had lived in Berlin but had been sent to her aunt and uncle in the village during the last days of the war for her safety. Sadly, her parents in Berlin had died during the Russian assault on the city, and now she had no other place to go.

He had faced enemy tanks and killed men at close range, but

being close to an attractive young woman turned his insides to mush. He had wanted to speak to her several times but words seemed to stick in his mouth, and his brain had become incapable of thinking. He had found the best way to deal with Gisela Joyner was to avoid her.

Gisela's eyes narrowed at the young man's silence and she grabbed the ex-captain's arm. "Nay! I will not let you get away with your arrogance. I know what you have done for us, but it is no excuse to treat me like a stone. I am talking to you, Herr 'great Captain,' and only ask a word in kind."

Axel was taken aback at her wrath but couldn't help but smile. Her anger did not become her beautiful face and made her attempt comical.

Gisela saw his expression and drew her hand back to slap him. Axel stepped back out of range and spoke softly. "You are beautiful when you're angry. And yes, I was trying to impress you."

Gisela lowered her arm and turned in a huff. She walked four paces before realizing she was marching in the wrong direction. She spun around and saw him waiting on her with the crooked smile. "You are a swine, Herr Mader," she barked indignantly.

Axel agreed with a slight bowing of his head. "Ja, but a lonely swine. Perhaps you would walk with me and we could talk during the walk home."

Gisela flung her head back. "Perhaps I will. But do not try and impress me, Herr great Captain. I do not impress easily."

Axel felt his heart melt seeing her head held high, proud and defiant. Her eyes were challenging him. He accepted the challenge feeling something he had never experienced before—he wanted to lose to this proud woman.

CHAPTER 4

1948

1 October

Major Jake Tallon of the U.S. Army Air Corps eased back on the throttle of big C-47 and spoke into his mike. "Give me thirty percent flaps."

The new copilot complied, but as he anxiously looked over the instruments, then out of the front window, he shook his head in disgust. "Goddamnit, Jake, this is fuckin' crazy. Why don't you just abort and try again tomorrow? We can't see a damn thing."

"Steady," Tallon said confidently. "Just a few more seconds and we'll bust out of these storm clouds and see the landing lights. Trust me, Buzz."

The copilot glanced over his shoulder at the navigator. "Is he always this crazy?"

The young navigator smiled. "Jake's the best. He knows this town. He bombed Berlin in 'forty-four."

The copilot strained to see the landing lights below. This is the last time I fly with vets, he told himself.

Jake eased back the throttle a touch more and nodded. "There it is, Tempelhof Airport."

The copilot began to breathe easier. "About time. Now let's just land this gooney, unload, and get our butts back to Bremerhaven. I got a waitin' piece of ass that has legs you wouldn't believe."

The navigator leaned over and patted Jake's shoulder. "Jake is the one who's gotta get back. His wife is about to have a baby. Right Jake?"

The broad-shouldered pilot smiled.

The plane taxied halfway around the huge field before rolling to a stop. The crew quickly unstrapped their harnesses and hurried to prepare the plane for unloading. Layover and turnaround were timed to seconds, and a crew that was too slow would get a royal ass-chewing from the airfield commander, not to mention a razzing from the other transport crews during the postoperations brief.

The airfield, nestled near the city's center, had made major changes since June, when the operation known as "Vittles" began. Berlin, like the rest of Germany, had been separated into military zones of occupation following the war. The old capital city was 130 miles inside the Soviet zone, virtually an island surrounded by the occupying Soviet armies. Berlin had been dependent for its survival on necessities brought in by rail and road transportation, but in June the Russians had blockaded all land-access routes into the city. The Soviets believed that the Berliners, faced with starvation, would force the Allies out of their zones of occupation. But the Russians had seriously underestimated the resolve of the Americans, British, and Berliners. Operation Vittles, which had begun with a few aircraft, had soon turned into the largest airlift in history. Everything from coal to milk was airlifted in by planes, which landed every three minutes. Tempelhof became the busiest airport in the world. The operation on the ground, which included refueling, unloading, and distribution, was just as massive and continued twenty-four hours a day.

With sleet beating down all around, Jake Tallon relieved himself under the wing of the plane. Then, as the last truck was about to pull away from the cargo door, he strode purposefully toward the plane's nose. Painted on the side of the fuselage was a smiling, half nude woman. The red and yellow letters painted over the figure spelled *Babe's Express*. Beneath the woman's bare legs were the words *Give me a call for a haul.* Tallon gave her a wink.

The copilot, sitting in the cockpit, motioned toward the window. "Why the hell does he always do that before we take off?"

The navigator grinned. "She used to ride on the nose of his B-17 during the war. It's for luck. He's telling the ol' gal he loves her. *Babe* has brought him through some pretty hairy shit. Remember, this is Jake's and my forty-third trip. We need all the luck we can get."

The copilot shrugged. "You guys are all fuckin' crazy if you ask me."

"Crank this sweet thang and let's get home! I have a date ta see my lady," Jake blurted as he came into the cabin.

The navigator gave his pilot the traditional half stick of gum and his headphones. "She had any labor pains yet, Jake?"

"Yeah, just before I left, but she wouldn't dare have our kid without me. We have a deal," Jake said with a wink as he slid into his seat. He leaned forward and patted the throttle affectionately. "Come on, *Babe*, one more time, ol' gal. Get ol' Jake home to Linda."

The copilot shook his head and mumbled under his breath. "Now he's talkin' to her. Shit."

Major Georgi Sorokin glanced up at the sound of a plane flying low somewhere in the dark clouds above. He shook his head in wonder at the Allied pilots. Flying in such weather was pure stupidity.

The ice-covered, rubble-strewn street called Karl-Marx-Allee was quiet, but he glanced in both directions before stepping into the little flower shop, pockmarked with bullet holes, that served as a safe house. The only employee, an old lady, glanced up, then immediately dropped her gaze from the thin, bespectacled customer in the ill-fitting raincoat. She padded toward the door and placed the Closed sign in the window. He immediately pulled back the soiled curtain that led to a storage room in the back. The room smelled of fresh plants.

Horst Volker appeared out of the back office and faced the man he thought of as his guardian angel. "What excuse are you going to give me this time?"

"I just returned from Moscow, where I briefed Minister Beria on the situation," Sorokin replied with irritation.

Volker arched an eyebrow. "Are we starting the project or not?"

Sorokin motioned to the small office behind the storage room and shut the door when both men were inside. He sat behind the desk and looked up at Volker, who remained standing. "I haven't seen you in a month. Please give me an update on your organization."

Volker snickered. "Why? Your leaders here in Berlin are so afraid of our starting a secret police that they will never use us."

Sorokin smiled patiently. "Things have changed. The update, please."

Volker discerned excitement in his mentor's eyes. Maybe something *had* changed. He took a seat and decided to cooperate. "Recruitment is finished. I have used the four SS officers whom you provided to me from Camp Viper as my section chiefs. We have modeled our organization on the Reich Security Main Office, but with five instead of six sections: Administration and Personnel; Equipment and Finance; Internal Security; Intelligence and Research; and finally, my Maintenance unit."

" 'Maintenance' unit?" Sorokin asked, wrinkling his brow.

Volker nodded. "Its function is to 'clean up' loose ends whenever necessary. It is located in another part of the city for reasons of security."

Sorokin allowed himself a small, ironic smile. "I assume you also gave your department an appropriate name?" he said.

Volker maintained his indifferent expression. "We are called the S Department. S for 'Special.' Now, tell me, are your leaders going to put my Special Department to work?"

Sorokin leaned back in his chair, avoiding Volker's searching look. "There are still a few problems that have not been resolved."

Volker threw up his hands and stood again. "Your leaders are bungling fools. They have started this so-called cold war, but they are doing all they can to lose it. First the Allies form the Federal Republic of Germany from their zones of occupation, and what do your leaders do? Nothing. Then the Allies rebuild to give hope to Germans in the West, and how do your leaders respond? They demand still more reparations and take coal and food from our freezing, starving people. The Allies in Berlin gave their people new currency so that they could *buy* necessities instead of trading cigarettes for them. What do your leaders then do? They cut off the city from the outside world and try to starve the people into submission. *Yes*, you have problems. You have idiots who don't know the German people in charge of your German policy."

Sorokin secretly enjoyed the lecture, as he had made almost exactly the same statements to his superiors in Moscow. "Since you are being so candid, may I conclude that you don't think much of our military's promise to Stalin to have the Allies out of the city by summer?"

Volker shook his head in frustration. "Your military leaders in Berlin are the biggest fools of all. They have already lost the western sectors. The airlift that they said would be impossible is working. The Allies are feeding the people and providing coal for their stoves. While your military uses Soviet action squads to intimidate and beat up politicians both in this and the Allied sectors, the West Berliners are laughing at you."

Sorokin leaned forward. "And what would you do?"

Volker looked at his mentor as if he had lost his mind. "I have said since my arrival that we need to consolidate our efforts in the

Soviet sector, form a new state, and get on with building a new Germany."

Sorokin smiled for the first time. "That is why I called for this meeting, my friend. After talking to my superiors in Moscow, it is clear that my government realizes it has made some mistakes. So you will have your new Germany. We even have a name for it: the German Democratic Republic. My government agrees that the military's attempts at coercion have been less than professional. So now those responsibilities will fall to you. You are to begin operations on our project immediately."

Volker sat down, searching Sorokin's face. "Your military will really allow Germans to begin tightening control over themselves?"

Sorokin raised an eyebrow behind his thick glasses. "They have no choice."

Volker eyed the thin Russian, not hiding his distrust. "But you say there are still problems?"

Sorokin's smiled dissolved. "General Wilhelm Zasser is trying to consolidate his power as Minister of the Interior. Your department will come under his control, but I will be your department's advisor. All of his orders will first go through me."

Volker let out an inward sigh of relief. "Then there is no problem. We know what must be done. You said yourself a year ago that we formed a perfect marriage of goals."

Sorokin sighed. "Yes, but he is still a problem. I am speaking now as your guardian angel. Don't trust him, and keep your distance. Don't tell him anything of importance unless you clear it through me. He must not know the workings of your department, and neither can any of the rest of your government officials. Your survival and that of the department is built on never allowing anyone to know your true activities. Knowing you exist is enough to worry them, and fear is your best defense."

Volker smiled again. "I am ahead of you. One of my informers is General Zasser's personal secretary. It seems she is a lonely widow and has found a young lover who is a university student and happens to be one of my security section's agents. I might not have followed your model of forming an organization, but I did learn the use of infiltration."

Sorokin laughed as he took out a folded piece of paper from his inside coat pocket. "We are a good team, Horst. This is the list of the four men I spoke to you about before I left. They are your first assignments. They must simply disappear. These targets are the first step in eliminating the troublemakers that could cause us problems in consolidating gains in our sector."

Volker took the paper and looked at the four names before refolding the note and putting it in his jacket pocket. "We have been planning their elimination for weeks, just for practice, awaiting approval. My maintenance section will take care of them within two days."

Sorokin stood and held out his hand. "Take care, Horst. We need you and your support to accomplish our common goals."

Volker grasped the major's hand. "You are forgetting my new name."

Sorokin smiled. "Yes, I'm sorry, Herr 'Wolf.' I was particularly proud of your new name since I picked it myself. Hagan Wolf has a nice ring. I hope Frau Wolf is doing well?"

Hagan Wolf dipped his chin. "Yes, Dagmar is doing well, thank you. Take care, my guardian angel. We Germans cannot afford to lose a voice of reason among your bungling bureaucrats. You and I will shape our country's future. We are Germany's hope."

Sorokin, seeing the resolve in Volker's ice-blue eyes, felt a chill run up his spine. He nodded in silence and turned around, opening the office door. Pushing back the curtain, he strode toward the door knowing he had given the death warrants of four men who had a large following. Their elimination would help, but what was most important was that his superior had approved the project of forming the new department within the Ministry of the Interior. It was what he, Georgi Sorokin, had been pushing all along. Now, with Volker having more power, it would be Germans tightening the controls and doing what was necessary.

Sorokin stepped out into the sleet and couldn't help but smile. He knew it was the beginning of what he had hoped for.

Out of the corner of his eye Jake Tallon saw the Russian fighter emerge from the clouds. He slammed the yoke forward to avoid a midair collision but the other plane, traveling at over three hundred miles per hour, had no time to avoid the C-47 that had suddenly appeared. The Russian fighter pilot's reactions saved him thirty seconds of life. By jerking the stick back, he lifted the Yak's nose enough to avoid plowing into the transport, but it still wasn't enough. The fighter's propeller chewed into the thin metal of the C-47 just behind the crew's cabin before shattering and sending the hapless fighter into a death spiral.

Jake had all of one second to react before the propeller tore into his bird. The sudden impact and horrific metallic screeching sounded as if a locomotive had run over the top of his plane. For an instant he thought he was dead. Then the sound vanished, leaving behind a howling echo. Jake realized it was no echo a split second later when the damp wind struck his face. He turned and saw gray sky through a gaping hole in twisted, blowing metal. The severed lower torso of the navigator lay in a pool of blood and hydraulic fluid; the rest of him had splattered against the far cabin wall.

The copilot, unhurt but stunned, screamed as he grabbed for the controls. *"Get us down, goddamnit!"*

Jake snapped his head back to the front and pulled the yoke back, trying to regain altitude. He yelled over the tearing sound of aluminum. *"We're still over the city. Got to keep her up till we're clear!"*

The copilot understood and released the controls. They could have landed on one of Berlin's wide boulevards, but anybody who was on the street would die. When the copilot turned to check the damage, he gasped in horror. Sparks from the severed wiring had caused a fire in the dead navigator's compartment, and the winds were fanning the flames like a giant furnace stoker.

"Fire!" he screamed, and tugged to free his seat-belt harness.

Jake held the stiff yoke in both hands, trying to keep the nose up. The copilot grabbed Jake's arm. *"We gotta jump! Abandon her, we're burning!"*

Jake shook his head and kept his grip on the shaking yoke. He knew that his plane would be a firebomb if it crashed with full fuel tanks into the suburbs of the city. "Come on, *Babe*, just a little farther. You can do it for ol' Jake."

The copilot yelled out for Jake to follow him before ducking down and dashing past the flames into the cargo bay. He slid back the door and hesitated before jumping, to see if Jake was behind him. He wasn't. Goddamnit! *Goddamnit! Where are you, Jake?* With heat searing the side of his face, he leaped out and pulled the ripcord. The chute opened seconds later. Under a full blossom of silk, he turned in the harness to see the burning plane slowly losing altitude. "Come on Jake, jump. *Jump goddamnit!"* He knew what Jake was trying to do—there was farmland just beyond the city— but even if Jake made it, it would be too late for him to get out. *"Jump, you stupid bastard. Jump!"*

Jake Tallon screamed in twisting agony as flames engulfed him and sucked the last breath from his burning body. *Babe's Express* crashed and exploded in a potato field just two hundred meters from the last houses of the Neukölln District of Berlin.

Brandenburg District, Soviet Sector, Berlin

Hagan Wolf, formerly Horst Volker, walked into the warehouse bay where the twenty-one men he had handpicked for his maintenance unit were seated and waiting. Two months before, he had screened the files and interviewed all those in the Ministry of the Interior's police force who had previously served in the Wehrmacht. Of the hundreds interviewed, he had found over thirty who had lied about their past and had actually served in the SS. It had been easy to determine, for he had each man strip to the waist. All former SS had their blood-group number tattooed under their left armpit. The best twenty men were recruited with the promise their pasts would never be revealed and that they would again be serving the Fatherland in a capacity where their previous skills would be used. Each man had been required to give an oath of loyalty, as they had in the SS training camp at Dachau, except this time it was not an oath of loyalty to Hitler, but rather to their leader, Hagan Wolf. They were also required to give a blood oath of secrecy about the existence of the organization known as the S Department.

Wolf halted in front of the seated maintenance soldiers and looked into their expectant faces. He grasped them with his hypnotic eyes and smiled. "We have been given permission to form the new department and carry out our first mission."

The men's faces immediately glowed, and they smiled and nodded to each other. Wolf raised his hand for their attention. "We have been training for weeks and we are ready. The four targets you have been watching are to be eliminated. Tomorrow night we will strike. Remember that the mission cannot be compromised by haste. Stay with the plan. No signs, no blood, no traces left behind. The waste disposal point is located as was briefed during the rehearsals. Are there any questions?" Knowing that there would be none, he turned to the young officer he had placed in charge of the special unit. "Captain Rink, please see me after you have issued the specific instructions."

The muscular blond officer came to attention and inclined his head. "Jawohl, Herr Wolf."

Ten minutes later Wolf sat regarding the twenty-one-year-old former Olympic shot putter and Hitler youth commander who had personally destroyed three Russian tanks in the closing days of the battle for Berlin. Max Rink was a big man, not in height, but in breadth, with his Herculean chest, shoulders, and arms that made him look almost like a Viking of old. He was saved from his brutish features by a boyishly handsome face that radiated a facade of innocence. He was far from innocent; behind the smiling brown eyes was a young man who had gone underground after the war and become a street killer of drunk or lost Russian soldiers. He was a werewolf, studying at the university during the day, but at night stalking the streets, seeking revenge for the rape of his mother and sisters by the Russians. All the men in the maintenance unit were older and more experienced, but none were as imposing or as intelligent. Rink had the traits Wolf needed in a leader, for his captain was street savvy, cunning, and had a gifted, mercurial mind that made him different from the others. He radiated confidence in himself and backed it up with action, not words. No one in the unit questioned the young man's authority for they knew he, Hagan Wolf, had trust in Max Rink as their leader.

Wolf furrowed his brow and spoke flatly. "You and I will supervise the disposal unit tomorrow night. If there should be any problems with any of the teams, I want your assurance the men know what they are to do."

Rink confidently leaned back in his chair. "They know what is expected. I have followed your instructions to the letter. I don't expect difficulties. The surveillance of the targets for the past weeks has made the mission easy, except for target number three. His wife will be accompanying him to the reception."

Wolf raised an eyebrow. "Does the team have a question about what is to be done with her?"

Rink smiled boyishly. "Nein, they understand their orders. The disposal unit has been informed and has made the necessary arrangements."

Wolf nodded. "Good. I can see you have been thinking." He rose and glanced at the map on the far wall, where the targets' homes were posted. "I will expect a few surprises, but nothing you have not thought of. Good night. I will see you tomorrow at the disposal point."

Rink stood and slapped his heels together as he dipped his chin. *"Guten Nacht, mein Führer."*

Linda Tallon smiled weakly as the nurse held out to her a baby wrapped in a light blue receiving blanket. "Mrs. Tallon, you've got yourself a seven-pound, eight-ounce, all-American, hungry boy. Congratulations."

"God, he's so beautiful," Linda Tallon said, tears in her eyes. "His daddy is going to be so proud."

The nurse laid the baby beside his mother. "You kept telling the doctor to wait. He said you were pretty darn upset about having your baby without your husband here."

Linda smiled as she touched her son's face. "We had a deal, but Jake will understand."

The nurse gave the adoring mother a grin. "What is his name? I have to make this official, you know, for the hospital's records."

Linda looked up at the white-uniformed nurse. "Daniel, after his father's granddad. Daniel Fitzgerald Tallon. God, it seems so long saying it."

The nurse smiled as the door behind her was pushed open. A stern-faced doctor, the chaplain, and the squadron commander came into the room.

Linda Tallon saw it in their faces the second they entered. She had been at the base for a year, and she knew why the chaplain and squadron commander would make such a late-night call, and it wasn't because of her new son. She steeled herself. "It's Jake, isn't it?

The squadron commander stepped forward, avoiding her wide, questioning eyes. "Linda, Jake's plane went down outside of Berlin. He didn't make it. I can't tell you how sorry I . . ."

Linda's eyes glazed over and she heard nothing else, even though the colonel's mouth was still moving. She was beyond hearing or feeling. Her thoughts turned to the smiling husband who had kissed her cheek just before he left early that morning. She remembered his last words: "I love ya, honey. Remember our deal. You promised."

The chaplain took her hand and spoke, but again she didn't hear. She was trying to remember every detail, the way he smelled and walked, that last gaze he had given her as he left, the lingering warmth of his lips on hers.

Linda Tallon's eyes suddenly focused and she grabbed the nurse's arm. She looked at the stunned woman and spoke with determination. "My son's name is Jake. Jake Tallon."

It was then Linda Tallon began crying.

2 October

Hagan Wolf stood by Havel Lake looking at the moon's reflection off the glistening water. Years ago he had stood in the same spot with his wife and had counted the many sailboats that had passed. He couldn't help but smile remembering that later that evening they had lain on a blanket and made love while listening to the sound of the gentle waves lapping on the shore. Hearing the approach of a vehicle, he broke from his reverie and turned around.

Captain Max Rink's large frame loomed out of the darkness as he walked up beside him and motioned to the path they were to follow. "All is prepared."

Wolf glanced one more time over his shoulder at the lake and made a promise to himself to bring his wife to their old spot. He wanted to see her smile and remember those good times with him.

The two men walked along the path to where the car he had heard had stopped beside a large boathouse. The team was dragging a gray-haired man from the backseat. Wolf and Rink ignored the activity and walked through the building's open side entrance. The inside of the boathouse was lit by a series of lanterns hanging from wooden rafters, the lanterns revealing a covered slip for a large motorboat. The pleasure boat was gone, replaced with a flat metal craft with a huge, exposed engine. Standing on the pier beside the strange flatboat were two of his maintenance men, who stood at attention.

Rink nodded and both men climbed down on the metal flatboat and lifted a hatch behind the engine. Rink motioned Wolf forward to see the arrangements for himself. "This was made specifically for our problem of disposal. As you can see, the wire-mesh fish hold is two meters by three meters, large enough for two large fish at a time. Just below the surface are two heavy-duty barge propellers driven by this diesel engine. Once the fish are in the hold and the propellers engaged, the complete disposal takes only a minute. The fish are reduced to pieces of only a few centimeters in size that will fall or drift through the wire-mesh cage. In experimenting with several animals, the drift time for some of the floating parts was several hours; however, no part could possibly be identified as either fish or animal."

"And clothing?" Wolf asked as he glanced at the powerful engine.

Rink frowned as if it were a personal oversight. "Yes, that is a problem. All clothing must be removed. Parts of clothing would float for a much longer period."

Wolf nodded and climbed back up onto the wooden pier where the two-man team waited, holding the chairman of the Christian Democratic party. The gray-haired old man was gagged and blindfolded.

Wolf turned and spoke disappointedly to Rink, who was climbing up to join him. "In the future we need the target incapacitated *before* coming here."

Rink shot an irritable glance to the team leader, who immediately grabbed the old man's head and violently twisted his neck until a loud pop was heard. The body fell to the wooden planks in a heap.

Wolf casually glanced at the body as he strode toward the door. "Prepare him."

A minute later Wolf stood on the pier looking down at the nude, white body of the chairman floating in the fish hold. Rink motioned for the metal cover to be closed and leaned closer. "The door must be secured because the force of the water once the propellers begin turning is quite intense."

Wolf did not respond as he watched one of the disposal-team men slide bolts into place, securing the hatch. Rink nodded to the second man, who turned a key on a box beside the engine, bringing the metal monster to life. The operator increased the power by pulling out a knob, increasing the engine's sound into a low roar. The operator glanced at Rink, who gave him a nod. He engaged the drive, and the pier immediately began to shake. The water in the slip beside the flatboat bubbled and turned white with froth. A loud thump came from something hitting the hatch cover, and the frothing water in the slip turned darker in the glow of the lanterns. Two more thumping sounds were heard over the monster's rumbling, then the engine's noise seemed to level out to a steady hum.

Wolf did not take his eyes from the slip as he watched the bubbling, churning water. Flecks of white and pink substance were all he'd been able to make out. He moved closer to Rink and spoke loudly to be heard over the rumbling engine. "And you say two fish can be disposed of at the same time?"

Rink nodded confidently. "Ja, easily. The propellers are recessed and are working in tandem. If one should become fouled, the system has an immediate shutoff. A second wire cage surrounds the housing so no debris is lost. We believe we have thought of all contingencies."

Wolf nodded, impressed as the engine was shut off and the silence again invaded the boathouse. The bolts were slid back and the hatch was lifted. The black water hold was empty except for a single one-centimeter length of sinew or muscle that floated like a thick piece of crushed noodle.

Wolf raised an eyebrow and looked at his captain. "It appears your system exceeds my requirements. You have outdone yourself, Max. Prepare the others immediately."

CHAPTER 5

1953

Düsseldorf

Gisela Mader held her daughter's hand as she walked to the construction site to find her husband. Axel Mader was looking at blueprints with the crew foreman when a worker nudged him and motioned toward the two approaching blondes. Axel folded the prints and patted the foreman's back. "Come back in thirty minutes and we'll talk about the south wing again."

He turned around just as his four-year-old daughter saw him and squealed with pride. "Papa, I helped Mama make your lunch. I'm a big girl."

Axel swept the little girl up in his arms and kissed her cheek. "Ja, you are getting bigger every day. I'm going to have to put a board on your head so you don't grow too fast."

His daughter's eyes widened. "But I want to be big and build a house like you."

Axel hugged his daughter and set her back down. "Nein, my princess. You will have young men build for you whatever your heart desires."

Gisela stepped forward and kissed her husband's sunburned cheek. "And what about me, great builder? Will you build me whatever *my* heart desires?"

Axel grinned and patted his wife's buttocks. "I know what you desire."

Gisela rolled her eyes. "You are a dreamer. Here is your lunch." She thrust a basket toward him and winked. "Maybe tonight we can talk about *other* things you do well?"

The family sat down in the shade of an oak and Axel unwrapped his rye bread, cheese, and sausage sandwich. He took a bite and motioned toward the half-completed structure. He glowed with pride over what he had accomplished since the Allies had nursed him back to health and released him to resume his life. "It will stand for a century and be the first of many built by the Mader Construction Company."

Gisela smiled, but she felt a tinge of jealousy, for he looked at his building in the same way that he looked at her. She put the feeling away and thought about the "talk" they would have tonight.

The Russian T-34 tank rolled to a stop beside the Brandenburg Gate and swiveled its turret toward a sea of screaming workers. The tank commander opened the hatch, stood up, grasped the machine gun's charging handle and yanked it back to load the first round. A rock hit the tank hatch door, and a bottle whizzed by the tank commander's ear. Over the sound of the rumbling engine he could hear the people chanting slogans as he brought his weapon to bear on the closest rioters. At the last second he raised the barrel and fired a burst over their heads. The bullets streaked over the workers without injuring anyone in the crowd, but two hundred meters away five innocent men and one woman, who were watching the riots from the street corner, were knocked off their feet by the impact of the bullets.

A crowd of horrified onlookers gathered around them. Two were dead, one was dying, and three were severely wounded. Some tried to help the wounded, while others could only scream and cry in outrage. Many picked up rocks and joined the striking workers.

One kilometer away a company of tanks from the Sixth Guards Regiment clanked their way down Stalin Allee in fighting formation. Marching toward the tanks were thousands of angry workers holding banners and placards that read: FREE ELECTIONS! *Walter Ulbricht* RESIGN. *Better standard of living and working conditions.* RETURN OUR GERMAN PRISONERS FROM RUSSIA! The riots had begun early that morning, soon after the striking workers had taken to the streets. The Volkspolice—Vopos—had been unable to handle the crowds, and the situation had quickly gotten out of hand. The First Secretary, Walter Ulbricht, leader of the German Democratic Republic, had been forced to call upon the Soviet Army to intercede on his government's behalf to regain control.

Undaunted by the approaching tanks, the workers had continued marching. Several had filled bottles with gasoline and stuffed rags down the necks for fuses. They used them against the lead tanks.

A tank machine gunner answered back with a long burst from his gun. The crowd panicked. People scattered in every direction, trampling those who had fallen and those who were too old or too young to move with the rolling human wave. Women screamed and men cursed as friends and fellow workers were struck down and left in the street dead or bleeding from gaping wounds.

Back at the symbol of Berlin, the Brandenburg Gate, a young man had climbed all the way up one of the massive gray columns. Thousands of people below held their breath as the seventeen-year-old ran along the top of the structure to the pole from which flew the Soviet flag. Vopos fired several warning shots, and the Russian tank gunners elevated their guns. The boy tore down the flag and screamed his defiance. The masses below roared back their approval and picked up more bricks and rocks.

Watching from a distance was an immaculately dressed, tall, dark-haired man standing in a crowd of onlookers. He shook his head and set off for his office. He had not been surprised by the "spontaneous" eruption of the workers, as reported on the radio. He had known the event had been planned and its leaders rehearsed weeks before, but nobody believed his reports.

The fools, mumbled Hagan Wolf to himself as he strode past a body lying on the sidewalk.

Walter Ulbricht, First Secretary of the German Democratic Republic, didn't rise when his guest arrived, but instead motioned to the chair positioned in front of his large desk. "Sit down, Herr Wolf."

Wolf took his seat and looked into the eyes of the tight-lipped, gray-haired man. It was his first summons to the party chairman's office, and the first time he had met his country's leader.

Ulbricht looked over his rimless glasses and nervously fingered his goatee. "I apologize for meeting you at this late hour, Herr Wolf, but I must tell you, I did not see your reports until a few hours ago. It seems that some of my staff took it upon themselves to disregard your warnings. I would not have known about your reports at all had I not received a call from our concerned Soviet friends asking why I did not take precautions to prevent the riots that occurred today. They *had* read your reports. Needless to say, I found myself in an embarrassing position. So I asked myself, how could the Soviets have read your reports before I did?" Ulbricht's eyes narrowed. "We both know the answer to that, don't we?"

Wolf's pale blue eyes remained unreadable.

The bearded man picked up a piece of paper from his desk, glancing at the typed lines. "Horst Volker, former SD officer in the SS. Hardly material for a good Marxist-Leninist. Yet your work for us has been exceptional."

"I am a good German, Herr Secretary. I believe Germany will one day be great again and will take its rightful place in Europe and the world. So I do what I must to rebuild our nation, even if some of our brothers have prostituted themselves to the decadence of the West."

Ulbricht dropped his gaze, unable to take the burning ferocity of Wolf's eyes. He had seen Volker's type before, and it scared him. He let the paper in his hands fall to the desk. "Herr Wolf, I believe it is time we moved you to the new Ministry of State Security on Normannenstrasse and gave you more people to perform your 'special' duties. You will be given whatever you deem necessary to guarantee the internal security of the state so that such events as happened today do not happen again."

"Ja, Herr Secretary," Wolf said flatly. He wanted to be careful not to show his elation.

Ulbricht leaned back in his chair. "Your activities will also include maintaining a presence in those countries that border us. I will tell General Mielke, your minister, that you are to be given any support you require."

The little man opened the top drawer of his desk and took out a folder. "Your first duty is to find those that caused the unrest today. In this packet are names provided by other organizations, but I'm sure your information is more current than mine. Those responsible for the riots are traitors and a threat to the state. You are authorized to eliminate that threat."

Wolf stood and took the packet from the frail hands of his leader. "The mission will be completed, Herr Secretary."

Ulbricht nodded in silence and turned to look out the window, signaling the meeting was over. Wolf smiled to himself and strode out of the office.

Lieutenant Colonel Georgi Sorokin glanced through the list of names before looking across his desk at his friend. "He must be running scared. He has done everything my superiors suggested, including moving you to the Ministry of State Security."

Hagan Wolf leaned back in his chair, raising an eyebrow. "He knows I work for you."

Sorokin shrugged and shook his head to make a point. "He failed to maintain control. Now he must pay the price."

"And the list?" Wolf asked with a sparkle in his eyes.

Sorokin handed the packet over the desk. "These should have been eliminated a long time ago."

Linda Tallon stepped out on the porch of her small home in Columbus, Georgia, with an armful of clothes to hang on the clothesline. She heard laughter and turned, seeing her five-year-old son chasing after the neighbor's six-year-old boy. Her son was wearing her husband's old flight cap and holding a stick as he yelled, "Bang, bang, bangbang."

The other boy was wearing a too-big Army fatigue shirt and his father's hunting hat.

Linda's face tightened. "Jake, come here!"

The boy's smile immediately dissolved. He knew all too well the tone his mother had used. "What'sa matter, Mom?"

"Don't 'what'sa matter' me, young man. You've been in my closet again, haven't you? I've told you a hundred times to leave your dad's things alone."

Jake raised his freckled face. "But Mom, I wanna play Army with Bobby."

Linda's shoulders sagged. He had that same puppy dog look as his father. She bent down and gave her son a hug. "Go ahead. I guess it's time we put your dad's things in your room anyway. He would have wanted it that way."

The boy grinned and turned to his waiting friend. "Bang! I got ya."

"Did not!"

Linda stuck two clothespins in her mouth, picked up one of her son's damp shirts from the pile and pinned it to the line. She reached for another but couldn't keep the tears back any longer. She saw so much of her husband in her laughing son that it made her heart ache.

She took a deep breath to get control again. She had made it through another spell. At least they weren't lasting as long. His image was fading more with each year. One day she might even be able to . . .

The tears welled up again. She didn't want to forget him. God Jake, I miss you. You'd be so damn proud of little Jake.

She took in another breath and sighed. Now it was really over. It was always better when she talked to him, that always did the trick.

Linda Tallon stuck two more clothespins in her mouth and went back to work.

Jake kissed his mother good night and walked back to his small room. Instead of getting into bed as he had promised, he opened the closet and took out the cardboard box his mother had put there. It was filled with his dad's uniforms. He picked up a worn leather flight jacket from the top and slipped it on. The arms almost touched the floor but it fit perfectly in his mind as he strolled to his plane and climbed in. Lying back on his pillow, he closed his eyes and flew over the bad-guy land, looking for targets. He saw one, a bad guy train . . . tat-tat-tat-tat-dow! Rattttta-tatatat dow! Got 'em!

Jake pulled up his plane and continued his search. He wanted to shoot 'em all and make his mom feel better.

He lowered his head to his shoulder and breathed in deeply, loving the smell of the leather. The jacket was warm, and he imagined how it would feel if his dad hugged him. He wished Big Jake had come home . . . It'd be real neat to play with him . . . He'd know and do all the things Bobby's dad did, except Big Jake would know a lot more. He'd play Army and build a tree house and play catch . . . and Mommy would be happy and we'd go ta movies and . . .

Jake drifted off to sleep, smiling.

Jorn Furman pushed himself along with his hands, ignoring the swarming flies that buzzed around his sun-darkened face. Around his neck was a leather strap holding four dead rabbits. Stopping by the bank of the small creek, he leaned forward and drank from a crystal clear pool. A Russian guard sitting close by casually glanced up. "German, you had a good day in the forest, da?"

Furman nodded without looking up and took another drink. The guard stood and leaned against a tree. "You might be going home soon, German."

Furman leaned back on his haunches and spoke back in fluent Russian. "Have you heard something, Ivan?"

The guard lifted and dropped a shoulder noncommittally.

"Maybe. I know another list is coming, but don't know if you are on it. I hope so, German. You have been here long enough."

Jorn agreed with a nod and began pushing himself back to the wagon that served as a kitchen. The road-clearing crews went out a month at a time to cut and haul trees out of the way and to make cart paths for farmers to reach the river that led to the larger markets downstream.

Jorn had made leather braces for his wrists, which extended down the front of his hands and covered his knuckles like fingerless gloves. To move forward and "walk," he would extend his arms, plant his knuckles and lift up with his shoulders. Lifting his half legs, he would throw his torso forward, replant his stubs and rock forward, starting the process over again. Over the past years, his shoulders and arms had become even more heavily muscled from the daily walks. Now, he could easily traverse ten to twelve kilometers a day. Every prisoner and guard in the Kadzhi POW Camp appreciated his special skills as a hunter. He would search the surrounding woods for plants, mushrooms, and anything else that was edible. He would also trap and snare small animals to add taste to the cook's two meals of goulash in the morning and evening. He had learned the skills from an old prisoner who had long since died. The old man had been a Forstmeister prior to the war and been called to duty in the last months, only to be captured in his first battle.

Jorn pushed himself to the camp kitchen fire and called out, "Sergei, I have mushrooms and wild onions."

The double-chinned Russian sergeant climbed down from the cook wagon caked in his usual dusting of flour. "Excellent! And hares I see. So the area is good hunting, da?"

Jorn took off the necklace of rabbits and his leather pack filled with the soup supplements. "Yes, but I saw bear tracks. I'll have to keep an eye out."

"Jorn, please don't bring a bear back tomorrow. The meal would spoil the prisoners and they would never settle for rabbit again."

Jorn faintly smiled as he opened the pack to take out the wild onions and mushrooms. "Ivan said there was a another list coming."

The sergeant erased his smile. "Da, but I'm afraid your name is not—"

Furman interrupted by picking up the string of rabbits. "I'll clean these and make some more snares."

The sergeant spoke with sadness toward the man's back as he propelled himself toward the forest. "I'm sorry, Jorn. I'm truly sorry."

CHAPTER 6

1961

Normannenstrasse 22, Ministry of State Security,
East Berlin

The black sedan turned left off East Berlin's busy Frankfurter Allee onto Jacques Duclos Strasse and proceeded up the bumpy road only a few blocks before turning right onto a quiet side street. Passing by a three-meter-high, brick-walled compound on the right, the vehicle slowed and rolled to a stop at the compound's side entrance security gate. Two heavily armed guards, warned of the arrival of the special visitor, pushed the gate back and snapped to attention as the sedan rolled past.

The passenger, seated in the back, leaned forward to get a better view of the enclosed complex of over forty buildings that comprised the headquarters, administration, schools, dormitories, and hospital of the Ministry of State Security, better known to the "outside" as Stasi. The Stasi minister, General Erich Mielke, reported directly to the Central Committee, which had given him the responsibility for the political, economic, and ideological security of the German Democratic Republic. Within the walls of the two-city-block complex was the secret world of over 31,000 employees whose duty it was to uncover all threats, in any form, to the state, and eliminate them as quickly and quietly as possible. Outside the walls of the compound, in fifteen districts and numerous locales, there were another nine hundred employees who investigated and reported on the citizens and their activities. It was a known fact that every government agency, major state-run company, town, village, club,

and organization in East Germany was infiltrated with Stasi informants. One particular department of the Stasi had quadrupled
in size. It was the chief of that department whom the passenger had
come to see.

Passing through a courtyard, the sedan rolled in front of the
newly constructed, seven-story headquarters building known as
"Haus One." The sedan stopped at the covered entrance where the
minister himself, General Mielke, stood to greet his special guest.
Without waiting for his door to be opened, the passenger got out
and shook hands with Minister Mielke, then climbed the short
flight of steps toward the glass doors held open by guards.

On the seventh floor in the main conference room, the minister's personal secretary hurriedly arranged bottles of mineral water
and apfelsaft. She was perturbed at receiving such short notice of
the special visitor's arrival, but she was also excited about having
the opportunity to meet the man who would probably be the next
First Secretary of the German Democratic Republic.

The main conference door opened and Minister Mielke led a
small, bespectacled, brown-haired man into the spacious room.

The secretary, who was somewhat overweight, curtsied clum-
sily as the small man's intense eyes fell upon her. He nodded without speaking and passed by the carefully arranged bottles to sit at
the head of the large conference table.

The minister began to sit to the right of the visitor, but the
small man held up his hand. "Thank you, Herr Minister, but you
won't be needed. As I told you on the phone, this matter is best
handled face-to-face with your department chief. Please understand."

The minister's jaw muscle twitched. "Of course."

"I'm sorry, Herr Minister," the visitor said, seeing the worry in
the general's eyes. "This matter is one in which the General Secretary has become personally involved. I am but his messenger. The
General Secretary will of course have much more information when
he discusses the matter with you personally at a later date."

Mielke was no fool. He nodded, forced a smile, and stood to
leave just as the door opened. Hagan Wolf stepped into the conference room. "You called for me, Herr General?"

Mielke knew that if his guest needed to see the chief of S Department, there was some matter that called for special attention.
Wolf's people were responsible for carrying out illegal intelligence
and counterintelligence activities, which often resulted in direct
action. They worked under the cover of a phony name: the Department of Scientific Research. There were over three thousand of

them, all specially selected and trained. Their duties were kept secret from the rest of the ministry's employees by an elaborate system of front offices and workers who actually conducted legitimate scientific collection and research.

Mielke gave Wolf a polite nod and walked out, closing the door behind him.

The small man sitting behind the huge table motioned to a chair to his right. "Herr Wolf, I am Erich Honecker. Please take a seat, and we'll discuss a project for which the First Secretary has given me responsibility."

Wolf strode to the end of the table and sat down, noting that the second most powerful man in the national government had not offered to shake hands. He liked that. It meant that Honecker reserved shaking hands for those he knew and trusted.

Honecker looked over his glasses. "Can I assume it is safe to talk in this room?"

The small man moved up another notch on Wolf's scale of respect. Honecker obviously understood the complexities of security; so many others in high positions did not.

"It is safe if you keep your voice low. The minister's secretary sits just the other side of the wall, and she is a hopeless gossip."

Honecker gave a hint of a smile and raised an eyebrow. "What I am about to tell you is classified 'Gold.' Only the First Secretary and myself are cleared for such information. I am passing it to you only to illustrate the importance of your assignment."

Wolf didn't show any emotion or hint of irony. He already knew what the small man wanted, for his mentor and personal advisor, Colonel Georgi Sorokin, had told him three days ago about the project.

Honecker softened his voice into a whisper. "As you know, the Vienna summit in the spring brought America's new President, Kennedy, and the Soviet party chairman, Khrushchev, together for the first time. During the private talks the party chairman attacked the amateur President, knowing how he had been weakened by the Bay of Pigs fiasco. Khrushchev told Kennedy he would be the last President of the United States unless he pulled his garrison out of Berlin. Khrushchev's ultimatum gave Kennedy six months to make the withdrawals. It was a calculated risk to test Kennedy's resolve and to see how important Berlin was to the Americans. The American President was stunned by the private ultimatum. However, he recovered very quickly and countered the threat by making a public address to his nation that Berlin would be held, even if it meant going to war. Kennedy surprised the Soviets by actually backing up his rhetoric when he called up additional forces and increased his country's defense budget. However, Khrushchev is a sly dog. He has another trick up his sleeve. As you are well aware, our country is hemorrhaging with the loss of trained workers and technicians to the West. One in six of our people has defected since the end of the war. With the recent tensions, thousands more are leaving monthly. Only yesterday the entire law school staff at Humboldt University failed to appear to teach their classes and were later seen in West Berlin. Khrushchev knows that either he must stop the flood to the West or our government will collapse. As a result, two days ago Khrushchev approved a plan to divide the city and stop the hemorrhaging. On August thirteen we will construct a wire fence around the one-hundred-three-mile perimeter of West Berlin. On the fourteenth we will begin building a permanent wall and enclose the capitalists so that they can stew in their own ferment."

A smile played across Honecker's face. "Our Soviet friends are rattling nuclear sabers to keep the western powers off balance, and the West is accommodating. The threat of war has the Americans planning hundreds of contingencies, but according to Soviet agents in NATO, they have no plans or policies to deal with a simple wall. Khrushchev will move his tank and motorized rifle divisions around the city early on the morning of the thirteenth to ensure that the Allies will think twice before interfering.

"Still, there is one major concern, and that is the reason you are here: security. If word of the plan leaks out, the Allies will invoke the Four Power Berlin Agreement that the Soviets signed after the war with the French, British, and Americans. As I'm sure you know, the agreement guaranteed freedom of movement throughout the entire city. The Allies could ruin our attempts at blocking the roads by running their military vehicles back and forth across the dividing line into the Soviet sector, invoking the access agreement. The barriers must be up *before* they have time to react. Once the streets are blocked, they can do nothing—the wall will be constructed inside the Soviet sector, and the Allies cannot tear it down. So as you see, only through total surprise and swift action can we succeed."

Honecker leaned closer, staring intensely at Wolf. "Soon many key people in our government will be told about the wall. Your job will be to use all of your agents in the West to keep you informed. If *they* hear anything of our plans, the source of the leak must be found and eliminated. You will also use your own local department assets to monitor government officials here. If any of our key people talk, you have the authority to arrest them immediately and to eliminate whomever they spoke to. You will receive whatever additional assists from other ministries that you need. Your minister will be told to support any requests you might have. Do whatever is necessary. Do not wait for authority or instructions from me."

Wolf waited for one more sentence, but it did not come: a statement of consequences to him should he fail. He was surprised but didn't show it. "I understand the assignment and will take the necessary steps."

"I know you have used the exodus of our people to infiltrate your agents into the West," Honecker added thoughtfully. "This, of course, will end on the thirteenth. I suggest you come up with an alternate plan. I have been very impressed by the information I have received from your informants in the Federal Republic. I hope the new barrier will not slow down the flow of information."

Wolf softened his stare into Honecker's eyes. "We have already in place over a thousand infiltrators that have been trained for just such a contingency, Herr Deputy Secretary."

Honecker rose and extended his hand. "I have great faith in you, Herr Wolf. Our government is fortunate to have such a dedicated professional."

Wolf shook the small man's hand and turned in silence for the door.

Five minutes later he closed the door to his own office and called in his second in command, the burly young Max Rink. "Assemble the staff," Wolf said with a smile. "We have work to do."

4 July,
Columbus, Georgia

Linda Tallon shook her head as she watched her twelve-year-old son through the back window. He was ridding the yard of its fire ants, as he did every year, by blowing away half of her newly planted grass with strategically placed firecrackers.

Jake held a lighted punk toward the fuse as an angry ant crawled up the small container filled with black powder. "Watch this one!"

Bobby Rawls, the next door neighbor, leaned closer to look. "I count only four of 'em," he said smugly.

The explosion sent pieces of ant and Chinese-rolled cardboard skyward, along with his mother's grass.

"Five! Beat that!" said Jake gleefully.

"Uh-uh, four ants is all I counted."

"Whataya mean? Ya didn't see that last one climb up?"

Bobby rolled his eyes. "Don't give me that crap, Tallon. Four and that's it."

Linda walked out on to the porch. "Come on, Jake, you said you wanted to see the parade this year, so let's go. We're gonna be late."

Bobby grabbed Jake's arm. "You ain't gonna go, are ya?"

Jake dragged his friend toward the back door. "Sure, it's neat. The Army marches and shows off all their guns and stuff. Come on, you can come with us."

Bobby motioned toward an ant pile with longing eyes. "But we ain't killed half of 'em yet!"

Forty-five minutes later Jake and Bob weaved their way through the crowd in front of Fort Benning Infantry School headquarters and sat down on the grass beside the reviewing stand. Jake looked around at all the uniformed men and their families. He had never known his father, but he almost felt as if he did. He had worn all his uniforms and his leather jacket, and had looked a thousand times through all the pictures his mother kept in a big, thick book. He also knew by heart all of the stories his mother and grandparents told him about Big Jake. It was in the hope of understanding his father better that he went to the parade. He wanted to know what his father had felt wearing a uniform.

A band passed by, then marching infantry units. Jake nudged Bobby. "My dad looked like those guys."

Bobby nodded and pointed at an approaching armored personnel carrier. "That thang is big!"

When the last of the military vehicles had passed, the band marched back onto the parade field, centered itself, and faced the reviewing stand. The deep-voiced announcer spoke into the microphone. "Ladies and gentlemen, please stand for the playing of the National Anthem."

The two boys stood with the rest of the crowd, and Jake felt his mother's hand on his shoulder. The band began to play. All around Jake uniformed men stood ramrod straight and saluted. He glanced over his shoulder. Tears were trickling down his mother's face. He turned to watch the band again, and for the first time began to capture some of the feeling in those beautiful notes. He brought his feet together and straightened his back like the soldiers. Remembering a picture in the book at home, he raised his hand and saluted in imitation of his father. A chill ran up his spine and he lifted his head higher. He knew somehow that his father was watching.

Düsseldorf, Federal Republic of Germany

Axel Mader moved the lamp closer and looked again at the blueprints of an apartment house he had won the bid on that afternoon.

Gisela walked into the small office having made her mind up. "Axel, your dinner is cold and still on the table."

Preoccupied, Axel only nodded as he jotted down the dimensions of the foundation to recalculate the number of meters of concrete needed.

Gisela picked up a book from a nearby shelf and tossed it on the blueprint in front of him. Axel looked up, startled. "Why did you—"

Gisela's eyes bore through him in anger. "I was talking to you but as usual you weren't listening. I said your dinner is cold! Princess and I have eaten alone for months and just once would like you to sit down and let us talk to you. Your daughter is worried her father doesn't love her . . . and so am I. You work all day and then come home and work most of the night. When is it going to end? When are we going to be a family again?"

Axel saw the tears welling in his wife's eyes and set down his pencil. Pushing back his chair, he walked around the table and took her in his arms. "I'm sorry. I'm just trying to get these last projects on track and—"

"You said that last year," Gisela replied, pulling away and quickly wiping her eyes. "We have everything we've always wanted. I don't need more things. I need a husband, and your daughter needs a father. Why do you push so hard? Why can't you relax and enjoy what you've worked so hard for?"

Axel pulled Gisela to him again and rested his chin on her shoulder, looking vacantly at the wall. "I . . . I don't know. I just have to be busy, but I will take the time from now on, I promise."

Feeling his sincerity, Gisela turned and kissed his cheek. "Your daughter is growing, and needs you to tell her she is still your princess. She is at that awkward age. . . . Her face has broken out again."

Axel walked with his wife into the kitchen and squeezed her shoulder. "Have I told you lately that you're still as beautiful as ever, especially when you're angry?"

Gisela smiled. "No, not for a long time, Herr great Captain."

Axel lay awake that night long after his wife went to sleep. He got up carefully from the bed so he wouldn't disturb her and padded into his study. Gisela's harsh reminder of his family responsibilities had hurt him deeply. She had been right; he had not given his family the time they deserved. But it was much more than that. Gisela

had asked why he was driven to work so hard. He sat down behind
his desk and lowered his head, knowing he'd been trying to forget
his past but had only been fooling himself. The memories were
always lingering in the back of his mind, waiting to be triggered.
That afternoon, he had picked up a dipper to drink water from a
pail and had remembered how thirsty he'd been in those last days
at the Alte Oder River. Driving home, he had passed a new Italian
restaurant and remembered the pasta he'd eaten before the Americans had attacked his platoon in Monte Cassino in 1944. There
wasn't a day that went by that he didn't hear, see, smell, or touch
something that reminded him of those days. The hardest part of
those memories was the guilt he felt. Every time he heard men
laughing, he thought of his brothers in heart and their promise.
He'd been trying to forget them too.

Axel closed his eyes. He knew the answer to the question Gisela
had asked of him. He drove himself, working long hours, so he
could keep the guilt away.

"What's wrong?"

Axel looked up at his wife, standing in the study doorway. He
tried to smile and say nothing was wrong but he couldn't. Deep
within him he was hearing, seeing, and feeling those days when he
had led men in war, the laughter, crying, screams of wounded. He
felt pride and humiliation and joy and sadness. Faces appeared that
made him want to laugh, and others that made him want to cry,
and always there were the images of his brothers of the heart who
begged to be remembered as he had promised them.

Axel's eyes began to water as he spoke in an anguished whisper.
"I . . . I have forgotten them for too long."

CHAPTER 7

12 August,
Northern East Germany

Jorn Furman took the small tree from his supervisor and set it beside the others he had loaded on the truck bed. Finished with his work, he grasped the rope tied to the end of the truck and climbed down hand over hand to his wheelchair.

With a sigh of frustration, the supervisor handed his workman all the money he had. "That's your wages and a little more. I'm going to miss you, Jorn. . . . Won't you change your mind? You've done a good job, and you have a future here. Things are getting better all the time."

Jorn stuffed the money into his shirt pocket and looked up with a scowl. "Rudi, things are *not* getting better! I was freed from the fucking Russian prison camp four years ago, and the damn train only brought me this far. I came home thinking, believing, it would be the Germany I knew. It isn't. This place is no better than the fucking prison camps! When I got off the train, our government officials only asked one question of me: Where were my identity papers? I spent twelve years, *twelve fucking years* of my life in the camps, only to come home to another fucking camp! Did our officials care that I'd spent a quarter of my life in prison? No, the bastards ordered me to work for the state. Ordered me! I couldn't do or go where I wanted because the fucking *state* needed laborers. Now I have served my time for the state, Rudi, just like I did for the Russians. They have finally given me my new papers . . . I am Jorn Furman again, but only in name. I have no past, but I damn well have a future. I can finally leave this place, and I'm going!"

Rudi patted his workman's shoulder in understanding. "Jorn, I know it's been hard, it has for us all, but where will you go? You can't leave the GDR and go home to Munich."

"Nein, I could never go to Munich again, but not because our state says I can't cross the border. I *will* cross the border, and I will find work somewhere else in western Germany. You and Frita should come with me. Look at yourself, Rudi. You don't own anything. Not your home, the tree nursery, or even this truck. The fucking state is your landlord, banker, and provider. Your wife has to stand in lines for everything, and still comes home with only half of what is needed to live. You are living a lie staying here."

Rudi waved his hand toward the house and farmland. "This is my home. I can't just leave it." He set his eyes in determination. "I'll work harder, and one day . . . one day things will change."

Jorn extended his hand to the supervisor. "I hope that 'one day' comes for you, Rudi. I truly hope and pray it does." Jorn picked up his small bag of belongings and placed it on his lap, then began pushing the wheelchair toward the road.

Rudi began to walk to the shed but spun around. "Jorn, I'll drive you to the train station. At least let me do that for you."

Jorn looked over his shoulder as he kept pushing. "Nein, you'd be an accomplice if anyone saw you drop me off. The border police are paying money to informers now. Good luck, Rudi. I'll always remember you, my friend."

Rudi lowered his head and walked toward the shed. He knew he would not be able to replace Jorn for all the younger men had already fled to the West. He would have to ask his pregnant wife to help him to at least get through the busy summer season. Next year it would be different, he told himself. Next year.

Normannenstrasse 22 , Ministry of State Security,
East Berlin

The basement operations conference room was filled with cigarette smoke and the stink of dried perspiration. Hagan Wolf sat behind a desk with a bank of telephones before him. He watched as his operations officer, with phone cradled against his ear, moved a red sticker to a new location on a huge map of Berlin while speaking into the handset. "Who is it you say he is talking to? . . . Are you sure?" He turned and looked at Wolf with widening eyes. "Wait while I talk to the chief."

Wolf was already on his feet. "Who?"

The operations officer spoke in a rush. "Lieser, the parliament representative from Brandenburg District, was seen talking to the British reporter from Reuters. The team leader wants to know if you want the official detained."

Wolf's lined face showed his long hours without sleep. "Of course detain him! Get him to headquarters immediately and have them question him on what was said. Then contact Colonel Rink and tell him I want him on that reporter *now!*"

Wolf spun around and walked five paces to the list of officials his teams were following, posted on the wall. He had four close calls so far that week, mainly from stupid politicians trying to impress mistresses or willing secretaries. None actually knew the whole plan, but they had pieced together enough so that he, the chief of "Operation Blanket," had to take action. The politicians and their lovers were now all in a prison in Potsdam.

Wolf took two steps to his left and glanced at the list of his agents in the West. They were identified by code names. Only he and Rink, his second in command, knew their names and locations. Surprisingly, all indications from them so far were that the Allies and the West Berlin police intelligence units knew nothing about the plan to close off the city. Only Agent Tiger, who worked in Bonn as a secretary for the chief of the West German Federal Intelligence Service, had any concrete information. Tiger had reported she had typed a memo from a Federal Republic intelligence source who had interviewed East German refugees who had crossed the border. The memo warned the U.S. Army Intelligence Center in Heidelberg that two border crossers had reported that large quantities of barbed wire had been moved from the outlying People's Army camps in the East and trucked to the outskirts of East Berlin.

Wolf turned and felt some relief as his Soviet guardian angel, Colonel Georgi Sorokin, entered the command center. Wolf quickly briefed him.

Sorokin then checked the list of agents and saw the note posted by code-name Tiger. He patted Wolf's back. "Your agent has done well. Don't worry about the report that was sent. Our agent in Heidelberg intercepted it."

Wolf smiled out of respect. Sorokin was head of the KGB for Berlin and the Federal Republic, and his agents were better placed than Wolf's own.

Sorokin motioned toward the wall map. "My only concern is these damn reporters who keep snooping around. The free-lance reporter from Reuters is not the only one. Another is that American from Associated Press, Robert Johnson. My agents have not been able to pinpoint him for the last four hours."

Wolf frowned worriedly. "That's too long. We'll have to assume he's found something." He swung his gaze to his waiting operations officer. "Inform the teams covering the phone terminals to monitor all calls from Americans out of the city. Robert Johnson doesn't speak German. Also inform the teams covering the wire services to pick up Johnson before he enters his office, and to take appropriate action."

Sorokin smiled. "Between us I believe we have the situation under control. You should get some rest and see Dagmar. You probably haven't been home for several days, have you?"

Wolf leaned closer, speaking in a whisper. "I may look worn, but I am enjoying this. This is the most important operation we have ever run. I have every agent in the field listening to everyone, even the janitors if they have a rumor to pass. So far, Georgi, it looks as if your leaders are to be congratulated. They have the western powers' intelligence community looking in the wrong direction."

Sorokin looked over his glasses with a crooked smile. "Thank you, but it is not over yet. I still worry about the American garrison commander in West Berlin. If he decides to take action without guidance from his superiors, we are in trouble. The Americans all think they must act like cowboys: shoot first and ask questions later."

Wolf shook his head. "Not him, he's no cowboy. General Clark is his superior, and he is far too worried about a nuclear war to let his garrison commander lift a hand without approval."

The operations officer picked up a ringing phone, listened for a moment, and spoke loudly to get Wolf's attention. "The team has the parliament representative. He told the British reporter not to leave this weekend on holiday, that a great event was going to take place. He said he owed the reporter a favor and didn't see any harm in giving him a tip."

Wolf spoke evenly. "Tell the team leader to drop the traitor off at the Vopo headquarters and tell Colonel Pfeffer what has happened. We'll let the police take care of him."

Sorokin looked at Wolf with concern. "And the British reporter?"

Wolf allowed himself a smile. "Rink knows where to find him."

Godfrey Tompkins unlocked the door to his empty office a block off Unter den Linden and strode straight to his typewriter. He had two hours to make deadline, and would just make it with luck if he started now. He loosened his tie and flipped open his notebook. He heard footsteps on the marble floor and looked up.

Max Rink lumbered into the office wearing American-style blue jeans and a short-sleeved dress shirt that exposed his bulging biceps. He reached behind him, took out a nine-millimeter CZ-75 pistol from the back of his belt and leveled it at the reporter's head.

"Sorry about the gun, but it is procedure," he said evenly, with only a tinge of an accent. "Would you please come with me? You are suspected of being a spy and are requested for questioning."

Tompkins swallowed hard. "Ridiculous. Who are you?"

Rink sighed impatiently. "I'm with the Ministry of State Security. Now please stand up, Mr. Tompkins, and follow me. If you can prove your innocence, you will be back to work in a hour."

Tompkins felt a little better. At least the Stasi agent was trying to be a gentleman. "I suppose you're just following orders. But your superiors are going to be issued a strong protest by my government for this absurdity."

Rink shrugged. "I'm sorry about all this, but as you know, orders are orders."

Tompkins straightened his bow tie and stood. He walked around his desk shaking his head. "I wish your people would talk to the Information Ministry and—"

Abruptly, Rink spun and punched the wide-eyed man in the stomach, doubling him over. Tompkins sunk to his knees in agony, gagging for air.

Rink replaced the pistol in the back of his belt and took an ink pen from his pocket. He pushed the clip forward, releasing a spring-loaded, four-inch needle. He bent over and grasped the gagging man's head, then twisted it so that the left ear was exposed. He carefully placed the needle point into the ear opening, then jabbed it into the man's brain.

Three kilometers away, Robert Johnson walked up the Kurfür-stendamm toward the Associated Press office in West Berlin. He had just left a young man in the Marienfelde refugee camp who had crossed into the West only the day before. The young man, who had been a driver in the East German Volks army, had said he had driven eight truckloads of concrete posts to different storage areas on the outskirts of the city. He had not thought twice about hauling the posts, but thought it odd that normally empty storage areas had been filled with barbed wire, posts, and wooden horses used for crowd control and roadblocks. The young soldier's story corroborated an East German Vopo police sergeant who had crossed two days before, saying the police headquarters' basement floor had been turned into a command center for some upcoming special operation. The sergeant said he had taken a clean-up crew into the center and saw maps of the city with a heavy black line along the East-

West city boundary. What was particularly strange was that key crossing points on the map had small stickers with unit assignment designations.

Johnson quickened his pace. He knew he had a scoop. He was only a block away from the Associated Press office when a young, attractive red-haired woman coming from the other direction stumbled and fell into him. Johnson caught her before she fell, but lurched back from a sudden stinging sensation in his side. He shoved the apologetic woman away and looked down to see if he had been cut. There was nothing on his shirt, but he rubbed the irritated spot as he continued walking. The damn girl must have been wearing something sharp, he thought. He had taken twenty more steps when he began to feel dizzy and disoriented. He staggered and as he tried to reach out for a lamp post to support himself, he sank to his knees and keeled over face first onto the pavement. Strangely, he felt no pain. He lay there with eyes open for only what seemed a second when a passing good Samaritan rolled him over and yelled for someone to get an ambulance. Johnson rolled his eyes up to look at the good Samaritan's face and knew then he was going to die. The good Samaritan was the young woman who had stumbled into him. Johnson opened his mouth and spoke the last word of his life. "Wh-Why?"

The young woman winked, then changed her expression and screamed again for the help she knew would be too late.

Eight kilometers from Stasi headquarters, Jorn Furman looked out of the window of his train car at the people who were assembling on the small town's railway platform, wondering why the passengers had gotten off the train. Five seconds later he got his answer when two uniformed Volkspolice entered his car and the senior officer barked, "All passengers get off and have your papers ready for inspection."

Two young men helped carry Jorn and his chair down to the platform and stood beside him. One of the teenagers disgustedly removed identity papers from his back pocket. "I heard they were doing this, but I thought we'd be checked after we were in Berlin. Now we'll have to walk to the nearest crossing point and avoid the damn Vopo patrols."

"What's happening to us?" Jorn interrupted before the other boy could reply.

The young man motioned to the distant Vopo sergeant checking papers. "It's a crackdown to stop border crossers. If you don't live in East Berlin, he won't let you back on the train."

The boy smiled at Jorn's look of frustration. "Don't worry, it's only three or four kilometers to the West Berlin border from here. The Vopo patrols are in cars, and they're easy to spot. You'll be free by this evening, if you take your time and keep your eyes open. I'd help you, but I have to be in West Berlin early to meet friends. I crossed twice in the past week. It's no problem."

"Which direction do I go?" Furman asked.

The young man pointed to the west. "That way. Follow the road. We're on the outskirts of the district of Pankow. Head straight west down that road until you enter the district of Reinickendorf. Once you cross the district line, you are in West Berlin. Freedom."

Jorn smiled and repeated the word that sounded so sweet. "Ja, freedom."

Thirty minutes later Jorn sat forlornly beside the road in his wheelchair. He had pushed himself only two hundred meters down the road before coming upon a roadblock. Behind Jorn were hundreds of sad-faced people standing with their beat-up suitcases and boxes tied with rope. Among them was the young man who had talked to Jorn at the railway station. Everyone's eyes were fixed on the East German Volks army soldiers who were standing five meters apart in a long line as far as the eye could see. The human barrier had been placed in position all the way around the train station to make sure no one made it to the city.

The young man saw Jorn and moved through the crowd to his side. "I'm sorry for telling you to go this way. I didn't know about the Volks troopers."

"Why do they do this to their own people? Don't they understand?"

The fellow passenger lowered his head. "They're trying to save a dying country."

An officer stepped in front of the crowd and put his hands on his hips before speaking loudly. "You are to return to the train station immediately. A train will be heading east in one hour. Collect your bags and begin walking. *Now!*"

A thin woman, weeping and holding a baby, stepped toward the officer. "My husband is waiting for me in the West. Please let me go on."

"No exceptions!" the officer barked.

"I have no money for train fare!" yelled an irate farm worker.

"We can't be forced to march like cattle!" an old woman cried out.

The officer lifted his hand as a signal. The line of soldiers took their rifles off their shoulders and held them across their chests as they slowly began marching forward.

Some of the mumbling, shaken people started back toward the station, while others stood defiantly and screamed at the oncoming soldiers. The crying woman with the child broke into a run and tried to get through a gap in the advancing line, but a sergeant quickly stepped in front of her. Where she sidestepped him and tried again to break through, a soldier lifted his rifle butt and roughly pushed her back, almost knocking her off her feet. She screamed hysterically and tried again. Again she was stopped.

Infuriated, Jorn yelled for the soldiers to let her go, as did other passengers who surged forward to help the terrified woman.

The officer withdrew his pistol, fired two shots into the air and yelled, *"Move to the station, now! Do not provoke me or my men any longer or you will suffer the consequences!"*

The first man to reach the woman pulled her back and tried to comfort her as he walked her away from the advancing soldiers. Jorn rolled his wheelchair in front of the officer. "You're separating a wife from her husband!"

The officer looked at the amputee with a glare. "Get out of my way."

Jorn didn't move and spoke with dripping disdain. "You are one of the reasons we are trying to leave this damn country!"

The lieutenant swung his hand to slap the cripple's face, but he was shocked by the speed and strength of the half man, who easily deflected the blow with a raised arm. Jorn reached for the officer's tunic but was struck from the side by a rifle butt, which snapped his head back and laid open his forehead.

The lieutenant slapped the stunned amputee's bleeding face. "Take this piece of shit to the station," he barked to the nearest soldier, "and personally make sure he gets on!"

At midnight the lights of the convoys lit the darkened streets as hundreds of trucks made their way through East Berlin toward their destinations. As the trucks rumbled by, prepositioned Vopos closed the gates of the twelve underground subway stations that crossed into West Berlin. They chained the gates and padlocked them. Simultaneously, other Volkspolice sealed off the entrances to the S-Bahn aboveground railway, which carried tens of thousands of Berliners across town daily.

A column of trucks pulled in around the Brandenburg Gate and East German officers got out of the vehicles, yelling commands to the unloading soldiers who quickly ran to form a human wall facing west. Behind the soldiers came more trucks, carrying border police and engineers who quickly unloaded rolls of wire, concrete posts, shovels, picks, and wooden horses for crowd control. Within minutes the sound of picks could be heard in the deserted streets as workers loosened cobblestones to dig post holes.

By twelve-thirty A.M. the people in the apartments near the border were awakened by the sounds of pounding and pneumatic drills jackhammering out concrete and stone. Alexanderplatz, the busiest East-West crossing point in the world, was a beehive of activity as heavy machinery rumbled and shook trying to break through the street pavement and loosen the trolley-car rails.

Five blocks from the center of East Berlin, a selected skeleton staff of the *Neues Deutschland* set type and worked on the special edition paper that would be circulated that morning to the people of East Berlin. The front page article would explain why the barrier was necessary. In part the lead article read: ". . . the traffic situation on the borders has been used by West Germany and intelligence agencies of NATO countries to undermine the economy of the German Democratic Republic. Deceit, bribery, and blackmail, by West German government bodies, military interests, and Allied exploitation have become intolerable. In the face of this aggressive adventurism by reactionary forces, the people's government has taken steps to guarantee the security of East Berlin. . . ."

By three-thirty A.M. the first rows of barbed wire were tied to posts that ran down the middle of streets, intersecting and separating neighborhoods, through cemeteries and churchyards, and down the banks of canals. Following the Soviet sector boundary line religiously, it crossed playgrounds, parks, roads, and railroad tracks, dividing the city into two distinct and separate parts.

Outside Berlin, two Soviet motorized rifle divisions and one tank division rumbled into positions on the outskirts of the city. They were not to take part in the construction, but rather to present an obvious threat that would worry the Allies into inaction.

Hagan Wolf was awakened at four A.M. as per his orders. A few minutes later, he entered the operations command center in the basement, which was bustling with activity. Six of his people manned phones to keep in constant contact with agents stationed at critical crossing points. Four more of his staff sat against the wall with phones to their ears, listening to reports from teams stationed in phone booths outside of the French, British, and American kaserne and the West Berlin polizei headquarters. Ten other staff members wrote summaries, studied reports, and updated maps.

The loud talking in the room turned into a murmur as the department chief strode in and took a seat in his chair. His operations officer began to give a report. He used a pointer to follow a black line drawn on a huge city map posted on a wall.

"Herr Wolf, the wire barrier has been constructed as per the plan with no complications. All critical crossing points have been barricaded. There has been no interference except for minor incidents at Alexanderplatz and Brandenburg Tor, where West German youths and drunks have insulted our soldiers and thrown rocks and bottles. The West Berlin police have since pushed the hecklers back behind a barrier they have constructed."

The officer pointed at the U.S. Army Kaserne at McNair Barracks, where the majority of the American soldiers were billeted. Wolf inwardly held his breath, waiting for the officer's next words.

"Our teams report the Americans, British, and French garrisons have not, I repeat, have *not* moved from their kaserne. It is reported that the Allies are still awaiting orders."

Wolf let out a sigh of relief as the smiling officer stepped forward and extended his hand. "Herr Wolf, you have done it. The operation was a complete surprise."

Wolf stood, shook the grinning man's hand, and turned to face his applauding staff. He waited until they stopped their applause and cheers before raising his hands. "I am not responsible for the success . . . rather *you*, my loyal and dedicated staff, have done it. Congratulate yourselves and your kameraden."

Wolf marched out of the command center and met Colonel Georgi Sorokin, who was walking down the steps. Sorokin smiled and put out his hand. "We have done it, my friend. Your First Secretary is very pleased, as is Khrushchev, whom I called only minutes ago. He asked me to pass on his compliments."

Wolf's blue eyes gleamed. "Today we have become a nation to reckon with."

Seelow, East Germany

Jorn Furman awoke in a room freshly painted white. He started to sit up but almost fainted from the sudden movement. Shutting his eyes, feeling as if his forehead had been caved in, he very slowly lowered himself back to the down pillow. He heard movement in the room and spoke rather than turned over to see who it was. "Where am I?"

A woman's voice startled him. "You are in my home, two kilometers south of Seelow, Herr Furman. You were found on the town's railway platform late last night."

A middle-aged woman came into view dressed in men's work clothes. Her face was thin, accenting her long nose. She did not help her looks, for she had pulled her chestnut hair straight back and gathered it into a bun at the back of her head.

She saw his expression as she set his washed and pressed clothes on the bed. "Yes, I am ugly, but you are no prize yourself, Herr Furman. I took the liberty of reading your identity papers. A policeman brought you here after some children found you."

Furman felt his nakedness and pulled the feather blanket up closer to his neck. When the woman had said the town's name, he had clamped his eyes shut in disbelief. Seelow was where he had been captured by the Russians in 1945. After the massacre at the bridge, he and Lieutenant Dieter had struck off to hunt down and kill the murdering SS officer. They had made it only as far as Seelow where the hunt had ended. There they found the main defense and were ordered into the line by desperate senior officers. The defense had held for two days before the Russians overran the last pocket of resistance on the heights just a kilometer south of the town on the 17th of April 1945. Now, he was back among the ghosts and memories that he had tried to forget. It had to be fate, he thought. Fate had brought him back to remind him he had failed in finding Volker.

"I would have thought you would want to ask more questions," the woman said. "They put up a barrier last night that will divide the city. Now they are beginning to build a wall. I envy you, Herr Furman . . . at least you made the attempt to escape. The rest of us shall always wish we had at least tried."

The panic-stricken face of the mother holding her child as she tried to break through the soldiers pushed into his mind. He knew the woman would never again see her husband, and he, Jorn Furman, would never see freedom. The state had won.

The woman lowered her head. He obviously didn't want to talk to her. Few people did anymore. But the stranger's silence was better than the accusing stares she usually got from people she knew. She patted his heavily muscled arm. "I will get you some food."

Minutes later she returned and placed a plate of sausage and cheese on the nightstand. "It's not much, I know, but it's all I have to offer."

Jorn avoided looking at the woman. "I will dress as soon as you leave the room, and be gone," he said. "Thank you for your help."

The woman turned for the door but she stopped and looked back over her shoulder. "I was a nurse during the war. It is my opinion you are not fit to go anywhere for at least two days. Perhaps in that time I can find you another wheelchair. Yours was found beside you, destroyed. It's your decision. I must go now. I have work to do in the fields. You can stay until you are stronger or you can leave."

She began walking when Jorn asked softly, "What is your name?"

She stopped again but didn't look at him. "Frau Ida Liebert."

Jorn shut his eyes to ease the pain in his head. "Thank you, Frau Liebert . . . and Frau Liebert, you are wrong. You're not ugly."

Ida left, hoping he would be gone when she returned. She didn't want him to find out how ugly her scars truly were—the scars that were inside, scars on her soul.

Columbus, Georgia

The newscaster on the television was saying something about Berlin. Linda Tallon stopped her ironing. She moved closer to the square-faced RCA and sat down on the worn couch.

It was Chet Huntley reporting that the East German government had erected a wire barrier around the 103-mile boundary of West Berlin, effectively stopping the flow of refugees. In a reassuring voice, Huntley stated that the Soviet army was not involved in the barrier construction and that American forces in Berlin had been placed on alert but were not yet deployed. The situation seemed stable. The White House had announced the President had been informed while on his father's yacht, the *Marlin*, in Hyannisport, and was in contact with the State Department. A strong protest would be made to the Soviet Union.

Linda leaned forward and spoke to the television in a tearful whisper. "Please don't let any more Americans die for that damned city."

Jake Tallon had walked into the living room and heard his mother's whispering. He did not want her to know he had seen or heard her, so he turned and tiptoed back to his room. Shutting the door, he strolled over to the worn scrapbook on his desk. Turning to the photograph glued to the first page, he saw his father and another man standing in front of an airplane with a half-nude woman painted on the fuselage. He looked past the airplane in the photo to the banner that was suspended from a plane hangar in the distance. The banner read:

WELCOME TO BERLIN—OUTPOST OF FREEDOM
Thank you, Army Air Corps, for keeping freedom's torch lit for the world to see.

The People of Berlin

Jake carefully turned to the last page, where two identical medals were taped. The citations beneath the awards identified them as Distinguished Flying Crosses. One had been given to his dad for bombing Berlin in 1944 and bringing back a shot-up plane and crew. The other was for his heroism in saving the lives of Berliners by staying with his burning plane to his death.

Jake ran his fingers over the cool metal, shaped into crosses, and shut his eyes to picture his father. For years he had looked through the pages studying every picture, trying to find out why his dad had given up his life for people whom he had once tried to kill. Didn't he know his wife needed him? Didn't he know she would cry? Why, Daddy . . . why did you die for somebody you didn't even know?

It wasn't fair. The Berliners had their freedom, while the Tallons had only a scrapbook. Like his mother, Jake hated Berlin.

Seelow, East Germany

The Seelow constable shrugged. "I offered, Herr Furman, I felt badly about leaving you here with the whore, but she was a nurse and the closest hospital is in Frankfurt an der Oder. We don't care much for her after what she did after her husband was killed. Nursing and fucking Russian officers will not be soon forgiven by any of us. Are you sure I can't take you back to the train station?"

Jorn leaned back on the pillow. "I'll stay until I feel better. Thank you for your concern."

The old man sighed and stood. "I am a veteran too, Herr Furman. We must take care of each other, for no one else will. I'll check on you in a few days. Auf Wiedersehen."

Jorn closed his eyes as the door shut. He could hear the woman crying in the living room.

Ida sat looking out through the window, wondering why she bothered holding on. She wiped her eyes and had begun to get up, when she saw Jorn in the hallway looking at her.

"So you know," she said. "Why didn't you just leave?"

Jorn planted his hands on the wooden floor and propelled his body forward to the window. He looked out over the overgrown yard and dilapidated outbuildings. "Why is there no garden?"

Ida wiped her tears with the back of her hand. "I asked you a question. Why didn't you go?"

Jorn seemed to ignore her. "You have no fruit trees," he said, "and you need hedges to block the wind."

Ida could take no more. "I don't want you here. Get out!"

Jorn turned slowly toward her. "Frau Liebert, I lost my legs and my freedom to the Russians. You lost your husband and you were used by them. There is nothing we can do to recover what we have lost. It's time to start planting and to begin life again. Tomorrow I will clear ground for a garden, then I'll go. I owe you that for taking me in." He lowered his head and pushed himself back toward the bedroom.

Jorn awoke, feeling, more than hearing, someone walk into the darkened room. He turned in the darkness and saw by the moon's reflection the robed woman standing by the open window. She looked up, as if searching for a particular star. Her hair flowed down to her shoulders and glistened in the moon's glow. She turned tentatively, as if trying to make up her mind.

She looked at him for a long time before whispering, "I have been alone for eleven years. I ache for someone to hold me. Tomorrow you may leave, but at least I would have this one night. I don't want to die never having been held as a woman again. No man wants a woman used by the Russians. Please, Herr Furman, don't refuse me this one night. Would you hold me?"

Jorn pulled back the blanket in silence. The woman let her robe fall to the floor and lay down beside him. She snuggled against his body like a frightened child.

Feeling her tremble, Jorn wrapped an arm around her shoulder and lay his head back on the pillow. Moments passed before the woman stopped shaking and seemed to melt against him.

Jorn closed his eyes. He felt content for the first time in over twelve years. In this woman's warmth, he realized, he had found hope again.

CHAPTER 8

1968

3 August
Dresden, German Democratic Republic

Forty-seven-year-old Hagan Wolf stood and strode out of the makeshift conference room that a week before had been a school classroom. Two morning briefers, referring to a large map of the GDR and Czechoslovakia, had outlined the invasion plans.

Wolf's temporary office was just down the hall. He was glad to be out of Berlin awhile, despite having to put on a show for the military, who were taking the invasion very seriously. It would be the first time a German army attacked across a neighboring border since the war.

Wolf walked into his office and was pleasantly surprised to see the gray-haired man seated by his desk. General Georgi Sorokin stood and greeted his old friend, with the usual crooked smile. "You're looking fit, Wolf. How is your tennis game?"

Wolf took his friend by the shoulders and grinned. "I can still beat you with one arm behind my back. What brings you from Moscow to Dresden?"

Both men sat down facing each other. Despite the pleasantries, Wolf knew the appearance of his friend meant something had gone wrong. Sorokin had returned to Moscow three years before to work as the KGB's chief of operations for the Eastern Bloc.

Sorokin looked over his thick glasses. "Wolf, I will come straight to the point. Party chairman Brezhnev is worried about the invasion. My agents reported to us some weeks ago that three Czech

generals had attained enough support from their subordinate commanders to force us into a fight that we don't want. I have been
given the mission of neutralizing the three generals." Sorokin leaned
forward with a look in his eyes that Wolf had not seen before. It
was the look of fear. "Wolf, this mission was given to me personally
by the minister himself. I don't have the assets to do it. My agents
have been compromised by a traitor who believed himself more
Czech than Russian. He compromised my entire network, and I
don't have time to infiltrate others. I need your help. I am asking a
personal favor from a friend."

Wolf leaned back in his chair. He couldn't turn down the request. He had informers in the Czech military and could accomplish the mission easily.

Wolf smiled to ease the tension. "What are friends for? Give me
the names of those that must be neutralized and the date the mission must be completed."

Sorokin breathed an inward sigh of relief. If Wolf had turned him
down, he would have had to report to the minister that he could
not guarantee the success of the assignment. He would have had to
submit his resignation at the same time. With Wolf's help, the three
Czech generals were dead men. Sorokin took a piece of paper from
his coat pocket. "The date of the invasion is August twenty. They
must be neutralized no later than a week before."

Wolf put the paper into his pocket without looking at the names.
He would now be able to report to his First Secretary the exact date
of the Soviet invasion. Even many of the Soviet leaders didn't have
this knowledge. He leaned back with a warm smile. "And how else
can I help an old friend?"

Feeling relieved, Sorokin gave his first real smile. "Nothing, but
I did read of the death of a man we both know. A Hauptmann Horst
Volker was listed as dead in a recent book published by your gov-
ernment. Did you happen to see it?"

Wolf nodded, feigning sadness. "Ja, it brought tears to my eyes."
He chuckled and patted Sorokin's leg. "What is going on in Moscow? I heard you remarried and . . ."

Minutes later Sorokin left the office and Wolf picked up the
phone from his desk. "Contact Colonel Rink and tell him I need to
see him."

Seelow, German Democratic Republic

Ida Liebert leaned over a pail, washing the dirt from her hands, and saw Jorn in the small wagon behind their plow horse, riding toward the road. She began to call out to him but stopped herself. He was in one of his quiet moods again and would want to be left alone. She was worried about him. The past seven years had been the happiest of her life, for Jorn had made her forget her past by giving her his love. His strength and determination had overcome even the people of the town, who now considered him one of their own. He had helped rebuild the school and church, and, only a few weeks after arriving, he had gotten permission from the state to start a flower nursery, using the land adjoining her house. Now the nursery was one of the largest in the region. Yet there were times when he was silent for days, lost within himself, as if he wanted or needed to be someplace else, someplace out of his past.

Ida walked to the house and looked down the road at the distant wagon. Jorn was still not hers.

Jorn pulled back on the reins, stopping the old mare just ten meters from the edge of a cliff that overlooked the beautiful Oder River valley. In the seven years he had been in Seelow, he had purposely stayed away from this spot. All around him were grass-covered mounds that seemed natural but weren't. Beneath the grass was blood-tainted soil. A few feet to his right was where his bunker had been. To his left was where he had shot his last Russian soldier. He was sitting exactly where he and Lieutenant Dieter had stood and raised their hands in surrender. The memory of Dieter caused Jorn to close his eyes and go back to those days in the spring before the last battle on the ridge. The beginning of the end had been only a few kilometers away. They had been such strong and determined men then. Death was real and living was the dream. He had known every man's name in his company and had felt a personal loss when one failed to answer the roll after a battle. The Alte Oder River had ended the war for him, for the enemy he had fought against for so many years had changed that day. As soldiers they had been prepared to accept the honor of a warrior's death in battle, but Volker, the Butcher, had taken that away. Volker had taken the lives of his colonel and his men to no purpose. They had died not as soldiers, but as animals led to slaughter. Volker had become his enemy that day. When he and Dieter had been forced to join the defense on the ridge, they had fought the Russians without hate. Their hate was reserved for only one man: Volker.

During all his time in the camps, Jorn had one dream: killing the Butcher. Then he had come to Seelow, and although for the past seven years he had told himself every day that he would leave and fulfill his dream, something had happened to him. His hate had been weakened by love. Ida had caused the memories of Volker to fade. Now, finally, the guilt he'd felt for not fulfilling his oath to kill the man was over.

Early that morning he had been to town. For the first time, all of the names of those German soldiers who had died in the war and prison camps were made available in a thick book in the post office. Both East and West Germany had worked together to compile, sort, and publish the information.

He had sat in his wheelchair in a long line with other towns-people and waited patiently until finally his turn had come. The first name he had looked up was that of Horst Volker. According to the book, Volker had died in June 1947, in Tomsk Prisoner of War Camp. The cause of death was listed as sickness, but so was Lieutenant Dieter's. There was no way to know. The Russian bastards lied about everything.

Jorn locked the wagon's brake and drooped the reins over the seat. He climbed down and gave the mare a gentle pat, then pushed himself closer to the edge of the cliff. "Farewell to you, Hans Dieter," he murmured. "It was here you and I last were true soldiers. Rest at last, my friend, the hunt is over for us."

Jorn looked back at the valley feeling sadness but also incredible joy. He had looked up the names of the men he had felt guilt about leaving and sending to the southwest that day on the river. Offering thanks to God, he had found that his brothers in heart were not on the list. Axel Mader and Lars Kailer had survived the war. He couldn't help but smile thinking about them. The Iron Men . . . yes, I have always remembered you as I promised . . . always. I've kept you with me, my brothers in my heart, and always will.

Jorn's reflective smile grew as he recalled the nights they had spent in Berlin drinking beer and singing the old camp songs before they had made the march from Gatow to Seelow and their final defensive position. His smile slowly faded and he looked out over the valley, knowing one or both men may have died after the war, though at least they had known living for a while, and perhaps had even forgotten their time in Hell. No longer did he have to carry the guilt of sending them back and of not fulfilling his last promise to himself of finding and killing Volker.

The sun had just set, leaving the land in darkening twilight as Jorn turned and glanced back at the grassy mounds. There was another name in the book he had looked up—his own. Jorn Furman was listed as dead. His wife and family in Munich would finally know he had died and would have peace. Backing up the old mare, he gave her the rein, knowing she would take him home.

Jorn pushed himself into the bedroom and woke the sleeping woman. He took her hand and looked into her eyes. "Ida, I have loved you for seven years, and yet you know nothing of me or my past. Tonight I want to start sharing my life with you for the rest of my life. I . . . I ask that you marry me."

Ida pulled back the blanket for him and patted the place where he had slept every night since coming to her house. "I accept, Jorn, now come to bed, I need to hold you and know this is not a dream."

Jorn took off his clothes and lay down beside her. She put her arms around him and kissed his cheek. "Welcome home, Jorn."

10 August,
Heidelberg, Federal Republic of Germany

Tears of joy and sadness rolled down Gisela Mader's cheeks as she kissed the bride's cheek. "I will miss you . . . come home soon."

The smiling young bride hugged her mother and stepped back, taking her husband's arm. "Mama, Richard and I will be back next summer to visit, I promise."

Captain Richard Hastings of the United States Army kissed his German mother-in-law's glistening cheek and gave her a gentle farewell hug. "Gisela, I love your daughter very much, and I will take good care of her. That's a promise."

Gisela tried to smile but began crying again. Axel put his arm around his wife and extended his other hand to the captain. "Richard, I wish you and my princess a happy life. Go on, you two must go and change or you will be late for your plane."

The bride's lips began trembling as she looked at her father, who was trying to hold back his tears. She opened her arms and they embraced for a moment before Axel gently pushed her back and looked in her tearing eyes. "I love you, my princess."

"And I love you, Papa," she whispered, trembling with tears.

Axel Mader led his wife to the sidewalk to join the other well-wishers, and they waved as the car pulled away from the curb.

When she could no longer see the car, Gisela leaned against her husband with tears rolling down her cheeks. "I don't know what I'll do without her."

Axel took the handkerchief from his pocket and dabbed his wife's cheeks. "I knew how you would feel, so I have a surprise for you. We are moving to your old home so you will be closer to your childhood friends."

Gisela's eyes widened in shock. "Berlin?"

Axel smiled. "You have talked of nothing else. With our princess gone, I thought it time I made your dream come true."

"Oh Axel! Berlin!" she cried and hugged him, burying her head into his chest.

A short, rotund man walked up behind them and tapped Axel on the shoulder. "Iron Man Mader, you always did get all the pretty girls."

The voice from Axel's past struck to his heart like a lightning bolt. The sudden jolt released a flood of memories, and although he had not heard the voice for twenty-three years, it seemed like only yesterday. Axel released his wife and spun around. He did not see a bald, well-dressed, forty-five-year-old fat man, but instead the third company commander of the Parachute Battalion 600. He looked into the eyes of the brother in heart who helped carry him from the Alte Oder River, and opened his arms. "Mein Gott, Lars!"

The two men embraced, pounding each other's backs as Gisela stood back in wonder. She had never seen her husband show such affection to a man before.

Seeing her expression, Lars Kailer stepped up to her and came to attention, clicking his heels and bowing. "Frau Mader, I deeply apologize for this intrusion on this special day."

Axel tossed his arms over his lost friend's shoulder. "Gisela, this is my old kamerad from—" He realized the other wedding guests were staring. He raised his hands. "Friends, I have lost a daughter today, but have found an old friend I have not seen in many years. There is still food and beer in the reception hall, so let's go back and celebrate some more!"

Minutes later Axel and Lars bumped beer mugs and forcefully whispered their toast to one another, "To the Iron Men!" and downed their beers.

Lars put down his stein and looked around at the guests, shaking his head. "One day, my friend, we will be able to shout to the world our pride and no longer keep our past a secret."

Axel smiled. "Don't worry about these Americans. They are

good people. They don't think that way about us. My daughter just married one."

"Where did you learn your English?" Lars asked. "I came late, and when I heard you talking to the guests, I thought for a moment it wasn't you."

Axel shrugged. "In the American prison camp they taught me some, and I learned more when working for the Americans. I am very happy that I did, for it has helped get many construction projects on their bases. That's how I met Richard, my daughter's husband. He is an engineer and was my site inspecting officer."

Lars grinned. "And you invited him to dinner to meet your daughter to make sure he would not give you any trouble. You are still a fox, Axel. You don't know how happy I am in finding you. You have given me hope I'll find the others."

Axel's eyes widened. "Others? You mean they—"

"Ja, haven't you seen the casualty book?" Lars reached in his coat jacket pocket and took out a folded piece of paper, handing it to Axel. "The government has finally compiled the information about our lost kameraden. When I saw your name and those of some other Iron Men were not on the list, I began the search for you all. I had my staff search every telephone book in the Federal Republic, and they found your name. I flew in from Hanover to surprise you, but you weren't home. A neighbor told me about the wedding, so here I am."

Axel looked up from the piece of paper with tears in his eyes. "Mein Gott, Thomas and Bernard live! I ... I didn't think it possible."

Lars's eyes misted as he nodded reflectively. "Ja, they live ... God, I wished Jorn's name was among those, but ... he and Hans Dieter were listed in the casualty book. They died in the Deblinka Russian Prisoner of War Camp in 'forty-seven."

Axel's jaw tightened and his eyes narrowed. "And Volker? Is that bastard alive?"

Kailer shook his head. "He died in the Russian camps."

"Who is Volker?" Gisela asked, uneasy at the hate she saw in both men's eyes.

Axel leaned back in his chair. Images from that day played in his mind. Just hearing the SS officer's name had triggered them. He shivered and slapped the table. "I will go with you to find the others."

Kailer gave Gisela an apologetic smile. It was obvious her husband was not listening to her. "Volker was a man we once knew and loathed, but now ... it doesn't matter. He's dead." He threw his arm over Axel's shoulder. "Ja, Hauptmann Mader, come with me. The Iron Men need each other to feel proud again."

Axel lifted his stein. "I have kept my promise, brother, I have remembered you and Jorn always. We must drink to our fallen brother. To Hauptmann Jorn Furman!"

Kailer lifted his stein. "To Jorn!"

12 August,
Klement Gottwald Military Academy, Czechoslovakia

The secret meeting of the senior military leaders of the country began precisely on time, as per the informant's message. The cleaning woman who scrubbed the corridor hall outside the conference room seemed annoyed at the disruption at such an early hour. Usually no one entered the building until seven A.M. The meeting this morning had begun at six, and the guard who was stationed outside the room kept walking across her newly scrubbed floor. She gave up. She collected her pail and brush and padded down the corridor to find something else to do.

During the first break of the meeting, the twelve officers split into small groups over coffee and rolls to discuss their views. The three generals who were arguing for the use of force in keeping the Soviets out of their homeland had enlisted two more commanders to their side. All five generals were now trying to convince a sixth, who was beginning to waver. It was this officer who suggested they all go to the more secure communications room, where they could discuss the matter without fear of being overheard. Once inside, he waited until his fellow officers were seated at a small table before stepping back and opening a door to a small side room. Through the door stepped the old cleaning lady and another identically dressed old woman. They both held silenced, short-barreled submachine guns. They swung the weapons, working from the outside to the center of the table in controlled bursts, shooting the startled officers. The officers had no chance to escape. Only the sixth general, who had thrown himself back against the wall, was unhurt. The women stepped forward and put a finishing bullet into the head of each general. The taller of the two women finished first, then turned her weapon on the man who had passed the information about the meeting. He nodded with a grimace and closed his eyes to take the bullet that would pass through his lower leg. The woman lifted the barrel and fired a quick burst that thumped into the man's heart. She spun immediately and fired another burst into her fellow assassin.

The woman then set her weapon on the table and pulled up her dress. Attached to a strap around her tanned thigh was a thermite grenade with a timer. She set the small device next to the closed curtains and pushed the button on top to start the three-minute countdown. Taking a breath to relax herself, she opened the hallway door, slumped her shoulders and stepped into the hall. The guard at the other end of the corridor gave her a bored glance and went back to the magazine he was reading. She slowly shuffled toward the opposite end of the hall to the back entrance of the building. Once outside, she raised her hand to her forehead, signaling the waiting staff car forward. The back door of the car had hardly opened when she slid in and got down on the floor. The driver pulled away slowly and approached the entrance gate to the academy, where a guard stood. The guard recognized the staff-car license plate as that of the commanding general of the Fourth Division and came to attention, saluting as the car rolled by.

A kilometer down the road, the old woman rose up and took off her scarf, exposing flaming red hair. By the time the car turned onto a dirt road and rolled into a barn, she had lost forty years of age by the use of cold cream and a towel.

Zehlendorf District, West Berlin

The couple opened the rusted gate and entered the overgrown yard of weeds and wild grass that were waist high. Walking carefully, for bricks lay hidden under the overgrowth, the couple moved up to the front door entryway of the gray, dilapidated house whose steps had rotted away.

Axel Mader climbed up to the porch supported by rotten posts and pulled his wife up to join him. He unlocked what was left of a door and entered the building. His wife walked ahead, stepping over piles of trash, and quickly inspected the large downstairs rooms. With a stern face she motioned him up the stairs and they walked through the upper rooms, which looked like the downstairs rooms, with their gaping holes in the walls and plaster on the floor from the partially collapsed ceilings. They walked downstairs together and she led her husband through the back door into the huge yard, which like the front, was overgrown in weeds. Undaunted, Gisela Mader waded through the growth, halting in the middle of the large yard. She turned to her husband and pointed at her feet. "The first thing I want you to do is plant an apple tree here." She pointed to a spot twenty feet to her left. "And one there, and another one on the other side at the same distance."

Axel put his hands on his hips. "What kind?"

Gisela smiled and waded back to him. "Bavarian greens, just like I told you I remembered." She joined him and turned, looking at the house. "I know you can't see its beauty, but I do. I remember this house, for it was my dream. We lived three blocks up the street and I would pass this house everyday on the way to school. I want you to rebuild it for me, Axel. Build my dream for me."

Axel put his arm around his wife's shoulder as he looked at the dilapidated structure. "It will take some time, for I'm a builder not a miracle worker. I'll have my engineers look at the foundation, but I think it will all have to be torn down and rebuilt from the ground up."

Gisela winced but nodded. "As long as it looks exactly the same, and don't forget the apple trees first."

Axel smiled, turned her toward him and looked into her eyes. "Why are the apple trees so important? Do you want to make me strudel the day we move in?"

His wife's lips quivered as she looked at the yard and thought back to a different time. "It was apples from this yard that I lived on for weeks before my parents sent me away to the village. There was no food, only the apples, and I—"

Axel leaned over, kissing her cheek, bringing her back from those days. "We'll go today and find trees at the nursery. I'll build your dream and we will sit here on the back terrace that I will build for you and we'll watch your trees grow until we are so old they will have to bury us here. That is a promise."

Gisela leaned her head against her husband's shoulder and shut her eyes. "My father always said that once you've lived in Berlin you could never leave. He was right. I feel like I'm home again."

Axel smiled and stroked her hair. "We are."

CHAPTER 9

1 December,
War Zone D, Republic of South Vietnam

Sergeant First Class Savage watched as a new lieutenant wandered down the path looking as if he were lost.

Savage shook his head with disgust. Shit, why do I always get the fucking kids? he thought to himself. Whydafuck do they give 'em to me? The sergeant sat up, away from the tree he was leaning against. "Hey, Loo tenant, over here," he barked.

The young officer's eyes widened in relief at the sight of the dirty soldier.

Savage motioned toward the ground as the lieutenant came up to him. "Take a load off. You must be our new platoon leader the ol' man radioed about."

The lieutenant sat and extended his hand. "Yep, that's right. I'm Lieutenant Jake Tallon, good ta meetcha."

"Savage," said the sergeant, grimacing in the officer's strong grip. "Platoon Sergeant Savage. What kind of experience ya got? What schools?"

Jake Tallon sat back proudly. "I was selected for Officer Candidate School out of Advanced Individual Training. After I was commissioned, I went to Jump School and then I volunteered for Special Forces. I went to the Special Forces thirteen-week officers course at Fort Bragg, then they sent me here to Vietnam."

Savage sighed. "How come you ain't in the Special Forces, then?"

The lieutenant lost some of his bluster and lowered his head.

"They thought I was too young for a team. They suggested I get some field experience then come back in six months."

Savage looked the officer over and grunted as he sized him up. Shit, he ain't over twenty, he thought. All-American type right down to the broad shoulders and Hollywood smile. That's all I need, another dumb-ass butter bar that don't know his butt from a hole in the ground.

Savage unwound his scrawny legs and stood up. "You got a map, Loo-tenant? All officers are suppose ta have maps to look like they know what they're doin'."

The lieutenant looked up meekly at the filthy soldier. "They just gave me this rifle and pack full of stuff and put me on the chopper. They didn't give me a map."

Savage rolled his eyes. "You know where you are?"

Jake got to his feet with a nod and smile. "War Zone D, right?"

Savage nodded, "Right, that's a start. Come on, Loo-tenant, I'll introduce you to the shitbirds in the platoon, then we've got some talkin' to do. We got an operation in the morning and you gotta know a helluva lot more than us being 'in War Zone D.' Oh, and Loo-tenant, don't say nothin' to the shitbirds just yet. Just nod and smile like ya know what you're doin'. I don't want ya ta scare 'em with all that knowledge ya got."

Jake followed like a puppy dog, but he wished the sergeant wouldn't call him by his rank the way he did. The sergeant said "Loo-tenant" like most people said "dumb-ass."

The early morning mist hung heavy on the ground as Lieutenant Jake Tallon led his twenty-three-man platoon toward the five waiting helicopters. Jake climbed on the first shaking bird and sat behind the pilot's seat. The grinning radio operator sat next to his new platoon leader and yelled over the whopping blades and screaming turbine engine, "Dig it, L-tee, da Delta Company, Second Batt, Seventh fuckin' Cavalry, is goin on a *charge*!"

Tallon smiled back faintly at the grinning soldier. He wasn't sure how to take him.

Seconds later the vibrating machine lifted off and dipped its nose to gain airspeed. Jake glanced at the five other men across from him. He tried to remember their names but gave up after two seconds; he couldn't even get past the first soldier. He had met all twenty-three men the previous afternoon, but he had only given each one a nod, as his platoon sergeant had instructed. Afterward Savage had used up quite a bit of time explaining how the airmobile operation would be run. By then the names of the men had already started to fade.

Jake leaned back, at once content and excited. He was finally doing what he had dreamed about for years—being a soldier. Despite his mother's protests, when he went to Baker High School he joined the junior ROTC program immediately. He had excelled in it, and in sports as well. He had strived to strengthen himself both in mind and body. By the time he graduated from high school, he had been an all-state halfback and had risen to the rank of captain in the corps. The next day he had walked down to the recruiting office. God, he'd never seen his mother cry like she had when he brought back the paperwork for her to sign.

He reached in his fatigue shirt pocket, took out a half stick of Wrigley's spearmint gum and put it in his mouth. His mother had always given him a half stick of the same brand of gum for luck just before his high school football games. She had told him that it was a family tradition. His father had always popped a half stick in his mouth before every mission he had flown during the war, and later when he had been switched from bombers to transports. His mother had said she sent gum to his father from the States until she finally had a chance to go to Germany after the war to give him the gum herself. Jake couldn't help but smile thinking about the first letter he had gotten from his mother months ago. Taped to the pages had been two sticks of gum.

Jake broke from his reverie and looked out of the open door of the Huey to the hilly, jungle-covered land ahead known as War Zone D. He felt the bird losing altitude and shouted for his men to get ready. Noticing that one trooper had nervously pushed his M-16's safety off, Jake leaned over, touched the young soldier's trembling hand, and motioned for him to turn the selector switch back to Safe. The soldier acknowledged with a quick nod and pushed the selector switch back into position.

The tail of the chopper suddenly dipped down in a flare, slowing the machine's forward airspeed. Jake scooted to the door and glanced behind him at the other choppers following in a diamond formation. He leaned out farther and looked past the front of the bird. Ahead was a three-hundred-meter-wide opening in the jungle, which would serve as their landing zone. "Lock and load," he yelled. "We're going in!"

The last gunships were pulling out, having expended their rockets, when Jake's aircraft began settling to the ground. The door gunners on both sides of the chopper announced the cavalry's arrival by blasting the woodline with M-60 machine guns. The skids had barely touched down when Jake bounded out of the bird into the waist-high grass and ran ten meters before throwing himself to the ground. He listened for incoming fire as Sergeant Savage had told him to, but he didn't really know what incoming fire sounded like. He hoped Savage's description of a distinctive popping noise was correct. The only thing he could hear was the rest of the choppers coming in.

The radio operator, still grinning, fell to the ground behind his lieutenant and held out the handset. "Ya better tell Six it's green, L-tee."

Jake cussed himself. He should have thrown a green smoke grenade as soon as he determined the LZ was cold. He began to grab for one from his harness, but by now one had already been popped and was billowing in the clearing. Somehow he knew it had been thrown by Savage, and he thanked him in silence as he snatched the black handset from the radioman. "Rawhide Six, this is One-six, LZ is green, over."

A matter-of-fact voice spoke back through the buzzing handset. "Roger, One-six, understand green. We're five minutes out. Keep your eyes peeled, out."

Jake tossed the handset back, vowing to himself not to forget another fucking thing. He forced himself to relax and think. He brought his head up after lying perfectly still for several seconds and called out for his squad leaders to report. His three buck sergeants responded in sequence. "First squad up!" "Second up!" "Third up!"

Jake got to his knees to see where his squads were located. They had followed his previous instructions from early that morning and formed a screen line facing the treeline. One machine-gun team was behind him, and the other was with Savage, who was kneeling thirty paces away. He felt a surge of pride and gave a nod to his platoon sergeant.

Savage ignored the gesture. "Watch your fuckin' front and keep them fingers on the triggers, shitbirds!" he growled. "The second platoon will be comin' in just a minute."

Jake could see his sergeant was still mad at him for ordering the men to stay in the open, as per the company commander's order. Savage had told him the company commander was new and didn't have his shit together, and that he should move the platoon into the woodline for protection.

Jake lowered his head. He would probably get in trouble for what he was about to do, but he felt it was worth it. He rose up to one knee and yelled, "Second squad move into the woodline on my command! First and third squads, cover their movement. Move out, second!"

Savage glanced over at his new platoon leader and nodded. The kid had potential after all. He was listening.

As the last squad settled into positions just inside the forest, another flight of Hueys came in and unloaded the second platoon, which fanned out and took up positions in the clearing.

Jake could see the newly arrived men clearly in the waist-high grass. They're nothing but targets, he said to himself. The sergeant was right. He stood, glanced down the line of his platoon, and decided to move forward a little more into the forest.

"We're going to move forward by squads another ten meters," he barked. "Second squad, you're moving first; first and third, you cover. Readdddy . . . move out, second squad!"

Jake hit the ground and rolled behind a large tree that had strange tentacles running out from its base. He rose up to his knee to check his platoon's position, but he was still not quite satisfied. Twenty meters ahead in the jungle was a small, thickly vegetated ridge that he didn't like the look of. He was about to bound the platoon forward again when Savage stepped up behind him. "Loo-tenant, don't move 'em anymore. That dumb-shit lieutenant in the second platoon is pissed 'cause you ain't in the clearing with him. He's calling the commander on the radio and makin' trouble, so just take the ass-chewin' and sit tight."

Just then the grinning radio operator held out the handset to him. "Six wants ya, and he don't sound happy."

Jake took the handset and pushed the sidebar. "Six, this is One-six, over."

"One-six, the Two-six just called me and told me you've moved your unit into the woodline. Do not, I say again, *do not* move into the woodline until I see what the situation is. Do you understand? Over."

Jake felt two inches tall as he answered meekly, "Six, this is One-six, we have already moved into the woodline but will proceed no farther, over?"

The captain's irate voice came back. "Roger, understand. I'll talk to you when I get there in about two mikes. Out!"

Jake handed the handset back to his RTO and looked at Savage with "aw shit" eyes. The sergeant grunted. "That's why you're wearing the brass. You have ta make decisions based on the situation as *you* see it. The commander ain't here to see this LZ, *you* are. You did what you thought was best. Just take the ass-chewin' and keep doin' what's right. Don't worry 'bout them smug-asses who always hide behind procedures."

Jake smirked. That was easy for the sergeant to say, since he wouldn't be the one getting the ass-chewing. He looked over his shoulder at the ridge and felt the hairs on the back of his neck stand up. Something didn't feel right. He kneeled behind the tree and stared at the thick vegetation, looking for signs of trouble. He couldn't see far through the thick lianas and creepers, but something was definitely wrong. He made up his mind and commanded loudly, "Break out entrenching tools and dig in. Team up, one man digs and the other man watches his front."

He heard groans and mumbling from the platoon and yelled angrily, "Do it, goddamnit!"

He turned, ready to listen to Savage tell him he was screwing up, but the noncommissioned officer was looking at him strangely. "What you see out there, Loo-tenant?" Savage asked nervously.

Jake glanced over his shoulder at the ridge. "I don't see anything . . . I feel something."

The sergeant had been in long enough to know about "feelings." "Dig, shitbirds," he yelled. "You heard the Loo-tenant!"

The third and final lift of helicopters came in with the third platoon and the headquarters element, which consisted of the company commander, a first sergeant, and two radio operators. The captain strode straight to his new lieutenant's position and immediately began his ass-chewing. "Goddamnit, Tallon, this isn't the fucking Special Forces, where it's every asshole for himself. This is the Cav, and we do things by the book. We secure the landing zone and then we clear the woodline by sending out patrols. You got it?"

"Yes, sir, I've got it," said Jake quickly, and motioned toward the ridge behind him. "Sir, that high ground is—"

The captain put up his hand, stopping further discussion, and was handed a handset from one of his radiomen. The commander spoke quickly, identifying himself, and listened to the message. He answered the caller with a "Wilco, out" and tossed back the handset. "The battalion commander is coming in and wants to bullshit for a while. Stay right here and don't move. I'll see what he wants, then we'll finish our little talk."

Feeling like a fool, Jake watched the officer and his entourage of radiomen and the first sergeant wade into the grass of the clearing.

Jake heard his radioman cussing and turned to see he was not making much progress in digging his foxhole. Jake took out his own entrenching tool and jabbed the blade into the ground, venting his own frustration. At least digging was something that didn't violate "Cav procedure."

The battalion commander's ship landed a minute later. A lieutenant colonel hopped out. Jake was too far away to see the officer's face clearly, so he went back to work on the hole. He saw Savage checking the other men's positions and wanted to do the same, but his captain had ordered him not to move.

Jake heard the battalion commander's aircraft increase power, and looked up just as the olive-drab Huey lifted off and began to shoot forward. He sighed. The captain would be on his way back. Jake tossed down his entrenching tool and put on his submissive look. The captain was approaching through the grass. Jake had just begun to get up when the air around him cracked and exploded in a thunderous roar of incoming rifle and machine-gun fire. He fell flat and tried to bury himself as bullets thudded into the tree, sending wood chips and fragments flying. He looked up and felt like vomiting. The exposed men in the clearing were jerking and twisting in a devastating maelstrom of bullets that scythed both grass and Cav troopers. B-40 rockets swooshed out of the treeline from his right, leaving a trail of spiraling smoke, and exploded among the men of the second platoon. A bullet cracked by his head, and he spun around to get in the hole. His radioman was lying in the shallow foxhole with only his hand exposed as it held the radio handset out to him. Jake crawled in and grabbed his lifeline to the outside world. He pulled out the map from inside of his fatigue shirt, and looked again to check the coordinates of the landing zone before pushing the sidebar. Just as he began to speak, a mortar shell made impact only twenty meters away, exploding in a *crump* and throwing out deadly white-hot shrapnel that tore through the tree limbs like razors.

Jake glanced back at the LZ. His company commander was rolling on the ground, smearing a path of violet blood over the grass. The commander's two radiomen lay in still heaps, and the first sergeant screamed in agony, having lost his hand and half his arm to ripping mortar fragments. Jake pushed the handset sidebar and yelled over the roar of battle, "Redhorse this is One-six, we're in deep shit! We got heavy incoming from all around LZ. Need fire mission ASAP, grid Yankee Golf two-six-two-one-seven-seven! I will adjust! Over!"

A calm voice responded along with a buzz of static. "Roger, One-six, understand. We will also contact gunships in your area and have them come up on this frequency. Wait, out."

A succession of mortar rounds exploded and threw up a geyser of dirt and a cloud of dust as Jake braved rising up to see his platoon. Not a single man was firing, for a hidden machine gun on the ridge would have shot anyone who moved. The enemy gunner was spraying Jake's men, then periodically raised the barrel and swept the clearing with long bursts to keep the second and third platoon survivors pinned down.

Jake saw the flashes from the machine-gun barrel and ducked, seeing the barrel swinging in his direction. He felt something heavy hit his back and thought for a split second he had been hit, but then he felt the heavy object squirming.

Savage rolled off his lieutenant and yelled to be heard over the din, "Did you call for arty?"

"Yeah, it should be inbound any second," Jake yelled, although he was only inches from the sergeant's face. Jake slapped the handset into the sergeant's hand. "You adjust the rounds. I spotted the machine gun. I'm gonna try and take it out."

"Don't be no hero, wait till the arty comes in!" Savage yelled.

Jake looked over his shoulder at the dead and wounded on the LZ. "Those troops can't wait that long, and neither can our platoon."

Jake pulled his leg up underneath him, about to jump up, when Savage grabbed him. "Wait till the gunner swings the gun toward the LZ again. He won't be able to see ya, but watch for snipers. I'll cover ya."

Jake had to wait for only a few seconds, for several men from the second platoon had jumped up from their exposed positions in the clearing and were trying to run for cover. Jake sprinted toward the expertly camouflaged bunker, keeping his eyes all the while on the blue flame at the end of the barrel. A sniper rose up and fired, but missed, and was about to shoot again when he pitched over, shot in the head by Savage. Jake had fallen into the thick vegetation to the side of the bunker and had already pulled the pin of a grenade. He let the spoon fly, counted two, and, rolling in front of the firing port, tossed in the grenade. A few seconds later the ground seemed to leap up under his body. He wasn't taking any chances. He pulled the pin of his second grenade, crawled back to the smoking opening and tossed it in. The muffled explosion was louder than the first, but he hardly heard it, as something else had caught his attention. Oh God! He ran back to his shallow hole. Savage was shaking his head.

"Goddamnit, L-tee, don't do that hero shit again. Get in the foxhole and—"

Jake pointed to the clearing. It had caught fire. Orange-red flames were engulfing the tall dry grass and sending a large, ugly, gray-brown smoke cloud skyward. The bloodcurdling screams from the wounded as they burned alive sent shivers up Jake's spine. He turned wide-eyed to his sergeant. "We've got to get those wounded out of there! Have the men lay down a base of fire into the treeline and keep the dinks' heads down."

Jake heard more screams, and knew he had no choice. He dropped his rifle, threw off his battle harness and helmet, and jumped to his feet in a dead run toward the clearing. He had dreamed too many nights of his father burning to death, and he couldn't take the pathetic cries from the wounded who were experiencing the same fate.

Breaking through a curtain of smoke, he was immediately taken under fire by North Vietnamese who had positions in a ring around the clearing. Jake dodged and cut left and right, like the days when he played on the gridiron, except that he didn't see any tacklers. He felt a slap to his shoulder, but he lowered his head and kept running toward the crackling flames and terrified screams. Just ahead a young trooper was trying to crawl clear of the flames that licked at his boots. Jake threw himself into a headlong slide through the grass to the soldier's side. He grabbed his fatigue collar, jumped up, and dragged the trooper behind him. His shoulder felt as if a hot coal had been placed under the skin and muscle, but he didn't stop. A nearby explosion knocked him off his feet, and he fell heavily on his side. He screamed in defiance and again got to his feet, though blood ran down from his brow, over his nose and into his mouth. He blew it out like a slobbering bull and continued to drag the soldier to the treeline.

When Jake finally fell behind a fallen tree, he rolled the moaning soldier closer to the thick wood for protection, then got up and ran back for another survivor.

Savage heard the whistling sound of the incoming artillery and tensed. Whooosh *ba-rooom*. It was the most beautiful sound he had ever heard. "Right two hundred and fire for effect with every fuckin' thing you've got!" he yelled into the handset.

When he lowered the handset, he saw his lieutenant dragging yet another wounded trooper to the safety of the woodline. He jumped up and screamed at his men, "Cover that fuckin' idiot!"

Jake heard nothing but the cries of the men he so desperately wanted to save. He jumped through a wall of flames and fell beside a blackened, screaming trooper whose face and hands were charred and cracked. The smell of burned flesh caused Jake to vomit. He spit the bile from his mouth and tried to grab the soldier's collar.

The young trooper tried to fight him off, but the blackened skin of his hands fell off when he grabbed the lieutenant's arm. He screamed, "Oh God! God! *God!*"

Jake retched again as he grabbed the man's collar. Choking in the smoke and feeling as if his own skin was about to burst into flames from the intense heat, he got to his feet and lunged forward through a wall of flame and into fresh air. He gasped and struggled for ten steps toward the treeline when suddenly he was knocked off his feet, hit in the chest by a burst from an AK-47. He lay on his back looking up at the sun, hearing and feeling nothing but a dull, faraway pain in his chest. Smoke engulfed him, and he shut his eyes. He knew he would soon be with his dad.

2 December,
236th Evac Hospital, Republic of South Vietnam

The nurse saw the patient's eyelids flutter as she rubbed crushed ice over his lips. She spoke, trying not to show her fatigue. "It's about time you joined us, Lieutenant. Come on, open those big eyes and look at me."

Jake Tallon felt as if he were submerged underwater with a fifty-pound weight on his chest. He tried to open his mouth but his tongue felt as if it were glued to the bottom. He managed to swallow and then to unstick his tongue.

The nurse dripped water between his lips. "You won't feel any too good for a while, L-tee. The doctors took one bullet out of your chest and two from your rib cage. You are one lucky son of a gun. Had another bullet gone through your lung, it would have been . . . well, you know. You've also got the makings of a pretty scar on your forehead, and you've got some first-degree burns on your face and hands that will take some time and cause some additional discomfort. The piece of shrapnel they dug out of your shoulder didn't mess up much muscle, so it'll be good as new." She smiled brightly. "Other than that, you're just fine." She patted his arm and dripped more water into his mouth. "You're going to be staying with us until the doctors say it's okay to ship you out, then you'll be flying to Camp Zama, Japan, where you'll do your recovery before going home."

Jake tried to speak but couldn't.

"Don't try and talk for a while," the nurse said. "You came in very dehydrated."

Jake's eyes widened and narrowed trying to communicate that

he wanted to know about his platoon. She knew what he wanted. They all wanted to know about their buddies. But in the lieutenant's case, it was better he didn't find out until he was stabilized. Delta Company had flown into the LZ with 116 men, and only thirty-six had been able to walk out after reinforcements arrived.

The nurse patted his unbandaged shoulder reassuringly. "Take it easy, Lieutenant, the war is over for you. In three or four months you'll be home." She lifted two medals that were pinned to his pillow. "You got yourself a Purple Heart and a temporary Silver Star. The general that came in said the Silver Star was going to be upgraded to a Distinguished Service Cross. You can write and tell your mom and dad they have a hero coming home."

CHAPTER 10

1971

Hanover, West Germany

Gisela Mader was trembling again. She often did these days. She had become a shadow of her former self over the past year. At least no one seemed to notice. The women were watching their men laugh and get drunk, as they always did when they met at their annual Iron Man reunions. But then Jutta Kailer leaned over with a worried expression. "What are the doctors saying about your illness?"

Gisela lowered her shaking hands to her lap and tried to smile. If Jutta knew, they all did. "Perhaps another reunion. I hope so. Axel lives for these times."

Jutta put her arm around the frail woman. "Marta and Anna and I will come up and visit you in Berlin every month from now on."

Marta Voss also leaned closer. "We pray for you, Gisela. We pray God will restore your strength and drive out the cancer from your body. God will answer our prayers, you will see."

Gisela looked into her friends' faces knowing their prayers were wasted. She had been told not go on the trip to Hanover by the doctors. They felt she was too weak. The tumors in her body were winning the battle and she had no strength left to fight.

Gisela forced a smile. "Thank you, my friends, you're right. God will give me strength."

Lars slapped Axel's back. "Tell us about that cabin you were building when we were all in Berlin last year. Is your masterpiece finished?"

Axel grinned. "Almost. Next summer I will invite you all up to join me, and we'll boat up the Havel and visit the Berlin nobody sees."

Thomas Seegar, a former platoon leader of the battalion, shook his head. "Axel, how can you take living in such a big city? It's noisy and polluted, and those damn liberals! Surely you don't like it?"

Axel smiled. "Thomas, Berlin is now my home, and I love it. It's in my blood, like being a paratrooper. Once you live there, you can never leave. My Gisela said that years ago, and she was right."

The mention of his wife's name caused the other Iron Men to lower their eyes in discomfort, for they all knew she was very sick. They had felt Axel's pain as he tried to act as if nothing was wrong. Axel broke the temporary spell by standing up and raising his stein. "I drink a toast to you, my kameraden and your lovely wives, who have come again together to remember when we were Iron Men."

They all stood, raised their steins, and cried out, *"To the Iron Men!"*

Lars Kailer had left the room five minutes before to accept a phone call. Now he returned with fixed eyes. He motioned his wife to join him in the hallway.

Jutta knew something was wrong the second she saw him, and excused herself. "What is it?" she asked him when they were alone.

He raised his bald head and stared past her toward the wall. "The call was from Axel's construction company president in Berlin. He got a call from a hospital in the States. His daughter and family were involved in a terrible accident. His daughter is critically injured, but looks as if she will pull through . . . her son and husband were killed. The company president thought it would be better if I told Axel than for him to hear it over the phone."

Jutta shuddered and shriveled. "Mein Gott, Gisela's grandson." Jutta thought of something Gisela had told her and looked up with hope. "Their daughter was pregnant. Did the—"

Lars shook his head. "She lost the baby as well. How am I going to tell them? How am I going to tell this horrible thing to my best friend?"

Jutta lifted his chin and looked into his eyes. "Because, Lars, *you are* his best friend."

Lars looked at his wife with tears running down his cheeks. "Why . . . why does it happen? Why is God so unmerciful to those who have already lived in Hell?"

Jutta shook her head as she took her husband's arm and walked him toward the room.

•   •   •

Tears streamed down Axel Mader's ruddy cheeks as he sat staring blankly at the table. Gisela was leaning against his shoulder, sobbing. The other Iron Men and their wives, all in tears, stood behind them and kept their hands on the couple as if trying somehow to give them strength.

Gisela raised her eyes to her husband. "Axel . . . bring my princess home to me . . . please bring her home, I need to hold her."

Seelow, East Germany

"Another increase in quota? Impossible!" Jorn Furman said angrily as he spun his wheelchair around, thrusting out his hand toward three dilapidated greenhouses. "I can't achieve what you demand now! This collective nursery is not a 'collective,' for no one else works here! How can you talk about increased production when you know I can't produce without more land and workers?"

The young district horticultural manager sighed and tossed his briefcase to the hood of his white Lada. "I have been given the authority to allocate you an additional fifty hectares from the farm collective that adjoins the north side of the nursery. I also have—"

"That is the land Borkman and Kahl work! That is their best field!" Jorn blurted, incredulous.

The young man shrugged his shoulders with indifference as he opened the briefcase. "The Cooperative Department of Crop Production reports they have failed to make their quotas for the past two years. They are unproductive. This collective nursery *is* productive. Now, as I was saying, I have been authorized to expand the nursery and build three more greenhouses, but larger, more modern ones. You will remain manager of the collective nursery, and a truck will be allocated to the collective along with appropriate wage increases for hiring workers."

Jorn lowered his head. "I can't take my friends' fields. It is all they have."

The young man rolled his eyes. "Herr Furman, it is not your decision, as it is not mine. The district cooperative manager is paid for those decisions and he has made it. If you feel obliged, hire the two farmers from the wages you will be receiving for additional workers. You are a successful manager and should be proud of your accomplishments. The state appreciates its hard workers and rewards them."

The young bureaucrat took a small cloth banner from the brief-case and held it up for Jorn to see. "I have the honor of bestowing on you the People's Production Award for a prosperous collective this year. You met all the production goals and exceeded monthly quotas twice. Congratulations."

Jorn took the banner and weakly shook the man's extended hand. He looked up into the man's eyes as he bunched the banner material in his callused hand. "Have you ever worked in the fields?" he asked with a searching stare.

The bureaucrat sighed. "Of course not, the state sent me to the university to learn management."

Jorn turned, looking at his nursery with a reflective glaze. "Did your studies teach you about people who work the land? Did they tell you about those of us who love the smell of the fresh-tilled soil and love watching life grow? Did it speak of the hours needed to prepare the soil and the experience needed to know when to fertil-ize and when and what to plant? Did your classes teach you any of those things?"

The young man closed his briefcase, knowing the cripple was trying to make some kind of point. "No, we were concerned with the results of your work. You produce a product, Herr Furman, and I manage those products for the district."

Jorn turned and looked at the young man as if feeling sorry for him. "Products are produced by people, Herr Manager. A manager does not just manage 'things,' he must also understand and manage people. I think about that the next time before you bestow a banner for 'things.' " Jorn tossed the banner back to the tight-lipped man. "If you knew people, you would know taking land away from others to give to me to improve *your* production is not a reason for giving banners."

The young man lowered his head, touched by the cripple's words. "I'm sorry, I'm . . . I'm just trying to do my job."

Jorn smiled. "Then there is hope for you. Come, let me show you how production could be increased with little investment by the state. Perhaps you will even get a banner from your district supervisor for the good ideas I will show you."

The bureaucrat returned the smile and walked alongside the cripple as he pushed himself on his hands toward the flower beds.

Ida Furman joined her husband and looked at the departing small, white car that was kicking up a dust cloud. "Was that the district bureaucrat again?"

Jorn was kneeling by a compost pile, removing branches. "Ja, he is not so bad once he leaves his intelligentsia briefcase behind. He actually listened to me today and has plans for expanding the nursery."

Ida put on her work gloves with a bitter frown. "And did he say how long before this miracle happens? The hothouses took two years to finish, and you and I had to build them because the builders would have taken another year."

Jorn laughed and grabbed his wife's arm, pulling her down to him. "Such faith you have in our state! Perhaps he is different."

She smiled. "And perhaps I will be a beauty queen."

Jorn kissed Ida's cheek. "You are a beauty queen to me."

2 June,
Da Nang, Republic of South Vietnam

The Military Intelligence colonel sat down and nodded for the officer standing in front of him to begin.

The nervous young captain rotated the pointer in his hand. "Sir, I'm Captain Franks from Fifth Special Forces Group. Material Assistance Command, Special Operations Group—MAC-Five-SOG— is our headquarters, and we are a subheadquarters known as MAC-Five-SOG North. Our primary missions are cross-border intelligence collection and interdiction operations into North Vietnam and Laos. A border-crossing team's size is mission-dependent but usually consists of a Special Forces captain, team sergeant, medic, Vietnamese interpreter, and five to eight handpicked, highly trained Rhade, Sedang, or Jari Montagnards. Most of the Yards have at least five to six years' experience. The missions of the teams vary from wiretapping, prisoner snatching, road watching, and trail mining, to ambushing key targets."

The colonel raised his hand. "I know all about how you operate, Captain. I'm the guy you send your intelligence reports to. I'm not here for briefings. I came here specifically to talk to the captain of team Snake. You did get my message, didn't you?"

The captain nodded. "Yes, sir, we did, but we thought you should know more about what we do and what risks are—"

"Damnit!" blurted the red-faced colonel. "I want to see the team leader who refuses to cooperate with my people."

The briefing officer sighed and nodded toward the sergeant at the back of the tent. The sergeant stepped outside.

"Sir, the Snake team leader will be here in just a minute," the nervous captain explained. "He got back from a mission last night, and he's catching up on sleep."

The irritated colonel rolled his eyes and sat back to wait. Five minutes passed before the tent flap opened to reveal a bare-chested man wearing camouflaged jungle-fatigue trousers and unlaced boots. The six-foot, broad-shouldered soldier yawned and patted his mouth.

The colonel's eyes narrowed. "This won't take long and you can go back to sleep, Captain. I've been told that you have not been cooperating with my people. I want to know what your problem is."

When the soldier lowered his hand from his mouth, the scars were exposed on his heavily muscled chest. The colonel noticed he had more scars on his shoulder and another that looked like a snake, which ran down his forehead.

The team leader ran his hand through his light brown hair as he walked over to the map of Victnam that hung behind the briefing officer. He took the pointer from the wide-eyed captain and tapped the northern portion of the map. "Sir, this is North Vietnam." He moved the pointer across the border and tapped again. "This, sir, is Da Nang, where you are now." He moved the pointer to the southern portion of the map and tapped again. "And this, sir, is Saigon, where your Military Intelligence boys are. I think that sums up the problem."

"What the hell is that supposed to mean?" the colonel blurted.

The captain shrugged. "Sir, your people aren't here, and they don't go with us up north. I think that pretty much says it all. If you want meaningful intelligence, I can and do provide it. But when some asshole in your organization calls up wanting to know the distance in inches across roads and the gauge of the wire we're tapping, and what kind of food the enemy is eating, I tell 'em to get screwed. If they want that kind of intelligence, they can come up and get it themselves. My job is to find 'em and report 'em so somebody can kill 'em. I don't give a flying fuck what they're eating, and I am not chancing the lives of my men to find out."

The colonel flew out of his chair. "That's enough insubordination from you, mister! I will not have you stand there and lie to me! My people do *not* ask those kinds of questions!"

The team leader calmly reached into the side pocket of his fatigue pants and pulled out four messages from Saigon. He handed them to the colonel. "I think you owe me an apology for calling me a liar, Colonel. This is all message traffic from your people requesting what I just told you. Oh, and there's one I forgot. The last message wanted to know what size slit trench the North Viets were using to shit in. Oh, and sir, look who signed off on those messages. I guess they got by ya, huh?'' The captain strode out of the tent without looking back.

As the colonel quickly read the first then the second message, his face grew red, violet, and by the time he finished the fourth, almost blue. "Goddamnit!"

He stormed out the briefing tent and bumped into the camp commander, Major Denton.

"That son of a bitch better pray I never sit on a promotion board. That is the most arrogant bastard I've ever met."

Denton nodded in agreement. "Sir, I've talked to him until I'm blue in the face. I can't get through to him."

"Fire his ass!" the colonel blurted.

The major's eyes widened. "Sir, Jake Tallon is the best cross-border team leader we've got. His team alone provides half the information we get. Last week alone the B-52 Arc Lights hit those camps dead-on and we received a four-hundred-man kill score from the aerial photo boys. The week before that he brought back the info on that base camp that we—"

The colonel sighed and waved his hand at the commander. "I know, I know, he's good, I've read about him and saw where he got a Distinguished Service Cross his first tour, but *Goddamnit, he pisses me off!* When's he going out again?"

"Black birds pick 'em up tomorrow night."

"So soon?"

"Sir, Captain Tallon loves it."

The colonel let himself smile. "Tell Captain Tallon for me that I apologize. I'm going to have to go back and kick some ass. It seems one of my majors has been signing message traffic for me."

The major shrugged. "Sir, with Tallon it wouldn't make any difference. He's so wrapped up in this snoopin' and poopin' shit, he scares me. The Yards say he smells and feels the Viets before ever seeing them. They believe he really is some kind of man-snake. They treat him like a god."

"How long has he been out here?"

The major turned and looked to the mountains in the north. "Sir, he's been here for ten months. Nobody before him lasted past six. He knows he's living on borrowed time, and it draws him in closer and closer to his men. He can't stand to be around any of the rest of us. They live like a cult. He wears the Yard bracelets and eats their food and even drinks their home-brewed wine. The guy has gone native. He's crazy in my book, but he's also special, sir. There's no gettin' around it. He's truly got the sixth sense, and that makes him bad news for the North Vietnamese."

The colonel lowered his head. "I wonder if a man like him can ever go home and lead a normal life?"

The major shook his head. "Sir, he is home."

Muggelsee (Lake), East Berlin

The driver slowed as he approached the ornate iron gate of the ten-foot walled estate. An armed guard stepped out of the guardhouse and approached the vehicle. He looked in the backseat window to ensure the passenger was in fact the director, and turned, nodding to a second guard inside the gatehouse, who was covering the car with an RPD machine gun that protruded through a gun slit. The second guard pushed a button to open the heavy gate.

Wolf lowered his passenger window. "Any visitors today?"

The guard smiled. "The usual lady guests to visit your wife, Herr Direktor. House security reported they went sailing."

Wolf nodded and rolled up his window as the electric gate slid back on rollers and clanged into place. He leaned back in the seat as the driver proceeded down the gravel driveway past the manicured grounds and toward a magnificent, three-story, seventeen-room, white stone house that had been given to the director as a reward for his exceptional service to the state. The estate had been built as a summer home in 1922 by a rich Jewish banker who then sold the estate to the Reich in 1934 for five hundred marks and an exit visa. The estate was turned over to the deputy director of the SD, who lived in the house until he was killed in the last days of the war. The Russians used the house and grounds as a regimental headquarters until 1949, then turned it over to the East German government. Wolf never ceased to be awed by the beauty of the estate nestled in the forest that surrounded the Grosser Muggelsee. It had been a perfect gift, for the estate was only twelve kilometers from his office, and yet far enough away from the city that it seemed as if he were living in the country. Because the lake was surrounded by forest, access was limited to only a single road that was closely guarded by the Volkspolice. The lake was the playground for the government's elite, and not just anyone could drive out to enjoy it.

Wolf's attention was focused on the lake, only fifty paces from the back of the house, where sailboats were gliding effortlessly across glistening water. He was happy his wife could enjoy the rewards of his position. She deserved the house and servants after the hard years she'd had to endure during and immediately following the war.

The driver stopped in front of the entrance and got out to open his superior's door. Wolf opened the door himself, anxious to change clothes and enjoy the last rays of sun on the back deck. He hastened to the door while speaking to his bodyguard and driver. "Check the security room before you go and see if the team needs anything. Pick me up tomorrow at the same time."

The driver snapped to attention. "Jawohl, mein Direktor!"

Wolf opened the door with one hand while loosening his tie with the other and entered the spacious marbled foyer. "Dagmar?" he called out.

"Out here," came a distant voice from the back deck. Wolf joined his wife a minute later, after hanging up his jacket and taking off his tie. Dagmar Wolf sat in a deck chair enjoying the sun, and looked up at her husband, beaming. "Summer is finally here."

Wolf smiled and sat down beside her. "Ja, you have always loved the summers. I understand you went sailing."

The tanned woman brushed back her graying blond hair and gave her husband a pout. "Must you know everything? It is one thing to have guards everywhere, but reporting on me is too much. They embarrassed me today when Margot and Frita were over visiting. We wore our new bathing suits when we sailed, and your men stared at us, ruining our fun. Won't you talk to them?"

"I would have stared too at such a lovely woman as you in a bathing suit," Wolf said with a wink. "But I will talk to them. They are new at the job and will be more discreet in the future, I promise."

Seemingly satisfied, his wife beamed again. "You won't believe what Frita heard. She was shopping and . . ."

Wolf watched his wife's lips moving but he wasn't listening. He was thinking of his handpicked security team, and was glad to hear they were doing exactly what he had ordered. He didn't want his wife unprotected for a second. The activities of the S Direktorate were expanding to the third world nations. Terrorists were being trained by his organization, and he could take no chance that one of the targeted nations would reciprocate and try some kind of direct action on him or his wife as a lesson. The Israeli Mossad was known for just such direct action tactics, as were the West Germans. The S Direktorate was making more enemies daily, for the silent war was turning more violent and not so silent. The chances of an attack were remote, almost zero because of his security, but he could take no chances when it came to Dagmar. She was his world away from the ministry's compound. She would have to learn to live with the stares of bodyguards who accompanied her everywhere. But perhaps he could do one thing to make the security seem less imposing. A female bodyguard. Yes, that would solve many problems. Wolf made a mental note to tell Max to select a female agent for his wife's personal security.

Wolf tuned his wife's conversation back in and smiled when she finished her gossip. He stood up and looked down at her. "Let's go for a sail. I'm jealous you went without me today."

"Now?" asked his wife, shocked at his suggestion, since dinner was almost ready.

"Ja, now. I need to enjoy the freedom of the wind and have you next to me. The summers are always too short."

Dagmar glanced toward the house. "What about your dinner?"

Wolf winked as he offered his hand to his wife. "Have the servants make up sandwiches. We'll have a picnic on board. I need you alone on the water. The stars will be beautiful and give me light so I can stare at you in your new bathing suit."

Dagmar smiled coyly. "I won't be wearing it once we are far enough offshore."

Wolf pulled her up and kissed her cheek. "Exactly what I was thinking. Hurry."

Dagmar took two steps toward the huge house but stopped and looked over her shoulder at her husband with welling eyes. "Horst, the past ten years have been the happiest of my life. Will the rest of our lives be like this?"

Wolf smiled. "Nein . . . it will be even better. Don't forget the wine." He watched his wife disappear into the tangible reward for honorable service to his country, then turned and looked at the sun's reflection on the glistening water. He had answered her honestly, for he had worked long and hard to achieve invincibility. No one said or did anything within the government that he was not aware of. The good life he and his wife had experienced over the years could not be threatened, not even by the outside world. The loyalty of his people was unquestionable, and the organization he had built ensured that his security was total. He was invisible to all threats, for he didn't exist.

Wolf smiled inwardly, knowing it was just the beginning. He now had the power and people to achieve what he had always wanted—a new Germany that once again would take its rightful place in the world.

PART II

1989

CHAPTER 11

Wednesday, 19 July,
Seelow, East Germany

Sixty-six-year-old Jorn Furman rolled over and kissed his sleeping wife lightly on the cheek. He grabbed the rail by his bed and lowered himself to the floor to start a new day. He did not often deliver his flowers to Berlin, but again the state transportation system was lagging behind. He would have to make the deliveries or the flowers would die, like the last shipment, which had sat in the distribution warehouse for a week.

Thirty minutes later he hauled his collapsible wheelchair up to the back of the old covered truck and secured it with rope to the tailgate. Then he climbed down and propelled himself on his callused knuckles to the cab. Once he was in the seat, he strapped on specially made boots which had carved wooden feet inside the bottom portion. They allowed him to reach the pedals and accelerator. It had taken him six months to learn how to drive using the boots, but over the years he had become an old hand. He placed his "feet" on the pedals and started the engine. He had looked forward to this trip, for he'd saved enough money to buy his wife a gift. He pulled out of the clay driveway and turned onto the dirt road. In minutes he would be on the highway that would take him to the capital.

West Berlin

Fifty-five miles from Seelow, sixty-five-year-old Axel Mader knocked on his daughter's bedroom door. "Princess, are you awake?"

He heard stirring and a sleepy voice. "Yes, now I am, Papa, thank you."

Axel continued down the hall, walked down the steps to the kitchen and put on the kettle. Twenty minutes later he was sipping tea and reading the morning paper when his daughter walked in buttoning her blouse. "Papa, could you button the top one for me?"

Axel put down the paper and quickly buttoned the blouse's top button and patted his daughter's behind. "You are much too thin. You must eat more and put some color back in your face. You'll never find a husband to take you off my hands if you look like a stick. You don't want to be alone when you turn old and gray like me."

The blond-haired woman patted her father's face lovingly. "You don't look a day past sixty."

Axel raised a white eyebrow. "Don't talk about age in my presence."

The attractive woman shrugged as she poured herself a cup of tea. "You're not getting old, Papa, just lazy. Are you going in to your office today or are you going to play 'semiretired' again?"

Axel tossed down his paper. "It so happens my old kamerad, Lars Kailer, is flying in for the afternoon. I'm taking him to lunch, and we're going to discuss the arrangements for the reunion this fall."

The woman eyed her father accusingly. "Papa, you don't need to make arrangements for the reunion, and you know it. You two are going to drink beer and act like fools just like you always do when he visits. I don't want you driving if you are going to drink like you did last time."

Axel growled. "Enough! You sound like a nursemaid."

The woman knew she had gone too far, and leaned over to kiss her father's cheek. "I'm sorry, Papa, I know how much you enjoy being with your friends, but please, I worry about you when you drink and drive. For me, please take a cab to pick up Lars."

Axel reluctantly agreed. "Only for you."

The woman smiled and kissed his forehead. "Thank you. Now I won't have to worry about you."

Axel patted his daughter's back. "I must go walk, and I will see you tonight when you come home."

The woman waited until he was opening the door before stepping out of the kitchen. "Papa, don't talk too long to Frau Schmidt. You need your exercise, remember?"

Axel dejectedly opened the door. "Will you grant me no vices to enjoy during my last days? Yes, Princess, I will walk and not stop too long. Now go to work and be sure to look for a husband . . . *please*, so I can live in peace."

Muggelsee, East Berlin

At the table in the breakfast room, Dagmar Wolf poured her husband his second cup of coffee as she regarded his profile. The years had been good to him . . . too good. His regal bearing combined with his swept-back silver mane and perfectly tailored suit made him look like royalty rather than a director for Stasi. Most of the other leaders were seedy and oiled like sewer rats. Her husband had always been the exception . . . and now that worried her. She sat down at the kitchen table across from him, began to speak, lowered her head to gather strength and lifted her chin again. "Horst, tomorrow you will be sixty-seven years old. I think it's time you told me when you are going to retire."

Wolf set down the paper he was reading and looked over his reading glasses. "You have never mentioned retirement to me before. Why now?" he asked, his voice soft, concerned, searching.

Dagmar avoided looking into his magnetic blue eyes, for they were too powerful and would sap her strength. "I have been talking to Frita, and she seems so happy since Kurt retired," she said, watching the steam rise up from the coffee cup. "They are planning a trip to Yugoslavia next week, and after that, South America." Her hands shook but she forced herself to go through with it. "I . . . I need to be with you more. I look in the mirror and see an old woman growing older every day, while you seem to . . ." She lowered her eyes, unable to stop the tears running down her cheeks. "I need you to be with me, Horst. I want to do things together and live our last years in happiness."

Wolf stood, tenderly lifted his wife's chin and softly wiped away her tears before leaning over to kiss her cheek. Then, taking her hands, he gently pulled her to her feet and walked her into the sun room with his arm around her shoulder. "Summer is here," he said, motioning to golden rays dappling the floor. "Let's sit on the back porch and enjoy the view."

He led his wife outside to the stone deck and sat down beside her on a rattan couch, patting her leg. "Now, what is really troubling you?" he asked gently.

Still afraid of his hypnotic eyes, she looked out toward the shimmering lake, trying to be strong. "Horst, you have accomplished everything you've wanted. The state will live without you . . . but I cannot. I need you." Her eyes began to well again, and she laid her head back on his shoulder. "It's my turn. Let's spend our autumn years together and enjoy the life you've provided us. Please . . . please come home to me."

Wolf rested his chin on his wife's head. "Ja, I have been working too hard . . . I'll come home earlier from now on, and we'll begin to spend more time together, I promise."

"But Horst, I need—"

He stood, but still held her hand and smiled. "We will go on holiday. Anywhere you want. Two weeks together to relax and get away for a while. How does that sound?"

Dagmar smiled wanly, knowing she was wasting her time. "Ja, that would be wonderful. When?"

Wolf patted her hand and walked toward the door to leave. "Late August, you select the place. Surprise me."

She lowered her head, hearing the door close, and looked at her liver-spotted hands. She said to herself what she wanted to say to her husband. Horst, will it ever end . . . will you ever be able to leave your precious direktorate? A moment passed, and Dagmar lifted her head to look back at the lake. She knew the answer and closed her eyes.

Tegel Airport, West Berlin

Pan Am Flight 603 from New York rolled to a stop at the Tegel Airport passenger tunnel and minutes later the weary passengers began the shuffle, bump, and grind routine of trying to hurry toward the door. The coach-class flight attendant stood beside the galley, watching the routine with amusement, but she noticed one of the passengers wasn't participating. She walked down the aisle to see who this sane person was and recognized the sleeping man in seat 36A. It was the sad-eyed Marlboro man who drank gin and tonics as if they were going out of style. If she had to cast a character for a movie to play a rugged bush pilot, he would have been it: late thirties to early forties, deeply tanned and lined face with a scar on his forehead, strong jaw, deeply cleft chin, and short but shaggy prematurely gray hair. He was perfect, right down to old leather flying jacket, faded chino slacks, denim shirt, and desert chukka boots. Still, she might not have noticed him if it had not been for his strongest asset, which had caught her attention when he had boarded in New York: his iridescent gray eyes, the saddest she had ever seen in a man. They were puppy dog eyes, lost and lonely.

She leaned over and lightly tapped the passenger's shoulder. "Sir . . . sir . . . we've landed."

Jake Tallon stirred and leaned forward in his seat, feeling as if his head were about to split open. He cursed his own weakness under his breath. He'd sworn off booze for good, then broken the promise he'd made to himself. He felt the flight attendant's eyes on him. His mouth felt as if it had been sandpapered, but he said thanks to her anyway.

The attendant smiled her best coach-class Pan Am smile. "First time in Berlin?"

Jake yawned before responding. "Yeah . . . and Germany, for that matter," he said as he fumbled with his seat belt and collected his briefcase.

She could tell by his tone he wasn't exactly thrilled with the experience. She waited until he stood in the aisle and opened the overhead compartment before her inquisitiveness got the best of her. "Hope you don't mind me asking, but are you a pilot by any chance?"

Jake's eyes squinted in pain, and he spoke softly so as not to disturb his swimming head any more than he had to. "Naw, I'm a lieutenant colonel in the Army." He glanced over his shoulder at the stewardess and tried to smile, but his head hurt too badly. "See ya."

As she watched him walk down the empty aisle, she felt disappointed and somehow depressed.

Jake cussed his lack of resolve once again as he walked down the tunnel walkway, and renewed his promise to himself that he was going to stay off the sauce. When he had called the assignments officer in Washington and pleaded not to be sent to Berlin, the personnel colonel had told him flatly that his options were either to go to Berlin or to submit his papers for retirement. The decision had been tough: go to the city that had killed his father, or retire from the Army he loved and try to start a new life in a civilian world he hated. Two weeks before, he'd made his decision in a bar. He'd known then, after his fifth gin and tonic, he'd have to try the assignment in Berlin. The Army was all that he truly knew, while his dead father was just a collection of pictures in an old book.

In the baggage terminal, a red-faced Pan Am representative was standing on the carousel speaking loudly over moans and gripes. ". . . as I said, the carousel is temporarily out of order and your baggage is in the process of being carried up. Please bear with us."

Jake took off the old jacket and moved to a corner of the crowded room, wishing he could somehow get the old excitement back. There had been a time when moving to a new job would have made him all tingly and nervous in anticipation. A new job had meant new challenges . . . but that had been when he was a star on a fast track with everything to look forward to. Those days were over now. He had let a failed marriage ruin his career, and now he was considered a loser. Shit. No matter how he tried to psyche himself up, he only felt more and more down. It was common knowledge that Berlin was a sleepy outpost with no real mission other than to show the flag. It was the place the personnel officers in Washington assigned washed-up lieutenant colonels to subtly tell them their services were no longer needed in the *real* Army. It was the end of both the line and a career. Shit.

The first load of bags was set on the carousel and the mad scramble began. Jake shook his head. If Berlin's airport was an example of the famous German efficiency, then he had reason for being depressed.

Slowly the crowd dwindled and the constant drone of bitching subsided into an occasional outburst. Jake pushed off the wall and made his way to the carousel. His two beat-up bags were not there, but a little sign resting on the rubber mat was. It read, "Last bag— if your bag is not here, see Pan Am representative." Just fuckin' great! Jake's shoulders sagged as he walked dejectedly toward the customs gate. He needed a drink, bad.

Thirty minutes later, after filling out a lot of paperwork, Jake strode down the terminal hallway looking for a bar. He sighed inwardly in relief when he discovered one up ahead, and quickened his pace. He stepped into the smoky room but came to an abrupt halt. What the hell do you think you're doing, Jake? Huh? The *new* start, remember?

With all his resolve, he gave one last longing look at the colored liquor bottles stacked behind the bar before walking out to find a cab. A minute later he stepped out onto the curb and couldn't help but smile. Finally, things were looking up. The line of waiting taxis were all Mercedes, painted tan. Hell, things couldn't be all bad if they use machines like these for taxis, he thought. He walked to the first cab and got in the backseat. "The American sector, Harnack House, please."

The driver turned with a puzzled expression. *"Was? Wo wollen Sie hin fahren?"*

"Huh?"

"Wie bitte?"

"What?"

"Sprechen Sie deutsch?"

"I'm sorry I don't understand. I . . . want . . . to . . . go . . . to . . . American—"

"Ach so, Amerikan, ja?"

"Yeah, I'm American . . . and want to . . . ah shit, never mind."

"Was?"

Jake opened the door and got out. "Thanks anyway."

It took him fifteen minutes to find a driver who understood enough English to understand that he needed to go the American sector. He had just leaned back in the cab when the car suddenly jumped into motion, fast. Jake grabbed for the seat belt, fearing for his life. Ahhhh Shit!

When the hair-raising ride ended fifteen minutes later, Jake got out and handed the driver a twenty-dollar bill. The driver shook his head.

"Nein, Deutschmark, bitte."

"Huh?"

"German money. Marks, please."

"Shit."

"No, German money, please."

Jake let the driver hold his briefcase hostage and went in to the Officers' Club to find someone who would exchange money. He found a young woman behind the reception desk who was very understanding and exchanged the twenty dollars from her own purse.

Ten minutes later Jake was in his room, all ten-square feet of it. Feeling washed out, he lay on the bed to think. It must have been close to seven or eight P.M. He glanced at the radio clock combination beside his bed and did a double take. The red digital numbers read 10:35 A.M. Great, just fuckin' great!

Jake threw the pillow over his head. Come on, Jake, regain control, my man, and face up to reality. You're here, and there's nothing you can do about it. You fucked up and now you're paying for it. Accept it . . . *accept it, goddamnit!* Stick to the plan. You've got to get back on your feet and make this assignment work. There's still an outside chance you can get back into the mainstream. You've still got friends who can pull strings; not everyone abandoned you because you screwed up. You can do it. Youcandoit!

Jake's jaw tightened and his eyes narrowed in renewed resolve. He swung up to a sitting position and took off his jacket. Now is as good a time as any to start, he said to himself. A three-mile run, push-ups, and sit-ups to start the new me. He took off his shirt and kicked off his desert boots. Not until he unbuckled his trousers and let them fall to his ankles did he remember that he didn't have his bags, which contained his running gear. Great, just fuckin' great! He fell back on the bed and looked up at the ceiling. He tried closing his eyes, but he had to fight off the old familiar image that caused the throbbing agony that attacked his mind and heart. He tensed and forced the image into the back of his brain, for he knew he couldn't handle it . . . not yet. Come on, Jake, don't give up. Don't let her get you down.

Jake clenched his teeth and rose up again. He quickly put his clothes back on and strode out of his room to walk and explore his new world.

East Berlin

Jorn Furman parked the old, battered orange truck beside the curb and unstrapped his boots. He waited until the sidewalk was free of passersby before opening the door and crawling down from the cab. He didn't like it when people stopped and stared as he "walked" on his hands. Minutes later he was in his wheelchair and pushing himself down the sidewalk of Unter den Linden toward the ticket office of the Stadt Opera House. His wife's dream had been to see a real opera. She deserved much more, but at least the tickets would begin to make up for the years during which he could offer her nothing but his love. The nursery he ran was one of the few profitable collectives in the district, and had become profitable to him personally when he started selling flowers on the black market. The state paid him by the month, a sum that he had barely gotten by on, but by selling them privately to dealers who in turn sold them to West Berlin flower shops, he made an additional twenty Ost-marks a week.

He sat in the queue for forty minutes. Most of the people in line were young students or nomenclatura, political elites. It was a typical state-run operation, meaning it ensured that common workers never got an opportunity to buy tickets. They were at their jobs when the ticket office was open, which was only three hours per day, three days per week.

When Jorn finally rolled to the ticket window, he asked the gray-haired old woman behind the glass for two tickets and explained that he needed his wife's ticket to be on the aisle so he could sit beside her in his wheelchair.

The old woman peered down at him. What she saw was a man

of the dirt, a farmer whose simple clothes and wheelchair could not hide his physical strength. His thick shoulders and bulging, exposed forearms were those of a man half his age. His face was tanned, weathered, and hard. His eyes showed no weakness. They were the eyes of a man who had never cowered. She recognized that look from a long, long time ago. It was a look of pride.

"Are you in the wheelchair because of the war?" she asked softly.

Jorn saw that her eyes were sad and searching. He put his hand through the small opening and patted her hand. "Mother, we were all wounded in the war."

She regarded him for a moment and slowly nodded. "I had forgotten my husband and son for a while today. You . . . you reminded me of them again. Their memory is all that I have."

Jorn shook his head. "Nein, Mother, you have me and every German who endured those times."

The old woman closed her eyes, squeezing his hand as if drawing strength. A moment passed, then she drew open the lower drawer and took out a book of season tickets. She pressed them into his hand and smiled. "From this 'one' to you, who understands. God be with you, my friend."

Jorn reached in his pocket for money to pay, but the old woman looked past him to the next person in line. "Ja, which performance please?"

Jorn rolled back to the truck, his eyes welling. A book of season tickets for two was something only the elite were allowed to purchase, and yet the woman had made them a gift to him. Such a present to his wife would make her cry. But that was not the reason for his own tears. He cried for the old woman and for himself and for countless others like them. The war would never be over for them, however the state tried to erase those years from their memories. They had taken away the churches and clubs where the old could find solace and perhaps peace. Talking about those days was considered "negative thinking that impeded the worker from progressive thought and production." It was just one among hundreds of subjects that the state did not want discussed. Spies enforced the will of the state by reporting such discussions to the Stasi. Nobody could be trusted. Neighbors turned in neighbors, and relatives turned in their own family members. Finally, the memories had faded; the war was forgotten.

Jorn rolled to a stop and looked up at the dark, angry sky. He spoke in a harsh whisper for the old woman, himself, and all the others: "I will not forget! *I will not* forget!"

West Berlin

Jake Tallon was hopelessly lost and soaked to the skin. He was standing in the pounding rain on a busy street corner. He had always prided himself on his sense of direction—until now. He shifted his eyes nervously. In the past hour he had almost been killed twice and had been yelled at another four times by angry German bicycle riders. He stepped forward to look down the street. Maybe he could recognize one of the buildings he had passed. Then he heard *ping, ping,* and spun just as a speeding bike rider flew past missing him by inches and yelled, "Dumkopf!"

Jake was about to yell back when he heard from behind him another warning. *Ping, ping, pingping.* He jumped back as four young children pedaled by, looking at him as if he were a complete idiot.

Jake was suddenly grabbed from behind and pulled back from the red brick sidewalk. He turned and looked into the face of an old woman who was shaking her finger at him. *"Was machen Sie da? Gehen Sie von dem Fahrrading runter!"*

Jake shrugged. "I'm sorry, I don't understand."

The old woman rolled her eyes upward and she waved her hand at him as shooing off a pest.

"Well, *excuse me!*" he barked as the little woman walked away.

Another woman stopped and spoke to him like a drill sergeant. "You stay off da bike path, ja. Nicht gut to disobey das rules. Nicht gut."

Jake felt one foot tall as he noticed for the first time the painted lines on the sidewalk. Of course, dummy, it's a bike path, *not* a sidewalk. Great! You're a perfect ugly American. He turned to thank the woman but she was already striding away. His shoulders slumped and he shivered.

He had learned two valuable lessons. The first was the weather in Berlin could change in minutes. When he left the Officers' Club it had been a beautiful sunny day. Thirty minutes later the sky had turned dark and released a torrential rain shower. Second, the bike paths were deadly.

Great. Now if he just knew where the hell he was . . .

Axel Mader lifted his beer mug and looked into the eyes of his old kamerad and fellow Iron Man, Lars Kailer. "Lars, I dreamed last night of Jorn. It was a strange dream because it was so real, like nothing I've ever experienced. We were on the river again staring at that butcher Volker."

Lars sighed and picked up his stein. "Jorn was the strongest of us all. He might be with us today if he had not tried to hunt Volker down. He's probably in Hell, making Volker's life miserable. Let's drink to him."

Both men drank deeply and slammed their pewter steins on the heavy wooden table, which caused the customers of the Gasthaus to turn and look in the direction of the two old men.

Kailer reached over and clapped his hand on Axel's shoulder. "One day, comrade, one day we will be able to go back to the river and erect a monument to those that fell. They deserve a stone with their names."

Axel smiled to lighten the moment. "Ja, with your money we should be able to erect a stone several houses high."

Lars laughed and pounded Axel's shoulder. "You talk of *my* money? You are the one who owns how many houses? Seven, eight? And how many construction companies do you own the controlling stock in? Three, four?"

Axel raised his hands in defeat. "I give up. We've been fortunate, but I tell you true, Lars, I'd give up all my houses and stock to have Jorn back. He was our closest friend. We are incomplete without him."

Lars leaned closer to his friend. "Always. Remember, we will always have him in our heart."

"Ja, always." Axel nodded reflectively and lifted his head. "I have an idea for our reunion in October. I think we should visit Gatow Air Base, the field where we started the march to Seelow."

"Is the airfield still there?"

"Ja, a British air base now. It will make a nice place for a small ceremony. I will arrange it, if you approve."

Lars patted Axel's shoulder. "Arrange it."

Axel picked up his beer mug and lifted it toward his friend. "I love you, Lars, even if you are an old, fat, bald goat."

Lars picked up his mug. "And I love you, old fox. We grow old but our hearts are still young. *Prost!*"

"*Prost!*" Axel said, lifting the mug to his lips.

Normannenstrasse 22, East Berlin

Hagan Wolf stood before the floor-to-ceiling window in his regal, dark-paneled office on the top floor of Haus One. His gaze moved over the compound and the city beyond.

"So, our Soviet friends are secretly going through our case files?"

Max Rink nodded his massive head. "My people have reported they are secretly entering the ministry's document room at night with a team from their embassy. Our old case files were destroyed years ago, but I don't like that they are sneaking around. We have always worked so closely before."

Wolf exhaled through his nose. "Times are changing. The Soviets' attitude toward us is changing as well. Dagmar asked me today when I would retire . . . perhaps it is not such a bad idea. I wouldn't have considered it a month ago, but after this past year's events, I believe my usefulness to the government has come to an end." He sighed heavily and looked at Rink. "The Soviets are weakening. They cannot be trusted anymore. Have the locks and guards changed at all entrances to the ministry. I'll talk to the new Soviet security advisor tomorrow, though I don't think I will find anything out. Like the rest of the breed that has infested their embassy lately, he is only interested in appeasing the West. I think, my old friend, that our country must begin to take steps to protect what we have gained over the long years."

Rink shifted in his chair and looked into his director's eyes. "Then we should start taking those steps now. We've never been stronger. What is this talk of retirement? We set up our own system of internal security in Angola, the Congo, Ethiopia, Libya, Yemen, and Syria because we are better than the KGB. We provided security advisors to Vietnam, Nicaragua, and Iraq long before the Soviets did. The KGB pales by comparison. Retirement? Nein, this is the time for the gray wolf to lead us in the kill. Chemical and heavy weapons experts are on their way to Iraq, as you ordered. Agents in South America report that several leaders are about to ask for our assistance again. The Soviets are weakening, but we grow stronger! How could you think of retirement, when we are so close to what we've always wanted?"

Wolf couldn't help but smile. "This old gray wolf just needed to know he was still needed. And you're right, the time to begin is now. Let's go visit our Soviet advisor and tell him we know of his activities. I want to see his face when he lies."

West Berlin

Jake awoke and peeked at the alarm clock. Thank God, it was finally evening. Hours before, he had finally found someone who spoke English, a young girl, who told him the directions back to Harnack House. There, he had taken off his wet clothes and fallen into bed. The nap renewed him, but when he got up to dress he found his clothes were still dripping from the shower bar where he'd left them. All he had in his handbags were a set of dirty jeans and a wadded-up shirt that he'd changed out of back in New York, after the flight from Fort Bragg. Screw it. He dug out the wrinkled clothes and put them on. He needed something to eat and a drink.

Minutes later he was told he could not go into the Officers' Club dining room in jeans, and he was directed to the basement bar known as the Fiddler's Green. As the maître d' informed him, "Short order meals are available at the bar . . . and of course they do have po-tato chips."

Jake mumbled an inaudible "Up yours too," and made his way down a flight of carpeted stairs to have himself some potato chips. As soon as he walked into the dimly lit room, he knew he had found himself a home: low ceiling, warm wood paneling, stained-glass windows, the smell of stale beer, a long oak bar, a bored bartender watching television, and not a single customer. My kind of place, he said to himself as he climbed up on the corner bar stool.

The small Korean bartender dressed in black slacks, white formal shirt, and black bow tie kept her eyes glued to the television that was fixed to the ceiling in the corner above the liquor bottles.

"What you want?" she barked.

Jake formed his mouth to say gin, but he felt the inner eye of his conscience staring harshly at him, then heard his inner voice warning him, *no hard stuff.* Jake pursed his lips and tried again. "Beer, please."

"What kind?"

"Lite."

The tiny woman turned and looked at him for the first time. "Lite beer? You sure?"

Jake shrugged. "Yeah, a Lite beer. Any kind will do."

The woman unglued herself from her spot and walked over closer to inspect him. "You in Germany, you know? You suppose to drink German beer."

Now it was getting personal. Jake gave her his best I'm-the-customer-and-you're-the-bartender look. "I prefer a Lite . . . please."

The small woman wearing the ridiculous bow tie was not impressed. She stared back hard, giving him a you-don't-get-it look. "You drink German beer, okay?"

"Nope, a Lite."

"Lite beer in storeroom 'cause nobody drink."

"Then go to the storeroom."

"Storeroom upstairs, long ways. I can't leave bar."

For some reason, Jake liked the woman. He wasn't sure why, except that maybe her bantering was helping to kill some time, and he had plenty of that. He smiled. "Okay, I'll go get the beer for you. I'll bring down a case 'cause I'm gonna be here awhile. Who do I have to see?"

The small woman returned a smile, making the room suddenly brighten. "My name Chong, what yours?"

"Jake."

"Jake, go upstairs to office and see Ernie. You tell him Chong say it okay, okay?"

An hour later Jake was on his corner stool nursing his fourth warm can of Miller Lite and watching television with Chong. It was nothing like he'd ever seen before. Armed Forces Network Europe was a real trip back in time—one year to be exact, as all the shows were reruns from last year's program schedule in the States. The best part was the commercials, or rather the breaks in the programming, when warnings were issued to the soldiers viewing to be careful about terrorism, AIDS, lurking spies, cleaning up after pets, crossing at crosswalks, fast trains, and bad checks. Jake lifted his can of beer to the screen. "And how about those bike paths?"

Chong placed another beer in front of him and looked closely at his face. She cocked her head to the side. "The scar on your head look like—"

"Snake. I know, everybody tells me that," Jake said. He had been told the same thing a million times.

Chong shook her head. "I not going to say snake. I gonna say *worm.*"

Jake gave her a look of indignation. "Nobody calls my scar a 'worm,' you got it?"

She cocked her head to the other side, still staring, still fascinated. "You right. Not worm. I think maybe noodle is bet-ter."

Jake was saved from further insult by "Wheel of Fortune," for Chong broke her gaze from him and returned to her viewing spot to watch the show.

The night and beer wore on, but Jake wasn't feeling tired or mellow enough to face going to his room and the darkness. He knew all too well what waited for him, and he wanted to hold off the assault as long as possible. He picked up his empty beer can and held it up for Chong to see. She didn't move until there was a break, then dug in the icebox and brought him another.

"You not married?" she asked, giving his left hand a sidelong glance.

Jake stared at the can. "Was, but not anymore. You?"

"My hus-bun spec four. He take *gooood* care of me." She looked over her shoulder at the TV. "Bad divorce, huh?"

Jake picked up the beer and took a drink. She waited for an answer for five long seconds before turning to him. "It was, I can tell."

Jake avoided the small woman's eyes. For some reason, he wanted to tell her about Helen and what she had done to him and his life, but instead he took another drink. "Let's drop it," he said quietly.

Chong shrugged and returned her attention to the television.

At midnight Chong poked his shoulder. "Jake, bar closed now."

Jake lifted his swimming head and looked around at the empty tables and bar stools. "Oh . . . oh, sorry. The jet lag must have got me."

She gave him a knowing nod. "Sure, Jake. You miss *gooood* movie. You go to bed now. I see you tomorrow. I have Lite beer for you, okay?"

Jake answered with a weak wave and put a twenty-dollar bill on the bar as he slid off the stool. He took a step and knew he was in trouble. The Lite beer wasn't as light as he thought. It must have snuck up on me, he told himself as he put his hands out to balance himself. He floated up the moving stairs to his room and entered the blackness that waited there. Flopping down on the bed, he shut his eyes to enjoy the spinning sensation, when suddenly that painful image that he so hated fought its way through the alcoholic haze and focused clearly in his mind. The pain of it ate into his heart and soul. He waved his hands to try and push the image away, but she remained staring at him accusingly. Tears welled up in his eyes and he moaned. Why, Helen? Why did you leave me?

CHAPTER 12

24 July,
Harnack House, West Berlin

Jake was awakened by someone knocking on the door. He got up and immediately fell back into bed holding his throbbing head. Oh, shit. He got up again, but much more slowly, and opened the door to reveal a smiling young man with two familiar beat-up bags resting at his feet.

Jake signed for the bags that had been God knows where on a Pan Am Clipper and closed the door. He struggled to the tiny bathroom and grabbed hold of the sink to keep from falling down. He looked into the mirror and shook his head. Great start, buddy! He looked again at the mirror, studying his scar. It did *not look* like a noodle. Not even close.

Forty-five minutes later, feeling a little better, he headed downstairs, but as soon as his queasy stomach growled a warning, he erased any thought of breakfast.

Berlin Army headquarters, he was surprised to hear at the front desk, was only a block away. Armed with a map the receptionist had given him—he was not about to take a chance after his last exploring trip—he went to look for the place where he would be starting his new life.

He showed his ID card to the guard at the side gate of Clay Compound, which served as the headquarters for the United States Forces, Berlin. The complex of buildings was surrounded by a tenfoot wall.

At Building One, the main headquarters, he had to show his ID card again at the door. The huge marbled foyer was magnificent, nothing like any headquarters foyer he had seen in his life. Oriental carpets covered the gray marbled floors of the massive room, and the fifty state flags of the United States lined the walls. At the top of a four-step landing was a seven-foot bronze soldier standing at parade rest with an M-1 rifle. His blank eyes stared at every visitor who entered, and reminded them of America's resolve to defend this outpost of freedom. Directly opposite the entryway and behind the statue were two spiral marble staircases which branched off on both sides of the raised landing and led up to the second floor. The glass wall behind the bronze soldier allowed sunlight to fill the giant hallway, the way church windows sometimes did.

Jake climbed the right stairway softly, so as not to disturb the silence. The second-floor landing was also huge and served as a half balcony. From the rail he could look directly down onto the bronze soldier below.

A prim, smartly dressed, middle-aged woman walked by, and he raised his hand. "Excuse me, could you tell me where General Thomas's office is, please?"

She looked at the name tape sewn to his camouflaged fatigues, then at his face. "You aren't the Colonel Tallon who is supposed to be here *next* week, are you?"

Jake was taken aback by both her question and her accusatory tone, but he still managed a smile. "Afraid so, but don't tell anybody, okay? I kinda wanted to get over jet lag before I got started. I'm just in checking the place out."

The woman's expression didn't change from her original pissed-off, schoolteacherly look. She finally pointed in the direction she had come from. "The general's office is that way, but I believe he is on leave. I suggest you stop at the G-3's office. There has been a change in your assignment. It's down the hall, first right and four doors down on the left." She went off in the opposite direction before Jake could thank her. He said it anyway and began walking.

The deputy G-3 introduced himself as Major Chad Evans. Jake accepted a steaming cup of black coffee, feeling as if it was a desperately needed transfusion.

"Okay, Chad, tell me what I'm supposed to do in Berlin," he said after he had taken a sip.

Evans shifted his eyes, obviously feeling very uncomfortable. "Sir, General Trout, the commander, selected someone else to take the job you were assigned. You're supposed to temporarily fill in as director of Plans and Operations until the new colonel gets here in three months. After the temporary assignment, you'll be the general's special projects officer. I'm sorry, sir, I thought you knew."

Jake shrugged, as if he wasn't bothered by being a stand-in, but he wanted to get up and put his fist through a wall. They must have found out about his past problems, he thought. That had to be it. The news was the final nail in the coffin of his career. He forced himself to speak as if he wasn't surprised at the news. "Temporary or not, what have I got myself into as the director of Plans and Operations for the Berlin Command?"

Major Evans sighed and leaned back in his chair. "Sir, you got yourself into a military-political mismatch that after two years I'm just beginning to figure out. Let me take it one step at a time and see if I can make it simple for you. Berlin is unique. There's no other way to say it. First you have to understand that we, the Brits, and the French are still an occupation force. What that means is that we run West Berlin. It is not a part of the Federal Republic. We, the Allies, still have occupation rights and can approve or disapprove any laws that govern the city. But we are not funded by the U.S. government. Our pay and the ammunition we shoot in training are about the only things Uncle Sam pays for. The Federal Republic of Germany foots the bill for our stay here to the tune of about six hundred million Deutschmarks a year."

The major took a sip of coffee and continued. "After the war the city was divided into four sectors, Russian, which is now East Berlin, and then the American, British, and French sectors, which make up West Berlin. Each Ally has its C.O.B., which means Commander of Berlin. Our two-star general in Berlin, Major General Trout, is the USCOB, or United States Commander of Berlin, and because he's the ranking U.S. officer, he's also the Commander of U.S. Army Forces here. The Brits have their two-star general, and so do the French. Over the years, the C.O.B.'s have let the West Berliners govern their own affairs on a day-to-day basis. They have a city government that has a mayor and elected officials, like the cities in the Federal Republic. But the C.O.B.'s have the right to veto any law at any time. Have I lost you yet?"

Jake leaned back in his chair, "No, so far you've told me we live off the Germans and pretty much run this place. The political side of what you told me, I'm not concerned about, 'cause it doesn't affect me."

The major wrinkled his brow. "I'm afraid that's not true, sir. You are going to be involved much more than you think. Let me go on and I'll get to your position and how you fit into all this. Berlin is unique in another way. As you know the American embassy for the Federal Republic of Germany is in Bonn. In Berlin we have something called a U.S. Mission run by the State Department.

West Berlin is the only place where the military commander is also the ranking State Department officer because the city is under military control. I gotta tell ya that really burns the State Department weenie's ass. Major General Trout speaks for the ambassador in Berlin instead of the Chief of Mission. Now again, it isn't what it's all cracked up to be. Mr. Fillmore is a good guy, and he handles all the political stuff, but he does have to get final approval on all cables and messages from General Trout before they go to Bonn or Washington."

Jake was getting antsy and leaned forward. "What's all this got to do with me?"

Evans stood and walked to a wiring diagram chart on the wall. "Sir, you are going to be wearing two hats. First, you are operations officer for the brigade, the combat force, and so you work for the one-star general. Second, you are the U.S. Berlin Command Director of Operations, which makes you the command's operations officer and means you work for the two-star, General Trout."

The major lifted his hand. "Wait, it gets better. The one-star, who is a soldier's soldier, is strong-willed as hell. The two-star is a political animal and thinks he's God's gift to the Germans, but you *also* work for a chief of staff who thinks *he* runs the command. You've got three bosses with three different missions, who don't do much talking to each other and don't necessarily agree on priorities. What I'm saying, sir, is you're always caught in the middle, and you never know who you're working for from one day to the next. In short, sir, to put it very simply, you're in a no-win situation."

Jake now realized why they had sent him to Berlin. They wanted to make sure he did *not* make a miraculous recovery and save his career.

A bushy-haired secretary leaned her head into the office. "Major Evans, it's Fay on the phone. She says the chief wants to see Colonel Tallon immediately."

Evans let out a groan. "Thanks, tell her he's on the way."

The major rose dejectedly. "I don't know how the hell he found out you're here, but he'll have my ass for talking to you before he did."

Jake patted the officer's shoulder. "Relax. I'm just temporary. I'll take care of it. Who is the chief, anyway?

"Colonel Harry Crist. I'll let you form your own opinion when you meet him. The only thing I can tell you is that he's different . . . definitely different. Come on, sir, I'll take you down to the head shed."

When Jake stepped into Crist's plush, ultramodern office, he sunk into an inch of thick carpeting. Sitting behind a desk was the plastic-faced woman he had met in the hall earlier that morning. She was smiling at him smugly.

Jake bowed his head. "And you must be Fay, the chief of staff's secretary, or is it personal assistant . . . or perhaps tattletale?"

"Secretary is fine. Go right in, the chief is expecting you," she said.

The chief's office had a twelve-foot cathedral ceiling. The walls were painted canary-yellow, and the lavish woodwork was flat eggshell-white. Large arched windows with brocaded white curtains made the room look more like a queen's bedroom than an office. Jake stood before an eight-foot, intricately carved, wooden desk and brought his hand up in a salute. "Sir, Lieutenant Colonel Jake Tallon reporting."

A short officer with salt and pepper hair was seated behind the desk.

"Do you swim, Tallon?"

"Excuse me, sir?"

Colonel Harry Crist rose to his full five feet eight inches and extended his hand. "I said, do you swim?"

Jake was confused. If the colonel had read his file as he was supposed to, he would have known Lieutenant Colonel Jake Tallon had attended the Special Forces Scuba School in 1974. Obviously the colonel either didn't care or had not taken the time to read his qualifications. What the hell difference did swimming make anyway? He shook the colonel's hand and spoke flatly. "Yes, sir, I can."

Obviously happy at the news, the thin-shouldered colonel walked around his desk and motioned toward two chintz wing-backs. "Good, that's important in this command. Sit down and let's get acquainted. Fay told me she saw you, and you can imagine my surprise that I didn't know you were in town. I make it my business to make sure my staff officers are welcomed properly and are briefed by me personally so that they start off on the right foot. Do you bike?"

Jake sighed inwardly as he quickly glanced at the pictures and certificates adorning the yellow walls. The certificates were for winning sporting events, and the pictures were all of Crist in running shorts or some other kind of sweat-soaked athletic wear. It was obvious he was one those hopeless physical fitness nuts who terrorized overweight or sedentary subordinates.

"Eh . . . I can ride one, if that's what you mean, sir."

Crist's eyes became intense. "No, I mean really bike. Remind me to show you my ultralight Scott. I have an old Collins you can borrow on Friday when we go out. It looks as if you're in pretty good shape, but I'll get you in a lot better. I have a philosophy I want to you to know about, so sit back. My philosophy is power down. You know what that means? That means I expect my staff officers to carry the ball and cross the goal themselves. Think of me as a coach who teaches you the basics but lets you call the plays. Remember that, Jack."

"Jake, sir, not Jack," he corrected, and nodded because he wasn't sure what else he was supposed to do.

Crist shook his head and his eyes suddenly narrowed as if in pain. "I got a call about you a week ago from one of my West Point classmates. He told me you had some troubles in your past assignment, something about a messy divorce and speeding under intoxication, striking a senior officer, and . . . can't remember the other one."

"The 'other' one was disrespect to a senior officer. The charges were dropped, as was the charge for striking the same senior officer. Did your West Point classmate mention that, sir?"

Crist shrugged. "He might have, but it doesn't matter because I judge a man by his work. I'm not interested in your past, only your future here with the staff of freedom. You like that? 'Staff of freedom'? I'm having a logo made and I'm going to put it on T-shirts for my staff. Good for morale. Now where was I? Oh yes, swimming. I conduct PT every Tuesday and Friday mornings. We assemble at Cole sports pool and swim laps for fifteen minutes, change, and then run four miles through the Grunewald, the park. You'll love it. Afterward, for those who want a real challenge, I take a group out biking for thirty or forty minutes. It's exhilarating, and I'm sure you'll want to join. Well, let's talk a minute about the job you're taking. The G-3 has the single most important job in the command except for mine. You control a ten-million-Deutschmark budget, and I will expect you to know where every pfennig is spent. There's the war plans and exercises and training area requests and on and on. You will not lack for work for the next couple of months. If you need my help or advice, my door is always open. The PX has bike shorts for sale this week. You ought to pick up a pair. They really do make a difference."

"I'm sure they do, sir," Jake said, wanting out of the office, bad.

Crist picked up a piece of paper from his desk. "To help you get acquainted with your fellow staff officers, I've made up an itinerary." He handed the paper to Jake. "The staff briefings will help you get a jump on how we do business in Berlin."

Jake read the first page of the heavy schedule and slowly shook his head. "Sir, this has me going to briefings, one after another, until six at night for three days. I just got off the plane yesterday. I'd like some time to get over jet lag and get settled before I get that 'jump.' "

Crist nodded without hearing his new colonel. He was looking out the window at the threatening sky. "Huh, oh yes, well, I'm glad you approve. You see those clouds? It means trouble. I didn't bring my rain suit with me this morning. I bike during lunch, and rain could change my plans." He faced Jake and put out his hand. "Don't forget, those bike shorts are on sale. Welcome to Berlin."

Jake shook the colonel's hand and walked out as fast as he could. He didn't slow down until safely inside his deputy's office.

The major looked up at his new boss and smiled. "Do you bike?"

Jake laughed only because he didn't want to cry in front of a fellow officer. He shook his head in exasperation. "Is that guy for real?"

The major motioned to a nearby chair. "Sit down, sir, we need to talk some more."

Jake was almost afraid to, but he sat down and faced the tall officer, who scooted his chair closer. "Sir, Crist will drive you crazy, but he's basically harmless as long as you don't ask for any advice. I strongly suggest you never, and I mean this sincerely, *never*, go to him with a problem. He'll only give you ten more."

Jake held up the itinerary as if it weighed ten pounds. "Looks like I have to see a Major Rodgers, political affairs officer. Where do I find his office?"

Evans shook his head. "He can wait. I need to fill you in on some more background before the staff gets their two cents in. You may be caught in the middle of a power struggle between three bosses, but make no mistake about it, the most important man in this command is the brigade commander, Brigadier General Clayton Thomas. He is a squared-away, no-nonsense leader. He focuses on only one thing, and that is training his soldiers to a razor's edge. He's good, damn good, and he knows his business better than anybody I've seen. I'm telling you this so you know who the straight shooter of this command is. The problem for us is that General Thomas is not the one who signs our efficiency reports. The US-COB, General Trout, does. He controls the staff by controlling the pulse on our careers through our efficiency reports. That means the staff does *not* support General Thomas or his combat soldiers in the brigade. It supports whatever General Trout or Colonel Crist think is important. So most of the staff are yes men. You, sir, as the

G-3, have to walk on the edge of a very fine line. You have to take care of the combat troops and make sure General Thomas gets all the support he needs to train his soldiers *and* at the same time please General Trout and not piss off his staff."

Jake felt a stirring deep inside him that had been missing in his life for a long time. The feeling was good, and warmed him like finding an old, lost friend. He felt challenged.

Seeing that his colonel was not as dejected as he would have thought, Evans took heart and felt better himself. He walked over to a large map of the city hanging on the wall. "Sir, we have three missions in West Berlin. We guarantee access into and out of the city via three flight corridors and one land route known as the 'Helmsted Corridor.' The second mission is to provide a presence in the city by having a well-trained, combat-ready force that knows how to fight in urban terrain and win. The third mission, in case the other two fail, is to defend the city in case of hostilities.

"From a practical view, we really have a political mission. We're here to show the flag and our resolve so that the Russians don't pull any shit like they did in the late forties, fifties, and early sixties. From a military standpoint, we're fucked from the get-go. Berlin is an island surrounded by the damn Berlin wall. Outside the wall are sixteen million commie East German civilians and 370,000 trained and well-equipped Russian soldiers. The Federal Republic of Germany is one hundred ten miles to the west. Poland's border is only seventy-five klicks to the east, and Moscow is only two hours away by air. We are sitting in the middle of communist East Germany showing the people what they could have had if they would have thrown the Soviet bastards out. Berlin is a symbol, clear and simple. The West Berliners go on about their daily business as if they were in the West, and we protect them and strut our stuff. Sir, we have damn good soldiers and leaders. Their worst real enemy, sad to say, is our own staff. So your real full-time job for the next three months is to protect our combat soldiers from their bullshit."

"Good morning, Colonel Tallon, I'm Major Rodgers, the political advisor for the command. The chief called me this morning and asked that I brief you about my job on the staff of freedom and what part I play in assisting General Trout with his dealing with the Berlin government. Let me first start by giving you some historical background and basic facts. First, the United States is an older nation than Germany. Most people don't know that, but it's the truth. Up until 1867, Germany as we know it was a collection of independent states all run by different forms of monarchies that had their own armies, money, etcetera . . ."

Jake's eyelids seemed to weigh fifty pounds each, and he couldn't fight their weight any longer. The jet lag monster had him in its grip. Jake's head slowly drifted down his chest.

Rodgers was just beginning to like the sound of his own voice when he noticed his one-man audience was snoozing. He sighed, walked over and gently nudged the sleeping colonel. "I'm sorry, sir, I know you're wasted after the flight, but it's the chief's orders. Let's skip the history lesson and get to stuff you need to know.

"Sir, the people of Berlin are proud of their city and for the most part support the Allies. Many of the older people remember the Berlin airlift as if it were yesterday and still thank our soldiers on the street. But the Berliners do *not* want to remember Nazi Germany. They try and erase those years from their memories. Children are told that the military is bad and they don't see the need for keeping the Allies in the city. They don't see the Russians as bad guys, and don't think we're worth the expense. They are more concerned with the environment and taking care of their people. The Green party just won big in the last elections, which means they are putting pressure on the Allies to quit making noise by shooting weapons on the ranges and driving our tanks down the streets. It's getting bad and it's going to get worse. You, as the G-3, will have to justify all the training we do in the city to the local politicians. The Green party people don't give a hoot about combat readiness. Their goals are simple: no pollution, no weapons, no soldiers, no wars."

Jake rose and shook the young officer's hand. "You and I have our work cut out for us. It's gonna be a pleasure working with you."

Jake walked back to the G-3 office and yawned in front of Major Evans. "The Z monster is getting me, so I'm going back to the O Club and go on a long run then take a little nap. I'll be in at seven tomorrow morning. Give me a rundown on my majors and then schedule a meeting so I can talk to them at eight. By the way, where is my office located?"

"Shit, sir, I'm sorry. I should have shown you your new home first thing. Follow me."

He led his boss through a series of interconnecting offices, past the fuzzy-haired secretary and into a large yellow room with a huge desk. It took Jake three seconds to glance over the spacious office, then he stepped back and faced the young secretary looking up at him through thick glasses. He judged her to be not more than twenty-two or -three. He smiled and extended his hand. "We didn't get a chance to meet, I'm Jake Tallon. I'm dumber than dirt and will sure need your help."

The woman stood up to all of her five feet and put out her hand. "I'm Maggie, sir. We've all heard a lot about you and we sure are glad you're here . . . this place is crazy."

Jake took the folded itinerary from his pocket and handed it to her. "Maggie, what I've seen and heard so far tells me you're right. Your first job for me is to call the people who were supposed to brief me and tell 'em I'm indisposed. Reschedule the briefings for the mornings over the rest of this week. I'd like my afternoons free."

Evans shook his head despondently. "Sir, the chief will be upset if you don't go to the briefing he has—"

Jake raised his hand. "The first rule is to take care of your soldiers. I am a soldier. The chief has violated the rule and has therefore forced me to take action to take care of myself. Plus, I'm just a stand-in. What's he gonna do to me, send me to Berlin as temp G-3?" Jake looked at his secretary. "Maggie, if that tattletale secretary of his calls and wants to know why I'm not following her boss's schedule, tell her the truth. I'm sick. Between us, I'm hung over and jet-lagged, but it's still sick. Got it, Mag?"

Maggie giggled. "Got it, sir. And sir, I already got a call from Fay. You have a chief of staff's meeting tomorrow at 1000 hours."

Jake looked at his deputy with a conspiratorial smile. "So, I finally get to see the staff of freedom in action, huh?"

Evans grinned. "You ain't gonna believe it."

CHAPTER 13

Tuesday, 25 July,
Clay Compound, West Berlin

Jake Tallon walked into the crowded conference room and found his place at the massive table. Place cards had been set out, identifying where the staff directorates sat. He looked around him with his lost, new-boy-in-school look in the hope that someone would break the ice and begin the introductions. The more he searched for a friendly face or glance, the angrier he got. It was as if he were invisible. None of the twenty-odd officers in the room acknowledged he was there. They were all in animated discussions, studying notes in their hands, or looking up at the ceiling.

Jake nodded to himself and pulled back his chair. It was obvious he was considered just a stand-in and Fay or somebody else had probably spread the word about his past troubles. He was tainted, and his fellow officers were following the time-honored tradition of the officer corps: avoid contact with a bad boy for fear of contamination. He understood perfectly. Fuck 'em! he said to himself as he sat down and opened the gift Maggie had given him that morning, a thick, professional, executive organizer. Maggie and Major Evans had filled out the monthly calendar inside of it so that he would know where the brigade was training, for what, and who was involved. They had also penciled in all upcoming important events and holidays.

Jake turned the divider to Meeting Notes and wrote down at the top of the page, "Temp G-3." He underlined the words then leaned back.

Two minutes later, Colonel Crist walked into the room and somebody barked, "Gentlemen, the chief of staff."

Everyone came to attention and Crist barked, "Take your seats." He tossed down a thick binder and stack of papers, and he pulled back his chair, but he didn't sit down. He looked at his seated staff as if they were a congregation and grinned brightly at Jake in the G-3's chair. He motioned theatrically toward the new addition to his staff. "The first order of business is introducing our new G-3, Lieutenant Colonel Jack Tallon, who has come to us from Fort Bragg, where he served on the, eh . . . where did you serve, Jack?"

Forty-two eyeballs swung in Jake's direction and he faintly smiled. "It's Jake, sir, not Jack. I served on the plans staff of the Special Operations Command, sir."

Crist nodded apologetically. "That's right, SOCOM. Well, let's give Colonel Tallon the ol' staff of freedom warm welcome."

The assembled officers applauded politely until Crist raised his hands for it to end. "We're lucky to have Colonel Tallon with us. As you can see, he is a qualified infantryman veteran of two tours in Vietnam and the Grenada invasion. I talked to him yesterday and found out that he swims and also bikes, so he will be a contribution to the staff of freedom PT program. Jack, on behalf of all of us, welcome to your first staff of freedom meeting. Do you have anything you want to say before we get started?"

Jake leaned forward in his chair and looked into the faces of the men around the table with a friendly smile. "Yes, sir, I would. I'd like to thank my fellow staff officers for being so kind before the meeting and offering me their support in getting settled in the command. I really appreciate it 'cause it made me feel like a member of the team already. Thanks, guys."

Crist beamed. He did not notice the general nervous shifting of eyes downward and squirming in seats. "That's great! I'm glad to hear you had a chance to get acquainted so soon, but it doesn't surprise me. My staff is like a family."

Crist, still smiling, picked up the first paper from his stack. "Okay, before we go around the table to see what everyone's doing, let me make sure the support is lined up for our staff PT this coming Friday. Jack, you'll need to talk to Major Evans about the troop support requirements. He knows what we need." Crist looked at the personnel officer. "Bob, make sure the running trails in the Grunewald are re-marked, I don't want anyone getting lost like last week. Sam, I want those refreshments to be on time this week, and see if we can get some real orange juice instead of the powdered stuff. Remember, everybody, 0630 Friday morning, Cole pool. Okay, that's it from me. Bill, tell us what's happening in the intelligence world."

Jake sat back and listened to each officer in turn talk about his specific area: intelligence, logistics, personnel, communications, community affairs, legal, contracting, resource management (budget), engineering, provost marshal, political affairs, protocol, and others. He heard about everything from terrorists sighted in Syria to the time schedule for serving lunch on Sundays at the club. The one thing he did not hear during the forty-minute update was any mention of what each staff member was doing to support the brigade's soldiers in their mission.

Jake had been briefed by his majors that morning and knew there were some upcoming training events that required the staff to coordinate for support.

When the updates ended, Crist looked over at him. "Jack, I skipped you because you're new and haven't got your feet on the ground yet. Usually you'll follow the intelligence briefing, but I—"

Jake raised his hand, interrupting. "Jake, sir, not Jack. As a matter of fact, I do have a few things for the staff." He flipped over a page where he'd made his notes. "I'm sorry, I don't remember everyone's names after the introductions this morning, so please bear with me. First, we have a battalion convoying to West Germany next week that needs logistical support and transportation help. Also, we have a field-training exercise coming up in September, so we'll need to start planning for it now. The staff will have to block out their calendars for four days so they can participate and—"

Crist broke in. "Eh . . . Jack, you don't need to mention those things in this meeting. You can make direct coordination with your fellow staff officers on an individual basis." Crist turned his attention back to the group. "Anybody have anything else?"

The logistics lieutenant colonel lifted his hand and stared hard at Jake. "What's this about blocking out our calendars in September? We have the golf tournament in September. I wasn't aware we were going to the field."

Crist smiled reassuredly. "No, we won't be going to the field during the tournament. Jack doesn't understand how the staff conducts field-training exercises. Okay, does anybody have anything else?"

The protocol captain meekly raised his hand. "I do, sir. I'm sorry I forgot. We have a CODEL coming in this week and will need support from the brigade."

Crist leaned back in his chair. "Who is it this time?"

"Sir, actually, it's three of them. The congressmen from New Jersey, Delaware, and Michigan. They are bringing wives but don't have any staffers with them."

Crist swung his head toward his new G-3. "Jack, get with Jim in protocol. The CODELs get top priority. We have a standard package of events for them that impacts in your area." Crist stood. "Okay, that's it. We've got to get to work. Don't forget, Friday morning I'll expect the staff of freedom to be at Cole pool."

The staff all rose and saluted. The chief threw back a salute and strode out the conference room. As Jake collected his calendar book, he felt the heat of angry eyes on him. He lifted his head with a smile and waited to see who would be first. No one came near him. He waited another full ten seconds before going on the attack with an extended hand to the closest stern-faced officer. It started a rush for the door. Jake shook the hand of the lieutenant colonel he had captured and found out he was the command chaplain.

The nervous padre looked around the emptying room and spoke softly. "I'm afraid you scared them."

Jake released the man's hand. "Why's that?"

The chaplain frowned. "I know what you're thinking about us, but you're wrong. We're just trying to survive and get our tours over with our careers intact. You might not know it yet, Jake, but as the G-3 you wield a lot of power that affects each of your fellow staff officers. We all know you're only going to be in the job a short time, and it's been said you had some trouble in your last assignment. To us that means you aren't worried about your career. You can work without worrying about your efficiency report or next assignment like the rest of us do."

Jake looked into the ruddy-faced officer's gentle eyes and realized he was only trying to help him understand the situation. Jake smiled. "Are you always so honest?"

"I try to be. Jake, take it slow. You're going to need help to achieve what you want. We all deserved the kick you gave us this morning, but you certainly didn't make any friends."

Jake's eyes saddened. "Does that include you, Chaplain?"

The corners of the officer's mouth slowly moved up in a smile. "No. I think maybe it's time we were reminded that our soldiers are the reason we're here. Good luck, Jake. God knows you'll need it."

An hour later, after attending a briefing on the command's war plans, Jake was stopped in the hall by Maggie, who grabbed his arm, turned him around and began pulling him in the opposite direction. She was talking twenty miles an hour as she tugged him along. "Boss, you're late for a meeting with Protocol on the CODEL visit. They called thirty minutes ago, but I couldn't find you. It's hot. I am taking you to their office now. Jeez, boss, you've got the building humming with what you did this morning at the staff meeting. Which reminds me, as soon as you're through with Protocol, come straight back to the office. General Thomas wants you to have lunch with him at his quarters. He's on leave this week, but he's sending his staff car for you."

Jake patted her back as they arrived at a door that she opened quickly for him. "Thanks, Mag, but I have a question. What the hell is a 'CODEL.' "

"Congressional Delegation, boss. Now hurry. You're late!"

Jake was escorted by a young woman into a conference room, where the meeting was already in progress. Jake strode straight to the small conference table without looking around.

Jim, the captain in charge of protocol, was writing on a butcher-pad board and turned around just as Jake sat down. "Oh, sir, I'm glad you made it, you missed the introductions, but we can do that later. I've written on the board the proposed intinerary from the U.S. Mission." The officer stepped back to show his list of events.

Jake checked the dates of each. He shook his head and looked up. "There must be some kind of mistake. The delegation arrives on a Thursday night, and you've got them scheduled for a State Department briefing the following morning at eight A.M., followed by an all-day tour of East Berlin. On Saturday, you have them on a shopping tour in West Berlin and a flying tour of the city until four in the afternoon. *Then* they visit our soldiers? For only *thirty* minutes?"

The captain nervously glanced at the six State Department officials seated at the table, as if to plead for their support.

Jake shook his head again. "I'm sorry, I guess I don't get it." He looked around the table at the group of four men and two women in business suits, all of whom looked like models for Brooks Brothers. All he got back were blank stares.

"Sir, what is it you don't 'get'?" the captain asked him.

Jake leaned back in his chair. "Jim, why are these congressmen coming to Berlin?"

A Harvard Law–professor type wearing a dark suit stood and adjusted his paisley tie. "Colonel, I think I'd better answer that one. I'm Rod Twining, the political affairs officer for the Mission. The delegation has specifically asked to see the soldiers of Berlin to assess their health, morale, and welfare. They are also very interested in the state of combat equipment. Detroit makes the tanks, you know?"

Jake nodded congenially. "Thank you, Rod." He noticed that all eyes in the group widened in shock at his daring to use the first name of the political affairs officer. He pressed on. "That was very helpful . . . and did the delegation also specifically ask to spend most of their time touring and shopping?" He heard a woman behind him stifle a laugh, but saw no humor on the appalled faces around the table.

Twining cleared his throat and brushed imaginary dust from his five-hundred-dollar suit. "Colonel, as a matter of fact, they did request some leisure time. They have had an exhausting trip, having visited other locations in Europe on their fact-finding mission. In fact, they are flying in to Berlin from Greece."

Jake wrinkled his brow. "Yes, except our Army has no tanks in Greece. Okay folks, let's quit beating around the bush. This is a junket, pure and simple. Now let's see how we're going to accomplish the mission. The first thing we have to do is reverse the schedule. They will see our soldiers training on Friday, not Saturday, and it will be for a half day, not thirty minutes. They will not have lunch in the Officers' Club. They will eat in the mess hall with the soldiers from their districts. Friday afternoon, they will take the chopper flying tour, and Saturday they will get the State Department briefing, tours of East Berlin, and shopping in West Berlin. Anybody have trouble with that?"

Again Jake heard a light chuckle behind him and began to turn around when Twining's voice boomed across the room. "Colonel, that's impossible. Helen, would you please explain the facts to our new colonel."

A prim, bespectacled woman of about forty began to get up but obviously thought better of it and sat down again. She sighed as if put out and began tapping her pencil to the beat of her words. "The tour of East Berlin must be on Friday because the stores are open on Friday and are closed on Saturday. The shopping trip on Saturday in downtown West Berlin must be in the morning because the stores are open only on Saturday morning and close at one. And we in the Mission do not appreciate the idea of a briefing on a Saturday."

"Thank you, Helen, for enlightening me," he said when he was sure that she was finished, "but I'm afraid you didn't hear what Rod said was the purpose of their visit." Jake erased his easygoing smile and looked around the table. "Folks, they asked to see soldiers and equipment, and that's exactly what they are going to do, *on Friday.* The soldiers and pilots in this command would not 'appreciate' being taken away from *their* families on the weekend to do a dog and pony show for congressmen. Their 'morale' would not be good and would reflect upon this command. The shopping and tour problem is yours. The military stuff is mine."

Twining sighed and rolled his eyes as if dealing with a dunce. "Colonel, you simply don't understand."

Jake rose up from his chair. "Rod, I understand perfectly! I've had to be a horse holder for hundreds of these congressmen. They don't make requests, their staffers do. The soldiers in this command will not put on dog and pony shows on weekends. Do not plan on them ever doing it again. Thank you, Rod, Helen, for this meeting."

Jake picked up his calendar book and gave a last look at the shocked group before marching out of the room.

He took a normal breath, once he was in the hallway, and strode straight for the chief of staff's office to warn him of a call from the Mission. Brushing past Fay, who tried to ask what he wanted, he walked into the "queen's bedroom" and saw Crist sitting on the thick carpet with his legs spread apart, stretching. "Sir, you're not going to believe what State tried to pull on us."

Crist looked up as he bent over his right knee. "Have you tried this before?"

Jake rolled his eyes up. "Yes, sir. Sir, I think you're going to get a call and—"

Fay stepped in. "Chief, it's Rod from Political Affairs, for you."

Crist sighed. "Just when my extensors were getting maximum effect."

Jake tried to step in front of his boss to get his attention, but Crist reached around him and picked up the phone. "Rod, how nice of you to call. What can I—"

Jake could hear the loud, angry voice booming out of the handset from where he stood. Crist's eyes narrowed and he looked at Jake as if he were a bad six-year-old. He nodded. "Well, of course I understand and will get personally involved myself, you can be assured of that. Colonel Tallon is new and . . . Yes, of course I'll explain that using your first name in front of your subordinates was . . . Yes, and you can tell Helen for me that this command does appreciate her work for us. Yes, of course. Thank you for calling."

Crist hung up the phone and sat on the floor again. He bent over his right leg and glanced up. "When you bend like this, you get maximum stretching effect on the lower quad extensors. Poor Rod really does need to work out more. He gets so excited that he becomes almost irrational. I think we should work with State on this and let them have their way, don't you?"

Every fiber of Jake's body was screaming, but he didn't show it as he sat on the floor in front of the chief. "Sir, I heard somewhere that if you turn your toes in and extend your arms out when you stretch over your leg, it enables you to get even more benefit. Like this." Jake did what he saw some aerobics instructor do on early morning television in the states.

Crist mimicked Jake and purred. "Yes, I can feel it."

Jake got up and peered down at the colonel. "Oh, sir, just to keep you informed, I'm having lunch with General Thomas this afternoon. I'll pass on to him that he'll have to block out his calendar this weekend so he can be there for the CODEL visit. I'm sure he had nothing planned."

Crist's head shot up. "Weekend?"

Jake raised an eyebrow. "Didn't Rod tell you he planned to let us take care of the delegation on Saturday? I'm sure it was an oversight on his part."

Crist stood and pulled on his chin nervously. "He planned for us to take them on Saturday?"

Jake nodded.

"Oh. Well, I think I'd better call him back."

Jake put his hand up casually. "That's all right, sir. I'll call ol' Rod and tell him we discussed this matter. No need for you to get involved in this one. Power down, sir, just like you said."

Crist sat back on the floor. "Yes, power down. You've got it."

Jake walked out of the office and wiggled his brows at Fay, who he knew had heard every word.

She nodded and whispered, "Slick . . . real slick."

As Jake walked out, he had to admit to himself that the exercise he'd shown the colonel really did stretch his lower extensors better.

The Mission's political affairs secretary glanced in both directions before stepping into a small cubicle where an attractive woman sat behind her desk pecking away on an old Wang computer. The secretary giggled. "Come on, tell me again what he said to Rod to piss him off so badly."

The blond protocol officer swiveled her chair and broke into a conspiratorial grin. "The colonel asked Rod if the delegation specifically asked for touring and shopping."

"He didn't?"

"He did and more. Once he knocked Rod off his high horse, he walloped Happy Helen. It was great!"

The smiling secretary sat down and scooted her chair closer. "Who is this colonel? Is he good-looking, tall, short, what?"

The woman shrugged. "Kinda tall, kind of good-looking, not married, kinda arrogant and kinda—"

"Whoa! Did I hear not married? *You* noticed? Come on, Kris, you don't look at guys the way I look at guys. What's this not married stuff? You must have liked him if *you* checked his left hand."

The blonde shook her head. "No, I don't 'like' him. I was sitting behind him and only got a glimpse of his face. I couldn't miss his hands because he leaned back in his chair with his hands on the back of his head. Actually, he seemed too arrogant for my taste and—"

"Whoa! Kris, you're forty years old."

"Thirty-nine."

"*Almost* forty years old. Thirty-nine-year-old unmarried women do not have 'taste' when it comes to eligible men. Hell, I'm thirty-two and my only standards are that they can breathe, walk, and talk. We're talking desperate here."

"I am not desperate!" protested the blonde, brushing back her hair with a swipe of her hand.

"Yeah, I ain't either!" said the secretary, using the same indignant tone. She stood and winked at her friend. "You liked him, didn't you? Come on, admit it to ol' Peggy Sue."

The protocol officer spun around and began typing again. Peggy stepped out of the cubicle and stepped back in. "You did, I can tell."

The blonde let her shoulders sag. "I did not 'like' him, but I will grant that he was interesting. Okay?"

Peggy nodded. "Okay, 'interesting' works for me."

Kris, the blonde, put her fingers on the keyboard and began typing with a smile.

Jake Tallon entered the huge house and was escorted to the back glassed-in breakfast room. Brigadier General Clayton Thomas sat at a small table reading through a stack of paperwork. Jake came to attention. "Sir, Lieutenant Colonel Tallon reports."

The general took off his reading glasses and rose to his five feet and ten inches. "Jake, it's been a long time."

Jake smiled and stepped forward with his hand out. "Yes, sir, about six years. You're looking great."

The two men shook hands warmly and sat down. Thomas leaned

back. "Let's see, the last time I saw you was when me and my boys finally made it to the presidential palace and found you with what was left of your team trying to hold off about three companies of pissed-off Cubans."

"And four East German advisors that nobody ever read about," Jake added.

The general lowered his eyes. "Nobody will read about you and your team having to hold out for those two days. God, we tried to get there sooner but . . ."

Jake shrugged. "Grenada seems a long time ago, sir. My time with Delta force was the best I've spent in the Army. I have you to thank for that."

The general nodded reflectively, then locked his eyes with his subordinate's. "I got the full report on what happened at Bragg. It was the reason I asked for you here in Berlin. I figured you'd just hang around there and get yourself in more trouble, and thought you'd need a change in scenery. You probably didn't wanna come, but I owed you at least the chance to get away and think straight for a while."

Jake lowered his head. "You were right, I didn't want to come, but . . . thank you, sir, for giving me the chance."

The general leaned closer. "Jake, I'm sorry about the change in assignment. General Trout decided he wanted his own man in the job. He heard what happened at Bragg. There wasn't a damn thing I could do. What really happened, Jake?"

Jake lowered his gaze to his hands. "Helen wanted a divorce after I got back from a short tour in El Salvador. I walked in the house after being gone for six months and found she'd cleared the place out except for a note pinned to the bedroom door. It said I loved the Army more than her . . . the usual stuff. I went to find her to talk things over, but never got past her lawyers. She was gone, and they wouldn't tell me where. It was all over, signed and sealed nice and official-like in less than a year. The day the divorce was decreed is the day she came back to Bragg with a six-month-old son that wasn't mine. She had been shacking up with a colonel from the hospital when I was in El Salvador. He was one of those smooth, young, long-haired types. She had been living with him the whole time, just twelve miles outside of the city. She married the bastard two weeks after the divorce was final. I fucked up and made a fool of myself during the wedding ceremony. The rest is history."

The general stared at him searchingly. "You off the sauce?"

Jake kept looking at his hands. "I'm weaning myself on Lite beer."

"Are you gonna make it, Jake, or do you wanna call it quits and take your retirement now? I can get you back to the States in a couple of months if you want."

Jake looked up. "I wanna try, sir. I know how to soldier, and it looks as if you need me, from what I've seen so far."

Thomas smiled weakly, as if it were a sick joke. "Jake, I've never seen such a fucked-up place. I'm fighting politicians, a lethargic staff, and a boss who is . . . I won't say it. I've got a good brigade, Jake, a damn good brigade, but I can't fight the bastards alone. I'm afraid I'm going to use you. I tried to get you the G-3 job, but General Trout wants another yes man. You've got three months to shake the bastards up and get them thinking about our soldiers for a change. After that, you'll work for me on some special projects that need your expertise. You and I know that no matter what you do in Berlin, you can't recover your career. But for that very reason, you're just the man I need. You can make waves and keep them looking over their shoulders. I can protect you on most things, but you're gonna have to play smart. I don't expect miracles, just a little relief."

Jake frowned. "I already had a few run-ins."

The general brightened. "I know, I heard this morning from two of my spies. Keep them all on their toes, Jake. Take care of my soldiers and use my name, if you have to, with the chief. He's out in right field somewhere, if you haven't noticed."

"I have, sir."

"Too bad. He has all the right schooling and assignments, but he just went off the deep end someplace along the line. Like I said, I'll protect you all I can, and if it gets too hot, I'll yank ya and you can start as my special assistant until I can get you back to the States. Fair enough?"

Jake stood and held out his hand. "Fair enough, sir."

A small woman walked into the room and flashed a wide smile. "Come here, Jake Tallon, and give me a hug!"

Jake returned the smile, lifted the small dark-haired woman off her feet and planted a kiss on her cheek. "You're looking beautiful as ever, Jenny."

She slapped at his chest. "You don't look half bad yourself, Jake. I was thrilled when Clay said you were coming. It'll be just like the old days back at Fort Benning. Remember those parties at the club?"

Jake smiled to conceal his pain, for Helen had been with him at all those parties. "Those were the good ol' days, that's for sure." He managed to make small talk for a few more minutes, but Jenny must have noticed his discomfort, as she changed the subject at once.

After he had gone, Jenny looked at her husband. "That bitch Helen was screwing around, wasn't she?"

The general nodded in silence.

Jenny looked down at the hall at the departing officer's back. "Is Jake gonna make it, Clay?"

Thomas sat down and looked down the empty hallway. "I don't know, but he'll sure give 'em hell trying."

Jake finished his second beer and set the empty can on the bar. Chong didn't move her eyes from the blaring television as she set another can of Miller Lite in front of him and wiped her hands with a dishcloth. They were watching "L.A. Law," on which Arnie was making moves on one of his clients.

Chong shook her head and talked to the screen. "Don't do it, Arnie. Don't do it, she bad for you."

Jake took a sip of the cool beer and toasted the screen. "Do it, Arnie."

Chong turned her head, glaring at her only customer. "You men all same."

Jake sneered back. "You women worse."

Chong looked back at the screen and moved slightly to put more of her back to her customer.

Jake suddenly felt something hard push into his spine and heard a harsh whisper. "You move you're dead, assho—"

Jake whirled in a blur of motion, knocking the object away from his back with his arm. He dropped to a half crouch and drew his other arm back, ready to deliver a blow.

The huge black man he faced tugged at his chin. "I'd give ya about a four on a scale of one to ten."

Jake grabbed the empty beer can from the bar and threw it at the man, who let it hit his chest, for he knew better than to duck and take his eyes off the Snake.

Jake was already in motion with a spin kick.

Chong was talking to the screen. "No, Arnie! Noooo!"

The black man stepped back, avoiding the boot that just missed his head, and spoke with a shrug. "That was about a five and a half."

Jake was closer now and jumped in the air, striking with his other foot. The man backed up but bumped against a chair and was hit just above the belt. He doubled over, holding his stomach.

Jake grabbed his hair and jerked. As the gagging man's head came up, he suddenly dropped to both knees and brought his hand up to strike his opponent's midsection, but Jake wasn't there.

Jake stood two steps to the man's right and peered down at him. "I'd give ya about a three, maybe four."

The man frowned. "Snake, you still ain't shit, man."

Jake opened his arms and both men hugged each other as Chong shook her head. "Arnie, you a fool."

Jake led his old friend to the corner of the empty room and pulled back a chair. "Sandman, what the fuck are you doing here?"

"Snake, don'tcha know about da detachment here, man? I'm a gen-u-ine spook now and gots me a cover and everything. Surely you heard about us."

Jake smiled, "Yeah, I knew Group had a bunch of losers here trying to play spy, but just seeing you tells me it's gotta be fucked up. I'm sure, Sandman, that you could put on Herm cloths and walk into East Berlin anytime you want. I mean there's black jigs in the East, right?"

"Fuck you, Snake."

"Yeah, that's exactly what I am, Sandman. You're lookin' at Mister Fucked."

The black man lowered his massive head. "Yeah, I heard, Jake. Sorry, man. It was a ride while it lasted, huh?"

Jake smiled sincerely. "Yeah, it was, Sandy. How you doin'?"

"Tolerable."

"And the old lady? Sissy still keepin' you straight?"

"Yeah, she tryin', Snake. Sissy been raggin' on me all evening to come get your ass and bring you over to see her. She makin' me beer money by workin' up in the headquarters in the G-4 shop and heard you was in town rufflin' feathers. She thinks da Snake is cool jus' cause he saved my ass in da Grenada action."

Jake stood. "Talkin' 'bout beer, I'll get us some. Whataya drinkin' these days?"

Sandman looked into his Jake's eyes. "Still can't take a compliment, can ya? You did save me, Jake. Me and the rest of the team is alive 'cause you put it down for us, man."

Jake shrugged. "You woulda done the same thing for me. Now, what you drinkin'?"

Sandman lifted his shirttail, exposing a beeper. "I'm workin', Snake, tethered to the 'thing' again."

Jake sat down. "You're really looking good, Sandy. What's your rank now?"

"Master Sergeant. I'm the detachment's ops NCO. We got lots of good shit here, Snake. The very best weapons and spook stuff for snoopin' and poopin'. The mission kinda sucks, but the livin' is good. Sissy likes it 'cause I'm home nights most of the time. Da thing can buzz me anywhere in town. Makes it easy."

Jake cocked his head to the side to see his friend's neck. "You healed up pretty good I see."

"Yeah, the scar gets me a beer now and then when I'm tellin' the young ones about da action. Hey, Snake, cut the shit, man. You really the G-3 of the command?"

"Yep, temporarily, or at least till I fuck up again."

Sandman's eyes became fixed on his friend. "You ever need anything, Snake, I mean anything, man, you call the Sandman. I owe you, man."

Jake put his hand on the soldier's thick shoulder. "You don't owe me a thing, Sandy. The Grenada action is history. I'm just glad to know you're in town. I'd go with you to see Sissy, but I'm working too. I have a stack of shit in my room to read for tomorrow. When I get settled, I'll give you a call, and we can all go out for dinner."

The Sandman rose and put out his hand. "We was good, weren't we, Snake? I mean, we really kicked ass and did it right. Ain't nobody can take that away, can they?"

Jake gripped the soldier's hands. "We did it right, Sandy, you can be real proud."

Sandman smiled and raised his hand in a fist. "Yeah, fuckin' A!" He strode for the door and disappeared, leaving Jake with the memories. Jake walked slowly back to the bar and saw that Chong had already put a fresh beer out for him.

"He friend, huh?"

Jake took a long drink and set the can down. "Yeah, the best. How did Arnie do? He score?"

Chong narrowed her eyes. "You men all same."

Jake winked at her. "I thought he would."

CHAPTER 14

Wednesday, 26 July

"Well?"

"Well, what?"

"How did your talk with the USCOB go?" Major Evans asked, searching his boss's face for some kind of clue.

Jake shrugged. "It's true what they say about little men."

"Come on, sir, what did he say?"

"Napoleon was small. Or maybe it was short. Whatever. Have you noticed that General Trout is small and short?"

"Bad, huh?"

Jake sighed, flopped down in the chair across from his deputy and looked toward the window as if longing to be outside. "It's for sure General Trout has never read *How to Win Friends and Influence People*. He told me up front he doesn't like the idea of having me do the job, not even temporarily, because I don't speak German and have had some 'problems.' He said he had also heard that I wasn't a team player and he only wanted team players on *his* team. He went on to tell me how he's loved by the German people and how he is going to change the way we do business in Berlin. He talked for about ten minutes and said 'I' about fifty times. I couldn't understand how come he didn't say 'we' if he believed in the 'team' approach. Anyway, it ended with him giving me a final warning about walking the straight and narrow."

Evans sighed and leaned back in his chair. "That's Trout, all right. They don't call him 'the Fish' for nothing. He treats his people like shit, and he's all smiles to the Herms. Wait till you see him in action."

Jake scratched his cheek. "Is he really in tight with the Berliners, like he says?"

Evans sighed again. "Sir, he only meets the bigwigs and money people who sweet talk him for their own benefit. He controls this city, remember?"

Just then Colonel Crist strode into the office, a huge grin on his face. "Jack, you're just the man I was looking for! You picked up those bike shorts yet?"

"Haven't had time yet, sir. And sir, it's Jake, not Jack."

"Make time, it's a great deal. The reason I came by was to tell you I've got a great opportunity for you. You're going to be the escort for the CODEL visit."

Jake's shoulders sagged inward. "By any chance did my ol' buddy Rod, from State, suggest me, sir?"

Crist beamed. "He sure did. You've made quite an impression on him, Jack. Oh, and I wanted to make sure the troop support was all lined up for our PT session on Friday."

Jake gave his deputy a conspiratorial sidelong glance before looking at the chief. "Sir, we've got a slight problem. Your request was for twelve soldiers from the brigade to help set up the running course and hand out drinks to the staff officers when they came in from the run. General Thomas thinks maybe we should use soldiers assigned from headquarters for that detail, rather than combat troops who've got training sessions to attend. I told the general that it was my fault and of course we'd use headquarters troops. I hope you approve?"

Crist seemed indignant. "Of course, that's what I intended in the first place. General Thomas is right. We don't want to interfere with the brigade's training."

"Yes, sir," Jake said with a long face.

Crist broke into a smile again. "Cheer up, Jack, you're learning." He turned around and walked out of the office.

Evans smiled with admiration. "That was good, 'Jack,' sir. Real good. Now all you have to do is talk yourself out of the escort duty."

Jake shrugged. "I think I talked myself 'into' that one."

The political secretary strolled into her friend's office holding a piece of paper and sat down.

The attractive blond-haired woman looked up from the envelopes she was addressing and saw the frown on the secretary's face.

"What's wrong, Peg?"

Peggy Sue was staring at the paper and spoke as if in a stupor. "I work hard. I live right. I even go to church, occasionally, and yet nothing good ever happens to me. It always happens to others. Why? Why can't it ever be *me*, just once?"

The blonde leaned back in her chair, knowing her friend was leading up to something. "What are you talking about?"

Peggy lifted her eyes and fixed her friend with a jealous stare. "You are the Mission's tour guide for the CODEL visit as usual, right?"

"Yes, of course, it's my job as protocol officer."

Peggy nodded and looked back at the paper. "This is the response from the military on Rod's request for an escort. Guess who the military escort is?"

The blonde shrugged. "Captain Jim Jenkins from their protocol office, of course."

Peggy slowly shook her head. "No, it's *him*! Mr. Interesting! Damn you, Kris, you have all the luck! I hate you for it."

The blonde took the paper from Peggy's hand and read the name to be sure who Peg was talking about. There it was, Lieutenant Colonel Jake Tallon.

"Now apologize to me for being so lucky," Peggy said. "Come on, it's the least you can do for this miserable unlucky divorcée."

The protocol officer looked into Peggy's eyes with the softest, gentlest look she could put on her face. "Peggy, from the depth of my heart I offer my deepest and most sincere . . . request that you leave now so I can get to work."

"Bitch."

"Unlucky!"

"Bitch."

"I know, but I'm an old lucky bitch," the blonde said with a wink.

"You wanna borrow anything?"

"How about that gold bracelet you wore yesterday? It will go great with the brooch I bought last week."

"You got it."

The blonde finally let the corners of her mouth move up in a smile. "Thanks, Peg."

Peggy sighed and walked to the door. She stopped at the frame and looked over her shoulder. "You have to tell me every last detail of how it goes."

The blonde rolled her eyes. "In your dreams."

Jake Tallon finally picked up the phone that he had been staring at for five minutes and dialed the number he had gotten from the command phone book. The phone rang twice before being picked up and a man's voice said, "Hullo."

Jake frowned. "Sandy, if that's your best German, you're in trouble, my man."

"Snake! How you doin'?"

"Sandman, I need some info."

"Shoot."

"Where does a guy find a, eh . . . what I want to know is if I was looking to find a . . ."

"You wanna get laid, huh?"

"Yeah, but no hookers or—"

"Yeah, Snake, I understand, you're looking to find a nice lady who doesn't ask what your sign is and can keep a decent conversation going. Doesn't have to be a great looker but at least a seven or eight. Right so far?"

"Yeah, exactly. I just wanna talk and—"

"Yeah, Snake, I got the picture. You wanna talk about world peace, feeding the Africans and cleaning up the oceans, and then you wanna have her fuck your brains out."

"I don't know about the world peace part."

"Wait a sec, Snake, let me check with an expert in the matter of matchmaking. Hey, Sissy, da Snake wants to find him some. Where do the single chicks hang out that are on the make in his neighborhood?"

There was a long pause while Jake listened to a distant woman's voice giving directions. Sandman finally came back on the line. "Snake, walk out the O Club front door, turn right, go up one block and you see a U-Bahn station, that's the subway, my man. Get on the train going toward Wittenbergplatz. Get off at the second stop. Walk up the steps of the station and look across the street. You'll see a honky-tonk called the Ey Shale. Sissy says the unmarried secretaries and German chicks who dig A-merican music hang out there lookin' for meat . . . I mean good conversation. Good luck, my man."

"Thanks, Sandman, and thank Sissy for me."

"Oh, Snake?"

"Yeah."

"The Herms wear their wedding rings on their right hand. Sissy wanted me to warn ya."

"Thanks."

"Good huntin', my man."

•   •   •

Jake finished his second recon of the crowded bar and strolled for the empty dark corner of the seedy tavern so he could dump the disgusting beer. It was real hard trying to be Tommy-too-Cool reconning chicks while walking and sipping warm beer that tasted like formaldehyde. He had made the mistake of trying the local beer known as Berliner Kindl, and the first sip was enough to know he had used the stuff in eighth grade to pour over a garden snake he had wanted to keep for a science project. The second local beer he had tried was Shultheiss. It was a little better in that he could at least feel his tongue after a few minutes. He dumped the warm beer on an unfortunate plastic plant that he swore wilted. He leaned against the wall checking his competition one more time . . . nothing to worry about. All the Herm guys tried to look and dress like Don Johnson, with rolled-up coat jacket sleeves, baggy slacks, and T-shirts. They had him down cold except they all wore white socks. Weird. Feeling like he had them beat in his Levi's and polo shirt, Jake looked over the target-rich environment of women. There were plenty, old, young, in between, plump, thin, and just right. His eyes took them all in for a final time, then he began the culling process: too fat, too ugly, too skinny, too tall, too young, too weird. That narrowed the field to about twelve candidates. It was strange, but it seemed that all German women smoked like chimneys and they all seemed to have red or blond hair. The redheads were the most interesting, for the shades of red started with violet and went all the way across the red spectrum to yellow-orange. The other thing German women seemed to love was high heels, not one-, two- or three-inch heels, but the four-inch spiked elevators. He also noticed German women liked to show off their bodies; short skirts, tight shirts, leotards, bike shorts, see-through slacks and shirts, revealing clothes that definitely made the room seem hotter than it was. The beer aside, he was beginning to really like the place.

The four-piece band took the small stage and started playing a tune that Jake recognized from the late sixties. It was his kind of music and made the place even better. He spotted a deeply tanned redhead wearing a short, tight, white skirt and sleeveless see-through collared shirt. She was holding her hand up with a cigarette between her knuckles in the European fashion that looked sexy. The redhead had that natural beauty that he had noticed in German women and admired. Unlike American women, the Germans didn't wear a lot of makeup and spend a lot of time with extravagant hairdos, and they didn't wear hose or bras either. They weren't advertising, but rather, seemed to be saying, "Here I am, the way I am." Jake liked that, the natural-woman look, yeah, the way nature intended, yeah, showing all that tanned skin, yeah. See-through blouse, yeah.

He went into his attack mode, pushing off the wall and walking his John Wayne walk directly toward his objective. He saw his target look to her right to another redhead and exchange nods. Jake slowed into a Paul Newman shuffle. The two women walked to the dance floor and began dancing together. Jake did his Michael Jackson backwards moon walk to the dark corner again. He was still cussing Sandman when the tanned redhead, still smoking the cigarette, gave him an "I'm interested, are you?" look. Awright, it was not what he'd thought, they weren't gay, they just wanted to dance, that's cool, that's European, that's natural, he said to himself. Yeah.

He winked at her and she smiled shyly. Good sign, shy he liked. The song ended and the couple went back to their bar stools. Jake repeated his John Wayne walk, crossing the dance floor, and leaned against the bar beside the golden-skinned redhead. He raised his hand for a beer then slowly turned his head as if to check out the band and saw the woman was looking at him, wetting her lips with the top of her tongue. He smiled his Burt Reynolds smile. She returned an innocent smile and somehow crossed her deeply tanned legs in the tight skirt. Instinctively he glanced down to admire her legs and suddenly froze in shock. Hairy legs? She had hairy legs! Be cool. It's okay, he could like a hairy-legged woman. It was European, he told himself, it was the natural way. He looked up into her soft eyes and dipped his chin wanting to say, "Your legs aren't that hairy." She had somehow gotten rid of the old cigarette and held an unlighted one toward him. Playing his part, he picked up a pack of matches off the bar and struck a match for her. She lifted her bronzed arm and bent forward. He stiffened; she had hairy underarms! Be cool! It was part of being natural. It was European, he told himself. He could maybe get used to hairy underarms.

The band started playing "Bridge Over Troubled Waters," and the woman cut her her eyes to the dance floor and back to Jake. He smiled with questioning eyes. "Would you like to dance?"

"Ja, bitte."

He took the woman's arm and guided her to the dance floor, where she turned and melted into his body. Be cool, it's European, Jake said to himself, feeling every natural mound and bone in her body press against him. Nice, real nice, been a long time since I felt a woman, he told himself. He let the music take him over and lowered his head and almost gagged. Ohooooo gawd! She did not stink, for women do not stink, they just smell different when they don't use deodorant. Be cool, it's European, it's the true natural woman, he tried to tell himself as he lifted his head as far as it would go and prayed for a breeze.

After the belly-rub dance, and soaked with sweat, Jake escorted the tanned Amazon to the bar and tried to smile as he motioned in the direction of the rest rooms. "Be right back."

Striding away, he cussed himself for being so set in his ways. He had to be more open-minded and change his old attitudes. He walked into the men's room and saw his reflection in the mirror hanging on the opposite wall. His image said, "Jake, what the hell ya think you're doing? Look at yourself, you're a forty-two-year-old American GI in a German singles' bar, come on, gimme a break. What are you and the Amazon going to talk about? Her tan, religion, price of wurst? Have a little pride, she is young enough to almost be your daughter, for Christ's sake!"

Feeling every bit of his forty-two years, Jake left the rest room and the bar. Thirty minutes later he walked into the Fiddler's Green and sat down on his old bar stool. Chong was scolding J. R. Ewing of "Dallas" for trying to swindle a poor farmer out of land that the farmer didn't know had oil beneath the rocky soil.

She set a Lite on the bar. "Where you been?"

Jake thought she was talking to the television. She broke her eyes from the screen. "Where you been?"

Jake sighed. "Trying to find some company."

She looked back at the screen. "You no Arnie, huh?"

Jake lowered his head. "Nope."

She told the farmer not to sell his land, but he did. Chong sighed. "What happen?"

Jake took a swallow of beer and lowered the can, shaking his head reflectively. "I guess it's gonna take some gettin' used to, that's all. I don't like cigarette smoke, dyed red hair, high heels, and hairy legs. I ain't very European, I guess."

"You in trouble. You don't like German beer either."

"Yeah, thanks, I forgot to add that one."

Chong looked back at the screen. "J. R., you big-time liar. Melissa, don't believe him. Walk away, Melissa . . . walk away . . . he lie lie lie."

In silence Jake rooted for J. R. because he knew women lied too.

CHAPTER 15

Thursday, 27 July

Jake strode into the office, only to find Maggie waiting with a pained expression. She held a cup of coffee for him.

He took the coffee first and drank two gulps before allowing her to give him the bad news. "Boss, the CODEL is coming in earlier than expected. The Mission is going to pick them up and get them to their rooms in the hotel, but you're going to have to go to dinner with them tonight to a fancy restaurant, and then you're going to the Ost Stadt O-per-ra."

Jake took the news like water off a duck's back. "Okay. What else?"

Maggie was stunned. Her intuition had told her the boss was not the opera type. She ventured a smile. "I think you'll enjoy it."

Jake nodded, sipped his coffee, walked into his office and suddenly stopped. "Maggie, what was that last part again, that Os-da-per-ra stuff. What is that?"

Maggie winced. "It's the East Berlin opera, boss."

"*Opera?* Uh-uh, no way. Tell them I'm sick, dead. Whatever you have to tell 'em, but no way."

"Boss, it's too late. Give me your room key, and I'll send the driver over to Harnack House to pick up your mess dress. It's formal tonight. He'll run 'em down to the cleaners and get a quick press job. I'll also call Mission protocol and find out all the details. You've got a briefing in one minute. Go on and don't think about the thing tonight. It'll be fine."

Jake lowered his head and mumbled "Yes, Mom" as he walked

to his desk. He picked up his calendar book and plodded out of the office like a little boy who had been told he had to go on to school.

The day went by fast for Jake. The series of briefings from the intelligence community had been interesting, not for their content, but for their incompleteness. As usual, the spooks painted a picture of doom, gloom, and evil lurking everywhere. When Jake had asked for specifics, however, he got the standard answer: he wasn't cleared for that kind of information. Jake had made himself four pages of questions that he would discuss later with General Thomas. Maybe *he* would give some straight answers.

Jake entered the office and was grabbed by Maggie, who turned him around. "Boss, you have to go home and change." She handed him his hat and a piece of paper. "On the paper are your instructions. The Mission protocol officer is with the CODELs and is running a little behind schedule. She asks that once you're ready, that you walk to her house, which is only three blocks from the O Club, and she'll pick you up there. Her father, who speaks English, is home and will let you in. Go, boss." She gave him a gentle shove.

That evening, Jake walked down the residential streets feeling like a one-man parade. The residents who were working in their yards stopped what they were doing and stared open-mouthed as he passed by. His mess dress uniform made him look like a gaudily attired band conductor. His navy-blue, short-waisted, waiter-style jacket had gold buttons, epaulets, and braids on the sleeves. The lapels were light blue, signifying he was an infantry officer, and on his left breast were his miniature badges and five rows of medals, which dangled and glistened ostentatiously. His slacks were blue with a large gold stripe running up the outside of each leg. A white, formal pleated shirt, black cummerbund, and matching black bow tie completed the ensemble.

A little boy rode by on his bike and nearly crashed into a tree. An old woman clapped. A man getting out of his car bowed. Jake pressed on, wishing he were invisible.

At the third block, Jake looked at the piece of paper with directions and made a left down a street called Annastrasse. He stopped at the gate of the second large house, which sat back off the street. He rechecked the paper to make sure it was the right address, then gaped in awe. It was a mansion. He was working for the wrong people, he thought. The house was huge, something out of *House Beautiful* magazine. White brick partially covered in green ivy climbed up one side of the front and across the eave. Heavy wooden shutters painted blue, flower boxes full of vibrant geraniums in every window, a red tile roof, and a lush green yard completed the picture. The house was a cross between a Barvarian château and an old English country home. If a protocol officer working in the State Department owned such a place, Jake thought to himself, the officer had to be selling dope on the side.

Jake pushed the button over the mail slot. Seconds later he heard a buzz and followed the instructions on the paper by pushing the gate open. He walked slowly up the brick path leading to the house, enjoying the serenity and beauty of the wildflower garden that lined the walkway. When he reached the entrance steps, he bent over and smelled some flowers growing in a large clay pot. Finally, reluctantly, he pushed the doorbell.

The door was opened by a thick-chested man with silver-white hair who was a little shorter than himself and looked to be in his sixties. He had the appearance of an outdoorsman: tanned, with a strong, square jaw and crystal-clear, dark blue eyes, and he was staring at Jake's uniform as if he were seeing a vision.

Jake stuck his hand out to break the spell. "Sir, I'm Jake Tallon."

The man still seemed totally fascinated with the uniform. "Ja . . . ja, I know, please come in."

Jake walked into the house and fell in love. It was as if it had been designed directly from his dreams of a perfect home: exposed rough beams, oak woodwork, warm-colored walls, and wooden floors. A man's house, he thought to himself, a house that made him want to take off his shoes and have a beer.

The older man led him into a den that again made Jake practically drool with envy. Oak bookshelves had been built in from floor to ceiling, and red leather furniture rested on a large Bacarra Oriental rug on a pinewood floor. The host still stared at the medals on Jake's chest and pointed at the first on the top row, obviously impressed. "This is an American Iron Cross?"

Jake glanced down at his left side. "Kind of, sir. It's a Distinguished Service Cross."

"It is for bravery, ja?"

Jake felt uncomfortable answering, and watered his response down. "Yes, sir, it is a combat decoration. The bottom three rows look pretty, but they don't mean much. Gosh, sir, you have a super house. And your English is—"

"So you are a warrior! In how many countries have you fought?" said the host, his eyes twinkling.

Jake shrugged. "Well, sir, never thought of it that way. Let's see, there was Vietnam, Laos . . . Cambodia, Grenada, and El Salvador. I guess that makes five. What kind of flowers were those on the steps, they smelled—"

"And were you wounded? Is there a way I could tell by looking at your decorations?"

Jake sighed inwardly as he realized he was not going to get his host to change the subject. He pointed at one of his miniature medals. "Sir, this is what we call a Purple Heart. It means I was wounded in action, and the little oak leaf on the ribbon means a second award."

"And this badge?" the man asked, pointing.

Jake looked down again. "Sir, that is a master parachutist badge."

The old man's eyes widened even farther, and he clapped Jake's shoulder as if he'd recognized a long-lost friend. "I was a parachutist in the war!" Taking hold of Jake's arm, he marched him toward the kitchen. "Come, comrade, let us go outside. We have much to talk about. But first a beer, ja? We will drink and talk soldier talk."

Minutes later Jake was seated facing his host, who was staring intently at him. "Where were you wounded?"

"In Vietnam. I was hit worst in the chest by rifle bullets, and shrapnel got me in the head and shoulder. In Grenada I got splattered in the thighs from grenade shrapnel."

The older veteran's eyes twinkled, and he began unbuttoning his shirt to reveal scars much like Jake's. "It is an honor to sit with you, Oberst Tallon," he said proudly. "We are alike, you and I. We understand each other although we have just met. We both wear the cross of iron." The old soldier grabbed the mug of beer sitting on the table and lifted it skyward. "To the Iron Men!"

Jake was not sure what the white-haired veteran meant, but he didn't hesitate, for he was moved by the veteran's pride. He picked up his beer mug and repeated, "To the Iron Men!"

They swallowed the contents and slammed their mugs on the table. The host leaned back with a strange, distant, reflective gaze. "Do you feel it, Herr Oberst? Can you feel the warrior spirits gathering around us? They have waited for us, my friend, they have waited for the coming together of warriors from different times and different armies. They wait to hear our words and laughter, to see our tears and feel our pain. It is all that remains for them . . . to be remembered."

Jake felt a chill run up his spine as he saw himself for a moment, an old man, alone, trapped with memories and no one to share them with. He understood perfectly the old veteran's words, which had pierced his heart. For reasons he couldn't explain, he reached out and put his hand on the old soldier's shoulder.

The host smiled at the gesture and placed his hand on top of Jake's. "We know the truth of war, don't we, my friend? No one knows but we who have been through it."

Jake looked into the veteran's searching eyes. "Yes, my friend . . . we know."

Ten minutes and another beer later, Jake was sitting spellbound as the veteran recounted how he had led his platoon in the battle of Monte Cassino in Italy. Jake could see the young platoon commander trying to hold off the American company that attacked straight up the mountain over the rubble of the old monastery and into the teeth of the platoon leader's defense.

A door slammed from inside the house and Jake heard a woman's voice calling, "Papa? Papa?"

The host stopped talking and his eyes focused, for he too had been there on the mountain in Italy. "Hier, draussen," he called out.

Jake heard footsteps and then the woman's voice again. *"Papa, ist der Herr Oberst bei dir?"*

"Ja, ja, er ist hier."

The woman's voice switched to English. "Colonel, I'm terribly late, so please go on while I quickly shower and change. The driver is waiting outside and will take you to pick up the CODEL and then to the restaurant. Please send the driver back, and I will meet you there later."

Jake exchanged looks with the old veteran, who shook his head and patted his back. "Women. They disturb everything. Go, Herr Oberst, we will talk again, ja?"

Jake smiled. "Sir, it's a deal . . . but please call me Jake."

The old soldier returned a warm smile. "And you please call me Axel. Former Hauptmann Axel Mader of Luftwaffe Parachute Battalion 600. Please come back, Jake. Soon."

Jake sat alone trying to ignore the six loud, sunburned people at the table next to his. He was trying to find a reason not to like them, but it wasn't working. They really weren't a bad bunch. They were not like some he had seen, perfect assholes with chips on their shoulders. These congressmen and their wives seemed like down-home types who were honestly trying to get a feel for where the United States soldiers were, what their jobs and missions were, and if they were worth the cost to the taxpayer. The congressmen themselves were all very outgoing types with quick smiles and quicker handshakes. Their wives were attractive, with the help of expensive makeup and Liz Claiborne clothes. They seemed to have formed a good relationship among themselves, for they chided and kidded the men at every opportunity. All in all it wasn't that bad a duty. In fact, he thought it might be fun.

He'd pierced a stalk of asparagus with his fork when a hush suddenly came over the crowd and took his attention off of his meal. A woman had entered and immediately stolen every man's appetite for food. Instead they feasted on her.

Jake lowered his eyes back to his asparagus. He had already sized her up in two words: classy, unobtainable.

A lady of her caliber was out of his league, and she didn't need another drooling idiot staring at her. Anyway, he had seen enough. She had short, blond hair styled in a bob, high cheekbones, a strong Aryan jaw, and an elegant smile. She wore a black brocade velvet jacket and a matching skirt with a white silk blouse, but it almost didn't matter what she was wearing. He thought her so poised that she could have put on a plastic garbage bag and still looked ready for a coronation.

Jake felt her coming nearer, then suddenly the congressmen were on their feet. "Hey, Krissy," one of them said. He seemed to know her. "We thought maybe you weren't gonna make it! Bill here was about to eat your appetizer."

Jake's mouth fell open in shock. The woman had stopped directly in front of his table. *She's* the protocol officer? he thought.

The congressman from Michigan spun around and took the chair opposite Jake. "Sit and tell me what the hell we've ordered. None of us speak or read a word of German." The couples laughed as the woman gave Jake an accusing stare and leaned over as if in casual conversation. "Why didn't you translate for them?" she whispered coldly.

"*Because*, I don't speak German," he fired back.

She gave him a look that seemed to say, Then what good are you? But she put on her happy face again for the congressmen and their wives.

Jake's eyes narrowed into slits. Whatever made him think that *she* was a classy broad? He wanted to scream, I didn't volunteer for this job, Miss Lady Fucking Astor! Instead he savagely thrust his fork into another asparagus.

The wives, feeling outclassed by the good-looking newcomer, needed reinforcements, so they focused their attention on the red-faced colonel at the adjoining table.

Jill, the wife of the congressman from Michigan, leaned back in her chair. "Colonel Tallon, please don't sit there by yourself. Won't you join us ladies? Our husbands seem to have forgotten we're here."

Jake forced a smile and pushed back his chair. He knew that the request was not a request. He brought his chair over and signaled the waiter he was changing locations. The women attacked him with questions about his medals, past, home state, and religion. So much for the fun, he thought.

•   •   •

Jake sat in the back of the van feeling like a fifth wheel as the congressional group listened to "Miss Astor" giving a speech from the front seat like a tour guide's. She had completely ignored him during dinner and had not said a word to him while loading the van. He pitied poor Axel for having to live with such a self-centered bitch.

"We're about to enter East Berlin through the famous Checkpoint Charlie," she was saying. "The military police know we're coming, so they'll wave us through. Then we'll drive into the East German border-police gate area. When we stop at the barrier, the border police guard will approach. You should all hold up your passports for him to see. Do not give him the passport. Only show it to him. Then he will motion for you to open it so he can see your picture. Once he checks our photos, he'll pass us through."

Fred, the round-faced congressman from Michigan, shook his head. "That's it, then. They won't let Jill in. She used a ten-year-old photo on her passport."

"Shut up, Fred! You've gained a few pounds yourself!" his wife retorted.

The group laughed and Jake sighed to himself. Great, everybody is a comedian tonight.

A minute later they drove by the tin military police building, which sat in the middle of a street, and passed a sign that read, YOU ARE LEAVING THE AMERICAN SECTOR.

They negotiated a series of barriers and rolled to a stop in a lighted area beside an ugly concrete building with darkened windows. Two stern-faced men wearing gray uniforms and peaked hats with green bands stepped off the curb and approached the van with hands resting on their brown leather pistol belts. One of the men raised his hand toward the driver, indicating he wanted to see an ID. The driver placed his passport against the rolled-up window glass, and the guard bent over to look at the document more closely. The group and Jake held their breath while the protocol officer smiled and spoke reassuringly. "This is their normal procedure. Now everyone please show your passports as I told you."

A minute later the van rolled out of the lighted border police checkpoint into a ghost town—at least it looked that way to Jake. The streetlights that lined the wide boulevard cast an eerie, almost unreal glow on the vacant sidewalks and spilled over onto the empty street. Five hundred meters behind them, the West Berlin traffic was bumper to bumper and people jammed the sidewalks at seven-thirty in the evening, but in the East it was if an alien ship had landed and sucked up all the life.

Jake and the rest of the group fell into a spell of silence. When a car's headlights suddenly shone ahead of the van, every head turned, as if they all needed to know they really were not the only humans left on earth.

The car putted past and Fred laughed. "What the hell was that, a sit-down lawn mower with a cab?"

The guide chuckled. "That is an East German–made Trabant. It's the dream of all East Germans to own one. It takes eight to ten years for them to save enough money to buy one. It has a two-stroke engine, much like a lawn mower, and runs on gas mixed with oil. It's a foul-smelling machine made of pressed wood and cheap metal."

"They're not going to be competing with Detroit anytime soon then," Fred remarked. The group laughed, and Jake rolled his eyes.

The van turned down another street, this one tree-lined, and Kris announced they were on Unter den Linden Strasse, under-the-lime-trees street, one of Berlin's most historically famous thoroughfares. She motioned to their front. "Coming up ahead is the famous Brandenburg Tor, 'Tor' meaning gate. You see it there, with the floodlights shining up on the columns. The Brandenburg Tor is probably the first thing you associate with Berlin, much like you would associate the Eiffel Tower with Paris."

The driver pulled over to the curb so the passengers could gaze up at the massive columned structure. The guide continued, "The gate was constructed between 1793 and 1797 by order of King Wilhelm of Prussia, who had a love affair with Athens and wanted Berlin, the capital of Prussia, to be the Athens of northern Europe. The Quadriga you see on top, the gold statue of the four horses drawing Victoria in her chariot, was added years later. It is interesting that the original Victoria was nude, but the Berliners of that time made fun of her because she was not endowed like a 'typical' German woman, so she was replaced with the Victoria you see now, who is wearing a flowing gown. Napoleon's army marched through the gate in 1809 after winning the Battle of Jena, and the great Bonaparte himself rode at the head of his victorious column. He liked the Quadriga so much, he ordered it taken back to Paris for display. It was not until 1814 that the Quadriga was brought back to Berlin after Napoleon's defeat and France's downfall. Germany's victorious armies marched through the gate many times in the past and included a 'victory' parade even for those who returned after World War One because the Germans did not accept their defeat. Probably the most famous photos you have seen are those of Hitler's Third Reich armies marching through the gate. It was here, where we are parked, that Hitler stood to salute his soldiers. Ironically, to the left of the gate and over a few hundred yards is where Hitler's bunker was located and where, in the last days of the war, he killed Eva Braun, then himself."

The guide looked back at the huge structure. "The street we are on was the main thoroughfare of Berlin that passed though the tor, but now of course it is blocked by the ugly wall that you see just behind the tor. Most of this area around us was totally destroyed in the war by Allied bombing, but like a wounded hero, the Brandenburg Tor stood scarred but defiant among the ruins and rubble."

She motioned for the driver to move on. "We are now heading east down Unter den Linden. On your right is the huge Russian embassy, and if you look closely behind the steel-barred gate you will see the lighted bust of Lenin."

"Yes, there it is!" squealed one of the wives. "It's big!" The group scooted closer to the right side of the van to see the huge lighted bust.

The guide motioned toward the gray massive stone building. "They say the Russian embassy is so large because it mirrors all the East German government offices that they still closely 'advise.' And up ahead on your right, on the corner, there is the famous Grand Hotel. Up ahead too is the Stadt Opera House where we will be going tonight."

The van pulled into a parking lot and rolled to a stop facing back toward the street. The group got out and their guide motioned to the building across the street. "That over there is the famous Humboldt University founded by Wilhelm von Humboldt in 1810. It was the leading university in Europe for some years before the Second World War. Now it is considered the Harvard of the East. The statue you see on the monument in the middle of the street is that of Frederick the Second riding his horse. Now if you'll let me have your attention for just a minute before we go in . . . There are some things you must know about German courtesy that are different from American. So as not to offend anyone when taking your seat, please face the seated people as you make your way down the row to find your seats. In Germany it is considered rude to scoot by with your back to them. When seated, you may talk before the performance, but very quietly. Loud conversation is also considered rude."

"Ya hear that, Fred?" blurted the Michigan congressman's wife. "Keep a lid on it. There's nobody in there who can vote for you." The group laughed, and so did Jake, who was now enjoying himself. The tour, despite the bitchy guide, was fascinating. He thought maybe that even the opera wouldn't be so bad. The new him could use some culture and refinement.

Jake followed the attractive protocol officer as she led the group into the building's ornate marbled and gilded lobby, which to Jake looked like a picture postcard. Soon he began to notice that the people gathered in the foyer were staring at him, or more specifically, his uniform. He now knew how Custer must have felt at Little Big Horn.

Jill turned and took hold of Jake's arm. "I've always wanted to walk into a castle with a prince, and here is my chance. You look absolutely dashing, Colonel, and obviously everyone here agrees."

Jake smiled, embarrassed. "Thank you, ma'am, but I'm beginning to wonder if my fly is unzipped."

She looked down at his trousers in spite of herself, and quickly glanced up red-faced, then gave him a gentle slug in the shoulder. "I like you, Jake. Men who don't take themselves seriously are rare these days."

Susan, the wife of the congressman from Delaware, turned and wrapped her arm around Jake's other arm. "That's not fair, Jill, I get some."

Both women laughed, causing the third congressman's wife to pout, "Aw, come on, girls, that's not fair. Isn't there enough to share three ways?"

Jake didn't see the guide turn around to see what the laughter was about, or the look of disgust she gave him.

Jake waited at the end of the row while the others were taking their seats. He tried to look around at the beautiful hall, but he couldn't take all the stares from the seated people. He lowered his head and smiled at an old man in a wheelchair who held the hand of a gray-haired woman sitting in the aisle seat.

The old man returned the smile and nodded, but kept his eyes on Jake's face.

Jake winked and turned to make his way down the row. Jill patted the empty seat between her and Susan. "Sit here, Jake. We couldn't get our husbands away from Cinderella."

Jake sat down, and Sue leaned across his legs to Jill. "Come on, Jill, Krissy is just doing her job." She glanced at Jake. "Isn't she, Jake?"

Jake shrugged noncommitally. "Don't ask me, ladies, I never met her, and still haven't, officially."

"You're kidding?" Jill said, shocked at the revelation.

"Nope, I'm newly assigned here, and tonight's the first time I've ever seen her," Jake said in a whisper.

Sue gave Jill a conspiratorial smile and patted Jake's hand. "Well, let us fill you in on her. We asked her lots of questions last night after she picked us up at the airport. She's German-born, of course, but she's also an American citizen. She was married to an American captain who was killed in a car accident some years ago. Ever since, she has lived in Berlin and worked for the U.S. Mission. Sad story for such a lovely lady, don't you think?"

Jake nodded, and was saved from any more gossip when the orchestra began playing.

Three rows back, Jorn Furman squeezed his wife's hand and felt her trembling excitement. She had been acting like a teenager anticipating her first date for the past week. He leaned over and kissed her soft cheek. She was his best friend in life, and to see her happiness gave him a feeling of bliss. He sat back to listen to the music and enjoy one of the most fulfilling nights of his life.

The van stopped at the front entrance of the Hotel Espalde, and the congressmen and their wives got out, thanking the tour guide and Jake. A minute later, after the last waves and a reminder that the van would pick up the group at eight the next morning, Jake climbed back into the van. He sat back feeling good about the evening and looked out the window as the van driver pulled away. The guide sat in the front seat, making notes in a small notebook. Ten minutes later and five miles away from the Harnack House, they still had not spoken to each other. Jake leaned up to the German driver. "Excuse me, could you please tell me what a *Ritterkreuz* is?"

The driver shrugged, *"Mein englisch ist nicht gut."*

Jake patted the man's back. "No sweat, neither is my German."

Another minute passed before the protocol officer spoke flatly. "Where did you hear about a *Ritterkreuz?*"

Jake was surprised by her voice, for it had lost the tour-guide inflection. He looked out the window to avoid looking at her. "Your dad and I were talking, and he mentioned he received one and—"

She transfixed him with a searching stare for an explanation of why he would ask such a question. "The *Ritterkreuz* means 'Knights Cross,' a medal for valor. Nazi things like that were not allowed to be kept. Why do you ask?"

Jake shrugged. "I don't know, I guess I wanted to see one, that's all." The van stopped in front of Harnack House, Jake got out saying "G'night," and strode toward the entrance, praying the bar was still open.

The driver pulled away and the woman lowered her head in confusion. Her father never talked about those days to anyone but his old kameraden; not her, or even her Richard when he was alive. Why would her father tell a man he didn't even know about his medal?

She lifted her head and felt suddenly weak. Papa is sick! He's having lapses and . . . no, he looked and acted fine when she had talked to him before she left for the restaurant. In fact, he was bubbling with excitement that he wouldn't give an explanation for. So why? Why would Papa tell the arrogant colonel?

"You play in band?"

"Come on, Chong, this is mess dress. I'm lookin' good, I went to an opera and everything."

"What was opera about?"

"Just give me a beer, huh?"

"You didn't like?"

"I tried, okay? Couldn't understand a damn thing."

"You miss 'Falcon Crest.' Old woman got new lover who really trying to get her money. Son knows and trying to make trouble but his wife helping lover."

Jake nodded, wishing he'd seen it. At least he would have understood the language. "Chong, did you know tor means 'gate'? You know, like the 'Brandenburg Tor.' "

"Sure, everybody know that. You drink German beer, maybe you learn language, huh?"

"Never mind."

"What opera about?"

"Singing."

"Come on, Jake . . . what it about?"

"This old woman got herself a new lover, but he's really trying to get her money and—"

"You right, never mind."

CHAPTER 16

Friday, 28 July

Peggy Sue waited in the cubicle behind her friend's desk and let out a whimper of anticipation when she walked through the doorway. "How'd it go?"

Kris set her purse and sack lunch down, then opened the window behind the desk. "The delegation? It's a good group."

"Not them! *Him!* Mr. Interesting! What kind of guy is he? What did you two talk about?"

Kris turned from the window. "Colonel Tallon does not speak German. Strike one. He is arrogant and self-centered. Strike two. He is totally without scruples. He made passes at the wives the whole evening. Strike three."

Peggy winced. "Ouch. That bad, huh? I hoped maybe he was different. How did he come on to you?"

Kris gave Peggy a look of indignation. "Me? He barely spoke a word to me the whole evening."

"But I thought you said he made passes at all the women?"

"No, just the wives. He smiled at everything they said and hung on their every word and—"

"Whoa!" Peggy said, holding up her hand. "Let me get this straight. He didn't make a pass at you?"

"No. The opposite, he completely avoided me."

"Uh-huh. And that, of course, is how you came to the conclusion he was arrogant and self-centered, right?"

The protocol officer's shoulders sagged a little and her tone became less confident. "Right. Well no, not exactly. You're turning things around."

Peggy nodded. "Okay, I think I'm getting the picture now. But tell me something. What does his not speaking German have to do with anything? I don't speak German. Hell, ninety-eight percent of the Americans stationed in Berlin don't speak German. Why is that a strike for the colonel?"

Kris forced a patient smile. "Peg, he is a colonel in a very important job. They don't put people in such positions without schooling them in the language. My Richard went to language school before he came to Germany, and by the time I met him, he was very proficient. Either Colonel Tallon didn't learn a thing at the school, or he chooses not to speak the language, which shows something about what he feels about Germans."

Peggy sighed and sat still for a full five seconds before pushing back the chair, standing up and shaking her head with disappointment. "Kris, you're a lost cause as long as you compare men with Richard. Richard was perfect and always will be. Just like your son was. But you have to let them go. They've been gone a very long time."

Kristina Hastings put her purse and lunch into the drawer and sat down behind her desk. Her eyes shifted to the picture of her husband and son beneath the desk glass. With welling eyes she looked at the wedding ring she still wore on her left hand. Maybe she *was* a lost cause, but what did it matter? She didn't even want to play the game. Richard, her husband, and Dirk, her son, were still with her in her dreams, and that was enough. She still had the dreams of her lost family to cling to.

East Germany

Jorn pushed himself in his chair straight down to the warehouse foreman's office on the dock. He was completely disgusted.

The foreman threw up his hands before Jorn could say a word. "I know, Jorn. The flowers died again because of a lack of water and light. It is not your problem. The state pays your salary no matter what happens to them. The state will even confer upon you another banner for exceeding production."

Jorn threw his arms up in frustration. "My plants are my children! I don't want meaningless banners, I want my children to live!"

"It is the same problem as last year and the year before that and the years before that," the foreman said in exasperation. "The priorities are food and fuel first. The food lines are getting longer, and the city workers are complaining to the transportation minister, who complains to the district transportation directors, who complain to the transportation bureaucrats, until it finally comes to the local distribution director, who complains to me! I have to listen to the complaints, but there is nothing I can do to help you or me . . . legally."

Jorn's eyes began to narrow. "Are you saying there is something else that can be done?"

The foreman looked past Jorn to the orange truck parked at the dock. "You deliver your flowers to Berlin on occasion now, don't you?"

Jorn shrugged. "Yes, but only when I have saved enough petrol coupons. The cooperative only receives a monthly allocation, and the collective shares them equally. I have had to make the deliveries myself on my allocation, for it is the only way to save my plants from your stupid bureaucrats."

The foreman pulled on his chin in thought. His gaze slowly lowered to the legless old man in the wheelchair. "I could put you on the transportation driver rolls. You would be paid wages for two jobs: nursery cooperative manager and transportation driver Second Class. You are really doing both anyway. The only problem is that you would also have to deliver some products to Potsdam as well as Berlin. It is more work, but you would make twice as much money."

Jorn looked at the foreman suspiciously, knowing there was a catch. "And how much for you?"

The man's lip curled back in a wolfish smile. "Fifteen percent. It is not much, considering you will become rich."

"And I will receive the necessary petrol coupons?"

"Enough to cover your trips, and some extra if you want to run a few trips on your own, if you know what I mean."

Jorn glanced down at his callused hands. It was the only way to beat the broken system. He looked up. "What else?"

The foreman made sure none of his workers were within earshot and spoke in a low voice. "I have certain goods that need delivering that will not be out of your way. The buyer you will deliver the excess goods to is very generous. You get twenty percent from me and whatever he gives you."

Jorn knew what the goods would be: hard-to-get food items for the black market. He stared hard at the foreman, then put out his hand. "I will give you *twelve* percent, not fifteen."

The foreman laughed and took the offered hand. "You are a shrewd man, Jorn. It will be good doing business with you."

McNair Barracks, West Berlin

Jake moved out of the way so that he wouldn't be in the background of the pictures taken with the congressmen and the young soldiers from their districts. It had been a good morning for everyone. The congressmen had learned about the readiness of the soldiers of the Berlin Brigade, and the soldiers had learned that their representatives were genuinely concerned about them. Jake felt good as he walked over to join the wives, who were seated in a stand of bleachers.

Jill patted the seat beside her, for the colonel to sit. "You see my husband? He's in hog heaven with all those future voters. Hey, where is Krissy?"

Jake shrugged with indifference. "She's off today. The military has the lead. Tomorrow she'll be your primary escort, and I'll be coming along for the tour of West Berlin."

Jill patted his arm with a sly smile. "Want me to put a good word in for you when I see her tomorrow?"

Jake grinned good-naturedly. "Come on, Jill, she's not my type. She's a widow."

Jill's eyes widened slightly. "Why's that so bad?"

Jake's smile faltered. "I've had firsthand experience. My mother is a widow. She dated a few times, but none of the guys could measure up. She could never let go of Dad." Jake realized he was being too serious and shored up his smile. "Jill, in ol' Jake's book of bachelor rules, it says on page one, 'Widows carry too much spare baggage around with 'em . . . ya can't compete with the past.' "

Jill realized she had tread on a sensitive spot and patted his arm again. "You hang in there, Colonel. My Fred saw the light and married me just four years ago, and it was the smartest thing he ever did." She looked deeply into his eyes and spoke almost in a whisper. "I was a widow, Jake, my first husband was shot down over Hanoi."

Jake's grin dissolved. "I'm sorry, Jill, I have a tendency for sticking my foot in my mouth."

She winked. "Don't be sorry, Jake. Just give us old widows a chance. It takes time to let the memories go."

Jake nodded, wishing he were someplace else.

Muggelsee, East Berlin

Dagmar Wolf was working in the garden with her assigned security guard when she heard a car on the graveled driveway. She rose up from her knees and shielded her eyes from the sun. "Renate, who is it? Can you tell?"

The young woman smiled. "Ja, it's Herr Wolf."

Hagan Wolf got out of the special, black Lada sedan and nodded to his driver. "Have a good weekend, Willi."

Dagmar kept her puzzled smile as she approached her husband. "This is a first, Horst, you being home so early. What is the occasion?"

Wolf looked past his wife toward the garden that she had planted every year since they had moved to the large estate. "I've come home to help you, my dear. I haven't ever helped you before in the garden, and thought it was time I did. You see, I *do* listen to you. I will be spending more time with you from now on."

She stared at her husband until his eyes shifted to her. Tears rolled down her cheeks as she walked toward him, holding her arms out for an embrace.

Minutes later as Wolf was changing his clothes, his green phone rang. He strode to the nightstand beside the bed and picked up the secure phone that was a direct line to his operations duty officer. "Ja?"

"Direktor, we have a walker."

"Who?"

"The number two in S and T. The deputy says the walker is very healthy."

"Is the walker covered?"

"Yes, since he began the stroll. The deputy requests a blue light."

Wolf's eyes twinkled. "You have the blue light. Call me when the light is out."

"Ja, Direktor. Guten Tag."

Wolf sat on the bed trying to place the face of the ministry's assistant director of Science and Technology. Of course, now he remembered. It was Thomas Weber, a young man brought up from the university because of his computer knowledge. Too bad he had walked. Being "healthy" meant that he knew too much. A man in his position should have known that he could not defect to the West without paying the consequences. But he was young. He didn't understand a lot of things. Maybe he actually thought he could walk away and leave his country and the Stasi. The fool.

Dagmar strolled into the bedroom. "Who was that on the phone, dear?"

Wolf stood, took hold of his wife's arm and guided her to the bed. "No one. Just a little problem at the office."

"Horst, what are you doing?"

"Undressing you. Has it been that long?"

She smiled coyly. "I should take a shower and—"

"I like the smell of the earth on you."

"But Horst we . . . oh . . . oooh."

Continental Hotel, West Berlin

Professor Thomas Weber and his wife shook the hands of the smiling men who were congratulating them for their bravery, though Thomas knew bravery was not involved. He had merely walked out of the West Berlin computer trade show exhibit hall, met his wife at the door, and took a taxi to the Marienfelde refugee center. It had only taken them minutes to sign in at the registrar's office and become citizens of West Germany. He had not told the center staff that he had worked for the Minister of State Security because they would have held them at the Marienfelde barracks for debriefings. He had told them he was a university professor, as he truly was prior to joining the Stasi six months before. Tomorrow he would tell them the rest of the truth and begin in-processing. Tonight he wanted to be free. His room at the expensive hotel was already paid for by the East German government, so he had seen no reason to let it sit empty. It was his wife's first visit to West Berlin, and she deserved some luxury after having to live at the Karl-Marx-Allee four-story apartment building's cramped three-room flat.

The men who were leaving his hotel room were friends he had met in the West at various trade shows. As assistant director for S and T, he was responsible for analyzing new computer hardware and securing the best and newest western software. He had agreed to join the Science and Technology Department of the ministry only because he'd thought he would be helping his country. He was convinced that by modernizing the government administration with computerization, progress could be made in improving the chaotic economic situation. Unless something was done to streamline the slothful bureaucracy, the system would collapse. His idealism disappeared when he learned that the ministry was not interested in his ideas. All they were interested in was modernizing their control of the people and improving military capabilities. He had made his decision to leave his country the day his wife had told him she was pregnant. He did not want his child to live in a decaying society where hope was only a dream.

Weber closed the door after waving farewell to his friends and excitedly turned to his wife. "Aren't they wonderful? They have helped us in so many ways."

Her expression was one of worry. "I'm frightened. My stomach is in knots, and I feel weak."

Thomas put his arm around his freckle-faced wife, who was five months pregnant now. "They will have me a job in a week in Stuttgart, and we will start a new life for our child. There is nothing to be frightened of. Our old life is over, and today we are citizens of the Federal Republic of Germany. 'Citizen.' Don't you love the sound of it?"

She lifted her willing eyes to him. "But our families . . . What will—"

"They'll be fine. We told them nothing, so they have nothing to hide. Please, darling, relax and think about how wonderful things will be for us. Everything you've always wanted is all around us."

He was interrupted by a knock on the door. The couple exchanged fearful glances. Thomas broke into a smile and patted his wife's shoulder. "We are forgetting we are in the West now. We don't have to be afraid of knocks at the door." He rose and walked to the door. "Who is it?"

"Room service for Herr Weber. Friends have ordered you champagne," said a woman's voice.

Thomas winked at his wife and opened the door. An attractive woman with dark red hair and wearing a man's tuxedo smiled brightly as she pushed the cart into the carpeted room. She took two crystal champagne glasses from the cart and offered them to the professor. "May I have the honor of pouring for you, Herr Weber?"

Weber took the glasses and gave one to his wife. "Please, that would be very nice."

The woman removed the already opened bottle from the silver ice bucket and made the formal presentation, displaying the label. "Dom Pérignon 1962. I hope you approve?"

She waited for the nod, took the white cloth from her shoulder and wrapped the bottle. She poured a small amount into Thomas's glass and took a step back to await his tasting.

The professor followed proper etiquette by smelling, swirling, sipping, and drinking before nodding. He had seen it done in a movie. "Delightful."

The waitress poured half a glass for Frau Weber, then poured the same amount for her husband. She placed the bottle back in the ice and wrapped the towel around the neck and top of the bucket. She waited until the couple toasted each other and sipped their drinks before smiling again. "Will there be anything else, Herr Weber?"

The professor was smiling at his wife and didn't look at the waitress. "No, that will be all, thank you."

The waitress picked up a small pad. "If you would be so kind to initial this form, please. The champagne was a gift, but I must have initials for the receipt."

"Of . . . of course," Thomas said, feeling suddenly heavy and sluggish. He had heard himself speak to the waitress but didn't remember his mouth moving. He stepped toward the woman who held out the pen and tried to grasp it but missed. His eyes went in and out of focus, and he felt himself falling forward.

Confused and scared, his wife moved forward to catch her falling husband, but her legs wouldn't respond. She fell facedown onto the carpet on top of him.

The waitress put on her gloves, then checked the still bodies, feeling their necks for a pulse. They had to be alive before she took the necessary final measures.

Muggelsee, East Berlin

Wolf picked up the green phone on the fourth ring. "Ja?"

"The light is out, no complications."

"Thank you. Good evening." Wolf replaced the receiver and glanced at his watch. He had given the blue light three hours and forty minutes before. During that time he had made love with his wife, worked in the garden, showered, changed clothes, and read two chapters of a mystery novel.

He thought about the young professor. Had he been patient, he too could have achieved great things for the state. All he had needed was to learn how to make the system work for him. He could have done such great things, but now . . . such a waste.

Wolf slipped on his shoes and strolled downstairs to join his wife in the kitchen. She was helping the chef prepare a salad with vegetables that he had gathered himself from the garden. He hummed a little tune. He felt the best he had in years.

Harnack House, West Berlin

"Don't divorce her, Elliot. She good for you. She love you. Think of children."

Jake had listened to Chong talk to the characters on "Thirty-something" for twenty minutes, during which time he had not made a single comment. The reason was simple, he didn't give a damn about what thirtysomething people did. He told himself if the show was about fortysomething people he would be interested, maybe. Television people, like movie people, always seemed to say the right things at the right times; he didn't. Oh, at night after a conversation, he thought of perfect comebacks, but it was always too late. He wished just once he could say the right thing at the right time. He raised his fifth empty beer can of the night, wiggling it. He was about to say "Beer, please" when Chong put one in front of him. *See, he said to himself, I can't even order a damn beer on time!*

He felt and smelled more than saw the woman walk in and sit down two bar stools down from him. He shifted his head and gave her a once-over. She was a six, no wedding ring, pretty face, big boobs, but a tad chubby and wore too much makeup. Obviously a Department of Defense civilian, for only military and DOD civilians were allowed in the club.

Chong shook her head at the "Thirtysomething" character, Michael, who had told Hope, the wife, to hang in there, her good-looking husband was just feeling down because his best friend, Elliot, was having troubles at home.

Giving Chong a sidelong glance, the auburn-haired woman slid off her bar stool and moved next to Jake. Motioning with her head toward the TV-infatuated bartender, she whispered, "Is it safe to order a drink when the bartender is like this?"

Jake wrinkled his brow and whispered. "Eh . . . not yet. Wait till Hope sees that Michael is upset because of Elliot . . . or when there's an Armed Forces Network break."

The woman looked into Jake's eyes to see if he was serious and saw that he was. The corners of her mouth turned up slowly into a smile and she looked around the empty bar. "How come there's nobody here? I thought this place would be rocking."

Jake shrugged and whispered again, "It's the same old story. The Officers' Club is trying to see how much money it can lose. The club won't let German women in unless they have an ID card. The people who are the would-be customers of this joint are mostly young, bachelor officers. No women, no customers, no business. The perfectly run Officers' Club."

She looked into his eyes again. "Are you a cynic by nature?"

Jake smiled. "I'm an old bachelor officer who knows how the system works—it doesn't."

She returned his smile but showed more teeth. "You must be a Capricorn, are you?"

Jake heard the warning bells go off in his head and quickly formed his mental defenses. "Eh . . . to tell you the truth, I don't know. I'm not into that sort of—"

"When were you born? I know all the signs. I'm an Aquarius, you know? You can tell because I talked to you first. We're very outward, as you can tell, right? I still think you're a Capricorn because we get along so good together and . . ."

Jake slowly shifted his body around so he could see the television as the woman kept talking. He was trying to think of the perfect line to tell the horoscope queen he was not interested in stars or her. He concentrated harder on his response and kept coming up with "Get lost," but that was too cruel. He thought harder.

". . . this morning I checked, and sure enough it said I would meet a stranger and we—"

Chong slammed down a mug on the bar, startling the woman. The small bartender with the big black bow tie gave the horoscope queen a squinting Korean glare and commanded, "Quiet! Hope talking to Michael!" Chong swung her head back to the television and told Hope to be patient, Michael would snap out of it.

Jake lowered his head with admiration. Chong was one of those people who naturally knew the right lines.

The indignant horoscope queen looked at Jake for support, but he joined Chong in talking to Hope. The horoscope queen slid off the bar stool and marched out of the bar.

During the next Army commercial Chong looked over her shoulder at Jake. "What fat lady want?"

"My sign."

"Really?"

"Yeah."

"She too fat anyway, Jake. You can do bet-ter."

"Really?"

Chong cocked her head to the side as if needing another angle of him to make a proper assessment. She straightened up and sighed. "I take back. Fat lady okay for you."

Jake picked up an empty beer can and brought his arm back to throw it at her. Chong smiled and turned back to watch the television.

CHAPTER 17

Saturday, 29 July

The van pulled to the curb and the sightseers got out to follow their tour guide to the island in the middle of a tree-lined boulevard. The warm sun shone down from a crystal-clear sky as Kristina motioned to her right. "You see there the Soviet War Memorial dedicated to their unknown soldier. It was built in 1945 by the Soviets to honor the thousands of unidentified soldiers who had perished in their attempt to take the city of Berlin. To many older Berliners, the memorial is known as the 'tomb of the unknown rapist.' Sadly, the undisciplined Russian soldiers raped thousands of Berlin's women and plundered the city after it was taken. The two Russian tanks at either end of the memorial are said to have been the first tanks to enter Berlin." She turned and faced to the east. "And there again is the Brandenburg Tor, which we saw Thursday night from the east side. It looks different from this side because of the wall. The street we are on is called Strasse des Siebzehn Juni, more commonly referred to as Seventeen June Street. The strasse was named in honor of the East Berlin workers' uprising of June seventeenth, 1953. The workers demanded economic reforms and de-Stalinization. Walter Ulbricht's regime used his Volkspolice and the Soviet army to suppress the demonstration, and almost five hundred people lost their lives."

Kristina paused a moment to let her words sink in before motioning to a huge tower to the east. "That tower you see behind and to the left of the tor is called the Fernsehturm, or simply the television tower. It took four years to build and is 365 meters high and has become the dominant landmark in East Berlin. The round dome you see near the top has television and radio transmitting systems and also a revolving restaurant. The West sent money to East Germany to rebuild its churches, but instead the communist government used the money to build the tower. In the West we call it 'the Pope's revenge.' You can see why by looking at the metal sphere. The sun casts a glare on the curved dome, forming a gold cross. The East Germans have done everything possible, even painting over the shiny metal with flat absorbing colors, but they cannot stop the sun from making its cross for all to see."

Kristina let the delegation take pictures for several moments, pointed out a few more landmarks, then piled everyone back into the van for a short ride to a huge building near the Brandenburg Gate. The van pulled to the side of the road. "This is the famous Reichstag. It was built in the late nineteenth century during the Wilhelminian Empire and was the seat of parliament during the Weimar Republic. The inscription above the entrance was added after World War One and reads 'Dem Deutschen Volke'—'To the German People.' The corner window you see on the right is where Philipp Scheidemann proclaimed the new German Republic on November ninth, 1918. Most of you will recall from your history books that it was here on February twenty-seventh, 1933, that the Reichstag burned. Hitler and his National Socialist party accused the communists of arson and used the fire as an excuse to declare himself dictator of all Germany. Some say it was Hitler's henchmen who were the arsonists. The truth will never be known."

Jill poked her husband. "You remembered that from your history books, didn't you?"

The congressman shrugged. "Eh . . . yeah, sure . . . kinda."

Kristina motioned for the driver to go on. "It's a museum now."

After another hour of sightseeing, Kristina turned in her seat. "We are now coming to the most famous street of modern Berlin, the Kurfürstendamm, better known as the Ku'damm. It is famous for its shops, theaters, cinemas, and over one hundred cafés and restaurants. Many of our American soldiers come here at night, for it is said that the pubs never close. Up ahead you see the symbol of West Berlin, the Kaiser Wilhelm Gedächtniskirche, the Memorial Church. The church was bombed by Allied planes, and the ruined tower you see stands as a memorial to the Second World War."

The driver drove past the church for a block and pulled into a no-parking area in front of a huge department store. Kristina smiled and motioned to the entrance. "And this, ladies, is the Kaufhause des Westens, better know as 'KaDeWe,' the largest department store on the continent."

The men all moaned in unison. Kristina smiled. "No, gentle-men, this is a store I think you will enjoy as well. It has six floors, and on the sixth is an entire floor of foods and small cafés featuring delicacies from all over the world. I might add they have a wonder-ful selection of beers on tap and wine available free for tasting. I will let you all out here so you can shop or roam the streets if you wish. Please be back here at the front of the store in two hours, and we will get you back to the hotel in time to pack and make your flight at three o'clock."

The wives pushed their men out of the van and in seconds had disappeared behind the department store's glass doors. Jake climbed out, walked around to the driver and patted his shoulder. "Gut job, Siegfried. You drove like a pro, my man."

Siegfried smiled and nodded. "Ja ja, I drive gut, Jake."

Kristina had ignored the colonel up to that moment, but turned in her seat when she heard the two men butchering both German and English.

Jake pulled a map out of his back pocket and a small German dictionary. "Okay, Siegfried, *Wo ist da flos mark.* I think that's right." He quickly turned the pages of the dictionary. "Eh . . . nope, *Vo ist de flo mart . . .* ya told me about?"

Siegfried nodded. *"Ja, ja, geben Sie mir die Karte. Das map, bitte."* He pointed at a spot on the map and toward the north.

Kristina leaned forward to look at the map. "What flea market are you trying to find?" she asked.

Jake stooped his shoulders to see. "Is there more than one? Sieg-fried and I were talking when you were showing the group inside the church this morning, and he said something about a flea market near a canal bridge."

Kristina leaned back in the seat. "Get back in, Colonel. We'll take you there."

"Naw, that's all right. I'll find it. You all better stay here and—"

"Get in, Colonel. We're in a no-parking zone," Kristina said in a voice that was louder than she intended. She softened her tone. "It's no problem. The market is very close. It will give us all some-thing to do for the next two hours."

Jake shrugged and got back into the van. "If you're sure it's not gonna cramp your style."

As the car began to move, Kristina fixed the colonel with a smug look. "How did you 'talk' to Siegfried?"

Jake could tell by her tone that it was intended less as a question than an indictment.

He looked out of the window to avoid her accusing gaze. "We

kind of used our hands and looked through the dictionary, but we got by."

"The German teacher you had in the language school must have not been very proficient."

Jake still kept his eyes turned away. "I didn't get a chance to go to the language course because there wasn't time. I only found out three weeks ago that I was coming here."

Kristina studied his profile. Perhaps her previous assessment had been too hastily made. He'd had no tutoring in German, but he was trying to learn. He wasn't the playboy she'd thought he was either. She had watched him closely that morning during the tour and had realized that he really wasn't overly attentive to the wives. He was just friendly by nature. His friendliness included a lot of touching—more than she'd seen from any other man, with the exception of her father. It was the colonel's way, as it was her father's, to pat people on the back, hold their arms, and even put his own arm around them. His style apparently worked. Not only did the wives and congressmen respond to him, but Siegfried did as well.

Kristina sat back in her seat. Peggy Sue said she was always comparing men to Richard. In the colonel's case that was not a problem. Richard had been a very quiet, sensitive man who possessed an inner strength that radiated love and tenderness. He was not a man's man, but rather a man who was an insightful, caring teacher. He knew the arts, loved poetry, and was a perfect father for their son. He could see and feel things others couldn't, and he cared deeply for people and their feelings. He was easy to know because he was always open, genuine, forthright.

The colonel was the complete opposite. His rugged good looks, devil-may-care smile, and outgoing personality made him easy to like, but hard to know. Although he touched people, he didn't let them get close. He listened well but didn't show his feelings.

She knew that she might just as well have been describing her father. The only time she had ever seen her father open up was when he was with his kameraden . . . they were like brothers.

The van pulled into a parking place just past a bridge over the Teltow Canal. Siegfried excitedly hopped out and opened the door for Jake, motioning toward an open-air market. *"Dort ist der Floh-markt das Siebzehn Juni. Alles klar, ja?"*

Jake patted Siegfried's back. "Alles klar, buddy."

The two men began walking toward the market when Kristina barked, "Be back in an hour and a half and don't be late."

Jake turned around. "Aren't you coming?"

Kristina wrinkled her nose. "They sell stinking old clothes and horrible junk. I'm going to walk along the canal."

Jake shrugged and fell in step with Siegfried again.

Kristina began to turn toward the canal but stopped and looked again toward the two men. Why not? she said to herself, and began walking quickly to catch up.

Jake was surprised when the protocol officer fell in step beside him. He slowed the pace, seeing that she had to strain to keep up. "That was a fast walk around the canal," he said with a playful smile.

Kristina let it drop. "I thought I might be able to help you with your German if you saw something you wanted."

Jake nodded with exaggeration. *"Ja ja, das ist gut, alles klar.* How was that?"

She rolled her eyes.

The open-air market was like a county fair, antique show, giant garage sale, and history lesson all rolled into one. The air was filled with the smell of wurst, fried potatoes, and excitement. The market had booths run by professional dealers, but also some run by school groups and by families who had cleaned out their garages or attics. Everything from seventeenth-century furniture to Mickey Mouse watches could be bargained for. Siegfried explained and Kristina translated to Jake the simple rules of flea market bargaining: never buy anything at the first asking price. Always offer half of what the seller wants. Somewhere in between a deal would be made. The idea was to walk away with both parties thinking they got the better deal. Siegfried was obviously a regular, for he seemed to know everyone and constantly stopped to shake hands and admire purchases. He also pointed out to Jake and Kristina the squat Turkish men and scarved women who roamed the market, and he warned the couple to stay clear of them. If the Turks spotted something they wanted, they would knock you down to get to it. They were not liked because they violated the rules of bargaining. They used intimidation and would shout and yak loudly if the seller didn't sell at ridiculously low prices. Kristina quickly translated the warning, then moved closer to Jake, but he didn't notice. He was having too much fun people-watching and browsing. There were old books, new books, coins, stamps, military paraphernalia, beds, trunks, lamps, and silverware. There was a booth filled with nothing but old phones, another with 1930s clothes, and another crammed with antique electric trains. He felt like a kid in a toy store. He was shown by a gray-haired woman how to wind up an old Victoria gramophone, and he was made to listen to one of her favorite records. He bought a World War II leather flying helmet and goggles from a young seller and modeled them for Siegfried and Kristina. She laughed and begged him to take it off before any friends saw them with the crazy person. Jake grinned back, for it was the first time he had seen the protocol officer laugh naturally.

His stomach began to growl from the smell of food, and he stopped at a tin and glass contraption on wheels that looked like a rolling Dairy Queen, complete with ordering window.

Kristina explained it was called an Imbiss, and the German answer to fast food. She read the menu painted on the side of the trailer and explained each item. He decided on roast bratwurst and an order of pommes frites because they looked safest. The roast bratwurst resembled a fat, foot-long hot dog, and the pommes frites were nothing more than french fries. When he took a bite of the bratwurst, he was surprised by the taste. It wasn't anything like any hot dog he'd tasted before. It was five times better. Siegfried ordered a curry wurst, and Kristina, a buletten, with a helping of potato salad. Jake eyed Siegfried's food and then Kristina's, even though his mouth was full. Seeing his look, Kristina offered him a taste of the meat patty with spices, which immediately started an exchange of bites and portions from Siegfried, who laughed and pounded Jake's back, proclaiming he had a German stomach.

Fifteen minutes later they had joined the crowd of lookers walking between a quarter mile of booths. Kristina had lost her previous attitude about the market and had become genuinely interested in Siegfried's explanation of which antiques were fake and which were real. Jake stopped at a booth selling military medals, then turned to Kristina with a puzzled expression. "There's a little of everything except for World War Two German medals. Are they that hard to get?"

Kristina shrugged and spoke German to the dealer, who looked in both directions before talking. Kristina passed on the explanation to Jake in a low voice. "He said it's illegal in Berlin to sell anything with a swastika, or Hitler's face on it. He says he has a World War Two German medal collection, but it's under the table. He sells them to collectors when police aren't around. He wants you to come around the booth and look at what he has."

Jake began to squeeze himself through the tables to see the collection, but Kristina and Siegfried took his arms, pulled him back, and quickly walked him down the aisle.

Jake looked at both of them as if they'd lost their minds. "Why'd you yank me away? I wanted to see 'em."

Kristina nodded ahead toward a green-hatted polizei officer strolling among the crowd. "You can thank me later," she said.

Kristina realized she was still walking arm in arm with the colonel and released him as if he were a hot potato. Not wanting him to see her embarrassment, she strolled over to a booth where a young couple was taking china out of a cardboard box. She recognized the design as that of old Meissen china, even though it was covered with dust, and asked the young woman how much she wanted for the set. The woman shrugged and looked at her husband, who shrugged back and spoke as if apologetic. "It is very dirty. We found it in my mother's attic when cleaning. Is fifty marks okay?"

Kristina almost fainted. The Meissen set was worth twenty times that. She reached for her purse and took out her billfold in three seconds flat. She was about to lean across the table to give the couple the money when two Turkish men pushed themselves in front of her and told the couple they wanted the china.

Kristina angrily elbowed herself between the two men and held out the money again to the wide-eyed couple. The older and bigger of the Turks shoved her aside and growled for her to get away. She caught her balance and began to fight her way between the two men again when the older Turk was suddenly spun around by Jake, who had grabbed the man's shoulder. He waved his finger in the Turk's face as if scolding a small boy. "Not good manners, my man. Not good at all."

The angry younger Turk menaced Jake, but Siegfried blocked him and warned him with a glaring look. Kristina walked up to the table and smiled as she handed the couple a fifty-mark bill.

The older Turk huffed and puffed and rattled Turkish and German at Jake, then tried to push him out of his way. Jake grabbed the startled Turk's hands and shook his head as he applied pressure. "Be nice, or this is gonna hurt real bad."

Kristina picked up the box of china just as two very heavy Turkish women wearing white scarves and long black shapeless dresses burst out of the crowd barking loudly in hysterical Turkish and attacked Jake with their purses and slaps at his body.

Jake released the squirming man's hands, and along with Siegfried, they made a strategic withdrawal under intense pressure from the unrelenting Turkish women. The crowd of onlookers laughed as the two men backed up, covering their groins with one hand from the low pokes and waving their other hands about their faces to ward off blows from the heavy purses. Finally the women gave up, but only because several of Siegfried's friends stepped in to help, allowing him and Jake to make good their escape. A minute later they caught up to Kristina, who was walking as fast as she could down the crowded aisle.

She sighed in relief when they came up on both sides of her, and then broke out in laughter.

Jake exchanged looks with Siegfried.

"What's so damn funny?" he snarled at her. "You see the size of those she-ayatollahs? They nearly beat us to death!"

She clenched her teeth at Jake's expression to keep from laughing again.

Jake shook his head and walked over to Siegfried, tossing his arm over the driver's shoulder. "Miller time, buddy. A beer, ja."

Siegfried nodded in understanding. "Ja, ve trink a beer."

"See you at the van in twenty minutes," Kristina called back as she walked away.

Jake waved his hand at her as if shooing off a pest, and followed Siegfried to an Imbiss trailer with beer signs pasted on the sides.

Jake waved good-bye to the congressional group a final time before they passed through the yellow doors of the airport's departure lounge. He turned to Kristina with a smile. "They were fun. If you ever need an escort again for a group like that, let me know."

Kristina sighed, obviously relieved of the responsibility. "I get about two CODELs a month. This bunch was ten times better than most, so don't be so quick to volunteer. Usually they come over for buying sprees in the East. We even had one senator have the audacity to write ahead to send someone over to the East and set aside crystal for his wife."

Jake walked alongside her as they approached the van that was positioned just outside. He opened the door for the protocol officer and patted her back as she got in. "Kristina, you do a heck of a job and I gotta tell ya I sure learned a lot about Berlin the last few days. Thanks."

She smiled shyly and closed the door herself. "Thank you for the compliment. That was nice of you to say."

Jake climbed in the back seat and leaned back. "And, if you ever go to the market again? Just let me and Siegfried know . . . cause we ain't!"

She laughed and quickly translated for Siegfried, who laughed with her.

Jake smiled at their laughter, but felt the familiar pain coming on. He shut his eyes, feeling the cocoon of loneliness slowly envelop him. The past three days had left him with good memories but he knew that tomorrow, next week, next year, and ten years from now he would not have anyone to turn to with a smile and say, 'Remember when we . . . ?' "

Jake's jaw muscle twitched thinking about Helen and the long night ahead. He wanted to scream and kick and shout to the world he was going to beat it, but deep inside he knew he wasn't. The knowing that the loneliness was always going to be there hurt and made made him feel very small and inconsequential. He turned and looked out the window, wondering what time the bar opened at Harnack House.

Minutes later Siegfried pulled the van to the curb in front of the Officers' Club, and Jake leaned forward and patted his back. "Danke, my friend, it was fun."

Siegfried turned and, with a big smile, rattled off several sentences in German ending with *"danke mein Freund."*

Kristina smiled and translated. "He said he enjoyed your company and hopes you'll drink beer with him again. He says he'll remember today for he made a good friend."

Jake shook Siegfried's hand then climbed out of van. He nodded toward Kristina. "Thanks. I hope I'll see you again sometime."

Kristina nodded back. "Thank you, Colonel. Good-bye."

Jake was walking slowly up the steps to his room when he decided to take a long run.

He changed clothes and was about to leave when the phone rang. He answered in his professional voice. "Lieutenant Colonel Tallon."

"Jake, this is Axel Mader. Good day to you."

Jake smiled. "Hello, Axel, how are you?"

"Not so good, Jake. I have a daughter who does not listen to her father. I asked her to invite you to the house tonight for dinner, but she did not because she thought you would have other plans. I thought she had better manners. Is it possible that you could join me for dinner?"

Jake answered immediately. "Sure, Axel, I appreciate the invitation. What time?"

"Seven will be fine."

Jake thanked the old veteran and hung up. At least he would have something to do. He opened the door to take his run, feeling better, for the night had just gotten shorter.

Axel Mader opened the door with a wide grin and extended his hand. "Good to see you again, Jake. Come in!"

Jake shifted the heavy grocery bag to his other hand and shook the veteran's hand. He stepped into the house with a cautious smile. "Axel, don't be offended, but I brought my own beer."

"What?" Axel said in mock indignation. He took the bag and looked inside. "You call this beer? It is bubble water!" He led Jake into the kitchen, where Kristina was cutting cheese.

She looked up with an apologetic expression. "How nice of you to come, Colonel." She changed her expression to annoyance with her father. "I'm afraid my father will not speak to me because I *failed* to follow *his* orders. He doesn't understand that you are a very busy man."

Jake, feeling the tension in the air, tried to be a peacemaker. "Axel, don't be upset with Kristina. It was all my fault. I mentioned to her this morning that I had a dinner engagement tonight. Lucky for me it was canceled. I'm sure she would have asked if I hadn't said something first."

Axel reached in the sack, pulled out the two six-packs of Lite beer and held them up for Kristina to see. "He has insulted me already by bringing *this*. I'm surprised he did not bring frozen dinners as well." He turned to Jake with a mischievous smile. "The way my princess cooks, it would have been a good idea."

"Papa!" Kristina blurted and threw a small piece of cheese at him.

Axel laughed, went to the refrigerator and took out a bottle of beer. "Come, Jake, bring one of your bubble waters and walk in the summer garden with me while my daughter burns our dinner."

Jake peeled off a can and quickly exchanged glances with Kristina, who mouthed a silent "Thank you." He winked and followed Axel to the back door.

Kristina put down the knife and walked to an open window that overlooked the backyard. The men were walking beside each other toward the apple trees that her father had planted long ago for her mother. Kristina felt a mix of anger and happiness gnawing at her. She was angry because it should have been Richard walking out there with her father. But she was glad that her father's eyes were twinkling again. It was a look she had not seen since her mother had died, and even then, only when he was talking to his old kameraden. The colonel had somehow brought the twinkle back.

The thought made Kristina feel yet another uncomfortable emotion: jealousy. She wanted it to be *her* walking with her father and listening to the stories he had never shared with her. She knew he loved her, but he would not share with her that part of himself. Yet he would with a stranger.

•   •   •

Axel sighed and looked up at the limbs of the apple tree. "I am sorry to hear about your wife, Jake. We Iron Men are not so strong as people think. We are fragile, for our hearts are somehow bigger and break more easily. When my wife died, I thought I could be strong and overcome the wound to the heart, but at times, even after all the years, I still bleed." He looked at Jake with a reflective smile. "I remember when I heard the war was lost when I was in the prison camp hospital. I thought I had somehow failed my country. I wanted only to die. An American doctor told me, 'Mader, your wounds will heal, but self-pity is a wound I have no medicine for.' It is strange, but until that moment I did not realize I felt sorry not for my country but for me. I had given so much, and yet it had all been for nothing. Perhaps, Jake, your wound has healed more than you think and the pain you feel is of your own making?"

Jake began to shake his head and say he had gotten over Helen, but instead he sipped his beer and looked into the old man's eyes.

Kristina stepped out the door carrying two bowls. "Your 'burned' dinner is ready, Papa."

Axel put his hand on Jake's back and walked him toward the patio table. "We must be brave and eat what she has cooked."

"I heard that, Papa!"

Axel rolled his eyes at Jake and whispered, "They only hear when they want to hear."

Jake was halfway through his schnitzel when he suddenly put down his fork and motioned to the breaded veal. "Axel, how can you eat this?"

Kristina looked up in shock and immediate anger, while Axel merely registered a blank stare. Jake motioned to his plate again. "How can you eat this terrific cooking all the time and not weigh three hundred pounds. This stuff is great!"

Kristina lowered her head in red-faced embarrassment.

Axel shrugged. "Because, Jake, my daughter only cooks like this when we have guests. But I must admit, the 'stuff' is very good." He reached over and patted his daughter's shoulder.

Jake smiled. "She's also very good at her job. She certainly wowed the congressional delegation this week. Even dumb me learned a lot about Berlin."

Axel waved off the compliment and grunted. "Princess showed you *tourist* Berlin. Next Saturday, I will show you the *real* city."

"Papa," she said, "the colonel probably has plans for next weekend."

Axel ignored her. "Jake, come over at 0830 and go with me."

Jake grinned. "I'd love to."

After the meal, Axel and Jake helped carry the dishes into the kitchen, then Axel got two beers and guided Jake to the porch again. "I want to hear about Vietnam. I never really understood that war."

Kristina stacked the dishes and moved closer to the open window to listen. The patio was just below the kitchen. The colonel was talking about the North Vietnamese soldiers' dedication to their cause. She quietly brought a chair up close to the window and sat down to listen.

The stories and beer wore on past midnight, but Kristina never moved an inch. She heard and saw battles that both men had fought. She cried softly to herself at her father's anguish when he talked about friends that had been lost, and she felt closer to him. Strangely, the colonel's stories were very much the same, and it struck her the two men were not so different. They had seen the same horrors and felt the same frustrations, pride, love, and guilt.

Tears welled up again and trickled down her cheeks. It was clear now why her father needed this younger man. Axel Mader needed to know that he and his comrades were no different from other soldiers. They were not the criminals, beasts, or Nazi superhumans that the world hated and despised. Not everyone was SS or Gestapo. Her father had needed acceptance from another soldier for what he had truly been—a man who did his duty and did the best he could for his beloved friends and Fatherland.

Jake set down his ninth empty beer can and shook his head as he flopped his arm over Axel's shoulder. "Ax, I know how ya feel. We lost our fuckin' war 'cause of da fuckin' politicians and fuckin' Jane Fondas and fuckin' generals who didn't tell the truth. We vets couldn't talk about the fuckin' war. I went to the Vietnam Memorial parade, and you know who was there? Just us vets, that's who. We had a parade to ourselves and said fuck da others, who didn't understand."

Axel swayed as he stood up and lifted his beer mug. "To the Iron Men who—"

Jake stood and put his hand up. "Wait. Wait a second, let's do this right." Jake dug in his slacks pocket and took out a small, thin box. "Ax, I picked up somethin for ya at the flo mart. When I met ya, I thought to myself ain't it a fuckin' crime this soldier didn't even have his . . . well, I mean we Americans wear all our medals around real proudlike, and . . . aw shit, I'm not sayin' it right. I know it ain't the one that was given to you, but by God, you deserve to have it and oughta have one."

Jake opened the lid and took out an original World War II Knights Cross with red, black, and white neck ribbon.

Jake came to attention and barked. "Hauptmann Axel Mader, Aaa-tench-*hut!*"

The old soldier's eyes filled with tears at the sight of the Ritterkreuz, but he snapped to attention at Jake's command.

Jake lifted his chin and spoke loudly among the apple trees. "Hauptmann Mader, for gallantry in action against your enemies, I present you, as one Iron Man to another, this award for valor and bravery above and beyond the call of duty. In keeping with the highest traditions of soldiers everywhere, who fought and understood, I present to you what is rightfully yours."

Jake steadied himself, stepped closer to the old soldier and put the ribbon around Mader's neck. He fastened the back and adjusted the medal, then stepped back, came to attention, and saluted. "Congratulations, Iron Man. It is an honor to know you and call you a friend."

Mader returned the salute, so overcome with emotion he couldn't speak.

Kristina turned away from the window, fearful that her sobbing would be heard. She had witnessed the rebirth of a man whom she loved more than life. Axel Mader, her father, the gentle man who had helped rebuild Germany, was tonight an Iron Man again, honored by another of his kind.

Still touching the iron cross, Axel sat down and looked up at Jake. "I . . . I can never repay you for what you've given me tonight," Axel said. He stroked the cross as if to reassure himself that it was real.

Jake saw in the guise of Axel his own father sitting before him. He leaned over and kissed his cheek, then patted the old man's shoulder and staggered into the house.

Kristina was sitting in the darkness on the front steps when Jake opened the front door. She stood and took his arm. "Come on, Colonel, I'll walk you home."

Jake held up a full beer can and took a long drink before shaking his head from side to side. "I . . . I'm fine, thank you, ma'am."

She nodded but kept her grip and helped him down the steps to the gate and down to the sidewalk.

"You sure are lucky having a dad," Jake said while crossing an intersection. "I mean really, really, really lucky. You cook good too."

"You bought the Ritterkreuz when I went back to the van, didn't you?" she asked softly.

Jake grinned drunkenly. *"Ja ja, alles klar."*

When they reached Harnack House, Jake tried to put his hand into his pocket twice before he successfully pulled out his key.

Kristina took it from him, looked at the number, and walked him up the stairs to the third floor, where she unlocked the door to Room 306. She set him on the bed, grasped his shoulders and pushed him back onto the pillow.

Jake smiled crookedly and shut his eyes. "I'm okay, really."

Kristina leaned over and lightly kissed his lips. "Good night, Iron Man . . . thank you," she whispered. She gave him one last look and turned out the light before walking out and shutting the door behind her.

PART III

CHAPTER 18

Monday, 31 July,
Normannenstrasse 22

The special phone resting on the corner of Hagan Wolf's desk buzzed softly. He put down the report he was reading and pulled a pad closer before answering. Only three people had his private number: his wife, the minister, and the General Secretary himself, Erich Honecker.

Wolf picked up the receiver. "Director Wolf."

His eyes widened in surprise. It was none of the three.

"The flowers are in bloom. A dozen would be nice for your wife," said the familiar voice. It was a recognition code he hadn't heard in years.

"Yes, a dozen would be perfect." When he heard the click at the other end, he wrote down, "Flower shop at 12 o'clock."

Why was his old friend in the city, he wondered, and why, of all places, had he wanted to talk in their old meeting place? He glanced at his watch. In two hours he would know the answer. An uneasy feeling came over him. Something was wrong. He pushed the button under the lip of his desk. The secretary knocked, then walked into his office.

"Ja, Herr Direktor?"

Wolf broke his stare from the wall and shifted his gaze to her. "Get me Rink."

Clay Compound, West Berlin

Colonel Crist rose from his chair. "General Thomas, I have the intelligence community chiefs here as you requested, and have asked the G-2 to lead off with the threat brief. I'm sure you'll be impressed by the work that Hank has put into it."

A thin, bookish lieutenant colonel wearing thick-rimmed glasses turned on an overhead projector. The first slide appeared. "Sir, as you can see, the numbers on this slide have not changed since we last briefed you several months ago. There are 370,000 Soviet troops still occupying East Germany, and the status of the six East German National Volks army divisions has not changed. The modernizing of the Soviet tanks from the older T-72s to the new T-80s with reactive armor is still going on, but—"

The brigadier held up his hand. "Hold it." He looked at Jake, who was sitting to his right. "Is this what he briefed you on?"

Jake nodded in silence. The general looked back at the puzzled face of the intelligence officer. "Hank, are you going to give me the same old briefing that basically says we're surrounded, outnumbered, and outgunned?"

The colonel quickly shuffled through his stack of over thirty slides and held up one with obvious pride. "Sir, this is *new* information." He placed it on the view graph. "This, sir, shows the exact locations of their Flogger, fighter-bomber air bases, and gives the estimated time in minutes of how soon they could reach Berlin in the event of hostilities breaking out."

The general rolled his eyes and shook his head. "Hank, I asked Colonel Tallon to take a look at our war plans to see if they needed updating. He needs updated intel estimates to establish just what the real threat is and how much warning time we will have to prepare for an attack. Hank, you and I both know that this material is not what he needs. He could get this info from *U.S. News and World Report*." The general shifted his eyes to the other men sitting at the conference table. "Gentlemen, for my benefit and my G-3's, could somebody in the intelligence community please tell me what the hell the *real* threat is and how much time we'll have if they decide to attack?"

The G-2 raised his chin with indignation. "Sir, Colonel Tallon is not cleared for any information above Top Secret and—"

"Don't pull that spook shit on me!" blasted the general. "Colonel Tallon was in Delta Force for four years and was the primary planner in Special Operations Command for the last two years. If you knew half the shit he did, your spook friends would have to kill you because you'd be a security risk. Sit down and answer the damn questions. I've let this bullshit go on for too long. Colonel Tallon has brought to my attention the fact that our war plans are flawed because we are basing them on old intelligence."

The general looked at the other men sitting around the table in front of them as he read the place cards. "In this room, I have representatives from the Intelligence and Security Command, the National Security Agency, Defense Intelligence Agency, Air Force Electronic Security Command, the Central Intelligence Agency, and the Berlin Command Military Intelligence officer. Gentlemen, I want some answers. Now again, what is the real threat to this command!"

Hank Ellis spoke up again. "Sir, the threat to Berlin specifically is the Soviet Western Group of Forces, whose headquarters is only thirty kilometers from here at Wünsdorf. Also the East German Motorized Rifle divisions located in Potsdam and Dessau, and the Seventh Tank Division in Dresden." Ellis shifted in his seat, giving Jake a smug "see there" smile.

General Thomas sighed. "Hank, am I going to have to spell it out for you? I don't want this bullshit answer that a horde is coming. The Western Group of Forces has eleven armored and eight motorized rifle divisions. I'm not a Clausewitz, but I sure as hell know the Sovs aren't going to use all those divisions to take little ol' Berlin. *Who*, goddamnit, is tagged to attack Berlin? Do we know what *their* war plans are?"

The CIA station chief, Burton Dawson, who was wearing a tan summer suit and regimental tie, cleared his throat and leaned forward in his seat. "General, based on information from a high-ranking officer who deserted and sought asylum in the Federal Republic, it is clear to us that Soviet ground forces have no intention of attacking Berlin in case of all-out war. The Soviets will use their fighter bombers to destroy the Allied installations, with special emphasis on the command, control, and communication nodes. That will take approximately ten minutes, as we have no hard sites. The result of such an air attack would effectively cut off our communications from our national command authorities and the outside world. In conjunction with, or prior to, the air attack, the Soviets would use East German forces to surround the city and begin a classic siege campaign. We estimate we could hold out in a best-case scenario for one month. The Allied troops in Berlin pose no threat to Soviet war plans, which are to knock out NATO forces prior to the arrival of follow-on forces from the States."

"And how much warning time would we have, Burt?" the general asked.

The station chief shot a glance at the G-2 colonel then back to the general before pursing his lips. "Based on recent information, we estimate we would be able to identify the Soviet Union's preparations for war at least thirty to forty days out, probably even as much as sixty days, depending on the Sovs' calling up their reserves east of the Urals. Sir, it is a simple fact that the Soviets could not sustain a major offensive with any degree of success without calling up their reserves, and we would definitely spot that kind of activity."

The general slowly shifted his eyes to the G-2. "Hank, our present war plans are based on a warning time of only forty-eight hours. That's a big difference from thirty to forty *days*. Why is it you made no effort to update the warning time and inform the G-3 that our plans needed revising?"

The G-2 colonel lifted his chin and spoke as if lecturing. "Sir, we in 'Military' Intelligence base our estimates on capability, not probability. Sir, the Soviets are fully capable of massing a huge force against us. With all due respect to our CIA friends, they didn't consider surprise attack. We did."

The general looked up at the ceiling as if in prayer. His eyes slowly lowered to the colonel, who was obviously impressed with himself. "Colonel Ellis, are you telling me you do not agree with the Central Intelligence Agency's estimates?"

Ellis lifted his brow. "Sir, again with all due respect to the agency, it is clear to me that based on the capability of the Soviets and our own vulnerability, we have no recourse but to plan for the worst case."

Thomas kept his stare on Ellis. "Hank, your wife has the 'capability' to kill you, but the 'probability' is, she won't. You have the 'capability' to make full colonel, but right now the 'probability' is you won't, *unless you pull your head out of your ass*! You are excused, and so is everybody else. I've heard enough."

The general motioned for the CIA's station chief and Jake to stay. Colonel Crist sat in his chair and bobbed his head. "Sir, you were right on target. When I saw the G-2's briefing two weeks ago, I said to myself it was lacking substance and made a note to myself to look into it. I'll work with Hank personally and get it up to standards and—"

The general gave the chief a sidelong glance. "Start now, please."

The chief didn't get the hint. "Yes, sir, I will get right on it first thing in the morning after PT. I'll assemble the intel community again and—"

General Thomas turned in his chair and pointed to the door. "I mean *right* now. Immediately!"

The chief collected his notepad. "Yes, sir, great idea. Get the work done now. I like it. Nothing like a challenge for the team, sir."

The general shook his head as soon as the chief had walked out. He turned to Dawson, who had taken a pipe from his pocket and was filling the bowl. "Burt, thank God we've got you here so I can get some straight answers. I didn't realize Ellis was so damn hard-headed. I want Jake to know what we're up against in this town, so please fill us in on what's been happening in your world for the past two weeks."

Dawson leaned back in his chair. "Sir, I was on your calendar for this afternoon because it just so happens last week was a busy one. There are four Libyan teams in East Berlin and another two teams from the Red Guard faction. West German surveillance has them, and it looks like they're getting training from the Stasi boys. Nothing serious. The big news is there was a hit on an East German couple last week in one of the local hotels. It's on wraps, and we're assisting the German Feds on it. It was a professional job made to look like a coke overdose. The victims were ID'd as crossers. The husband didn't tell Marienfelde he worked for Stasi. Big mistake. He was their deputy assistant director for Science and Technology. He was making the West trade shows to pick up the usual off-the-shelf software, but he must have known something important, as it was an extreme measure to knock him off, even for Stasi. The Berlin polizei forensic boys smelled something fishy when they saw how the bag of coke had been opened. It was ripped, not cut. A cokehead will cut a bag just enough to fit the spoon, and then he'll use Scotch tape to close it. The forensic boys called the Herm Feds, who brought in the works to sweep the place. The bodies were sent to Frankfurt for special autopsies. Both crews came up with the same conclusion. It was a hit. The pathologists found that a drug had been used to knock them out before bad coke was blown into their noses. They also found that only the back portion of the nasal passages of both victims contained constricted membrane cells, meaning the victims' heads were bent far back when the coke was introduced. The victims were supposed to look like they'd used a spoon, but you can't use a spoon with your head back. A straw or something like was used to do them. The forensic team was just as successful. They found traces of the knock-out drug on the carpet, along with traces of champagne. They also found three strands of long red hair on the victims and one on the pillow behind the female, who was blond and very pregnant. Based on a DNA on the hair samples, the pro who did them was a female, middle-aged, with natural red hair, blood-type A. The M.O. has been run through the computers looking for possibles. So far none have been found. Whoever she is, she's damn good, 'cause we have no record of her."

Dawson shifted his gaze to Jake. "We're dealing with some bad folks in this city. I went into too much detail, but it was so you'd know my people are not like your G-2. We know what we're doing, and so do the German Feds. The general asked about the threat in case of war. I see the biggest threat being from the East German Stasi. We know of at least a hundred suspected Stasi agents in West Berlin, which means there's a helluva lot more of them we *don't* know about. In case of war, you wouldn't be able to move without them knowing about it. They could block roads, blow bridges, kill your leaders, and cause untold havoc to your operations. The Stasi is good . . . probably the best in the world. They don't play by the rules, and that makes them very dangerous. When you rewrite your war plans, keep the Stasi threat in the back of your mind. It's real, and they're already in the city."

East Berlin

Wolf walked down the sidewalk of Unter den Linden Strasse toward the flower shop that was on the next corner. At the intersection he waited for a car to pass and checked to see if he could spot his people. He was satisfied, for he couldn't. Thirty seconds later he opened the front door of the shop and casually looked around. He saw only two customers and the young woman who now managed the store. The woman acknowledged him by cutting her eyes toward the curtains leading to the storeroom. He blinked once and walked toward the back room.

Seventy-year-old Georgi Sorokin rose from the office chair with a faded smile.

The two men embraced and patted each other on the back, then Wolf grasped his old mentor's shoulders.

"You've lost weight, my friend, but you're still looking fit. What brings you to Berlin?"

Sorokin closed the office door as Wolf sat down in a side chair. The Russian smiled again. "I'm here to see an old friend whom I owe very much." Sorokin sat down behind the desk, facing Wolf. "And how is Dagmar?"

Wolf frowned. "She wants me to retire like you did."

Sorokin lowered his eyes to his arthritic hands. "I am not retired. I was recalled to duty six months ago as a consultant for the

General Secretary's Eastern European Affairs committee. I was brought in as a consultant for the German question."

Wolf got the uneasy feeling again. "What question?"

Sorokin leaned forward and spoke softly. "Hagan, the policies of my government are changing. Mikhail Gorbachev has brought in a new breed of politician. They do not seek reform, they demand it. Perestroika and glasnost are not words, they are facts. When I saw these young men, who had fire in their hearts and disrepect in their eyes toward those who stood for the old ways, I knew that to be a survivor, I had to nod with agreement when they spoke. Thus I have been accepted as a reformer. I believed, at first, that it was all a finely orchestrated masquerade, conducted by a genius of propaganda. But it is not. It is real. They are dismantling the very system we tried so hard over the years to preserve. It has all come about because my country is on the verge of economic collapse. The old ways have been set aside to save us from ruin."

Sorokin paused as if pained. "I have come now, Hagan, as a friend, to warn you. I have been to the meetings and have heard what the future holds for your country. The German question has been decided."

Wolf kept his piercing eyes locked on Sorokin. His Soviet intelligence desk had kept him informed, of course. He was well aware of the Soviets' internal problems and loss of control over the Warsaw Pact. It had been evident years before, when the Polish reformers were allowed to speak out and rise up to strangle their government. But that was Poland. The Soviets' staunchest ally and primary economic trading partner was the German Democratic Republic. The GDR had no vocal dissenting parties or spokesmen, for he, Hagan Wolf, had personally seen to it. The Soviets would not abandon the flagship of Eastern Europe and the rock of the Warsaw Pact.

Sorokin read the look of confidence in Wolf's eyes and shook his head. "Within days the Hungarians will open their borders. Their delegation came to Moscow and gave us the date. In early September they will renounce their agreements with the GDR which restrict your citizens from crossing into the West. Understand, Hagan, the Hungarians did not come to Moscow asking for permission. They came to *tell* us it would happen. And Gorbachev *thanked* them for the courtesy."

Wolf's eyes glazed and his jaw muscles rippled. Sorokin had just described the beginning of the end of everything he, Hagan Wolf, had worked for. The neck artery of the GDR would be slashed. The young and technically skilled workers in his country would abandon the Fatherland for higher-paying jobs and better standards of living in the West. His country would be bled dry within a year.

Sorokin's voice deepened. "It is over. Gorbachev has accepted the invitation of Erich Honecker to attend your country's fortieth anniversary on the seventh of October. After the parade, he will advise Honecker to step down as General Secretary. Gorbachev believes Honecker is out of step with the new world order and Soviet policies on rights of self-determination. He will also inform Honecker that Soviet forces stationed in the GDR will not interfere or be a party to the oppression of any opposition parties that might arise. Wolf, Gorbachev is abandoning your government."

"You are certain of this?" Wolf asked in a raspy whisper.

"I am the one on the committee who presented the German question to Gorbachev." Sorokin leaned forward in his chair and spoke softly. "Hagan, I am here as your friend and mentor. What I have told you, no one in your government knows or will know. Neither does anyone in my government know I am giving you this warning. I am trying to give you time to do what is necessary, to clean up loose ends and protect yourself from embarrassments when your leader and government fall from power. You have until seven October. You and Dagmar deserve to retire in peace, free from those who would try and accuse you of wrongdoing."

"I will do what is necessary," Wolf said icily.

Sorokin stood and extended his hand. "I will be back in Berlin on the thirteenth of October. I am to speak with our ambassador and give him a letter for Honecker if he has not stepped down by that time. In the letter, Gorbachev *tells* him to resign. I will meet you here at the same time on the thirteenth. I cannot contact you until then. Take care, my friend, and use the time wisely."

Wolf strode into his office, where Rink stood waiting for him. He sat down in his old chair behind his desk, looking past his deputy director. "Was he followed?" he snapped.

"Nein. He came alone with no protection or surveillance."

Relieved, Wolf leaned back to think how he would execute the plan he had formulated while walking back to his office. He felt no regret or guilt, only exhilaration, as he had in the closing months of the war. While others had fallen into despair, he had stepped forward and led, as he would do now. This was not the end. It was the beginning.

U.S. Mission, Clay Compound, West Berlin

"Mrs. Hastings, you have a visitor from the military," Peggy Sue announced.

Kristina, her back to the doorway, was watering her variegated spider plant. At the sound of Peggy Sue's voice, she turned and almost dropped the plastic water bottle. Colonel Tallon was standing behind her grinning friend. He was the last person she would have expected.

Kristina forced a smile. "Thank you, Miss Jabowski. Colonel, are you here volunteering for another CODEL?"

Jake sat down without being asked and looked over the small room. It was typically female, uncluttered, organized, lots of pastel colors, pictures of family on the desk.

Kristina glanced at Peggy Sue who was still standing there giving the colonel a sideways look. "Thank you, Miss Jabowski," Kristina repeated more forcefully.

Peggy Sue reluctantly made her exit. The colonel was staring at a picture on the wall.

"That's our cabin on the Havel," Kristina said.

Jake looked at the picture more closely. "Cabin? Looks more like a hotel." He faced her, but lowered his eyes. "I came by for two reasons. The first is to thank you for walking me home the other night. I woulda probably got lost, or worse, gone to sleep on a curb or something."

Kristina smiled. "You remember me walking you home? You were in better shape than I thought, then. Looks like you recovered."

Jake frowned as looked into her laughing eyes. "I was one hurtin' puppy. I'm still cussin' Lite beer. How is Axel?"

Kristina rolled her eyes up then back to him. "When I got home, I found him asleep under the apple trees clutching the gift you gave him. I couldn't get him up, so I rolled him onto a blanket. He slept like a dog until almost noon Sunday."

Jake felt a pang of sadness for the old soldier.

Kristina saw the strange sadness in his eyes and wondered if he understood the significance of the trees. "What was number two, Colonel?"

Jake took a crumpled card out of his pocket. "I got an invitation to dinner last week from my British counterpart. He invited me and the French G-3 to the Brit O Club for a similar number dinner. I tossed it and told Maggie to send my regrets, but then I got to thinkin' that maybe I really should go and meet them socially. The problem is, they're all married. I don't know anybody yet . . . uh, I mean any ladies other than you, and . . . well, I was wondering if . . . ya see, I thought maybe you'd . . ."

"Are you asking me to go to dinner with you?" Kristina asked, to save him from further embarrassment.

Jake brightened. "Yeah, that's it. Are you doing anything this Friday night?"

Kristina flipped open her desk calendar to Friday and looked at the blank page as she tried to make up her mind. Her eyes slowly moved to Richard and her son's pictures beneath the glass.

Jake knew what she was looking at. He had seen the pictures while scanning the room. He could already see the answer in her eyes. He stood. "I'm sorry, I shouldn't have asked." He checked his watch. "Damn, I've got a meeting to go to. I'll see ya . . . and again I'm sorry for asking. It was dumb." He headed for the door, cussing himself for violating his own first rule: never date a widow.

When he walked into his office, Maggie was waiting with a handful of messages and a phone call on line one.

Jake picked up the phone on his desk. "Lieutenant Colonel Tallon."

"Colonel Tallon, I would like very much to go to dinner with you . . . on one condition."

Jake smiled. "What is it?"

"You don't drink beer with your dinner."

"No deal."

"Colonel, the British are very proper, and you would insult the host by drinking beer."

"Thanks for reminding me. I'll bring my own. They probably only have that German stuff."

"Colonel, you're impossible!"

"You going?"

"Yes."

"Can you pick me up at 1900 hours?"

"What?"

"I don't have a car yet, 'cause I haven't taken the international driver's license test. Can you pick me up? Otherwise, I can walk over, and we'll call a taxi."

"I'll pick you up! Anything else, Colonel?"

"No. Yes . . . thank you, Kristina."

"Bye, Colonel." She hung up and looked at Peggy Sue, who was bobbing her head up and down.

"You did it! God, at last! The bitch got herself a real date!"

Kristina forced a smile.

East Berlin

Jorn Furman climbed down from the truck tailgate using a rope and lowered himself into his wheelchair. The shocked buyer shook his head as he withdrew a wad of Ost-marks from his pocket. "I never would have believed it. You are very strong for an old man."

"You mean legless old man," Jorn said pointedly as he pushed himself forward to take the money.

The buyer kept his smile. "Ja, you are the perfect delivery man. The Vopos would never believe you capable of delivering goods by yourself."

Jorn quickly counted the marks and looked up at the younger man. "I can deliver again this Friday at the same time."

The buyer glanced over his shoulder at the stacked boxes in his garage. "That will be fine, but no honey next time. I need all the meat and vegetables you can haul. The meat I can sell in an hour, and the vegetables in two. Honey doesn't move fast enough."

Jorn put the money in his front shirt pocket and looked at the buyer with narrowed eyes. "How do you sleep, knowing you sell food that should be going to the markets? You are one of the reasons the people must wait in lines."

The buyer laughed and motioned to Jorn's bulging shirt pocket. "You take money from me and say *I'm* the reason for the lines? Look at yourself. You have a truck. You could volunteer to haul food from the distribution warehouse. You could do your part for the state. But why should you? What will the state give you in return? I sell food to people who don't have time for lines because they work two jobs so they can buy clothes for their children or food for their parents. The state is the problem, old man, not me. If the state provided something other than slogans and higher production quotas, you and I would not be doing business. We, old man, we the people support the system by waiting in lines without complaining and producing new quotas without a word of protest. We the people deserve the state. We are sheep. Nein, worse. We follow the rules of the state *knowing* they are leading us to ruin."

The buyer strode over to a box and took out a smoked ham. He tossed the ham to Furman and snickered. "Take that as a gift so your wife won't have to wait in line. She would never see a ham like that even if she did wait. Only the privileged and political elites can buy ham like that."

Jorn climbed down from his chair to collapse it and leave. The guilt he had felt in taking the money was gone.

Normannenstrasse 22, East Berlin

The windowless room was lit by fluorescent lights that hung from a sound-absorbing ceiling. A thin, blue cloud of cigarette smoke floated like wispy fog above the large conference table where the five members of the Shadow Committee sat in session.

At the head of the table was Hagan Wolf, telling the other four men of the impending downfall of Honecker and their government. When he had finished, he paused to let his words sink in. Like Rink, who sat to his right, the other three men were specialists in their fields and had served him faithfully over the years. Sitting next to Rink was Eric Fisher, a former SS officer and currently the shadow Finance and Administration department chief. He provided the administrative support, funds, and documention for all S Direktorate activities. Sitting directly across the large table was Markus Grober, the Science and Technology shadow. He provided the equipment, ordnance, explosives, and expertise in technical matters for the Direktorate. To Grober's right and Wolf's left was Ernst Mantel, a lawyer and the Direktorate's Internal Security shadow manager. He had served with Goebbels in the last two years of the war as his personal legal advisor.

Wolf motioned toward the empty chairs around the table and spoke solemnly. "We five men *alone* are the reason our government survived for forty years and the reason there has been peace. That is why the others were not called to be here. We have a patriotic obligation to make the transition to a new leader and government succeed. Our methods of operation under Ulbricht and Honecker may be questioned, or worse, construed as embarrassing to new, more liberal, democratic leaders. We cannot let that happen. We have until seven October to eliminate the embarrassments and insulate ourselves. We will ride out the storm and wait to be called upon to serve the new leadership. It will happen, my friends. The new government will still have to deal with the Soviets, for the political reality is that four hundred thousand Soviet soldiers and advisors are stationed in our country. The new government will have to accept the Soviets' presence . . . and they will realize they will have to have us to survive. No government can live without a means to protect its security from outside threats."

Wolf let his last words linger in their minds and swept his gaze over their faces. "But we will be called upon to serve our new government *only* if we are looked upon as honorable men."

Wolf turned to the man on his left. "Ernst, for our benefit please explain what constitutes a criminal act or activity."

Mantel pushed his glasses back farther up his nose and lowered his hand, holding his American-brand cigarette. "Herr Direktor, I believe it is germane to know the conditions necessary to prosecuting a criminal act. There must be a victim, victims, or witnesses who will come forth and report the crime to legal authorities. They must then charge the person or persons who committed the offense. However, documentation can be presented by authorities in a case in lieu of victims and witnesses who are not forthcoming."

Wolf leaned back in his chair. "My friends, we cleaned our offices some years ago and took steps to protect ourselves. This cleanup will be different. Before, we assumed a new government would share many goals and objectives with the old. That assumption is no longer valid. We must clean up by scraping the walls and floors and removing all traces of our special activities. We must become invisible. Our mission is to eliminate all possibility of criminal prosecution. This includes eliminating any witnesses, victims, and documentation that can be traced back to this committee and our direktorate. We have sixty-five days. To assist us, I will convene the S Direktorate Department chiefs in this conference room tomorrow morning. I will tell them there is a major security leak, that an agent from the West has penetrated our organization. They will be told to immediately activate emergency measures. All files and records that are sensitive in nature are to be accounted for and turned in to the documentation branch."

Wolf set his eyes straight to the front. "You will all furnish a list of those who know directly of our activities. The lists will be given to Max, who will consolidate them and take whatever action is necessary. I am also concerned about those outside our circle who know of our activities. I want their names as well. I will need the lists within three days."

Wolf leaned back in his chair, directing his unreadable eyes to Eric Fisher of Finance and Administration. "Eric, what are our current funds in cash?"

"We have a little over eight million Ost-marks in discretionary funds, and another nine million in accountable funds."

Wolf drummed his fingers on the table for a moment. "Place a million marks each in separate Swiss accounts for the Shadow Committee members. Take the money from the discretionary funds. From the accountable funds, provide whatever Max needs to hire outside support, and list them as training costs." Wolf swept his gaze over the shocked faces of the group. "You deserve a reward for your faithful service to me and our country. I also want each of you, for precautionary purposes, to see Eric and secure whatever documentation you need to emigrate from the GDR if it becomes necessary. That is all for now. Remember, sixty-five days. Good night, kameraden."

Wolf met with his deputy in his office following the departure of the other Shadow Committee members. He poured Rink and himself a drink from a bottle of vodka he kept in his bottom desk drawer. "Max, we will be very busy for the next two months. Our first priority will be eliminating all the risks to us. Our second will be planning what assets we need to keep in place and which assets must 'disappear' until the new government is in place and we can once again form a new organization."

Rink leaned forward in his chair. "Are you that sure the new leaders will have a need for us?"

Wolf allowed himself a small smile. "The Russians will see to it. It is in their best interests—it's the reason Sorokin gave us advance warning, I'm sure of it. He wanted to ensure we were clean and acceptable to the new leadership when they took power."

Wolf's brow knitted. "I know you can handle the necessary elimination of risks, but I'm concerned about our den chiefs in the West. Their early retirements must be planned very carefully. If only a few are retired, the others will go to ground. I believe it will have to be a simultaneous strike to ensure complete eradication."

Rink took a sip of his drink and set the glass down. "I'll prepare a plan and get your approval. Don't worry, the task will be simple. I can handle it." He looked into his superior's eyes and spoke softly. "And the Shadow Committee members?"

Wolf met his stare. "Nein, they will not be on my list . . . not yet."

Harnack House, West Berlin

Chong turned to the customer in the corner during a commercial about the benefits of U.S. Savings Bonds. "You quiet tonight."

Jake looked up from the pamphlet he was studying. "I don't like 'China Beach.' I never saw women like that in 'Nam."

" 'China Beach,' goood story. My husband watch all time."

Jake nodded, giving her a good-for-him look, and picked up his can of beer. Chong squinted at him. "You flunk driver test again, huh?"

Jake sighed. "Yeah. The damn signs got me again. I'll tell ya somethin', Chong, I don't think I wanna drive in this town anyway. I've learned Germans are pretty good folks, except when they ride bikes or drive cars. I've never seen anything like it. You'd think the roads were a raceway."

"You buy bike, it safer. I drive car one time, then quit. It scare me baaaad. Buy mountain bike. They on sale at PX."

Jake searched Chong's expression to make sure she wasn't a spy for the chief of staff. "I'll think about it."

She squinted at him again. "You find girlfriend yet?"

Jake set down his beer can. "Don't have time, 'cause I'm with you."

She shook her head. "No, you with Lite beer."

Jake picked the can up and kissed it. "She don't argue, and she's always there when I need her."

Chong's right brow lifted. "What about Mission lady? I hear you ask her for date."

Jake nearly fell off the bar stool. He had asked Kristina only five hours before, and already the word was out. The internal gossip network at Clay Compound must have been working overtime.

He lowered his beer and looked into Chong's sparkling, questioning eyes. "I asked her 'cause she's nice, okay?"

"She drink Lite beer?"

"No, she's German."

Chong furrowed her brow. "Then you in big-time trouble."

Jake began to reply, but the bartender's words sunk in. He looked at the can and lowered his head. "You're probably right."

CHAPTER 19

Friday, 4 August,
Rose Range, West Berlin

" 'Bout damn time you came. I been tellin' these Rambos they ain't seen shit till they seen the Snake and da Sandman in action."

Jake nodded at the small group of waiting men, all dressed in civilian clothes and wearing shoulder holsters, then fixed his accusing eyes on the big black man. "How much you bet 'em, Sandman?"

Master Sergeant Washington wrinkled his brow. "Come on, Snake I wouldn't do—"

One of the men stepped forward and handed Jake a nine-millimeter automatic and tossed his head toward the other five men standing behind him. "We got twenty bucks apiece ridin' on it."

Jake sighed, giving Washington an I-thought-so look.

Sandy Washington growled at the traitor. "Cap'n, I told ya ta keep yo' mouth shut."

The captain rolled his eyes and handed Jake two magazines. "Sir, please excuse the master sergeant. He lost his fuckin' head. He's been tellin' us you and him were the record holders for the pop-up course, and . . . well, sir, we think he's blowing smoke up our ass. No offense, of course. I know you've been out of the business awhile, and we caught you cold, but we'll give ya a couple practice goes and then spot ya four targets for record."

Jake pursed his lips and looked skyward for a moment before

212

casually looking back at the captain. "Tell ya what. How about you go forty apiece and I skip the practice and the spot. We do it now. Your best against me . . ." He looked at Washington and winked. ". . . and this old has-been."

The captain's eyes narrowed as he studied the eyes of the overly confident lieutenant colonel. Was he bluffing?

Washington squared himself to his fellow sergeants, who were standing behind the captain. "Put up or shut da fuck up."

The five Special Forces NCOs huddled around their team captain and began whispering.

Jake stepped back and leaned closer to Washington. "What the fuck you got me into, Sandman? When you called, you said it was urgent, so I canceled two meetings and came out here. This is what you call urgent?"

Washington shrugged. "Shit, Snake, I figured you was bored. The fuckin' kids was raggin' on me. I told 'em we was a team back in the good ol' days, and they called me on it. What da fuck else could I do?"

"Ya coulda kept me outta it. Shit, Sandman, I haven't been on a pop-up in two years. I—"

"You're on," said the captain. "We think you're bluffin'—no offense, sir, but you and the sergeant ain't spring chickens. We're gonna spot ya two for your age . . . it's to make us not feel so guilty, ya understand."

Jake bowed and swept his hand toward the enclosed range. "Please, your team goes first."

The captain returned a head bow. "It will be our pleasure." He looked up, all business. "There's thirty-two computerized pop-ups. They could come up single, pairs, or triples. Any one stays up more than two seconds, you're dead."

"What speed?" Jake asked as he slapped a magazine into his pistol.

"Max, of course. The record is twenty-six on this course with a buddy team at that speed." The captain showed his teeth as he smiled. "Sergeant Simpkins and I hold that record."

"Do it," Jake said.

The captain turned, motioning to a broad-shouldered young sergeant wearing blue jeans and pink T-shirt. "Come on, Sim, let's show the old-timers how it's done."

The two men withdrew their automatics from their holsters as they strode toward the entrance of the building and disappeared inside.

Jake and the others walked over to the scoring tin building behind the enclosed range and focused their attention on the console where a computer screen and bank of television screens displayed the eight cubicles inside the covered range. The range operator pointed to the computer screen. "The computer will score it and show us how they're doing on this monitor. When the targets pop up, you'll see a blinking, man-shaped icon on the screen. If the target is hit, it stops blinking. If it blinks for more than two seconds, the computer automatically activates a siren, ending the shoot."

Sandy Washington leaned over to Jake and whispered, "It's a piece 'a cake, relax, Snake. It ain't shit compared to the Bragg course."

Jake rolled his eyes. "Sandman, I ain't believin' you got me into this . . . but he shoulda never said we weren't 'spring chickens.' I still got it . . . I think. It's you I'm worried about. You lookin' kinda gray around the edges."

"Fuck you, Snake."

The operator glanced at the first TV screen that showed the two-man team standing in front of a doorway. He picked up a microphone. "The range is clear . . . firers may proceed at their discretion."

Inside the range, the captain nodded to his partner, took in a breath, raised his pistol up, cupping it with the other hand, and rushed inside the small room.

Jake didn't watch the TV screen. Instead he focused on the computer monitor as he heard the distinctive muffled ka-booms from the fired pistols. The screen showed eight rectangular boxes. Inside the first box four blinking icons had suddenly appeared from different locations. Now none were blinking. The team had "killed" them all.

The operator nodded. "One is cleared . . . but it gets harder as they progress into each room."

Jake yawned and stepped back outside. Washington saw him walk out, tore himself away from watching the action and followed. "What's wrong, Snake?"

Jake ran his fingers over the pistol in his hand as if touching a woman's skin, and put the sound of the shooting out of his mind. "I was just thinkin'. It's been a while, Sandy . . . I've missed it. It's tough knowing we really are gettin' too old."

Sandy smiled. "Yeah, but we gonna have some stories ta tell at the old soldiers' retirement home, ain't we?"

The siren's blare turned both men's heads toward the shack. A sergeant stepped out of the scoring shack with a grin. "They matched their top score, twenty-six. They got to the seventh room before they bought it."

"The range is clear . . . firers may proceed at their own discretion."

Jake winked at Sandy. He listened for it and faintly heard the hum. It got steadily louder, and his eyes slowly began to narrow. He felt it now, the machine's gentle vibration rippling though his body like a stone cast in a still pond, the first small wave expanding outward, perfectly symmetrical, growing. Ready now, he nodded to his partner and stepped into the room. He didn't know why he knew, it was just the way it was . . . the way it had always been, since he'd found he had the gift in Vietnam. He fired, spun and fired again. Few had it. The little people did—the Montagnards— and the Sandman had it . . . the inner machine. It took over, and once on, it didn't want to let go. The Sandman was there. He felt him, didn't see him. His machine's vibration was distinct, gentle, tuned. Jake heard him fire but didn't look. He didn't have to. The vibration was right.

The range operator grinned. "You believing this shit!" The captain and Simpkins exchanged "aw shit" glances. The operator started rocking in his chair, his eyes fixed on the monitor. "They cleared seven, going into eight . . . target down . . . downdowndown. Fuck me! They did it!"

The captain waited with the five others. He watched them come out and saw it in their walk and eyes. He'd seen it a couple of times before in other men. Those with the gift were both blessed and cursed, but today, more blessed. He sighed and held out the money.

Jake shook his head. "Naw, it'd be like taking candy from kids. Us old-timers would rather just have ya buy us a beer sometime."

"Bullll-shit," Washington blurted, snatching the money out of the officer's hand. "They been givin' me a ration 'a shit for days! This is revenge money, Snake. When they reach for the billfolds, they gonna think twice about raggin' on the Sandman."

Jake wrinkled his brow to the captain in apology. The officer smiled. "Howzit feel . . . to know when you're in the groove?"

Jake handed the officer his empty pistol and patted his shoulder as he walked toward his staff car. "Good." He walked on and didn't look back.

Washington puffed out his chest, looking at the six men. "What'd I tell ya?"

Normannenstrasse 22, East Berlin

Max Rink set a typed piece of paper on the desk in front of the S direktor and sat back in his chair. "As per your instructions, that is the consolidated list from the Shadow Committee. Twenty-two fish."

Wolf glanced down the list of names, some of which were men he had known and worked with for over thirty years. It was ironic, he thought, that three of the targets' wives were at that moment at his house with Dagmar for the weekly bridge game. He shifted his eyes back to the big man. "What's your plan?"

Rink smiled, pleased with himself. "The navy recently received an intelligence-gathering ship from the Soviets. In two weeks the ministry is flying up a team of experts to the Rostock naval base to advise naval intelligence on the use and employment techniques of the sophisticated equipment. Thirty members of the ministry are going on the trip. Fourteen of the fish on the list will be on the plane."

Wolf's eyes widened in disbelief. Rink raised his hand. "I know what you're thinking. A bomb going off in the plane would be an obvious purge tactic, and our direktorate the most likely suspected. I assure you, Herr Direktor, that will not be the case. The third fish on the list is secretly having an affair with the wife of Colonel Hoff, your counterpart in the Ministry of Defense."

Wolf glanced down at the list. The third name was that of General Norbert Sommer, the defense minister's deputy. Wolf smiled. Like so many of the others, Sommer was a fool. All the principal leaders who dealt with Stasi and had contact with the West understood they were considered a security risk, and therefore watched . . . yet they still persisted in their childish games, believing they would not be caught.

Rink held up some Xerox papers. "And these are photocopies of Frau Hoff's and General Sommer's letters to each other. It seems they enjoy writing about their fucking as much as doing it." He leaned back with a distant stare. "Wouldn't it be tragic if Colonel Hoff were to find out about the affair going on behind his back? All kinds of things might happen—murders, suicide, the deaths of innocent men on a plane."

Wolf raised an eyebrow. "Can you arrange everything in only two weeks?"

"I have begun."

Wolf smiled to himself in satisfaction, knowing the mission was in good hands. He looked back at the list of names. "You have told me how fourteen of the fish will be taken care of. What of the remaining eight? Wait . . . I see here on the list General Bosch of the Border Guard Command. His son is a navy officer stationed in Rostock. I think he would appreciate an invitation to fly up on the ministry's plane to visit his son."

Rink's lips curled up in admiration. "Ja, and that leaves only seven. Two are quite old. Pohl, from Finance, and Strauss from Communications and Security, are over seventy. Heart attacks are planned. Ulrich will have a fatal accident during holiday in Yugoslavia, and the bachelor Steir will die on the operating table while undergoing a routine gall bladder operation in late September. The remaining three targets are retired from the ministry and will be no problem. Two are alcoholics and the third is very sick."

Wolf locked his eyes with Rink's. "And the den chiefs? Are they on a separate list?"

Rink's jaw muscles twitched but his eyes did not falter. "Ja. There are nine den leaders that must be early retired. They will be taken care of on the second of October in a simultaneous strike by third parties who will know nothing of where the mission came from."

Wolf's stare softened. The hits on Max's den chiefs represented a personal tragedy to him. Rink had worked for thirty years perfecting his network of agents. Those to be retired would be his oldest and most valuable. Retiring them would be like eliminating members of family.

But Rink was a professional. He would not let his personal feelings stand in the way. Wolf folded the list of names and handed it back. "Keep me informed. It looks as if this summer will be a very sad one for Dagmar. She gets very upset at funerals."

Hangelsberg Forest, East Germany

Jorn Furman turned right off the highway onto a bumpy logging road and drove for half a mile before stopping. He smiled to himself as he picked up the wrapped gift for his wife from the seat beside him. He knew the present would make her very happy. That morning he had delivered his flowers to stores in East Berlin and dropped off another five boxes of black market goods to the buyer. With his profits he had bought a used cassette player from an electronics store and picked up two cassette tapes from a music shop. The tapes were music from his wife's favorite operas. Jorn locked the present in the glove compartment. Leaning over, he unstrapped his boots and picked up the worn leather pack from the passenger floorboard. Two minutes later, with the pack on his back, he propelled forward on his hands toward the darkness of the forest. Twice a week he went on his "walks" to get away from state quotas, small talk, rude stares, and looks of pity. He loved his wife, but the forest was his next closest friend. The trees didn't care if he had no legs. In the forest he was an equal. There he felt most alive. It made him whole again, heightened every instinct and sense, made use of his every fiber and muscle. In its darkness he was confident and strong. Among the trees and animals he was young again.

Ida Furman threw a handful of corn out to the chickens and geese that had gathered by the small runoff pond. Seeing a man-made dust cloud approaching from the south, she smiled. Jorn was coming home. She would wait at the side of the house to see him drive up in the old orange truck, which they both affectionately called "Der Panzer." Of course, it didn't look like a real tank, but it had a menacing quality, with its large protuding bumper that made "tank" seem an appropriate name. Jorn had gotten the old converted army truck from the state years ago. He still cussed it every day, but she thought it was more from habit than true feelings. It was strange, but like everything else on the small farm, even Der Panzer seemed like family.

As Ida watched the truck approaching, she couldn't help but feel as excited as a little girl. He had left early that morning without waking her or giving her a good-bye kiss. After being with him for so many years, she could read him like a book. Her husband loved making her happy, and she was certain that he now planned to surprise her with a gift.

The truck pulled off the dirt road and into the long driveway, rumbling up the dusty path that led to the back of the house. She waved and followed Der Panzer, trying to contain her excitement.

Jorn turned off the engine and opened the door to look down at his wife. "Why are you grinning like a schoolgirl?"

Ida kept her grin. "Because I'm happy to see you."

Jorn furrowed his brow. "Why is it I can't keep a secret from you?"

"Because you have slept with me every night for twenty-eight years . . . and you talk in your sleep."

Jorn bristled. "I don't!"

Ida laughed and stepped up on the running board to look in the cab. "Where is it?"

Jorn picked up his pack from the floor and handed it to her. "Here, I brought you wild onions, mushrooms, and herbs."

Ida took the bag and looked past him toward the seat and floorboard. "You bring me the same thing twice a week. Don't you have something else?"

Jorn rolled his eyes and quickly unstrapped his boots. "Get down and turn around. Don't look until I tell you to."

Holding the pack, Ida turned her back to him. Thirty seconds passed and still he had not spoken, although she had heard paper rattling. Another thirty seconds passed, and then, almost as if the angels were calling, she heard music. Soft, like a whisper. The music became louder and louder and she spun around. "*Oooh*, Jorn!"

With tears of joy still in her eyes, she walked beside her husband as he pushed himself to the porch in the wheelchair. She held the cassette player in her hands as if it were precious china. She was still unable to speak.

Jorn lifted himself from the wheelchair into the porch swing, and Ida sat beside him and lowered her head. "Jorn, it costs so much. You shouldn't have."

"You deserve it. Play it for us and let's sit here forever and listen."

Ida leaned over and kissed his cheek. "Jorn," she whispered, "you don't need to give me gifts to make me happy. I have you."

"And now you have your music. Play it. Make me happy as well."

Ida looked into her husband's eyes with concern and love. "I will, but you must promise me you will be careful when you walk in the forest. I know you must do it, but I worry about you. What would happen if you were to fall and hurt yourself? I wouldn't know where to find you. I wait every evening, looking toward the south to see the dust cloud when you make the turn onto the road. My stomach churns and I think of a hundred bad things that could have happened to you until I see that brown cloud. Jorn, you are not a young man. It is dangerous to be out there in the forest alone. Promise me . . . promise me! You'll be very careful, and you'll come home to me every evening."

Jorn smiled. "I walk so that I'll live longer to be with you."

Ida leaned back against Jorn's shoulder and pressed the start button. She closed her eyes and began rocking in the swing as the music floated like a soft breeze and caressed the evening stillness with its wonder.

Jorn closed his eyes, feeling his wife's head resting on his shoulder. He thought about the promise he had made to her, and about another promise he had made long ago to his brothers in heart. He smiled inwardly and lifted an imaginary stein of beer in his mind. He had not forgotten. To you, my brothers. You'll be remembered always . . . always.

West Berlin

Jake Tallon stood awestruck. He was looking down at a woman behind a silver Mercedes 350 SEL convertible that had just pulled to the curb.

"Are you getting in or are you going to just stand there?"

The spell was broken. Jake closed his open mouth and looked down the street as if not hearing the woman. He slowly turned his head back toward the driver, catching her eyes, then looked up the street again. "Sorry, I don't go with strangers. Did you see a cute little gal named Kristina by any chance when you were driving up this way? She's kinda simple and wouldn't be as dressed up as you are."

Kristina opened the door and got out. She joined him in looking down the street. "I didn't see her. If she doesn't show up, what will you do?"

Jake shrugged, looked at his watch then back down the empty street. "I'll give her another two seconds, then decide."

Jake waited five before he turned, looking at the ravishing woman beside him. She had looked terrific when she dressed up for the CODEL dinner, but tonight she was *really* dressed up. The strapless, dark blue, sequined evening dress perfectly set off her golden tan and sun-streaked hair. He didn't know what he liked most, the dress that showed off her slim, perfect figure, or her exposed shoulders and tanned cleavage, which made him swallow to keep from drooling. It was a tough decision, so he opted to make no decision and like it all. He slowly lifted his eyes to her radiant face and put on his lost little boy look. "Eh . . . I'm Jake Tallon. Would you like to go to dinner with me?"

Kristina was still getting over shock herself. She could see that, unlike most Army officers, Jake Tallon knew how to dress. His dark suit fit him perfectly; it was cut to accent his broad shoulders, yet was subtle enough, blending just the right amount of dash with the sublime. He looked like a blue blood cursed with a perpetual silly grin. "Colonel, I'm beginning to feel foolish standing on the sidewalk like this."

"Does that mean you'll go?"

Kristina sighed. "Yes, Colonel, if it will get us off this side-walk."

Jake opened the Mercedes driver-side door and bowed.

Kristina's eyes narrowed. "I thought you were going to drive."

Jake's face squinched as if in pain. "I flunked the driver's test again."

Rolling her eyes as if she'd expected the response, Kristina slid in behind the wheel as best she could in the tight-fitting dress. Jake loved every embarrassing second, figuring now they were starting off on an even playing field. He had *not* expected her to show up in a Mercedes convertible, and he most certainly had *not* expected her to look so . . . so . . . "edible," came to mind, but he changed the adjective in his mind to "stunning." It was one thing to ask a classy lady out to dinner, but something else again to take a stunning one. He wanted to impress his allies with his good taste, not have them drooling. Worst of all, he had made the fatal error of showing his surprise. The one thing Jake Tallon prided himself on was not ever, ever, ever being caught surprised, and worse, show-ing it!

He got in the car as Kristina eyed him suspiciously. "Why are you acting so strange?"

Jake felt a wave of relief. She had said "strange" rather than "surprised." Maybe she didn't see my open mouth after all, he thought. With all his leftover resolve, he forced a smile. "Strange? No. It's just, I haven't been picked up by a exceptionally good-looking woman in a convertible in the last couple of days. It struck me that I was a very lucky guy, that's all."

Kristina seemed to ponder the response before finally smiling. "I'll take that as a compliment. Sit back and relax, I love driving with the top down, don't you?"

Before Jake could answer, the car squealed away from the curb and he was pushed back into the seat by g forces that made his head hurt and chest pound.

Fifteen minutes later the car stopped in front of the British Of-ficers' Club. Jake took his first normal breath since leaving the front of Harnack House and pulled himself out of the deep indentation he'd made in the leather seat. Only then did he glance at Kristina, who was looking at herself in the rearview mirror, checking her unmussed hair. She winked. "This thing really moves, doesn't it?"

Jake got out of the car, thanking the heavens for surviving the ordeal. He felt an uncontrollable urge to kneel down and kiss the solid, stable, unmoving ground beneath his feet. If he ever had any doubt about how it felt to be in the seat of a jet fighter traveling at mach one, it was gone. Never had he been so scared while trying to be so cool in all his life. He was still speechless as he took Kristina's arm and led her to the club's entrance.

Kristina smiled as she held Jake's arm. "That was the most fun I've had in long time. They were all wonderful people. And the meal . . . it was superb."

Jake was feeling no pain from the wine, and the Guinness beer his British counterpart had insisted they drink after the meal. "Yeah, Ian and Lionel were good guys. They weren't as stuffy as I thought they'd be. I had fun."

Kristina giggled and playfully slapped at his arm. "You all acted as if you knew each other for years, the way you kidded each other. The stories were hilarious. I didn't realize, Colonel Tallon, that you were such a funny storyteller. You had the wives in stitches."

Jake chuckled. "Ian is the one who cracked me up. When he used that uppity British accent to describe visiting the United States, he tore me up." Jake abruptly stopped and pointed at Kristina. "I say, dear boy, you colonists eat the most bloody awful foods. How does one properly eat barbecue ribs, corn on the cob, and fried chicken with any sort of deportment and proper etiquette? Why don't you Yanks prepare proper food known to the rest of the civilized world, which requires the use of silverware?"

Kristina laughed and backed up a step, remembering Jake's response. She pointed back at him and lowered her voice. " 'Cause when we lick our fingers, it reminds us of lickin' you limeys."

Jake grinned and put his arm around her. "God, I love hearing myself when I'm on a roll. I'm flattered you remembered."

His light feeling ended abruptly when they reached the convertible and Kristina opened the driver's door to get in. He very slowly walked around to the other side, gathering strength. He opened the door and sat down in the leather seats that had nearly suffocated him on the previous trip. Swallowing his pride, he pleaded, "Kris, could you take it slow this time? I really did enjoy the meal . . . but I'd rather not see it again."

Kristina eyed him coldly. "You don't like the way I drive, Colonel?"

Jake shrugged. "Hey, I like the way you smile, and I like the way you look, talk, and walk. I especially like the way you laugh. But no, I don't like the way you drive."

Kristina stared at him a full five seconds without so much as twitching an eye before she turned in the seat and started the engine. The car crept onto the road and very slowly pulled out into the right lane. Thirty minutes later, without another word communicated between them, she drove past the Harnack House entrance and parked in the parking lot. She glanced up at the stars for a moment, then at Jake. "Did you really mean what you said?"

Jake figured by her silence during the drive that he'd hurt her feelings and ruined the evening. He lowered his head. "I'm sorry, it's just I don't like going fast. I—"

"No, not that. I meant what you said about liking the way I looked, walked, and talked."

Jake slowly lifted his eyes to hers. "Kris, you made the evening one I won't forget for a long time. Thank you."

She held his gaze for a moment before sitting back and gazing up at the stars again with a sigh of contentment. "I don't want to say good-night . . . not yet. I feel like . . . like I'm floating."

Jake leaned back with her and looked up. Five minutes passed before he spoke again. "Are the nights always so beautiful in Berlin?"

"I'd forgotten there were nights like this." She leaned over and kissed his cheek. "Thank you for this wonderful evening, Colonel."

Jake accepted the kiss without a word and opened the door. He got out and looked down at her. "When you gonna quit calling me by my rank?"

Kristina started the engine and smiled. "Good night, Jake. I'll see you tomorrow."

Chong was surprised to see her best customer sitting in his usual spot when she turned from the TV, but she didn't show it. She reached in the icebox, took out a Lite beer and set it in front of Jake. "How was date?"

Jake shrugged and picked up the beer. "How was TV?"

Chong searched his face and slowly began to smile. "You like Mission lady, huh?"

He shrugged again. "What happened on 'Falcon Crest'? Did the ol' lady knock off the guy who was trying to blackmail her into selling the winery?"

Chong kept her smile. "You like Mission lady, Jake. I can tell 'cause your noodle turning red."

Jake's face tightened. "It's not a noodle, damn it! It looks like a snake *and* it's not turning red. Watch TV, damn you!"

Chong shrugged. "Old lady hire hit man to take out blackmailer, but he too smart for that. But she no dummy either. She won't sell winery, and . . ."

CHAPTER 20

Saturday, 5 August,
East Berlin

The seventy-one-year-old director of finance for the Ministry of State Security, Gottfried Pohl, walked arm in arm with his wife through the Tierpark, as he did every Saturday morning. They had left their house on Waldrow Allee only ten minutes before and were on a path that wound through the trees toward their favorite duck pond. He was keeping his eyes on his Rottweiler and saw him sniffing a shrub. Pohl glanced to his left, where a young couple were sitting on a park bench. The young man was pulling the girl to him with the hook end of an umbrella, and having brought her close, kissed her passionately. Pohl frowned as he turned to his wife.

"The young have no morals anymore."

His wife smiled. "And we didn't kiss in the park?"

Pohl gave her a reluctant smile. "Not at seven in the morning we didn't. They must have been up all night. Where do they get their energy?"

His wife was about to smile when her husband was bumped forward. The young man with the umbrella quickly apologized and ran off, followed a second later by the girl, playfully chasing him. Pohl had felt a stinging sensation in the back of his calf just as the man bumped him, and now he reached down to check his leg.

Pohl's wife regarded him with concern. "What is wrong?"

He rubbed his calf and looked at the young man, who had turned around and was taunting the girl, keeping her away by playfully jabbing at her with the umbrella. Pohl straightened up and shrugged. "A bee must have stung me."

The old couple continued walking for several hundred meters along the path toward the small duck pond. Pohl stopped and called his dog, to keep the Rottweiler from chasing the ducks. He reached for the approaching dog's collar and suddenly felt hot and faint. He straightened up, gasping for air, and tried to lift his right hand to grab his wife's arm in order to steady himself, but he couldn't move his arm.

His wife looked at him strangely and stepped closer. "What is wrong with . . . ?" Her eyes widened, seeing him attempt to talk, his mouth quivering. She shrieked for help and reached for her husband, but he was already falling.

Gottfried Pohl lay on the ground looking up into the brown eyes of his dog and died.

Four hundred meters away the young couple who had been watching Pohl quickly strode back to the Tierpark autoplatz and got into a yellow Trabant. Seconds later the small car rolled onto Befreiungstrasse and headed west toward the city center. The young woman who was driving motioned to the umbrella by the young man's side. "Keep the tip clear of the floor, a bump could trigger it."

The young man picked up the umbrella and pushed the side release. The spring-loaded hypodermic needle popped into place in the hollow metal tip. He pushed the release back, and the needle receded into the casing. He grinned. "They think of everything, but what would we have done if it had been raining?"

The girl shrugged.

West Berlin

"What a beautiful morning! This, Jake, is the *real* Berlin! The Café Moahring is where I come every Saturday precisely at nine to have coffee and apple strudel. You can not see Berlin from a van, you need only to sit here and watch it pass before you."

Kristina gave her father an accusing glare. "Be honest, Papa, you come to the café to watch the women pass by on the Ku' damm."

Axel shrugged. "That too. It is all part of the atmosphere of an outside café. You are supposed to look at the women to make them feel like women. Is that not so, Jake?"

Jake leaned forward in his chair as two young women passed by wearing black combat boots, short leather skirts, leather-studded jackets, black lipstick, and pink-orange hair cut in a Mohawk. He turned to Axel. "Those two must feel like women who just got off a spaceship."

Axel raised a silver eyebrow. "Actually, they're from the district of Kreuzberg. All the strange ones live there: skinheads, artists, communists, neo-Nazis, and pacifists. It is the hotbed of dissent against everyone and anything. They have a demonstration there at least twice a week for or against something. You see, Jake, since Berlin is not officially a part of the Federal Republic, there is no draft here. The young idealists in the West who don't want to be drafted, come to Berlin and go to the university. Berlin has always been a liberal city, but has managed to keep the strange ones in one district. To walk down a street in Kreuzberg is better than a trip to our zoo."

"Papa, it's not that bad. You don't like Kreuzberg because of the Turks. Admit it."

Axel threw up his hands. "I admit it." He looked at Jake with a worried frown. "The Turkish have overrun the city. It is our own fault, for they work the menial jobs a German won't these days, but they have bred like rabbits. Soon every other Berliner will be a Moslem praying three times a day to Mecca. One day they will take over the government and order the beer halls closed and our women veiled. I tell you, Jake, I'm worried. The day the Berlin women wear long dresses and scarves is the day I leave."

Jake nodded in agreement. "Yeah, I'll go with ya, no beer and no women is definitely not my kind of place."

Kristina had enough. "Stop it, both of you! People may hear you bigots talking."

Axel winked at Jake and scooted his chair back to allow room for the approaching waiter, who was carrying a tray. "Jake, this is what I come here for. Once you've tasted the strudel, you will be a slave to it forever."

The waiter set plates of thick, hot, sliced strudel in front of Kristina and poured steaming white sauce over it.

Kristina spooned some of the sauce. "This is hot vanilla sauce. Papa is right. Once you've had strudel with white sauce, you're hooked for the rest of your life."

Jake took a bite of pastry and his eyes rolled back. No words he knew could describe how incredible the taste was. He chewed slowly, wanting to savor every bite and make it last as long as possible.

Axel winked at his daughter. "I think he likes it."

Afterward, Axel drove his big Mercedes 580 SEL down the Kurfürstendamm, heading west. "Jake, I am now going to take you to the cabin, where we can sit in the sun and enjoy the real beauty of the city."

When they got to Havel Lake, the Mercedes pulled into the parking place in front of a boat dock. Axel got out and pointed at the closest slip, where a forty-six-foot cabin cruiser rocked gently in the water. "What do you think of her?"

Jake swallowed hard. "That's yours?"

Axel grinned. "The benefits of hard work. Come, we have to prepare her."

"Hold it! We've got provisions in the trunk, remember?" Kristina said, patting the trunk lid.

Axel tossed his head toward his daughter. "She brought you some of that disgusting beer you drink."

Ten minutes later the *Defiance*'s twin diesel engines were rumbling and churning the water as she headed for the open waters of Havel Lake.

Axel had a bottle of beer in one hand and steered with the other. He had donned a white navy captain's hat and was playing the part for all it was worth. Kristina ignored him, but Jake played along, thoroughly enjoying Axel's cussing when sailboats cut across their bow. "Look at that bastard! He doesn't know a jib from a spar. They do what they please on the water, like undisciplined children. What I'd give for a cannon! Jake, we are heading north, and on your right is the Grunewald, which borders most of the lake. On the left is the British sector, and just past the shore is Gatow Air Base. *Damn that fool!* You see him tack in front of me on purpose? I want a cannon!"

Kristina pointed out the Wannsee Yacht Club docks on the right and tried to show him the public beach, but Axel shouted, "Quiet on deck! No tours on my ship! Cabin ho, two points off the port bow!"

Kristina pointed out the cabin to their right. "It's the *starboard* bow, Papa," she said snidely.

"That's what I said!" Axel blurted. "Cabin ho off the starboard bow!"

Jake had seen the picture on Kristina's wall, but he was still not prepared for the reality. Sitting on a small finger of land and nestled back in the trees was a two-story log house that looked like a Swiss château. He had thought he was pointing out a hotel, not a home. It had a sharply angled roof that extended far out over the basic structure, making it resemble a ski resort, complete with wooden decks. Axel cut the engines and glided toward the dock. "Prepare to cast lines! Move lively now!"

Kristina hurried out of the enclosed bridge and took the catwalk to the bow, where she picked up a heavy rope. Jake had followed her, not knowing what else to do, but she pointed to the rear of the boat. "Go aft and get ready to jump on the dock and tie us off."

Jake hurried back along the catwalk to the rear of the cruiser and mimicked her by picking up the end of a curled rope.

Axel spun the wheel and yelled, "Prepare to dock! Prepare to tie off lines on my command!"

"Shut up, Papa!" Kristina yelled, having enough of his commands.

"Aye aye, Skipper!" Jake yelled.

When Jake entered the cabin, carrying a case of Lite beer in his arms, he shook his head in wonder. Then he wandered from room to room, so awestruck that he forgot he was still carrying the case of beer.

Kristina finally found him in the great room, staring out at the lake through the huge glass door.

He turned and looked at her with wide eyes. "There are people out there on the beach and . . ."

Kristina opened the slider and walked out onto the deck. She glanced at the people lying on the beach only fifty paces away. "They walk and ride in on their bikes. It's a beautiful beach, don't you think?

Jake tentatively joined her, still carrying the case of beer. "Yeah, but they're not wearing anything."

She turned and looked at him as if he were an idiot, then strode back through the doorway.

Jake gave one more lingering look at the beach, then hurried to catch up. "Hey, where do I put this beer?"

A minute later Jake strolled out to the front of the cabin, where Axel was reclining in a lounge chair. Jake stopped dead in his tracks. His friend was nude.

Axel laughed at his shocked expression. "Welcome to the real Berlin, kamerad. The sun is the next thing to God to us Germans. Take off your clothes and enjoy its healing powers."

"I . . . I don't have a bathing suit."

Axel sat up. "Bathing suit? Nobody wears a bathing suit here. Keep on your underpants, if you're modest."

"I don't wear underwear," Jake said meekly.

"A soldier for sure! I don't wear the damn things either. Get a beer and another for me. There's some shorts in the hall closet for timid guests."

Relieved, Jake did an about-face and hurried to the closet. Minutes later, wearing a pair of boxer-style shorts that almost came to his knees, he carried out two beers. He had taken the belt off his slacks to hold up the extra-large trunks.

"You are an American, that is for sure," Axel said, shaking his head. "Give me two months with you, and I'll make you into a German."

Jake sat down on the lounge chair and leaned back. His head had just rested against the sailcloth when he thought he saw a vision pass in front of him. He blinked and it was gone.

"Nice costume," Kristina said sarcastically as she sat down on a lounge chair beside him.

When he turned to reply, he nearly fell out of the chair. She was also nude, except for a string bikini bottom. If there had been any doubt in his mind about her being tanned all over, it was gone now. He looked straight into her eyes, willing himself not to drop his gaze a fraction of an inch. "Eh . . . thank you. Axel let me borrow some big guy's underwear." He clamped his eyes shut and leaned his head back.

"Jake, are you embarrassed, by any chance?" she asked.

"Me? Naw. The sun feels great, huh?"

"You want some lotion?"

Jake was not about to look at her again. "No thanks, never use the stuff."

Axel shook his head. "Princess, I fear Jake isn't used to our customs."

Kristina sighed and got up. A minute later she returned and lay back down on her chair. "Better?"

Jake looked toward her with squinting eyes. She was wearing the other half of the skimpy string bathing suit, which just barely covered her nipples. He nodded, and with all the resolve he could muster tried not to look shocked. "Hey, it didn't bother me the first time. When in Rome, do as the Romans, I always say."

She leaned back and lowered the sunglasses that had been perched on the top of her head. "Nothing worse than a liar. Your face is red. Better get used to it. You're in Berlin."

Jake took a long drink of his beer and lay back. He couldn't help but notice her only flaw. She had an ugly pink scar that ran from her lower right hip around to her stomach. He assumed it was from the car accident the congressional wives had told him about.

Ten minutes later Jake nodded off in that special, relaxed state in which he was thinking but his body was sleeping. The combination of the warm sun and apple strudel had taken its effect. He had rationalized in his mind the nudity, for it was obvious he was the only one embarrassed. He had told himself he would adapt . . . later, but that he would not ruin his friends' weekend by being a stick-in-the-mud. The sight of Kristina's small but firm breasts in that split second had totally undone him. He had forced the thoughts of her lithe, perfectly shaped body and tanned, supple skin to a back cavern in his brain. He didn't want all that exposed skin to make him feel any different about her. She was a special woman who had unlocked something inside him, and he didn't want his hormones to screw up a friendship that he felt was building between them.

He slipped past the thinking phase into the sleeping phase, and dreamed he was on a deserted island with nothing but naked native women. He was a stranded soldier wearing fatigues and was trying to convince the giggling natives he was not a war god, he was a love god who wanted to spread love at the earliest opportunity. The natives insisted if he was what he said he was, he had to take off his clothes. He had decided to be the best war god on the island.

"Jake? Jake, wake up, you're getting burned."

Jake blinked once, then twice, then bolted upright. Kristina was holding out a plastic bottle of suntan lotion.

"Better put this on, you've been sleeping for thirty minutes and you're looking awfully red, especially the scars. Mine is sensitive to the sun, and you have a lot more than me."

He squinted up at her because the sun was directly over her shoulder. She pointed to his thighs. To his embarrassment, his shorts had ridden up to his crotch, where ugly, dark purple scars criss-crossed like fat worms just under the skin. He hated them. He took the bottle and squirted warm cream into his hand. "Looks like between you, me, and Axel, we made the guy who invented stitches awfully rich. I guess we should start a club and compare scars." He heard snoring and looked over at Axel, who sounded like he was sawing logs with a chain saw. "You're really—"

"Really, really, really lucky to have a dad. I know," Kristina said with a smile.

He dipped his head. "I already told you, huh?"

"About ten times. What happened to your father?"

Jake rubbed the lotion on his legs. "He went down in a plane here in Berlin during the airlift. I never saw him, except for pictures. He would have been about Axel's age. I guess that's why I like being around your dad so much. I've never had any dealings with men your dad's age, so it's . . . it's kinda special." He looked up at her for only an instant as he handed the lotion back. "Thanks."

She took the bottle, peering down at him, seeing a different man than before. "Lay back and I'll put some on your chest and arms."

Jake closed his eyes as she sat down beside him. The touch of her body against him, and her hands on his skin, was like the strudel, beyond description.

Kristina spread lotion over the scars on his chest and shoulders. "Have you visited the place where your father's plane crashed?"

He didn't want to break the spell by talking, but he didn't want her to know what she was doing to him either. "I wouldn't know where to look. It doesn't matter, my dad was just a dream to me anyway."

She rubbed the lotion over his other shoulder and down his arms, then touched his face and put some on his cheeks, nose, and forehead. "Jake, this scar on your forehead looks like a sna—"

"Yeah, a snake. Everyone says that." He thought of Chong. "Well, almost everyone."

She smiled and patted his stomach. "I think you're properly protected now."

"Thanks," he said, hoping she would get up. Her being so near was driving him crazy.

Kristina stood and gave him another long look before putting the cap on the bottle. She made her mind up. "Let's take a walk, and I'll show you around."

Jake sat up and motioned to his shorts. "I'm not going to embarrass you like this, am I?"

She took his hands, pulled him to his feet and backed off a pace, looking him over. "I think you should at least roll up the legs, they're a little long."

Jake did as she suggested and stood at attention. "Better?"

A smile played on her face. "A little."

They strolled around the cabin, and she pointed out a large, moss-covered cement blockhouse just ten paces past the back deck. "Papa calls that his bunker."

They walked closer, and Jake could see it had firing ports and a narrow step-down side entrance, which was covered with cobwebs. "It's all that's left of a flak battery that used to be in this area. It was some kind of guard-post bunker. Papa cleaned it out years ago and had a new metal door made. He uses it as a wine cellar." She continued walking and turned toward the beach.

Seeing where they were headed, Jake shortened his stride and hung back, as if interested in the surrounding pines and maples.

She slipped her arm around his and tugged him toward the grassy shoreline. "Come on, you'll get used to it."

Jake cringed. "What if somebody sees me walking along a nude beach?"

She sighed. "Jake, almost all the beaches on the lake are optional. Germans are not offended by nudity. It is natural, and we enjoy our freedom. Come on."

She was right. Within fifty yards, he had seen every shape and size body imaginable, from old men, to baby boys, to grandmothers with breasts that hung to their stomachs, to young girls who would have made Hugh Hefner drool. He walked along trying to act as if it was a normal stroll through a park that it so happened was full of buck-naked people. The hardest part was passing the women who smiled, waved, and greeted them with *"Guten Tag."* He thought to himself, after the first time, how the hell do you smile and say "Good day" back to two nipples, a very hairy crotch, and a smiling face? Damn, it was asking too much from a guy. And the men! Shit, how can you pass by one without checking the equipment to see if you stacked up, or even rated? Shit, why am I looking at the guys? he wondered. And then it hit him—sure, it was the American trait of competitiveness. American men would never accept nudity because they would be too worried about being outsized by another. And no American woman in her right mind would prance out and show off her little ta-tas to the whole world. The American clothing industry would collapse if people didn't care how they looked in public, wearing nothing but their birthday suits. After all, clothes were supposed to accent the positive and hide the negative, and naked people don't care either way. It was clear that in Berlin the concession on bathing suits was losing money big-time because the people preferred to let it all hang out and stick out and droop. The only commodity whose stock he would buy in Berlin would be suntan lotion—Berliners had a lot more places to protect.

Kristina glanced ahead and picked up her pace. "Do you play?"

Jake saw what she meant, and halted as if he had hit a wall. It was true! Nude people did play volleyball!

She stepped back, grabbed his arm and pulled him toward the small open area where laughing, bouncing people tried to keep a ball going over a net. The first nudie magazine he'd ever seen as a young boy had pictures of a nudist colony, and the black and white photos were almost all of people playing volleyball. He took one look and knew it was much better in living color. He couldn't help himself, he began laughing. It was a young boy's dream come true!

Kristina looked at him, misreading his laugh. "Come on, I'll play on the other side."

Jake very reluctantly joined the bouncing people, feeling like a freak wearing the shorts, but nobody around him seemed to notice. The ball sailed toward him and he began to send it back over the net when a buxom woman brushed past him and jumped up, slamming the ball over in a spike. For a moment a round brown nipple was within one inch of his nose.

He looked at Kristina through the net for moral support, but she was diving for the ball that a player had blooped up. It was a great save, but her string top had slipped down beneath her breast during the effort. That's it, he told himself, I'm outta here! No red-blooded all-American guy could take the mental punishment. The ball sailed in his direction. He had taken a step to leave the court but couldn't let the big-busted woman outdo him again; it was a matter of pride. He jumped up and spiked the ball into the corner. A young man tried valiantly to pop it back up into play, but it careened off his arm. The players all clapped, and a gray-haired old lady with drooping breasts patted his back. "Super! Wunderbar!"

Feeling like a star, Jake thanked her with a "danke," and decided a couple of more plays wouldn't hurt anything, plus he could show the nudies how it was done in the good ol' U.S. of A.

Kristina walked ahead of him with a scowl. He spoke to her back pleadingly. "Hey, so we whipped ya three straight games. There's always another day. You missed a few shots, it's no big thing."

She spun around and burned holes through him with accusing eyes. "You deliberately hit those spikes at me!"

"No I didn't. Really, come on, it was just a game and "

Kristina couldn't take his hangdog look and broke out in laughter. "The big American showing off, was what you were! You should have seen yourself, strutting around in those ridiculous shorts."

Jake's jaw twitched. "I was good My team appreciated me."

Kristina broke up again, seeing his serious expression. "We all loved you. We haven't laughed that hard this summer. You were the perfect American, big, loud, and totally crazy. Jake, you do not slap people's behinds in Berlin."

"I was firing up the team, getting them motivated."

"Jake, you motivated only the women. The men probably thought you were ga—"

"They did not! Okay, so I got a little excited."

Kristina frowned again. "And what was with the chant you had your team yell? That 'We're number one! We're number one!' chant. Jake, it was not a football game. It was a friendly game of volleyball

where no one cares who wins or loses . . . until you started playing."

Jake threw up his hands, "You play to win, not to have fun,
every American knows that. I was just trying to instill a little pride
in beating the crap outta you guys. We'll be even tougher next
weekend, if I can get rid of Greta. She giggles too much."

Kristina shook her head and took his arm. "You are impossible!
But . . . it was fun, wasn't it?"

Jake withdrew his arm from her and put it over her shoulder,
giving her a gentle squeeze. "Lady, it was great. I mean, heck, apple
strudel, the boat, the cabin, and nude volleyball? How could a day
get any better than this?"

"What is going on?" Axel demanded with an angry scowl as he
stepped in front of the returning couple. "I go to sleep and wake
up, and no princess or kamerad." He looked directly at his daughter.
"You did not wake me to make me turn over, and I sunburned
my—"

Kristina tried not to laugh. "Papa, not again!"

Axel held up his hand. "You should have awakened me. It is
your fault! Do not laugh. I'm an old man who needs his daughter
to remind him of things."

Jake tried to keep a straight face. "Damn, Axel, does it hurt? I
mean, how can you walk in those slacks?"

Axel eyed the tall American who was biting his lip. "You are
laughing too? Jake, my kamerad? Please, as fellow soldier, help me."

Jake wrinkled his brow. "Wha . . . what can I do?"

Axel broke into a huge grin. "Get me a beer!"

Hangelsberg Forest, East Germany

Jorn Furman rested his head on his wife's lap and looked up at
gnarled limbs of the old oak. "Now do you understand why I come
to the forest?"

Ida stroked her husband's forehead and faintly smiled. "I've always known why, Jorn, I'm just happy that today you've shared
your forest with me. Thank you for this picnic. It means more than
all the other gifts you've given me."

He shut his eyes, contented, but felt her hands trembling. He
rose up and looked at her. "What is wrong?"

Ida's eyes began to well. "You are black-marketing, aren't you?"

Jorn sighed in relief and laid his head back on her lap. "It is
nothing. I deliver leftover food to a buyer. Don't worry. I'm not

going to get caught. And if I do, what can they do? Take away the only nursery collective manager who is making the district agricultural director a profit? They would do nothing but make me go to rehabilitation classes."

She lowered her eyes to him. "Jorn, what happens if a member of the collective turns you in? They will do it out of jealousy. I know some who have turned in members of their own family!"

"The collective members won't turn me in. They profit as well. Don't worry, I am an old man making eighty marks a week more than before. If they want my old bones, they can have me. At least we will know one system works in our government."

"Jorn, look at me, I'm sixty-six years old. My hair is gray, my body is shriveling. I would be lost without you, what would I do?"

Jorn sat up again and brushed a tear from her cheek. "I am only one of hundreds in the district who sell on the black market, and I make far less than the others. They would have to arrest all the workers and managers in distribution warehouses before they got to me. Don't worry."

Ida leaned over and kissed his cheek. "Take care of yourself, my husband. I could not live without you."

Muggelsee, East Berlin

Dagmar Wolf rubbed suntan lotion on her husband's forehead, waking him.

Wolf took his wife's hands and pulled her down to him, then softly kissed her lips. She sat with him. "I'm sorry I woke you. I just didn't want you sunburned."

He sat up and stroked her cheek with the back of his hand. "Don't say 'I'm sorry' to me. You could never do anything to be sorry for. It is such a beautiful summer, the best and warmest in years. You should put on a bathing suit and join me."

She blushed. "I don't have the figure for it anymore."

"Nonsense, I love that figure. Go into the house and change. We can enjoy the sun as we used to."

She motioned with her head toward the nearest security camera perched on a pole at the water's edge. "I hate those things. I'm embarrassed to lay on my own porch and sunbathe. The security men see everything."

Wolf frowned. "No, my darling, they watch the water to see who approaches the estate from the lake. The other cameras on the corners of the walls do the same. They can't see us. Go change now."

Dagmar glanced at the camera, then her husband, still not convinced. "Let's go sailing. We'll throw out the anchor once close to
the far shore, and then lay in the sun, but not in our suits. We will
enjoy the sun like we used to, remember?"

Wolf rose, and kissed his wife's forehead and smiled. "I could
never forget."

They walked down the steps from the stone porch toward the
dock, arm in arm. Dagmar leaned over, resting her head on his
shoulder. "I remember like yesterday the first time we lay together
on the shore of the Havel. We were so young and so timid. I thought
you would never kiss me. I was so happy that day when you finally
did. I fell in love with you that very moment."

Wolf smiled reflectively. "I fell in love with you months before.
I dreamed of you every night, and it took all those weeks to finally
find the courage to kiss you. I didn't know what you would do . . .
I was afraid."

She stopped and looked into his eyes. "I didn't think we could
have made each other happier than we were that day, but every
time we make love, it is better."

Wolf gently touched her cheek. "Get in the boat and let's see if
we can make it even better."

"Direktor! You have a call."

Wolf turned toward the familiar voice of Renate, his wife's security guard. "I'll be right there. Help my frau prepare the *Eagle*."
Wolf patted his wife's arm. "I will see who it is and be right back."

The call was from the ministry's duty officer, informing him of
the tragic news that the director of finance, Gottfried Pohl, had died
of a heart attack that morning. Wolf thanked the young major and
asked him to call the S Direktorate's operations duty officer and
have him call the residence in two hours.

As Wolf walked down the porch steps, he tried to decide what
expressions he would use and what words would sound sincere to
Dagmar. He would receive the call when they had returned from
sailing. He would have to look shocked and saddened when he told
her that their close friend, Gottfried, had died. Poor Dagmar. The
next sixty days would be filled with sadness for her. She deserved
at least another two hours of happiness before the effects of the
clean-up operation began. He smiled. And he deserved her body
writhing on him. Dagmar was a lady with clothes on, but without she was . . . yes . . . he felt the tingling sensation in his loins
building.

West Berlin

Axel unlocked the door to the house and threw his arm over Jake's shoulder, walking him inside. "Next weekend we will motor up the Havel to the old citadel, then follow the Havel River up to . . ."

Kristina followed the two men inside, knowing Jake would be coming next weekend, not wanting to miss the opportunity to be with her father. She smiled to herself for she was glad. The two men needed each other, and she didn't mind sharing her father's love with such a man.

She walked into the kitchen and was surprised to see the colonel shaking hands with her father.

"Thanks, Axel, it was a great day. I'll see you next Saturday at the same time."

"You sure you won't stay and eat with us?"

Jake smiled. "Naw, I've really got to get going. I haven't done laundry since I got here, and have a stack of reports to read." He put his hand on Axel's shoulder, seeing his disappointment. "I really have to go. I'll see you next week for sure, that's a promise."

Axel smiled begrudgingly. "Next week, then."

Jake gave Kristina only a nod as he strode toward the hall. "Thank you for putting up with me today."

She turned to walk out with him, but he had already opened the front door and stepped out.

She turned to her father with a look of puzzlement.

He returned a sad frown. "I think our friend is very lonely and can only take so much of us, for we are living in a different world than he is. I used to feel like that after your mother passed away. I had a very hard time understanding how life could go on. It will take time for him to give up what he has learned to live with—his loneliness."

Kristina knew the feeling all too well and put her arms around her father's neck. "Papa, I'm happy that I have you to keep me out of that world."

Axel kissed his daughter's cheek and looked deeply into her eyes. "We all hold on to our pasts, but we cannot live there. I think you too must let go of some of those memories and make room for new ones." He smiled. "I liked seeing you laugh today. It made me happy seeing you happy."

Kristina blushed and lowered her eyes. "We all had a good time."

Seeing his daughter's discomfort, Axel patted his stomach. "How about making your old father feel good again and feed him? I'm starved."

·   ·   ·

Jake's jaw muscles rippled as he strode up the sidewalk toward Harnack House. He'd felt the heavy cocoon wrapping itself around him when they'd driven back from the lake. He'd had no choice. Axel and Kristina had made it through their own personal trials and losses and had achieved some happiness. They sure as hell didn't need someone like him screwing up their evening with petty personal problems that he wasn't able to handle.

He hurried through the Officers' Club entrance, bounded up the steps to the third floor and into his room. Slamming the door behind him, he strode into the bathroom to face himself in the mirror. It hurt facing the truth, but he had to admit it: Jake Tallon was holding on to self-pity. That was all he had left of his relationship with Helen. It wasn't her. He didn't give a shit about Helen anymore. It was their dreams of a future that he'd wanted to hold on to. When she had left him, she'd taken his dreams with her. They were all he had . . . just dreams, stupid fantasies of having kids and being able to teach his son how to ride a bike, throw a ball . . . It wasn't all that much, but for someone who hadn't had a dad himself, it had meant something.

Jake noticed the man in the mirror had tears running down his cheeks, but he didn't pity him any longer. He knew deep inside it had not all been Helen's fault. The man in the mirror hadn't spent enough time with her, hadn't talked, really talked, to her. He hadn't even asked her about *her* dreams.

Jake turned away from the mirror feeling gnawing guilt and remorse. He had been lying to himself for too long. He had always known deep inside that he'd loved his dreams more than he had his wife.

"Hi, Jake, oh . . . you sunburned bad. You big-time red."

Jake nodded in brooding silence and took a swig of the beer Chong had placed in front of him. She looked back at the television but slowly shifted her eyes back. "Bad day, huh?"

Jake shrugged. "Naw, in fact it was a great day. I played volleyball, boated, and—"

"Sunburn your noodle."

"Chong, come here. Take a closer look at this scar. . . . See? It's not even close to looking like a noodle."

Chong waved her hand toward his head. "I think you getting bald too. I have friend who has lotion. It work! My husband use. His hair grow so much he need a haircut a week, you know."

Jake took another long drink before feeling the top of his head.

"See, it getting thin. You want me to talk to friend and get you bottle?"

"Might as well get me two."

"Where you go to get sunburn?"

"Havel Lake."

". . . They no wear clothes at Havel."

"Yeah, I noticed."

Chong's eyes narrowed. "You men all same."

Jake picked up his beer can and watched the drops of condensation drip down its side. "Some of us are trying to change."

CHAPTER 21

Saturday, 19 August,
Seelow, East Germany

Jorn Furman raised his wrist and looked at the luminous hands of his watch. It was five A.M. He lay for a moment gathering strength before carefully getting out of bed so as not to wake his wife. He had just placed his hands on the floor to propel himself to the bathroom when she raised her head from her pillow. "Jorn, what are you doing up so early? This is your day off."

He turned on the lamp by the bed and picked up his shirt. "It's nothing," he said softly. "I need to repot the geraniums before their delivery next week, and prepare the ground for planting the fall crop. Go back to sleep."

He began to reach up and turn off the lamp, but Ida sat up. "Eric and Hermann will do those things on Monday. Come back to bed and—" She stopped speaking when she saw the look in his eyes. "Oh, Jorn, no, they wouldn't have left you. I talked to them yesterday. They understood that we had to get the summer crop in."

Jorn lowered his head. "I talked to them too. I told them they should go while they still could. They are leaving at first light this morning for Hungary." Jorn raised his eyes to his wife. "There is nothing for them here. Word that the Hungarians have taken down their border fences with Austria has spread like wildfire. I couldn't ask them to stay . . . the West is their only hope for a future."

"What about the crop? You can't do it all alone!" she exclaimed incredulously.

Jorn looked out the window toward the flower beds and greenhouses. "I'll just have to work a little harder, that's all. I can do it."

Ida's face turned to stone. She pushed the down cover off and swung out of bed. "Not by yourself you won't. I will help you."

Jorn couldn't help but smile at her, standing there wearing her worn flannel nightgown and stern scowl. He reached for her hand. "I am the luckiest man on earth, having you."

"Don't sweet talk me, Jorn Furman. Let's get to work!" she barked.

Pankow District, East Berlin

In the back of a van parked in an alley, Max Rink looked at his watch and set down his cup of coffee. He picked up the telephone that had been strung to the van the previous night and dialed the number written on an acetate board in front of him.

Colonel Rolf Hoff had to grope for a moment in the darkness before finding the receiver and answering. After listening a few seconds, he sat up and spoke in agitation. "Ja, ja, I'll go the office and pick it up. I'll be there in twenty minutes and deliver it to the general before he departs. Don't worry."

Renee Hoff lifted her head from the pillow when her husband angrily slammed the receiver back into the cradle. "Who's calling at this hour?" she asked sleepily.

Hoff stood, turned on the lamp, and began to look for his socks. The clock read 6:10 A.M. "It was the weekend duty officer. General Sommer is leaving on a flight for Rostock this morning at seven and forgot a package he left in the office. He called the duty officer from the airport. He wants it delivered to him before the plane departs. The duty officer couldn't leave his post, so of course the general told him to call me. Damn Sommer! He must be getting senile, the way he forgets everything!"

Renee Hoff laid her head back on the pillow, thinking about Sommer. He had been in the bed with her only three days before. Thoughts of their recent liaison made her feel hot and tingly.

Five minutes later Colonel Hoff turned off the lamp by the bed and leaned over to kiss his wife's cheek. "I'll be back in an hour or so. Go back to sleep."

Four blocks away, inside the van, Max Rink lowered his binoculars. His target had just left the house. He picked up the phone and dialed a number at the airport, a private line.

The chief of security for Schönefeld Airport picked up the receiver. "Ja?"

Rink spoke in a flat monotone. "He will be there in thirty to forty minutes. Be sure you follow all instructions to the letter. The general must not see him or know of the delivery."

"I will handle the matter as you ordered," the security chief nervously whispered.

Rink hung up and turned to the man he was grooming to be his replacement, Lothar Rossen, a veteran of fifteen years in Rink's Special Operations Department. "Take care of him once the investigation is complete. He is a loose end. Never leave loose ends."

Colonel Rolf Hoff stormed to his car still fuming at the treatment he had received from the airport security agents. He gave the distant aircraft a last glance as it climbed into the clouds, then angrily jerked open the door to his Trabant and slid in behind the wheel. Imbeciles! Incompetent morons! Hoff took a deep breath to control his shaking and shut his eyes to try and remember every detail for the report he would write to the chief of security. He had arrived with the box of documents in plenty of time, but the uniformed agents would not let him personally deliver the package to the general. They wouldn't even let him see the general. He'd had to sign the box over to the plane's crew chief, who wasn't even cleared to get near secret documents from the Ministry of Defense! Still writing the report in his mind, Hoff pulled out of the parking lot. He would be home in less than twenty minutes.

Ten miles away Renee Hoff awoke to something cold and hard touching her forehead. She opened her eyes just as her mouth was covered by a gloved hand.

Max Rink spoke softly and reassuringly as he lowered the pistol barrel from her head. "I am from Stasi, Frau Hoff. You won't be hurt if you do exactly what I tell you. Please do not scream as I take my hand from your mouth. I will then explain why I am here and what you can do to help us. I assure you this matter deals with our national security and needs your complete cooperation. Nod if you understand."

The wide-eyed woman tried to nod, but the weight of his hand had her pinned to the pillow. Rink felt the attempt and slowly lifted his gloved hand. He smiled and backed up a step, keeping the pistol down at his side. "Thank you, Frau Hoff. Now, if you would please sit up, we will discuss a security problem we have concerning you and General Sommer."

Rink saw her already fear-filled eyes grow wider, but he was interested only in getting her into the proper position. She tentatively rose, clutching the down cover to her neck to conceal her nakedness, and sat back against the headboard.

Rink stepped back as if he were going to sit down in the chair behind him, then suddenly grabbed the bed cover, yanked it down, raised the pistol, and fired a bullet into her forehead. The silenced weapon had made a report slightly louder than a man spitting, and had sent a nine-millimeter bullet through her skull, which blew out the back of her head and splattered blood and brain tissue over the headboard and white-painted wall.

Rink's upper lip curled up in satisfaction as he regarded his work. But there was still more to be done.

In the cargo hold of the ascending VIP flight carrying General Sommer, the altered altimeter's small, watchlike hand passed the 8 representing the eight-thousand-foot mark and continued to move slowly upward toward the 9, where a small copper pin had been recently inserted. The thin metal hand moved slightly, and then again, touching the pin. This completed an electrical circuit to a blasting cap, which in turn detonated twenty kilos of plastic explosive that lined a cardboard box in the cargo hold. A horrific roar of unleashed heat and energy instantly vaporized wiring, conduits, cables, aluminum flooring, and baggage. The upper flooring, seats, instrument panel, and two pilots were ripped to pieces by the monstrous force and blown through the top of the cockpit into a three-hundred-knot gale.

General Sommer and nine other passengers in the rear of the plane had time only to gasp and instinctively clamp their eyes shut before the plane began to plummet. The torn metal skin shrieked and flapped as the mangled fuselage fell at just over one hundred miles per hour. The hurricane-force wind pinned the passengers to their seats. Their screams were trapped in their throats, and conscious thoughts were frozen in their brains for eighteen endless seconds before their agony ended, abruptly.

Colonel Hoff parked in his home's small driveway and got out of the car. The ride had calmed him down, and his thoughts now were on getting undressed and into bed. He unlocked the door to the house, and walked down the hallway. He noticed that the bedroom door was open and the lamp was still out. He quickened his stride.

He stopped abruptly just inside the doorway. The room smelled with a sickening coppery odor. Just as he saw his wife sitting up with her head dangling down, he felt a gun barrel press into his temple.

"Freeze! Don't move a fucking muscle," Rink said coldly. "Do exactly what I say. Move toward the bed, *now!*"

Hoff heard the words but was incapable of doing anything but staring at the grotesque sight of his wife, nude, her head dangling over her chest, and behind her, blood splattered on the wall. His eyes moved over the bed sheet, which glistened with a dull sheen of coagulated dark blood around her white buttocks.

Rink pushed the stunned man to within a foot of the bed, keeping the pistol pressed against his temple. Hoff gagged and, shutting his eyes, began to shake uncontrollably. Rink withdrew from his jacket pocket the latest letter Hoff's wife had written the general and slapped the folded pages into Hoff's left hand. "Read it! So you'll know why," Rink hissed.

Without opening his eyes, Hoff mechanically lifted the letter. Rink pulled the trigger.

A few minutes later, Rink stepped back into the hallway, took in a deep breath, and ran through a mental checklist. Woman in the proper position. Altimeter faceplate, parts, wiring, packing tape, and necessary tools hidden in upstairs study. Hoff in proper position, holding letter and weapon. Finger on trigger, rest of letters in bedroom. Suicide note and pen. Satisfied, Rink walked to the front hallway and flipped on the porch light, then picked up his empty canvas bag in the kitchen. When he left, he was careful to close the door behind him.

Havel Lake, West Berlin

The captain of the cruiser stood behind the wheel and ordered his first mate to start the powerful inboard engines. Jake Tallon obeyed with an "Aye aye, Skipper," and turned the key in the ignition switch.

"I think it is time you were the captain," Axel said, with a gleam in his eyes. He took off his hat and placed it on Jake's head. " 'Captain,' you are in command of the *Defiance*."

Jake rolled his eyes up at the hat, then looked down his nose at the other mate, Kristina. "Bring the captain and the junior captain beers, then prepare the ship for—"

"You two are impossible!" she barked, and stormed out of the bridge.

Jake shrugged his shoulders, "I thought I sounded pretty good."

Axel handed him a beer from the cooler behind him and motioned toward the open waters of the lake. "Women don't understand men's fun."

Kristina erased her counterfeit frown and felt inwardly pleased as the cruiser pulled away from the dock. Her father was the happiest she'd seen him in years. He appeared to have grown younger over the past three weeks; at least he seemed always to be smiling or laughing.

She too had experienced a change since the colonel had come into their lives. That morning, the two men had talked for hours at the café, and would have continued for hours more if she hadn't reminded them that they should be going. The two of them had been drawn as close together as two men could get. She envied them for what they had.

"Look at the bastard!" she suddenly heard Jake yell. "He cut across our bow to test us! Get the cannon and blow his ass outta the water!"

She laughed aloud and walked back inside the bridge cabin to join the fun.

Jake knew it was now or never. He held his breath and walked out the cabin door praying Axel and Kristina wouldn't even notice his new bathing attire that he'd bought at the PX.

"Mein Gott! What the hell is that you're wearing?" Axel blurted, sitting up in shock.

Kristina raised her head from the lounge chair and whistled, then clicked her tongue. "The volleyball team will love those."

Jake thrust out his chin and continued on to his lounge chair, trying not to show that he was dying inside. "They were on sale, okay?"

"You wasted your money," said Axel, lying back down.

Kristina nodded. "I can certainly see why they were on sale."

Jake sat down glaring at Kristina who was only wearing her string bottom. "Give me a break, will ya? It takes time to change old ways."

Kristina wiped the sarcastic grin from her face. "They look fine, I was just kidding. I think you're making progress."

"I think they look like the Italian underwear sissies wear," Axel piped in.

Jake flushed and spun his head toward the old soldier. "Yeah, but at least I won't have to worry about the sun burning my you-know-what!"

Axel smirked and put on his sunglasses. "Don't expect me to

play on your side today. I don't want my friends seeing me playing volleyball with a man wearing sissy Italian underwear."

Jake popped a top to a beer and looked back at Kristina with a tight grin. "He's gonna be sorry he said that. We're gonna kill them."

Kristina leaned back in her chair and pushed down her glasses from her forehead. "What's this 'we' stuff. I have friends too, you know? I think I'll play with Papa's team."

Jake nodded, took a drink of his beer and continued nodding. "Okay. I understand. It's war, then. This sissy against the birthday suits. I can handle that. In fact I like that. You are both going to be very sorry. Jake the Snake is gonna cut no slack."

Seelow, East Germany

Ida Furman slowly rose, straightening her aching back, and wiped sweat from her brow. She looked down the long row of weeds yet to be pulled and glanced up at the sun. She knew if she did any more work, she would pass out. She glanced at her husband, who was soaked in sweat from digging out the long roots of thistle weed in the next row. "Jorn, let's finish later this afternoon, when it's cooler."

Jorn pushed himself over to his wife, and they walked to the shade of a lime tree and sat down. He looked toward the south and sighed. "If we were twenty years younger, we would be driving through Czechoslovakia toward Hungary."

Ida leaned back against the old tree. "Would you really want to leave our home?"

"It is not our home. It is the state's home. We have the privilege of working their land only as long as we can produce their quotas. The farm will be taken away when we are too old to work. Yes, I would want to leave here . . . if I were younger."

Ida looked up at the branches. "I have heard of protests. The churches are speaking as one to the government about allowing the people to have a voice. Perhaps it is a beginning, as is the Hungarians taking down their barriers to the West."

Jorn lay back on the grass, putting his hands behind his head. He shut his eyes and spoke in a whisper. "Perhaps."

Muggelsee, East Berlin

Hagan Wolf put his arm around his weeping wife and gave her a gentle hug. "You must be strong for the others. I'll have Willi and Renate take you to their homes, and I'll join you as soon as I can. I've been called into the office by the minister. He too is very upset at the news of the crash. He wants me to become personally involved in the investigation."

Dagmar lifted her hand to her husband's face. "I will do my duty. Go on, I understand." She lowered her head. "It is so terrible. All of my dearest friends' husbands are dead. First Pohl, and now this. Is God punishing us all?"

Wolf lifted his wife's chin so she could see his tears. He spoke with a tremble in his voice. "We have each other, and we will find new friends. We have had to do it before, and we will do it again. Be strong, my darling, for you are my strength. I cannot stand to see you sad."

Dagmar patted his hand. "Go, do your duty, and I will do mine."

Minutes later Wolf got in the back seat of his sedan and the driver accelerated. He put the thoughts of his wife's tears away and turned them toward the meeting he was going to attend. The minister had called an emergency meeting to discuss the plane crash and to let the directors know about the preliminary investigation.

Wolf couldn't help but smile inwardly at the thought of his minister telling the same story that Rink had told him two weeks before. The incredible outcome would be that the defense minister would have to humble himself and ask the Stasi to help keep the awful secret of the bombing and messy affair from the public.

Wolf bit his lip to keep from laughing aloud.

Havelsee, West Berlin

Axel slapped Jake's back and handed him a beer. "You played brilliantly, kamerad. It's just too bad your team didn't win."

"You gave me the old women and giggling Greta, ya cheater! You stacked the deck against me, and you damn well know it!"

He patted Jake's shoulder in mock consolation. "Maybe next week you'll do better, when I'm not here to choose the teams."

Jake's eyes widened. "What do mean, you won't be here?"

Axel seemed confused. "Didn't Princess tell you? I'm leaving on Wednesday to visit my kamerad Lars Kailer, in Hanover. Every summer we go fishing in the Baltic for several weeks on his boat and catch nothing but colds. Lars is a rich old goat who owns at least twenty newspapers in the Federal Republic. But he is also an Iron Man." Axel could see the disappointment in Jake's eyes, and smiled. "You and Princess will have the lake to yourselves."

Jake furrowed his brow. He didn't want to be left alone with Kristina. It was one thing when Axel was around. It would be totally different with just her and him and the sun. He looked at his friend apologetically. "Axel, I'm afraid I can't. I got word yesterday that they have an apartment for me, and I'm moving in next week. I'm gonna need the next couple of weekends to get the place squared away."

Kristina walked out the cabin door with a plate of cold cuts and bread. "What have you two been talking about?" she asked as she set the food down.

Axel gave Jake a sidelong glance. "I was just telling Jake about my fishing trip with Lars. Jake tells me he'll be busy the next few weeks, so, my princess, you'll have to come by yourself to the cabin."

Kristina's smile vanished. She nodded mechanically as she arranged the bread. When she finally looked up, she gave Jake an icy stare that chilled him to the bone. Then she turned and walked back into the cabin. A moment later she strode past the two men as if they weren't there and headed for the dock with a beach towel in her hand.

Jake looked at Axel, who was making himself a sandwich. "What's wrong with Kris? Is it something we did?"

Axel shrugged. "I'm afraid she's slipped back into her old world again. She gets like this when she knows I'm leaving. She doesn't like being alone."

He and Jake watched as she climbed up on the boat and spread out her towel on the deck. She slipped off her string suit and lay down facing the sun.

Axel sighed heavily. "I worry about her when she is like this. I believe she thinks of her lost family. It is very difficult for women to lose their children. You notice she avoids the children on the beach? I think it is too painful for her to face them."

Axel paused, as if making up his mind about something. He raised his eyes toward Jake again. "Would you look out for her when I'm gone . . . as a favor from one Iron Man to another? I will not be able to enjoy myself knowing she is alone and feeling the way she does."

Jake stood up. "Of course I will. I don't blame you for being worried. I'll . . . I'll think of something as an excuse to come by and

see how she's doing. I'm not going to be *that* busy." Jake looked
again toward the boat. "I'm going to go talk to her and keep her
company. Save some food, huh?"

Axel smiled to himself as he watched Jake walk toward the boat.
His plan was working perfectly.

Jake looked down at the glistening nude woman and was about
to speak when Kristina opened an eye. "You're blocking my sun,"
she said harshly. "Why are you here, Colonel? Aren't you embarrassed at my nudity?"

Jake sat down and faced her. "I'm not embarrassed," he answered honestly. "I came over to tell you that your dad wasn't quite
right about my being busy. I'm moving into an apartment next
week. I'm finally getting out of Harnack House. I can't come to the
lake, and I hoped you wouldn't either. I'd like you to help me fix
my new place up. I don't know anything about decorating or fur-
nishing, and I'll need to get the place presentable. . . . I'll even pay
you for your time by taking you out to dinner."

Kristina's scowl had slowly dissolved as he was speaking. She
sat up and took off her glasses. "What would my friends think of
me, coming and going out of your apartment?"

Jake motioned to his suit. "I'm the sissy in Italian underwear,
remember?"

Kristina laughed and flung back her hair. "Okay, but I don't
work cheap. It will have to be a nice restaurant. Not Burger King."

Jake winced. "How about McDonald's?"

"No. A German restaurant, expensive."

Jake lowered his head, then abruptly raised it again. "I got it!
Steaks at my place. We'll buy a barbecue grill and cook out, invite
Sandman and Sissy over, drink good wine that even has a cork."

Kristina rocked her head in thought. "Maybe. You're getting
close."

Jake looked at her as if exasperated and threw up his hands.
"Okay, I'll throw on some wurst with the steaks, and we'll have
some sauerkraut with the corn on the cob."

He waited for her next comeback, but she couldn't take it anymore. She burst out laughing.

Axel Mader heard his daughter's laughter, followed a second later
by Jake's. He got up and strolled into the cabin's darkness and whispered, "Do you hear them, Gisela? Do you hear the sound of their
happiness? I am a meddling old fool, but sometimes, like today, I
can still work a little magic." Despite his smile, tears trickled down
the old Iron Man's face as he shut his eyes. "I miss you, Gisela.
I . . . I miss you so very much."

Muggelsee, East Berlin

Exhausted from a long meeting, Wolf started walking up the steps that led from his marbled foyer to the bedrooms.

"Direktor, please, could we speak a moment?" It was Renate, his wife's security guard. For a change she wasn't wearing a shapeless dress and didn't have her hair severely pulled back in a bun. In fact, standing below him in the muted light, she looked like a vixen. Her blond hair flowed down over her bare shoulders, and her short silk nightgown revealed every fold and form of her willowy body.

"What is it?" he asked softly.

She lowered her head. "Your frau has been very upset . . . much more even than at the Pohl funeral. I had to give her something to help her sleep."

Wolf could see that Renate was upset as well, and retraced his steps back to the foyer. With his arm around her shoulder, he walked her up the staircase. "You did the right thing. It is a very trying time for us all. You are going to have to take good care of her, for events are going to keep me very busy for the next few months. You need to—"

"The holiday will be canceled?" she asked, her accusing eyes impaling him.

Wolf nodded dejectedly. "Ja. I know she has planned the trip but—"

"Herr Direktor, she lives for this holiday. Lately she has spoken of nothing else. And today has so terribly shaken her . . ."

Wolf reached the top of the stairs and looked deeply into the woman's eyes. "I have responsibilities to the state that you and my frau cannot imagine. A storm cloud is brewing that could ruin all of our lives unless I do something about it. Dagmar, you, all of us, must be strong to face what lies ahead. Do you understand? I need support, not tears. I will make it up to her later. Now I must do what has to be done for our country." He took her hand and stroked it.

Renate was caught in his mesmerizing blue whirlpools. "I'm sorry," she whispered. "I was only thinking of Frau Wolf. I understand."

Satisfied, Wolf walked Renate down the hall to her room and opened the door. "Good night, Renate . . . remember, be strong, help my frau and me get through the storm . . . we need you." He patted her cheek tenderly and gave her a last lingering look before turning and walking down the darkened hall as if bearing a heavy weight on his shoulders.

Renate, feeling as if his hypnotic eyes were still upon her, watched him until he disappeared into the darkness.

CHAPTER 22

Friday, 1 September,
West Berlin

Jake Tallon rolled over and took two swipes at the buzzing clock radio before finally hitting the off button, which he wished was the kill button. He hated Friday mornings. It was chief of staff PT day. Crist called it "staff of freedom PT," but it wasn't. It was Crist showing how fit he was. Jake had learned how to avoid Crist at work. It was easy, as Crist didn't know what was going on and didn't seem to care. But PT was different. The chief of staff's Tuesday and Friday PT sessions were torture. Not because they were particularly demanding, but because of Crist's never-ending lectures on fitness and his stupid demonstrations of exercises that would make a contortionist cringe.

Jake dressed in his running gear, put on a heavy sweatshirt, set his shoulders, and headed for the apartment door. He couldn't help but smile with pride at how good his place looked. Kristina had put her touch everywhere.

It was a four-block run to the Cole pool. When he got there, the rest of the "staff of freedom" were already on the deck. They were biting their lips to keep from laughing as they watched the irate chief of staff pace in front of them. He stopped and yelled, *"Who would do this? Why? Why would anyone want to do this?"*

None of the staff moved a muscle. Fuming, Crist turned around to glare at the swimming pool's light blue water, on which were floating cow-patty chips. The culprit had a sense of humor, for every other bobbing cow patty had an ice cream stick and paper sail sticking up from it.

Crist spun around and gazed into each man's face, trying to find someone with guilty eyes. They all looked guilty. He put his hands on his hips.

"This . . . this is *sabotage*! Someone is trying to get out of PT and is making everybody else suffer! If I find that someone, I'll . . . I'll charge him with defacing government property!"

Crist pointed at the provost marshal. "Call your people and get them over here and check for evidence." He pointed at the G-2. "Hank, I want your people checking around the offices and keeping an ear to the ground." Crist faced the rest of the staff. "I'm going to find the pervert who ruined my PT session! Everybody get dressed for the run . . . we'll run five miles instead of three to make up for losing the swim!"

Ten minutes later Jake was jogging down Hüttenweg toward the turn off into the Grunewald. He heard heavy breathing and was about to look over his shoulder when Crist ran up alongside him. "Jake, I want . . . you to help . . . me find who . . . it was. . . . We can't let . . . this happen. . . . PT is important."

Jake nodded. "Yes, sir, I'll keep my eye out . . ." He wanted to finish with, "for someone carrying around bullshit."

The chief patted Jake's back. "I knew you . . . would understand." Crist fell back to a slower pace and let his temporary G-3 run ahead.

East Germany

Jorn pulled Der Panzer into the distribution warehouse loading area and was about to back up to the dock when he heard his name being called by the dock foreman. Jorn saw the approaching man and knew something was wrong by the look on his face.

The foreman stepped up on the running board, talking loudly, as if he wanted the entire warehouse to hear. "Hullo, Jorn. Sorry, but you'll need to pull your truck out. We're waiting for trucks to make pickups. Park your vehicle in the field and come and join me for a cup of coffee." The foreman then whispered, "Stasi is here."

When Jorn pushed the wheelchair up the ramp onto the loading dock and headed for the office, he spotted the two Stasi agents immediately in their identical blue windbreakers and western-style faded jeans.

The foreman closed the office door firmly behind him. "Jorn,

I'm sorry about the delay, but these local Stasi bastards are snooping around trying to scare my workers out of going to Hungary. If they were looking for black-market goods, I'd be in jail by now. Your load is sitting under the tarp there on the dock."

Jorn accepted a cup of coffee and set it on the desk. He picked up the sack from his lap and handed it to the foreman. "These are mushrooms I gathered in the forest yesterday. Have your wife slice them thin and cook them in butter."

"Thank you, Jorn. I love fresh mushrooms. I—"

One of the Stasi agents opened the office door and strode in. "We're finished here. I don't think you'll have any more problems with loss of workers. I explained to them the state is not issuing any more visas and within thirty days no one will be allowed to cross the Czech or Polish borders unless he's on offical business. Thank you for your cooperation."

As soon as the agent had gone, the foreman snickered. "The stupid bastard. Does he think the people will stand for being locked inside their own country?"

Jorn shrugged. "What can we do but complain?"

The foreman sat down with fire in his eyes. "Last week the Poles did more than complain! They voted the communist bastards out. Tadeusz Mazowiecki is the first democratically elected non-communist premier in the Russian-occupied countries. It's the beginning. I'm tired of having Russians on our soil. They destroy our fields with their exercises, and yet we have to trade them our best produce, and all we get in return is their soldiers and lousy shit products no one wants. Our government is corrupt as long as it makes deals with the Soviets. And the Stasi is the worst form of the government. They are worse than the old Gestapo."

Jorn couldn't help but smile at his friend's wrath. "What has caused all this rhetoric? I would think an outspoken foreman would be frowned upon."

The foreman opened the lower drawer to his desk and took out a West Berlin paper. He tossed it in front of Jorn. "We have never been allowed to read western papers or even have them in our possession. Now I know why. Take it, Jorn, read it. I get them twice a week from a friend who works with the railroad."

Jorn sighed and rolled his chair back. "I don't need to read what I already know. Besides, my friend, I am too busy working to read. I must bring the truck up and load the goods for my trip. I'm already behind schedule."

The foreman raised his hand. "Wait, Jorn. I have something for you in return for your gift of mushrooms." Again the foreman reached into his lower drawer. This time he took out a slender box and handed it to his friend. "I think you'll be able to use it more than I."

Jorn opened the lid and smiled. Inside was an eight-inch sheath knife with an antler handle. "It's beautiful. I can't accept such a gift."

The foreman pushed the box back toward Jorn. "Take it, I have a dozen more that were accidentally sent here in a shipment that should have gone to the Strausberg distribution warehouse for export. The system is so bad they will never know of the mistake. Take it. It's German-made by skilled craftsmen who get nothing for their work and can't even sell their products to their own people. It is a gift to remind you that perhaps you should read the papers."

U.S. Mission, West Berlin

Peggy Sue sipped her coffee and looked over the cup at Kristina. "Well? You've been alone with him two weekends in a row. Surely something has happened?"

Kristina rolled her eyes. "Peggy Sue, we have *not* been alone. His friends Sandy and Sissy Washington have been over, and we've been to dinner together."

"You know what I mean! Don't hold out on ol' Peggy Sue. I can tell something is happening. I see it in your face."

Kristina lowered her eyes. "Something is happening but I don't know what it is. He treats me more and more like a . . . friend. It's hard to explain."

Peggy Sue worriedly scooted closer to the table. "Watch that buddy-buddy stuff. Don't let him treat you like one of the boys. I went with a softball player like that. It was the worst experience of my life. After games he'd take me to the team bar, where he expected me to join him and the boys in drinking beer and singing rugby songs. You shoulda smelled them! God, it was horrible! All they wanted were groupies to stand around and tell them what great athletes they were. Never, and I mean never, let a man treat you like a buddy."

Kristina smiled. "I don't think the colonel plays softball, but thanks for the warning. I got the impression he's been trying to look out for me, like a big brother. He hasn't said or done anything that . . . well, you know."

Peggy Sue nodded. "Yeah, he hasn't come on to ya. Hmmmm . . . sounds like you're gonna have to make the first move. I went with a major like that, never would give the right signs, so I ended up taking the initiative."

Kristina waited for the rest of the story, but Peggy seemed to have finished. "Don't stop there, did it work?"

Peggy Sue winked. "Sure did, but things didn't work out 'cause he got orders for the States. He writes now and then, but I know if I'd had just another couple of months with him, I wouldn't be here sitting talking to you."

"I'm sorry it didn't work out, but I'm glad you're here. Oh, Peg, you used to work for the Air Force at Tempelhof, didn't you?"

"Yeah, met a few zoomies too. Why?"

Kristina dug in her purse and pulled out a note she'd made to herself. "I heard there was an historian over there who knows all about the Berlin airlift. Could you get some information for me? I wrote down what I need on this."

Peggy Sue glanced at the scribbled handwriting, then back to her friend. "His dad was named Jake too?"

"Yes. Will you do this for me?"

Peggy Sue got up. "Sure. God, I hate Fridays. It means a weekend, which means finding something to do for two days. You and Mr. Interesting going to play house again?"

Kristina shook her head. "Papa comes back today."

Maggie met Jake at the door as he strode into the office. She handed him a cup of coffee and followed him, reading from her steno pad, as he made his way to the desk.

"Boss, General Thomas wants to see you in ten minutes to discuss the upcoming field exercise. At ten you've got a meeting with Resource Management to discuss the budget, and at ten forty-five you've got a training meeting with the battalion representatives. The driver's testing office called and said you did better . . . you missed passing by only one point. I've got you rescheduled for this afternoon at two."

Jake slapped the desk. "I knew that question on the right-of-way got me! I know the damn test by heart. The answer has to be C instead of B."

"Boss, I'll go over the pamphlet with you before you—"

"Excuse me, are you Colonel Tallon?" said a young man who had just barged into the office like he owned the place.

Jake's eyes narrowed. He knew within two seconds that any man in an out-of-style polyester suit, white socks, and black low-quarter government-issued shoes had to be from the Army's Criminal Investigation Division.

Jake rolled his eyes. "Don't whip it out, I know who you are. Just see my deputy about whatever you came for. I'm busy."

"Colonel, it's procedure," the agent said as he whipped out his badge and identification. "Agent Rawlins of the two-eight-seven criminal investigation detachment here in Berlin. I've been instructed by the chief of staff to question all participants in the physical fitness session this morning who might have knowledge of the illegal contamination of the pool by use of—"

"*Out!*" Jake blurted, pointing at the door.

"Sir, I have been instructed by the chief of staff and—"

"*Out!*" This time Jake had come to his feet, burning holes through the shivering agent's forehead. Agent Rawlins backed up grudgingly.

Maggie giggled. "I heard about it. Everybody in the building knows."

Jake sat down and collected his calendar book. "Maggie, when you approach an intersection, you always yield to the car on the right. Right?"

"Yes, boss, unless you're on a primary road, and you can tell that by the little signs with the yellow diamonds."

Jake got up and walked toward the door to make his way to the general's office. "What about bikes? Do I have to yield for them too?"

Muggelsee, East Berlin

Wolf stepped into the foyer and looked into the worried eyes of Renate, who had been waiting anxiously for his arrival. She put her finger up to her lips, signaling for him to be quiet.

His eyes narrowed and he was about to speak when he heard strange laughter coming from the back portion of the house.

He motioned Renate closer and whispered, "I came as fast as I could after you called. What is wrong with her?"

The twenty-five-year-old agent motioned for him to follow. She led him into the library and stopped at the double doors leading into the sun room. She leaned close to him and spoke softly. "I'm very worried. Frau Wolf is playing a game of cards . . . with ghosts." She opened one of the doors for him to see.

Dagmar laughed as she poured herself another glass of wine and looked across the card table at Maria. "Your stories are always so funny. I was out just yesterday and—"

Wolf threw back the door and strode in. "What are you doing?"

Dagmar's glazed eyes lifted slowly to him. She smiled drunkenly as she motioned to the empty chairs. "I'm enjoying the company of my friends. Join us."

Wolf could see the bottle was almost empty. He set his shoulders. "Come, dear, you must be very tired. I'll help you upstairs and we'll—"

"No, join us. Sit down. I have slept half the day. I called Margot but she is busy at work . . . like you always are. I have no one else to talk to. My . . . my friends are *all* here." She waved at the empty chairs and lowered her head.

Wolf steeled himself, pulled back a chair and sat down. He leaned over and took his wife's hand, which was bloodless and cold. "Dagmar, we have both been through a lot this summer. We have lost our dearest friends and—"

"No. You have your precious work. What do I have, Horst?" Her eyes were locked on him, searching, pleading.

"We'll find new friends. We'll have a grand party and invite all of my department chiefs, deputies, and their wives so you'll be able to meet them."

Dagmar's eyes rolled back. "Ja, a party . . . like the old days . . . a large dinner party. I will use our best china, of course, and we'll bring in additional staff, and I'll supervise the . . ."

Wolf slowly got up as he listened to his wife rambling, and motioned Renate to help him. He took Dagmar's arm and gently lifted. Her head lolled to the side and she looked at him with a faded smile. "I'll have to have a new dress, and matching shoes. I will look my best for you and . . ."

He and the young woman walked Dagmar up the steps, down the hallway and into the bedroom. He motioned Renate out with his head and led his wife to the bed. She smiled coyly, slapping at his chest. "Horst, it's so early."

He lay her back on the pillows and began unbuttoning her silk blouse. "Close your eyes, my dear. Things will be much better in the morn—"

"Ja, I don't care if it is early . . . undress me and love me like you do, Horst. I need you inside me . . . love me hard, push into me deeper than ever before." She reached for his trousers and fumbled with his belt.

Wolf began to push her hands away, but saw the desperation in her eyes.

Still wearing his robe, Wolf stormed down the stairs and into the kitchen, where Renate sat at the small table. Startled, she snapped her head up from the book she was reading.

"How long as she been drinking like this?" he whispered harshly.

"The last two weeks, Herr Direktor. She has been very depressed. I thought she would get over it, but it seems to be getting worse."

"Why didn't you tell me?" he hissed.

The young woman looked at him accusingly. "I thought you knew, Herr Direktor. In any case, this afternoon was the first time she has drunk so much, and I called as soon as she began talking to herself. I dismissed the house staff so they wouldn't see her, and told the chief of security to keep his men downstairs."

Wolf shut his eyes. The young woman had done everything she could have. It wasn't her fault—it was his. He had hardly talked to Dagmar in days. He turned around and strode back into the hallway. He'd taken only four steps when he heard a whisper behind him. "Direktor, you must be very hungry, as you missed dinner. I have prepared a meal for you."

Wolf glanced over his shoulder. "Thank you. And thank you also for calling me so promptly. I'm going to check my frau, and then I'll be back. Get Carl up here from the security room. I want to speak to him."

He continued walking and quickly retraced his steps back to the bedroom. Dagmar was curled up like a little girl, asleep on the bed. He leaned against the doorframe, trying to erase the thoughts of their lovemaking. She had tried too hard to please him . . . it had been pathetic. He forced the thoughts out of his mind. He knew his Dagmar would be fine. She would be strong and get over her temporary depression . . . he would help her. He left her room, promising himself as he walked down the hall that he would make the time to take care of her. Nothing was more important. Everything else could wait . . . except the clean-up.

West Berlin

Jake pushed the button on the gate and shifted the sack of beer to his other hand. When the gate buzzed, he pushed it open and went to the front door. He was about to knock when Kristina threw the door open.

"Well, it's Colonel Tallon. Are you checking on me like my *father* asked?" she said angrily.

He began to reply, but she stepped menacingly closer and growled, "Jutta Kailer, Lars's wife, called me an hour ago and said my father would not be home till Monday. She said he was having a wonderful time and has decided to stay longer. Do you know why he decided to stay longer, Colonel Tallon? Because he knew his daughter was well taken care of. He said he had asked a friend to look out for her. I wonder who that could be?"

She looked like she was going to start swinging. Jake backed down one step. "It's not—"

"*My father had no right!* I'm not a little girl! I'm a grown woman! I don't need you or anybody else watching over me! I'm sorry, Colonel Tallon, you thought you had to be my babysitter!"

Jake saw her eyes tearing, and he did the only thing he could think of. He threw the sack of beer over his shoulder, pulled her to him and kissed her passionately. Still holding her arms, he looked into her eyes. "You're right, I was watching you . . . but not because Axel asked me to. I *wanted* to. I wanted to see you smile and talk and move. I like watching you. Hell, I *love* watching you. I'm sorry I kissed you. I shouldn't have done that." He released his grip, turned and walked down the steps.

Kristina stood trembling on the porch and called out to him, "Don't go, please."

Jake looked over his shoulder. "Go? I'm not goin' anywhere. I'm just gettin' my beer."

She shook her head and walked inside, leaving the door open.

Jake helped stack the dishes, then took Kristina by the hand into the cool night air toward the apple trees.

Kristina leaned into him and he put his arm around her. "What are you thinking about?"

"You."

"What are you thinking about me?"

Jake kept silent.

She looked up into his face. "What?"

Jake lowered his eyes to her. "I don't want to spoil our friendship by saying or doing something stupid. I like the way we are."

Kristina lowered her head. "I like being friends with you too . . . but what could you say or do that I might think is stupid?"

Jake kept silent for several moments, not wanting to tell her, and yet needing to. "I'd say things like I wanted to be around you more and wanted to . . . damn, Kristina, you know what I'd say."

She raised her head and they locked eyes. She leaned forward and pressed herself against him, feeling his warmth and strength. Jake softly, tentatively, kissed her lips. When she didn't resist, he grasped her tighter. At first he felt as if they were floating, but then, slowly, they began sinking together, into each other, lost in each other.

Jake awoke in Kristina's bed and felt her warm body against his. He kissed her bare shoulder and snuggled against her to make sure he wasn't dreaming. Kristina stirred and turned over, pressing herself to him. He kissed her cheek and wrapped his arm around her. He never wanted to let go of this wonderful feeling.

She felt his desire growing, then rolled on top of him and smiled. "I like this better than being just friends."

Jake leaned up and kissed her chin. "Me too."

CHAPTER 23

Friday, 29 September,
Grunewald Forest, West Berlin

Axel Mader climbed out of the camouflaged military vehicle and patted the hood. "What is this called again?

Jake spoke as he buckled his combat harness. "It's an HMMWV, a high-mobility multipurpose wheeled vehicle. We call it a 'Hummer.' "

Axel walked with Jake up a forested slope. "When you told me you wanted me to see 'your' Berlin, I had no idea what you were talking about."

Jake slowed his pace. "I thought after all the weekends that you showed me your city, the least I could do was show you the Berlin I know. We've been out in the Grunewald and in Doughboy City for two weeks, training as if we were at war. Doughboy City, our training area, is in Parks Range and is made up of about thirty buildings we had built to simulate an actual small town with streets, sewer systems, and buildings. We had two major battles there last week, and this week we're fighting out here in the Grunewald to practice conventional tactics. Tomorrow is the last day of the exercise; we're ending with a big attack tomorrow morning."

The two men topped the crest of the ridge and could see on the other side a platoon of soldiers digging foxholes and laying concertina wire. Jake motioned down the ridge, speaking softly so the soldiers wouldn't hear him. "We've ordered a company to defend this ridge. There's another platoon off to the left, and another one behind us in a reserve position. Tomorrow morning at 0700 an OP-

FOR—opposing force company—is going to attack them, but they don't know that. I'm here to evaluate the company and see if they defend properly. I know the main attack is going to hit this platoon, so I wanted to see how the young platoon leader has his defense laid out."

Minutes later the two men were walking along the line of freshly dug foxholes. Axel stopped behind the position where an M-60 machine gun was located. He squatted down to see the gunner's fields of fire and glanced up at Jake with a confused expression. "Why is the machine gun here and not on the flank?"

The young, nineteen-year-old gunner heard the question and pointed down the slope. " 'Cause if'n they gonna come, they gonna come right up that draw and try and sneak up on us. When they do, I got 'em."

The platoon's lieutenant, noticing the colonel and the stout, silver-haired man standing by the machine-gun position, walked over. He heard the last of his gunner's explanation.

"Sir," he said, "I'm prepared to brief you on how I've laid out the defense, if you're ready."

"Before you brief me, Lieutenant Beavers, I want to introduce you to Axel Mader, a former captain in the German paratroopers who fought on the western and eastern fronts. He's my guest and I'm showing him how we train. You might want to ask him a few questions. He's actually fought the Russians."

The lieutenant looked at Axel with awe. "Herr Mader, it's a pleasure to meet you. I've never met anyone who's fought Russians. Did you ever have to defend against them on a slope like this?"

Axel was almost speechless. He had had no idea Jake was going to introduce him as a former officer, and he was doubly shocked by the young officer's respect for his military experience.

"Yes, my young friend, many times," he ventured. "Once, I defended a ridge much like this one."

The lieutenant's eyes opened wider. "How did they attack, sir?"

Axel shifted his gaze down the slope and recalled a day forty-four years before as if it were only yesterday. "First they send their reconnaissance units to strip away your scouts and snipers and to find your main defenses. They then use their mortars and artillery to keep you burrowed in your holes while they form into battle formations and begin to advance en masse. They don't care about casualties, so they will only lift their artillery once their first ranks are hit by their own shell fragments. By then they are almost on top of you. That is when they yell like demons and try to overrun your positions."

"How . . . how did you stop them?" asked the spellbound officer.

Again Axel looked down the slope. "Our scouts and snipers would stay well-hidden and let their reconnaissance units pass. When they saw the main attack formations, they would immediately call in our artillery and begin the slaughter. My snipers would shoot the leaders, for their soldiers were all conscripts, and without leaders they became confused and scared. By the time their main attacking units hit my defense, the artillery had decimated their ranks and they were forced to strike piecemeal. Again my men were instructed to shoot the leaders first. My machine guns did not fire and give away their positions until the Russians were in the wire or mine fields directly to our front. Once the battle was over, we hastened to lay more mines and quickly passed out ammunition, for a second attack always followed the first. When the second attack came, their soldiers had to make their way over their own dead, which both slowed and scared them. Again we stripped away their ranks with artillery and shot their leaders as they approached. We held our ground with grenades, and our machine guns, positioned on the flanks, threw up a wall of steel across our front. Death was everywhere. Their screams were drowned out by our own, and like ghouls coming out of our holes, we rushed forward screaming like banshees. The Russians tried to run then, but no one in Hell escapes the devil."

Axel's distant eyes focused and he looked at the platoon leader with a penetrating stare. "*You* are the devil, and you must think like him. Your enemy must never be allowed to follow his plans, for without a plan they become cattle. Break up his formations with obstacles, make him go where you want him, and kill him . . . kill him . . . and keep killing him."

The young officer closed his open mouth and stood looking down the slope. Several moments passed before he turned and spoke quickly to the colonel. "Sir, I take back what I said about my defense being ready. I'll come and get you when I'm prepared to brief."

The officer turned to his men and barked, "Squad leaders, report to me! Platoon sergeant, get me the artillery forward observer and pick me out four riflemen as snipers!"

Jake stood and pulled Axel to his feet. "I would have liked the story better if I had had a beer."

Axel lowered his head, embarrassed. "I always get carried away. I never would have thought they would listen to an old man."

Jake smiled and put his hand on Axel's shoulder. "You're not just any old man—you're an Iron Man, and that makes you special."

Minutes later the two men were walking toward the Hummer.

Jake opened the door and took out a rucksack. "Axel, I'll have my driver take you back. I really appreciate you coming."

"You're staying the night?" Axel asked.

"Yeah, I've got to check the other platoons and walk the line tonight to make sure they're keeping their men awake. And the attack hits tomorrow morning."

"I want to stay with you."

Jake stepped back to the vehicle and spoke to the driver. "Go by the office and pick up my extra sleeping bag. Then tell Maggie to call the Mission protocol officer and tell her her father is going to freeze his ass off with the U.S. Army tonight."

East Berlin

Jorn knew something was wrong as soon as he saw the buyer approach. The man opened the cab door and helped him down. "Good to see you, old man. It's good to see a friendly face for a change. I've been questioned by the Stasi the past few days and was worried about you. They are cracking down everywhere."

Jorn propelled himself to the back of the truck and climbed the rope into the back. He pushed the first of ten boxes of meat toward the tailgate. "Something is wrong . . . what is it?"

The buyer took the box and set it down to the side. "I'm quitting, old man. It's over for me. The people I wanted to help can no longer buy because the prices have gone too high. It is a sign things are getting worse. I'm going to the West at the end of October. I have a visa for Hungary. I cannot stand to see my country collapse. I love it too much to watch it fall apart. The Russians will not help this government, the people are slowly realizing that. Perhaps another year, maybe two, it will end. I will come back and help rebuild when the time comes."

Jorn smiled as he pushed another box forward. "Why are you waiting? You sound like you're already there in your mind."

The buyer tossed his head toward the apartment. "My wife is about to have a baby—a son, I think, because he kicks so hard. My son and I will be back, old man. We will be back and you can come and work for us."

Jorn looked into the buyer's eyes. "No, my friend, you can come and work for me. This old man is going to stay and watch."

Normannenstrasse 22

The Shadow Committee stood as Hagan Wolf entered the already smoke-filled basement conference room. He motioned the four men to take their seats and turned to Ernst Mantel, who was nervously arranging a small stack of papers. Mantel had just arrived from Moscow. Wolf had ascertained from an abbreviated discussion with him over a nonsecure phone that an emergency had arisen and a special meeting was needed.

"I have been to visit my counterpart in the KGB Documents section," Mantel began. "It seems they are housecleaning, as we have been doing. All documentation linking the KGB to us has been destroyed or altered. But when I asked about the disposition of our personnel files, I could tell by Dmitri's expression that something was wrong. He was very apologetic, but it seems that files describing our prior service with the SD were taken by members from the General Secretary's office and have been turned over to the Nazi Era Historical Documentation Section of the Soviet Supreme Court."

Wolf felt an uneasy feeling building in his stomach as Mantel turned to another page of his notes.

"The Soviet Union is bowing to pressure from the West to open their captured SS files so that the West's 'Wanted Book' can be updated. As you know, the United States Army captured a majority of the SS records prior to the war's end in Bavaria and have stored them in Berlin. What the West does not know—yet—is that the Soviets captured photocopies of those files, but much more complete files, for they were updated until the very last days. The Soviets also have historical documentation of SS and SD operations written by an unnamed professor, and it is more accurate than anything the West has in its possession. *All* documentation will be available to the West on the first of December. Our personnel files will be included. The KGB, however, has removed all references to themselves, recruitment from Camp Viper, training and handling over the years. All of us in the Shadow Committee except Boris were listed as killed in the Russian prisoner-of-war camps, and given new identities by the KGB. The West will now read that a mistake was made and that we were released, not killed in 1947."

Wolf relaxed his tense body. "What is your concern? If our connection to the Soviets has been removed, then we have nothing to fear. Almost all the SS changed their names after the war. We are no different. We are not wanted by anyone."

Mantel looked into Wolf's eyes. "Herr Direktor, you will be listed in the Wanted Book, just as the rest of us will."

Rink spoke for all of them. "What is this 'book'?"

Mantel pulled out another piece of paper and glanced at it as he spoke. "In the Federal Republic, each of the sixteen provinces has an Attorney General's office, a department of which is called Crimes of Violence Committed During the Nazi Era. Each province has responsibility for a given area. A Wanted Book sits in every one of the Attorney Generals' offices. It is a book of those during the Nazi era who committed a crime, and it includes full names and dates of birth. We are all listed because SS and SD 'friends' who were captured by the West turned traitor and told of our activities to save themselves."

Mantel nervously shifted his eyes to Wolf. "For example, Herr Direktor, you were charged by four German prisoners of war, captured by the Allies, with the killing of their commanding officer and members of their battalion while you served as a collection company commander."

Wolf remained impassive.

"Only Herr Rink need not worry about the book," Mantel went on, "as he was only a Nazi youth leader at the war's end."

Wolf spoke calmly. "You say the documentation section will be opened in December. How much time do you anticipate we will have before we are placed on the active list?"

Mantel nodded, knowing the question would be asked, and looked again at his notes. "Herr Direktor, there is an organization in Ludwigsburg, West Germany, called the Central Federal Agency for the Elucidation of Crimes of Violence Committed During the Nazi Era. They call it the Zentrale Stella for short. They are professional Nazi hunters. Members of their staff have already made arrangements to be in Moscow on the first. They are bringing a twelve-man team who will concentrate on updating the Wanted Book. I believe that with so large a staff, they will read our files and place us on the active list within days."

Wolf swept his gaze to the others. "I think we owe our kamerad our thanks for bringing this matter to our attention. We have served with honor and will leave with honor. We will simply make the necessary arrangements prior to December first. I suggest we all plan to retire by November and take extended vacations out of the country." Wolf motioned toward the man seated by Rink. "Eric can provide passports and documentation for changing your identities. I need not remind you that you have more than adequate funds available to live very well wherever you desire. But remember, your wives *cannot be told* of this until you are out of the country." Wolf's expression changed. "While we are here, we can also thank

Boris for his handling of those we placed on our housecleaning list. Now, does anyone else have something for the committee to address?"

Grunewald Forest, West Berlin

Bone-tired and cold, Jake spread out his poncho and unfolded his sleeping bag. Axel unrolled his own bag and looked up at the stars. "It has been a long time, mein kamerad . . . a long time."

Shivering, Jake took off his boots and put them under the head of the bag to use as a pillow. "I've been doin' this off and on for twenty years, Axel. I don't think I'll miss it. The hardest thing is gettin' all nice and warm and then havin' to get up and piss. Nope, I don't think I'll miss that part one bit."

Axel looked around at the trees and darkness, absorbing the smells of the night. He sat down on his sleeping bag and looked up again at the stars. "Yes you will, Jake. You will miss the faces of these young men you teach."

Jake slid into his bag and lay back. "I miss Kristina, that's who I miss. I guess you know I think a lot of her, Axel."

Axel smiled in the darkness. "And I thought it was me you came to see every night. I'm disappointed in you, Jake. I thought you would have found a woman with some meat on her bones . . . but I'm also glad. Very glad." Axel sighed. "Speaking about my princess, I need some advice from you."

Jake rose up on an elbow, surprised at Axel's downcast tone. "Sure."

Axel sighed again before speaking. "While I was with Lars, fishing in the Baltic, he showed me a letter he had received from the wife of an Iron Man, Jorn Furman, who was our closest friend. We were all together in earlier campaigns and during those last days. He was captured by the Russians in Seelow and later died in the Russian camps. The woman's letter asked Lars if he would write and tell her about Jorn and those days we served together. She hadn't asked before because so many husbands didn't come home, and it had been a time of rebuilding lives, not remembering the tragedies of the past. She remarried, but her second husband has passed away now, and in her autumn years, she wants to know the answers to the questions that have always torn at her heart.

"That night, Lars and I wrote the woman a letter. When it was done and I read it, I knew that it was not written just to her, but to all the families of the Parachute Battalion 600. Lars agreed. On the eighth of October, one week before our reunion here in Berlin, the letter will be printed all across the Federal Republic and here in West Berlin. Lars has sent me a finished, typed copy. His editors added an explanation and history of the battalion, making it a rather large article. When I showed it to Kristina, she became angry and called us fools for opening old wounds. She wants me to tell Lars not to print it. Jake, I'm not sure what I should do."

"Do *you* want the story told, Axel?" Jake asked softly.

"I want Jorn's wife and all the others to know the truth. They . . . my kameraden would have wanted the truth known. They deserve at least that."

Jake lay back down and closed his eyes. "I think you and the other surviving Iron Men would want it that way too. Good night, Axel."

Axel reached out in darkness and patted Jake's shoulder. "Gute nacht, mein kamerad. Thank you."

Normannenstrasse, East Berlin

Wolf poured vodka into a glass for Rink and leaned back in his worn chair. "I am not worried by the information Mantel gave us this evening. My Russian mentor destroyed my personnel file years ago. I will remain dead." Wolf sighed and swirled the vodka in his glass. "It's sad the others did not have similar guardians to look out for their interest."

Rink understood and took a drink before asking the only thing he needed to know. "When?"

Wolf wrinkled his brow and thought aloud. "They are very worried, so they might try and leave the country before November. I think we should retire them immediately after Honecker resigns. A few days after at the most."

Rink took another drink. "What about the money in their accounts?"

Wolf shook his head. "It's too late to touch the money without raising suspicion. Besides, they are honorable soldiers. Their widows deserve to live comfortably."

Rink stood and put on his jacket. When he had gone, Wolf's smile began to dissolve. What Mantel had reported disturbed him. Four men had written charges against him for the incident on the Alte Oder River. The only survivors he knew of were the men who had faced him that day so many years ago. Old emotions he had not felt in years began creeping back and eating into his soul. The four who called themselves Iron Men knew he had broken his word of honor.

Wolf walked to the window and looked out at the dark horizon. He knew those memories would haunt him until he could be sure every witness against him was dead.

CHAPTER 24

Monday, 2 October,
Normannenstrasse 22

Max Rink studied nine locations indicated by red pins on the maps of West Germany and West Berlin he had pinned up weeks before. Feeling depressed, he turned around and strolled back to his desk. The Ministry of State Security had over 3,500 agents and informants working in Europe and other countries in the world, including the 1,900 he managed in the Federal Republic and West Berlin. They had infiltrated virtually every sector of society, especially the military and political institutions. Over the last ten years, the network had expanded into western European high-technology corporations. The huge network had taken him and his director years to put into place. Today's retirements would effectively wipe out a quarter of that work.

Rink sat down and, as he sipped a cup of coffee, thought about his twenty-eight den chiefs, each of whom had his own pack leaders responsible for a network of subagents. Of the twenty-eight, nine had the misfortune of being recruited years ago by himself or his director. Losing nine den chiefs meant he would lose their packs as well, for only the chiefs knew the identity of their pack leaders, and only the pack leaders, in turn, knew their networks of informants and collaborators. All these people would go underground after the purge and wait to be contacted. In this case, that would never happen. All these valuable assets would be lost.

Rink raised his thick wrist and looked at his gold Rolex. It was 0658 hours. In less than two minutes, the retirements would begin.

He opened his bottom drawer and took out a bottle of schnapps, then poured himself half a coffee cup full.

At 0700 he stood, raised his cup toward the maps and whispered, "To you, my foxes, who served with honor . . . I am proud of what you did for your country. *Auf Wiedersehen, meinen Kameraden.*"

Three hundred forty miles from Rink's office, the fifty-two-year-old assistant manager of Frankfurt International Airport pulled his new Mazda 626 into his assigned parking place fifty meters from the administration office entrance. He picked up his morning paper and sack lunch from the car seat and began to open the door when a man walked by. He waited till the dark-complexioned man passed before opening the door, and only saw the blur as the assassin spun around and fired a small pistol. The den chief responsible for twelve pack leaders fell back, grasping his neck where a bullet had lodged in his throat. Blood poured between his fingers as he fought for a breath, not seeing the gunman raise the pistol and fire again. The bullet passed through the chief's left eye, snapping his head back.

At the same time in Bonn, the deputy police chief for the city walked out the front door of his house and began the ten-minute walk to his office. His network was one of the oldest and most reliable, with agents placed in every defense ministry directorate. He was shot dead as soon as he stepped onto the sidewalk by two gunmen in a parked BMW.

Nine kilometers away, the Esso station manager unlocked the front door and nodded toward his night shift employee, who sat behind the counter. At night the door to the station and convenience store was locked, the transactions done through a small window just large enough to pass through a six-pack of beer and take money for gas.

The fifty-year-old den chief walked straight to his desk, interested in the list of cars that had already been dropped off for repair. He was expecting a special car that would be left for servicing. In the headliner of the black Volvo would be the plans to the new antitank rocket developed by the Swedes. One of his pack leaders assigned to NATO headquarters in Brussels had called the night before wanting a "tune-up," and said he would drop the car off that morning.

The night clerk yawned and began to stand up to let his boss sit down, when he noticed an approaching customer reaching into his coat jacket. The den chief heard his young clerk gasp, and began to turn his head when the first bullet from the gunman's pistol struck the Esso manager and former GDR citizen above the ear and blew out the other side of his head, splattering and shattering the plateglass window. The night clerk only had time to lift his hand to protect himself before a bullet passed through his palm into the bridge of his nose.

In Berlin, a professor of economics at the Free University, and chief for twelve pack leaders, was stabbed to death as he rode down in the elevator from his apartment. Three miles away, the police chief of the Berlin district of Steglitz opened the door after kissing his wife, and was startled to see two men standing on his front porch. He began to speak when he was shot at point-blank range. The chief's wife screamed for only a second before she too was struck in the face by bullets, crumpling on top of her husband and den chief, who had been responsible for subordinates that had infiltrated every major city government agency in West Berlin.

Seven kilometers away, the head Forstmeister for the Berliner Forest in the southern Grunewald stood on the banks of Havel Lake looking across the water toward East Germany. As den chief, he had five pack leaders who were responsible for the receiving and processing of infiltrated agents arriving by boat and barge from the East during the evenings. He turned, hearing men approach, and was shot three times in the back. He died before hitting the ground.

In downtown West Berlin, across the street from the Teltow Canal, the night manager walked out of the Esplade Hotel, where she had worked for twenty-one years. The fifty-three-year-old den chief was responsible for nine pack leaders who received and passed hard information from traveling agents that came in from the West. Reaching the Ku'damm U-Bahn station, she was about to grasp the handrail to go down the steps when she was bumped from behind and tumbled forward. She was able to keep her balance before falling, thanks to a neatly dressed man who appeared from behind her and grabbed one of her flailing arms. Another good Samaritan behind her also grabbed for her, but had a straight razor attached to his palm, which he swept across her throat. The woman was released as her blood spurted out in a gush with each beat of her racing heart. She gurgled instead of screaming as she toppled over and fell down the stairs, clutching her throat.

At 0740 the owner and manager of the second-largest nursery in West Berlin pulled her red Mercedes into the parking lot of her store on Clay Allee. The fifty-four-year-old manager and den chief of fourteen pack leaders took out her keys and unlocked the door. She was responsible for the direct-action agents that worked the Berlin city government officials. Their work was looking for opportunities for blackmail, using the fear of prosecution, disgrace, or divorce. Her pack leaders were all attractive women, except for four gay men. Presently all her pack leaders had lovers in very high positions.

Pushing the door open, she turned to relock it from the inside but saw a couple standing in front of her, holding pistols. The den chief only had time to close her eyes before she was blown back inside the building by the force of the first bullets striking her chest.

Twelve blocks from the flower shop, Jake Tallon felt a light kiss on his cheek, stirred and opened one eye.

Kristina backed away and tossed her purse to the floor. "I thought you Army men were light sleepers. I unlocked the door and walked right in here without so much as a peep from you."

Jake slowly closed the one eye.

"Come on, Jake, wake up. I haven't seen you in two weeks because of your stupid field exercise. I called your office this morning and they said you had the day off. I told my boss I had to check on a sick friend and hurried over to see you. Talk to me."

Jake coughed once then twice as he tiredly raised his head from the pillow. "I . . . I'm sick."

Kristina's expression changed to one of worry. "What's wrong?"

He dropped his head back to the pillow. "Heartsick, need tender loving care . . . baaaaad."

Her eyes narrowed. "You're faking."

Jake lifted one eyelid again. "You came to see a sick friend, so I'm sick. Come here and take care of me."

Kristina sighed and began taking off her clothes. "I think it's terrible that after two weeks you won't even talk to me first. You take Papa to the woods, but you wouldn't take me. That says it all, doesn't it? It's not fair . . . not fair at all."

As she spoke, Jake moved his hand, which was under the pillow and holding the nine-millimeter Beretta. He pushed it to the crack between the mattress and headboard and let it drop to the carpeted floor. He'd heard the front door opening and out of instinct had been cautious. Within seconds he'd known it was Kristina because of the sound of her walk. It was dumb, he told himself, but he couldn't get rid of years of training overnight.

She stepped out of her skirt and let it drop to the stack of clothes she had already taken off. Seconds later she stood nude before him. "Say something to me?"

Jake threw back the covers, revealing he was naked as well. "I missed you. Now come here."

She raised an eyebrow as she looked him over. "I can see you *did* miss me."

Jake sat up, grabbed her hips and pulled her to him. Kissing her flat stomach, he began working his way up to her firm, erect breasts, but she started laughing and pushed him away. He sat back, his shoulders sagging dejectedly.

"Great, I lose my touch in two damn weeks."

She smiled as she pushed him back on the bed and lay on top of him. "Sorry, Colonel, but it's hard to take you seriously when you have green grease paint on the back of your ears."

Jake rolled her over on her back. "Sorry, I guess I didn't get it all off. Want me to take another shower?"

She smiled as she stroked his face. "No. I've missed you too."

Jake moved down to her stomach. "Now, where was I?"

An hour later Jake and Kristina were seated at the kitchen table drinking coffee. Kristina glanced at her purse. "Oh, I almost forgot the other reason I came over." She pulled a folder from the side pocket of her purse and handed it to him. "That's a copy of an article my father and Lars wrote. Read it, then please talk some sense into him. He listens to you."

Jake began reading. Minutes later he lowered the last page and looked up. "It's a very touching and sad story. Why do you think your dad is foolish in wanting it printed? It talks about love and comradeship, and it tells me your dad and Lars miss their friends very much."

Kristina's face reddened. "I should have known. You Americans don't understand what the war did to us. I was not even born then, and yet I carry guilt, as does every German. Papa and Lars should let the past stay buried. It serves no purpose to relive those terrible years that every German abhors. It would not be printed if Lars weren't so influential. Lars is a fool, and Papa is a bigger fool if he thinks it will make any difference. I feel sorry for Papa, because despite what he thinks, it will only serve to make the guilt worse for all of us."

Jake put his hand on Kristina's and looked into her fiery eyes. "Don't feel guilty. Be happy for your dad. This is his catharsis, his chance to tell the world that a madman killed his men, his friends. All those years of not telling—can you imagine his frustration?"

"And what about the rest of us?" Kristina asked. "Do we have to be reminded again and again about our past? I had nothing to do with it, Jake. What about me?"

Jake spoke softly. "It's the families of the battalion that he is speaking to, not you."

Clay Compound, Building 8, 10:35 A.M.

CIA station chief Burton Dawson held the secure phone to his ear and waited until his superior in Bonn finished speaking before responding. "You only had four in Bonn. Shit, I've got seven stiff Herms littering the neighborhoods here in the city! Mine were all hits, clear and simple. We're supporting the locals and the Herm Feds. They've got all the scenes locked down tight, and they've brought in all the high-tech shit. None of the hits here were clean. They were noisy and messy, definitely not pros, most likely hired-out cheap labor, so that means whoever ordered them was desperate for quick action. One of our stiffs was a suspected Stasi mole, and on another one they found some coded notes, so we're assuming the rest were all moles too. But I gotta tell ya, that's not good news. If they were Stasi, the Herms have got themselves some big-time problems. The victims had been in business for a long, long time. The locals will have to assume lots of damage has been done. We knew there were plenty of Stasi moles, but we sure as hell didn't know they were so respectable. We've got our eyes on two other suspects, but they're both strictly business as usual. It stinks of a purge. All the stiffs are over forty-five on my end, what about yours?" Dawson listened, nodded. "Okay, then let's assume they were knocking off the old-timers. Why? Why the older ones and why now?"

He listened for several seconds and sighed. "I know you don't have the answers. Shit, neither do I, but if it was Stasi knocking off their own people, there has got to be a reason. Something has spooked them into heavy action, which means something big is going on. Better send me up some help. Once you cable this info to Langley, all hell is gonna break loose. The Herms have already begun to panic. They're using everything they've got in the field to tear this town apart looking for the hit teams and leads. The Brit MI-6 and French SDECE boys in town have already asked for a meet to talk the situation over. Everybody is asking the same question—why?"

General Thomas looked up from the report he was reading and took off his glasses. "Sit down, Jake."

Jake knew by the sound of his superior's voice that the general didn't like what he was about to do. Jake sat down and looked into the senior officer's eyes.

Thomas sighed. "I'm sorry, Jake. I tried my damnedest, but Trout won't budge. The colonel who's taking your place got in three days ago while we were in the field. Trout told him to start as G-3 . . . tomorrow."

Jake nodded in silence. He had already heard a rumor, and figured that's what Thomas wanted to talk about.

Thomas slapped the desk. "*Goddamnit! It sucks!* You just don't treat people like that! You've done a hell of a job, and all you get outta him is twelve hours' notice and a kick in the ass. It's typical, Jake. Trout is a pompous ass who doesn't give a shit about anybody."

Jake remained stoic.

Thomas stood, moved around his desk and glared out the window. "I'm sorry, Jake, real sorry." He turned and softened his expression. "At least I have a little good news. I have a job for you that gets you away from Trout, the chief, and this headquarters. Burt Dawson from the CIA needs some help. He called me an hour ago. He couldn't say much on the telephone, but he asked for you by name, if it's any consolation. At least he and I know you're a damn good man."

Jake stood. "When does he want me to report, sir?"

Thomas knitted his brow. "Ten minutes ago. I'm sorry, but he needs you right now. My driver is standing by to take you to him."

Jake came to attention and saluted. "Very well, sir."

He was about to execute an about-face without waiting for the general to return his salute, when Thomas barked, "Hold it! I know I just kicked you in the nuts by telling you you were canned, so get mad and scream. I wouldn't blame you if you did. We can go drink a beer if you want and talk it out."

Jake put on a false small smile to make his friend feel better. "You know I did a good job. That's enough. I'd better get going."

The general lowered his head and went dejectedly back to his chair. He heard his door shut and kicked his trash can across the room before sitting down.

Jake sat in the back of a big Mercedes, staring out of the tinted window. He knew in his heart that he wasn't the second-rater that some people thought he was, but Trout hadn't even given him time to say good-bye and pack the few things he had in the office. Maggie at least deserved a hug.

"Sir . . . *sir*, we're here."

Jake broke from his reverie. The driver, a young sergeant, was staring at him as if he were deaf. The car had stopped in front of an old, three-story, brick barracks. Jake got out and turned to ask the driver if he was sure this was the right place, but the car was already in motion. Jake looked around. He was in the small kaserne known as Roosevelt Barracks. It was only six blocks from Clay Compound and served as barracks and headquarters for signal units, or so he had thought.

As Jake stood there, the door of the barracks burst open and Master Sergeant Sandy Washington stepped out, scowling. "God-damn it, Snake! Get your ass in here! I've been waitin' like a ugly girl on prom night!"

To Jake, seeing his old friend, hearing his bitching, was like a shot of hope in his veins. He faked anger by threateningly pointing his finger at the approaching bear of a man. "Hey, I got news, Sand-man! I ain't late. You're early!"

Master Sergeant Washington broke into a grin and grabbed Jake's hand, pumping it as he pulled him into the building. " 'Bout damn time you made it. I was gettin' worried that I was gonna be the only grunt." He lowered his voice and spoke out of the side of his mouth. "We need ya, Snake, the spooks have fucked up things enough."

Before Jake could ask his friend what the hell he was talking about, Burt Dawson stepped out of an office into the hallway and took a pipe from his mouth. "Hi, Colonel, glad you could join us. Please follow me to the briefing room, and I'll explain why you're here."

Minutes later Jake was seated behind a table in a "clean" room, meaning there were no windows and the walls were covered in sound-absorbing material to thwart electronic eavesdropping de-vices. Dawson sat down across from Jake and drew back an eye-brow. "I heard what Trout did to you, but if it's any consolation, you wouldn't have been in the job another day anyway." He lifted a paper from the desk and held it up. "You and twelve other men I requested from the military and other organizations have been or-dered to work for me temporarily on a special project. This request was signed by the U.S. ambassador to Germany, Laverne Walters, an hour ago. This is a faxed copy. I would have given it to Trout if he had balked."

Jake didn't like being temporary help again, but he had to admire Dawson. Mentioning the ambassador certainly got his attention. Walters was the U.S. government's top representative, and ruled supreme in all matters with respect to Germany. Although hardly used, his powers included supremacy over the U.S. military, short of war.

Dawson handed another piece of paper across the table. "I know you've seen these disclaimers before. You'll have to sign it."

Jake signed it. It was a standard government form that stated he could not divulge his association with, activities for, or intelligence information received from the Central Intelligence Agency without their written approval. He pushed the signed contract over to Dawson and leaned back, knowing what would come next.

The station chief slid the document into a folder and began the standard briefing that was to the Company what Miranda rights were to cops. "Do you understand that your employment with us is in the national interest of the United States of America and that you cannot communicate the matters, material or anything else related with your work other than to those designated as cleared and essential to this project on a need-to-know basis only? Do you understand that if questioned about your work or activities, you will use the cover story that will be provided? That if questioned by superiors, you will use the cover story provided? That you will not now or ever communicate your association or specifically use the name or nickname, or refer to the organization by which you are employed, to anyone without the express written approval of the employer, and should you violate the contract, you could be prosecuted to the maximum extent possible?"

Jake nodded. "I understand."

Dawson patted the folder. "That makes it official, then." He stood and walked to the end of the long table, where an overhead view graph and slide projector were sitting side by side. A screen hung on the wall. Dawson turned to Jake. "Colonel, up front, so as not to raise any expectations, I want to make clear that your involvement with us will be ninety percent overt. The other ten percent may entail some very low-key surveillance work. The job will not be sexy, high-speed, or remotely dangerous. I'm telling you this now to put your mind at ease. I'm gonna give you a rundown on our current situation, then tell you what you're going to be doing and who is going to be working with you. Once I'm finished, I'll take you upstairs to your work area, where you can get filled in on more details from Sergeant Washington."

Dawson put a view graph on the overhead and motioned to the color map of East Germany displayed behind him. "Colonel, unlike Russia, East Germany is not perceived as a threat by most Americans or even by the average West German. That perception is a mistake. It is a threat because of the Stasi. Since our last discussion about Stasi, some things have changed and heated up the waters."

Dawson put on another view graph. "In the last fifty-six days there has been an inordinately high number of deaths within the

Ministry of State Security. As you see on the slide, they began on four August with the death of their director of finance, followed a week later by the death of their director of communications. On nineteen August the Stasi VIP aircraft, an An-26 with thirty-six passengers, crashed seven miles north of the Schönefeld Airport. The GDR press said it was an accident. Our experts who reviewed the GDR television film coverage as well as satellite photos of the crash site, say that due to the scattering of wreckage, it is clear the aircraft sustained major damage prior to crashing. In other words, it was bombed. As far as we can determine by reading the obituaries, Stasi lost twenty-two people, sixteen of whom were heavy hitters, including their director and deputy director for reconnaissance and security, and their deputy director for administration. The others were mostly experts in surveillance, surveillance equipment, and intelligence analysis. The crash also claimed the deputy of the Ministry of Defense and a high-ranking general in the Border Guard Command. The same day the plane crashed, the defense ministry's chief of intelligence and internal security committed suicide along with his wife."

Dawson motioned to the screen. "You can read the rest if you want, but the bottom line is that the Stasi has either had a helluva lot of bad luck recently or something is happening to cause all this turnover. You might ask yourself why it should concern us that the opposition might be whacking each other. Today, between 0700 and 0800 hours, four civilians in the Federal Republic and seven West Berlin citizens were shot down or had their throats slashed for no apparent reason. At least that's what the press has been told. The fact is, three were innocent bystanders, and the other nine were leading citizens, all over forty-five, established in West Berlin for over twenty-five years, and Stasi moles . . . with God knows how many more agents working for them. Of the nine agents hit, our organization and the West German intel community had only suspected one. It suffices to say that we have a problem. As you can imagine, I'm being asked lots of embarrassing questions, and my crew is jumping through their asses trying to find answers. The West German Feds are panicking, the Brit and French intel community is panicking, Langley is panicking. Soon the Senate intelligence committee will be panicking. In my business, like yours, there is a saying that goes, 'Shit rolls downhill.' Well, it's rolling, and I'm up to my ass in it."

Dawson picked up the slide projector's control. "That pretty well sums up the situation and my problem at present. Langley is sending support, but it's not going to help in the current investigations.

That brings us to you. I asked my chief for some specially trained help that can take up the slack until this fiasco has cooled down. He got the ambassador's okay and cleared it with the military and the Defense Intelligence Agency to use military experts. Colonel Tallon, you will head up a task force comprising two handpicked, experienced, Special Forces personnel from the Berlin detachment. As you probably know, they have been conducting covert training operations in East Berlin for years and know the city like the back of their hands. They have also had a lot of practice in low-level photo surveillance. Late this evening you will also be receiving two men from the National Reconnaissance Office in the States. They'll have the latest reconnaissance satellite photos, and they're both imagery and interpretation experts. You'll also receive two eastern Europe intelligence analysts and two experts on East Germany from U.S. Army European Command in Heidelberg. You will also be getting one behavioral scientist and one management consultant from Washington, D.C. They are both contracted. Master Sergeant Washington, whom you already know, will serve as your ops NCO and take care of administration requirements. One of my men will be with your unit for a few days to brief you and your people on what we need and how we got the information in the past. That brings me to the mission of your task force."

Dawson pushed the control button and the first picture flashed up on the screen of an organization chart. "This is how we think the Ministry of State Security is organized. I said 'think,' because we can't be certain. Stasi has never been penetrated by us or anyone else. They are good. They have had no defectors, except for low-level types. The few mid-level defectors that tried to make it to the West were terminated or kidnapped before we could get to them. We have no hard information on their organization except what we can get by research, photos, monitoring phones, electronic eavesdropping, etcetera, etcetera. We've been able to piece together most of it, and we used to know who the key players were and where they worked, but with all the recent changes we haven't been able to keep up. Here's where your task force comes in."

Dawson pressed the projector control button, and a color slide of a typical government building flashed on the screen. In quick succession Dawson showed six more slides of different buildings. "What you are seeing is where Stasi works." He pressed the button again and the screen displayed an aerial satellite photo of a six-block section of East Berlin. Stepping toward the screen, Dawson took out a collapsible pointer from his shirt pocket and pointed to the center of the picture. "This, Colonel, is Stasi headquarters in downtown East Berlin. It is surrounded by a ten-foot wall. Actually, it's two compounds connected by a soccer stadium. Between the two compounds the Stasi organization covers two and a half square city blocks, comprising more than forty-three buildings, including these four high rises, a hospital, administration buildings, schools and classroom buildings, cafeterias, gift shops, an athletic field, a park, four motor pools, underground parking facilities, more offices, and here, the real headquarters, Haus One, the heart and brains of the ministry . . . we think. On top of this building and these other two, you see state-of-the-art radio communication equipment, including sophisticated satellite communications disks and radio antennas. Over eighty thousand people work in these compounds, and at any given time their schools house three to four hundred students, who learn everything from making simple bombs out of fertilizer to organizing state security organizations of their very own. They come from Iraq, Libya, South Yemen, Ethiopia, Angola, North Vietnam, the Palestine Liberation Front, the Red Faction, Hezbollah, SWAPO, and the ANC just to name a few. Outside the compounds are the Stasi district and local offices. Outside the borders of East Germany there are a couple thousand agents . . . our best guess. There are also thousands more on the Stasi payrolls as informers and part-time help. Stasi is in every East German embassy and every trade delegation. There are Stasi advisors in all the countries I previously mentioned, plus Algeria, Cape Verde, Guinea, Zambia, and many other interesting places. Bottom line, there are lots of the fuckers, and they are up to no good."

Dawson pressed the button and another aerial photo appeared, this time a close-up. "This compound and the other one are very closely guarded by posted and roving guards, and TV security cameras. If you were to drive within a three-block radius of these compounds in a foreign-plated car, you would be spotted by posted guards who would radio the information to other guards positioned within a block of the compounds. If you were to keep driving, you would be stopped before making it to within a hundred meters of the compound wall. You would then be searched, and if they found cameras or surveillance equipment, you'd be questioned, detained for hours, and then thrown out of the country with a stamp in your passport that would prohibit your entry into East Germany again."

Dawson flashed up on the screen a picture of a large group of people gathered around a flowered grave. "This picture was taken at the latest funeral of a Stasi high roller who died 'accidentally' during routine surgery last week. The people you see, primarily the men, are key players, bigshots in Stasi. A lot of them are new faces.

Your mission is to find out which ones have taken the place of those who died. It's not an easy task, but do-able. I will be very happy and consider your mission a success if you can identify a third of the people and tell us where they live, what time they leave for work, what kind of car they own, their license numbers, what time they get home, if they are married, have kids, etcetera."

Dawson looked at his watch with a grimace. "I'm expecting a call from Washington in five minutes. More shit rolling downhill. Do you have any questions before I take you upstairs?"

Jake stood. "Yes, just one. Why did you pick me? There are a hell of a lot of people around more qualified than I am."

Dawson smiled for the first time. "In 1971, I was a helo pilot in 'Nam with the Company's special ops blackbird unit. I know you don't remember me, but I remember the Snake. I picked you and your team up twice from up North, and each time, you brought everybody in your team back alive. I remembered you because you always got on last, after your team members were safely on board. It might not sound like a good enough reason to some . . . but it is to me. You really gave a shit about your people."

Dawson winked and strode for the door. "Come on, I'll hand you off to Master Sergeant Washington and you can get started."

A minute later Jake was on the third floor in a large open bay down the center of which twelve empty desks were spaced five feet apart in a rigid line. Dawson waved to Washington, who was posting a map. "Sergeant, will you show the colonel around and fill him in on the task-force members?" Without waiting for a reply, Dawson turned to Jake. "Colonel, I have to go. I'll talk to you again once you get your people on board. You can brief me then on how you plan to accomplish the mission in three days. Needless to say, I wish you the best of luck."

Jake waited until Dawson had walked down the stairs before he looked at Washington. "What da fuck is really going on?" he snarled.

Washington motioned for Jake to follow him into a small office at the end of the bay. There, the big sergeant flopped down into a chair and gave his old friend a faint smile. "What makes you think Dawson didn't give you the whole story?"

Jake sat down and raised an eyebrow. "We worked with the Company in Grenada, remember? They never tell you everything."

Washington grinned. "The Snake still got his sixth sense, huh?" The grin dissolved. "Did Dawson happen to mention the Stasi has big-time connections with the KGB?"

Jake sighed. "I figured, but he didn't mention it."

"Did he happen to mention we aren't allowed to do anything without his approval?"

Jake's face tightened. "No."

Washington nodded. "He will, once you brief him. I've already been through the files and photos they gave us. It's the typical Company shit that ya gotta be a rocket scientist to read and understand. They have some good stuff, but nothing high-speed. I figure there's a lot more that we're not cleared for. I've been talking to Jim, the Company dude that's supposed to get us info and brief us on techniques, equipment for surveillance, and all that. He's friendly enough, but strictly a low-level operator. It's obvious we're just cheap hire-ons that can do some menial labor to get them caught up while their big boys are busy. They don't want us to ask a lot of questions—just do what we're told and keep out of the way. I tried getting some ELINT info from them, but they went into their 'You don't need to know that' routine."

Jake shrugged. "It's all right by me. The mission sounds easy enough. You got a rundown on the people coming to us?"

Washington motioned to a stack of files on the corner of the desk. "Their records say they're all qualified. I'm not sure why we need a behavioral scientist, but all in all, we've got a good team once you get them organized. I figure we can knock this assignment out in three to four weeks, but in case ya didn't know, we can't cross the border till after the eighth cause of the East's fortieth anniversary parade. The streets are gonna be all blocked off for rehearsals until the activities on the sixth and seventh. Till then we can get organized and plan our attack."

Jake stood, took in a deep breath, exhaled slowly, and faced his friend. "I'm ready. Show me what they have and let's get started."

CHAPTER 25

Tuesday, 3 October,
Roosevelt Barracks, West Berlin

After the twelfth member had introduced himself, Jake pushed himself from the wall he'd been leaning against and faced his task force. "Okay, now you know who everybody is." He motioned to the wall behind the seated men. "That is our mission."

He walked around their chairs to a row of six white butcher-paper sheets, which he and Washington had taped to the wall the night before. Each paper was labeled at the top in Magic Marker with the name of a Stasi directorate. Below the titles they had drawn in a blocked organizational chart. Inside some blocks were color photos of known leaders. Inside others were large question marks.

"Phase one is to fill in the blanks. You will notice that some pictures are marked with a red X. It means that leader is dead and has been replaced, so we'll have to find out who the replacement is." Jake motioned to an enlarged aerial photo taped to the wall beside the butcher charts. "That photo shows the two Stasi compounds. We put numbers by each building in the compound. Below the photo is a listing that tells you where the Company thinks the directorates are located. Once we know who the leaders are and where they work, we begin phase two of the operation. We will find out where the leader lives, if he's married, has kids, his schedule, the usual background stuff."

Jake smiled as he looked into the faces of his men. "I know from personal experience how you guys feel having just flown in from the States. The jet lag monster is kicking your ass. Don't worry.

This morning is only an overview to get your minds tuned in to the project. In a couple of hours you can go back to Harnack House and rest. I have handed out a folder to each of you. Inside you'll see which directorate you've been assigned. You'll also see that I've assigned you a buddy. The two of you will work as a team. Also in your folder is all the information our employer has on your assigned directorate. Now I'm going to have Dr. Higgins, our behavioral scientist, stand up and give you the little briefing that he gave me on the way back from the airport this morning. After Dr. Higgins speaks, I'm going to have Bob Johnston, our management consultant, stand up and give you some organizational facts that also might help."

Jake nodded toward a balding middle-aged man dressed in a hopelessly wrinkled suit that was twenty years out of style. "Doctor."

Higgins took off a thick pair of glasses and stood up. "Gentlemen, I have been studying Warsaw Pact organizations for some time, and I have learned that their governments are not much different from ours in one aspect: their reward system. This is particularly true of Germany, which as a whole is a product of its militaristic past. The typical German, East or West, has been brought up with great respect for authority. Keeping that in mind, I offer three criteria for identifying those in leadership positions within Stasi. One, a true sign of status is being chauffeured. The type of car that is driven will determine the leader's status in the hierarchy of leadership. The bigger the car, the higher position the person will have. Based on our employer's files, all directors and deputy directors are chauffeured. That fact alone should narrow your field considerably. Two, location of homes. Homes in East Germany are state owned. Homes provided to high-ranking Stasi leaders will usually be larger and farther away from the compounds than those of lower- or mid-level employees. Three. Location of parked cars in relation to their office building. The closest parking places are status symbols. Those on your organizational chart who do not rate chauffeured cars *do* rate parking within the compound. Thus, the chairman of a specific organization subordinate to a director can be easily identified by ascertaining how close to his office he parks his vehicle."

The doctor paused in thought, then shifted his eyes toward Jake. "Colonel, the criteria could be expanded to include the entire Stasi organization. Logic tells me that if one were to apply the criteria to the ministry as a whole, one could categorize the directorates by order of importance. I should think by studying the location of motor pools, types of official vehicles, and the condition of various office buildings, it would be very easy to determine which director-ates are considered more important than others."

Jake knew that was not part of his mission, but he instinctively liked the idea. He nodded. "I think you're on to something, Doc. How about tomorrow, after reading through your file, you come and talk to me."

Jake turned toward the management consultant, who was thirty pounds overweight but had a perpetual, cheery smile and was im-peccably dressed. "Bob, what have you got that might help us?"

The consultant shrugged and stood up. "Dr. Higgins pretty much stole my thunder, but there are a few minor details that might help. If these Stasi guys are like typical senior ranking leaders in corpo-rations, there are some perks that typically go with the job. Lunch breaks for example. CEOs, if they bother with lunch, usually sched-ule longer breaks than their subordinates do. Another thing I'd look at is their clothing. I'd say it would be safe to assume that the better dressed they are, the higher position they hold." Johnston was about to sit down but popped back up again. "Shoes. I almost forgot. Shoes are important. People who have money or status often buy expen-sive shoes. It's an ego thing."

Jake stood. "Thanks, Bob. Okay, you've heard some criteria that might narrow the field. I want everyone to link up with their as-signed partners as soon as I'm finished. Get acquainted, then read over your folders and go through the photos. I want everyone to sleep on it tonight. Tomorrow come in and talk over the possibili-ties with your partner. Narrow the field as best you can. We'll have a group discussion at ten in the morning, and you can explain your rationale for elimination or selection to the rest of us. I want a free exchange of ideas and thoughts. Doc Higgins and Bob gave us all something to think about, but I realize you won't be able to get inside the compound to find out where people park. Does anybody ha   "

"Excuse me, sir, but yes we can."

Jake recognized the redheaded, pimple-faced kid who had inter-rupted him; he was one of two imagery experts from the National Reconnaissance Office. They had arrived from the States only thirty minutes before the meeting had started. Jake didn't like being in-terrupted. He furrowed his brow and spoke in a restrained snarl. "Did you wanna say something?"

He had tried to make it a warning to the punk to shut up and wait his turn, but the kid came to his feet and faced the shocked task force members, who knew their commander's authority had been trounced.

"Colonel, what ya said about not being able to get in the compound isn't true. Me and Ski"—he motioned to another kid in the front row, who was chewing a wad of gum—"we studied a four-day run from our bird, just before we got word and hatted up to fly here. There were a few cumulus clouds, but you can tell by the bird's flicks where the cars are parked. Shiiit, we can even show you what cars, their color and make, drove into and out of the Stasi compounds if ya want. We can even tell ya what building the dude goes into."

Stunned, Jake took a step back to regroup. He didn't know whether to hit the redhead or kiss him. "What the fuck are you talking about? Talk English, for Christ's sake!"

The young man seemed genuinely shocked at the outburst and looked at his friend, Ski, for support, but good ol' Ski had figured out his new red-faced task-force commander was pissed. Ski lowered his head, leaving his buddy stranded. The redhead rolled his eyes up and raised his hands to the group. "Sorry, dudes. I forgot this is contract work." He looked at the colonel and put on an apologetic look. "Colonel, I apologize. Let me start over. The 'bird' is our European stationary reconnaissance satellite. She'd been shooting flicks for the Company for four days prior to our getting notified we were tagged to come over and help out. She was put in orbit by the shuttle two months back. She doesn't take stills. She's a CBD—Cecil B. DeMille. That means she takes frames every two seconds and transmits them to our base computer for storing. We brought our computers and disks, and we can pull up a run of anything from ten seconds to all four days if you want. It'd be like watching a jerky movie, but you sure as hell could track a man getting out of a car and follow him. We can even enlarge the frames and zoom in to get detail—right down to the color of his shoes and which side he parts his hair on. The bird is hot shit."

One of the men spoke up. "How wide is the angle? Can you track the leader's car to his home if it's within the city?"

The pimple-faced redhead bobbed his head. "Sure. On the run we brought with us, the radius from the focal point is thirty kilometers. We get distortion after that, but you can still identify objects as big as cars at fifty klicks."

All the task-force members seemed to speak at once, wanting to ask the same question. Jake raised his hand to quiet the excited group and asked it for them. "Where was the satellite's center aiming point?"

The redhead seemed surprised. "Shiiit, I thought you all knew—it's where the Company requested we put it, the Palace of the Republic . . . five kilometers from the Stasi compounds. With the run we brought, we can track a single car for the entire four days any-where in East Berlin."

Jake exchanged glances with Sandy Washington, who was grin-ning ear to ear. The kid was telling them he had almost all the answers they needed. Jake couldn't help but smile. This was going to be a high-tech cakewalk.

Jake walked the seven blocks from the brick barracks to Har-nack House to unwind after the day's events. Despite his telling his men to take off, most had stayed and reviewed the satellite's pictures on the computer, until he had been forced to order them out so he could leave and lock up. He looked at his watch. It was past nine P.M. He knew he ought to call Kristina and tell her he was no longer the G-3, and he even picked up his pace, but slowed again after only a few steps. He needed a few beers first.

With a quick glance, Chong saw the customer walk in, but swung her eyes back to "Night Court."

Jake climbed onto his stool and waited patiently. Seven minutes passed before the show was interrupted by an Armed Forces Net-work commercial.

Chong reached into the icebox and took out a Lite. She sat the beer on the bar and lowered her eyes. "I hear you no longer G-3. Sorry, Jake."

Jake inwardly shriveled. If Chong knew he'd been canned, the word was already out in Clay headquarters. He covered his pain with a shrug and forced a give-a-shit smile. "No big deal. How you been doin'?"

"I not sell much Lite beer since you move away from Harnack House. How come you don't come and see me? Is it 'cause of Mis-sion lady?"

Jake took a drink of the beer and put back on his plastic grin. "Yeah. I found something better than Lite beer."

Chong gave her customer a faint nod. "I glad to see you happy. Mission lady drink Lite beer yet?"

Jake lost his fake happy-go-lucky expression. "Not yet."

Chong sighed and adjusted her bow tie before slowly moving her eyes to him. "I very sorry about your job. I think general make big mistake."

Jake looked at his beer can reflectively and shrugged. "Naw, he did the right thing." He took another drink and scooted off the bar stool. "I think I'd better get some sleep. Been a hell of a day."

Chong watched her customer until he disappeared, then turned back to the television hoping the show would make her laugh. Somehow she knew it wouldn't.

Ten minutes later Jake walked into his apartment and began unbuttoning his shirt. He glanced at the telephone. He should make the call to Kristina, but he didn't know what he would say. He needed more time to digest the situation and somehow find a way to make it more palatable. Walking back into the bedroom, he noticed his fatigues lying on the floor. The sight of camouflaged material hit him like a ball bat in the forehead; it reminded him he was no longer a real soldier. He had worn a field uniform for over twenty years . . . but now those days were over. The thought was so depressing, he flopped down on the bed, staring up blankly at the ceiling. His eyes began to water, and he rolled over and buried his head in the pillow.

Axel glanced up from the book he was reading and saw his daughter staring at the phone. He shifted his gaze back to the book and coughed to get her attention before he looked again in her direction. "Princess, why don't you call Jake? He would probably like to know you are concerned about him."

Kristina had abruptly broken her stare from the phone when her father coughed and had picked up her knitting again. She kept her eyes on her work. "No, I don't want him to know I know. If he wants to talk about it, he'll call."

"He won't call and tell you he was fired by an idiot," Axel said, more loudly than he intended.

Kristina looked at her father accusingly. "I should never have told you. Jake wasn't fired, Papa, he was always just temporary. He will call when he's ready."

Axel tossed his book to the light stand. "Don't you understand how he feels? He is an Iron Man. The general has taken from him what he loves most—his soldiers. Call him!"

Kristina stared at her father defiantly. "I understand only that I shouldn't have told you what I heard today. It's not your concern. Jake will call if he wants to talk."

Axel's eyes narrowed. "An Iron Man will not talk about his pain!" He got up and strode to the hallway. He stopped at the doorway to look over his shoulder. "If you knew him as well as you thought you did, you would understand that."

Kristina remained silent.

Muggelsee

Dagmar heard Renate come into the bedroom, and closed her eyes. "He's going to be late again, isn't he?"

The young woman sat down on the bed and took Dagmar's hand. "The director is preparing for Gorbachev's visit. You know how important this event is. I talked to his secretary. He should be home by midnight. Come, we will have dinner and write out the invitations for the party."

Dagmar closed the book she had been reading and listlessly shifted her welling eyes to the young woman. "We've had to change the date for the party three times because of my husband's schedule. I don't think we'll ever have it. Go on . . . I'm not hungry. Make sure Greta puts a plate away for him. He'll need to eat something."

Renate got up. She was irritated. Frau Wolf seemed to have aged ten years in the past two months, and Renate felt sorry for her, but also angry at her lack of understanding for how busy the director was. "I will bring you something," she insisted in a monotone. "You need to eat and get your strength back."

Dagmar knew the woman didn't understand her pain and never would. Renate was a product of the system her husband had helped build, where the greater good of the state always came first. Feeling sorry for the young woman, Dagmar lay back on the pillow, shut her eyes and said a prayer for her soul . . . but she knew it was too late. Renate, like her husband, was past prayers.

CHAPTER 26

4 October,
West Berlin

Jake awoke after tossing and turning all night. He was still dressed in his clothes. He cussed himself for allowing his emotions to overcome him, and glanced at his digital clock. It read 6:12. He cussed again, knowing he'd have to cut his run short to make it to work before seven-thirty. He swung his legs off the bed to stand up, but again saw his fatigues, still lying there in a heap where he had left them days before when he had come out of the field. Steeling himself, he leaned forward, scooped them up, and went into the bathroom, where he tossed them into his closet. He would not be weak again, he told himself. The past was past. He had a task force to lead and a mission to accomplish.

His thoughts turned to the reason he'd had such a fitful sleep. It had been Dr. Higgins's words at the end of his briefing: "Logic tells me that if one were to apply the criteria to the ministry as a whole, one could easily categorize the Stasi directorates by order of importance." Jake had gone over the sentence again and again during the night, especially the seven key words that echoed in his head: ". . . one could easily categorize the Stasi directorates . . ."

He turned the faucet on and looked in the mirror. His eyes narrowed and his jaw muscles rippled. The bastards knew. They knew who ordered the hits.

Roosevelt Barracks

Master Sergeant Washington raised his hands for protection from his commander's wrath and bad breath. "Whoa, Snake. You're upset, calm down and chill out. Sure the Company knows. We both know the Company didn't give us all the info about Stasi. There are two directorates missing from the info they gave us. Their man said the Company didn't need or want us to worry about those two. It was pretty damn clear to me they didn't want us to find anything out about them. We aren't supposed to know they know, but we got smart people so we figured it out. Don't rock the boat. We complete the mission of plugging the holes of the six directorates they need info on, and then we forget it."

Jake backed off and sat down behind the office desk. "What if they don't know? What if they've been too damn busy spying on the Soviets, confirming data for the upcoming CFE talks?"

Washington sat down, looking at his boss worriedly. "You get any sleep at all, Snake? Sure they know. Dr. Higgins and his 'criteria' figured it out, didn't he? Da Company got plenty of behavioral scientists. Forget it."

Jake's eyes blazed as he leaned back in his chair. "It's just like when the Company said there *wasn't* any opposition in the Presidential Palace on Grenada. We lost five men, and seven of us were wounded by the fucking 'opposition' that weren't *supposed* to be there! I gotta know the bastards know this time!"

Washington shook his head in warning. "You gonna step on your dick if you tread on their turf, Snake. You know how the Company is. We contract pukes can't ask questions or try and play in their big game. We gotta act like we just fell off the turnip truck and only do what they ask for. Nothing more. Let it be, Snake."

Jake's eyes kept their penetrating stare on Washington, until the soldier gave up under their unrelenting intensity. "Okay, let's say you do find something. How you gonna tell 'em without stepping on their egos?"

Jake's expression changed and his eyes suddenly softened. "Sandman, I want you to take Higgins's place on the team that's looking at the administration directorate. Higgins and I will take a look at the other two directorates that the company conveniently left off the list. We'll see if we can figure out who has the real bad boys pulling triggers. We have to brief Dawson tomorrow at one on what we found so far. After that, if Doc and I find something, I'll brief Dawson myself in the office so nobody else takes the heat. If Dawson knows, he'll tell me to back off. If he doesn't, then we've done our part for the good ol' CIA and U.S. of A. Either way, I'll feel better."

Washington smirked. "You have a little problem." He stood and opened the office door and motioned toward the bay. "You'd better take a look at this."

Jake walked around his desk and followed the big man as he strode down the bay floor toward two large Tectronic computer monitors and the imagery experts seated behind them. Washington tapped the redhead's shoulder. "Tell the colonel about the 'little' problem we have."

The pimple-faced wirehead motioned to a large box of disks by his desk. "Sir, you asked for all four days of the run. I don't think you realize how much information you're talking about. The bird shoots as long as it has enough light, then automatically shuts off. What I'm saying is, we have fourteen hours of photos from each day of shooting, which equates to fifty-six hours of stored information. Remember, our bird takes a picture every two seconds. That's thirty frames a minute, eighteen hundred frames an hour times fifty-six hours. Sir, we have 10,080,000 frames."

Washington looked at Jake. "Boss, what the wirehead is saying is that we got ourselves an information overload problem. Ain't no way to make all them frames into glossy eight-by-tens. 'Course, if you do, let me know 'cause I wanna buy me some Kodak stock first."

Jake looked at the monitor where a frame was displayed. The picture of the city of Berlin was crystal clear. He leaned forward, looking at the screen more closely, and spoke to the redhead. "Zoom it down to one of the compounds."

The kid pecked the keyboard, and the picture changed to a tight shot, as if taken from a helicopter directly over the main compound. The redhead motioned toward the screen. "Sir, we usually work right off the screen and only print when necessary. The trouble is, we only have two monitors to show the runs to the teams. Everybody wants their turn to check their directorate, but once they're on it, it takes a long time to track a car or man."

Jake backed up in thought. Ten seconds passed before he faced Washington again. "Starting now, the teams work in shifts. Half work during the day, the other half at night. Train two men per shift on the use of the computer and keep one of the imagery experts on each shift to provide technical advice." Jake glanced behind him at the pieces of butcher paper. "Priority goes to the biggest directorates first." Jake turned to the redhead. "Going through all the frames is a waste of time. Use only the photos between 0630 and 0900, when Stasi comes to work in the morning, eleven-thirty till one for the lunch bunch, and between 1630 and 1800 hours for when they go home. That ought to cut the time the teams stay on the computer."

Washington smiled and nudged the redhead. "That's why da Snake's in charge. He fixes 'little' problems."

Jake began to walk back to his office when Washington tapped his shoulder. "When do you want me to schedule your time on the computer so you can check out what we talked about?"

Jake spoke over his shoulder as he strode to his office. "Put me on when everybody else has finished."

Axel Mader walked up to the apartment door and put the letter into the mail slot. Turning around, he strode back to his car and got in. He didn't feel that he was meddling, as Jake was his friend. How his daughter felt was her problem. He only knew he could not sleep nights knowing how Jake must be feeling, and wanted him to know he had a friend. It was the least one Iron Man could do for another.

Axel pulled away from the curb already feeling better.

Muggelsee

Wolf walked out onto the large stone deck and looked across the lake to the forest on the far shore. It had been a long day of attending meetings, going over the security arrangements for Gorbachev's visit, and he needed time to think. Before leaving the office, Rink had given him a folder that contained copies of the charge sheets filed against him for war crimes. The names of his accusers had been whited out long ago by the Allies. All four documents claimed he had murdered, in cold blood, the colonel of the battalion, badly wounded a captain, and ordered the killing of at least a hundred men of the Parachute Battalion 600. Wolf smirked. The only surprising news was that the captain he had shot in the chest had survived.

Wolf thought about that river bridge only seventy kilometers due west from where he stood. Whenever he saw that bridge in his mind, he felt a gnawing ache deep in his soul. After all these years and all he had done for the security of the state, that single event was the only one he felt regret for. No one else knew or cared that he had failed the Führer, had let some traitors escape, but he, Captain Horst Volker, cared. In forty-nine years of service to his Fatherland, only once had he let his country and leaders down. Staring out across the lake, he whispered, "Where are you, Iron Men . . . where are you?"

Dagmar came out to join him. "What are you thinking about?" she asked.

"I was wondering about our future," Wolf said. "Have you thought about where we will live when I retire?"

Dagmar's eyes widened with hope. "You have submitted the papers?"

Wolf looked at her as if she should know better than to ask. "Of course not. There is still much work to be done, but perhaps in two, maybe three years, I will. Now is the time to make arrangements for acquiring a new home for us. Where would you like to live?"

Dagmar covered her disappointment by turning her back and walking toward the door. "This is our home. We could never leave it."

Wolf lowered his head. "It's the state's home. Once I retire, it can be taken away."

Dagmar stopped and looked over her shoulder. "Erich Honecker gave it to you for your hard work. He is your friend. He would never take it away. Why are you talking so foolishly? Come before your dinner gets cold."

Wolf followed his wife, although he didn't feel hungry. He knew Dagmar would soon be very distraught . . . again. Erich Honecker and the house would soon be just memories.

West Berlin

Jake set the other letters aside and opened the one from Axel. He smiled. The lines were poorly written and the English was even worse, but it had obviously been a labor of love from his friend. Axel had found out from Kristina that he had lost his job, and Axel wanted him to know that his old kamerad was there if he needed him. The last line invited Jake to the house for an informal dinner on Friday night, the sixth, to meet Lars Kailer, who was flying in to help stock the cabin for the Iron Man reunion the following week.

Jake folded the letter and picked up the phone. He hoped it wouldn't be Kristina who answered on the other end.

He was lucky. It was Axel. Jake thanked him for his letter and told him he would be there Friday night. He also asked if he could bring two friends whom he wanted Axel to meet.

Axel laughed. "Of course, so long as they drink German beer."

Jake felt better when he put the phone handset back into the cradle. He waited only a few seconds before picking up the phone again to call Sandman.

Harnack House

Chong began to reach for a beer for her customer, when Jake held up his hand. "Just a Diet Coke. I gotta go back to work in a while."

"How is new job?"

"Okay," Jake said, shifting his eyes to the television in the hope she would drop the subject.

"I win car on 'Wheel of Fortune' tonight. I know answer. It was phrase. 'The bigger they are the harder they fall.' I win. Vanna White clap and everything."

Jake lifted an eyebrow. "What kind of car?"

"Red."

"Win me one, will ya?"

Chong put her elbows on the bar and supported her square face with her hands. "Why you here instead of with Mission lady?"

"I like your company."

She rolled her eyes. "You lie. You using hair lotion?"

"It stinks," Jake said, wrinkling his nose.

"You bet-ter use. Your hair getting thinner. . . . When you going to see Mission lady?"

"Friday."

"That long, huh?"

"Maybe I can grow some hair by that time."

Chong shook her head and backed up. "You men big-time stupid. Mission lady good for you."

Jake looked at his glass filled with Diet Coke and ice. "She don't drink Lite beer, remember?"

Chong sighed and faced the television. She watched "All in the Family" for only a few minutes before turning and giving her customer another accusing squint. "You better give Mission lady a chance . . . she good for you."

Jake picked up his glass and sighed, knowing he would have to deal with it and call Kristina . . . tomorrow.

CHAPTER 27

5 October,
Roosevelt Barracks, West Berlin

Master Sergeant Washington expected to see five very tired men in the work bay. He smiled to himself at finding only one. A glance told him the lone soldier had been there a long time.

"Damn, Snake, how long you been at it, and where the hell is the night shift?"

Jake broke his bloodshot eyes from the screen and leaned back, stretching. "What time ya got?"

Washington glanced at his watch. "Just a little past six."

Jake yawned and stretched again. "I got here around midnight. The night crew had everything they needed by two A.M., so I sent 'em home to get some sleep."

Washington stepped closer, thinking he hadn't heard right. "They're finished . . . already?"

"Almost," Jake said tiredly. "They've got a few more low-level leaders to track, but I figure we can wrap up the first phase in a couple of days. The day shift almost got finished too, right?"

"Hell if I know," Washington said with a shrug. "I ran around Berlin most of yesterday trying to find special paper and processing fluid so they could print pictures. Then I had to go to Burger King to pick up lunch for everybody, and later again for dinner. Shit, Snake, I'm the administrative gofer, remember? I make the coffee and keep shit paper in the latrine. I ain't had time to check nothin'. I don't know what the hell they're doin' on the computers."

Jake smiled and pulled a chair up beside him. "Come here and sit down, 'gofer.' I'll tell ya how the teams broke the code so fast."

Washington reluctantly walked around the desk and wrinkled his brow before sitting down. "Snake, I'm tellin' ya up front, my man, I hate computers . . . never even liked the people who used them. You ain't gonna make me no wirehead, are ya?"

Jake leaned back in his chair. "Naw, just listen and watch so ya know how the teams are doing it. It's easy." He motioned to the monitor. "A team sits down here and runs the disk that shows the change of work shifts in the morning at Stasi headquarters. First they pick out their assigned directorate's building and zoom in on it so they can see all the entrances. Then they start the frames rolling until they see a car pull up to one of the doors and a chauffeur get out to open the back door for his passenger. Bingo, they have their man. Ya see, not just anybody can drive into the compound. Just the high-level staff and the leaders. So then the team reverses the frames, kinda like instant replay, back to just before their man gets out of the car, and they zoom in for more detail. When they run the frames forward again, they watch as he gets out and walks to his office building. They wait for a good shot of their man and freeze it. They then take their folder and compare the Company's funeral pictures with the person on the screen. So far, we've found every directorate and deputy director that way. Hell, one of the directors was wearing the same suit and tie."

Washington grinned. "Ain't this some shit? We gonna put James Bond out of business with all this high-tech satellite gee-whiz stuff."

Jake smiled. "It gets better. Remember the freeze frame I talked about? Well, all the team does next is hit the print button, and the computer sends the frame to the processor there in front of you. In less than a minute out comes a color picture. Now comes the fun part: they reverse the frames and follow the car until the guy is picked up at his house. Bingo again. Now they know where he lives. They take a picture, then zoom out to see where the house is in relation to the compound. A couple of the teams already know if their directorate is married or not by zooming in on the clotheslines in their back yards. We even got a picture of the wife working in the garden and his two girls leaving for school."

Washington sat back with a Cheshire grin. "And to think Dawson is coming for his briefing this afternoon to see how we plan on accomplishing the mission. Shit, Snake, you gonna be able to tell him you're almost done. He's gonna shit a brick."

Jake's expression changed when he heard Dawson's name, and

he looked back at the frame on the screen. "We still have a few more to identify."

Washington knew the look and tone of voice. "What'sa matter, Snake? You couldn't find anything on the directorates you were checking out?"

Jake pressed the keyboard keys and zoomed in on a silver-haired man getting out of a black car. "It took all night, but I found them all right. I wasted an hour on the first directorate and found out why the Company didn't want us to work on it. Its only purpose is training and recruiting." Jake pointed to the silver-haired man on the screen. "But the other one—the one this bastard is in charge of—is what I was looking for."

Washington leaned closer. "He looks like Cary Grant from this angle."

Jake picked up the folder beside him, took out one of the CIA's photos of a funeral and held it up next to the screen. "Can you pick him out of the crowd around the grave?"

Washington looked at the monitor then the photo and pointed. "Yeah, it's this tall guy with his arm around the old lady in widow weeds. Same silver hair and big shoulders. Looks like he's in pretty good shape for an old-timer."

Jake tossed his head in the direction of the other computer. "Doc Higgins came in about three this morning, and I had him go through the disks, concentrating on this guy. I call him the Silver Fox. Doc worked at the computer till about five, and then told me he was gonna do some kind of comparison study. He's in my office now. If he comes to the same conclusion I did, then I think we've found the special ops organization in Stasi. Doc wouldn't tell me anything, so I've been sittin' here waiting and—"

Washington held his hand up. "Looks like your wait is over, 'cause here he comes."

The disheveled doctor was approaching in a hurry. He pulled up a chair and glanced at Washington before speaking to Jake. "Do you want me to wait and brief you later?"

Jake waved his concern away. "Naw, don't worry about Sandman. He's in this special project with me."

Higgins held up a folder. "I made a complete evaluation. You can look through this or I can quickly summarize."

Jake was too tired to read, and he wanted Washington to hear it. "Go ahead, Doc, tell me what you found."

Higgins opened the folder and glanced at the summary page for a moment. "I have gone over the satellite runs as well as the other team folders to make a comparison. Based on what I've found, I can say without a doubt that the man you referred to me as the Silver Fox is the director of a very unusual and powerful organization within the Stasi. Based on my criteria, he fits the model of a leader in all respects. He is chauffeured in a black, tinted-windowed, Lada 2300, equaled by only the minister's car. The only other director who comes close is the director of reconnaissance, who is chauffeured in a Lada 1600, a full step down. The Fox is picked up at his house in the morning and driven to the compound. He enters the side gate and is let off in the back entrance of Haus One, the principal Stasi headquarters building. He is the only director to use the back door, which I find unusual."

Higgins paused long enough to withdraw a computer-generated, blow-up photo from the folder, and he handed it to Jake. "Our Fox lives in this walled-in estate on the Muggel Lake. The lake is situated east and south of the city, but within the city limits. As you can see by the picture, it is surrounded by a huge park and forest to the west. The estate comes complete with guards, and note the sailboat tied to the pier behind the house. I have looked at the other directors' residences, and nothing compares. It is clear this Fox fellow is very highly thought of by the ministry. Now, using the same criteria, but expanding the scope of analysis, I found the following."

Higgins took another satellite photo from the folder and held it up. "First, cars. You can see the parking lot behind Haus One where the car of the Fox is parked. If you look closely, you will notice that all the vehicles, with the exception of those of the directors, are of the same type, and each has an extra antenna for a two-way radio. This parking lot is, in fact, a motor pool of nothing but new Lada 210-S's and these two rows of Barkus vans, which also have two-way radios. I think it's safe to assume that the vans are used for eavesdropping or phone-tapping equipment. The only similar vans within Stasi are in the other compound. The Company files indicate that the other compound's motor pool services two directorates: Directorate for the Security of the Economy, and Directorate for the Struggle Against Suspicious Persons. You can see for yourself that the vehicles in this bigger motor pool are the much cheaper Trabants and Wartsburgs, and only very few have two-way radios. I used the computer and watched the motor pool behind Haus One and within an hour saw a definite pattern. Two-man teams use the cars and vans, and seventy percent of the teams came from the building across from the motor pool. It is one of the newest buildings, and it is the most heavily guarded in the compound. It also has radio antennas and satellite disks on its roof. While I was watching the frames, I stopped several times to zoom in and see who was going into and out of the new building. It was in one of those shots that I saw our Fox, with two other men, enter the main entrance. The guard in front came to attention and saluted. The guard had never before saluted anyone else. My conclusion is that the motor pool behind Haus One and the new building belongs to the directorate under the leadership of our Fox."

Higgins took off his glasses and wiped the lenses with his handkerchief. "I have gone through all the photos provided by the Company, and it is clear Herr Fox's organization is the one most likely to be engaged in illegal activities. The reason is what is *not* in the photos. I have searched back photos of public and official government events, and unlike the other directors, Herr Fox is not in any of the photographs. Why? And why all this special treatment and special equipment?"

Higgins put his glasses back on. "It is obvious that the answers to those questions point to a very, very powerful man."

Jake exchanged glances with Washington, then shifted his eyes to the doctor. "Do you think the Company knows?"

Higgins's eyebrows shot up. "Of course. It's the reason they didn't give us any information on this directorate in the first place. The information on Herr Fox and his organization is obviously very sensitive and has been compartmentalized."

Washington gave Jake an I-told-you-so look, but Jake ignored it and pressed on. "Doc, I'm going to find out for sure. I plan on briefing Dawson on what we found. I agree the Company probably does know, but for my own peace of mind, I have to find out for sure."

Higgins looked concerned. "They are very touchy about these things, Colonel. I agreed to work with you on this for the purely selfish reason that I wanted to test the limits of my criteria." Higgins lowered his head. "But I must admit this fellow Herr Fox did get to me. To think the man actually attended the funerals of those he had purged, and even had the audacity to escort the widows, is . . . is utterly repulsive." Higgins looked into Jake's eyes. "I can understand your concern in wanting to make sure. So do I."

Jake stood and put out his hand. "Thanks, Doc. We'll know this afternoon. Go get some sleep, and I'll see ya here at noon when the teams prebrief me."

Higgins smiled tiredly as he shook Jake's hand. "I suggest you get some rest yourself, Colonel."

"There's a few things I have to check, then I'm on my way." Jake waited until Higgins had walked down the stairs before picking up the doctor's folder and his own. He handed them both to Washington. "Sandy, I'm gonna take the doc's advice and crash for a couple of hours. Do me a favor. Combine the stuff in both folders into one and make me a copy."

Washington grimaced. "Damn, Snake, ya know making copies of this kind of stuff violates Company policy."

Jake rolled an eyebrow up. "The copy is to cover our ass, just in case."

"You still don't trust them, do you?" Washington said softly.

"Do you?"

Washington lowered his eyes to the folder. "I'll make the copy."

Peggy Sue strolled into Kristina's office holding a cup of coffee. "You two kissed and made up yet?" she asked as she sat down.

Kristina glanced up from the list as if put out by the interruption. "There is nothing to 'make up.' He just hasn't called or come by lately, that's all. I have no idea where he is or what he's doing."

"And you still haven't called or gone by to see him?"

Kristina's eyes narrowed and she tossed the list to the side. "I'm seeing him tomorrow night, if you must know. Papa has invited him to dinner, and he's bringing guests. Okay?"

Peggy Sue's brow arched. "Hey, I didn't 'have to know' anything, Kris. I just wanted to know if you two were on speaking terms. I got that information you wanted from my Air Force friend at Tempelhof about Colonel Tallon's father. I came in here to find out if you still wanted it. Sorry I even asked. Okay?" Peggy Sue got up and strode toward the door.

Kristina's lip quivered and her eyes began to water. "No, don't go. I . . . I'm sorry, Peg. It . . . it's just that I don't know what to do. I'm not any good at this. I know losing the job crushed him, but I don't know what to say to him."

Peggy Sue came back and put her arm around Kristina's shoulder. "You don't have to say anything. All you gotta do is let him know you care. Men's egos are beyond our comprehension, so don't try and figure out the perfect thing to say. It will probably be wrong. The best thing is just let them know you're there for them." Peggy Sue chuckled. "I heard that on 'Oprah Winfrey' last week, so don't think I'm an Ann Landers or somethin'."

Kristina smiled through her tears and stood up, wiping her eyes. "Come on, show me that information about his father."

Jake strode toward the stairs and met Dawson just as he reached the top step. He was about to welcome him when he noticed, to his surprise, a short, well-dressed civilian following behind the station chief.

"Colonel Tallon," Dawson said, "meet my West Berlin counterpart, Kurt von Kant. I've asked him to join me for the briefing. Kurt and I have been working together a long time on Stasi. He is very interested in how you plan on accomplishing the tasks we gave you."

Jake shook the German's hand without speaking. Dawson had not mentioned bringing a visitor, and that fell into the category of a surprise. Jake hated surprises, especially when he knew the CIA didn't do anything without a purpose. With his internal warning bells going off, Jake led the two men to the bay where the task force sat waiting.

Washington quickly brought up another chair to the front row for the German. Jake waited until both men were seated before directing his prepared comments to Dawson. "Sir, we have done the preliminary work, and by a process of elimination we have already identified all the directors and their deputies and matched them with their directorates. All we have left to do is to fill in a few holes in the lower-management tiers."

Dawson shook his head as if he'd just been slapped. "Did you say you have *already* positively identified the first two levels of leadership?"

Jake motioned to the task-force members. "Sir, the men behind you did it with the help of the SRS. I'm going to ask each team to come up and brief you on their assigned directorate. But first I'm going to have Dr. Higgins come up and explain his analytic criteria, which made the job much easier for us."

Jake began to motion to Higgins when the German spoke up. "What is SRS?"

Dawson leaned closer to his counterpart. "SRS is the Stationary Reconnaissance Satellite I told you about."

The German nodded. "Ach so, ja. I'm familiar with its capabilities." He motioned to Jake, "Please, continue."

An hour later and without further interruption, all the teams had finished briefing.

When the last team sat down, Jake prepared to make his closing remarks, but the German stood up with a wide smile.

"Splendid work. You are doing a great service for our country, and I can assure you your efforts are appreciated by our government. I am delighted to have . . ."

Jake glanced at Washington. He knew they were getting smoke blown up their ass. The kraut's words were right, but his body language said something else.

Dawson stood next and shook the hand of each task-force member, then thanked them all for their good work. "Very impressive," he said to Jake. "I had no idea you would finish so quickly. I had expected that some fieldwork would be necessary."

"It still might," Jake said. "I don't want to say we can get everything you need from satellite photos. We might need to do a few stakeouts to get particulars for the background folders. It's too early to tell."

Dawson nodded. "Whatever you decide, let me know, and I'll arrange the support requirements with the help of Kurt's in-place people."

Dawson was about to guide von Kant to the stairs when Jake stepped in front of the station chief, motioning him down the bay toward his office. "I have one more briefing, which will take only five minutes. I have some information that might be of interest to you."

Dawson looked at his watch, then to von Kant, who shrugged. "Okay," Dawson said. "Five minutes is about all the time we've got."

Jake led the way, and seconds later the two intelligence officers were seated and looking up at Jake, who stood in front of a piece of butcher paper covered with sailcloth. "By chance, we stumbled onto a man in Stasi who seems to be very powerful." Jake removed the cloth, revealing a blow-up photo of his Silver Fox getting out of a black car. Before Jake could say another word, von Kant was on his feet as if he'd been poked with a hot iron. "What is this!" he angrily barked at Dawson. "I thought we agreed Wolf was my responsibility!"

Dawson stood. "We did." He took two steps, ripped the paper from the wall and handed it to von Kant, giving Jake a warning glare. "This is not *your* area. I appreciate your efforts, but stick to the mission I gave you and nothing more. Give me everything you've got on this man, please."

Jake knew his boss was not a happy camper, and his "please" was not a real please, it was a demand. Jake picked up the folder from his desk and handed it to Dawson. "I just wanted to make sure."

Dawson's gaze softened in understanding. "We know about him."

Von Kant took the folder from Dawson's hands and shifted his burning eyes to Jake. "Who else knows?"

Jake didn't like his tone. He glared back. "Just me and Dr. Higgins. I've followed procedure and kept it compartmentalized."

The German looked back at Dawson and spoke with the same

commanding, cold inflection. "I need your personal guarantee on this."

Dawson visibly tightened. "You've got it, but don't push, Kurt. We've agreed to stay out because of your government's request, but we still have our national security interests to keep in mind. I don't want this blown out of proportion. The task force stumbled over it, and that's all. I don't want to get any calls from my boss on this, you understand?"

Von Kant stiffly nodded once. "Very well, but I suggest you watch your hired help more closely. They are cowboys." He gave Jake a parting don't-mess-with-me look and strode out of the office holding the wadded-up butcher paper and folder.

Dawson sighed. "This didn't happen, understand? You know nothing about nor have you ever seen the man in that picture, and neither has Dr. Higgins. You heard me give my personal guarantee."

"I understand," Jake said, answering in his best humble voice.

Satisfied, Dawson turned to go, but stopped and winked. "Good job. This whole thing stinks. It's above my level and all mired in politics. The kraut is an asshole. But Jake, I'm serious, forget everything."

As soon as Dawson left the office, Jake opened the bottom drawer and removed the folder Washington had prepared for him. He opened it to the first page and picked up a pen. He wrote at the top of the page in big letters, Herr WOLF, and closed the file.

Higgins cocked an eyebrow. "I told you they knew."

Washington nodded. "And I told you too."

Jake couldn't help but smile. "Yeah, but now I know for sure. Remember what I told you, it's forgotten. We don't say anything else about it, that's Dawson's orders."

Washington held up his hand. "Wait a minute. Doc, the thing I don't get is why the Company is lettin' the Herms take the lead on the Fox action?"

Higgins's eyes seem to focus on something in the distance for a moment. Jake had noticed it before and knew the computer in the doctor's head was busy sorting and sifting information. Higgins lowered his head and began pacing in deep thought. Fifteen seconds passed before he stopped and seemed to nod to himself. "It's logical that West Germany would consider the Stasi its primary opposition and would want the lead. After all, it's in their best interest for national security reasons. But the discussion the colonel overheard between Dawson and Kant is a little disturbing. I would think the Company would work independently of the West Germans and that the two intelligence organizations would cooperate and share information. The only logical explanation is that what the colonel heard was probably a turf battle at the station chief level. I'm sure the Company is still very much involved in monitoring the situation, but must keep the sensibilities of the West Germans in mind. As I told Colonel Tallon before, this is a very touchy subject for both intelligence communities. It always is when there is so much to be gained . . . and lost, with careers on the line."

Washington threw his hands up. "What the hell, it's not our concern anymore. We'll just follow orders and not worry about it. Right, Snake?"

Jake forced a smile to cover his uneasy feeling. "Right. Now let's get back to work. Doc, would you please tell the task force that today and tomorrow they're to keep working and get all the info they can for their background folders. Tomorrow afternoon at one we'll have a meeting and see where we stand, and I'll decide whether or not fieldwork is necessary. Sandman, I want you to show me what we've got in the way of surveillance equipment in case we decide it's a go."

"Are you sure you want me to tell the task force what to do?" Higgins asked nervously.

Jake patted the doctor's back. "As of right now, you're my deputy. I'd like you to work with the teams and see how they're coming and give me an evaluation if you think we have what we need without having to go into East Berlin."

Higgins straightened his back and raised his chin. " 'Deputy Task Force commander' has a rather nice ring. I think I prefer it to Doctor."

Washington opened the office door and gave Higgins a warning stare. "Don't get any fancy ideas, Doc, I'm the guy who is really in charge around here and don't be forgettin' that or you ain't gonna have no coffee or shit paper."

Jake followed Washington down into the basement of the building. Washington had to unlock two doors and finally came to a steel security walk-in vault. He spun the combination lock as he spoke. "This is one of the Company's contingency ops vaults. They put our surveillance gear in here. It's all the top-of-the-line stuff. We should be able to handle the action with no problem."

The last tumbler clicked into place and Washington pushed down the steel handle and swung back the door.

Jake stepped in and abruptly halted, seeing the rack of weapons.

"Contingency ops? For what, World War Three? Damn, look at all this shit!"

Washington walked over to the storage shelves where the cameras and tele-photo lenses were stored. "Forget you've seen that stuff. It's the Company's idea of playing soldier if the shit hits the fan in an emergency. They got four other cache sites like this one in the city. You know how they are . . . got more plans and money than people to carry anything out. I don't think they've even zeroed the rifles."

Jake looked at the boxes of ammunition and stack of flak vests and shook his head. "I thought they'd have more fancy gear. This is all basic Government issue. M-16s, night-vision gear, nothin' really high speed."

Washington lifted up a camera. "Come on, Snake, don't worry about their shit, they got their high-speed gear with 'em in the basement of their other building. This is what you came to see."

Jake inspected the surveillance equipment, and minutes later was standing behind Washington as he shut the vault. "You still comin' to dinner tomorrow night?"

Washington turned for the stairway with a scowl. "Yeah, but you owe me big time. I gotta take Sissy to KaDeWe tonight to buy a new dress. You gonna owe me fifty big ones."

Jake threw his arm over Washington's shoulder as they walked up the steps together. "Sorry, Sandman. I didn't wanna go to dinner by myself. I don't think I could explain our cover without you. Anyway, you'll like Axel."

Washington snarled. "You still owe me fifty for the dress, and if I gotta drink German beer, you gonna owe me another ten."

Jake passed by his apartment and walked on to Harnack House. He thought a few beers and a little verbal swordplay with Chong would get his mind off of business, Kristina, and the asshole he'd met that afternoon. Kurt von Kant had gotten to him. He didn't like being talked down to by anyone, especially when they didn't wear a uniform and had a von in their name.

Jake knew things were looking up when he walked into the bar during an armed forces commercial.

Chong set a beer in his spot before he even sat down on the bar stool. "You looooookin' good, Jake," she said brightly.

What is wrong with this picture? Jake asked himself. Chong never said he looked good. He began to ask her what was wrong when he smelled the approaching woman coming up behind him. Chong's smile said the rest.

Kristina sat down on the bar stool and gave him a casual glance. "New in town, stranger?"

Jake glared at Chong's sly grin, then gave the woman next to him a cursory look before turning his attention to the beer can in his hand. "I been around for a few months. You come in here often?"

Kristina swiveled in her chair and looked around the empty club. "All the time. I like the action."

"Yeah, it's rockin' tonight. Can I buy you a drink, pretty lady?"

"Sure. Say, that scar on your forehead . . . it looks kinda like a noodle, doesn't it?"

Jake snapped his head to Chong, who looked up at the ceiling. He took a drink of beer and set down the can. "Naw, it's a snake. *Some* people are blind and can't see it."

Kristina nodded absently and leaned back on the bar. "What's your sign, handsome?"

Jake slammed the beer can down and reached across the bar for Chong, who was giggling uncontrollably. She backed away, batting at his hands. "You two better than TV!"

Jake broke off his attack, hearing Kristina's laughter. He sat down again and leaned over, kissing Kristina's cheek. "I missed you, pretty lady."

Kristina grabbed his neck before he could get away and pressed her lips against his. A full ten seconds later she leaned back and looked into his eyes. "I missed you more."

Jake tossed his chin toward the door. "Let's go to my place and argue there."

"Do I get kiss too?" Chong asked, putting her hands on her hips.

Jake smiled without taking his eyes from Kristina. "You gonna get more than that for setting me up." He stood and offered his arm to Kristina, then glanced at the still-smiling bartender. "I'll be back one day and wring your neck with that stupid-looking bow tie."

Chong winked. "I be here, tough guy."

CHAPTER 28

Friday, 6 October,
West Berlin

Sissy Washington leaned over to Kristina and whispered, "I think it's time we went to the kitchen and found something to do."

Kristina glanced at the four laughing men at the other end of the dinner table and pushed back her chair. "I think you're right."

Minutes later the two women sat at the kitchen table with full cups of coffee. Sissy exhaled through her nose as if put out, and motioned to her new dress. "I don't know why I even bothered. No offense, but I thought this was going to be a real dinner, not a gathering to tell war stories. I can only take so much. They laugh and joke about it, but I can tell ya, I wasn't laughing when Sandy was gone. I worried myself sick."

Kristina instinctively patted Sissy's hand. "The good thing is, all that's past. At least you don't have to worry about him going off to some war now."

Sissy looked at Kristina as if she had told a bad joke. "Are you trying to be funny . . . or don't you know?"

Kristina was shocked at the sudden change in her guest. "Know what?"

Sissy sighed and nodded and she lowered her head. "Did you buy the story Jake told you about what he and Sandy are working on?"

"Well, I did think it a little strange to have a colonel in charge of making an Army information film about Berlin. Usually protocol is brought in to provide assistance, since we make tours regularly."

Sissy nodded. "Exactly. It's a cover. They're into something. I see it in Sandy's face. He's playing a good game, but I know him too well. It's probably nothing dangerous, but it's heavy enough to need a cover story, which worries me. I wait every night for him to come through that front door, and only then do I finally relax."

Kristina rolled her eyes up. "I can't imagine what they would be doing that could possibly be dangerous in Berlin."

"Good. Neither can I. I'm not really worried at this stage, just concerned. Now, what was the name of those wonderful red berries you fixed?"

Jake strode into the kitchen and yelled over his shoulder, "Here they are!" He bowed and motioned toward the dining room. "The ladies are requested for an announcement."

When the two women walked into the room, the men were all standing behind their chairs.

Axel put down his stein of beer and motioned to the short, rotund man to his right. "I am honored tonight to have my old kamerad, Lars Kailer, with me to see what wonderful friends I have. I would like now to share some good news with my friends and loving daughter. Lars has informed me that the article he and I wrote will be published in this Sunday's papers throughout West Germany and here in Berlin. Please join me in a toast to the kameraden Lars and I loved. They deserved that the truth be told. To truth!"

"To truth!"

Everyone drank and was about to sit, but Jake raised his glass. "And I would like to propose a toast to Hauptmann Mader and Hauptmann Kailer, both true Iron Men. To the Iron Men!"

"To the Iron Men!"

Jake leaned over to Kristina after everyone was seated and whispered, "Thank you for drinking to the toasts. I know you're not happy about all this, but it meant a lot to him to see you drink with the rest of us."

Kristina looked down to the other end of the table, where both her father and Lars were still wiping away tears. She nodded. "Thank you for making the last toast. It was sweet."

Axel walked Sandy and Sissy Washington to the door. "I'm so glad you could come. It is wonderful meeting new friends."

The sergeant shook the old soldier's hand. "It was a great dinner and the beer wasn't half bad. Thanks, Axel. Sorry we had to turn down the invitation to go to the lake with you tomorrow, but like

I said, Sissy promised to look after some neighbor's kids. I'd really like to see the place."

Sissy elbowed her husband in the ribs. "Axel, *he's* the one who volunteered us. He likes to tell the kids war stories."

Axel took Sissy's hand. "I'm sorry we must have bored you tonight with our stories. We warriors sometimes forget our manners."

Sissy smiled. "It was a wonderful evening. I enjoyed myself. Thank Kristina again for me. I'll be looking for the paper Sunday and read your article."

Axel kissed Sissy's cheek and shook Sandy's hand again. *"Auf Wiedersehen, meinen Freunden."*

In the kitchen, Jake came up behind Kristina, who was washing dishes. He tapped her shoulder, and when she turned, he kissed her. She pushed him away only after she felt the kiss ending. "Jake, you act like you haven't seen me in weeks instead of last night."

Jake winked. "I can't get enough. Ya need some help with the dishes?"

"You've never asked to help before," she said, eyeing him suspiciously.

Jake picked up a dishcloth. "I want to be next to you, that's all."

Kristina thought about what Sissy had told her, and began to ask if he liked the new job, when Axel walked into the kitchen and put his arm over Jake's shoulder.

"Lars has gone to bed and the Washingtons have said good-night. I need just one more beer. Let us take a walk and visit the apple trees."

Jake could not decline, for Axel had already steered him toward the back door. Kristina also didn't complain. She knew by her father's tone that it had not been a request, but rather a very gentle demand. She took out two beers from the refrigerator and handed the bottles to the men as they passed by.

When Jake reached the barren apple trees, he halted beneath the branches and looked up at the stars. Axel joined him but remained silent. Jake rested his hand on the trunk of the tree, keeping his distant gaze. "I wish I had a place to come to like this."

Axel looked about him. "Yes. Here I always feel as if my Gisela is with me. She loved these trees. When will you be leaving?"

Jake lowered his head. "You know, huh?"

"Ja, as soon as I heard you were moved from your position. A soldier cannot remain where he is if he's not wanted by his superior."

Jake sighed. "I haven't told Kristina yet." He faced his friend. "You know also I want her to go with me?"

Axel nodded. "Ja. I will miss her, but I know she will be happy."
"You think she'll say yes?"
Axel smiled and wiped a tear from his eye.

CHAPTER 29

Saturday, 7 October,
East Berlin

Wearing a black topcoat and matching hat, Erich Honecker, the leader of the Socialist Unity Party of Germany, and General Secretary of the German Democratic Republic, walked up the steps of the bannered reviewing stand and took his place at the rostrum overlooking the wide boulevard of Karl-Marx-Allee. Following Honecker came Mikhail Gorbachev, wearing a gray topcoat but no hat. He stood to the East German leader's right. Standing behind the two men were the East German Council of Ministers, and behind them were the members of the Central Committee. Seated with their wives and families in the special bleachers next to the reviewing stand were the members of the Politburo. To the front and below Honecker's raised platform was a single row of seats for heads of state from visiting communist countries. Honecker glanced over the scene with pride, for the leaders had come to pay their respects to his country and him. He'd had breakfast with the Czechoslovakian leader, Milos Jakes, and his old friend and ally Nicolae Ceausescu, leader of Romania. They both had vowed their continued support. He had met briefly with Nicaragua's president, Daniel Ortega, earlier that morning and found him brash, but not foolish—he would learn soon enough. Yasir Arafat, chairman of the Palestine Liberation Organization, had come seeking funds, as usual, and China's vice-premier, Yao Yilin, seated to Arafat's left, had declared upon his arrival the day before that he had come to show his nation's gratitude for the GDR's official support during the Tiananmen Square affair.

Stepping up to Honecker's left was the stiff-backed Minister of Defense, General Heinz Kessler, who came to attention and signaled the massed military bands on the street in front of the reviewing stand to begin playing. As the musicians brought their instruments up, Honecker looked over the stands along the street. As far as he could see, they were filled with his country's workers, there to show their respect to the socialist state on its fortieth anniversary. He felt the power of the state in their resolute faces.

Erich Honecker stood tall. His country, after all, was the frontline bastion of socialism and the most prosperous state in the communist world. In three hours he would be talking to his mentor and friend, Mikhail Sergeivich, in private discussions before the Soviet president departed for his homeland. He, Honecker, was confident that Mikhail Sergeivich would present him with a solution to the Hungarian border problem. Had not the Soviet General Secretary promised him as much when they spoke the previous day?

The bands began marching down Karl-Marx-Allee. A single tear trickled down Honecker's cheek as the first army unit snapped their heads and eyes in perfect unison to the right and began their goose-step march, honoring him and the nation he led. It was the proudest day of his life, he thought to himself. It was truly the beginning of another forty glorious years!

Everybody had an armful of provisions to carry to the cabin. Jake held two cases of beer. "Are you stocking up for a month?" he yelled ahead to Axel, who was carrying two sacks of groceries.

"Lars wanted us to make sure the cabin was properly stocked for the reunion in two weeks," he called back. "We will all be staying here."

Kristina, carrying two cartons of soft drinks, walked by Jake. "They get too loud when they're at the house, and the neighbors complain."

Jake joined Kristina. "I can bring a sleeping bag and we could share it," he whispered.

She stopped and narrowed her eyes, then laughed and began walking again. "Come on, we've got ten more sacks of groceries. We'll discuss the sleeping arrangements later."

Axel led Lars and Jake down into the wine bunker and turned on the light. Jake whistled. "Damn, Axel, I thought this was a musty wine cellar." He walked deeper into the spacious pine-paneled room, which looked more like an apartment than a wine cellar, except for the near wall, where shelves of bottles rose from the floor to the ceiling.

Axel glanced around the room with obvious pride. "Yes, this is my hideaway."

Lars added four bottles to the bottom shelf and looked over his shoulder at Jake. "Don't let him give you that 'hideaway' talk. He picks up women on the beach and brings them here so his daughter doesn't know. Why do you think there is a bed in the corner?"

Axel winked at Jake. "Wishful thinking."

The three men were strolling back to the cabin when Lars stopped and motioned across the Havel toward the far bank. "Axel, isn't that the Gatow over there?"

Axel joined his friend and looked across the lake. "Ja, are you thinking about those days again?"

Lars broke his gaze and began walking again. "I am glad our article will be coming out soon. It will be like a weight lifted from my shoulders."

Axel patted Lars on the back. "Yes, we will have done our duty then. Come, we had better help my princess put away the groceries before she begins complaining again."

The three men started toward the back deck of the cabin, but two polizei officers hailed them from the beach. The officers strolled over and started asking questions in German. Jake listened without understanding a single word until Axel motioned to Jake and used the word "Amerikanisch." The officer nodded. "Excuse my English please," he said. "Have you seen people here you do not know?"

"He wants to know if you've seen any suspicious-looking people since we've arrived," Lars explained.

Jake shrugged. "I haven't seen anybody at all."

"Thank you," the police officer said, as if he had expected the answer. "I must ask everyone this question. Please understand." He turned and spoke to his partner, and they both continued down the beach.

"What was all that about?" Jake said.

Axel sighed. "They're still looking for suspects in the shootings five days ago. It was terrible. I knew one of those killed. Frau Schroeder owned the nursery only four blocks from our house. We talked many times . . . it is hard to believe that in Berlin such things could happen. The papers said it had to do with drugs."

Lars snickered. "The story in the papers was a cover. One of my investigative reporters found out from a police source that those killed were somehow involved with the Stasi. It has been impossible to get the truth from the police, for the cases are being handled by the Federal Republic's special investigation service. It is the biggest story in years, and we can't touch it. Chancellor Kohl called me personally and asked me not to print anything without first getting clearance. He said it was a matter of national security . . . and I believe him."

Axel lowered his head. "I cannot believe Frau Schroeder was involved with the Stasi. She has been here longer than me. . . . There has to be another reason."

Lars glanced at Jake. "Axel believes in people. I do too, but in my business I see everything, and every day my faith in man is shaken. And to think the killings were done with guns. It is unheard of."

"Why are shootings so unusual?" Jake asked. "It happens every day in the States."

"We're not allowed to have guns in Berlin," Axel said. "The occupation laws still apply here."

Lars nodded. "In the Federal Republic we can keep shotguns and rifles in our homes for hunting, but no pistols or automatic weapons of any kind."

Kristina stomped out on the deck and put her hands on her hips. "Do I look like a slave to you? It's not *my* reunion, so why am I doing all the work?"

Axel exchanged a glance with Jake. "And you like that woman?"

Jake chuckled. "I think she looks great when she's mad. With a little more training, she'll be a super galley slave."

Axel exchanged a glance with Lars and winked.

The black four-door Lada stopped by the curb and the two men waiting on the sidewalk stepped forward. One opened the door and the other leaned over to speak to the passenger. "Direktor Wolf, will you please follow me."

Wolf was not surprised by the call he had received late that afternoon, although he was surprised at how late the meeting was to take place. It was only a few minutes before midnight. His escorts led him up the stairs and into the back entrance of the Palace of the Republic, down the marbled hallway and into a waiting room. He waited only a few seconds before the side door opened and a thin, long-nosed man motioned him inside, then left, shutting the door behind him. Wolf approached the desk where the pallid General Secretary sat looking as if he had aged twenty years since Wolf had seen him on television that morning.

Erich Honecker moved his glazed eyes toward the visitor and spoke in an anguished whisper. "He told me to resign."

Wolf sat down without being told. Honecker unfolded his hands and looked at them as if they were soiled. "I sat there listening to a man I thought I knew. He said things to me that I didn't believe were possible from a leader of the Soviet Union. He talked about world peace and an end to the cold war . . . and he told me to resign . . . *me*! The Russian bastard told me to resign for the good of my . . . *my country*!"

Wolf saw the drool forming on the gray man's lower lip, but remained silent.

Honecker rose and shook his head. "I will not do it! I am the last hope for a true socialist state! My people will follow me . . . they will support me. We will show the Soviet Union we don't need them. We can begin programs immediately to expand trade with the West and . . ."

Wolf did not move a muscle or blink an eye. The gray man ranting before him was a mere shell, an empty container trying to regain strength, not with substance, but with words, air. He went on about crackdowns, tightening controls, increasing the size of the police and internal security units. He rambled on about reorganization, streamlining, and restructuring, more air.

Exhausted, Honecker finally sat down and lifted his dead eyes to Wolf. "You can put these programs into effect immediately, can't you?"

Wolf nodded without a change of expression. "I am a loyal servant, Herr General Secretary."

The small man managed a weak smile. "Yes, together we can hold this country together. We . . . we have worked for forty years to build our state into what it is today. We can be proud."

Wolf rose, bowed his head to his leader, and walked out of the opulent room.

Twenty minutes later he was back in his office, where Rink sat waiting.

"What did he say?" Rink asked.

Wolf thought for a moment before answering honestly. "Nothing."

CHAPTER 30

Monday, 9 October

Wolf's secretary met her boss at the office door. "Herr Direktor, Herr Mantel has been calling since early this morning. He wanted to see you as soon as you came in. He said it is an urgent matter."

Wolf handed his topcoat to the slim woman. "Bring me a cup of coffee first, then call his office and tell him I am available."

Wolf wondered what could be so urgent. Mantel could not possibly know he was targeted, for Rink was handling the action personally.

The secretary came in with his coffee and set it on the desk. "He is here, Herr Direktor."

Wolf took a sip of the hot liquid and nodded.

Ernst Mantel closed the door behind him and strode toward the desk. He looked worried and held up a copy of *Der Morgen*, a West Berlin paper. "Did you see this?"

"I don't read western papers. I have a staff that does that," Wolf said in annoyance.

"Did they show you this article that came out in the Sunday edition? It mentions you by name."

Wolf felt a wave of nausea as Mantel set the paper in front of him. The quarter-page article was titled WHAT HAPPENED TO THE IRON MEN? He read the first lines and went back forty-five years to the bridge. His emotions raced along a maze of taut, tingling nerves that seemed to terminate in his pounding heart. Hot and flushed, he read the last paragraph before letting the newspaper fall from his hands.

Mantel had never seen Wolf show his emotions before. "I'm . . . I'm sorry, Hagan, I should have told you the paper used your old name."

Wolf didn't hear the apology, for in his relief and joy, he was incapable of hearing or seeing anything but a fuzzy mental picture of that day on the bridge when the surviving Iron Men had challenged him. He had forgotten their names, but the paper had listed them. He closed his eyes for a moment and saw the first captain step forward. "I am Hauptmann Axel Mader, butcher! I am the man who will kill you. . . ."

"And I am Jorn Furman. If Mader doesn't kill you, then I will. . . ."

"Hagan? Hagan, are you all right?" Mantel asked, putting his hand on the director's shoulder. Wolf broke from his reverie and nodded with a distant stare. "Ja, I feel the best I have in years. Thank you, Ernst. I will have a copy of the article made and send the paper back to you. Thank you for bringing it to my attention."

Wolf stood and walked Mantel to the door with his arm over his shoulder. "Thank you again, my friend." He waited until Mantel had gone before turning to his secretary. "Have Max come and see me immediately. I want no interruptions when he enters my office. Reschedule or cancel my appointments and bring me another cup of coffee."

U.S. Mission, West Berlin

Peggy Sue took one look at Kristina and nearly dropped the coffee cup she was holding. "What the heck happened to you?"

Kristina glanced with bloodshot eyes at her friend. "Come on, I'll tell you."

Peggy Sue frowned. "Hold it. You need to go visit the ladies' room before anyone sees you. Your blouse is inside out. My God, you look like you just got up. You'd better brush your hair too."

Kristina showed no embarrassment or surprise. She merely turned around and walked out of the office, as if in a stupor. Peggy Sue shook her head and followed her.

"What's happened?" she said when she caught up to her in the hallway.

"I've been up all night answering phone calls from family members of Papa's old army unit. They read Papa's article and called to thank him."

Kristina pushed through the powder room door and walked to

the sink. Turning on the water, she splashed her face and looked at Peggy Sue's reflection in the big mirror. "I was wrong about Papa's article. You should have heard the people I talked to. They were so . . . so thankful, and yet it was very sad. They broke my heart."

"What about your father, didn't he talk to them?"

Kristina began unbuttoning her blouse. "Yes, he and Lars, his friend, talked all Sunday morning from about seven in the morning till late in the afternoon, when Papa had to take Lars to the airport."

"How'd they get your number?" Peggy Sue asked.

"The last two paragraphs of the article has Papa's and Lars's telephone numbers so that members of the family could call about the reunion this coming Saturday."

Peggy Sue gave Kristina a quick inspection. "You look presentable now. I think if I were you, I'd get sick at lunchtime and go home and get some sleep. You'll never make it the whole day. Oh, did you tell Colonel Tallon about his father?"

Kristina put her brush in her purse. "Not yet. I told Papa, and we're doing something special to make the surprise even better."

"What?"

Kristina smiled for the first time. "It's a secret. I'll tell you next week when it's done."

Max Rink looked up after reading the article and raised an eyebrow. "All of them in one place. It couldn't be more perfect."

Wolf's eyes were glazed as he paced in front of the large office window. "I want your best on it. There isn't much time. The ceremony is Saturday morning at Gatow. Everything you need to know is in the paper. I don't care how it's done or who else is in the way, I just want it done. The border fence is only a kilometer away from the ceremony, and I plan to be there to hear it when it happens."

Jake Tallon held up his notepad as he addressed the task-force teams. "Okay, I'll try and summarize what I've heard. Interrupt me if I screw up. First, second, fourth, and fifth directorates are good-to-go. We need fieldwork in third and sixth directorates only. The third has one man, and the sixth has two men. That makes a total of three surveillance subjects."

Dr. Higgins raised his hand. "I don't think it's necessary to put a team on the subject in the sixth directorate. He is only the head of the department of administration for the propaganda directorate. We have a good photo of his house, and we know he's married. I think that's sufficient information for his folder. We were truly unable to determine the status of the other two, so they should have priority."

Jake looked at the other seated men. "Anybody disagree with Doc? . . . Okay, we drop him and go with what we've got. That's it, then. Two subjects. I'll see you tomorrow morning. I'll assign missions and brief you on the equipment and rules then. Good job."

Five minutes later Jake was in his office with Washington and Dr. Higgins. Washington was taping a piece of butcher paper to the wall. Two subjects and their homes were glued to the paper. "Piece 'a cake," he said. "We sure as hell don't need the whole task force for this little bit of work."

Jake sat down behind his desk. "Agreed." He shifted his gaze to Dr. Higgins. "Doc, I think—"

"I know," Higgins said, lifting his hand in submission. "I'm not going to be needed. You don't have to worry, I prefer to stick to my theories and studies anyway. I was never very good with a camera. I'll tell our consultant to make plans for leaving tomorrow."

Jake stood and held out his hand. "Doc, it was good working with a pro. You can be very proud. It was you that broke the code for us."

Higgins nodded as he shook Jake's hand. "It's been fun." He smiled and turned to Washington. "Sandy, you've taught me a very important lesson. Always look for the man who puts the shit paper in the latrines . . . he is the true boss."

Washington laughed as he pumped the doctor's hand. "Yeah, Doc, you got it. You *did* learn something."

Jake sat down again when the doctor left and shut the door. He looked at Washington and sighed. "Who else we gonna drop off the task force?"

The black Porsche rolled to a stop in front of the guard shack at the gate of Gatow Air Base. The RMP walked to the driver side. "ID please, ma'am." The blond woman took the British dependent's identity card from her purse and held it up for the guard to see.

The guard had never seen the attractive woman before on the base. The card said she was the wife of a retired colonel. "What would be your business here at Gatow, Mrs. Warrenton?"

The woman held up a paper clipping and spoke with a slight accent. "I drove up from Hanover to see my parents and to see where this reunion ceremony will be held. My husband is now an historian and will be flying in on Saturday morning to interview some of the men who survived. I hoped to find out exactly where the ceremony will be held, because my husband will be on a very tight schedule."

The guard gave the card back. "You had better be coming early on Saturday, then, ma'am. We are expectin' quite a crowd." He pointed to the intersection just past the shack and gave her directions to the hangar where the ceremony would take place. "Drive carefully, ma'am," he said when he had finished.

"Thank you, I shan't be long," she replied, and rolled the car forward.

CHAPTER 31

Friday, 13 October

In the chill of the early morning, Ida Furman's breath formed long, white vapor clouds as she carried crates filled with flowers to Der Panzer. Her hands were numb from the cold and her joints were aching as she picked up the last crate. In the east the horizon burst in a dazzling display of red, then red-orange light. She stood watching and shivering as the tip of the sun rose higher and the colors became softly muted. The sunrise somehow made her discomfort worthwhile. She tossed the crate, which contained twelve mums, into the tailgate. Jorn stacked it carefully before climbing down, his sweat-soaked shirt exposed to the frigid air. He shut the tailgate and made sure his collapsed wheelchair was securely tied down.

"Put this on, Jorn, before you catch your death," his wife said, and tossed him his light red wool jacket.

He slung it over his shoulder. "What would I do without you worrying about me?"

Ida leaned down and kissed his glistening forehead. "You'd probably think something was wrong if I didn't act like an old hen." She walked with her husband as he propelled himself on his gloved hands toward the cab. Opening the door for him, she saw his walking bag on the passenger floor and frowned. "No walking today," she said as he climbed up into the seat. "You will have had enough exercise after this day is done."

Jorn leaned out, kissing his wife's cheek. "Do I hear the hen clucking again? I love you, I'll be home before five."

Twenty minutes later Jorn backed the truck up to the loading dock of the distribution warehouse. He opened the door, climbed down, and propelled himself toward the ramp. At the top of the ramp the foreman stepped out of the office and motioned for him to come inside.

Jorn's friend, from behind his desk, held out a newspaper toward him.

Jorn could see it was the West Berlin *Der Morgen*, and waved the offer away. "I told you, I think they are dangerous."

The foreman flipped through the pages and walked around the desk. "I got this three days ago, but I've been keeping it for you. There is an article in here that caught my eye. I read it thinking it could not be about a man I know, for it says the man died. I think you should read it."

Jorn reluctantly took the paper and glanced at the page. When his eyes caught the title, he suddenly felt hollow. Trembling, he forced himself to read on.

Tears rolled down his cheeks as he looked up at the foreman after rereading the article for the third time.

The foreman lowered his head. "You don't have to explain anything to me, Jorn. I just wanted you to know. Keep the paper." He walked to the door. "Your kameraden must have cared for you very much. You're lucky to have such friends." The foreman strode out to the dock to begin loading.

Jorn wiped the tears away with the back of his hand. He thought of Helga, his first wife, whom he could still see in his mind waving good-bye at the train station that last time. Slowly the image faded, and he saw Ida smiling at him as he left that morning. No regrets, he said to himself, and straightened his back. No regrets. He turned around, pushed himself to the dock and looked to the west. He couldn't help but smile, knowing his two old friends were still alive and prospering. "The Iron Men," he said to himself. "I have missed you too, my friends. Thank you for remembering me and our kameraden. I have always remembered you . . . always."

Hagan Wolf glanced at his watch then over to Rink. "We have security on the flower shop and eyes to follow my guardian angel?"

"Everything is arranged," Rink said. "Our people at the airport saw him arrive with the delegation from Moscow this morning and followed them to the Hotel Stadt Berliner. He and the others checked in, put away their bags, and called the Soviet Embassy. They were picked up an hour ago and are in the embassy now. My people will call Operations when he walks out of the embassy, to ensure he isn't followed."

Wolf nodded. "He should be pleased with what he hears from his ambassador. Minister Mielke called last night, sounding very distraught. He told me Honecker is resigning for 'health' reasons. Egon Krenz is going to be voted in as new General Secretary when the Central Committee meets to accept Honecker's resignation."

Rink's eyes widened. "Krenz? He's Honecker's protégé. The people will never accept him."

Wolf raised an eyebrow. "It's just a temporary change to give the government time to clean up its loose ends, as we have done. Krenz won't be able to crack down on the reformers and marchers. They will increase in number until they force the government to fall. What that means to us is, we must distance ourselves from this temporary government. Find out who the new liberal leaders are and put surveillance on them. We need to start now so we'll know who we will be dealing with when they eventually come to power." Wolf swiveled his chair and looked out the window. "Does Mink have everything that is required?"

Rink nodded. "The equipment she requested was delivered last night by boat. We had a slight setback in our time schedule because our receiving teams were under the control of one of the den chiefs who was retired. I had to make arrangements with one of our maintenance teams to perform the duty. Mink sent word this morning that the targets will be hit during the early part of the ceremony. I suggest you be at the border to listen at ten."

Wolf leaned back with a satisfied smile.

Jorn Furman rolled the money tightly and secured it with a rubber band, then unscrewed the metal cap of his hollow wheelchair armrest. He placed the money inside and replaced the cap.

The buyer watched the procedure with a smile of admiration. "I see you are taking my advice. Have you had a run-in with the Stasi yet?"

"No, but I've seen them, and you were right, they are easy to spot. I'm sorry that you haven't been able to leave for Hungary as you had planned, but if the marches get any bigger, the government won't last much longer anyway. You'll be able to watch with me and begin rebuilding sooner than you think."

The buyer pointed to the bruise on the side of his neck. "I'm not watching, old man. I marched in the demonstration in Leipzig on Monday. There were fifty thousand of us. Fifty thousand leaders chanting for democracy. I didn't get this bruise from a Vopo's club. It was from an old woman hugging my neck so hard I thought she was going to break it. Jorn, it's happening. The people are rising up, and the Vopos and Stasi bastards can't do a damn thing about it. There are too many of us. We're marching again, but this time it's going to be here in East Berlin. Join us. Learn how wonderful it is to feel like a real man again."

Jorn smiled and looked down at his stumps. "How about half of a real man? I'll think about it. Take care, my friend, and I'll see you next week."

The buyer shook his head. "No, I'm finished black-marketing. My wife is about to have our baby, and I can't take any more chances. This is good-bye, Jorn. I wish you happiness and freedom very soon."

Jorn shook hands with him. "I have always loved the word 'freedom.' Good-bye my friend. I wish you and your family 'freedom' too. Auf Wiedersehen."

Minutes later Jorn turned the Panzer off Friedrichstrasse onto Unter den Linden to make his first delivery to the flower store on the corner only three blocks away.

As Jorn Furman made the turn, General Georgi Sorokin walked into the flower shop at exactly one minute before twelve noon and browsed among the potted ivy for several seconds as an excuse to check the customers. Besides the store manager behind the counter, there was only a woman, with her small child, picking out cut flowers for an arrangement. Sorokin walked past the counter and pushed back the curtains to enter the back storage room.

One minute later Wolf strolled into the shop and stepped out of the way of the customer and her daughter. They left with a bouquet of white and yellow mums.

The young manager cut her eyes to the back room. When Wolf had disappeared through the curtain, the manager turned the sign around on the door.

Jorn turned right off Unter den Linden and made an immediate left into an alley that served as the unloading area for the flower shop. He was about to unstrap his boots when his cab door was opened and a man standing below him barked, "Move on!"

Jorn was shocked more than angered. It took him a moment to recover and realize it was probably another deliveryman. Jorn motioned to the back of the truck. "I'm delivering flowers. If you want to come into the alley, I'll back out and let you in."

A second man, wearing a blue nylon jacket, walked up and stared at Jorn as if he were a piece of rancid meat. Then he stepped up on the running board and inspected inside the cab with his eyes. Jorn knew at that moment the men were Stasi. No one else would issue commands so arrogantly, and no one else would be wearing a shoulder holster, which Jorn could clearly see as the man bent over to look under the seat.

The security man stood back, erect, and patted Jorn's chest then sides. "Delivering flowers, is that what you said?"

"Ask Emma inside about me," Jorn said confidently. "Tell her it's Herr Furman from the Seelow nursery. . . . She is expecting the delivery."

Hearing the name Emma changed the security agent's expression. "Wait here and don't move. I'll check." He stepped down from the running board and spoke to his partner, who had just lowered the tailgate. "Heinz, watch him. I'm going to talk to Emma."

Minutes that seemed like hours passed before the blue-jacketed agent appeared and waved Jorn down from the cab. "You can unload, but don't use the back door. You'll have to go through the front."

Both men stepped back and were shocked to see the old man unstrap his boots and leave his lower legs in the truck. They both exchanged glances that said they knew they had wasted their time. A cripple was no threat. They separated and went back to their watch positions.

Minutes later Jorn had lowered four boxes of yellow mums, his wheelchair, a dolly, and himself by rope to the ground. Stacking the crates of flowers on the dolly and folding out his wheelchair, he was now ready to begin the shuttling. He would have to make two more trips to finish the delivery. Inserting the dolly handles into the specially designed arms attached to the wheelchair frame, he climbed into the chair and began rolling toward the door. Years of practice made the routine easy for him. The dolly rolled behind his chair like a wagon.

Emma waited and held the door open. "I'm sorry about this, Herr Furman, but the back room is being used right now. Just stack the boxes by the counter, and I'll move them into the storeroom later."

Jorn looked over his shoulder, then motioned the young store manager closer. "Are you in trouble with the Stasi?" he whispered.

The woman smiled as if he had told a joke and backed up. "Nein, they are just checking around for black marketeers. Don't worry about it."

Jorn nodded, presuming that the Stasi must be watching her store for illegal deliveries of flowers. He was lucky. His next delivery was to a store that did just that—took his flowers and sold them to the West for hard currency. He told himself he would drive around the next store a few times to make sure the Stasi weren't watching there as well. He rolled to a stop by the counter and climbed down to start work.

"I knew you had destroyed my file years ago, so I had nothing to worry about. You've taken very good care of me," Wolf said with a smile.

Sorokin nodded reflectively. "We've made a good team, Wolf. We have done all we could for our two countries. It's time we let the younger men take over with this new world order they speak of. We have been fighting the secret war for too long. They think they will bring an end to the cold war, but you and I know there is no such thing as an end to our kind of fighting. The goals will change but the result will be the same. Somebody will have to do the job that our leaders have performed to ensure survival of the nation."

Wolf leaned forward in his chair. "Georgi, we are going to build an even better organization than before. We have cleaned our house and stand ready to help the new government when called upon. With your help, you will be able to convince the new leaders that we—" He stopped in mid-sentence, seeing the discomfort in Sorokin's face. "What's wrong?"

Sorokin lowered his head for a moment, as if gathering strength. He looked back at Wolf, grabbing his eyes. "You will not be working for the new government. You'll be working for us . . . temporarily. We want you to turn over your organization to a new director, who has already been chosen. My government cannot afford the loss of the critical information that only you can provide. Your informers in the high-technology European corporations are much too valuable to us. We need them for our survival."

Wolf sat upright, his eyes burning through Sorokin's forehead. "*Your* government is telling me what I must do?"

Sorokin met Wolf's glare. "Hagan, you must hand off your organization to a new director. He is a young man in your Ministry of Trade untainted by the old regime. It has been arranged."

Wolf's jaw muscles rippled. "My file wasn't destroyed, was it?"

"It will be . . . in December, once the handoff is completed," Sokorin said, feeling the heat from Wolf's burning stare. "Don't feel betrayed. You weren't. The world we knew has changed in just months. My government is only doing what is necessary to survive.

Compromises and agreements have been made that I never would have dreamed possible. I've taken care of you, my friend. Your past with the SD and activities with the S Direktorate will be erased. Your name has already been removed from the Wanted Books in the West. Arrangements have been made for Minister Mielke to accept responsibility for any activities that may in the future be deemed illegal. Your name will never be mentioned. You may retire in peace and emigrate wherever you desire. We guarantee your—"

"Bastard," Wolf hissed. "You've made a deal with the Federal Republic, haven't you?"

Sorokin's stare wavered.

Wolf snickered with contempt. "Anything to ensure the survival of your country . . . I should have known. We're dying, bled dry by your fucking parasitic country, and now you need another host. The Federal Republic, Georgi? The fucking Federal Republic? What kind of deal have you made? What are you afraid of that makes you deal with—" Wolf stopped, a tight smile slowly playing across his lips. "Of course. Your biggest fear. Reunification! One Germany. You know we will ultimately reunify!"

Sorokin raised his head to speak, but Wolf cut him off with a sardonic laugh. "There's nothing you can do about it, is there? Your great General Secretary tried to open the floodgate to reduce the pressure, but he was too late. The dam burst beneath his feet. He's drowning and grabbing for anything to try and save himself."

"You think you could reunify without our approval?" Sorokin snapped back. "We occupy your country, Herr Direktor. We still 'protect' you."

Wolf slowly shook his head, keeping his icy stare. "It's over. You know it. You can't stop reunification, you can only delay it. What deals have you made, Georgi? What are you getting from the Federal Republic to allow them to take us over? Guarantees, loans, grants, what . . . *what?*"

Sorokin sighed. "After all these years . . . and this is what I get in return? Your distrust?"

Wolf leaned forward menacingly. "You *got* forty-three years of security for Mother Russia. What was the deal, Georgi? What have you traded to ensure your 'survival'?"

Sorokin's eyes locked with Wolf's. "You."

Wolf's face lost its color. Sorokin raised an eyebrow. "You and your organization are part of the deal. You're right, we can't stop the reunification, but it could take years . . . and your brothers in the West are impatient. They want it now. We will give it to them . . . for a price. They are not different from us. They too are concerned about their future. They know where the next war will be fought—in the world market. Survival will not depend on armies, it will depend on the production of goods that the people will buy. The old war is over, but the new one is beginning. It will require a new kind of S Direktorate to meet the challenge." Sorokin smiled cruelly. "I'm still your protector, Hagan. We have offered your West German brothers a secure economic future. With the agents you have placed in high-technology corporations all over Europe, the Federal Republic will get all it needs to keep at the forefront of the race for markets. But, of course, it will be a cooperative effort. Russia has the raw materials, West Germany has the production capability. A perfect marriage. You have underestimated yourself. You are one of the greatest soldiers that has ever fought in the secret war. The organization you built is the best in the world. Your country will prosper and grow because of what you leave behind. It is a true legacy. What more could a man ask than to help his country become a world economic power and once again achieve greatness?"

Wolf's face became stoic. "It never changes, does it, Georgi? The leaders and governments change, but we soldiers still remain mired in the filth."

Sorokin stood. "Your fight will soon be over, my friend. You and Dagmar can live the rest of your lives in peace and with honor. I will contact you next week so you can meet the new director and our new western counterpart."

Wolf rose, maintaining the same stoic expression. "I will make the necessary arrangements."

Sorokin offered his hand, but Wolf turned his back. Sorokin lowered his arm and turned for the door in silence.

Jorn Furman dropped down from his wheelchair and picked up the top box of flowers from the last dolly load. He set the box on the floor and, out of the corner of his eye, caught the movement of the curtains behind the counter. He turned just as a thin, old man wearing glasses walked out. Jorn thought it strange, for he hadn't seen the man enter and knew he wasn't an employee. Probably some kind of inspector, he thought as he picked up the next box. He was about to put the flower crate on top of the other when a tall, silver-haired, regal-looking man pushed the curtain aside and strode out of the back room.

The store manager was waiting and handed him a bouquet of flowers. "For Frau Wolf, Herr Direktor. I hope she enjoys them."

Jorn's heart and body froze stone-cold, for he had seen that arrogant face a thousand times in his dreams. He blinked, thinking his eyes were deceiving him. Then the tall man looked directly at him, only for a moment, but long enough for Jorn to see the piercing blue eyes. Jorn knew then it wasn't someone who looked like the bastard—it was him! The blue-eyed monster who had killed his men in his nightmares over and over again for forty-four years was standing only two meters from him. The Butcher, Horst Volker, was alive!

Wolf had taken the flowers and glanced to his left, having caught a movement out of the corner of his eye. He'd been surprised to see a filthy old man kneeling on the floor and holding a crate of flowers. He made a mental note to talk to Max about his security team and started for the door, but he bumped into the side of a wheelchair. He sidestepped the obstacle and glanced over his shoulder, then realized that the old man was not kneeling, but was rather a pathetic double amputee, standing on stubs encased in leather cups. He felt a chill, for the cripple had pierced him with a strange stare.

Jorn shook with pent-up rage and propelled himself toward the blue-eyed monster, but the young woman stepped in front him. "Herr Furman, aren't we going to do a joint count of your delivery?"

Wolf stood next to the curb and ran his hand through his silver hair, signaling that he wanted to be picked up. He looked over his shoulder again, upset that security had allowed a delivery during the important meeting. The amputee was obviously harmless, but it was a breach nevertheless. His thoughts turned back to Sorokin and his eyes began to blaze.

Furman brushed past the woman and had to shove the dolly out of his path. Lowering his head and thrusting his arms out, he shot forward and made it to the entrance just as the Butcher got into a black Lada sedan and shut the back door.

Jorn faced the wide-eyed manager and growled, "What was that bastard doing here?"

The frightened woman backed up. "Jorn, stop looking at me that way. You're scaring me."

Jorn began to move toward her when his shoulder was grasped from behind.

"What are you doing to scare Emma?"

Jorn turned and looked into the face of the agent wearing the blue nylon jacket. Jorn screamed inside himself that he must regain control and survive. He widened his eyes and yelled up at the man. *"I'm not a freak! I hate it when people look at me like I'm a freak!"*

Surprised by the outburst, the agent backed away, holding up his hands. "Take it easy, old man. Take it easy and relax, nobody is calling you names." The agent glanced over at the woman. "What was he doing to scare you?"

The woman stared at Jorn as if he had gone mad. "He was looking at me like a wild animal, and called the direktor a bastard and wanted to know why he was here."

Jorn growled, pointing at the woman. "She's looking at me like a freak, just like that tall bastard did. They're all bastards! I can't stand that look! *I'm not a freak!*" Then, mumbling incoherently, Jorn slowly began shoving himself to his chair, shaking his head side to side.

The agent looked at the woman for her opinion. She rolled her eyes, pointed a finger toward the side of her head and moved it around.

The security agent agreed with a nod. He followed Jorn to his chair and picked up the dolly for him, sliding the handles into the metal loops. "You feeling better now? You calmed down enough to drive?"

Jorn lowered his head. "I . . . I'm sorry . . . I just can't take it. . . . I can't take the stares." Jorn looked up at the agent. "You're not one of them. You have good eyes."

The agent nodded with exasperation. "Ja, I'm a good eye man. Go on now, it's lunchtime, you must be hungry. Go on and get yourself something to eat."

The agent took out a few coins and put them into the chest pocket of Jorn's jacket. "Drink a few beers and take it easy."

Jorn smiled crookedly, widened his eyes and bobbed his head as he pushed himself toward the door. "Ja, ja, a beer, two beers." Once out of the place, he pushed faster, knowing he had barely saved himself. When he'd seen Volker, something inside him had snapped. He'd lost total control of his emotions. The crazy act had saved him from his own stupidity, but for how long? he asked himself. Had the Butcher recognized him?

Jorn hurried into the truck and quickly backed out of the alley and onto the street. He went over the events in his mind as he turned down Unter den Linden, trying to put distance between himself and the store. He had driven only three blocks before abruptly pulling the truck to the curb. Emma knew Volker; and she had called him "Direktor." The security agents, the big car—they were all Stasi! Volker was a director in the Stasi! Mein Gott, what if he *did* recognize me? Ida!

Jorn slapped the gear into first and pulled back onto the road. He and Ida had to get out of the country as fast as possible. There was no choice now. But first there was one thing left that had to be done.

Wolf slammed the door to his office. Rink was there waiting for him.

Wolf walked to his chair but didn't sit down. He had sat in that old chair as the S direktor for over half his life. The leather was worn paper-thin on the arms and the seat . . . but it was still comfortable and served its purpose. His secretary had tried to replace it, insisting it was worn-out and unfit for the office, but like him, it was still functional.

Now he sat down in the old chair, listening to it creak. It was a sound he had learned to love. He snarled and pounded the desk. "Fuck the Russians, I'm staying."

Rink sat down, unsure if he should nod or shake his head. Wolf's eyes shifted to him coldly. "First, your security team at the flower store violated procedure. They let an old man, a double amputee, in to deliver flowers during the meeting. Pick him up. I want him checked to see if he heard anything. Second, I want that security team made an example of. Third, my mentor wants us to turn over our high-tech assets to a stooge *he* has selected as my replacement. The Russians have made a deal with the Federal Republic to 'share' our information. We are going to show the Russians who they are dealing with." Wolf stood. "Now get out and take care of points one and two. Think about the third and come back in ten minutes. We have work to do and not much time."

Jorn Furman was waiting impatiently at a light on the outskirts of the city. It would take at least an hour to get back to Seelow and another thirty to forty minutes to pack what they needed for the drive to Czechoslovakia and freedom. He knew the border points were closed, but unlike the East German border into the West, there was no wall along the Czech border. He would find a way, the Panzer didn't need roads, he would go cross-country. "Freedom," he said to himself again. *Freedom!*

The operations officer of the S Direktorate tore off the pink mission slip from the pad and walked into the ready room where two special action teams sat watching television. He held the note up. "Who's up?"

A heavyset man half asleep on the couch folded back his eyelids and slowly stood. "Me and Arno."

The ops officer handed the agent the pink paper. "This is a routine pickup, Reich. Get over to the flower shop on Unter den Linden—the address is on the sheet—and talk to Fräulein Emma Stammer. She's our people, so be polite for a change. She will give you a description of the subject and an address where he can be found. Our deputy director wants to talk to him personally, so make it fast."

The agent's eyes opened wider, and he threw back his shoulders, straightening up. "Goddamnit, why didn't you say it was important in the first place?" He snatched the paper from the smiling operations officer and glanced at his partner, who was already standing by the door. "I'll drive, you navigate. And don't get us fucking lost like last time!"

Max Rink listened and his face flushed. He waited until Wolf finished telling him everything Sorokin had said at the meeting before shaking his head. "The KGB would terminate us as soon as we turned over our information. We would be loose ends."

Wolf shook his head. "No, we think that way, but they don't. They'd fear we had kept something back and wait until our informants began providing information. And then, ja, they would retire us. It doesn't matter. We will turn nothing over. If the West Germans want what we have, then they will get it from only us. Nothing will change except for the location of base of operations, and we will be protected by the same government that has tried to destroy us for so many years. Ironic, isn't it?"

Rink leaned back in his chair, thinking aloud. "We would only need to be a very small cell. No need for more than twenty, maybe thirty trusted employees. The den chiefs would remain invisible and . . . we will have to resurrect the den in West Berlin that had infiltrated Siemens Corporation. It can be done. I still know of at least two pack leaders." His eyes suddenly focused and he looked at Wolf. "We must be very careful. They will never trust us."

Wolf nodded. "Ja, and that is why it will work. We will never trust them."

The manager of the flower store glared at the fat team leader who was leaning against the counter and looking her over as if she were undressed. "His name is Jorn Furman, he's in his sixties, and he's crippled. No legs from the knees down. He lives in Seelow, about seventy kilometers east of here on Highway One. I don't know where the collective nursery is in Seelow, but I'll call the district agriculture office and have them meet you at the entrance of the town with his address. . . . Watch him, he acted crazy today. And stop looking at me that way! I don't appreciate it."

The special action team leader sighed and glanced at his young muscular partner. "Arno, you think you can handle an old cripple? I'll drive and you direct me to this Seelow. This shouldn't take long. I want to get back and talk about flowers to this lovely Fräulein."

The woman shifted her unsmiling eyes to Arno. "Get him out of here before I stick a 'flower' up his big ass."

The team leader pushed off of the counter. "I'll be back, flower lady. Keep it nice and warm for old Reich. He likes them hot."

The woman shook her head in revulsion, wondering how such a man had been promoted to team leader. Jorn Furman may have been crazy, but the special agent wasn't that far behind him.

Jorn slapped the steering wheel, seeing the line of cars stopped ahead on the highway. He had just passed through Muncheberg, only eighteen kilometers from Seelow, when he had to slow down because of a traffic backup. He rolled the Panzer to a complete stop behind a dirty yellow Trabant. Not now! he thought in anguish. Please not now!

Ten agonizing minutes later, the cars began to move again. Two Trabants up ahead had collided and had finally been pushed out of the way. Jorn didn't look inside the cars as he passed for he knew when the poorly made fragile cars were involved in accidents the passengers were almost always killed or maimed horribly. The pressed board bodies of the death traps splintered and always impaled the trapped occupants.

When Jorn finally reached open road, he sighed in relief. He drove for five more kilometers before turning off to make the one necessary stop before going home. Turning off the engine, he climbed down and propelled himself toward the warehouse ramp.

"Jorn, what brings you back?" the surprised foreman asked, looking up from his deck.

Jorn took the paper the foreman had given him that morning from his belt and tossed it onto the desk. He picked up a pad of paper and pencil and spoke quickly as he wrote a note. "I am in trouble. I am leaving the country as soon as I get home and pack. You have been a good friend, and I need one last favor from you."

Jorn paused from his writing and looked up. "I must get this message to West Berlin to the man whose name and telephone number is in the paper. Axel Mader. You said you knew someone who often went to the West on business. Can you have him please call my old friend and read him this note for me? It is very important."

"What kind of trouble, Jorn? And what is this about leaving? What has happened?"

Jorn finished writing, ripped off the top page of the pad and folded it. "I have no time to explain. The Stasi is after me. I am a dead man if I stay. It has to do with the article. Believe me, please. Take the note and make sure it is sent. I beg you."

"Mein Gott, Jorn, of course I'll help you in any way I can. But what about money? I have some money and a few contacts, I—"

Jorn thrust the note out to him. "Just this, my friend. It is enough."

The foreman took the paper. "I'll make sure. I'll miss you and I'll pray that one day you can return."

Unable to speak, Jorn grabbed the foreman's hand and kissed it. He spun around, thrust out his hands to the concrete and shoved himself toward the open door.

Jorn slowed the truck upon reaching the hedge and held his breath until he drove past the driveway and looked past the barren apple trees to the distant house. He nearly wept with joy and relief when he saw that the curtains in the front windows were all open. His gnawing fear had been that the Stasi had called ahead to their district office and sent men who would be waiting in the house. He braked and backed the Panzer up until he was once again past the driveway, then put the gear back into first. He sped up and drove up the long path toward the house, honking the horn.

Ida heard the noise and put down the bread dough she had been kneading. As she stepped out onto the porch, she saw her husband climbing up to the tailgate. He disappeared inside the covered truck bed, and seconds later a crate of flowers flew out the back and crashed to the ground. Shocked, she stepped off the porch just as another crate sailed through the air.

"Jorn, what are you doing?"

Jorn tossed another crate out and looked down at her. "Pack warm clothes and food for five days. We're leaving in thirty minutes for Czechoslovakia."

"What are you talking about! Moving? What is wrong with you?"

Jorn threw out another crate of flowers before stopping and looking down at her again. "Ida, Volker is alive. I saw him today, he's a Stasi director of some kind and I don't know if he recognized me or not. We can't take the chance."

Ida saw the fear in her husband's eyes and hurried into the house.

The heavy special action team leader glanced at his passenger after passing a car on a curve. "How much farther?"

Arno looked down at the map on his lap. "Fifteen, maybe twenty minutes to Seelow. If we make it! Would you mind slowing down?"

The heavy man grinned and increased his speed.

The district agricultural collective manager strode up to the white sedan and leaned over to talk to the driver. "You just missed the district security team. They drove out to the Furman place to hold him until you arrived."

The team leader glared at the bureaucrat. "Who called the district office? It was to be our pickup."

The manager took a step back from the car to put more distance between himself and the foul breath of the agent. "The woman who called me from the flower shop thought it would be necessary because of the distance you had to travel to get here, but it didn't make any difference. The district team took an hour to respond. They are only several minutes or so ahead of you."

"Where's the house?" the team leader asked impatiently.

The manager pointed down the road and gave them directions. The team leader stomped on the accelerator.

Jorn climbed into the cab and glanced at his watch. He was twenty minutes behind schedule. He strapped on his boots and turned the ignition. "Don't cry, think about being free by tomorrow," he said, patting Ida's hand.

Ida sniffed back her tears and set her shoulders. "I'm ready."

Jorn shifted the truck into first gear and rolled from behind the house onto the long driveway.

"Oh, mein Gott! Noooo!" Ida cried, pointing at the Trabant that was skidding into the driveway and blocking their exit.

Jorn was already accelerating. "Hold on!"

The district Stasi team did not know they had made a mistake in pulling into the tree-lined driveway until they saw the orange truck barreling toward them. With no room to turn around, the frightened driver braked hard, causing the light vehicle to skid at an angle, and threw the car into reverse.

Both men realized at the same time it was too late to back out, and frantically pulled at their door handles to get out of the death trap.

Jorn gritted his teeth and clutched the steering wheel tighter just as the Panzer's heavy bumper, with two tons of steel rolling behind it, tore through the top of the Trabant like a knife through butter. The terrified district agents had only been half out their doors, and ducked down at the last instant, which saved them from decapitation but not death. The force of the heavy truck smashed the body of the tiny car like a sledgehammer hitting an aluminum can and shoved the hulk the entire twenty meters back to the road.

Jorn slapped the gear into reverse and backed up. He stopped only after he was sure the bumper wasn't tangled up with the wreckage. His wife was sobbing.

"It's over, Ida. Lie down on the seat until I check them."

Jorn quickly unstrapped his boots and climbed down. He pushed himself along, unperturbed by the wide trail of dark blood, dust-covered intestines, and oil left on the road. Lying partly out of the wreckage, the driver looked unmarked until Jorn got closer. Then he saw that from the waist down the man was nothing but mangled flesh twisted and entwined with the crushed door and frame. Jorn ignored the pungent odor of death and the bulging, unseeing eyes as he tore off the agent's shoulder holster and put it over his own neck. He looked inside to locate the other man's weapon, but the passenger had ducked back inside the car and had been crushed beneath the dashboard.

Jorn began to turn for the Panzer when he saw the dust cloud signaling another car approaching at a very high rate of speed. He spun around on his stubs and propelled himself as fast as he could for the truck.

The special action team leader's eyes narrowed. In the distance he saw wreckage at the right side of the road and an orange truck backing up, then disappearing from sight. He snarled as he let up on the accelerator. "Looks like trouble."

The blond agent had already pulled out his pistol. He jacked a round into the chamber. "He's just a cripple."

The team leader could see the wreckage more clearly as they got closer. "Tell those district assholes that!" he snapped. He braked hard and skidded the car to a stop alongside the road fifty meters from the driveway. He knew what had to be done. "The wreckage is blocking the driveway. He can't get out without backing up and gaining enough speed to knock it out of the way. The bastard is in his truck, hiding behind the house, waiting for us to pull up so he can knock the wreck into us. Get out and flush him toward the—"

The orange truck burst through the hedges only thirty meters away and came barreling toward the two stunned men.

Jorn Furman had been taught long ago the best defense was attack, and that is exactly what he was doing. He had backed the truck up far enough behind the house to give him room to gain speed. He'd cut across the yard and carrot patch and smashed through the hedges at a speed of thirty-five kilometers.

Yelling to his partner to get out of the car, the team leader, Reich, hurriedly opened the door, jumped out, and pulled his pistol to meet the assault. His panicking partner was still fumbling with his seat belt.

"Get out, fool!" Reich yelled.

His partner freed the belt and shoved the door open. Taking only a step away from the Lada, he jerked his automatic up and began firing at the roaring, oncoming truck, which was almost on top of them.

Jorn screamed in defiance and kept his boot on the accelerator despite the bullet-shattered windshield that had crystallized and blown back, showering him and Ida with glass. He grasped the steering wheel tighter, focusing his attention on the left front fender of the white car as he yelled over the whining engine for his wife to stay down.

The heavy team leader fired his pistol twice at the orange blur before hearing the sickening impact. He snapped off one more shot that hit just behind the passenger side door as the truck righted itself and sped away, leaving him alone in the billowing dust cloud.

Jorn looked into the door mirror, grinning in elation. "We're free, Ida. You can get up."

Trembling, Ida slowly raised her head from the seat and tried to speak but instead coughed up blood.

Reich looked into the grimacing face of his partner. Arno had been struck by the Lada when the truck had knocked it sideways. Both of his legs were lying at odd angles beneath him. The team leader smirked. "You should have stayed in bed this morning." He glanced down the road, about to holster his pistol, but froze. The truck had come to a stop only two hundred meters away.

Ida lay on her side on the seat as Jorn frantically tore at her blood-soaked clothes, trying to find the wound. He pulled back her wool sweater and heavy work shirt. A small bullet hole oozed blood from her lower back. He prayed as he gently rolled her over, knowing he'd only found the entry wound, which couldn't have caused the massive blood loss. As he began to pull up the sticky sweater from over her stomach, she shivered and spoke in a weak, faraway voice. "I'm cold, Jorn, hold me . . . pleeeease hold me."

He quickly pulled the sweater back, exposing her work shirt, which had once been blue but now was a glistening, dark maroon. Shaking uncontrollably, he began unbuttoning her shirt when she weakly raised her hand and stroked his cheek. "I . . . I love you Jorn. I . . . never told you . . . enough."

With tears running down his cheeks, he grasped her hand and leaned forward to kiss her blue lips. "Freedom, Ida . . . think of that word. I'm taking you there."

Her eyelids slowly closed and she softly smiled. "I see it . . . I . . . see. . . ."

Jorn closed his tear-filled eyes and leaned back, still holding her hand to his face, when he heard someone approaching. The huffing team leader jumped up on the running board, leveling the pistol through the open window at the back of Jorn's head. *"Freeze, asshole!"*

His back to the agent, Jorn slowly lowered his wife's hand to his chest, bumping the holstered pistol that hung there.

The agent shoved his automatic inside the cab and jabbed the barrel against the back of Jorn's head. "Raise your hands where I can see them. *Now, shithead!"*

Jorn released his wife's hand, which fell to his lap, and slowly raised both hands.

"You fucking idiot," the agent snarled, "did you really think you could get away from us? Don't move a fucking muscle."

Reich withdrew the pistol from the open window and grasped the handle of the cab door. As soon as he pushed the handle down, Jorn flung himself backward into the door. The team leader fired as he was knocked back by the blow, but the bullet went high, striking the inside top of the cab. The agent grunted in pain as first his buttocks, then his head hit the road. Jorn grasped the doorframe to stop his own fall, then quickly pulled himself inside and yanked the pistol free from the holster.

The stunned agent lay helpless in the road, for the shooting pain in his back and head was so intense he was blacking in and out of consciousness.

Jorn screamed in rage as he aimed at the groaning man's head and pressed the trigger. Nothing happened. He pressed again, but still nothing happened. He jacked a round into the chamber, flicked off the thumb safety and raised the weapon again. He fired once and missed. He fired again and hit the agent's earlobe. Grasping his shaking hand with the other hand, he fired again and again, to try and ease the agony that boiled inside him, and again, to bring Ida back somehow, and again, wanting to see the faceless bastard jerk, and again, and again, and again.

Twenty minutes and fifteen kilometers past Seelow, heading west, Jorn turned the clanking, smoking truck off Highway One and onto a logging path for fifty meters into a meadow surrounded by oaks and pines. He turned off the engine and looked at the gray face of the woman lying on the seat. He gently patted her shoulder. "Sleep well, the forest will protect you."

Jorn unstrapped his boots for the last time and leaned over to pick up his walking pack from the blood-jelled floor. The setting sun was about to disappear below the treetops. He climbed out of the truck, put on the pack, and looked back once. Tears rolled down his cheeks as he bid his Ida a final farewell. "I have to go now, the Iron Men are waiting. . . . I—I will miss you."

Jorn took in a deep breath and promised himself no more tears until it was over. Then he continued west, toward Berlin.

Wolf slammed the car door and strode straight toward the entrance and down the basement steps into the hallway. He passed the operations room and turned into the planning room where Rink was waiting with a sullen scowl.

Rink motioned irritably toward a cloth divider that he'd used to pin up a map. "I have questioned everyone involved. The best source was the manager of the flower shop. She had provided the information to our team. The cripple's name was Jorn Furman. Yes, the same name as the man in the western newspaper article. Obviously he is not dead and must have recognized you."

Wolf's jaw muscle twitched as he seethed in anger. He had been within four feet of him. He could have had the coward had he only recognized his . . .

"Direktor?" Rink said, seeing his superior wasn't listening. "Herr Direktor, we have every available team looking for him. He can't get far. The borders have all been blocked and the guards briefed on who to look for."

Wolf's eyes slowly focused on Rink and he spoke in a rasping whisper. "I want Furman alive. I will take him with me tomorrow to listen to his friends die. I want to see his face when he hears the explosion."

Feeling a chill run up his spine, Rink motioned to the map. "He can't have gotten far. Our agent in the flower shop says he drives an old orange truck, which should be easy to identify. We'll find him. How far can a cripple go?"

Mink stroked the small cylindrical blasting cap a final time before gently pushing it into the vagina of plastique she had formed to accept it. Smiling, she closed the pliable lips around the shaft and ran her hand up the firing wire to the shunted end. The lovers were sleeping, she told herself as she slowly, soundlessly, coiled the wire so as not to disturb them. She stood and stepped back to admire her work. It was one of her best, a masterpiece that combined male simplicity with female complexity into a single instrument of destruction. Soon the male part would wake and its desire would demand release. The female part would give it to him. She would give it to them all. She would give them death.

CHAPTER 32

Saturday, 14 October,
Hangelsberg Forest, East Germany

Jorn Furman awoke with a start at the sound of a helicopter flying overhead toward the east. Telling himself he had to keep moving, he rose up stiffly from under the rotted log where he had burrowed himself. After marching most of the night, he had slept for only a few hours. Sleep wasn't as important as distance. The farther away he got from the truck, the better his chances would be. Despite the cold, he took off his red wool jacket because an aircraft spotter would easily see the color in the daylight. Most of the leaves were gone from the hardwood trees, and there weren't enough pines deep within the forest to cover his movement. He rubbed dirt into the material until it was dark reddish-brown, then put the jacket back on and began to reach for his pack. He stopped as he noticed the unaccustomed weight of the pistol on his hip. The simple reminder caused him to look up and scan the immediate area around him. He was no longer a nursery collective manager, he told himself, but rather a soldier, and he had to follow the proper procedures. They were the same procedures he had drilled into his men so many years before. Security is always first. Make sure your position is secure. Once you've established security, check your men, weapons, and equipment. Plan before you move. Know where you are before moving.

Jorn listened to the forest a full minute for warning signs before drawing the pistol from its holster. He pushed the magazine release to count the bullets. Six in the magazine and one in the chamber.

It was enough for the mission, he told himself. After slapping the magazine back into the grip, he faced the high ground to the southeast. He had done a good job of navigating in the darkness during the night. When he had left the truck, he had headed west for two kilometers, bypassed north of the village of Muncheberg, and cut back south to avoid the swampland there. At two that morning he had crossed Highway One and begun the southeasterly march that would keep him in the Hangelsberg Forest all the way to the outskirts of Berlin. The route was longer, but avoided towns, roads, and low ground that was marshy this time of year. He was now about three kilometers from the highway and at least nine kilometers from the truck.

Jorn swung the pack up to his shoulders and planted his fists into the soft soil to start the new day's march. He wanted to reach the railroad tracks, which were five to six kilometers away, before resting again. He shook from the cold and his stomach growled, but he consoled himself with the thought that he had been much colder and hungrier before. A soldier could expect only misery. Hope and dreams of a better time were a soldier's only cause for pushing on. Jorn fixed his eyes to the front and pushed himself forward, knowing deep inside that all his hopes and dreams had died in Der Panzer but one: that of finding his kameraden.

Jake Tallon woke at six-thirty and rolled out of bed. He'd told Kristina he'd go with her to pick up Lars's wife, Jutta, and Frau Furman, who were coming in on the seven-thirty flight from Hanover. He had just reached the bathroom when he heard the front door opening. Only one person other than himself had the key. "I'll be right there, Kris!" he yelled. "Make us some coffee!" He began to turn on the faucet when Kristina stormed in.

"Have you looked outside?" she exclaimed almost hysterically. "It's going to rain, I know it. It's going to ruin everything."

Jake glanced at her reflection in the mirror as he turned on the water. "Relax. I called the weather station last night. It's going to cloud up, but it's not supposed to rain till after twelve or so. The ceremony will be fine."

Kristina nervously tapped her foot. "You haven't been outside; I have. What are we going to do if it rains? They can't move that many chairs inside and—"

Jake turned around and put his finger to her lips. "Shush. It's going to be just fine. Once we pick up the ladies and drop them off at the house, we'll go to Gatow and supervise, okay? Now go make us some coffee and calm down."

"Easy for you to say," Kristina said, pouting. "You could at least be a little bit worried."

Jake shook his head and splashed his face with water before looking at her reflection again. "You're doing enough worrying for the both of us. Make us some coffee."

At 0700 the duty officer knocked on his director's office door. Wolf rose fully dressed from the couch where he had been lying for the past three hours after monitoring reports from the all-night search. He strode straight for the door and five minutes later was seated in the operations room for an update.

The operations officer motioned behind him toward the map. "Herr Direktor, at first light this morning, one of our helicopters spotted Furman's truck parked in a small meadow off Highway One. The vehicle was hidden from the road by trees. The helicopter crew made radio contact with our communications and control van, which then notified all our teams and search units. The helicopter landed and made a preliminary search. They found the body of a female in the cab of the vehicle. They estimated her to be in her late sixties. We suspect it was Furman's wife. She had been shot in the lower back, obviously during the escape attempt. The site commander, Colonel Grober, has reported he is in the process of sealing off the area for five kilometers in all directions and is assigning zones for the teams to begin their search. Colonel Grober has requested the standby company from the Feliks Dzierzhynski to assist in the search, since the area is heavily wooded."

Wolf stood up and moved closer to the map. "Yes, send him the guard company and whatever else he requests. Where was the truck found exactly?"

The officer turned and studied the map for several moments before pointing his finger. "Here, Herr Direktor. As you can see, it is just off Highway One in the Worin Forest area, fifteen kilometers west of Seelow."

Rink, who had been sitting in the back of the room, stood and stretched his arms above his head. "Herr Direktor, our worst fear is passed. He didn't cross the border into Poland or Czechoslovakia. A double amputee can't get very far in the forest. They'll find him within hours, if not minutes, once the search begins."

Wolf tried to picture the face of the dead woman. He had not thought of Furman being married. He turned to the duty officer.

"Check to see if the Furmans had children. If so, pick them up. Also contact the Vopos, give them a full description and tell them to warn the townspeople within twenty kilometers that a very dangerous criminal is on the loose and they should report him if he is seen. We have roadblocks on the highway in both directions checking passengers, correct?"

"Jawohl, Herr Direktor, since last night when Herr Rink ordered it at 1800 hours."

Wolf nodded, satisfied with the arrangements. "I will be in my office." He motioned to Rink to follow him and waited for him in the hallway. As soon as the big man stepped through the door, Wolf began speaking in a half whisper. "I know you're doing everything possible. They will find him sooner or later. I'm going home to shower and change clothes before driving to the Gatow border fence." He winked. "I wouldn't want to miss the ceremony."

Jake glanced at his watch. It was already nine. In an hour the reunion would begin, and maybe then Kristina would calm down. He shook his head in pity for the two men Kristina was supervising as they tried to put up the bunting around the raised stand. He strode over, gently took hold of Kristina's arm and walked her toward the first row of chairs. "Will you please sit down and just let everybody do their job?"

Breaking his grip with a yank, she glared at him coldly. "They weren't putting in enough staples. Did you check if the plaques were here? And what about the caterers?"

Jake put his arms over her shoulders so that she had no option but to look at him. "Listen to me. The plaques are here, I told you that ten minutes ago. The caterers are in the hangar and are setting up the tables with food. Everything is fine, so take it easy, will ya? Everything is going according to plan."

Kristina's eyes softened. "I'm sorry. It's just that I want it to be perfect for Papa. He and Lars have worked so hard in trying to make this a memorable event."

Jake released her and motioned to the wooden platform, raised a foot off the ground. "See, the bunting looks great."

Kristina began to agree but then stiffened. "They forgot to decorate the podium!" She made for the workmen before Jake could grab her.

Jake lowered his head in defeat. He had started back to the hangar when an attractive, raven-haired woman carrying camera equipment stopped in front of him. *"Entschuldigung, wo ist die—"*

Jake raised his hand. "Sorry, *ich bin Americanischer. Meinen Deutsch ist sehr schlecht.*"

The woman smiled and shifted the heavy camera bags that criss-crossed her shoulders. "Yes, I was wanting to know exactly where the Iron Men will be sitting, please? My paper wants a picture of them all together during the ceremony."

Jake turned, motioning toward the wooden stage. "You see those first six chairs in the front row on the stand? That's where they'll be sitting, and behind them will be their wives or family."

"But I thought there were only four survivors," she said, looking deeply into his eyes.

"You've done your homework," Jake replied, smiling. "The base commander, Colonel Gibbons of Her Majesty's Royal Air Force, will be sitting in the center with Frau Furman, the widow of Iron Man Jorn Furman. Frau Furman is being honored because it was her letter that made this event possible. Can I help you with those bags? They look heavy."

The woman flicked her head to the side to keep the bangs from her eyes. "You are so kind, but thank you, no, I'm used to it. Thank you for the information."

Jake watched her walk to the platform, admiring the way her tight jeans showed off her perfectly proportioned backside. Her paper must be paying her good money, he thought to himself. They were all designer wear, right down to her hundred-fifty-dollar white leather Reebok walkers. And her perfume! It must have been expensive. It took everything he had to keep from leaning closer to smell more of her.

Suddenly his view was blocked and he was looking into two very angry brown eyes. "Do I have to supervise you too?" Kristina snarled.

Jake managed a weak grin. "She needed directions."

Unimpressed, Kristina growled, "It's a long walk back to your apartment, Colonel."

Jake raised his hands. "I'm just trying to help."

Kristina glanced over her shoulder at the photographer, who was bending over and setting up a small tripod in front of the platform. "She can't take pictures there! She'll block everybody's view."

"You want me to tell her?" Jake asked, knowing halfway through the sentence he'd made another big mistake.

Kristina's incendiary eyes snapped back to him. *"No!"* She turned and marched toward the woman like a miniature tornado.

Jake wanted to watch, but saw Axel approaching down the aisle and couldn't help but smile at the way his friend bounced with excitement.

"Jake, can you believe it has finally come true? Please show me how it is all arranged."

After Jake had shown him the caterer's food layout in the hangar, he walked with him back to the stage to explain how the chairs were arranged. Jake was surprised to see the small tripod, camera, and camera bag still positioned in front of the stand. He looked over the crowd, which was growing by the minute, but didn't see Kristina.

Axel looked about him. "It's perfect. I just hope the rain will hold off till after the ceremony."

"There you are!" Kristina cried as she strode up behind the two men. She gave her father a hug, then took his arm and tugged him toward the crowd. "Bernard and Thomas are here. They want to go through the sequence of events again before the ceremony begins."

As soon as Jake was left alone, he turned to find the boxes of plaques, and in so doing bumped into the raven-haired photographer. She lowered the camera she had held to her eye and smiled in recognition. "So we meet again."

He motioned to her camera in front of the platform. "I see you're all set up. I hope you won't be blocking anyone's view."

She took out a black, plastic control box from her pocket. "This is the latest. It's a laser remote control that triggers the shutter. You'll never see me."

"Neat," Jake said. "I haven't seen one before. My friend was worried you might be in the way of the family members."

The dark-haired woman chuckled as if it were an inside joke. "Yes, I met your 'friend.' She was very adamant that I move, but once I explained how the remote control worked, she said it would be all right."

Knowing he was asking for more trouble, Jake broke off the conversation by lifting his hand in a farewell wave and started for the hangar. "Good shooting."

"Thank you," she replied.

She lifted one of the cameras hanging from around her neck and took a picture of an old woman being escorted down the aisle by a young girl. Backing up to get a different angle, she snapped another, then turned around to prepare the special camera that rested on the tripod. Smiling to herself, she unzipped the large leather bag sitting beside the tripod and withdrew a thin, black plastic-coated cable. She inserted one end of the cable into the back of the mounted camera and the other into a large crescent-shaped battery pack inside the camera bag. She dug into the side pocket for film as she moved the angle of the bag so its right side would face the front row of chairs on the stand only five meters away. She took out a canister of film and slid it into her pocket, then zipped the bag closed. The claymore-type mine had been prepared for detonation the instant she had plugged the cable into the battery pack, which was ten times its normal size. The pack was encased in a hard plastic shell packed full of plastique explosive. The mine was eighteen inches long, twelve inches high, ten inches deep, and its right side was embedded with marble-size steel ball bearings.

Mink lifted another camera dangling from her neck and began snapping pictures as she moved away from her masterpiece.

The driver opened the door and Wolf got out of the black sedan. The two young border guards who manned the concrete watch tower exchanged worried glances and rushed down the steps to see who the unscheduled visitor was.

The driver explained his passenger was a high ranking official in Stasi and wanted some time alone in the tower to observe the Gatow Air Base. Both guards knew the request violated procedure, but they also knew better than to bring the subject up. The power of the Stasi could overrule any procedure or law.

Wolf climbed the last step and strode over to the huge glass windows facing south. The view was spectacular. Past the ten-foot-high, chain-link fence was a no-man's land where the dog runs were located, and past that was the antivehicle ditch, then another twenty meters of plowed ground, and finally another ten-foot, chain-link fence. Wolf looked past the border obstacles and could see in the distance the airfield and the roofs of the distant hangars, although because of the rolling terrain, he couldn't see the actual ceremony site. He stepped closer, opened the hinged window, then pulled up a stool. Facing the open window, he sat down and glanced at his watch. It was almost ten, and almost the end of his sleepless nights.

Lars Kailer looked at the crowd seated before him and leaned over to the man to his right. "It begins, my friend."

Axel patted Lars's leg. "We've held them in our hearts always. We can be very proud."

Lars rose and walked to the podium situated to the right of the VIP chairs. The crowd of over three hundred fell silent. Lars looked into the faces of the widows and mothers in the front rows and bowed his head in respect. He began speaking into the microphone. "Fellow Kameraden, family, and friends of Parachute Battalion 600.

We are gathered here today to pay our respects to those men who on this spot forty-four years ago, began their march to the east to try and hold back the Russian advance. Five hundred and forty men began that terrible march, knowing they might never see their loved ones again, but they went. They went with their heads held high. They went willingly to try and save their beloved Fatherland. Sadly, only a few more than half survived the gauntlet of terror from the skies before reaching . . ."

Although Jake could not understand a word of the German, he could tell by the silence and the absence of movement in the audience that Lars's words were touching home. Already people were using handkerchiefs to dab their eyes. He glanced at Axel. He knew his friend was with his soldiers again, standing on the tarmac making the last-minute checks before getting the word to start the march. The other faces of those seated on the platform were also filled with emotion. Frau Furman had tears running down her cheeks. The RAF colonel seemed mesmerized, and the other Iron Men, Bernard Foss and Thomas Gertig, had the same distant gaze as Axel. Kristina, with a melancholy expression, sat behind her father. Jake wished he were beside her. He supposed there would be plenty of time to hold her later. He began to walk around the audience to get into position. His part in the ceremony was to stand to the far right of the platform and hand Axel and Lars the plaques to give to the wives and family members. Piece of cake, he said to himself.

Mink stood to the left of the audience, taking pictures with six real photographers from various papers and magazines. She had purposely not spoken to any of them and tried always to look busy to avoid their asking questions. Backing away from the others, she took one more look at the Iron Men before taking the remote control from her pocket. She moved another step to her left to get a clear view of her tripod camera, then aimed the control and pressed the single white button. A small red light on the side of the distant camera instantly flashed on, indicating activation. Mink checked her watch and began walking to the back of the crowd that stood behind the seated audience. She had only three minutes.

Mink picked up her pace as soon as she was safely behind the crowd of onlookers. She glanced at her watch again and reached in her pocket for the keys to the rented car. She now had only two minutes and thirty seconds.

". . . now it is time to honor those families whose husbands and sons did not return." Lars motioned behind him toward the two seated men left of Frau Furman. "Bernard Foss and Thomas Gertig,

Battalion 600 survivors and former officers, will make the presentations."

Lars sat down as the two Iron Men stood and walked over to the other end of the platform, where they picked up a free-standing circular floral arrangement with a large iron cross in its center made from sprayed flowers. They moved the arrangement over next to the podium. Bernard removed a banner from his pocket and unfurled the large red-, black-, and white-striped ribbon representing the German colors they had fought for. He draped the banner over the arrangement and came to attention, saluting. Printed on the ribbon were the words: WE SHALL ALWAYS REMEMBER.

Axel and Lars stood and exited the platform to their right, where Jake was standing with the first box of plaques. "It's going great," Jake whispered.

Axel winked as he took the first plaque from the box and handed it to Lars, speaking quietly to his old friend, reminding him of the sequence. "We wait here until Thomas calls us forward for the presentation."

Thomas Gertig approached the podium microphone as Bernard walked over to Frau Furman and offered his arm. Thomas spoke as the couple approached the center of the platform. "We would like to introduce Frau Helga Furman, the widow of Hauptmann Jorn Furman, commanding officer of the second company of the battalion. He was a . . ."

Jake watched as Axel and Lars began to step forward with the plaques. Suddenly everything became a blur and an earsplitting roar erupted. Jake was hit by a huge invisible moving wall traveling at the speed of sound, which knocked him off his feet and swept him back as if he were made of wheat chaff.

Stunned, he lay motionless on the tarmac. His eyes fluttered and he wheezed in a labored breath as a thick, dust-filled black cloud settled down around him like a heavy, oppressive blanket. He blinked and kept blinking, for it was the only movement he could perform. He could feel nothing, and all he could hear was a loud, steady ringing. He strained in anguish to regain control of his mind and body. His lips twitched, then his toes began tingling, then his fingers. Somewhere, he thought, above the horrible ringing that pounded in his head, he heard shrieks and screams. He blinked again and again to focus his eyes.

Abruptly, he was turned over. He realized only at that moment that he had been lying facedown. He saw a blurry face above him and felt hands feeling his body. The person was a man, and he was moving his mouth. Slowly, as if the voice were being turned up by a volume controller, Jake began to hear German words, but he didn't understand them. Then, as if shaken awake from a nightmare, he suddenly knew where he was and fought to sit up. He shook his head, still unable to focus his eyes, and squinted to relieve the horrible pounding in his head. The screams came from behind him. He turned and gasped. The nightmare was real. Ten feet away, the smoking wooden platform was shattered, its wooden planks sticking up at odd angles. Bodies and metal chairs lay mangled at the rear of the structure as if a giant hand had swept them back. *My God! Axel, Kristina!* He tried to get up but still couldn't get his legs to respond. He screamed, trying again, and managed to get to his feet. He took one wobbly step and nearly cried in relief when he saw Axel crawling on his hands and knees toward the platform. Lars was behind him trying to sit up and was crying out for his wife. Jake stumbled over to Axel to check for wounds, but he saw no blood and continued on toward the mass of mangled and torn bodies. From among them came pathetic pleas for help. God, please let it be her . . . *please!* Kristina, please let it be you!

Wolf got up slowly, keeping his eyes on the dissipating black cloud in the distance. He could hear the wailing sirens, and he closed his eyes, savoring the moment. A few seconds passed before he reopened his eyes and walked toward the spiral stairway. It is almost over, he said to himself. Now there was only one more loose end to clean up. Jorn Furman.

His hands covered with blood, Jake finished wrapping the leg wounds and glanced up at Axel, who was cradling his daughter's head.

"Axel, a doctor is here. Let him see her now."

Sobbing, Axel looked up at the young British officer whose dress uniform was already splotched with blood. "Her head wound is very bad. We stopped the bleeding from her leg and thigh, but we . . . we . . ." He leaned back, exposing her blood-splattered face. A piece of wood debris from the platform had blown back, hitting the right top portion of her head and peeling back her scalp. "We didn't know what to do for . . ."

The doctor knelt down and quickly examined the still bleeding head wound. His expression didn't change as he spun around, looking up at his assistant. "Get her to the ambulance immediately. Start an IV with Ringers and call ahead for a neurologist to be standing by." He faced Jake. "Your wife?"

"My daughter," Axel said, patting Kristina's shoulder.

The doctor kept a stoic expression. "I can't tell you anything yet about her chances. She's stable, thanks to both of your efforts. Help us move her to the stretcher."

Jake quickly took off his jacket and laid it over Kristina's shoulders as the stretcher team set the canvas litter beside her limp body. Jake, Axel, the doctor, and the litter team picked her up and gently set her down on the olive-drab material.

Jake patted Axel's back. "Go with her. You need to be checked."

Still crying, Axel looked around him at the carnage. "Why, Jake? My God, why?"

Jake put his arm over the veteran's shoulder and guided him to the ambulance. "I don't know. Just be thankful that Kristina and Jutta Kailer are still alive."

Two British soldiers took Axel's arm and helped him into the back of the ambulance. They returned for Jake, but he waved them away. He stepped up to the back of the van and gently stroked Kristina's cheek. "I never got the chance to tell you . . . I love you."

The attendants closed one door and moved Jake back as they shut the other one.

Jake watched until the wailing vehicle disappeared from sight before he turned and looked at the overturned chairs, bodies, and rows of wounded being attended by Royal Military Police and soldiers. He felt dizzy and closed his eyes.

He had found Kristina under the ripped body of Bernard and nearly went crazy in anguished pain, seeing her blood-soaked clothes. It had taken everything he had to force himself to check her pulse. Miraculously, it had been strong and regular, and he had become all business in trying to save her. He discovered the head wound when he turned her over. Axel had dragged himself over by then. He was still half stunned, but coherent enough to help stop the bleeding of the other tearing wounds. While he and Axel helped Kristina, Lars and others from the audience had attended to the only other survivor on the stand, Jutta.

Jake opened his eyes, feeling incredibly weak. He stepped closer to study the direction of the blast and understood why the two women had survived. Thomas, Bernard, and Frau Furman had stood in front and taken the brunt of blast, shielding Lars's wife almost completely, but only partially protecting Kristina.

Jake felt sick and lost as he stepped over part of the body of an old woman who had been seated in the audience in front of the platform. She, like the five others who still lay sprawled on the blood-covered tarmac, had been killed by the back blast. The medics and people from the audience had gotten most of the twenty or thirty wounded moved to the triage area by the hangar, but the dead still lay in their blood.

Jake couldn't stand seeing the woman's eyes looking up at him, and he bent down to close them.

A young captain reached out, stopping him. "Sorry, ol' boy, don't touch her, please. I say, have you had an orderly look at the bump on the side of your head? It's quite nasty."

Jake yanked free of the officer's grip, leaned over and gently closed the woman's eyes. He looked up at the frowning captain. "Can't you at least cover them?"

"Of course, as soon as my team is finished taking the necessary pictures. It is important to the investigation. Please don't touch her again." The officer's expression softened. "The bloody Irish have gone too far this time."

Jake stared at the officer incredulously. "Irish? The IRA did this?"

"Sorry, I thought I told you. Yes, the bloody bastards called head-quarters just after the explosion and said they were responsible. While we were on our way here, the Smuts Army Barracks was hit as well. It's just down the lake, you know. I received an initial report that four of our Royal Guards Regiment lads were killed and seven others were wounded. The buggers sure made a mess of this one. They got the C.O. and his wife, but an awful lot of civilians as well. The bloody bastards will burn in bloody Hell for this one. I say, you really should have that knot on your head attended to."

Jake began to walk away but saw a crushed camera lens beside the body. He spun around to the captain. "The bomb was in a camera or the bag sitting in front of the platform! A woman, about forty, attractive, black hair, five-foot-five or six, wearing photographer's clothes, was the one who set it up. I talked to her. I—"

The officer nodded and looked at Jake with concern. "Right. You told me twenty minutes ago. I checked, and the gate guard remembered her going out the gate just before the explosion. Others have also given us a description. We ascertained it was the camera bag after talking to you and the photographers. Don't you remember telling me after you put your friend in the ambulance?"

Jake shook his head, feeling disoriented, and raised his wrist. He had thought it all had just happened minutes ago, but his watch told him it was now almost eleven-twenty. At least an hour had passed since the explosion. He looked up at the officer, but he had become a blur. Something was wrong. He had never seen the captain before, and yet he said . . . Jake blinked at the sight of soldiers walking by with plastic bags half full of flesh and pieces of clothing.

God! God no! Frau Furman, Thomas, Bernard, the RAF colonel, their wives . . . They were in the bags! Jake staggered back, closing his eyes, and suddenly felt himself falling.

Jorn Furman had heard raindrops striking the tree limbs above him before he felt any. He had also heard a train in the distance and knew he was close to the railroad tracks that would guide him to Berlin. Although exhausted, he felt better than he had that morning. The rain would keep the helicopters from the sky and the dogs from finding his scent. He stopped for a moment to rest beside an old oak. He knew the long rest stop that he had planned would have to wait. The rain and wind that were beginning to toss the limbs overhead were his chance to put more distance between himself and the truck while it was still light. Taking in a deep breath, he pushed himself forward. Soon he would be soaked, and his own movement would be the only thing that would keep him warm. He didn't want to think about when he would finally stop and rest. The shakes would start first, then the teeth chattering. Rest would only come after a long, miserable night.

Wolf strode into the operations room fully expecting good news, but saw by the expression of the operations officer the search had not turned up Furman. He proceeded into the back office, where Rink was pouring himself a cup of coffee.

"Do we have a confirmation yet?" Wolf asked.

Rink looked up tiredly. "We won't be able to get confirmation until tomorrow or possibly later. Using the IRA as a cover and our maintenance team to plant the diversion bomb was good, but it also worked against us in a way. The borders are closed down tight and security has been increased everywhere, especially in the hospitals. The British aren't releasing any information until after the investigation, and they are taking no chances. Our people can't use their usual contacts without raising suspicion. We'll have to be patient."

Wolf forced himself to agree. Trying to find out now who had died would only cause compromise. He glanced toward the television in the corner. The West Berlin stations would have something on later, and he made a mental note to watch them when he got home. The thought of home reminded him he had promised Dagmar he would take her out to dinner tonight.

Wolf reached out and took the coffee cup from Rink's hands.

"Go home and sleep. I'm leaving now, and so should you. They will call when word comes."

Rink forced a tired smile. "I told you Mink was our best."

Wolf nodded as he slowly walked for the door. "Ja, the ceremony had a very loud ending. Congratulate Mink for me."

CHAPTER 33

Sunday, 15 October

Jake rolled over, knowing he was in a hospital before opening his eyes. He had spent a lot of time in such places, and the antiseptic smell of the stiff sheets was a dead giveaway. He glanced around the dark room and figured out within seconds he was in a private room of a U.S. Army hospital. Nobody else but the Army decorated hospital rooms with cheap cardboard prints of ocean scenes in even cheaper frames. He rose up slowly, testing his movement and not quite sure why he was there. He felt a bandage taped over a very sensitive raised knot above his right ear, but otherwise he felt no worse than he did after a bad hangover. He glanced at his watch, did a double take, and nearly screamed. It was almost six A.M. He had been out for almost eighteen hours. He swung out of bed and strode for the door, cussing at every step.

The ward nurse looked up from behind the counter when the door across from her opened. She smiled tightly at the grumbling patient. "Good morning, Colonel . . . now please go back and lie down. You are not supposed to be out of bed."

Jake ignored her as he strode to the counter and picked up the telephone. He dialed a number and held his hand up when the nurse tried to protest. He heard three rings before the party answered.

"Hullo."

"Sandman, come and get me. I'm in the Army Hospital."

"Shit, Snake, man am I glad to hear your voice. I came over yesterday as soon as I heard, but they wouldn't let—"

"Sandman, hurry," Jake said, cutting him off and hanging up. He glared at the nurse, who was wearing captain's bars. "Captain, get whoever has to release me. I'm walkin' outta here in fifteen

358

minutes. One way or the other. Make it easy on yourself."

Jake strode back into the room and turned on the light. He opened his closet but shut it again as the smell of blood on his unwashed clothes hit him. In that single second he had seen the chaotic scenes all over again and had broken out in a cold sweat. Feeling sick to his stomach, he marched back out to the nurses' station. She was on the phone ratting him out. He stared her down and she hung up. Jake eased his glare and leaned on the counter. "Look, I just want to find out how my friends are who were hurt in the bombing. I've been out for eighteen damn hours, and I need to know. Kristina Hastings, the protocol officer for the U.S. Mission, she was one of those injured. Do you know where she is?"

The captain preferred this nicer tone of voice and responded in kind. "She's not here, so she must have had an injury we couldn't take care of. What kind of wounds did she have? That will tell me what hospital she was taken to."

Jake had a hard time producing the words. "She had, eh ... a very bad head wound."

The nurse nodded. "Oskar-Helene-Heim, then. They have the best neurologists."

Jake picked up the phone but saw two men approaching down the hall. The sight of them caused him to grind his teeth in seething anger. He reluctantly put the phone down and walked back to his room to wait. They entered seconds later, and Jake slammed the door behind them from his position against the wall. He stabbed a finger in the taller man's chest. "The biggest threat is the Stasi? You fucked up, Dawson! The whole goddamn 'community' fucked up! Who the hell was supposed to be watching the fucking IRA!"

Unfazed, Burt Dawson backed up and looked around as if he were in the market for hospital rooms. Kurt von Kant was the one who seemed offended. He thrust his chin out. "MI-6 is responsible for tracking the IRA! They had no indication of any attacks in Berlin, or we would have known about it!"

Dawson waved his hand downward at his German counterpart. "Kurt, the colonel is justifiably upset. Let him vent his anger. It's about all any of us can do right now."

Jake felt as if he were going to explode. He wanted to smash his fists into the wall, the ugly picture, the two men's faces, anything to release his anger, guilt, and frustration at being so helpless. Unable to stand still, he paced in front of his bed like a caged animal.

"Have you at least heard how Kristina Hastings and Axel Mader are doing?" he snapped at Dawson as he walked.

Dawson nodded as he took his pipe from his coat pocket. "Mader is doing fine. You and the protocol officer are the reason I'm here. The IRA trying to blow away two U.S. citizens pisses off the U.S. of A. My people checked on her. She underwent surgery last night, and she's still in the recovery room as we speak. Her chances of making it are very good, but whether she sustained brain damage is still unknown. They'll have to run a CAT scan to find out. Was she a friend of yours?"

Jake grabbed the collar of Dawson's sport coat, jerking the startled man forward. "Don't you dare say *was*, goddamnit!" he snarled.

Dawson exchanged glances with von Kant before looking at Jake apologetically. "I'm sorry, I didn't know she wa—is more than just a friend. Come on, Jake, let me go. Please." Jake released him and backed up, breathing through flaring nostrils. Dawson backed up too.

"Jake, I'm not the enemy, and there is nothing I can say that will make things any better. All I can do is assure you that everybody in the community is as outraged as you are. Why don't you sit down and relax. Kurt and I need to hear what happened. You're rested and probably thinking a hell of a lot straighter than you were yesterday."

Jake didn't move an inch. Dawson sighed, knowing it was not going to be an easy task to get him to settle down. He spoke softly but kept his professional tone. "Look, the Agency is on this as well as Kurt's organization. The Brit MI-6 chief here in Berlin has called for a meeting at eight this morning to discuss a coordinated operation. London sent in some IRA experts last night, and we're all going to compare notes so it's not a half-assed hunt, and so that nothing, or no one, slips through the cracks. We want the hitters as much as you do, but MI-6 has got the lead because the hit on the ceremony happened on a Brit base. They've got jurisdiction, and they're calling the shots."

Dawson motioned toward the German. "Kurt and I interviewed five eyewitnesses last night. We're here to hear what you saw, all of it, every detail that you can remember. You're the only U.S. witness able to tell us anything. I know that it won't be easy, but it's goddamned important. You might have seen something the others didn't. . . . You've had field experience, and you can pick up on the little things."

Jake's jaw muscles rippled as he tried to make up his mind if it really would do any good. He lowered his head, clearly seeing the dark-haired photographer's smile. "I bumped into her about nine-fifteen, maybe nine-twenty. She was carrying a camera tripod and . . ."

Thirty minutes later the two intelligence chiefs stepped out into
the hallway. Sandy Washington was leaning against the nurses' station counter talking to the captain. He followed Company procedure and didn't act like he knew the two men. He waited until they
were five steps down the hall before excusing himself and strode
into the room. He wasn't sure what to expect, and he was relieved
to see his friend sitting on the bed, staring vacantly at his hands.
"You okay, Snake?" he whispered.

Jake looked up. "Yeah, good to see your ugly face. Come here."
Jake got up and hugged the big bear. He knew he was losing it, and
hadn't realized until that moment how bad he'd needed to hold
someone who understood and cared. The simple act of touching his
old friend unleashed his emotions. He started to cry and couldn't
stop.

Sandy Washington remembered back to Grenada when the roles
were reversed. He had been hit in the neck by shrapnel and thought
he was going to die before the relief force arrived. He had clutched
his team leader, and friend, who was also wounded. Jake had held
him tightly and told him he couldn't die till he was back in the
States because he still owed him money . . . and he'd promised Sissy
he would bring him back in one piece. In a way, his old team leader
had talked him out of dying and made him believe in living.

Jake finally released his grip and stepped back, wiping his eyes.
"Sorry, Sandman, it's just that it's all my fucking fault. I talked to
the bitch who planted the fuckin' bomb . . . even told her where
the VIPs would be seated and—"

Washington put his arm over Jake's shoulder and gave him a
hard squeeze. "Stop that bullshit! You couldn't have known, man.
It was a pro job. There wasn't nothing you said or did the hitter
couldn't have known or couldn't have gotten from anybody else.
Shit, Snake, you know that. Get off the fuckin' guilt trip. You jus'
gonna have to turn it, man. Turn it and think how lucky you are
that Kris is alive and Axel wasn't hurt bad. You know how glad I
was, hearing your voice this morning? Well, I'll tell ya. I got down
on my knees and thanked the big jumpmaster in the sky. You made
it, man. And here you are playing 'what ifs' in your mind. There
ain't no what ifs. It fuckin' happened, and it's over, and thank God
I ain't trying to identify your ass in some morgue. You know how
I hate fuckin' funerals."

Jake lowered his head and spoke hoarsely. "Thanks, Sandman."
He suddenly looked up toward the door. "I gotta get outta here and
be with Axel when he sees Kris. Where is he, ya know? How's he
doin'?"

Washington pursed his lips. "I went to see Ax last night after I came to see you. Both trips were wasted. They had you both knocked out like lights. But I did manage to get a report on him. He's got a fucked-up right eardrum, but nothing else that a few Band-Aids won't cover. The Kailers are in the same hospital, and they're both covered with big-time bruises, but I found out Axel and the Kailers will be released at nine this morning." Washington lowered his head. "Krissy ain't doin' as well, buddy. She has a major leg wound and they're running tests this afternoon on her head injury to see how bad it is. I'm real sorry, man . . . real sorry."

Jake changed the subject before he lost it again. "How's the task force?"

Washington seemed surprised by the question. "Didn't Dawson tell ya when he was here?" He saw by Jake's expression that he didn't. "He pulled the plug, Snake. I got the call late last night. Dawson said to give what we had to his assistant and sent the task force home."

"He say why?" Jake asked, wondering why Dawson hadn't told him.

"He said they had enough info, and with what happened with the bombings, they couldn't provide any support for our surveillance work 'cause all his people would be working this new action. I'm supposed to stay on a week longer to clean up and make sure all the stuff we got is handed over properly."

Jake knew he really didn't care about the project anymore anyway and motioned to the door. "Let's get out of here, I gotta get some clothes and something to eat. I'm starved. Then we'll go get Axel and the Kailers."

Washington made no move to get up. "It ain't that simple, my man. The nurse says the on-duty doctor ain't releasin' you till your tests come back clean. They playin' by the book on this one, Snake. State Department and Dawson want you here to make sure you're A-okay."

Jakes's eyes narrowed as he slid off the bed and headed for the door. "Come on."

Jake walked out into the hall in his bare feet and hospital gown. He gave the captain a nod and kept walking. She came to her feet. "Where do you think you're going, Colonel? You're not supposed to be walking around."

Washington was following his leader, and turned around, shrugging. "I'm just followin' orders, ma'am."

The nurse came around the desk and yelled angrily, "The doctor says you can't go!"

She thought she heard "fuck the doctor," but she wasn't absolutely sure.

Hagan Wolf reached out for his wife, but she wasn't there. He pushed back the feather blanket, wondering why she had gotten up so early. He rose up from the bed irritably after tossing and turning all night waiting for the phone to ring. He knew that not getting a call meant one thing: they hadn't found Furman. It also meant the search would need more people and more equipment at the same time the damn protestors were draining off resources by their ever bigger marches. So far the minister hadn't asked any questions about the search, but he would if more men and equipment were requested. Wolf lifted his eyes to the window, telling himself there was nothing to be worried about. Furman would be found. No man could hide from the Stasi for long. Yet he felt an uneasy churning in his insides, knowing that Furman, despite his being an amputee, had somehow eluded him, even years ago when he had searched the camps and eliminated those who had known he'd broken his word of honor. And Furman had somehow survived for years in the wretched camps, where so many others had perished.

Wolf closed his eyes to go back to the flower shop and see the coward's face again. A moment passed, then he shuddered. A cold, tingling sensation, emanating from his testicles, ran up his spine, spread across his shoulders, up his neck and down to his tightening chest. Gasping for a breath, he felt his legs wobble. He sat back on the bed and forced himself to breathe in deeply to try and regain control. Five seconds passed, then ten, before his pounding heartbeat finally slowed. For an instant he had seen Furman, but it was not in the flower shop. It was as if had been right there in the room, only a few feet away. The amputee had been pushing himself forward on his hands and stumps, coming directly toward him with a feral grin and black lifeless eyes, like a preying animal about to strike.

Wolf stared out of the window and past the lake to the distant forest. His searching eyes glazed. Abruptly, he knew Jorn Furman wasn't trying to escape—he was coming for him.

Downstairs, Dagmar sat fully dressed at the kitchen table, staring vacantly at the wall. She had been sitting in the same position for over two hours. She had realized at last that the day she had hoped and prayed would never come was finally upon her. The lie was over. For years she had chosen to ignore the rumors about what her husband was doing in the service of the state. It didn't matter.

She had known since the beginning. It was just part of the lie. But slowly over the past months, the lie had begun unraveling. First it was the Hungarian border opening, the flight of so many of the young and the educated. Then, within weeks, so many of the husbands of her friends had died. Layer by layer the lie became more exposed. The marches, the Vopo crackdowns, the closing of the borders, and the most evident sign—the people. The people she had known for years, the grocer, the saleswomen where she shopped, the cobbler, the baker, cashiers, waiters, cooks, and even servants, had all changed. Their eyes showed anger, hate, frustration . . . and hope for change. They looked at her as if she were the enemy. The final layer was gone. The lie was exposed even to the people. It was over.

Dagmar wiped the tears from her eyes and stood up. She had to at least say good-bye to Margot Honecker, wife of Erich, the General Secretary. Margot and her husband had been Dagmar's rock, her hope that things would always remain the same. But now the government was crumbling. The lie, the state, was dying, and they were all going to perish with it.

Dagmar turned and nodded to Renate, who sat in the shadows, waiting. The agent got up and hurried to the front door to get the car.

Jorn Furman slowly inched his hand forward. Sensing danger, the male Canadian goose sleeping on the bank lifted its head from beneath its wing and managed one squawk to alert the flock, but it was too late for him. His powerful wings beat the ground and the water's edge in a final death throe, for his long slender neck had been broken. The early morning mist that rose from the pond swirled in eddies as the panicked flock flogged the air in their desperate effort to escape. In seconds they were gone.

Jorn picked up the heavy bird by its neck and pushed its head under his belt. Planting his fists, he shoved off toward the ravine where he had made his temporary camp.

Thirty minutes later skinned goose legs and thighs were roasting over a small fire. The rest of the meat had been picked from the bones, rolled in mud balls, and now rested in the coals. Jorn sat back eating the male's heart and watching the smoke that rose straight to join the heavy curtain of fog that hung over the barren treetops. He knew he was taking a risk, but an acceptable one. He had traveled another ten kilometers during the night, and now was the time to rest and regain his strength. Later that afternoon he would need both, for he was going to try and catch a train.

•   •   •

Jake saw them coming and took three steps toward the door before stopping to wait. Axel pushed open the hospital glass door and walked straight for him. He stopped a foot away. They both communicated all they needed to without speaking. Then they hugged each other. Axel patted Jake's back one more time and turned to help keep the door open as Lars pushed his wife out in a wheelchair. Washington pulled up to the curb in his black Chevy four-wheel Suburban and got out to help. Minutes later the vehicle pulled away and joined the light Sunday traffic.

Across the street from the hospital entrance a young man sitting in a black BMW lowered his camera after taking pictures of those who had come out. He turned to his partner in the passenger seat. "Control is not going to like this."

The passenger lifted an eyebrow. "Ja, it seems that either the dead have arisen, or the living were very lucky."

The driver sighed and started the engine. He pulled out quickly, and within seconds spotted the Chevy. It was stopped two cars ahead at a traffic light. The young driver shook his head. "You know what this means, don't you?"

The passenger kept his eyes on the vehicle. "Ja, we're going to be busy."

Max Rink put down the phone and slowly got up. He walked into the outer office and motioned for his assistant to come in and shut the door. Seconds later Lothar Rossen stood before his deputy director.

"We have a touchy situation that you must take care of with the greatest of care," Rink said. "I just received a call that the direktor's wife, Frau Wolf, was picked up early this morning by a Vopo security detachment outside of Honecker's residence. She had tried to get in to see Frau Honecker and became hysterical when the security men wouldn't let her. Frau Wolf had to be restrained. Her assigned security guard, Agent Renate Lafkee, called an ambulance and had the Frau taken to our hospital. Renate is there now with the doctors, and she is very worried. I want you to go over and report to me what is happening before I call the director and inform him of the situation."

Silently Rossen came to attention and then walked out.

Rink stared at the wall knowing it was not going to be a pleasant day for his director or for him.

.   .   .

Jake cut the engines and guided the *Defiance* toward the dock at the cabin. Standing ready, Sandy Washington jumped off the bow deck onto the small pier and quickly secured the line. Jake and Axel exchanged looks, having watched the sergeant. They both knew what the other was thinking—it should have been Kristina. Neither man spoke as they helped carry the wheelchair and Jutta Kailer to the dock.

Jutta sighed in relief as soon as Jake, with her husband Lars at her side, rolled her into the cabin. "You hear that, Jake? No phones ringing."

Lars picked up an ottoman and set it before the small, fiery woman's feet. "Elevate your legs like the doctors said, Jutta. Blood clots can be dangerous. I'm sorry we had to move from the house, but now you can relax and rest."

The little woman's eyes narrowed. "Stop treating me like an invalid. I'm fine. And don't be sorry for moving me from the house. The telephone was driving me crazy. We should have known that everybody would be calling to find out how we were." She looked over her shoulder at the black man carrying her bags in. "We all thank you, Sergeant Washington. If you had not offered your beeper to us, we'd still be listening to the damnable ringing. The hospital could have never gotten in contact with us if Kristina's condition changed."

Washington smiled. "No sweat, ma'am."

Jutta returned his smile and looked at Axel, her expression changing. "I want to go with you when you see Kristina."

Axel frowned. "Nein, you have been moved around enough already. Jake and I will go. The doctor said Kristina's tests would be complete by noon. We'll have to leave in just a few minutes. You need to follow the doctors' orders and rest."

Lars sat down by his wife. "We have already discussed this before. You must stay off your feet. Sergeant Washington will stay with us while they are seeing Kristina's doctor. I called the office last night while you were sleeping and talked to Berg. He understood. He has contacted our family and told them we are fine. We just need a few days, then we can go home."

Jutta reluctantly agreed and reached out to take Axel's hand. "She will recover, Axel, she is strong like you." She squeezed his hand tightly, willing her confidence and faith into him.

Axel forced a smile he didn't feel.

•   •   •

Rink walked past the operations situation room, made a right, passed by a guard who came to attention, and made another right through a steel vault door into the special ops center. The center was the most closely guarded secret in East Germany, the heartbeat of Rink's network of agents and maintenance teams outside the borders of the GDR.

Behind a console of computer screens, telephones, and blinking lights sat the special operations center officer. He held up a piece of standard notepaper as soon as he saw Rink. "I called for you because of this. I received it over an open line only minutes ago from one of our West Berlin surveillance teams. It looks as if Mink was only partially successful."

Rink took the note with a sinking sensation. He read the hand-written lines and knew the day had gotten worse.

. . . . . . *Urgent* . . . . . .

The delivery was flawed. Upon inspection found all pieces but two were damaged beyond repair. Inspectors on site and await your instructions on disposition of undamaged goods.

Inspector Six

Rink lowered the note after rereading it twice. He looked at the special operations officer, who had swiveled his chair around to a lighted wall map of West Berlin. "I have already contacted our maintenance assets, teams three, four, and five, to establish a blanket over the two targets. We have an unsecure line to pass instructions over, and I have appointed the leader of team six as overall mission commander. He is the most experienced. I have a secure phone on its way over the border now so we can communicate freely with him and pass your instructions on to him."

Rink nodded. "Ja, that is good. Get me the confirmation pictures. Inform the commander he has the mission and to finish it with the support of the other teams. He has till midnight tomorrow night to make it as clean as possible." "Clean" meant it was to look like an accident, which required surveillance, planning, and special equipment.

The officer nodded and picked up one of the handsets from the console. Rink began to turn around, but stopped, realizing he had a loose end to clean up. It was a difficult decision, but with the change in events, Mink had outlived her usefulness. He put his hand on the duty officer's shoulder. "Mink failed me. Send a special action team over to convey my disappointment."

• • •

Jake sat rigidly on the edge of his seat as he watched the doctor's face for a sign of hope. He was beginning to regret he hadn't taken the time to learn more German. Finally the doctor's face began to lose its somber expression, and his lips actually moved upward in a slight smile.

When the doctor finished speaking, Axel looked as if a hundred pounds had been lifted from his shoulders. "Our princess is out of serious danger and the tests indicate no permanent brain damage," he said, but then his voice and eyes lost some of their excitement. "Herr Doktor says she is still unconscious because of bruising and swelling of the brain, and that more tests are needed once she becomes conscious. He says her leg injuries are quite serious, and we must understand that it will take some time for her to recover."

Jake had prepared himself for the worst. Tears of relief and joy clouded his eyes as he reached out for Axel's hand and squeezed it tightly. He tried to speak but found he was incapable. He swallowed and tried again, and his words came out in a whisper. "Can we see her?"

The doctor surprised Jake by speaking in almost perfect English. "Herr Mader can if he wishes, but I'm afraid you can't, Colonel."

Axel shot to his feet. "Ja, please, I want to see her."

Several minutes later a nurse guided Axel through the double doors. "I'm sorry you can't go in," the doctor said to Jake, "but it is the rules in such circumstances that only family members can see the patient. I wanted to speak to you anyway, Colonel. I'm sorry about the earlier discussion. I thought you spoke and understood our language. It is obvious that you are close to Herr Mader and his daughter. It will be a very difficult time for them both. Progress in such cases can be never be predicted. As I told Herr Mader, it appears there is no permanent brain damage, but she did sustain a severe blow. We were able to save most of the skin above her forehead and scalp, but there will still be considerable scarring. Her leg wounds were quite nasty and required removal of a considerable amount of muscle. We have done all we can do for the time being . . . now it is a matter of time. My concern is that the slight disfigurement of her forehead and major skin damage to her legs may cause Kristina severe mental trauma."

Jake looked into the doctor's eyes. "Scars don't matter . . . her living is all that counts."

The doctor nodded. "Yes, of course, for you and Herr Mader, that is all that is important. Kristina is going to live, Colonel, but how she accepts the result of her injuries will be determined by those she loves."

Jake straightened his back. "We'll get her through it."

The doctor put his hand on Jake's shoulder. "Yes, you and Herr Mader are very strong, as you must be . . . but I warn you, the trial is yet to come. When she becomes conscious, the true test will begin for both of you."

Wolf looked past the doctor standing in front of him, toward his wife. "Why is she strapped down?"

"Your wife was hysterical when she was brought in, Herr Direktor, and we had to sedate her. The restraining straps are merely a precaution to keep her from hurting herself. As you can see, she is now resting comfortably. Now please, let us return to the office, where I can ask you some questions about her medical history."

The doctor gently reached for Wolf's arm to guide him out of the room, but Wolf pushed his hand away. "Don't touch me. I'm staying here," he snarled.

"My staff and I cannot help her if we don't know what caused the hysteria," the doctor replied matter-of-factly. "Is she taking any medication?"

Wolf kept his eyes on his wife. "I don't know."

"Has she experienced a loss of a loved one or—"

"Out! Get out and leave us alone!"

The doctor seemed unfazed by the outburst. "As you wish, Herr Direktor, I'll be in my office."

Wolf waited until the door shut before walking to the side of the bed. Trembling, he reached out and touched Dagmar's hand. "Why?" he asked in a pleading whisper.

Jorn Furman put his ear to the track and heard an unmistakable hum. The freight from Frankfurt an der Oder was on time. Many times, while on his walks, he had seen the old train. He backed off the raised track berm and pushed across the gravel service road into the trees to wait. He still couldn't hear the distinctive chugging, but he would soon enough. He leaned against a tree trunk, looking left and right. It was as good a place as any. Just to the west lay one of the few bends in the track. He couldn't see far beyond because of the trees, but neither would the train's engineer once he had gotten beyond the bend. If he could get close to the tracks without being seen, Jorn thought, he might be lucky and find a way to grab onto something as the slow-moving freight cars passed by. It was a long shot, but it was worth a try.

Suddenly he heard laughter and froze. He moved his eyes back toward the west and saw, walking around the bend, two young soldiers with their caps on the back of their heads. One had a cigarette dangling from his lips, and as he hopped from one railroad tie to the next, his friend hopped along, trying to light the cigarette.

Jorn lowered himself behind the tree. He was in no danger from these two. He watched them as they drew closer, then heard the train coming in the distance.

Both men heard it too. "It's coming!" one yelled.

Jorn heard a voice respond from around the bend. "Good! Show your flags and make sure the engineer sees you! We are ready here!"

The young soldiers took small yellow flags from their back pockets and picked up their pace, moving down the tracks toward the east.

Jorn backed up farther into the forest and headed west as fast as he could plant his fists.

A minute later he could see the train to his left between the trees. It was slowing. He pushed harder. The high-pitched squeal of the locomotive's brakes echoed through the forest as he veered toward the tracks. He stopped behind a large pine and lay down to crawl around its thick trunk. Gently separating the tall yellow grass on the edge of the gravel service road, he saw that the smoking locomotive had stopped just past the bend. As he suspected, not ten meters away was a small camp. The detachment of six soldiers was already searching the first freight cars. Jorn knew this was his chance, and quickly backed up.

The sergeant walked alongside the tracks as his men inspected the undercarriage of each padlocked car, knowing they were wasting their time. Only two of the front cars were unlocked and they had both been empty. Their doors were left open to air out the stink of some hogs unloaded ten kilometers back.

The sergeant stopped at the last freight car and took out a cigarette from his field jacket pocket. He smoked until his men had finished their inspection. "Well, did any of you see an old man with no legs?"

A young soldier motioned to the front of the train. "No, but I smelled him."

The sergeant laughed and raised his arm, signaling the engineer to continue. The locomotive's huge wheels began rolling forward and the cars groaned in unison as the couplings clanked into place with the strain.

In the dark shadows of the back corner of one of the hog cars, Jorn Furman sat with his pistol at the ready.

•   •   •

Dagmar stirred, then her eyes fluttered.

Wolf rose from his chair where he had been sitting for hours, gently stroked her cheek with the back of his hand and spoke softly. "I'm here, darling."

Dagmar's eyes focused and they nervously cast about the small room before looking into her husband's eyes. Her lip quivered as she lifted her hand to him. "I . . . I'm sorry, Horst."

Wolf smiled reassuringly. "Don't be sorry for anything, dear, you're just tired. I'm the one who is sorry for not seeing you were troubled. I will take you home and everything will be fine, I promise."

"No, we must leave here, Horst. We must go far away. Tomorrow. Please, get me away from this city . . . please get me away."

"We will be leaving, my dear. I promise. But wonderful things have happened. We still have work to do, you and I. Germany needs us. We will—"

Dagmar shook her head like a small girl. "No more lies . . . no more lies."

Wolf's face tightened but he kept his voice calm, reassuring. "I would never lie to you about anything. We'll go home and—"

Dagmar stiffened and her eyes opened wider as she bolted upright. *"No more lies!* I can't stand it. *You hear me? No more!"*

Wolf stepped back in shocked horror. She had never raised her voice to him, let alone looked at him that way. He patted her shoulder, wishing he had not removed the restraints. She was like stone to the touch.

Dagmar pushed his hand away and swung her legs out from under the covers. Her stare was cold and accusing. "You didn't tell me Erich was being forced to resign or that our government is falling apart. Why?"

Wolf's jaw muscle twitched. "Because it didn't matter. It won't affect us."

She smiled sardonically. "Won't affect us? We will have no hope when the government falls, no state, no life. Won't affect us, Horst? Do you think I am a fool?"

"Quiet yourself, dear. Haven't I always taken care of you? We do have a home here, temporarily . . . but we will move to another. You will learn to love it just as you did at the Muggelsee. You and I are going to take part in the building of a new Germany, what we've always wanted. We will have new friends and you'll be—"

Dagmar snickered. "Walter Ulbricht is dead. Erich Honecker is dying along with our state. What Germany, what leader, is it be this time? What name will the Russians give us?"

Wolf lowered his voice, speaking calmly but forcibly. "I have never been a sycophant for the Russians. I have always worked for the greater good of Germany. What I have done for our nation has all been to make her great again."

"Ah, German greatness? Is that it?" Dagmar turned away in disgust. "You must face the truth, Horst. It is over. The people know. They look at us differently. They know who I am. They might not know what you do, Horst, but they know who you are—Stasi, their enemy. You do nothing for our people. You threaten, beat, and kill them. I know, Horst! I know you are the notorious S Department Direktor who always does his job and never asks anything in return. The Great Honorable Soldier just doing his part for the greater good. You are nothing but a—"

Wolf drew back his hand and came within an inch of striking her across the face. She smiled cruelly. "Yes, hit me, I deserve it! Hit me! *Hit me!*"

Wolf lowered his hand, feeling sick. He turned away, shaking his head. Dagmar spoke, dripping disdain: "The *people* are Germany . . . and you don't even know them. You've worked on the compound fourteen hours a day and come home to a walled-in asylum. Your friends, the ones you haven't killed, are fellow elites. Don't dare talk of helping Germany, Horst. You don't know what Germany is anymore."

He spun, grabbing her shoulders. "*Shut up!* You don't know what you're saying!"

She smiled a little girl's smile. "Time for truth."

Wolf backed away from her, shriveling inside. "I've worked my whole life for you . . . don't you understand? My whole life I've wanted nothing but to make you happy."

Dagmar's eyes shot up and suddenly softened. She raised her hands out to him, speaking in a pleading whisper. "Then make me happy, Horst, now. Take me away from here, and we'll go to any country you want. Let's start our lives over again while we still can."

Wolf looked into her eyes and saw an old woman, one he didn't know.

Dagmar nodded with tears in her eyes. "You can't, can you? You can't give up the lie."

Wearily Dagmar lowered her head and lay back on the bed. "Go away, Horst. I can't bear you any longer. Leave me, tell them whatever you want . . . just leave."

Only when she heard the door shut did she begin to sob.

•   •   •

Rink rose up from the waiting room chair, seeing his director come down the hallway toward him. He saw by his walk that something was wrong.

Wolf halted in front of his deputy with a distant stare. "Have them send my frau to the hospital in Rostock. She is very sick. Call the residence and inform the house staff to pack some clothes and whatever else she might need for a long stay."

"What . . . what has happened, mein Direktor?" Rink asked, not believing what he was hearing.

Wolf's blue eyes turned to ice. "She has had a mental collapse. I'll walk back to the office while you make the arrangements. Be sure they have her out of Berlin by nightfall."

Wolf adjusted his tie and straightened his back. He set his eyes to the front and began walking down the empty hallway.

Jorn could not see the passing countryside from the corner where he stood in the shadows of the freight car, but knew he was running out of time. He could not stay where he was until the train stopped or he would be caught. Making up his mind, he lay down on his stomach in the straw and pushed himself along the vibrating wooden floor toward the open door.

When he looked out and saw the buildings in the distance, his heart sank. He had waited too long. The train was entering the outskirts of Berlin.

He sat back away from the door. He didn't know if the train made stops before reaching the main station at the city's center. The first building passed by, then another. He moved closer to the door, pulling the shoulder straps of his pack down tighter to ready himself, in case he saw a good place to make his jump. He leaned out again and saw a sign pass by: FRIEDRICHSHAIN 1 KM. He prayed the train would stop there. He waited. Seconds ticked by. He leaned out again, and although the train was not slowing, he saw ahead a mound of dirt beside the track just ahead. He was readying himself when suddenly he heard the metallic squeal of the brakes engaging. The car jerked. He caught his balance by throwing his hands to the floor to steady himself. The train was pulling in alongside another. He saw no one. He grasped the lower door rail and lowered his body. Dangling in air only a meter from the passing ties, he waited until the train almost stopped before dropping. His stumps hit between two ties, but the forward momentum still pitched him over. He fell on his shoulder and rolled down a slight gravel embankment. Quickly getting to his stumps, he pushed himself over the tracks and beneath the undercarriage of the other train. Leaning against a steel wheel, he slowly peered around it to look for an escape route. Directly in front of him, just below the gravel embankment, was a worn path leading through a rusted fence. Beyond the fence were blackened warehouses. One looked occupied, the other's roof was partially caved in, its windows broken and all of its doors gone.

To the left was the small station ahead and two men in railroad uniforms walking in the opposite direction. To the right he saw no one. He planted his hands and shoved off for the inviting darkness of the bombed-out warehouse.

The newly appointed operational commander looked through his binoculars at the cabin a kilometer and a half away across the lake. He turned to the thin, hawk-nosed man he knew only as Adler, leader of team five. "Have you found us a boat?

"Ja, I rented a small one, but it is fast."

The commander nodded and backed away from the window. "I should think a fire would do it. It's clean."

Adler cocked his head to the side. "There are two entrances and large windows. How will you keep them inside?"

"How do you know there are two entrances and big windows?"

"I took the boat over and got a closer look. The house sits back on a small finger of land surrounded on three sides by water. I didn't have to leave the boat to see everything we need to know. There are no roads, only trails leading to the cabin from the forest. It's going to be easy."

The commander shrugged and walked for the door. "If there are big windows, then it won't be completely clean. They'll be dead before we burn it. Come, take me over on this fast boat of yours. There's still time for a look before it grows dark."

Jake idled back the engines and let the boat glide to the dock. He held the wheel with one hand and shook Sandy Washington's hand with the other. "Thanks, Sandman, sorry about ruining your weekend. I'll be in tomorrow to get my stuff out of the office."

"Take another couple of days, Snake. Rest up and drink some beer. You still look a little pink around the gills to me."

Jake smiled for the first time without a conscious effort. It felt good. "Naw, I want to come in anyway and call Dawson and see how the investigation is going."

Washington motioned over his shoulder. "Watch it going back,

Snake. It's gettin' dark. See ya tomorrow. Want me ta come and pick you up?"

Jake pointed at the parked Mercedes in the parking lot. "I'll be driving Axel's car. He insisted."

Washington jumped to the dock and turned around. "He know it took you two months to get your license?"

"Don't rub it in, Sandman. Give Sissy a hug."

Minutes later Jake was pointing the *Defiance*'s bow for the cabin. He saw four men in a small boat in the distance cruising by the cabin's pier at low speed. Reporters, he thought as he pushed the throttle forward. Why can't the bastards leave people alone? As he closed in, he saw the boat lift up and shoot forward. Jake slowed, glad he wasn't in the small boat. He hated going fast.

Wolf walked into the house and was surprised to be met by his wife's security agent in the foyer. She took his coat.

"Good evening, Herr Direktor," she said with a warm smile. "Your dinner will be ready in forty minutes. Perhaps you would like to relax in a hot bath before your meal? I have prepared the bath just in case, and would like to demonstrate my abilities as a masseuse."

He gave her a cautious glance and saw the unmistakable glint in her eye. He knew Rink must have talked to her, but it didn't matter. His best soldier was only trying to take care of him. She would do.

CHAPTER 34

Jorn Furman awoke looking up into the face of a drooling Irish setter. The inquisitive animal lowered its head, sniffing the pack beneath Jorn's head. Flicking his hand at the big dog, Jorn sat up, worrying where its owner was. The vegetation was sparse where he had spent the night under the boughs of a drooping pine, and anyone who got close enough would be able to see him.

"Here, Runny, come here!" cried a distant voice.

Jorn leaned over and hissed at the animal. Runny whined as he scampered off toward his master.

Jorn quickly put on his pack and parted the branches to leave, but saw he had to cross an open soccer field. The eastern sky was just beginning to turn light, and already he could make out three people walking their dogs in the semidarkness. He cursed and stepped back. The night before, he had been able to travel for only two hours. He had wanted to go farther, but he could not move fast enough or find enough dark shadows to hide from the headlights of passing cars. He'd had two very close calls before finding the park and making camp. Unlike the forest, where he was in his element, he found the city alien, filled with too many unknowns. Here he was stripped of his natural defenses: smelling and hearing. The city was filled with constant noise, and the air stank of sulfuric coal. He felt helpless.

He was ready to give in to defeat when a runner caught his eye. Jorn pushed himself forward again to watch the young man sprint across the soccer field. He envied him, remembering when he too

376

had been able to move so effortlessly. The runner disappeared in the darkness, as had Jorn's fears, for he realized that he'd been thinking like a nursery collective manager again instead of like a soldier. He smiled to himself, remembering what he had always told his men. When in doubt and the situation seems hopeless, do the unexpected. Attack!

The sleeping taxi driver awoke hearing a light tap on his window. He turned his head but didn't see anyone, so he shut his eyes, thinking he must have been dreaming. It had been a long night. He'd picked up most of his fares from the airport. After the last drop, he had pulled into the Volkspark autoplatz to sleep for a while. It was understood by all the drivers that sleeping on the job was acceptable as long as it wasn't obvious, which meant hiding on back streets or in park autoplätze. The state paid the same, no matter how many fares were picked up, and no one tipped except foreigners.

He had just made himself comfortable again when he heard another tap, but this time on the hood. Kids, he thought to himself, and opened the door to shoo them away. He had placed one foot on the ground and was about to step out when, to his horror, an apparition rose up from the earth, grabbed the door from him and swung it, knocking him back inside.

Jorn quickly pulled the door wide open and pressed the pistol barrel to the wide-eyed driver's nose. "I am a desperate man being hunted by Stasi," he said calmly. "If you were to scream or try to escape, I would have to put a bullet in your brain. I need only information and a ride. Do as I say, and you will have a thousand marks. If you don't, you will die. The decision is yours. The money for your time or a bullet?"

Shaking uncontrollably, the driver closed his eyes and stammered, "Th-The—The money. I'll take the money. Don't kill me—please, please, don't kill me."

Jorn lowered the pistol. "Good choice." He opened the back door and climbed in, keeping the driver covered and stationing himself on the edge of the seat. "I'm not going to hurt you, friend, so please stop shaking and open your eyes. We need to talk. Do you like goose?"

Wolf awoke feeling his manhood being gently stroked. He raised his head, looking at Renate, who was sitting by his hip as she worked her magic. She spoke huskily. "I thought perhaps the direk-tor might like a little massage before taking his shower." Her eyes shifted to her work. "Ah . . . and I can see you approve."

Wolf felt renewed, having had his best sleep in years. The young woman's evening performance had drained him to the point of blissful exhaustion. He reached out and ran his hand up her inner thigh. Renate murmured as his fingers explored inside her. Thrust-ing her hips forward, she moved to and fro, using the same rhythm as her moving hands. Wolf placed his hand behind her head and gently pulled downward. She needed no more cue than that. He lay down again, arching his back, feeling her flicking tongue tease him.

The forest's morning stillness was disturbed by a lone, sweat-soaked runner on the twisting path. His feet crunched the brittle leaves and his labored breathing echoed softly among the red ma-ples as he pushed harder, trying to forget.

Jake had not counted the miles, for he didn't care. All he wanted was the deep satisfaction of feeling the pain in his heaving chest and throbbing legs. He increased his pace as he came to the trail that led to the distant cabin. Pumping his arms and legs, he kept his eyes focused on the wood structure and ran in a full-out sprint. Every muscle and fiber screamed in agony, but he pushed on, trying to forget the explosion, carnage, and Kristina's blood on his hands. The cabin was now only fifty meters away, but he didn't want to stop. Then suddenly his vision blurred and he stumbled. Catching his balance, he slowed to a jog, knowing deep inside there would never be enough distance. He had to think of the future, not the past.

Jake slowed to a staggering walk, placed his hands on his hips and threw his head back, sucking in air to feed his starving lungs. After a few moments he was able to take a normal breath, and felt the afterexertion high coming on. He closed his eyes to savor it. A full minute passed before he opened his eyes and turned to walk back up the beach.

Across the lake in a rented house, the commander walked into the living room and laid a sketch map on the floor. He motioned for the seven waiting men to sit down, and rolled back his thick shoulders. "As you already know, I have been appointed the overall operational commander for the mission. Teams one and two are presently in position, watching the house where the targets are staying, and will keep us informed of their movements. My team, team six, and team five will comprise the assault force that will conduct the attack. Team four will remain here at our base and maintain constant security and monitor the operation on the radio."

When the commander had finished his detailed operations briefing, he issued his final orders to his men. "By ten this morning I want all weapons, silencers, magazines, and ammunition cleaned and oiled. The weather report for this afternoon and tonight is rain. Check and waterproof flashlights and radios, and be sure to install new batteries. Peter, you will be exempted from weapons cleaning. As soon as this meeting is over, you are going to take the auto into the city and buy a dog. I want you to drive as close as you can to the lake, then walk the dog to the cabin, but keep a safe distance away so as not to be suspicious. Check for a position where you think it best to secure our rear while we are conducting the clearing operation. Also, I want you to familiarize yourself with the route that leads from our initial landing location to the position you select. Tonight it will look different in the darkness, and . . ."

Mink reached in her purse for her keys as she approached her decorating boutique. She stopped in front of the glass door and bent over to insert the key. It was within a fraction of an inch of the lock when she froze, seeing a small, thin, red and white wire running up the metal door frame on the other side of the glass. Her heart pounded as she backed up slowly and spun around to spot the eyes that she knew would be watching. She saw him across the street a half a block away, getting out of his Mercedes. She felt no fear as she turned and quickly walked in the other direction. The watcher was just that. She would easily lose him. She quickened her steps at first but abruptly stopped when she noticed a man approaching from the other direction. His eyes locked with hers. A coat lay over his arm and hand.

Mink smiled to herself and turned, retracing her steps back down the sidewalk. She heard the assassin's steps behind her and increased her pace to keep out of the killing range of the silenced pistol she knew he carried. The watcher and assassin had closed to within ten feet of her from both directions to block off her escape, when she stopped. Standing in front of her shop, she faced the assassin with a feral grin. "Idiot."

He began to raise his hand beneath the coat but she spun around and held the key within a breath of the lock. Both men froze. She smiled at their fear, then snarled. "I'll see you both in Hell." She inserted the key and disappeared in a roaring blast cloud that blew out the front of the store into the street, killing her and the two men.

Across town, a West Berlin customs officer stooped over to look at the one-day visa, to ensure that it was stamped and that the picture inside matched the face of the East German citizen inside the car. The customs officer was only going through the motions in case his supervisor was watching, for he knew the weekly visitor from the East. He smiled as he handed the paperwork back. "Another meeting, Ernst?"

Ernst Radtke sighed. "Ja, I will be berated by your transport company officials again, for my government still cannot accept the responsibility for maintenance of the trains."

The officer nodded. "Ja, ja, it is terrible that our two Germanies cannot even agree on a common rail system. Perhaps this week it will happen, ja?"

Ernst knew it wouldn't but nodded anyway. "Ja, perhaps this meeting. Danke."

Waved on through the checkpoint, Ernst drove the Chech Skoda up Prinzenstrasse and turned right on Blücherstrasse. He saw an outside phone booth by an Esso station and pulled the car to the curb. His friend, who was a dock foreman at a distribution warehouse outside of Seelow, had asked that he call a man whose name was on the note he had given him. He, Ernst, was to read the note to the man and tell him Herr Furman was being hunted by the Stasi and that the man should pray for his friend. It was a strange favor and even a stranger note, but the warehouse foreman had given him a ham as a favor to call. What were friends for unless they could help each other? he thought to himself.

Ernst found the name in the phone book, and after depositing twenty pfennigs, dialed the number. He let it ring ten times before hanging up. Shrugging, he began to walk back to his car, but heard the coins drop into the tray. Turning back and reaching for the money, he glanced down at the name again, and saw the address was in Zehlendorf, the same district where the meeting was going to be held. Well, it's not that far out of the way, he said to himself. If Herr Axel Mader isn't there, then I'll just write him a note with what I was supposed to say and attach it to the original note and drop them in his mailbox.

Ernst put the twenty pfennigs in his pocket and walked back to his car, noticing that the cold wind was picking up. He glanced up and frowned. He had not brought his umbrella, and it looked as if a storm was coming in.

Jorn Furman looked up through the boughs of the green pines at the threatening sky then back to the cab driver, who had introduced himself earlier that morning as Rudi. Rudi had become, in the course of the past three hours, a very talkative companion, for he had five hundred Ost-marks of Jorn's money in his shirt pocket, and they had discovered they had a common enemy, the Stasi.

"You see? It's perfect," Rudi said, referring to the thick forest of evergreens about him. "We are south of the city. This is the last stand of trees we can hide in and still watch the border fence without being seen. The state cleared the forest from the border years ago. This section of the wall is the best to make your escape, for as I told you, there is no real wall, only two chain-link fences." He patted Jorn's shoulder. "But please reconsider. At least sixty people have died over the years attempting to cross into the West."

Jorn replied by planting his hands in the soft soil and pushing himself forward to see the wire barrier beyond the trees. Rudi had pulled off the dirt road minutes before and guided his new friend up a trail. Jorn pushed ahead, not worried that Rudi would try to escape or turn him in. When Jorn had told him he was trying to escape into West Berlin, the driver's eyes had lit up like Christmas bulbs. Rudi had immediately volunteered to help. His brother had crossed before the wall went up in '61, and his sister's son and family had escaped through Hungary only two months before. He too had received a visa for himself and his family for Hungary, but Stasi agents had come to his house and slapped him and his wife around, threatening them and taking their visas away.

Jorn lay down and crawled to the edge of the treeline. He raised his head up to see over the brown grass. Five hundred meters away were two parallel, three-and-half-meter-high, chain-link fences running as far as he could see. The wire obstacles were separated from one another by a hundred-meter plowed field, and inside the plowed area, spaced a half a kilometer apart, loomed concrete guard towers.

Rudi crawled up beside him. "It is an abomination," he whispered. "A wall not for the protection of a nation, but for keeping its people locked in. It is a scar on my heart." He looked at Jorn with admiration. "I would go with you if it weren't for my family. God be with you, Jorn. Be a free man, but don't forget us." He broke his pleading gaze and pointed. "On the other side of the barrier is

Lichterfelde, the southernmost district in West Berlin. You see that tower straight ahead? It is unmanned because of shoddy construction. The unmanned tower is five hundred meters from the one to the right, known as Tower Twenty-two. It has two guards, as do all the towers."

Jorn kept his eyes on the ugly structure. "How do the border guards get to the tower?"

Rudi motioned to the plowed field. "There is a road in the death strip. A small truck patrols it and also brings in each shift. You see the small houses in the center of the strip? They are doghouses for Alsatians. The dogs are leashed to cables that allow them to run fifty meters in either direction. The truck brings the dogs food and water twice a day."

"Do the guards in the towers communicate to each other by radio or telephone?" Jorn asked, still making mental sketches.

Rudi grinned. "Radio. I know because the son of a friend was a guard there until he crawled over the wire to freedom. The boy always complained that they were very poorly equipped for their duty. They had no phones and their toilet was constantly broken. They carry only Kalashnikov rifles, no machine guns. My friend said the guards are told to shoot anyone within the strip, if they won't stop after being told once to do so, but if you make it over the last fence, they are not allowed to shoot. It is against international law and they abide by it for political reasons."

"Mines?" Jorn asked, continuing his mental checklist.

"Nein. Many times I've seen patrols walking back and forth in the strip, checking the fence and the dogs."

Jorn studied the terrain between him and the first fence, noting the yellowish-tan color of the soil. He knew it would not be easy, but it could be done.

The first raindrops driven by the wind slapped the limbs overhead. Jorn looked up toward the north and saw dark thunderclouds spreading like a black ink stain, coming in their direction. He glanced at his watch and motioned Rudi back. "We have to do some shopping."

Rudi sighed and pursed his lips. "I suppose it comes out of my money, eh?"

Jorn took the last of his life's savings from his pocket and handed the wad of bills to the shocked driver. He had no use for the money. Within hours he would be dead or he would be free.

Axel Mader stepped off the double-decker bus into a driving rainstorm. Pulling up his jacket collar, he hurried to the protection

of a large pine just off the road. He had come in with Jake on the
Defiance that morning, and then driven to the hospital to be with
Kristina. He had given Jake the car once they arrived at the hospital.
Jake was to take it, and Axel would take the bus back to the Gru-
newald, then walk the one kilometer to the cabin.

Wet and shaking from the cold, Axel now wished he'd made Jake
take the bus instead. He looked up and saw no sign of a let-up in
the deluge. Turning around, he began walking down the trail that
would take him to the lake.

Five minutes later Axel slowed his pace, for he found himself enjoying the solitude of the forest. He found he didn't feel the
cold or rain as he strolled among the trees, for he had been talking
to Gisela, telling her how he was holding up under the strain and
that he needed her help in giving their princess the strength to
recover.

When the rain and cold wind finally made him shiver, he looked
about him and realized he had wandered off the path. He knew that
if he walked downhill, eventually he would come to the lake. In
only a few minutes he saw the lake and the cabin off to his right.
He hoped Lars had kept the fire going. He was close to home when
he pushed aside the branches of a pine and saw a young man ahead
dragging a poor soaking-wet spaniel on a leash. The dog was obviously tired and didn't like the cold rain. Feeling pity for the animal,
he walked over to the young man, who had his back to him and
seemed to be very interested in the cabin. "Your dog is going to get
sick," he said.

The stranger spun around wide-eyed, but Axel kept going. He
had said all he would to someone who abused defenseless animals.
He stopped instead by the dog and leaned over to pat its head,
speaking loud so the drenched man would hear. "The first chance
you have, run away from this fool." Axel looked over his shoulder
and gave the wide-eyed man an icy glare, then strode for the cabin,
hoping the bastard got pneumonia.

Hagan Wolf spread out the papers they had been working on
since he arrived late at the office that morning. He backed up with
a nod of satisfaction. "I believe we have a very impressive bargaining chip. Wouldn't you say?"

Rink was still amazed at his director's ability to concentrate
after what had happened to his wife. Not even Rossen's negative
morning report on the search for Furman had distracted him.

Rink walked down the length of the table nodding as he read

aloud the title at the top of each page. "Aerospace . . . Chemicals . . . Communications . . . Computers . . . Plastics . . . Plant and Manu-facturing Equipment . . . Engineering and Optics . . ." He turned, looking at the director. "Ja, I believe they will be very impressed."

Wolf picked up a book from his desk and tossed it to Rink. "I should just give them this and tell them we have people in place in all the western European corporations that are of interest to us."

Rink turned the book over reading the title.

INTERNATIONAL CORPORATE 1000
The World's Leading 1000 Corporations

Smiling, Rink set the book down on the table and retraced his steps, looking at the papers again. "You would not be exaggerat-ing," he said. "Has Sorokin set up a meeting yet?"

Wolf began picking up their work. "No, but he will soon. The minister has a meeting scheduled in one hour with all of the direc-tors. The purpose is to discuss a massive cleanup of all the ministry files."

Rink smirked. "He's a little late."

Wolf turned, raising an eyebrow. "Don't underestimate our new First Secretary. Herr Krenz has promised our minister at least a month, before he gives the government over to someone else more in line with demands of the protestors. Honecker was a fool only at the end of his reign for not understanding Gorbachev. Honecker still had the power even in defeat to ensure Krenz was named as his successor. It was Honecker's last gift to his loyal staff."

"But the government will still fall, ja?"

Wolf continued picking up the papers and putting them in fold-ers. "Ja, it will fall, and the West will rush in to reunify the coun-try." He looked again at Rink. "And we will be sitting in back, watching it all. Our western brothers will come in with promises and then they will rape the people. They will take over the plants, factories, stores, and anything else of value. Unemployment will skyrocket, frustration will grow, and then, my friend, the govern-ment will need control measures." Wolf smiled. "You see, Max, loyal soldiers like you and I will always have our job to do. But this time we will let others fight the internal security war. While the new Germany is struggling with its identity, we will be looking to the future and ensuring the survival of the Fatherland. One day . . . one day, mein kamerad, we will be a power like no other on earth. Germany will once again make other nations tremble as we take our rightful place in the world."

Rink's skin broke out in goose bumps, seeing the truth in the intoxicating but clear blue eyes of his leader. He knew beyond a doubt he was in the presence of a man who could make the dream come true.

Wolf glanced at his watch. It was already past three. "What time does the operation begin tonight?"

"It begins at nine, and should be complete by ten. Should I tell Rossen you will join him in the special ops center this evening?"

Wolf turned back for the door and spoke while going out. "No, just call me when it's over."

His wet hair plastered to his head from the rain, Jake viciously kicked the door and tried the key again. This time the lock clicked and the door swung open effortlessly. He kicked the door again anyway, hating, despising, and wanting to kill the bastard who made the fucking lock that required so much patience and time to open. Goddamn German know-how obviously didn't understand tired, wet, upset Americans!

A pile of letters lay on the floor. Shit. Remind yourself, Jake, he thought, get a fucking mailbox instead of a door slot. He reached down, moved them around, and turned a few over to read who they were from. One made him tighten. It was from General Thomas. It didn't have a stamp, which meant his driver had dropped it off. Opening the envelope, he saw that the one-page handwritten letter was on the general's official stationery. He began reading.

> Jake, I've been trying to get in touch. I went by the hospital as soon as I heard, but they had you knocked out. I went back yesterday. They said you walked out without a release—not smart. Don't worry, I told them you were on special assignment and reported directly to me. I saved your ass again, so you owe me. I know you're hurting because of Kristina. I know about your relationship with her because the wife picked it up on the gossip circuit. If you want to talk about it, come over and we'll drink a beer. Please.
>
> Dawson called and says the task force did a super job. Thanks. I knew you would. The offer still holds to get you back to the States when you're ready. Let me know. Jake, take care of yourself. Get things worked out and check back in next week, or see me sooner if you want. You are on official recuperation leave till then. I signed the paperwork this morning.
>
> Thomas

Jake took in a deep breath and tossed the letter to the floor with the bills and overdue subscription notices. Thomas was one of the good guys, but seeing Burt Dawson's name in the letter had made him smolder again. Jake walked into his bedroom and pulled open the closet door to get his yellow Goretex running suit and extra clothes. He snatched the suit from the hanger and tossed it to the bed, wishing it were Dawson's neck. He had gone to the brick barracks office to get the few things he had left there and had tried to call the station chief to see how the investigation was going. It was clear within seconds he was not a player anymore, for he had not gotten past the secretary.

Jake threw a pair of jeans and a sweater on the bed, knowing Dawson would never call back. Dawson was like the Army. They wanted Jake Tallon's talents for as long as he was useful, and when they didn't need him anymore, they dumped him. Right! Fuck them! He picked up an athletic bag from the floor of the closet and strode to the small pile of clothing on the bed. He stuffed the clothes into the bag and angrily reached over and picked up his pistol from the nightstand. He aimed the Beretta at the closet door, wishing it were the raven-haired bitch. He fired the whole magazine in his mind. Feeling only a bit better, he lowered the pistol. His thoughts turned from the killer to Kristina, whom he had tried to see once he had left the barracks. Again he had not gotten past the ward nurse because the rules could not be broken. The doctor, however, did talk to him, and told him her condition had not changed—they were still waiting for her to become conscious.

Jake tossed the pistol into his bag for no other reason than it felt good holding the weapon and dreaming about killing that black-haired bitch. It would give him something to do, he told himself.

Jorn Furman was on his back in three inches of mud as he slithered through the small opening he had cut in the fence. Turning over, he hooked the wire cutters to his belt and began crawling again. He had been dropped off by Rudi two hours before, and because of the blinding rainstorm, had moved up his schedule to take advantage of an early darkness brought on by dark thunderclouds. Every part of his body was covered in tan clothing that matched the wet soil. Even his face was smeared with brown grease. Beneath his clothes he wore wool long-handled underwear, and on his head a wrapped piece of brown burlap. Rudi had bought him the new heavy work clothes, gloves, and a pair of wire cutters.

Jorn raised his head and wiped his eyes, trying to make out the guard tower in the rain. It was now only thirty meters away. He had seen the guard shift change while he'd been waiting, and knew the walking patrols would stay indoors until the rain let up. He had

to take out the guards in the tower. If he tried to crawl past and
the rain stopped, he would be seen or the dogs would bark, warning
the sentries. He knew he had to make sure that there were no guards
to see him crawl to the far fence. Lowering his head, he began
crawling again.

Sergeant Pieper walked to the plate-glass window and shook his
head as he looked out into darkness. "I still can't see a damn thing."
He turned to his partner, who had his feet up on the console while
he read a magazine. "You want to play cards, Lutz?"

"Nein, you cheat," Lutz said with a smile, and turned back to
his article on resorts in Yugoslavia.

The sergeant grunted and glanced up as the red lights that were
supposed to improve their night vision flickered. Like everything
else electrical in the tower, it had a short. Reaching up, he gave the
fixture a tap. No change. He tapped harder and still nothing happened. He turned around to the control panel and pushed the auxiliary power button. The light immediately stopped flashing.

"I fixed it," he said with a smirk.

"You'll burn out the wiring using the auxiliary power," his partner said flatly.

"Good, then they'll have to come and fix the whole system,"
the sergeant said smugly, but he glanced back at the panel to make
sure the searchlight and siren buttons were all glowing green. They
were. He picked up his rifle, which was leaning against his chair,
and looked out the window.

"The whole Volks army could march by and we wouldn't see
them," he said in exasperation. He turned around and looked out
the window facing West Berlin. The border fence lights were on,
but in the storm they looked like fuzzy yellow balls suspended in
space. It was useless to try and keep watch under these conditions.
He sat down to clean his rifle.

He was about to press the magazine release when he heard
something. He listened closely but could only hear the steady hum
of the radio above the control panel, and the rain slapping against
the windows. He pushed the magazine release and took out the
banana clip.

"Freeze!" a voice suddenly commanded.

Both men turned their heads at the same time.

Jorn spoke with all the authority he could muster. "I'm sorry,
but I must ask you both to lie down on your stomachs and—"

The sergeant, to Jorn's right, spun around and raised his rifle. Jorn hesitated for a split second. He did not want to kill the man,
but he heard the unmistakable click of the safety being pushed off.

Jorn grimaced and pulled the trigger. The sergeant pitched backward, hit the counter and fell to the floor. The red lights began blinking again.

While the sergeant had been making his move, the guard on the left had dropped the travel magazine and scooped up the rifle that rested against his leg. The sound of the pistol going off had only made him more frantic to get the rifle pointed at the intruder. He swung the weapon up and pushed off the safety in one motion. He was about to press the trigger when he heard the second deafening explosion. Then he was on the floor, dying. He closed his eyes, wishing he had seen the Yugoslavian beaches just once.

Shaking, Jorn lowered the pistol in revulsion at the smell of cordite and blood. Tears welled in his eyes, for he knew that had he been in their position, he would have done the same thing. They had just been soldiers trying to do their job.

By the time he had reached the bottom step of the tower, Jorn had forced all thoughts of the two young soldiers out of his mind. It was time. He didn't look left or right, for it didn't matter anymore. He was past the point of no return. If the truck or walking patrol came, there was nothing he could do. His only hope was to get through the last fence, which was now fifty meters ahead of him. The rain came down in sheets as he pushed himself forward. Then he halted abruptly. A black object was moving toward him. He drew his pistol as the dog closed quickly and silently. Only its chain singing on the wire cable and the splash of its feet signaled its attack. Jorn waited and squeezed gently, taking the slack out of the trigger. The animal planted its front paws, lowered its head, and hunched its shoulders for a leap at Jorn's throat. The shot rang out, and the animal, having just cleared the ground, crumpled in midair. Unable to move fast enough, Jorn was knocked to the mud by the forward momentum of the Alsatian's dead body. He managed to push the beast off him, then got up and set his eyes on the fence, which was now only thirty-five meters away. With the other dogs barking and wailing, he pushed forward, his hands sinking deep in the mud. Plant and push, he told himself, plant and push. Twenty meters, plant and push. At fifteen meters he saw the lights perched on poles above the border fence clearly and realized the rain was letting up. He veered toward the darker area between the lights. Ten meters more, five, the glow of West Berlin beckoned him. Finally it was before him, glistening—the last barrier. The sound of a siren from one of the towers didn't faze him as he placed the wire cutter's jaws on the first link and pushed the long handles together. A searchlight in the next tower suddenly came on and bathed the wire and ground around him in ghostly white light. He kept cutting. One shot rang out, then another. The barking of the dogs became frenzied and thunder rumbled across the sky, adding to the din. Men shouted, there were more shots, but he never stopped cutting the shiny white wire. A bullet grazed his ear and another sent sparks flying off the fence. He didn't care. He would die like those in the tower, trying. It would be a soldier's death. He cut another link, and the small section, still held by one last loop of steel, partially fell. Jorn heard the boots splashing in the mud, but also the crunch and clink as the jaws split the steel of the last link. The rectangle he had cut had fallen back and left a black hole. He planted his hands for the last time in East German soil and dived into the dark void, toward freedom.

Jake tied off the *Defiance*, picked up his briefcase and athletic bag, and headed for the cabin. The rain had slowed to a drizzle, but the black, boiling clouds were rumbling ominously. He was about to knock at the door when it flew open.

"Set the table, he's here," Lars yelled into the room. He turned to Jake. "Hurry! Jutta wouldn't let us eat until you arrived. I have prepared a gourmet's delight for us tonight."

Axel glanced at the stack of mail on the floor that Jake had given him before dinner. He had not gone through it yet. He was not ready to receive the cards and notes from sympathetic friends. He wanted only to know that his princess would be better. Glancing away from the stack, he pushed back his chair. "How about bridge tonight?"

Jutta shook her head and reached over, patting Jake's arm. "Jake promised me he'd show us how to play the game Kenny Rogers sings about . . . you have to know when to hold 'em, and know when to—"

"Poker," Jake said, smiling. "Sure, but you won't have a dime left when we get through playing. I'm good."

"Dime?" Jutta asked with a quizzical stare.

"Ten pfennigs," Axel said.

Lars stood up to clean the table. "You talk big, Jake. But you don't know your history. We Germans invented gambling while your country was still an undiscovered wilderness."

Jake eyed the rotund man and got up to help. "Yeah, but we did what we always do: stole it and perfected it. Five card stud made

America great. Look at Kenny Rogers. He made a mill just singing about it."

"Mill?" Jutta repeated.

"Lots of pfennigs," Jake said, winking.

The mission commander walked down the row of assault force members, inspecting their uniforms and faces to ensure that nothing shiny was exposed.

"Lock and load your pistols and place them on safe," he suddenly barked. "Rolf, get a blanket to cover you. The polizei insignia on your raincoat reflects light."

He checked his watch and turned to the leader of team four. "It's eight-forty. We're going to load the boat in five minutes. Did you get a radio check with surveillance teams one and two?"

Four's leader nodded, not taking his eyes from the glistening road. "Ja, team one reported that the cruiser pulled in at seven at the cabin's pier, and no one has left the house."

The commander smiled in the darkness. "Then it's as good as done."

Jorn propelled himself from the door, having been told to leave before the irate man called the polizei. It was the third house he had tried and the third time he had been cut off before he could explain he needed help. But refusing to give up, he pushed himself to the next house and knocked on the door.

When the door opened, a little boy no older than seven stared at him, wide-eyed. Jorn forced a smile and tried to contain his shaking. The cold had seeped into his bones.

"Ja?" the boy said.

Before Jorn could speak, a young woman stepped up behind her son and pulled him back. "What do you want?" she said, her voice cracking with fear.

Jorn lowered his head. It was no use. How could he speak without scaring her more? He shook his head and began to back up when another voice spoke softly. "What is it you want?"

Jorn looked up at a man who appeared to be a few years older than himself. The woman and boy now stood behind their grandfather, staring at Jorn as if he were a carnival freak. But the man's eyes showed no fear.

"I have just escaped from the East, and I need to call a kamerad to come and help me."

The old man's face cracked in a smile. "Ja, that is a good story. I suppose you want just a few pfennigs too, ja?"

Jorn shook his head. "Nein, I want nothing. Please, I will wait out here or on the street if you want. Just call Herr Axel Mader for me. He is a kamerad from the war. Tell him it is Jorn Furman, and he will come."

The old man's expression changed. "The war? What unit?"

Now Jorn felt some hope. He suspected he was talking with a fellow veteran. "The last unit I served with was the Parachute Battalion 600."

The old man spat at him. "You think I'm a fool? We all read the papers! Don't use newspaper stories to gain pity for your lies! Go away and don't dare use the names of good men for your begging."

The old man grabbed for the door to slam it, but Jorn shot his hands out and propelled himself forward. He took the blow on his shoulder and shoved the door back with his powerful arms. The woman shrieked and pulled her son to her. The old man took up a stance to protect his family. Jorn pulled the pistol from under his coat, leveling it at the man, then flipped it up and caught it by the barrel. He tossed the weapon toward the startled veteran. "I am *not* lying, kamerad. Shoot me if you don't believe me, but never call Hauptmann Jorn Furman a liar."

The woman was already at the telephone, but her father looked Jorn over, then held up his hand to his daughter. "Wait, Erika. I want to hear what he has to say."

Jutta looked into Jake's dancing eyes and spoke confidently. "You are pretending."

Lars sighed. "Dear, it is called 'bluffing.' "

Jutta kept her stare. "Ja, bluffing, I know you have nothing, Colonel."

Jake raised an eyebrow. "Put your money on the table and find out."

Jutta picked up four wooden matches and tossed them to the center of the table on top of a small stack. "Now, Colonel, I believe it is your turn. I call."

Jake's eyes narrowed as he looked at the cards, then back to the woman.

Axel grinned. "Could it be our Iron Man has met his match?"

Lars chuckled at the expression on Jake's face. "Ja, as the song says, 'You have to know when to fold them.' "

Jake tossed the cards down in exasperation. "I need a beer!"

Jutta chuckled as she raked the pot toward herself. "You need luck, not beer. And you should get yourself some more matches."

"Bring us all beer," Axel yelled.

Lars motioned to the stack of mail by Axel's foot. "Axel, would you go through those and see if there is anything for me? I gave the office your address before I came to Berlin."

Axel picked up the letters and quickly began scanning through them. "Here is something for you." As he handed the envelope over, a small folded note fell to the floor from among the letters. His name was handwritten on the outside. He picked it up and opened it, and another smudged piece of paper fell to the table. He read the note in his hands first.

> Herr Mader,
>   I was asked by a friend in East Germany to give you the enclosed note. It is from someone you know, who, I'm afraid, has gotten into serious trouble and is being hunted by the Stasi. My friend told me it has something to do with an article you wrote. I am sorry about the news, but my friend said it was important to Herr Furman that his note reach you. Pray for him.
>
> A fellow German

Jutta put down the cards when she noticed Axel's face. She thought for a moment he was having a heart attack. She grabbed for her husband's arm. Lars too took one glance and knew something was dreadfully wrong.

Axel picked up the second note and unfolded it with trembling hands.

When Jake came in with an armful of beers, he swallowed the words he was about to speak and hurried to the table. He could see something had upset everyone.

Axel looked up from the second note and passed it to Lars, who sat rigidly, having read the first.

"Jorn is alive?" he said, and then his expression changed. "Volker!" he snarled.

Jutta gasped. "Mein Gott."

Axel clenched his jaw. "The bastard lives." Shaking with rage, he lowered his head and whispered almost inaudibly, "Jorn . . . mein Gott, what have we done to you?"

Jake had seen hate before, but never like he saw in the eyes of the two men across from him. He reached over and touched Jutta, who had just finished reading both pieces of paper.

"What's wrong?" he whispered.

Jutta began to give him the notes but remembered he didn't speak or read German. She read the first one and translated aloud, then began the second.

". . . Jorn says Volker is a director of some kind in Stasi and is using a new name, Herr Wolf, and . . ."

Blood drained from Jake's face. He sat without hearing another word as the name Wolf reverberated through his mind like a bell clang. He shoved himself back from the table, almost knocking it over, then spun around and picked up his briefcase. He slammed the case on the chair and flipped the releases. He took out the top folder, and from it produced a color picture which he tossed on the table. "Is that Volker?"

Axel and Lars needed only a glance. "Where? How did you get this?" Axel demanded.

Jake tossed the entire file on the desk. "He's in charge of the Stasi directorate that ordered the deaths of those people killed here in the city weeks ago."

"Mein Gott, he's the one!" Lars cried out. "He wants us all dead! He ordered the bombing!"

His words sent a shiver up Jake's spine. He had not made the connection until that very second, but it had to be true.

Axel made the connection too, and looked out of the huge window. "There was a man today at the back of the house and—"

"The four men in the boat!" Jake blurted. "I saw four men yesterday close to the dock. And today there were the two men at the dock sitting in a BMW beside Axel's car."

Lars stood up suddenly and looked around as if he were trapped. "We've got to get to a telephone!"

"I'll get the boat ready," Axel said. "Get your coats and we'll—"

"Stop!" Jake blurted. "Lars, shut all the curtains. Axel, don't go outside until I've checked around. Jutta, push yourself to the bathroom and lock yourself in until we come and get you. Stay away from the windows. Move, Lars, get the curtains closed! Axel, help him and turn off all the bottom-floor lights, but leave on the ones upstairs."

No one moved at first, for they were almost in shock at what they knew was happening. Axel was the first to move, and grabbed Lars's arm. "Come, we must do what he says."

Jake lifted his hand in warning. "No more talking, only whispering. I'm going out the front. I'll knock three times before I come back in. Everybody be near the bathroom and ready to leave." He strode to his bag and unzipped it. He took out the black Beretta and jacked a round into the chamber, then moved quickly toward the door.

The old man looked away from the road to his brooding passenger. "I'm sorry for not believing you at first, Herr Furman. It is so incredible that you, of all men, would show up at my doorstep . . . I'm sorry too for having to be the one who told you about the horrible bombing."

Jorn's eyes still misted from the tears he'd shed when he heard about Helga, the two Iron Men, and the mothers of the men he had led. He had not thought he'd been capable of any more tears of remorse, yet now he felt as if his heart would break. Only his seething hatred kept him going, for he knew who had ordered the killings. Only one man was capable of it, and only one man had the motive to do it: Volker.

The old man pulled the Audi to the curb and motioned to the house. "This is the address of Herr Mader. Even if he is still not at home, we can at least ask some of his neighbors where we might find him."

Jorn reached out and took hold of the man's arm. "Thank you for helping me."

The old man nodded. "I know how it feels losing kameraden, my friend. I served with the Afrika Korps. Come, let's see what we can find out."

Jake, moving with his back against the deck and searching the darkness, heard the unmistakable sound of a motorboat off to his right. He froze. He was unable to see anything, but he could hear the engine idling. Then, standing perfectly still, not even breathing as he listened, he heard the fiberglass body of the boat scraping the sand on the beach. He dashed to the front door, knocked three times, and quickly entered. The burning embers in the fireplace and the upstairs lights gave off enough light for him to find his way into the hallway, where Axel and Lars sat waiting on the floor. Both men had fashioned short spears made from knives tied to the old ski poles that had hung by the fireplace.

Jake sat. "Somebody just landed in a boat about two hundred meters down the beach to our right," he whispered. "If it's them, they'll be hitting us once they get into position. We could make a dash for the boat right now, but if we're caught in the open, we're dead."

Axel shook his head in the semidarkness. "We need to stay in our defensive position. They don't know we know about them, so surprise is on our side."

Jake put himself in the mind of the commander of the hit team. "They'll have to cover both entrances. So will we. I'm going out and wait on those that come to the front. You two wait by the back entrance, but don't get close to the door, and stay low. They may blow it and try a rush. Stay as calm as you can and stick anybody in the legs who comes. Try and get his weapon. One of you do the sticking and the other the cover, in case more come."

"The fire extinguisher!" Lars whispered excitedly. "We can use it to blind them."

"Good idea," Jake said. "If you think of anything else, use it, but stay low to the floor whatever you do. They won't expect an attack from below. I gotta go. Good luck."

Jake got up, but Axel reached out and touched him. "Take care, son."

Jake patted his friend's hand in silence and moved toward the door.

"Leader Four, Security is posted," the commander whispered into the radio. "I am now moving into position, out."

Across the lake Leader Four lowered his radio and picked up the telephone connecting him to the special ops desk officer in East Berlin. "Peg one in position. Second peg is moving."

Jake heard a second motorboat's grumbling engine from the direction of the pier. He tightened his grip on the pistol, knowing his worst fear had come true. It would be a coordinated attack. Whoever they were, they knew what they were doing. He slipped away from his position against the house and crawled along the side of the wooden front deck, which was surrounded by a short hedge. He had moved only five feet before he stopped and raised his head to peer over the thick hedge. He could easily see across the glistening wood planks and beyond, for the bedroom light on the second floor cast its diffused light over the front of the house. Behind him there were only shadows, so he knew he couldn't be seen as long as he made no sudden movements. He had a perfect field of observation and fire, unless someone came up behind him. It was a risk he would have to take.

The passing seconds seemed like hours. Jake heard what he knew were the sounds of men trying to be quiet. They were moving slowly, but every time they lifted their feet, he heard the distinctive soft patter of dripping water off their boots. Then he saw the first one. The figure was just a dark shadow against the background of the shimmering lake, which reflected the glow from distant, lighted docks. Another shadow joined the first, then both disappeared behind the redwood picnic table opposite him, only six meters away.

Jake's heart pounded so loudly he thought they would surely hear it as he slowly, carefully, pushed the Beretta's safety off with his thumb, not allowing the telltale click.

A quiet, almost inaudible voice, combined with static, told him they had a radio. That meant there were others. Instinctively he tightened his back muscles, waiting to be shot from behind. He heard more whispering, then one of the shadows appeared and strode straight for the door. He walked into the light, and Jake held his breath, hoping he was real. He was wearing a polizei uniform. But as the officer got closer, Jake's jaw tightened. In the officer's right hand was a flat black pistol with a silencer. The man stopped and nodded to the other shadow before knocking on the door. Jake waited, torn, knowing that once he fired, the other man would see his muzzle flash. The other shadow would hose him, if he had a submachine gun.

The policeman knocked again and backed up, looking up at the bedroom light, keeping his pistol hidden. "Herr Mader," he barked loudly, "it is Leutnant Gother from the polizei. I have a message for you from my captain."

Jake held his breath and prayed for the killer to go back up just one more step so he would block the other shadow's view from his own position in the hedge.

The man backed up and filled his lungs to yell again. Jake fired and rolled.

Leader Five jumped at the loud report and watched in horror as his fellow team member reeled backwards and hit the wet ground like a limp doll. Leader Five froze. The instinct not to move saved his life for four seconds, after which he made the mistake of overriding his natural inclination. He felt he had to do something, so he rose up and scanned the dark shadows in front of him.

Jake aimed and fired from his new position along the hedge. The leader was lifted from the ground by the impact of the bullet, which had drilled a hole between his eyebrows. His body flew back and made a splat when it hit the soft ground.

At the rear of the house the commander's head had jerked upward at the first shot. He had known it was not fired by his own men, which meant the mission was compromised. He sat perfectly still for a moment, listening for signs of immediate danger to himself, then he heard the second shot. Getting up, he backed slowly across the deck toward the stairs, straining to see in the darkness. He heard an anxious whisper asking for a report in his ear receiver, but ignored it. The back door was opening. He raised his pistol and fired three rounds into the door. The reports made only small, muffled pops, but the expended shells clattered loudly on the wooden deck. He lowered the weapon and ran. Bounding off the steps, he lifted the radio's small mouthpiece and screamed, "We've been ambushed! I'm coming to you—"

He didn't hear the crack until after he felt the bullet tear through his back and out of his chest. He stumbled and hit the concrete bunker he had passed earlier. The blow knocked him onto his back. He lay unable to move, drowning in his own blood.

Jake, shrouded in darkness, looked down at him and kicked the pistol from his hand. Axel and Lars came out of the darkness, Lars kneeling by the shot man, placing a hand on his chest. Immediately the team leader was able to take a breath.

Jake turned, hearing a soft noise. He bent over and pulled the small radio from the man's vest pocket, then yanked out the earpiece cord. Immediately the sound came over the small speaker. "What is he saying?" he whispered to Axel.

"He is wanting a report on the situation," Axel said softly.

Jake pressed the transmit button and whispered, "They're dead, asshole!" He picked up the silenced pistol and handed his own weapon to Axel. "Come on. We've got to clear the area all the way back to the forest. I'll take the left side of the beach and you take the right. We'll work ourselves toward the center and then up the finger. Lars, there are two dead in the front. Get their pistols. You guard the back and have Jutta keep the front covered. Axel and I will holler when we're coming back in. Shoot anybody else who doesn't identify himself." He motioned to the wounded man Lars was attending. "We'll need him to answer questions, so get a good airtight bandage on him."

Jake nodded to Axel. "Take it slow and easy."

Jorn had heard the shooting in the distance as he made his way down the forest trail. The old veteran and he had gotten the information they needed from a house across the street from Axel's. The professor who lived there had been wary at first, for he had been asked the same question by reporters. Thankfully, when Jorn had told him about himself, the professor had believed him, although only with the corroboration of the Afrika Korps veteran. The old veteran had then driven him to the Grunewald, following the professor's instructions, and had let him off at the bus stop only a kilometer from the cabin. He had volunteered to wait to make sure Axel was there, but Jorn had told him he had done enough.

Jorn threw out his hands and swung his body forward as fast as he could, hoping he was not too late. He heard a twig snap and froze. A moment later he heard heavy breathing and suddenly a man burst through a thicket only ten meters in front of him. The man stopped, taking in tortured breaths and looking over his shoulder. He raised his left hand and spoke into it. "Leader Four, Leader Four, this is Security, over."

Jorn could hear no one respond.

The frightened man spoke again. "Our assault force was ambushed trying to take Mader's cabin. No one from the teams is reporting. Only a voice speaking English responds. The mission is compromised, I say again, compromised. I think they are after me. I am not far from the Havel Chaussee. Pick me up! I will be hiding by the bus stop. Hurry! Out." The man began running directly toward Jorn, who had taken out his pistol. He had heard all he needed to know.

The agent saw what looked like a stump on the trail just ahead. He changed direction to avoid it and nearly fainted when the stump commanded, "Freeze!"

Jorn didn't hesitate this time. When the man's right hand came up holding a pistol, Jorn fired point-blank and enjoyed the sound of the bullet thumping into the man's midsection and the grunt that escaped his throat. Jorn felt no remorse or guilt, as he had when he'd shot the soldiers. This time he felt wonderful.

Jorn put the barrel on the writhing man's forehead and squeezed the trigger. He smiled and pulled the trigger again and again. He kept pulling the trigger, oblivious to the fact that there was no report or recoil. He pressed the trigger for Ida, Helga, Thomas, Bernard, and the mothers who had gone to the ceremony to honor him and his men. The hot barrel smoked and stank with burned blood and flesh but he kept pulling the trigger, wanting to kill the man forever. Suddenly he was jerked onto his back by an arm around his neck, choking him. He struggled, but the grip became tighter. He felt the attacker's face and hot breath on his cheek. His vision blurred and his clawing hands fell to his side. He knew he was dying but didn't care. Ida and all the others were waiting for him.

Jake relaxed his grip when he felt the man go limp. Within seconds he was conscious again, and Jake jerked his arm tighter for a moment to let him know who was in control.

"Who the fuck are you? Why'd you kill him?" Jake snarled.

Jorn didn't understand a word but he knew it was an American's voice because he'd heard American POWs during the war. Relief flooded through him, giving him strength and hope again.

"*Wie heissen Sie?*" said another voice from the darkness.

Axel stepped forward. He had come on the run when he heard the shots.

Jorn tried to speak but his larnyx felt as if it were crushed. "Jo . . . Jo . . . Jorn . . . Fur-man," he finally managed to gasp.

"Mein Gott!" Axel blurted, rushing forward.

Max Rink stood staring at Rossen, who lowered the phone from his ear and looked up. "Leader Four reports rear security reported to him over the radio just minutes ago. The others have been ambushed and someone speaking English has control over one of our radios. Teams one and two were monitoring, and all report the same thing: a voice said 'They're all dead, asshole,' in English. The remaining team member requested pickup, but he has not responded to Leader Four's calls for the past five minutes. Leader Four requests instructions as to whether he should send a man out anyway."

Rink's eyes widened. "*Nein!* The imbecile should know better than to ask! He is to follow procedures on compromise. Surveillance teams must move to new locations and change to the alternate frequency. We must assume the targets have contacted the polizei by now. Have the teams report as soon as the West Berlin polizei arrive at the cabin. They will undoubtedly take the targets in for their protection."

Rossen brought the phone up to give Leader Four his instructions as Rink walked over to the desk with the secure phone. He stared at it a long moment before picking it up and beginning dialing.

Wolf rolled off Renate's oiled body and picked up the ringing green phone. "Ja?"

Renate saw her director's body suddenly tighten as if he had been slapped. His face screwed up in anger, then shaking rage. Only his eyes remained blank.

"I will be in at six tomorrow morning to hear the complete report of the failure," he said coldly. "Find out from our polizei informers where the cowards will be taken and how they knew about our assault. I will make the decision on how it will be done."

Wolf hung up, feeling a tingling surge of energy course through his veins. He savored the exhilaration of knowing that no matter what they did, they would die. Either the assault team had acted foolishly or the cowards had been very lucky. It didn't matter. The polizei and special units would soon have them under their protection . . . and then he would finish them once and for all.

CHAPTER 35

Jake flipped the body over with his foot. It was there, just as it always was, the special look of violent death. The face was gray, contorted, frozen in time; the eyes were wide open, but the pupils were dull, sharklike; a coppery smell hung heavy and low to the ground.

Jake felt the first warning tremor. The machine was running out of adrenaline. When he had waited to fire at his first target, he'd felt the hum of the machine kick in. The oiled parts—instinct, training, experience—churned, and the machine hummed. Time had become suspended and conscious thought ended as soon as he had pulled the trigger. Blurs, flashes, and a few fuzzy snapshots taken by his mind were all that were left . . . except for the bodies. There were always the bodies to remind him.

Jake heard voices. He broke from his reverie, realizing he had been hearing them for some time. He felt another tremor run up his arm as he looked at his watch. Yeah, time had stood still for a while. It was almost ten-thirty. He had lost an hour under the machine's control. The voices were those of the Iron Men. Jorn Furman was back with his friends.

Jake felt eyes on his back. He walked over to the woman sitting in the wheelchair on the front deck. She had been watching him, silently.

He patted her right hand, which was holding the pistol. "You know how to use it, Jutta?"

She kept looking into his eyes, searching. She blinked and lowered her head, regarding the pistol, then raised her eyes back up to him. "It . . . it is a nightmare."

Jake patted her shoulder, trying to get her back. The shock of what had happened was settling in. Reality. He had wanted her to guard the front, but knew it would take her more time to regain control of her anguish.

Lars removed the piece of plastic from the prisoner's sucking chest wound. The man wheezed and pink bubbles frothed and gushed from the red hole.

Jutta pushed herself away. The others stood watching, unfeeling, as the man clawed the deck trying to take a breath that wouldn't come. Finally he shook his head from side to side and gurgled in his throat. Lars hesitated, then covered the wound with the plastic.

The Stasi commander opened and closed his mouth, taking in air like a fish out of water. Axel leaned forward, repeating the questions the man had refused to answer before. "Who are you? Who do you work for?"

Jake moved back and sat beside Jutta in the corner of the deck. "Tell me what he's saying, Jutta."

She listened and translated only the prisoner's answer, as if she were in deep tunnel.

"He says he is Stasi, leader of the assault force. . . . There are no other units scheduled to attack, no other units available. . . . Three teams remain, but they are surveillance. . . . Orders come from Stasi headquarters in East Berlin. . . . He doesn't know from whom, he only gets orders from messages or calls from people he does not know. . . . Yes, he had been involved in bombing, but not at the ceremony. . . . His team had set the bomb up at the gate of the British army base and had been given instructions to blow it once they'd heard the explosion at Gatow."

Jutta listened to the next question from Lars and gasped at the wounded man's response. She turned, looking at Jake. "He said we're all dead, no matter what we do. It is just a matter of time."

Jake saw the body bouncing and heard the gurgling as the Iron Men backed away. Furman tossed the plastic bandage into the darkness. The interrogation was over.

Jake strode toward the wounded man, but Axel stepped in front of him. "No. He dies. When you were checking the bodies, Jorn told us about his escape from the East. Men like this commander killed his wife Ida. They had been married twenty-eight years. He dies, Jake. Jorn has ordered it."

Jake stepped back.

•   •   •

Axel leaned against the rail, looking up into the darkness. He turned around slowly. "Jake, can you tell us what you know about Volker and his organization? Is it true, what the Stasi commander said? Are they so powerful we are dead no matter what we do?"

Jake knew he was going to violate the rules, but to the Company, Dawson, and people like von Kant, the Stasi was just the "opposition." To the survivors on the deck, Stasi was the fuckin' enemy that had tried to kill them twice in the past three days, leaving a wake of dead or wounded friends and family.

Jake told them the truth.

When Axel finished the translation to Jorn, everyone fell into a heavy, oppressive silence.

Jutta shifted in her wheelchair and turned around to face the men. "I know what you are thinking, all of you. Don't worry about me. Go someplace so you can talk and decide. I'll stay here and watch."

"The bunker," Lars said.

Jake pushed off the deck railing to follow, but Axel put his hand out. "Jake, this doesn't concern you any longer. You saved us tonight, but now it's over for you. Leave and take Jutta, before it is too late."

Lars turned around. "He's right, Colonel. There is nothing more you can do. The decision is for only Axel, Jorn, and me. Please take Jutta to safety for me."

"Hold it!" Jake said angrily "What 'decision' are you talking about it? There is no decision. We are all leaving tonight, and I'll get you to the U.S. Mission. My government will protect you."

"We are not running," Axel said gently. "Go on, take Jutta in the *Defiance* and leave us."

Jake stood his ground. "I'm staying here until I find out what the hell you're talking about."

Lars took Axel's arm. "Come, he can stay with Jutta. We'll explain to him later."

Axel reluctantly turned and walked down the steps, leading the other two men into the bunker.

Jake knelt beside Jutta. "What's going on?"

The small woman wiped tears from her eyes. "They are old fools, Jake. They made a vow a long time ago and . . ."

Jake listened as the thunder rolled across the sky.

The candlelight played over the three stern faces of the men seated at the table in the bunker. Lars shifted in his seat, his eyes settling on Axel. "What can we do?"

Jorn pounded the table. "Do? You know what we must do! We attack! The bastard expects us to cower and won't anticipate us. We have no choice."

Axel leaned forward. "Jorn is right, we have no choice. Volker will kill us all. You heard Jake. The murders that happened only weeks ago included the district police chief, who was a Stasi agent. We can't go to the polizei, and we can't stay here."

Lars looked into both men's faces. "Do you really think we could find him? I can destroy him within days just by printing what we know in the papers. The people of both Germanies will be outraged at what he has done to us and his countrymen."

Jorn shook his head. "We can't be sure of that. Even if somehow you were able to live long enough to give your paper the information, he would find out and flee to another country."

Axel nodded. "Lars, Volker will declare war on us once he finds out about the destruction of his assault force. I say attack. I made a vow, and it is time to carry it out."

Lars thought of his wife, but also of his fellow Iron Men and their wives, mangled and torn on the platform only two days before. Then his eyes glazed and he went back to that day on the river. "Attack," he said.

Jorn looked into the faces of the other men. "It's time for the hunt to begin."

Axel's jaw muscle twitched. He stood and slapped his hand on top of Jorn's. "The hunt!"

Lars pushed back his chair and slapped his hand on top of the others'. "The hunt!"

Jake had silently walked down the stairs of the bunker a minute before and stood unseen in the shadows. Although he did not understand a word of their German, he saw the decision in their faces. He pushed off the wall and strode straight for the table. He held up his hand as he approached, looking directly at Axel. "You're not going without me. That's final. I'm in, and there's no more discussion."

Axel began to speak, but Jake slammed his hand on top of Jorn's and repeated the words he'd heard them say. *"Die Jagd!"*

PART IV

CHAPTER 36

Jake slipped the last weighted body over the side and into the lake just as the rain again began to fall. He hurried to the bridge of the *Defiance* and spun the wheel to head back to the cabin. He had volunteered to drop the bodies so that he could be alone for a while. He needed time to think. The decision to find Volker had been made, but the hard part would be finding a way to do it. The three men back at the cabin were doing just that, coming up with a plan. He had provided them with his file and hoped it would help, but he knew the chances of making it back from the mission were in the minus category. There simply wasn't enough time. In training with Delta Force he had conducted at least ten such training missions, but each one had taken weeks to plan. He and the Iron Men would go in without extensive planning, prior reconnaissance, or rehearsals. They had decided to go in tomorrow night, reasoning that it was best to do it as soon as possible, before Volker's jackals could find them. There was no other choice for them—die trying or die running. They had to try.

Jake slowed the engines as he approached the pier. He searched his soul for fear or doubt but found none. He was at peace with himself and his decision. Months before, he had come to Berlin as a self-pitying loser. He had blamed Helen for ruining his career, but the fault had really been just as much his. The Army and his loneliness were all he had left until he'd met Axel and Kristina. They had made these past months the happiest of his life. It was ironic, for Berlin had taken his father, but it had also given something back—a man and a woman he loved dearly. Volker would have to die for what he had done to Kristina and the others. But it wasn't just that—there was another reason. He had no regrets he couldn't live with, but knew he would if he let Axel go without him.

Jake hailed Jutta in the darkness to let her know he was approaching the cabin, and he heard her respond. He strode to the back deck and found the tough little woman sitting in her wheelchair under the small awning, trying to stay out of the rain. He patted her shoulder, walked into the cabin and came out a minute later with blankets and Axel's slicker. "I'm sorry about all this," he said, wrapping the blanket around her legs. "You shouldn't be out here."

Jutta grabbed his arm, looking into his eyes. "Jake, Lars told me of their decision. Tell me the truth. Will my husband come back to me?"

Kneeling down, Jake took her hand in his own. "I don't know, but at least this way he has a chance. If we don't go, we're all dead anyway."

Jutta squeezed his hand. "Not you, Jake, they're not after you. Why do you have to go? Doesn't Kristina mean more than wasting your life trying to find Volker? She needs you."

Jake returned the squeeze and stood. "She needs her father back."

Jutta kept her grip, staring at him. "Kristina told me you and Axel had become close, but until I saw you both together, I didn't believe it possible. You're going because of Axel, aren't you?"

Jake leaned over, kissed her forehead and backed up. "It doesn't matter. I've never believed in causes, only people. Axel, Kristina, you, and Lars are good people, as were those who came to the ceremony. The others are gone, Jutta. I don't want to lose you and my remaining friends."

Jutta released his hand. "Then there's hope that my Lars will come back. They are going for revenge . . . but you, Jake, are going out of love. Bring them back, Iron Man . . . you are their only hope."

Jake stared at her a moment, then turned and silently walked down the steps.

The bunker had changed into a tactical operations center while Jake was gone. Berlin city maps in various sizes and aerial photos from the file were pinned to the paneled walls. Axel taped up pieces of tablet paper with checklists printed in German and English, while Lars and Jorn huddled around one of the large maps, drawing circles and highlighting routes. He saw in their faces that the cold, hard truth of the odds against them had set in, but he also saw their steel-eyed determination.

Axel glanced up as Jake came in. "Did we weight them enough?"

Jake nodded silently. Axel took his arm. "Come, we have made a preliminary estimate of the situation and narrowed our options."

Jake sat down facing the large map, as did Axel and Jorn. Lars remained standing, his eyes locked on Jake. "We are old, Colonel, but we have not forgotten the rudiments of planning. We are well aware that the time is too short for much discussion. I will brief you on what we think is a plausible plan. Axel will translate any questions you may have to Jorn. If you do not like the plan, tell us and we will change it. I'm telling you this because we have all agreed that you should be our leader."

Jake began to protest, but Axel leaned over, putting his hand on Jake's arm. "Nein, don't refuse. You know as we do that there can be only one leader, and we have agreed that it should be you."

Jake glanced at Jorn, who nodded, as did Lars. He looked back at Axel. "Okay, but you're my second in command."

"It would be a pleasure, mein Oberst."

CHAPTER 37

The door finally opened after Jake had knocked five times.

"Sandman, have I got a deal for you," he said, walking past the big man, who wore only boxer shorts.

Washington looked at his watch then at Jake. "Christ, Snake, it's five-fuckin'-fifteen in the mornin'." He wiped the sleep from his eyes.

Jake held up the Mercedes car keys. "I know. But I got a deal ya can't turn down. Listen to me. That new Mercedes 580 SEL outside at the curb is yours. Give me your Chevy Suburban and it's an even swap. I also need the keys to the barracks. Don't ask me any questions. Just take the car, and give me the keys. It's important."

Washington's eyes narrowed. "It's an action. I can smell it on you, man."

Jake looked around, hoping to see the keys somewhere. "I can't tell you anything. It's for your own good. Just get me the keys. I'm running on a tight schedule."

Washington shook his massive head, trying to make sense of what was happening, and opened his mouth to speak, but Jake cut him off. "Get me the fuckin' keys, Sandy."

Washington went into the bedroom and came out with the keys to the Suburban and the barracks.

Jake held up the second set. "You gave these to me yesterday when I came by to borrow the Chevy. You don't know why I wanted them, but you didn't think a thing about it, since I was your task-force commander. That's the story you'll give if anybody asks, and they most definitely will, sooner or later. Go in late today, and leave early. That way you won't need the keys. Don't take the Mer-

410

cedes. Don't go into the basement or the vault for any reason. If anybody asks about me, you haven't seen me since yesterday morning."

Jake took an envelope from his pocket and set it on the nearby television. "If you don't hear from me in the next forty-eight hours, cash the check in the envelope and put it in your savings account." Jake put out his hand. "Take care, Sandman, and give Sissy a hug for me."

When Jake had gone, Washington stood staring at the door for a long time.

Jake swung the heavy vault door closed and locked it. Minutes later he walked away from the barracks entrance carrying two heavy bags. He hoped the Company didn't need their cache of weapons anytime soon, because they were now short four M-16s, some ammo, and four pairs of night-vision goggles.

Standing on the pier, Axel sighed in relief seeing the *Defiance* emerge from the fog and darkness. He spun around and hurried to the cabin. "He's coming!" he whispered as loud as he could.

Lars rose up from the front porch picnic table and picked up his wife's overnight bag, which sat by his feet. He strode to the back deck, where Jutta and Jorn were sitting in the darkness watching. "Anything?" Lars asked, breaking the silence.

Jorn shook his head. "With this ground fog, a sniper would have to be within five meters to see us. It's safe for now."

Lars handed the bag to his wife and took hold of her wheelchair handles. "It's time to go. The colonel is back."

As soon as the boat was loaded and everyone was on board, Jake began to signal for Axel to reverse engines to pull away from the dock, but a shout out of the darkness froze his blood. Jorn spun around with his pistol ready, but Jake stepped in front of him, shaking his head. Jake heard the shout again and turned. "Here, goddamnit!"

A huge dark figure emerged from the mist and leaped up on the deck. Jake wanted to hit the man, knock him overboard, or shoot him in the leg. Instead he snarled, "You stupid sonofabitch."

"Fuck you, Snake! I came to get my Chevy back. Sissy don't like the color of the Mercedes."

Axel hurried down from the bridge. "Does he know what we're doing?" he asked nervously.

Jake shook his head. "No, he's just here saying good-bye. Right, Sandman?"

Washington took a wider stance, challenging them all. "Nope, I'm in this action. Sissy dropped me off on the road behind the cabin. You got some company up there, if you didn't know it. They was sittin' in a Volvo talkin' on a handheld radio when I snooped and pooped by 'em."

Axel motioned toward Jorn, who still held his pistol ready. "He could have killed you."

Washington snickered. "Him? Shiiiit, I smelled him before I saw him. I been waitin' and listenin' to you all packing up."

Lars had come up from the cabin to see what the delay was. Jake turned to him.

"Lars, escort Sergeant Washington below to the cabin with you and Jutta. Don't tell him anything, just watch him. We'll decide what do with him when we get to the new base. And tell Jorn who he is before he shoots his black ass."

Jake motioned Axel back to the bridge. "Get us out of here. I'll be up and join you in a minute."

Jake turned to face the black man, and softened his voice. "Go with Lars, Sandy. I know why you've come, but you're out of this one. Go on, we're pressed for time, and it's too dangerous to leave you here. I'll talk to you later."

Washington shrugged. "I'll go with him, Snake, but you ain't talkin' me outta shit. You and me is a team, remember? You need the Sandman." The engines grumbled as the cruiser began moving. Jake looked into his friend's determined eyes for a long moment before turning in silence to join Axel on the bridge.

Nineteen kilometers away, Director Hagan Wolf strode down the stairs past the guards and into the special operations center, where Lothar Rossen was waiting for him. Wolf sat down, glanced around, then fixed his stare on Rossen. "Where is Max?"

Rossen came to attention. "Herr Direktor, Herr Rink will be here shortly. He is on the phone with the city southern Border Guard commander. It was an urgent call."

Wolf's eyes narrowed. "Start, from the beginning."

Rossen had already posted a large map, and pointed to a small red circle on it. "Herr Direktor, this is where the targets were staying on the Havelsee, in Herr Mader's cabin. The assault force began their . . ."

Wolf listened in brooding silence as the department chief explained what had happened.

Halfway through the briefing, Wolf became impatient and shook his head. "Ja, ja, the force obviously walked into a trap. Have you determined how the targets knew the teams were coming?"

"Furman told them."

"What?" Wolf blurted, turning around.

Rink strode forward with a scowl. "I just got off the phone with the idiot commander of the southern Border Guards. Last night he phoned his report in to his headquarters, thinking they would send it to us. The idiot didn't follow procedure of notifying us about crossers using weapons."

Rink saw the fire building in his director's eyes and knew this was no time for explaining bureaucratic foul-ups. He got to the point. "Furman killed two guards and a dog early yesterday evening during the rainstorm and cut his way through the fence into West Berlin. We have to assume he reached the others. It's the only way they could have been prepared."

"How did they know it was Furman who crossed?" Wolf snapped, not believing a word of it.

Rink sat down and leaned back in his chair, trying to remain calm. There was a bigger problem than Furman. "The border guards *don't* know who the crosser was, but the report stated they saw what appeared to be a man with no legs cutting the wire. They fired shots but missed, and the man escaped. The killings were done with a nine-millimeter pistol. The agent Furman killed in Seelow carried the same kind of pistol, and it was never found."

Despite Wolf's outward show of anger, he felt inner relief. His premonition of Furman's coming for him was now just a bad dream. Wolf's icy stare shifted from Rink to the map. "So, they are all together again . . . touching."

Wolf smiled to himself. Furman, the little amputee who continued to amaze him with his tenacity, was now with the others. Perfect. For all his efforts, he would be rewarded by dying with his kameraden.

"Have our polizei informers reported on where the targets have been taken?"

Rink shook his head as he stood and walked to the map to explain the dilemma. "Herr Direktor, as strange as it may seem, it appears the polizei were never notified."

Wolf stiffened and his eyes widened. He had assumed the cabin would have been crawling with polizei looking for evidence and answers. His prey had done the unexpected.

"The dock surveillance team reported that the American motored to the dock early this morning," Rink continued. "He left in Mader's car and returned in another vehicle an hour and ten minutes later. He carried two large bags to the boat and departed. They were unable to determine if he returned to the cabin, because of the darkness and fog."

Rink stared at the map, shaking his head. "We had assumed the targets would notify the polizei. They didn't, and that leaves us unprepared. We don't have enough maintenance teams in West Berlin to do the job. The special unit I sent to eliminate Mink for her failure was reported killed by their own bomb, and we've discussed the assault force losses. I have already ordered four of our teams from here to cross the border, but it will take time to hide their weapons inside the bodies of cars and—"

"They're gone," Wolf said flatly. "If they knew about the attack, then they know how far our reach extends. They probably used the American as a decoy. While he motored to the docks, they took the assault team's boat and motored up the lake. They are hiding now, trying to decide where they can go and be safe."

Rossen stood. "I'll have the surveillance team in the Grunewald check the cabin."

"Ja, do that," Wolf said, "and have them get rid of the bodies of the assault force."

Rink looked at his director worriedly. "How do they know of us?"

Wolf thought of what Dagmar had told him in the hospital about the people knowing what he was. He smiled sardonically. "Furman knows. He might have even been spying on me. It doesn't matter. Now we have to find them. Use every informer we have in West Berlin. They can't go far. Kailer has family, and Mader's daughter is in the hospital."

"And the American?" Rink asked.

"Ja, he is the mystery. Perhaps a friend of Kailer or Mader; again, it doesn't matter. He dies with the rest of them. Go on with your preparations of sending over the additional maintenance teams. They will be needed once we find them."

Rink shifted his eyes back to the map. "I underestimated them. It won't happen again."

Wolf's brow furrowed as he stood. "It is war. They won only the first battle. Use every asset we have. Find them . . . and finish them."

Inside an enclosed slip, the men of the *Defiance* were all seated at the table in the main cabin. Jutta was pulling guard duty on the bridge. Lars had just finished briefing his phase of the operation.

Jake turned to Washington. "You've heard the plan. You sure ya still want in?"

Washington shrugged. "Got nothin' else better ta do."

"What about Sissy?" Jake asked, watching Washington's eyes for the slightest glint of doubt.

"She just told me ta make sure everything works when I get back. She also told me ta bring your ass back."

Jake looked at Lars and then Axel, who had just translated the black man's response to Jorn. All three Iron Men nodded their approval.

Jake picked up the checklists. "It's settled, then. Let's get down to it."

"Eh, could I make a few suggestions?" Washington asked.

Jake leaned back in his chair. "Shoot."

"Well, first thing is, I better be the one who finds us a place to stay, not Axel. He ain't got fake ID, and usin' his real name ain't smart. Next, Axel and Lars shouldn't be rentin' no cars until we're ready to go in. Again, they gotta use their real ID and driver's licenses to get transportation. By waitin', it cuts down on the opposition knowing they're around. I'll go rent a car and a couple of rooms in my name, then come back and get you all. Once I get you all put away nice and safe, I'll go get my Chevy and leave the rental. I'll be buyin' and gettin' equipment while the rest of ya rest up. I had a full night's sleep. None of you have. And the last thing is, I'll drive into the East and not you, 'cause it's *my* truck."

Impressed, Jake lifted an eyebrow. "You been around the spooks too long, my man. You're thinkin' like 'em."

Washington stood up. "I'm goin' to find a cab and get to the airport and get us some wheels so we can get this action rollin'." He looked at his watch. "I got 0937 hours. I'll be back within an hour." He turned to go but stopped and faced the table again. "Sorry, guys, I'm a little short on money."

Axel and Lars both reached for their wallets, and within seconds Washington was holding over nine hundred marks. He stuffed the bills in his pocket and winked. "I'll get us some nice rooms."

Wolf sat in the smoke-filled minister's office listening to a man at the end of his rope. Mielke had aged ten years in the past ten days. His fingers and teeth were nicotine-stained dark yellow from chain-smoking eighteen hours a day, and his drawn face had the gray pallor of a dead man. He paced nervously behind his desk, shaking his head from side to side as he spoke. "We're running out of time, Wolf, out of time. I'm to fight the rear guard action for the government, and yet they tie my hands. I've asked for help in the destruction of the files from the army, but that pompous ass Kessler has the nerve to say it's *my* problem. We're running out of time . . . out of time."

Wolf calmly brushed lint from his blue cashmere jacket sleeve. "But I've noticed everyone carrying on business as usual, Herr Minister. Don't you think it's time you focused *all* your available manpower on destruction of the files? I should think a few days of concentrated effort would do it."

Mielke stopped abruptly and looked at Wolf as if he had lost his mind. "We are Stasi. We will work till the end to do *all* our duties."

"There are over nine million files, Herr Minister," Wolf said flatly. "You are running out of time if you think Administration can destroy that number in a month."

The muscles of Mielke's neck popped out as he sucked in deeply on his cigarette. Holding it a moment, he eyed Wolf, then his face became obscured in a cloud of exhaled blue-white smoke. He began pacing again. "You were the smart one, Wolf, you planned ahead. I don't have to worry about your direktorate, do I? Nein, I have never had to worry about the infamous S Direktorate. You did your dirty tricks so cleanly, you were praised and revered by the Secretary General himself. And the rest of us—the rest of us were fools running out of time. I have been told I'm to be the scapegoat for the government. I alone am to be held responsible while the others save themselves. Even Honecker has made a deal. The Russians have promised him he will be able to live his years out on the Black Sea. The goddamn Russians! A deal!"

Mielke halted again for another suck on the noxious weed. He exhaled through his nose and walked straight to where Wolf was sitting. "Help me, Wolf. Make sure they find nothing that will incriminate me."

Wolf wanted to laugh, but instead played his part. "I will take care of you, Minister, as I have always have. They will have nothing. But you must destroy the files. Their existence alone makes you an accomplice in the eyes of the liberals. Use every man and woman within Stasi, but destroy those files before you run out of time."

Mielke's trembling lips drew back in an effort to smile, but it was beyond him. Instead he put his hands on Wolf's shoulders. "Thank you, Wolf. My wife was frightened that I would be taken and . . . Thank you, my friend, thank you." Mielke released his grip.

Wolf rose, bowed his head slightly, and made his exit. Once outside, he brushed the ashes from his shoulder. He stank of smoke.

He returned to his own office just as his private phone buzzed.

"Ah, my friend," said the voice on the other end, "sorry to disturb you. I just wanted to thank you for the invitation to your house this evening. I hope you don't mind, but I'm bringing two friends who very much want to talk to you and Herr Rink, and of course meet your charming wife. I think you said around eight?"

Wolf forced himself to speak calmly. He had not expected to hear Georgi Sorokin's voice. Neither did he like the way he had just been ordered to furnish his house for a meeting about which he had not been forewarned. Still, he tried to make his voice sound congenial. "I am sorry, my dear friend. Sadly, my wife has taken ill. Perhaps another evening would be better."

Sorokin's voice rushed back. "Excellent, eight it is, then! One of the guests is with me now. He sends his thanks. See you at eight. Good-bye."

Wolf slammed down the phone and pressed the button below his desk. His secretary knocked and came in seconds later. He leaned back in his chair. "Call the residence. Tell the chef I have four guests coming over at eight this evening. Also inform my chief of security to tell the rest of the house staff . . . and tell the chief to make arrangements for additional guards."

"Jawohl, Herr Direktor."

Wolf lowered his head as soon as the secretary left. Of all times, he thought to himself. Why now? He looked at his watch. It was already past one o'clock. He picked up the phone and pushed the direct line button to Rink. The phone only rang twice before the deputy director answered.

"The meeting we've been waiting for is tonight," Wolf said quickly. "Come to the residence at seven. Yes, the residence, bring the information we prepared for them." Wolf hung up and leaned back, feeling the energy begin to build. Hours before, he had received word that the Havelsee cabin had been vacated, as he had predicted. There were no bodies and few signs of battle. He had been right, the cowards had gone into hiding.

Turning slowly, Wolf smiled. He would have wanted it no other way. They were challenging him just as Sorokin was, trying to manipulate him into giving up his power. They were all such fools.

Jake was awakened by a gentle nudge. He focused his eyes and saw Washington looming over him. "Time to practice, Snake."

Jake sat up, looking at his watch. It was almost 1400 hours. He couldn't believe he'd slept for over three hours. He hadn't thought he was capable of sleeping. He remembered just closing his eyes to rest them after going over the plan for the third time, but . . .

"Come on, Snake, Axel and Lars just got back with their rental cars. I'm gonna brief everybody on the equipment, then we can go."

Jake got up and walked out of the plush hotel bedroom and into the sitting room, where the team was waiting. They weren't much to look at, he thought to himself, but he felt a tingle of pride being with them.

Washington stood in front of the team and motioned to the canvas bags that lay in front of them. "As you can see, your equipment bags are marked with fluorescent paint so you'll be able to find them in the dark. According to the plan, we'll have to change quick, so listen carefully. Open your bags and we'll take it one step at a time. The first thing you see is your black jumpsuit. Some of you have the ones the Stasi team were wearing. When you put 'em on, make sure you unzip the legs first so you can get your feet through without having to take off your shoes. Do it now. . . . Good. As you can see, I cut Jorn's suit legs off. . . . Yeah . . . it fits fine. All right, now take out the watch cap from the bag and put it in your left rear jumpsuit pocket. Now the gloves . . . they go in the side pockets. Now take out the pistol belts and suspenders and put them on. Adjust the belts so they . . ."

The team followed the instructions, storing the equipment in the jumpsuit pockets and attaching the various pouches to the belts, which held the silenced pistols and spare magazines. Then Washington had them take off the pistol belt and harness and jumpsuit. As they would have to dress in just under two minutes, they would need more practice. The first attempt took a little over three minutes, the second only two minutes and thirty seconds, the third less than two minutes. He nodded in approval and had them take out the M-16s in each of their bags. He showed them how to load, operate, and dry-fire the lightweight assault rifle. When the weapons were put back in their bags, he had the men take out the small cases that held their night-vision goggles. He showed them how to fit the devices on their heads, turn them on, and adjust the focus. A minute later the training was over and Washington ordered everything packed in order of sequence of use.

Jake waited until his team was ready and Lars had said good-bye to his wife, then he held up his wristwatch. "We're on schedule. I've got 1435 hours. Phase one begins . . . now."

Axel and Lars picked up their bags and followed Washington out the door to stow their bags in the Suburban. Jorn climbed up into

Jutta's wheelchair and picked up his bag. Jake raised a finger. "Ein moment," he said, and strode into the adjoining room, where Jutta sat on the couch with her legs propped up. She was staring at the blank television across from her with tears running down her cheeks.

Jake leaned over, kissed her forehead and took her hand.

"Sissy will be picking you up in less than an hour. She'll have another wheelchair, and the both of you will be going somewhere nice and safe. Don't worry."

She looked up at him, speaking softly. "Bring them back, Jake."

He turned, rolling back his shoulders, and walked for the door. It was time.

Jake helped Jorn get up into the backseat, realizing for the first time how heavily muscled the old man was. It had been like picking up a boulder. Jake got into the front passenger seat and looked toward the back compartment. "Where's all the gear?" he asked Washington as he got in.

The sergeant grinned. "Creative packing. If they've changed the rules at the border, we gonna have a long vacation in Leavenworth prison."

Jake winked at Jorn and held up his thumb. *"Alles klar, ja?"*

Jorn raised his thumb. *"Ja, alles klar."* Jorn lowered his hand and looked over the interior of the truck. It was, like everything he had seen in the West, beyond his dreams. Colors, smells, even the taste of the hotel fruit that he had ordered were all beyond description, and it saddened him. He thought of how much Ida would have enjoyed all this. For so many years she had accepted such a dreary existence. Now it all seemed a waste. Tears welled in his eyes, not just for Ida, but for all his people who had been prisoners for too long.

Axel pulled the Audi to the curb as directed by the border guard and got out, holding his papers.

The guard motioned to the drab gray building behind him. "In there."

From the corner of his eye Axel saw Lars pulling up, but he kept walking. He stepped inside the small office, where a uniformed woman sat behind a battered desk and held out her hand without looking at him. "Papers."

Axel handed her his Berlin identity card and rental car papers, then held his breath as she looked at his name and quickly thumbed through the booklet beside her. She began speaking as she shut the booklet and picked up the current list of those who were to be stopped or detained. "You must exchange twenty-five marks for Ost-marks. The rate is currently one to three. You are restricted to not over one hundred marks of purchased goods per day that can be brought back. Upon leaving the GDR you are forbidden to take out everyday articles such as food, clothing, shoes, etcetera that you may have purchased in our country." She set down the paper, having not seen his name on the list, and from a stack picked up a booklet, which she handed to him. "The rules are printed in this for your convenience. Obey them, please." She handed back his papers and only then looked up at his face. "Enjoy your visit. . . . Next!"

Axel exhaled, feeling his stomach quivering. Outside, Lars stood behind his car with the trunk open, acting as if he were looking for his papers. He saw Axel scratch his face upon leaving the office. It was the signal that they were to proceed. Shutting the trunk, Lars took out his passport and headed for the office, telling himself to act natural.

Two kilometers away, Washington turned the truck down Kochstrasse, drove for a block, then made a left on Friedrichstrasse. After only twenty meters he slowed to approach a tan metal building in the center of the street with a large sign over it proclaiming CHECKPOINT CHARLIE.

Washington gave the passenger beside him a sidelong glance and spoke calmly. "Just do like I said, Snake. The MPs are in there. Our unit goes through all the time on recons. They even know our cover is that we're construction contractors working for the government, so they won't say nothin'. I do this all the time. Piece'a cake."

Jake sat back and tried to be calm. All doubts about accepting Washington on the team had long ago been erased, and this again proved his worth tenfold. What bothered Jake in retrospect was knowing that he might not have been able to do the job without him.

Washington pulled into the center lane parking space and got out. He had taken only four steps when an MP sergeant stepped out of a side door of the tin shack.

"Hey, Sandy, how ya doin'?" he said.

Washington smiled and raised his hand in a wave. "Hangin' in. Ya still ain't got a job, I see."

The young military policeman chuckled. "You should talk." He looked at Jake in the front seat then back to Washington and grinned. "Ya goin' sightseein' again?"

"Yeah, I dig the museums and all that culture shit."

The MP turned around and spoke over his shoulder as he walked back for the door. "I'll log ya in. Go on. Good luck, huh?"

"Thanks, I owe ya." Sandman strode back to the four-wheeler and got in. He smiled at Jake as he started the engine. "What I tell ya? Piece'a cake." He reached back, patted the blanket behind him and whispered, *"Alles klar, Jorn, nur fünf Minuten mehr."*

Jorn whispered back, *"Gut."*

Jake set his eyes forward, steeling himself for the next hurdle and hoping Sandman had been right. He had whispered to Jorn, "Only five minutes more."

Washington pulled the truck out and waved at the MP behind the window, then passed the large sign that said, YOU ARE NOW LEAVING THE AMERICAN SECTOR.

Washington took in a deep breath and exhaled as he weaved the truck around the first of two red-and-white-striped pole barriers. "This is it. Get your passport ready and look bored."

The East German border guard waved the vehicle to him and stepped off the platform. He jotted down the license number and the number of people in the vehicle, then strolled over to the office alongside the road and passed the paper beneath a chest-high darkened window. Inside, the guard checked the license against those of known spies. It was on the list, but had a blue circle around it, meaning the passengers were harmless spies. It was common knowledge that the Americans dressed their military intelligence stooges in civilian clothing and sent them to take pictures and snoop around. They were harmless as long as they obeyed the rules and stayed away from military and Stasi buildings. The guard passed the paper back to the outside guard and barked, "Cleared."

Strolling back, the guard lifted his hand, palm up, and turned it, indicating the passengers were to show their passports and then to open them so he could see their pictures. Both passengers complied, and he gave a cursory look. He nodded and motioned them through.

Jake shut his eyes and let out a deep breath of relief. Washington just smiled, turned down a side street and increased speed. Waiting until he covered a full kilometer, he slowed and nodded to Jake, who turned around and lifted the blanket. *"All ist gut."*

Jorn sat up and put on the baseball hat Washington had given him, as his disguise to make him look like an American.

Jake motioned him forward with a smile and adjusted the cap so the bill was positioned correctly over his head. "Now ya look like a real Cincinnati Reds fan."

Jorn forced a smile and leaned back, feeling a chill. He was back in the sad land. He was home again.

•   •   •

Axel sat in the rental car, watching the rearview mirror, waiting. Five parked cars away Lars was doing the same. The black Suburban pulled off Neue Krugallee into the rose garden parkplatz. Both waiting men got out of their cars and began walking to the garden that overlooked the Spree River.

Jake nodded when the Iron Men came down a path, and he held up two fingers to Jorn. "Phase two begins."

Washington took out the wheelchair as Jake helped Jorn out of the backseat. In minutes they were heading up the rose-garden path.

Axel, ahead of Lars by ten meters, pretended interest in the shrubbery as he watched for any other vehicles that might have followed the American truck. He stopped, let Lars pass him, and pulled on his ear. Jake breathed easier and turned right onto another gravel path.

Washington motioned over his shoulder. "Just behind us is Treptower Park, where the Soviet War Memorial is. Five thousand Soviet soldiers who died taking the city are buried there standing up. If you get a chance, you need to come back sometime and see it. It's really somethin'."

Jake nodded in silence, knowing he would never come back even if he could. They followed the path along the bank of the Spree, stopping now and then to look across at the east bank, as if they were visiting tourists. They were getting the lay of the land. Directly across from them was the southern finger of land that formed the inlet off the Spree, the Rummesburgersee, where the patrol boats were docked.

They continued down the tree-lined path for four hundred meters until they came to a grass-covered promontory with park benches facing the river. Behind them the park was a maze of small paths leading around geometrically landscaped gardens and hedges. Lars posted himself a little way down from the promontory and scanned the empty grounds before pulling on his ear. Washington pushed Jorn's chair to the side of a bench and sat down. Axel remained standing with Jake and spoke in a normal tone as he motioned with his head toward the two-hundred-meter-wide entrance to the inlet. "There they are."

Jake could see the docks clearly. They were only six hundred meters away, nestled at the base of the inlet. The ugly, gray, squat patrol boats were facing away from him, but he could see their flat-roofed pilot cabins. The water behind one of the boats frothed white, and dark diesel smoke boiled up as one of the craft began backing out of its slip. Jake looked at his watch to mark the time. It was exactly 1600 hours.

Axel watched the boat turn around and head directly toward them and the mouth of the inlet. "Ja, she's a ten-meter, twin diesel inboard Haifisch." He turned to Washington. "To use your phrase, 'a piece of cake' to drive."

Jake smiled without taking his eyes off the boat as it increased speed, heading up the Spree in the same direction they would go tonight. He noted the two uniformed men on the bridge and the one on the rear deck stowing the line. He looked at Washington for his opinion.

The sergeant winked. "No sweat."

Jorn took the tourist map from his pocket and spread it out on his lap. He pointed out the inlet on the map to Axel. "The patrol boat will go upriver for only two kilometers, then turn south into this small access waterway, which leads to the Teltow Canal. There it will begin patrolling. Our route tonight takes us past the access all the way up the Spree River to the Muggelsee. We don't have to worry about any patrol boats once we're past the access. They patrol the border only where the canal divides the city. All we need to do is establish the times for their shift changes. We should wait here until one more boat leaves, note the time, then drive to the other side and make a reconnaissance of the docks."

Axel translated to the two Americans, both of whom gave Jorn a thumbs up.

CHAPTER 38

Muggelsee

In the master bedroom of the Muggelsee estate, Renate laid the last of the dresses in a box and knelt in the closet to start collecting the shoes. It was a strange feeling, removing another person's past, especially when she was trying to replace that person. The director had told her that morning to remove his wife's things and all reminders of her. Renate knew the clothes would be easy, but there were so many other things in the house that were uniquely Frau Wolf's: the plants, knickknacks, the arrangement of furniture, even the gardens outside. She wondered if it would really be possible to erase a person who had lived in the same house for over thirty years.

Renate felt someone watching her and turned. The security chief stood in the bedroom looking at her. He glanced at the three boxes beside the bed and lowered his head. "It is very sad. I will miss her."

Renate collected two pairs of old-style high heels and tossed them toward the box. "I will need at least another carton. Did you want any of this for your wife?"

"No, it wouldn't seem right. I hoped the frau would return . . . but when the director ordered her clothes removed . . . it is very sad."

Renate tossed two more pairs toward the carton. "Did I see additional guards?" she asked, to change the subject.

The chief looked away from the boxes, for they sickened him. "Ja, four temps for tonight. You'd better hurry. The director will be back soon. I'll send the standbys up and take what you've collected to the basement."

Renate collected an armload of shoes and dumped them. "I understand Herr Rink will be here tonight. Who else is coming?"

The chief's eyes narrowed. "That's not your concern anymore. You have new responsibilities, remember? Make sure you do them well." He couldn't help the look of revulsion he gave her before he walked out.

She picked up the last of the shoes and threw them on top of the others before standing and looking at the empty side of the closet. She wondered how the director would ever fill such an empty place again. Then suddenly she felt dirty and went to wash her hands.

Twelve kilometers from the residence a cloud of diesel smoke still hung over the dock as the three-man crew from Patrol Boat 5 climbed up the ladder to the pier. Standing back on the dock, watching, was a stocky old man hunched over a cane. The first crew member off the ladder, a middle-aged first engineer, noticed the old man and waved him back. "You're not supposed to be here. Move on."

The old man waved his hand in disgust. "Ja, ja, I am going. It's sad when a citizen can't even look at the Spree anymore." Lowering his head, Axel Mader padded down the creaking planks.

Sitting in a rental car parked in a lot facing the harbor, Jake and Lars exchanged glances of relief.

An hour later the entire team sat behind a small knoll in Pionier Park, four kilometers from the boat dock. Jorn sat on top of the raised ground pulling security as the others huddled around the tourist map.

Lars took the light. "Thanks to Jorn's information, this park is perfect for our return base. The Spree River is only a hundred meters behind us. When we return, we'll beach the boat on the bank and walk back up here to our rental cars parked in the autoplatz. The routes to the border crossing points will be just as we planned. No changes are necessary."

Jake raised his wrist. "Everything so far is going well. It's 1840 hours now. We'll all leave here in the Chevy in twenty minutes."

The others nodded in silence. Axel and Lars stood. They walked up the knoll and sat down beside Jorn, putting their arms over his shoulders.

Lars gave his friend a gentle squeeze. "You planned well. There are no changes. We'll be taking the eight o'clock crew."

Jorn closed his eyes, savoring the feeling of his kameraden's closeness. "No man has put his arm around me since the war," he said softly. "I'd forgotten what it was like to have such friends."

Axel patted Jorn's back. "We'll always be together from now on, Jorn. When this is over, we'll have the rest of our lives."

Jorn nodded with a distant stare as he hugged the two men to him. "Ja, the rest of our lives. Always."

Muggelsee

Rink stood when his director walked into the library. "Any news on our prey?" Wolf asked, waving Rink back down and sitting across from him in his green leather chair.

Rink took three five-by-seven color photographs from his sport coat pocket. "We received these this afternoon. They were taken at the hospital when Mader and the Kailers were released. You can also see the American in the picture."

Wolf felt a chill seeing Mader's face. He did not recognize Kailer, but seeing Mader was like seeing a ghost. His face was fuller and older, but it was unmistakably the man who had first challenged him so many years ago. "You didn't answer my question."

"Mader and Kailer both rented cars at 1330 hours from Hertz at Tegel Airport. One of the cars was found back at the parkplatz at the Havelsee docks at 1530, so we assume a switch was made. The airports, train stations, and autobahn crossing points have all been covered. They have not left the city to try and escape to the West. Our people are still checking all the hotels and pensions, but as of yet we have found nothing."

"And the families and friends have heard nothing?"

"No, all their phone lines are tapped, but so far nothing. And the hospital where Mader's daughter is has a team watching as well, but again, nothing. However, one of our informers does report that the hospital contacted the polizei, trying to contact Herr Mader. It seems his daughter is conscious and is asking for him."

"It won't be long, then," Wolf said, smiling to himself. "Send an additional surveillance team to the hospital, and keep all the entrances under close watch. I believe Mader's daughter is your best lead." Wolf shifted his gaze to the folders Rink held in his hand. "Ah, yes, our bargaining chips. It should be an interesting evening. Do we know who Sorokin's guests will be?"

Rink's lip curled up. "Yes, our informants in the Ministry of Trade tell me Sorokin visited with the deputy minister today in private. It appears that Jens Hergler is Sorokin's choice to be our new director." Rink lifted one of the folders and handed it to Wolf. "We had surveillance on all the likely candidates. This is his file. Clean, except for some problems with his wife, as you will read."

Wolf thumbed through the file for a moment, then raised an eyebrow. "And the other guest, from the West?"

"Rossen is handling the surveillance himself. He will call and tell us as soon as he knows."

Wolf looked back at Hergler's file and shook his head, snickering. "Sorokin trying to keep secrets from me is very foolish. He should know better."

Rink let himself smile. "The student surpassed the teacher years ago."

Wolf chuckled. "We shall see."

Washington pulled off the main road into the alley, cut his lights and rolled into an old repair yard. The passengers unloaded with their bags, and within fifteen seconds the Suburban was pulling back onto the main street.

Jake stood watch while the others changed into their battle gear beneath a shed. "We are ready," Axel whispered minutes later.

Jake turned around and felt a tremor of pride run up his spine. They were standing like dark statues, head to foot in black, rifles slung across their backs, night-vision goggles perched on top of their heads, faces covered with black camouflage paint, pistols in hand. They were *ready*. He smiled, unseen in the darkness, as he unzipped his bag.

The crew of Patrol Boat 7 straggled one at a time into the locker room in their headquarters building to change into their uniforms. By seven-forty they had all dressed and picked up their weapons from the arms room. They walked together into the adjoining operations and dispatch office for the usual briefing from the operations sergeant, whose additional duty was to brief them on the most recent rules of engagement. Tonight it was the same as it had been since Honecker had resigned. They were not allowed to shoot or fire at crossers. If they saw someone trying to swim the canal, they were to "physically restrain" the swimmer. The crew went through the ritual of flipping ten-pfennig coins to see who would be tagged for the unthinkable duty of jumping into the ice-cold canal to carry out the order. The chief pilot and the first engineer smiled in relief when poor Sebastian, the second engineer and youngest of the crew, flipped to the side of his coin showing the compass and hammer, the state's national symbol.

The chief pilot clapped his young engineer on the back. "Don't worry, Sebastian, I have an extra set of clothes in the boat."

The first engineer chuckled, but Sebastian remained sullen. The three men walked down the dark pier to boat-slip number 7 and lined up behind the single ladder to begin climbing down to the gently rocking craft. The chief pilot went down first, then the first engineer. The pilot planted both feet on the deck and turned around. He suddenly gasped—something hard had been jammed into his stomach. He looked down, startled to see the shape of a man kneeling in front of him. A harsh whisper ended all doubt. "You speak, you die!"

Still standing on the pier, Sebastian had seen the black shadow rise up from the deck behind his pilot. He spun around, but faced a dark figure holding a pistol within an inch of his face.

The first engineer looked down, then up from his position midway down the ladder. He thought about yelling, but something cold pressed against the back of his head, and then he heard a whisper. "Climb down very slowly and you won't die."

Two minutes later the engines of the patrol boat rumbled to life. Jake bent over, checking two of the prisoners whose mouths, legs, and hands had been secured by Lars with duct tape. He walked back to the bridge, where Axel was backing the boat out of the slip. Lying on the deck by his feet was the chief pilot, whose hands and feet were taped. Jorn held a knife to the pilot's throat. Jake could see by the panel lights that the pilot's neck was bleeding where Jorn's knife was pressed against the skin.

"Is he going to cooperate?" Jake whispered.

Axel nodded. "Ja, he already has. Right after Jorn convinced him he would gladly cut his jugular. He told us the radio is not used except for emergencies."

Jake sighed in relief. He had worried about hourly commo checks to the dispatcher. He took the roll of tape from the snap link on his belt and quickly made two wraps around the pilot's head, covering his mouth. Jorn rolled the man out of the way.

Axel motioned ahead and turned off the running lights. "We're entering the Spree."

"Lock and load your rifles," Jake commanded his team.

The familiar metallic sound of the M-16 bolts slamming forward reminded Jake of one last preparation. He took out a half stick of gum from his pocket and stuck it in his mouth.

The bell rang and the maid waited the required five seconds before opening the large oak door.

Georgi Sorokin stepped into the foyer with a wide smile and extended his hand toward his waiting host. "Good to see you, Wolf. You're looking extremely fit."

Wolf wouldn't lie and return a similar compliment, for Sorokin, dressed in a cheap, brown suit that hung from his skeletal frame, his sunken face freckled in gray-white splotches, looked as if he had one foot in his grave. Wolf forced a pleasant smile. "So good of you to come."

Behind Sorokin was a middle-aged, heavyset man wearing an expensive Italian-made suit. "Wolf, I would like to introduce Herr Jens Hergler, Deputy Minister of Trade."

Wolf recognized the face from the photo in the file Rink had given him earlier. He smiled as he shook the bureaucrat's plump, soft hand. "It is a pleasure, Herr Deputy Minister. How is your wife Suzanne? I was so sorry to hear about her sickness."

Hergler's eyes widened. "Eh, yes, she is doing well, thank you. She is recovering nicely."

Wolf maintained his plastic smile, thoroughly enjoying the man's questioning look. Hergler was surely wondering how he, Wolf, knew his wife was drying out at a private hospital on the coast.

Sorokin then said as a small man entered, "I would also like to introduce . . ."

Wolf felt the pent-up energy inside himself explode and rush through his veins. He stepped forward and finished the introduction himself. "Herr Kurt von Kant, Special Internal Security Chief of West Berlin. Yes, I know Herr von Kant by reputation. And from our photographs of him, of course. It is a pleasure."

Von Kant's eyes didn't show surprise. Instead he returned a barb of his own. "Direktor Wolf, I have seen your photos as well. At funerals, I believe. It is a pleasure to finally meet you."

Georgi Sorokin clapped his hands together. He did not like the feeling crawling up his spine. "I need a drink."

Wolf motioned toward the living room. "Please, this way, gentlemen." He turned to the deputy trade minister. "I believe you drink only tonic water, am I correct?"

"Eh . . . yes, how did you know?"

Wolf exchanged looks with von Kant, then Sorokin, before smiling at the unsettled bureaucrat. "It is my business to know everything, Herr Deputy Minister."

Sorokin lowered his head. Von Kant's eyes sparkled.

Washington waited along the bank, listening. He heard the muffled engines but didn't see the dark shape until it loomed out of the darkness only a few meters ahead. He waded out to his waist in the cold water and grabbed hold of the boat ladder extended over the side. Immediately, the engines increased power with a churning rumble.

Jake reached over the rail and grabbed the pack on Washington's back, then pulled the big man up and onto the deck as the bow lifted with the increase in speed. Within seconds the darkened craft was plowing through the water at twelve knots, leaving a wake that splashed against the banks. From his position at the wheel, Axel could see the river ahead clearly through the night-vision goggles.

Behind him, like two knights, Jake and Sandy donned their suits of neoprene rubber, while their squires, Lars and Jorn, prepared their weapons by dropping them into Ziploc bags.

Axel turned and barked, "Checkpoint two on the right. Six more kilometers."

Wolf cocked an eyebrow at Sorokin after showing him the typed, four-page list of high-tech corporations in which he had planted informers. "So you see, Georgi, Max and I aren't ready to retire. We will need to 'assist' the new director for quite some time to achieve what you desire. There is so much yet to be done for the new Germany."

Sorokin looked into Wolf's eyes. There was no choice. The information that could be derived from just a quarter of these companies would be enough to assure the Soviet Union's economic survival for years. The cost, however, would be Wolf, a man he couldn't control. Wolf had been an ally in the old, secret wars, for they had shared a common enemy, the West. But in the economic war, they would eventually compete against one another. And in competition, Wolf always went for the throat.

Sorokin's expression hardened. "I see only a man who believes he is indispensable. My superiors may think differently."

"Ah, but they would lose so much." Wolf said, still affecting a cordial smile. "I'm sure you will explain how my new arrangement is in the best interests of both of our nations." Wolf's smile dissolved and his stare hardened. "Won't you?"

Sorokin shifted his eyes to von Kant, who had picked up the list of companies and scanned the names.

"He is blackmailing us," Sorokin stated flatly. "I didn't know he would want to become personally involved. Will you still agree to our deal if he's in?"

Von Kant looked at Wolf with a searching gaze. Slowly, he began nodding, but he kept his eyes locked on his host. He stood. "I believe you have a beautiful view of the lake from your back veranda, Herr Wolf. . . . Why don't we stroll out and see it. Just you and I."

Sorokin's face flushed and he quickly stood. "No, I demand that whatever is discussed be said here."

"Sit down, Georgi!" Wolf commanded, coming up out of his chair. "You are a *guest* in my house, and in my country! You make no demands here. Your government's influence ended with Honecker!"

Sorokin's eyes bulged behind his thick glasses as if they were going to pop out of their sockets. His whole body shook with rage and frustration. He knew what the two men wanted to discuss.

Wolf gave a slight nod to Rink, who got up, gently took the Russian's arm and assisted him back to his chair. Wolf's icy gaze shifted to Hergler, who sat with an open mouth, unsure of what was happening but very sure it wasn't good. "I believe you should go and find Greta, my maid, and ask for another drink for your friend. He looks as if he needs it."

Sweating, Hergler got up and made a wide detour around his host as he walked into the dining room.

Wolf motioned for von Kant to follow him. "If you'll follow me, I'd be happy to show you the view."

Wolf led the way back across the foyer and through the library and sun room. He opened the back door for the smaller man.

Von Kant took in a deep breath of the night air as soon as he stepped out on the stone deck. He exhaled and chuckled lightly. "The Russian had thought he would keep control with his 'new' director and be able to save his country from economic ruin."

Wolf kept his eyes on the dark shimmering waters. "The Russians are most dangerous when in turmoil. You know that. Don't play games with me, von Kant. I know your government is making deals with them, just as we had to."

Von Kant gave his host a measured stare. "You were their puppet, were you not?"

Wolf moved his head slowly, pinning von Kant with his narcotic eyes. "Are you the Americans' puppet?"

Von Kant smiled. "We both have had to dance on the razor's edge. I am very impressed with the assets you have available. I knew you had infiltrated some areas, but hadn't dreamed you'd been successful in so many."

Wolf's eyes gleamed. "You're playing games again. Sorokin knew of my assets. He told you, or you wouldn't be here. What have you come to offer?"

Von Kant's jaw muscles twitched. He was dealing with a man who had over thirty years of experience in subterfuge. He'd confirmed what he had thought all along. Wolf could not be bluffed or manipulated "I came to offer a united Germany," he said softly.

Wolf stepped closer, pressing. "That will come within months, no matter what happens. The people will settle for nothing else. Why are you here?"

Von Kant didn't give ground. He met Wolf's glare. "I came for the future. You hold it. I represent not West Berlin, but those in our government with political vision. We believe that with your help, Germany can again become what she once was. The men I represent offer you a place with us. Your past will be cleansed for the greater good of our united nation. You will be given a new life and a new direktorate, not here in the East, but in Bonn, at a growing electronics company that needs a research and development director. You are offered that position immediately."

Wolf stared at von Kant for a long moment. Von Kant was his counterpart in West Berlin, the power behind the scenes pulling strings for the politicians who thought they ran the government. Von Kant would know that he, Hagan Wolf, was the man to deal with in East Berlin, not Sorokin.

"I will need some of my staff," Wolf said. "They must be part of the deal."

"Of course, we planned for thirty or forty additional specially qualified employees to come with you. It will be arranged."

"And Hergler and Sorokin?" Wolf asked, as if it were an afterthought.

Von Kant sighed. "Sorokin came to us, before Honecker resigned, to offer us his deal on behalf of his government. He has since lost his usefulness. As you said, we did make some deals with the Russians, but only for short-term loans and grants in exchange for the Soviets' pulling their troops out in four to five years. They will get a few bones of intelligence, but it is not your concern. I will deal with the Russians and the KGB. Your new job is much too important to waste with them. Hergler is a Russian puppet. He goes when the government falls. We've already seen to it."

Wolf felt a twinge of pity for Sorokin. He had always been loyal to his country, and always, like himself, Sorokin understood that his nation's survival came first, no matter what the cost. The cost had been high.

Von Kant put out his hand. "Do you accept our offer?"

"There is a condition. I want to be able to give Sorokin information for the next two years. He has done much for us both. To send him back with nothing would not be wise. The Russians are still very powerful, and it is best to wean them slowly from the breast. If it becomes dry too quickly, they will bite it off and try and kill the mother."

Von Kant kept his hand extended. "It is done. To the new Germany."

Wolf grasped the man's hand. "To the new Germany."

Axel throttled back, bringing the engines to a low, churning rumble. "We're entering the Muggelsee," he said.

Jake and the others peered through the bridge at the distant western shore. It was dark except for one lone, large, three-story house.

Jake brought up his binoculars. "She's seven to eight hundred meters away. Sandman, where are the winds coming from?"

The sergeant stepped back from the bridge and looked up at the wind vane on the communications mast. "It's a blowin' from southeast to northwest at about seven to eight knots."

Jake still held the binoculars to his eyes. "Axel, bring her in from the northwest. They won't hear the engines until you're within a hundred meters. It looks like the floodlights on the poles at the end of the walls are both angled toward each other—not pointed out toward the lake. Their coverage overlaps along the bank at the retaining wall."

Jake shifted his view slightly. "The light on the pole at the end of the pier isn't a flood, it's a standard bulb. The sailboat is still on the northern side of the dock. So far, it looks better than we expected." He turned, handing the glasses to the sergeant. "Whataya think?"

Washington studied the dock, then shifted the glasses to the back of the house. "Yeah, nice an' dark under the dock, like we thought. Plenty of dark places next to the house too, once we're away from the floods."

Jake took the aerial photo of the house out of Axel's uniform back pocket and set it against the control panel lights so the others could see as he pointed. "The dock comes off this retaining wall. From the retaining wall the grounds go back for only twenty meters to this lower bricked area beneath the porch at the back of the house. Probably a walkout basement door beneath the deck somewhere. These steps lead up to the large stone porch to the main back entrance of the house. Based on what I see so far, we go with the plan. We take out the guards on the outside first, seal the house, then clear the rooms until we find and kill him. Remember, we don't kill the house staff once we're inside, but don't take any chances. If you have to kill, shoot 'em in the face. These silenced .22s won't bring a man down with a body shot, unless it's in the head, neck or heart. Don't use the rifles unless you hear gunfire. If we can, we wanna stay with the silenced pistols the whole mission."

Jake looked back at the lighted house in the distance. "Phase three begins . . . now. Axel, take us in nice and slow."

Jake nodded to Washington. The sergeant picked up his swim fins, mask, and snorkel and walked to the rail, where he pulled down his neoprene hood.

On the opposite side of the boat, Jake also took up his position. He spat into his diving mask to make sure it wouldn't fog.

Axel brought the bow around, keeping the speed steady, and headed straight for the objective. Jake patted his chest, feeling the pistol in the Ziploc bag beneath the neoprene suit, then reached behind himself to make sure the small pouch that contained his equipment was attached to his belt. He held his hand up, and Lars handed him extra-heavy neoprene gloves. Jake slipped them on and nodded he was ready.

Washington waved, signaling he was also set. They waited. Seconds ticked by. When Axel estimated that they were within five hundred meters from the house, he throttled all the way back to idle and whispered over his shoulder, "Stand by."

Jake and Sandy lowered their masks, put their snorkels in their mouths and climbed over the rail, facing each other across the back deck. The boat glided in. Axel waited until they were within four hundred meters, and whispered again, "Go."

Both men lowered themselves into the dark water.

•   •   •

Wolf returned a smile to Sorokin, who was searching his face for answers. "Come, my friend. Let's you and I go to the library and chat for a few minutes while the others retire to the dining room."

Rink took his cue and led the other two out as Wolf walked his old friend across the foyer.

Wolf motioned to the green leather chair and sat down opposite Sorokin. "Georgi, I have not abandoned you, my friend. You will receive the benefits of our life's work. I have made a deal, but we will give you what your government desires. It seems, now, I am *your* guardian angel."

Sorokin took in a deep breath in relief. "I won't ask for how long . . . for I know you too well. It is enough . . . for now. The world is changing, Wolf. Your new Germany will not be a threat to us only. The whole world will be watching with worry. And they will take the necessary measures to keep your new nation contained. As your old friend, I give you my last advice. Remember the past. Germany has been destroyed twice by men like you and von Kant."

Wolf smiled. "I do remember our past and I have learned from it. Come, Georgi, our dinner will be cold."

As Sorokin got up, he noticed some photos beneath the lamp. He paused for a moment to look at the top picture before taking his host's arm.

Jake kept his arms to his sides as he kicked his legs to propel himself forward. His protective layer of neoprene had warmed the numbing cold water trapped next to his skin, and by constantly opening and shutting his gloved hands, he had finally brought feeling back to his fingers.

Five meters away Sandy Washington struggled to keep up. He watched his leader's short-barreled snorkel skylighted in the glow of the floodlights ahead. When it suddenly disappeared, Sandy gave another kick, took in a deep breath, and submerged into the blackness. He kicked with all his strength, putting his hand out to his front to ward off the pier's huge pilings. He kicked until his lungs felt as if they were going to burst before gliding toward the surface. His head broke above the waves and he spit out the mouthpiece to take in a quick breath so he wouldn't pass out. He saw his leader a few feet in front him with just his mask above the water. They were directly under the end of the pier.

Jake pointed to the wiring that ran beneath the deck above

them. He nodded silently and submerged, leaving Washington in the semidarkness holding onto the moss-covered support pole.

Jake came up for air twice, hiding in the long shadows of the pilings as he made his way toward shore beneath the dock. He hadn't seen or heard the guard. He went under for the last time and swam until he touched the retaining wall. When he surfaced, he found that he was only in waist-deep water, but his head had only a couple of inches' clearance from the bottom of the dock planking. He peeled off his hood and listened. A moment passed, and then he heard footsteps off to his left, along the graveled path beside the retaining wall.

Jake took off his gloves, removed the penlight from the pouch on his belt and flashed it twice toward the opposite end of the pier. Then he took out the pistol and silencer.

At the signal, Washington took out his penlight and flashed it twice toward the northwest part of the lake, then went back into his pouch for a pair of small wire cutters. He climbed the first two rungs of a three-rung wooden ladder, reached up to the wiring cable and snipped it. The pier became dark. He lowered himself back down and withdrew his pistol to wait.

Both guards' heads snapped toward the dock when the pier light went out. The new guard was closest. He turned to his partner. "Friedrick, are there more bulbs somewhere?" he asked.

Friedrick walked closer so he didn't have to talk so loud. "Check the light before I call it in to the security room. The bulb may just need a tap or tightening."

Surprised at hearing two voices, Jake cussed. He hated fuckin' surprises. There had only been one guard in the photos. Fuckin' Murphy's law was alive and well. He heard the first man walk overhead. He waited, getting the rhythm of the footsteps, then slowly moved toward the retaining wall, straining to hear where the other man was.

Friedrick shifted his feet, and fished a pack of cigarettes out of his pocket. He shook one loose and put it into his mouth, then snapped the lighter lid back. He had only begun to flick the flint wheel when he saw a movement directly ahead. Instantly he knew it was too late, and instinctively shut his eyes.

Jake fired and turned. The other guard was still walking toward the end of the pier, keeping the same rhythm. Jake rolled over the retaining wall, got into a crouch and lowered his hand to the dead guard's jacket collar. He walked backwards, keeping his eyes on the pier as he dragged the body out of the lighted area, into the grass and over a small English-style hedge. When he had dropped the body, he glanced left and right. Both security cameras were stationary, and like the floodlights, were facing at a forty-five-degree angle toward the retaining wall and shoreline. The left camera was closer to the pier, but its angle didn't cover the end of the dock. The farther camera's did. He looked back at the guard, who was still walking down the pier, and made his decision, knowing he was running out of time.

The guard looked up at the bulb, knowing he couldn't reach it. Now how in the hell was he supposed to check it? He smiled to himself. Friedrick was playing games with him. A joke. Shit. He'd fallen for it. He began to turn around for the long walk back, but he heard a sound coming from the lake. He turned, straining to see what it was. The low grumbling noise got louder. He saw a shape loom out of the darkness and wondered why the chief hadn't mentioned that a patrol boat would be on the lake. No matter, he said to himself. They had obviously come to investigate the light. Good, they could fix it. The grumbling engines stopped. Only the waves hitting the dock made a sound. The boat glided closer, then he heard the planks behind him creaking.

Putting on a scowl, he turned to accept a ribbing from the other guard, but instead he saw a huge black figure. His eyes widened in terror and urine flooded down his leg. He saw the small flash but heard no sound and felt no pain as he fell forward. Then something hot pressed against his head.

Washington squeezed the trigger and stood back just as the rope from the patrol boat sailed toward him.

Delayed by the hedges, Jake broke the rules and hurried toward his target when he saw the boat pulling up to the end of the pier. He stopped, kneeled, aimed at the camera and fired.

The guard sitting behind the console broke his gaze from the television in the far corner of the room, where on the screen a man was undressing a woman. The security room at Muggelsee was famous for its porno tapes. The guard looked back at the monitors and saw on the bottom right screen nothing but static fuzz. He tried adjusting the picture, but nothing worked. He glanced at the other camera's picture. It seemed darker. He sighed and looked up at the television again. "Olf, check camera seven."

The backup got up, stood in front of the other backup agent, and stretched.

"Get out of the way. I can't see the TV!" the second man said.

Olf snorted through his nose, and taking his jacket from a peg, opened the door and stepped out.

Jake spun as the door opened, and saw a man only six feet away walking with his head down and zipping up his jacket. Jake waited only a moment before squeezing the trigger. The man's head snapped back and the rest of his body turned limp. He fell in a still heap. Stepping over the body, Jake stayed low and looked through the dirty window of the door. Then he grasped the knob and prayed he wasn't too late.

The guard sitting at the console adjusted the brightness of screen eight, but it didn't help. He was about to give up when in the upper right-hand corner of the picture he saw three men walking on the dock. He blinked, for a short ape appeared to be following them on his hands. He touched the pan right and close-up buttons. The camera shifted and the lens zoomed in. He gasped. The men were carrying rifles on their backs. Then he saw the dark shape at the end of the pier. A boat! He reached for the alarm button but suddenly felt something slap his forehead.

Jake fired again, aiming lower, and spun around toward the man he had sneaked by seconds before, who was sitting on the couch with his back to the console. The agent had not heard anything over the panting and cries of ecstasy from the television. Jake fired.

Washington sighed in relief as Jake stepped out of the walkout basement door. His leader held his thumb up, but then gave a time-out signal. The sergeant turned and whispered a warning. "Hold it. Nobody move. We got problems."

Seconds later Jake kneeled down with black-faced men, hidden in the shadow of the stairs. "There are more than we thought," he whispered. "Change in plans. Lars, you and Jorn go in the basement door. There are guards sleeping in the back rooms. Keep an eye on them until we get back. Let anyone come downstairs or in the back door, but don't let them out once they're in. The rest of us are going to go with the plan. First we eliminate the guards, then we finish it. Let's do it."

Wolf leaned back in his chair as the maid cleared away the first empty plates. "Tell me, Herr von Kant, what has been keeping you busy lately? As you know, we've had some internal problems, and I've been out of touch with what you've been doing."

The West Berliner raised an eyebrow as he dabbed his chin with his napkin. "I hardly believe you are 'out of touch' with anything, Herr Wolf. As you probably know, we experienced a terrible IRA terrorist attack on Saturday. The British are handling the investigation, and we are supporting as best we can."

Sorokin set down his fork. "I am the one out of touch, being in Moscow. I didn't hear of it. Who were the targets?"

Von Kant gave the Russian a pained frown. "The British guards at Smuts Barracks and an RAF commander at Gatow Air Base. Sadly, they killed the commander with a bomb during a reunion of one of our old German parachute units, the Iron Men. What was left of them anyway. Many Germans were killed and wounded."

Sorokin's eyes snapped accusingly to the host.

Wolf winked at his old friend and motioned to the woman bringing a tray with the second course. "I hope everyone is hungry. We will be having seven courses tonight. Nothing is too good for friends."

On the path beside the house leading through Dagmar's garden the first guard crumpled to the ground. The second turned to see why his partner had tripped, then pitched over, joining his kamerad. A small hole had been drilled through his temple. Washington lowered his pistol and listened for a full five seconds before signaling that he would take care of the guard standing under the light at the front entrance. Jake stepped away from the corner of the house, nodding. He motioned that he would get the two drivers leaning against the cars in the driveway.

Jake turned and waved Axel up to him. "You take the one on the right," he whispered. "I'll take the other. Wait till I shoot first."

Axel followed Jake around the front of the house, always keeping in the shadows of the trees. They stopped only ten meters from their targets, then they separated and began crawling.

Axel was shaking so badly he could hardly make himself move. His heart felt as if it were pounding through his chest, and he couldn't seem to get enough air. He prayed he would be able to hold the pistol steady. His target lit a cigarette. The tip glowed as he drew the smoke into his lungs, then a cloud escaped his lips and floated upward as he looked up at the stars. Axel glanced left at Jake's target, who was leaning against his staff car, holding a small flashlight to read by. Jake was already on the opposite side of the car, looking toward the front entrance and waiting for Washington's target to fall. His own target took the cigarette from his lips and mumbled; no, he *sang* softly. Axel crawled closer and rose up to one knee beside the fender of the car.

Washington kept his eyes straight ahead, trusting the others to watch his back. He took one step up the stairs, then another, and he saw the top of the guard's head. He raised his pistol and took another step. The guard saw him just as Washington fired. The guard's head jerked back and his knees buckled.

Jake saw the man fall. He rose up, took two quick steps to his right for a clear shot, and squeezed the trigger. The muffled cough sounded sweet, but he cringed as the expended cartridge clattered off the hood. The reader slid down the side of the car, but his head caught between the sideview mirror and the door. The lights from the house reflected grotesquely off his dulled, protuding eyes.

The other driver sang, and rocked his shoulders as if to his own beat, without seeing or hearing anything else. Axel rose up from his knee and aimed. His hand was steady. He put a bullet just a millimeter left of the driver's Walkman earphone.

Axel began to lower his pistol, then froze. Someone was approaching from his right. A man appeared, zipping up his pants as he walked out of the shadows of a barren oak. The man stopped abruptly at the sight of the driver lying on the ground. A black figure stepped toward him. He reached inside his coat for his gun, but a bullet tore through his jaw. The man flinched with the blow and looked back at the black-uniformed man as if confused. He grasped the grip of his nine-millimeter and pulled the weapon clear of the holster, but another bullet struck him just below his right eye. For a moment he stood as if in disbelief. Then he toppled over.

Jorn Furman carefully opened the door of the last room and listened. Hearing only the sounds of a sleeping man, he planted his hands and entered the darkness. At the bed, he took the bloody antler-handled knife from his belt and laid the blade across the man's throat. He waited until the man moved before shifting his weight down and back, slitting his victim's throat. As he felt the hot wetness flow over his hands and heard the sickening gurgling noise, he leaned over and whispered, "For Ida."

Lars, watching the stairs and the monitors, heard Jorn before he saw him. "Are they still sleeping?" he whispered.

Jorn pushed himself forward from the small hallway. He stopped looking up at the stairs, then turned his head slowly to his fellow team member. "They won't be a problem."

Lars saw the blood on Jorn's uniform and the freckles of dull red splattered across his darkened face. He looked back at the stairs and spoke softly. "*They* didn't kill Ida and Helga, Jorn."

Jorn's upper lip curled. "No, but they protect the man who did."

Lars closed his eyes, praying for their souls. The sound of the upstairs door opening and then footsteps brought them open again. He motioned Jorn back and raised his pistol.

The chief of security, holding a plate of sandwiches, was halfway down the steps when he smelled something that caused him to stop in mid-stride. It was the faint smell of cordite from a fired pistol or rifle. It lingered distinctly, like a light perfume. Internal warning bells clanged in his head and his senses perked. He couldn't hear the usual sounds from the television, and he heard no one talking. He slowly squatted to put the tray down on the steps behind him, when he saw a movement at the bottom of the stairway. He saw the flash and instantly felt a stabbing pain in his groin. He fell back, and the tray and sandwiches tumbled down the carpeted steps with him. Groaning in agony, he grasped for the banister.

Lars fired three times as he ran up the stairs, trying to stop the man's horrible sounds. Each bullet had hit flesh, but he still groaned. Closing within a meter, Lars raised the pistol, steadied his hand, and pulled the trigger. The chief's taut body suddenly relaxed and slowly began slipping down the steps, leaving a deep crimson trail on the beige carpet.

Lars looked at the body in horror as it slid past him, but heard a harsh whisper behind him. "The door! Check the door and see if anyone heard!"

Cursing himself for his weakness, Lars quickly moved up the stairs and listened at the door. He heard low voices, but none were excited. He turned, holding up his thumb, and sighed inwardly.

Jake nodded to Washington, then opened the gatehouse door. The guard turned to see who had entered, and was shot in the face.

Outside the gate, in the guard shack, the lone security guard listened to soft music from the transistor radio sitting on the plywood counter.

"We need your help," said a voice, startling him. He got up and stepped out of the shack to see who had spoken from inside the estate. A man was standing behind the gate, in the shadows. "What do you want?" the guard asked, stepping closer.

Axel didn't need to speak again, for he heard the muffled pop and saw the man topple over to the ground. Washington rose from his firing position by the gate's ornate ironwork. The gate clanked as it rolled back a meter. Washington hurried through the gap, grabbed the dead man's collar and pulled him out of the light and into the estate grounds. The gate clanked shut as the sergeant dropped the body beside the near wall and faced the two approaching men. All three exchanged glances in silence and slapped in new magazines. They faced the distant house and began the long walk to finish the job.

CHAPTER 39

The deputy trade minister leaned back with a contented look. "That was excellent, Herr Wolf, I must talk to your chef and find out how he made the delightful béarnaise."

Wolf couldn't help himself. "Yes, you are a gourmet cook. I had forgotten."

Hergler smiled meekly, lifted his wineglass and told himself to just enjoy the meal and not to make small talk again. He didn't want to know what else his host knew about him.

Sorokin decided to see if he could make the host feel discomfort for a change. "Wolf, I couldn't help but notice a picture on the table when we were in your library. Are you interested in photography or was it business?"

Wolf smiled dryly. "It was a picture of some old veterans. I'm afraid they have been diagnosed with a fatal disease. I don't expect them to be with us much longer."

"And the younger man in the picture, he was dressed like an American. Is he also sick?" Sorokin asked, raising an eyebrow.

Wolf shrugged with a pitiless frown. "The disease is very contagious."

Von Kant gave Wolf a warning look. "I hope your discussion is not about what I think. I would not, if I were you, Herr Wolf, involve an American in any 'business.' I have been successful so far in keeping them out of your affairs. It would be unwise to raise their ire. The recent terrorist attack has made them very angry. I would not want that anger turned toward your organization."

Wolf smiled indulgently. "My friend, when I do business, it's always handled professionally. Fatal accidents and diseases are quite

443

common. I wouldn't concern yourself. This matter is of personal interest to me."

"All the outside guards have been eliminated," Jake whispered to Lars and Jorn. "Axel is at the back entrance, and Washington is covering the front. The house is sealed. We'll clear the kitchen, then the room at the back entrance, so we can get Axel. There is something going on in the house, maybe a dinner party. There were two staff cars in front. We'll follow the plan for now. We clear all the rooms one at a time until we find him."

Lars translated to Jorn, then motioned toward the door at the top of the stairs. "The kitchen is to the right. I heard people talking and pans clanking. I think it was the cook and maid."

Jake pointed at the roll of duct tape dangling from the snap link on his team member's belt. "If we can, we'll use that, but if they give us any trouble . . ."

"I know," Lars said, and began walking up the stairs. Jake held his hand out. "I'd better go first."

Lars gently pushed his hand aside. "You don't speak German. I'll lead." The old man set his shoulders and continued up the steps.

In the master bedroom, Renate slipped off her bra and picked up the towel she had laid on the bed. She stepped closer to the window as she wrapped it around herself and looked out toward the lake. She saw that the pier light was out and a border patrol boat tied to the end of the dock. She mumbled an obscenity under her breath at the chief, for he had not told her about any additional security measures. She knew why he hadn't told her, just as he wouldn't tell her who the guests were. She recalled his repulsed stare again and shook with anger. I'm just following orders! she thought furiously, and hurried into the bathroom to shower, wanting to be fresh and clean for her director when he returned. Turning on the water, she dropped the towel and looked at herself in the mirror. She saw another woman looking back at her. One much older . . . the one who wore all those clothes and shoes. The woman she wanted to replace.

Renate smiled at the reflection, knowing she could defeat her.

In the kitchen, the maid was reaching for the third dessert goblet when she was suddenly jerked backward. The chef turned and saw only a blur before being struck in the throat. The second blow, in the solar plexus, doubled him over. Jake spun around. The woman's face was turning blue. Her body became limp. Keeping his grip around her neck, Lars lowered the unconscious maid to the floor before releasing her and grabbing for his roll of tape.

Jorn held his automatic, covering his team members. His eyes were in constant motion toward the three entrances that led into the kitchen.

On the back porch, Axel tried looking through the windows, but all the curtains were drawn. He moved back to the door and put his hand on the latch. Pushing down, he felt it give, and he very gently pushed it forward only a crack to listen. Nothing. He waited.

On the front porch, Washington reached up and removed the glass globe. Setting it down gently, he spat on his fingers and reached up to unscrew the bulb. His reward was darkness on the second turn of his hand. He put his ear against the door and slowly opened it an inch so he could hear anyone approaching. He sat on the doorsill and waited.

Jake heard voices coming from behind the door to his left. He saw by the looks on Jorn's and Lars's faces that they heard them too. He whispered a warning: "Follow the plan. We have to be sure the other rooms are clear so our backs are safe. Lars, do you understand?"

Lars, staring hard at the left door, reluctantly nodded once and translated to Jorn, who looked unhappy at what he'd heard. Jake knew how they felt, but it had to be done his way for their own safety. Jorn holstered his pistol and extended his hands to the floor to propel himself toward the opposite door. Jake exhaled in relief and patted Lars's back, motioning down the hallway toward the front door. "Watch for us."

Lars lifted his pistol and motioned toward the sounds. "If I think they hear you, I'm going in, Jake. Volker is not getting away."

"They ain't gonna hear me," Jake said confidently. "Take care of yourself." Jake stepped over the two bound people lying on the floor by the stove. He moved to the door and listened. Hearing nothing, he nodded to Jorn, who pushed the door open from his position against the wall.

In a shooter's crouch, Jake stepped into the lighted room, his eyes and pistol moving in sync as they searched for a target. It was a large sun room filled with curtained windows, ferns hanging from the high ceiling near the far wall, white rattan furniture, a tree in a huge pot in the corner. The room smelled fresh, clean, empty of humans. The arched double doors leading into the next room were open. He could see it was a library or study. He moved with his back against the rear wall, his eyes focused only on the other room. Each step revealed more of the interior of the library, the green leather chairs, bookshelves, desk, more books. He stopped, tapped the rear door behind him, and kept moving.

Axel heard a gentle knock. He paused for a moment, whispering to Gisela, asking her to give him strength. He pushed the door open and crept in. He saw Jorn first, to his right, his face and uniform splattered with dried blood. He was standing in an open doorway, a kitchen behind him.

Axel pushed the door all the way back, revealing the rest of the room, and saw Jake moving toward the opened arched doorway of another room.

Jake stopped, turned slightly and looked at Axel. His eyes were like those of a panther, cold, unreadable. He motioned for the Iron Man to move forward and cover him. Jake stepped into the library. Axel followed him.

Upstairs, Renate stepped out of the steaming shower and began drying herself with a towel. Moving out to the bedroom to cool off, she passed by the window and saw that the light at the end of the pier was still out. She moved closer to see if the guards were doing anything about it. Searching the path along the retaining wall, she didn't see anyone. Then she lowered her gaze and froze. A man was lying on the ground behind one of the hedges. He was lying at an odd angle, as if . . . Her stomach knotted. *Mein Gott!*

Her eyes darted to her clothes, then to the handbag on the door-knob. She grabbed the handbag and pulled out her .32 automatic. With shaking hands she jacked a round into the chamber; the metallic chuck-link sound stopped her trembling. She looked back at her clothes but shifted her gaze over the bed to the green phone on the nightstand. One call to Operations would bring a reaction force to the residence within minutes. Yes. She lunged across the bed toward the phone.

They were in the foyer. Jake watched the stairway and landing as Axel walked silently down the long hallway and looked into the open doorway of the small bathroom under the stairwell. Empty. He looked back at Jake and shook his head, then turned in the opposite direction and raised his thumb to Lars. Lars nodded.

Jake moved over to the front door, tapped it once and opened it all the way back. Holding his M-16, Washington stepped in backwards, keeping his eyes and weapon on the distant front gate.

"Right side is cleared," Jake whispered. "Lars and Jorn are covering the back from the kitchen. There's a dinner party going on. We heard them."

"How many?" the sergeant whispered.

"I heard three voices, could be more, all male. I can't leave Lars alone in the back, so Jorn is staying with him. You'll have to watch the stairs until we've finished."

The sergeant broke his gaze from the gate for just an instant. "Take care of yo'self, Snake." He stepped back out onto the porch.

Von Kant chuckled and drank the last of his wine as Sorokin told about his first meeting with Gorbachev. Wolf glanced impatiently at the empty plates in front of his guests. He leaned toward Rink and whispered, "See what's taking Greta so long."

Rink immediately headed for the kitchen. Wolf shifted his gaze and attention back to Sorokin.

". . . he was just Seevglivich then. A good practical joker who could . . ."

Lars didn't hear Rink's approach. The carpet muffled the sound of his footsteps.

When Rink pushed the swinging door, he felt it hit something and heard a clatter. He backed up, feeling sorry for Greta, and caught the edge of the door as it rebounded. He was about to step in to help her when he saw an all-black figure bend over and reach for a silenced pistol on the floor. Behind the crouching man was another on his knees, and in his hand was a nine-millimeter automatic.

Lars screamed as he fell back to let Jorn fire. *"Axeeel!"*

Rink swung the door as hard as he could at the man who yelled, then fell to floor and grabbed for his own pistol. Bullets exploded through the door, showering him with wood splinters. Hergler, seated with his back to the kitchen, slumped forward to the table with three bullets stitched up his back. Wolf, at the opposite end, was grazed in the arm and fell to the floor clutching his wound just as Rink began shooting.

Axel had only been four steps into the living room when he'd heard Lars's scream, and he broke into a run as Jorn's first shots reverberated through the house. He'd been almost into the dining area when he'd heard the thunderous cracks of return fire from just inside the room. He saw the shooter kneeling beside the far wall, but the man had seen him too and was spinning around. They fired at each other at the same time.

Jake, just behind and to the left of Axel, saw him go down. Still running, Jake screamed and fired as fast as he could pull the trigger. The shooter's large body jerked spasmodically with each hit, and fell back against the wall.

Jake tossed down his empty pistol and withdrew his Beretta from his belt. He leveled it at the silver-haired man on the floor and began to squeeze the trigger.

"No, Jake!" Axel barked as he got up from the floor. Jake nearly cried, hearing the familiar voice, and turned around. Axel's thigh wound was oozing blood, but his eyes were clear and focused on the man he'd come to kill.

The bullet-shattered door opened and Lars walked out, his left arm dangling at his side. His shoulder and arm wounds had soaked the black material of his jumpsuit. He looked with grave eyes at Axel. "Jorn is hit very badly."

Jorn pushed himself into the room, the front of his uniform glistening with blood. He grabbed Lars's leg to stay upright. Glaring at the man on the floor, he growled to Axel. "Finish it."

"*Snake?*" Washington yelled anxiously from the porch.

Jake turned and yelled over his shoulder. *"We've got some friendly WIA, but we're okay. Stay in position."*

One of the men cowering on the floor under the table lifted his head up when he heard the English words. He rose up holding his hands in the air and looking at Jake in disbelief. *"You!"*

Jake recognized von Kant the second he raised his head. Jake's whole body shook with rage as he raised his pistol, pointing it at the German's head. He hissed, "Get your buddy under the table and get against the wall. I'm gonna deal with you later. *Move!*"

Jake walked over to pull Volker to his feet, but the director pushed the American's hand away and got to his knees on his own. He looked at the three Iron Men and stood up, facing them defiantly. His lips drew back as he felt the energy building inside. He knew he was facing his ultimate challenge.

Axel limped a step forward and leveled his pistol at the chilling blue eyes. "I am Hauptmann Mader, Volker! I have come to fulfill my vow."

Lars stepped forward, forgetting his pain and straightened his back. "And I am Hauptmann Kailer, Butcher. I have come to fulfill my vow."

Jorn's face was gray but his eyes burrowed into the ex-SS officer's forehead as he planted his hands and scooted his legs forward. "I'm Hauptmann Furman, you bastard. I am back to fulfill my vow."

Volker let his incendiary gaze move from one Iron Man to the next as they spoke. Then he slowly shifted his eyes back to the first man. "Kill me, Mader, but know this: your daughter is now conscious and asking for you. I know, for I have people watching her." He fixed his stare on Lars. "Kailer, your son and daughter are both worried about you, as are your grandchildren. They are being watched and their conversations listened to every time they speak. Kill me, cowards . . . and they will all die, your daughters, sons, their children . . . all of them. Kill me and you will have nothing left to go back to."

Jorn pulled the pistol from his belt. "What about me, Butcher? Who have you not killed that I have loved?"

Volker looked at the half man with disdain and snickered, "*You* killed them, coward, forty-four years ago when you deserted."

Jorn raised his pistol.

Volker looked in panic to Axel. "She will die, Mader! Your daughter will die!"

Axel raised his pistol and fired. Volker staggered back with a look of shock. He touched the wound in his side. "I will kill them all! You can't kill me! Don't you understand? You can't!"

Lars lifted his pistol, squeezing the trigger. Volker's right shoulder jerked with the impact of the small bullet. Axel fired again, the bullet ripping through Volker's arm. Lars fired. Volker reeled back, screaming in agony from the bullet shattering his wrist.

"Stop this!" Sorokin yelled, stepping away from the wall. "You don't understand what you are doing. I will guarantee your safety if you—"

Axel turned and put a bullet just over Sorokin's head. Lars aimed and shot Volker's right kneecap. Axel turned and shot the other one. Volker fell back on his buttocks, his face screwed up in anguish and pain.

"Tallon, stop them!" von Kant screamed.

Jake fired from the hip. The slug thudded into the wall beside von Kant's right ear.

Jorn raised his pistol.

Volker looked into the amputee's eyes, and seeing the hatred there, smiled through his pain. "I . . . I've been waiting for you."

Jorn whispered softly. "For Germany." He pulled the trigger.

Sorokin jerked with the sound of the pistol's report and gagged as blood and brain tissue splattered the back wall. He sunk to his knees crying, not for Volker, but for his country and what it had lost.

Von Kant stared at Jake with loathing. "Am I to be executed too?"

Jake ignored him. "We gotta move," he barked at the other Iron Men, who stood watching the pool of blood expand behind Volker's head.

"*Jake! We got company at the gate!*" Washington yelled from the front porch. His M-16 cracked, punctuating the warning.

Jake spun, pointing his pistol at von Kant. "You'll live if you and your buddy help my friends to the boat on the back pier." He looked at Lars. "Cover them, and if they do anything stupid, kill them. Move!"

Von Kant remained stationary. The sound of gunfire increased outside. Jake looked into the German's eyes as he aimed the pistol at his forehead. "Decide."

Von Kant knew the American would do exactly what he said. He broke his stare and told Sorokin to assist the amputee. Jake patted Axel's back. "Get the engines started and cast the lines. Sandman and I will be right there. Go!"

The living room windows shattered with incoming fire. Axel didn't flinch as he took the M-16 from his back and handed it to Jake. "We won't leave the dock without you."

Jake took the rifle and ran toward the front door.

Washington slapped in a new magazine and aimed at the dark figure running toward the cars parked in the driveway. He squeezed the trigger and rolled to the other side of the door just as bullets from assault rifles slammed into the wall and doorframe. The man he had shot in the chest fell back.

Another soldier jumped up from behind a tree and made a dash as two others laid down covering fire. Washington saw him coming, but the bullets were hitting just above him. He was about to bring his rifle up when he heard the distinctive popping of another M-16. The running soldier pitched backward, stitched across the chest.

"How many more?" Jake yelled from the living room.

Washington ducked back inside the door. "At least four. They came in a truck that stopped at the gate. I—" Washington felt more than heard the movement behind him and turned.

Renate shot the huge man in the back and dropped to a crouch, facing the living room, where she'd heard the other foreign voice. Bullets slammed into the front of the house, breaking glass, shattering wood, and chipping stones as she crept forward.

Jake was hunched down below the window, his body covered in shards of glass from the shattered windows. He saw her just as she raised her pistol. He jerked back, firing as she squeezed the trigger. The bullet smacked the wall a breath away from his head. The woman was propelled backward with the impact of the M-16 rounds blowing through her neck and face. Still firing the pistol, she landed on her back in the foyer.

Jake screamed as he got to his feet. *"Sandeeeee!"*

The Sandman lay on his stomach with a bullet hole just below his right shoulder blade. He was reaching for the rifle with his left hand. "Goddamnit! Goddaaaamnit!"

Jake fell beside him and pushed the rifle into his hands. Washington nodded toward the entrance. "Another truckload of 'em just pulled through the gate."

Jake brought the rifle up to his shoulder. "Hang tough, buddy."

Washington let a wave of nausea and pain pass before lifting his rifle. "Go on, Snake. It just takes one to hold 'em off. Get your ass outta here."

Jake pressed his face against the stock and aimed. He squeezed the trigger and knocked down a man running toward the side of the house. He looked over the stock at his friend. "We're a team, remember?"

A line of men rose up from the shadows in front of them as a machine gun opened up from their right.

Jake pulled the big man back as bullets shredded the wood around the door and chewed up the stairs behind them.

Jake got up as soon as the machine gun shifted its fire to the living room windows. He pushed the selector to automatic and pressed the trigger, spraying across the line of advancing men in a single long burst. Half the men fell, the others ran for cover. The machine gun quickly shifted back toward the muzzle flash and ate away again at the front entrance.

Jake dragged Washington farther down the hallway and sat him up against the wall. "We're gettin' the fuck outta here. Can you walk?"

Washington put out his hand. "Just get me to my feet."

•   •   •

Axel had the engines running and looked toward the house. Von Kant shook his head with a smile. "They'll never make it. None of you will."

Axel swung his pistol barrel around and struck the disbeliever in the head. Von Kant fell to the floor of the bridge in a heap. Axel yelled to the end of the dock where Lars and Jorn were positioned behind a stone bench. "Do you see them?"

Lars saw the rear door open, but he waited until he was sure, then yelled, "They are coming!" Lars turned to the Russian, who was staunching Jorn's wounded stomach with his jacket. "Take him back to the boat."

Jorn shook his head. "You know I'm dying. Let me die in my homeland."

Lars grabbed the Russian's arm and shoved him toward Jorn. *"Take him!"*

Sorokin shook his head. "Grant your friend his request. He isn't going to make it. I'll stay with him."

Jorn rested himself against the stones of the bench, feeling very tired, and nodded toward to the distant stairway where Jake was helping the sergeant down the steps. "Axel loves that American like a son. I got what I wanted, old friend. Make sure Axel gets what he wants—his son back. Go, Hauptmann Kailer, as your senior officer I ask you to carry out my last order."

Lars set his M-16 on the bench in front of his friend and withdrew his pistol. He looked at Jorn with tears glistening his cheeks. "Good-bye, my kamerad."

Jorn smiled. "Good-bye, Iron Man Kailer."

Lars ran toward the two men.

Jake saw Kailer and waved him back. "Get on the boat! They're right behind us!"

Kailer saw men coming out of the door and raised his pistol, firing.

Jake spun around and shot his entire magazine. He reached for another but Lars stopped him. "Get on the boat, *now*! Jorn is covering our withdrawal! *Move!*" Lars shoved the two men toward the boat. "Hurry, before it's too late!"

Jorn turned to face the team running down the pier. He slapped a new magazine into the butt of the pistol and jacked a round into the chamber before glancing at the Russian who knelt beside him.

Sorokin looked into Jorn's eyes. "There's been enough killing. It's over."

Jorn squeezed the trigger. The bullet passed within an inch of Sorokin's face. "Get away from me," Jorn said, dropping the pistol and picking up the rifle. "Get down behind the wall and stay down.

As you said, it is over." Jorn looked back and saw three men dash away from the right side of the house. He aimed and fired high. Men from inside let loose a fusillade of lead. Jorn ducked down behind the protective stone and saw the Russian slipping over the retaining wall. He smiled to himself when over the boat's grumbling engines he heard Axel yelling, *"We'll always be together, Jorn Furman . . . always!"*

"Ja, always," Jorn whispered. He rose up and fired a long burst at the stars. He felt no more hatred. The Russian had been right. There had been enough killing. Return fire ricocheted off the stones, but he didn't hear it. Then something struck him in the chest, but he didn't feel the pain. He slowly slid down the side of the bench, closed his eyes, and rested his weary body.

CHAPTER 40

The dark patrol craft cut quietly through the waters of the Muggel-see. The bridge floor was slick with blood as Lars held the penlight toward Axel's exposed thigh wound. Jake placed a bandage over the oozing hole and tightly wrapped and tied the last length of gauze around it. There was nothing else left in the first-aid box but Band-Aids. He shined his penlight on Washington to see if he was still conscious. He was. The sergeant was sitting against the rail holding an M-16 in his lap and staring out at the dark water. Jake brought the light back to Lars. He was a tough old goat, but like the others, he was going into shock. Their adrenaline was gone, and pain and stiffness were taking over.

Jake got up from the vibrating floor and checked on von Kant, who sat against the bridge cabin wall. He was bleeding from his split cheek. "Give up, Colonel," he snickered. "You are finished. Your friends need medical attention now."

Jake ignored him and stuck the penlight into his belt. He put his arm around Axel's shoulder. "How ya doin'?"

Wearing night-vision goggles, Axel was biting his lip to keep from screaming in pain—both from the wound and the loss of Jorn. Jake felt his friend's body trembling. He patted his back. "I'll take the wheel, Skipper. Give me your goggles and get one of the rifles and rest near the rail."

Lars's head lolled to the side in the darkness. "Jake, none of us can drive our cars. What are we going to do?"

Jake slipped on the goggles and focused the lens. "What was Plan B, if we couldn't get back to the cars?"

Lars lowered his head. "There was no alternate plan."

454

Jake turned, pushed the throttle all the way forward and barked over his shoulder, "There is now! We're going home. We're gonna do what Jorn would have done. *Attack!* We're not going north on the Spree like we came in. We're going south to the Teltow Canal. We're gonna beach this baby on the West Berlin bank."

"It's full of patrol boats," von Kant said in shocked disbelief. "You'll have to travel three kilometers up the waterway before you reach the portion of the canal that borders the West. There's no way you can get to the west bank! The patrol boats and machine guns in the guard towers will stop you."

Jake barked over his shoulder, "What's your vote, Sandman? Fight or Stasi prison? Von Kant thinks we're fucked."

Washington gritted his teeth but smiled to himself through his tears of pain. It was like Grenada all over again. He and the team had thought it was over ... except the Snake. He'd cussed and sworn they weren't defeated as long as they believed. Washington slapped his M-16. "Fuck what da spook says, man. *Attack!*"

"Lars?" Jake asked.

Lars lifted his head, knowing what Jake was doing. He'd done it himself back in the old days. His leader was trying to get them thinking and moving so they wouldn't go into lethargic shock. He growled and straightened his back, *"Angriff!* Attack!"

Von Kant shook his head and slid down the bridge cabin wall to his buttocks. "Fools! You're all fools! We're all going to die!"

Washington took a fresh magazine from Lars and spoke for all of them. "Shut da fuck up!"

Sorokin walked along the long row of bodies laid out on the front lawn, shaking his head at the waste. He stopped at the last body and spoke aloud to the dead man. "You were so close, my friend ... so close to obtaining what you had always wanted—your old Germany back." Sorokin bent over, closing Volker's eyelids, and turned to find his last hope. He saw him lying on a stretcher in the driveway. Just ten minutes before in the house, he'd thought the man was dead, but then saw his fingers twitching. The big man had been hit four times with bullets, the last in the head, but the small bullet had glanced off the skull and cut a path under the skin from above his right eye all the way to the back of his head before exiting.

Sorokin kneeled and placed the man's hand in his own. Leaning over, he spoke reassuringly. "Hold on, my friend, the ambulances will be here in just a few minutes. You are going to live."

Max Rink's dulled eyes moved slowly toward the Russian. "Is the director . . ."

Sorokin squeezed Rink's thick hand. "You did all you could, Max. He died bravely. I was there with him at the last."

Rink's lip quivered. "Who . . . who were they?"

"The Iron Men," Sorokin said softly. "They came for revenge, but paid dearly. It is over, my friend. Revenge is not worth the consequences. Look what it did to your leader, who devoted his energies in trying to kill them. It is self-destructive. You must recall your teams. Don't continue the madness. Concern yourself with only your country's future. You are your country's last hope. Von Kant is gone, as is your leader. I, as always, am still here. We can continue together and fulfill your leader's dream."

Rink's eyes came into focus and looked up at the old man. "Is . . . is it still possible?"

Sorokin smiled. "With the help of a guardian angel, anything is possible."

Jake tore off the goggles and yelled, "Patrol boat bearing down on us dead ahead!"

Washington motioned skyward. "We got helicopters coming in behind us, Snake!"

Axel glanced at the oncoming patrol boat. "Only one more kilometer to the canal border."

Jake flipped every switch and pushed every button on the control panel. The running lights came on, as did the searchlight, siren, and revolving red warning flasher on top of the bridge.

"We're gonna tell the folks in the West we're coming home! Lars, man the searchlight and blind the oncoming boat! Sandman, forget the choppers, they're not armed. I'm gonna pass the patrol boat on your side. Blow away their fuckin' bridge! Axel, help him!"

Jake looked down at von Kant, who was staring at him wide-eyed. "Get below and pray we make it. If we don't, asshole, you don't."

Von Kant shook his head and came to his feet. "What can I do?"

Jake motioned toward the fire extinguisher on the wall, "Break the windows in front, hurry!"

Von Kant grabbed the fire extinguisher just as Lars directed the searchlight beam toward the patrol boat's bridge only a hundred meters away. Von Kant smashed the windows, as Jake had told him to, and then broke the others around the cabin.

A helicopter's searchlight suddenly illuminated their boat. Jake lifted his M-16 from the console and rested the barrel on the sill of the broken window. The oncoming craft was was only fifty meters away and coming straight for them. He began firing in short bursts.

Washington pulled back the trigger of his assault rifle, spraying the bridge as the boat closed within twenty meters. Three seconds later his weapon was empty. Axel then hosed the deck and cabin with thirty rounds of searing lead.

Jake heard no incoming bullets as he sped by the riddled craft. It was dead in the water. He began to relax his grip on the wheel, but his jaw tightened when he saw another two patrol boats turn on their lights just two hundred meters ahead. "Reload! We got two more!"

He set his eyes on the boat closest to the west bank and tuned out the maddening, whining siren, the magazines clinking into place, the beating whop-whop-whop of the chopper blades, and the screaming of the engines. He nodded to himself knowing this was it. *"We're going home! Attack!"* he yelled.

"Come on *motherfuckerrrrrs!*" Washington yelled over the din and raised his rifle.

Bullets cracked and popped overhead as Jake bore straight for the boat on the right. He had already loaded a new magazine and was firing with one hand. Lars directed the searchlight at the bridge of the boat and lifted his head yelling, *"Angriiiif!"*

Von Kant ducked down. Tracers from the oncoming boats were zipping past like huge green meteors. "You're crazy for trying it!" he screamed at Jake.

Jake saw the right boat veer toward shore out of control. He swung the bow toward the remaining challenger. He grinned. "Piece'a fuckin' cake!"

A bullet cracked over Jake's ear, but he kept grinning.

The pilot of Border Patrol Craft 4 saw his fellow pilot veer off from the attack and cursed him. Suddenly his bridge window shattered from a hail of bullets. More cracking lead zipped and zinged past him, thudding and ripping into the wood panels behind him. Glass crystals had covered his face so that he was afraid to blink. He glanced behind and saw his first engineer sprawled on deck. He looked back at the boat. It was coming, bearing down like a freight train. It was live or die. He spun the wheel. He wanted to live. His boat plowed into the shore at twelve knots and came to a crunching halt.

Just ahead were the glistening, empty waters of the canal and the lights of West Berlin. Jake turned off the siren and throttled back, steering the craft toward the West Berlin bank.

Von Kant stood and smiled in relief. "We made it."

Jake spun around and threw his forearm into the smiling man's face. It was satisfying to feel the jaw crack with the blow. He had promised the traitor his life but not his teeth. On the bank above people were lined up, yelling hysterically.

"What are they saying?" he asked Axel.

Axel spoke wanly. "They think we're an East German boat crew trying to defect. They are yelling for us to hurry before more boats come or the tower across from us begins shooting."

Jake cut the engines to glide in when suddenly the bridge seemed to disintegrate. A blue tongue of flame was erupting from a machine gun in a guard tower directly across from them on the east bank. The bullets were moving toward him, eating away the cabin. Axel stood and brought his rifle up to return fire. Seeing the old soldier exposed, Jake screamed and lunged across the deck to push him down. He winced, feeling the first bullet strike. The second hit a split second later. Axel cried out as the taut, jerking body next to him went slack. "Jake! Mein Gott, Jake!"

Lars spun the searchlight toward the tower to blind the gunner as Sandman screamed in anguish and fired at the concrete structure. The onlookers from the west bank shouted and shoved, running for cover. The tower machine gunner saw the boat touch the beach and immediately ceased fire, as were his orders. Jake didn't hear or see any of it. His head had slipped down and was resting on Axel's shoulder. His arms had fallen limply down to his sides. He closed his heavy eyelids, feeling the old man hug him to his chest and rock him back and forth as if trying to will life back into him. Jake tried to tell him, but he couldn't get his words through the bloody froth.

The old man nodded, putting his cheek against Jake's. "I know, son . . . I love you too."

Jake smiled inwardly and let the cold darkness take him.

Burton Dawson slapped twice in the darkness for the ringing telephone on the nightstand before grasping the handset. He brought the device to his ear. "Yeah?"

He listened and bolted upright. "What? . . . Shit! I'll be there as soon as I can. Don't send this up to Bonn until I check what the fuck is going on. Get von Kant's deputy and have him meet

me at the hospital. . . . Yes, do as Sergeant Washington wants.
Put them all in the American Army Hospital and make sure
you post additional security. . . . Just fucking do it! I'm on the
way."

CHAPTER 41

The emergency room's double doors slammed back and Burton Dawson entered like a dark storm cloud. The field agent stood and braced himself to face the oncoming fury.

Dawson stopped only inches from the man. "How bad is Tallon hit? Can he talk?"

"He's on the table now. It doesn't look good."

Dawson's eyes widened. "What the fuck happened?"

The surgeon sat down tiredly. "We were only able to remove one bullet from Colonel Tallon's back, and we nearly lost him doing it. He is much too weak to proceed with the second operation until he regains his strength. The other bullet is lodged next to the spinal cord and will require a specialist."

Dawson sighed. "Is he out of immediate danger?"

"No. The remaining bullet is causing paralysis because of its location. He's very weak, and it will be difficult for him to regain strength because the pain will be such that . . ."

Dawson listened patiently until the doctor was finished. "And the others?"

The surgeon picked up a clipboard. "Mader is out of danger, as are Kailer and Sergeant Washington. They are all stabilized. Washington wants to talk to you, and won't let us operate until he does. You'd better see him now so we can get to the bullet."

Dawson was already heading for the door.

•   •   •

Sandy Washington grimaced in pain, but he kept his eyes on Dawson. "I want your guarantee."

Dawson's brow furrowed. "If we confirm what you've told me, you've got it. In the meantime, I'll get Kailer's family and Mader's daughter secured with our people."

Washington grabbed Dawson's jacket and pulled him closer to the gurney, snarling, "Don't trust a fuckin' German spook or cop, Dawson—none of 'em. They're in deep. Real deep."

Dawson nodded to indicate he understood. Only then did Washington release him. Dawson motioned toward his agents to push the gurney into the surgery room and looked back at the sergeant as he was wheeled by. "They're doing everything possible for Jake. I want you to know that."

The sergeant's eyes clouded. "He's going to make it . . . he has to."

18 October

Burt Dawson brought up a chair beside Washington's bed and sat down. "You look a helluva lot better than you did last night. The doc says you'll be all right. Mader and Kailer are holding their own and out of danger."

Washington's eyes asked the question.

Dawson leaned back. "Jake is the same . . . he's got a fifty-fifty chance. They're sending in a specialist. They'll operate once he's strong enough . . . maybe a couple of weeks."

Washington stared at the station chief. "Your people find anything?"

"Yeah," Dawson said, relieved that Washington didn't ask more about Tallon. "Phone taps and some of the Stasi surveillance boys were policed up. The West German Feds are real embarrassed by all this . . . especially with it comin' from us. They're protesting, but not too loud just yet. They're running backgrounds on all their people."

"And von Kant?" Washington asked, locking eyes.

Dawson took in a deep breath and exhaled through his nose. "He walks. He's part of the Federal Republic's intel community board. His meeting with Wolf was sanctioned. We're not in a position to dictate policy when it comes to the internal affairs of other governments . . . but we'll be watching the little bastard."

Washington shook his head in disgust and closed his eyes.

Dawson didn't want to end the conversation so negatively. He forced a thin smile. "I have some good news. Mader's daughter is conscious and doing very well. We're moving her to this hospital, both for security reasons and so she can be closer to her father."

Washington's eyes swung to Dawson. "How is she taking the news about Jake?"

Dawson looked at his watch and stood up. "She doesn't know about any of this yet. I'm going to tell her when they get her situated in her room. Hey, I gotta go. Your wife is outside waiting to see you. Just make sure you don't tell her anything about what happened. We're still trying to figure out how we're gonna handle it. Ya got it?"

Washington nodded.

Dawson began to walk for the door but stopped and looked over his shoulder. "I'm breaking the rules, but I thought you might wanna know. I got a call, an unusual call, from the East. It was a Russian who used to advise the Stasi. An old fart named Georgi Sorokin. He wants to have a meet. He says he's acting as a go-between so that this affair can be discussed between me and Wolf's replacement, a man called Max Rink. To show good faith, the hit orders on the Iron Men have been rescinded. He said it's over."

Sandy closed his eyes. "Thank God."

3 November

Jake felt the racking tremors beginning and opened his mental scrapbook. They were blurs mostly, pictures he had snapped in his mind during visits of those who had come to see him over time, a few words, sentences recorded with each photo, to be treasured and taken out like an old scrapbook to keep the pain away. They were his only memories of the past weeks . . . or maybe even months. He didn't know, didn't care, they were just there; a few bad that hurt, but mostly good. He liked them all. They made the tormenting pain and strange feeling of helplessness go away for a while.

"Hey, Jake, it me, Chong. Arnie not doing so hot now, he not score long time. J.R., he try get his ranch back from old wife and causing big-time trouble. I miss you and your noodle. You hear me, don't you? I save plenty Lite beer for you 'cause nobody else drink. You get bet-ter soon . . . okay? You hear me, Jake? Okay?"

"Snake, my man, lookie who I brought. Sissy, it's okay. Talk to him, he can hear you. I know he can."

"Say, hey, Jake. Sandy and I been real worried and . . . oh God, Sandy, you really think he can hear us? His eyes seem so blank."

"Sure he can! Lookie here, Snake, they got me almost patched up. They shipping me and Sissy out, man. Seems you and me ain't wanted around the city anymore. The Company made me sign some fuckin' cover story, you know the deal. Never talk about it and . . . fuck 'em, Snake. Fuck 'em . . . we did it right. We can be real proud, man. We . . ."

"Tallon, it's General Trout. I hope you can hear me. I want you to know you have embarrassed this command and me personally. I may have to follow the ambassador's orders on this matter, but you are ruined . . . you hear me, Tallon? I have a long memory. I am getting you out of here as soon as you recover enough to walk. You're going to be on the first plane out of *my* command and out of *my* city."

"Sir, I don't think he hears you."

"It doesn't matter. His kind never do. I only came because the ambassador told me to personally check on him. Well, I've seen him. Let's go."

"Sir, aren't you supposed to leave those flowers? I thought they were sent by the ambassador?"

"Eh, yes, thank you I forgot. . . ."

"Hi Jake, do you recognize me? It's General Thomas. . . . The doctor said you might be able to hear me. Can you move your eyes or blink so I know . . . don't worry about it, Jake. I just came to tell ya how sorry I am about all this. I never should have gotten you over here. I'm sorry, troop . . . so goddamn sorry. I'm not supposed to know, but goddamn, Jake, you kicked their ass. Must have been like the old days, huh? Sorry, Jake . . . I'm really sorry. I called your mother and she wanted to fly over, but her doctors advise against it. She had a minor stroke when she got the notification about you. Don't worry, she's doing fine, nothing serious. She wants you to know she loves you and is praying every day for you to get better. She says to come home to her, Jake. She needs you. I'll keep you posted and . . ."

"Colonel, it's Dawson. I hope you hear me. It's official. The hit on Wolf's residence was done by an unknown terrorist group. That is the official release to the community. Your friends have all been debriefed and have signed the necessary paperwork. There was no assault team, no attack into the East. Their injuries were caused by an auto accident. Shit, Jake, you really fucked things up. You got the Herm Feds all pissed off. It's gonna take all the ambassador's blue chips to calm this goat screw down. . . . If it's any consolation, he told me to tell ya good job, but get the fuck outta Germany. Me? I say you took too many fuckin' chances, but what the hell, huh?

You accomplished the mission, right? Oh yeah, von Kant has lost about fifteen pounds. He's still on fluids and can't eat through all the wire holding his jaw together. Just thought you'd like to know. Hey, I gotta go."

"Jake, it's me, Axel. Look who I've brought! Don't cry, Princess, he can hear you, talk to him."

"J-Jake, it's Kristina. I . . . I've missed you so much. I've been worried sick about you and . . . oh, Papa, he looks so weak. I . . . I can't stand to see him like this. . . ."

"Jake, she's too upset to talk. . . . I'm taking good care of her and we're both waiting for you to get better so we can all be together again. Princess looks good, doesn't she, son? The bandage comes off her head in just a few more weeks. I can walk now, and they're letting me go home. I'll be back every day to see you and . . ."

"Jake, it's Kris. . . . I love you. . . . Do you hear me? I love you."

Memories, thought Jake as he closed his mental scrapbook. It reminded him of the book he used to look through as a boy, the one with pictures of his father. But the pictures in his mental scrapbook were becoming more and more faded, distant, harder to tell what was real and what was imagined. He had been fighting the agonizing pain, but it made him helpless. He wanted more than anything to reach out and touch them . . . to speak to them all, but he couldn't. Pleeeease God! It hurts so bad!

The neurosurgeon pulled off his blood-smeared gloves and tossed them into the basket. He slipped his sweat-soaked mask down to his neck, took in a deep breath, and exhaled slowly. The U.S. Berlin Hospital chief of surgery had been observing the operation.

"He was lucky," the specialist said. "It was a hair's breadth away from penetrating the spinal cord. These past weeks must have been torture for him."

"What's your prognosis?"

The specialist nodded tiredly. "There will be swelling for the next few days, but I'd say in five to six days you should see dramatic improvement in your patient. He'll recover with time."

The colonel sighed in relief and motioned toward the double doors. "There are some people outside in the waiting room who will be very relieved to hear that."

9 November, six A.M.

The ward nurse turned on the light and glanced at the patient as she picked up the chart at the end of his bed. She saw his eyes were open, as usual. She smiled. "You're looking much better without those feeding tubes in your nose. How you doin'? The same, huh? It won't be much longer. You had us worried for a while, but since the surgeon got that last bullet out a week ago, it looks real good. You're going to have to cooperate with us. You should be able to start feeling again, and without those tubes, you'll be able to start talking to us and eating again so we can put some weight back on you. You're going to have to try real hard to start moving your fingers and toes. I'll be back a little later and we'll start work, okay? . . . Come on, keep those eyes on me and blink a couple of times. Not yet, huh? Okay, but work on it, will ya? Mr. Mader and his daughter have been here every day to see you and sure would like you to show some improvement. All of us would."

Midnight

The night nurse walked into the room, turned on the television, and looked at her patient. "I wanted you to see this, Colonel. It's unbelievable. The wall came down tonight at around eleven P.M. Can you believe it? Look at that! Look at all those people standing on the wall in front of the Brandenburg Gate. I . . . I never thought I'd see this day. . . . Sorry, I don't usually tear up, but it's really something. My God, there must be thousands! Their faces, look at those faces . . . God, it makes me so . . . so proud being a part of all this."

The nurse turned and was surprised to see her patient's eyes were on the television. It was the first time his eyes actually seemed focused. Before, when his eyes were open he didn't seem to know or understand, but now his eyes were . . .

"Can I come in, please?"

The nurse turned, looking at a small Oriental woman in the doorway. She was wearing a large black bow tie and was carrying a brown paper bag.

"I come after work to see Jake. He friend, you know. I bring him present to celebrate." Chong took a can of Lite beer from the small bag and held it up.

The nurse frowned. "Alcoholic beverages aren't allowed in the hospital." She broke into a smile. "But come on in and join us. I think the colonel is really seeing the television. . . . *Look!* He's looking at you!"

Chong smiled and lifted the can of beer. "No, he lookin' at beer. Hi, Jake, you noodle lookin' bet-ter. My husband, he TDY, you know. I want to share this big-time special night with friend, you know. I come see old friend. It big day, huh?"

The nurse tilted her head. "You hear that?" She went to the window and opened it. Horns were honking and people were yelling and laughing. The din filled the night air.

Chong smiled. "Yeah, it big party outside. Everybody in street. Like New Year party. I wanna make sure Jake know it happening. He help make it happen and—"

"It . . . it's not a noodle."

Shocked, both women snapped their heads toward the patient. Jake's lip quivered as it crawled up in a weak smile. "It's a snake."

24 December

The uniformed Army chaplain looked around the small hospital room filled with poinsettias and smiled at the assembled guests. "I've married couples in unusual places, but this is a first for me." He walked to the bed and winked at Jake before turning and facing the audience. It comprised a bartender, nurses, doctors, Mission secretary, General Thomas, and a German couple. "Will the father please escort the bride forward?" he said, to get the ceremony under way.

Red-faced from too many precelebration beers, Axel pushed his daughter forward in a wheelchair. Wearing a green dress and hat, and a red ribbon around her elevated, bandaged legs, Kristina kept her twinkling eyes on the groom.

Jake broke his gaze from his bride to wink at Chong. She was beaming. General Thomas and Peggy Sue gave him a thumbs up, and both Lars and Jutta Kailer dabbed their eyes with handkerchiefs. Jake looked back at Kristina and held his hand out to her as the chaplain opened the bible and looked upward. "On this special Christmas Eve day we have gathered here to . . ."

4 January, 1990

Axel pulled his new Mercedes to the curb and turned off the engine. With misted eyes he looked at his passenger. "Jake, Kristina and I have already said our good-byes. Jutta and Lars have taken her and the bags to the airport to check in. She'll be waiting on the plane. Bear with us, Jake, it's easier this way for me. Before I take you there, I want to show you something. It is Kristina's surprise, but she thought that perhaps I should be the one to show it to you." Axel motioned out the window toward a park. "Go down that path and you'll see it. I'll be with you in just a moment."

Jake opened the door, picked up the two canes by his side, and began the painful walk. He loved the smell of the wood burning in the fireplaces from the houses across the street and the evergreens in the park. It was his first time out of the hospital, and he wanted to see and feel the wonders of the outside world, which he had so desperately missed. He walked along the path, enjoying the crisp air, but suddenly stopped. Ahead of him was a white, marble, five-foot monument rising out the ground. Etched in the top of the stone was a side view of a C-47 cargo plane. He stepped closer and saw a half-nude woman on the nose of the plane's fuselage. *"Babe's Express,"* he said softly, reading the words above the figure. The first five engraved lines below the aircraft were in German, but the rest were in English. He leaned on his canes and read the words in a whisper.

"During the Berlin airlift, on the first of October, 1948, Major Jake Tallon, United States Army Air Corps, perished in flames in his plane *Babe's Express* at this location. He died so that Berliners would live. His country awarded him a Distinguished Flying Cross for heroism and selfless devotion to duty. We Berliners shall not forget his sacrifice. He is one of us now, an Iron Man enshrined in our hearts. As long as men are free, his memory shall live."

"He's one of us, Jake . . . an Iron Man."

Jake turned to the old soldier and tried to speak but failed. He looked back at the monument. A moment passed before he had composed himself enough. "I . . . I know he appreciates this."

Holding two long-stem roses, Axel walked stiffly forward and laid one of the flowers at the monument's base. He turned, handing Jake the second rose, and forced a smile.

"Jake, you and your father have given us more than we can ever repay. Thank you, Iron Man."

Jake took the flower and knelt down on the ground where his father had died, feeling as if he were touching him for the first time. Tears trickled down his face as he laid his rose beside the other, knowing now how Big Jake could have given his life for others.

Thirty minutes later, the two men walked into the airport.

Axel hugged Jake to his breast, then pushed him back. "Go on, my princess is waiting for you on board."

Jake turned to go, but then hugged the old soldier one more time. "You said once you lived in Berlin, you could never leave. We'll be back this summer, Axel . . . that's a promise."

Axel's eyes watered again. "There is so much I want to say."

"I know." Jake walked through the yellow doors without looking back.

The lady at the small counter smiled as she took his ticket. "You almost didn't make it."

Jake looked over his shoulder at the man pressed against the glass. Teary-eyed, he turned, facing the old soldier, and came to attention. Bringing his hand up in a salute, he whispered, "Goodbye, Iron Man . . . I love you."

Axel Mader smiled. He came to attention and returned the salute. "Auf Wiedersehen . . . my son."